THE WAR
AGAINST THE
CHTORR
INVASION

THE WAR
AGAINST THE
CHTORR

INVASION

A MATTER FOR MEN
A DAY FOR DAMNATION

David Gerrold

NELSON DOUBLEDAY, INC.
GARDEN CITY, NEW YORK

Published by arrangement with
Pocket Books, a Simon & Schuster
Division of Gulf & Western Corporation
Simon & Schuster Building
Rockefeller Center
1230 Avenue of the Americas
New York, New York 10020

Printed in the United States of America

CONTENTS

Chtorr (ktôr) *n.* 1. The planet Chtorr, presumed to exist within 30 light-years of Earth. 2. The star system in which the planet occurs; a red giant star, presently unidentified. 3. The ruling species of the planet Chtorr; generic. 4. In formal usage, either one or many members of same; a Chtorr, the Chtorr. (See **Chtor-ran**) 5. The glottal chirruping cry of a Chtorr.

Chtor-ran (ktôr-en) *adj.* 1. Of or relating to either the planet or the star system, Chtorr. 2. Native to Chtorr. *n.* 1. Any creature native to Chtorr. 2. In common usage, a member of the primary species, the (presumed) intelligent life form of Chtorr. *(pl. **Chtor-rans**)*

> *—The Random House Dictionary*
> *of the English Language,*
> Century 21 Edition, unabridged

A MATTER FOR MEN

Acknowledgments

The following people have provided valuable support
and made significant contributions to this book:

Dennis Ahrens
Jack Cohen
Diane Duane
Richard Fontana
Harvey and Johanna Glass
Robert and Ginny Heinlein
Don Hetsko
Rich Sternbach
Tom Swale
Linda Wright

ONE

"MCCARTHY, keep down!"

"Yes, sir."

"—and shut up."

I shut. There were five of us climbing up the slope of a sparsely wooded ridge. We angled diagonally through high yellow grass so dry it crunched. July had not been kind to Colorado. A spark would turn these mountains into an inferno.

Just before each man reached the top he sprawled flat against the slope, then inched slowly forward. Duke was in the lead, wriggling through the tall weeds like a snake. We'd topped five hills this way today and the heat was getting to me. I thought about ice water and the Jeep we'd left back on the road.

Duke edged up to the crest and peered down into the valley beyond. One at a time, Larry, Louis and Shorty moved up beside him. I was the last—as usual. The others had thoroughly read the land by the time I crawled into place. Their faces were grim.

Duke grunted. "Larry, pass me the binoculars."

Larry rolled onto his left side to unstrap the case from his right hip. Wordlessly, he passed them over.

Duke inspected the land below as carefully as a wolf sniffing a trap. He grunted again, softly, then passed the binoculars back.

Now Larry surveyed the scene. He took one glance, then passed the binoculars on to Louis.

What were they looking at? This valley looked the same to me as all the others. Trees and rocks and grass. I didn't see anything more. What had *they* spotted?

"You agree?" asked Duke.

"It's worms," said Larry.

"No question," Louis added.

Worms! *At last!* I took the glasses from Shorty and scanned the opposite slope.

A stream curled through ragged woods that looked as if they had been forested recently. And badly. Stumps and broken branches, ragged sections of trunk, huge woody slabs of bark, and the inevitable carpet of dead leaves and twigs were scattered unevenly across the hill. The forest looked as if it had been chewed up and spit out again by some rampaging, but finicky, prehistoric herbivore of gargantuan proportions and appetite.

"No, down there," rumbled Shorty. He pointed.

I put my eyes to the glasses again. I still didn't see; the bottom of the valley was unusually barren and empty, but—no, wait a minute, there it was—I had almost missed it—directly below us, near a large stand of trees; a pasty-looking igloo and a larger circular enclosure. The walls of it sloped inward. It looked like an unfinished dome. Was that all?

Shorty tapped me on the shoulder then and took the binoculars away. He passed them back to Duke, who had switched on the recorder. Duke cleared his throat as he put the glasses to his eyes, and then began a detailed description of the scene. He spoke in soft, machine-gun bursts —a rapid monotone report. He read off landmarks as if he were knocking items off a checklist. "Only one shelter—and it looks fairly recent. No sign of any other starts—I'd guess only one family, so far—but they must expect to expand. They've cleared a pretty wide area. Standard construction on the dome and corral. Corral walls are about . . . two and a half—no, make that three—meters high. I don't think there's anything in it yet. I—" He stopped, then breathed softly. "Damn."

"What is it?" asked Larry.

Duke passed him the binoculars.

Larry looked. It took a moment for him to find the point of Duke's concern, then he stiffened. "Aw, Christ, no—"

He passed the binoculars to Louis. I sweated impatiently. *What had he seen?* Louis studied the view without comment, but his expression tightened.

Shorty handed the glasses directly to me. "Don't you want to look—" I started, but he had closed his eyes as if to shut out me and the rest of the world as well.

Curious, I swept the landscape again. What had I missed the first time?

I focused first on the shelter—nothing there. It was a badly crafted dome of wood chips and wood-paste cement. I'd seen pictures of them. Close up, its surface would be rough, looking as if it had been sculpted with a shovel. This one was bordered by some kind of dark vegetation, patches of black stuff that clumped against the dome. I shifted my attention to the enclosure—

"Huh?"

—she couldn't have been more than five or six years old. She was wearing a torn, faded brown dress and had a dirt smudge across her left cheek and scabs on both knees, and she was hop-skipping along the wall, trailing one hand along its uneven surface. Her mouth was moving —she was singing as she skipped. As if she had nothing to fear at all. She circled with the wall, disappeared from view for a moment, then reappeared along the opposite curve. I sucked in my breath. I had a niece that age.

"Jim—the glasses." That was Larry; I passed them back. Duke was unslinging his pack, divesting himself of all but a grapple and a rope.

"Is he going after her?" I whispered to Shorty.

Shorty didn't answer. He still had his eyes closed.

Larry was sweeping the valley again. "It looks clear," he said, but his tone indicated his doubt.

Duke was tying the grapple to his belt. He looked up. "If you see anything, use the rifle."

Larry lowered the binoculars and looked at him—then nodded.

"Okay," said Duke. "Here goes nothing." He started to scramble over the top—

"Hold it—" That was Louis; Duke paused. "I thought I saw something move—that stand of trees."

Larry focused the binoculars. "Yeah," he said, and handed them up to Duke, who scrambled around to get a better view. He studied the blurring shadows for a long moment; so did I, but I couldn't tell what they were looking at. Duke slid back down the slope to rest again next to Larry.

"Draw straws?" Larry asked.

Duke ignored him; he was somewhere else. Someplace unpleasant.

"Boss?"

Duke came back. He had a strange expression—hard—and his mouth was tight. "Pass me the piece" was all he said.

Shorty unshouldered the 7 mm Weatherby he had been carrying all morning and afternoon, but instead of passing it over, he laid it down carefully in the grass, then backed off down the slope. Louis followed him.

I stared after them. "Where're they going?"

"Shorty had to take a leak," snapped Larry; he was pushing the rifle over to Duke.

"But Louis went too—"

"Louis went to hold his hand." Larry picked up the binoculars again, ignoring me. He said, "Two of 'em, boss, maybe three."

Duke grunted. "Can you see what they're doing?"

"Uh uh—but they look awfully active."

Duke didn't answer.

Larry laid down the binoculars. "Gotta take a leak too." And moved off in the direction of Shorty and Louis, dragging Duke's pack with him.

I stared, first at Larry, then at Duke. "Hey, what's—"

"Don't talk," said Duke. His attention was focused through the long black barrel of the Sony Magna-Sight. He was dialing windage and range corrections; there was a ballistics processor in the stock, linked to the Magna-Sight, and the rifle was anchored on a precision uni-pod.

I stretched over and grabbed the binoculars. Below, the little girl had stopped skipping; she was squatting now and making lines in the dirt. I shifted my attention to the distant trees. Something purple and red was moving through them. The binoculars were electronic, with automatic zoom, synchronized focusing, depth correction, and anti-vibration; but I wished we had a pair with all-weather, low-light image-amplification instead. They might have shown what was behind those trees.

Beside me, I could hear Duke fitting a new magazine into the rifle. "Jim," he said.

I looked over at him.

He still hadn't taken his attention from the sight. His fingers worked smoothly on the controls as he locked in the numbers. The switches made satisfyingly solid clicks. "Doesn't your bladder need emptying too?"

"Huh? No, I went before we left—"

"Suit yourself." He shut up and squinted into his eyepiece.

I looked through the binoculars again at the purple things in the shadows. Were those *worms?* I was disappointed that they were hidden by the woods. I'd never seen any Chtorrans in the flesh.

I covered the area, hoping to find one out in the open—no such luck. But I did see where they had started to dam the stream. Could they be amphibious too? I sucked in my breath and tried to focus on the forest again. Just one clear glimpse, that's all I wanted—

The *CRA-A-ACK!* of the rifle startled me. I fumbled to refocus the binoculars—the creatures still moved undisturbed. Then what had Duke been firing at—? I slid my gaze across to the enclosure—where a small form lay bleeding in the dirt. Her arms twitched.

A second *CRA-A-ACK!* and her head blossomed in a flower of sudden red—

I jerked my eyes away, horrified. I stared at Duke. "What the hell are you doing?"

Duke was staring intently through the telescopic sight, waiting to see if she would move again. When she didn't, he raised his head from the sight and stared across the valley. At the hidden Chtorrans. A long time. His expression was . . . distant. For a moment I thought he was in a trance. Then he seemed to come alive again and slid off down the hill, down to where Shorty and Louis and Larry waited. Their expressions were strange too, and they wouldn't look at each other's eyes.

"Come on," said Duke, shoving the rifle at Shorty. "Let's get out of here."

I followed after them. I must have been mumbling. "He shot her—" I kept saying. "He shot her—"

Finally, Larry dropped back and took the binoculars out of my trembling hands. "Be glad you're not the man," he said. "Or you'd have had to do it."

TWO

I ENDED up in Dr. Obama's office.

"Sit down, McCarthy."

"Yes, ma'am."

Her eyes were gentle, and I couldn't escape them. She reminded me of my grandmother; she had had that same trick of looking at you so sadly that you felt sorrier for her than for yourself. When she spoke, her voice was detached, almost deliberately flat. My grandmother had spoken like that too, when there was something on her mind and she had to work her way around to it. "I hear you had a little trouble yesterday afternoon."

"Uh—yes, ma'am." I swallowed hard. "We—that is, Duke shot a little girl."

Dr. Obama said softly, "Yes, I read the report." She paused. "You didn't sign it with the others. Is there something you want to add?"

"Ma'am—" I said. "Didn't you hear me? *We shot a little girl.*"

Her eyes narrowed thoughtfully. "I see. You're troubled by that."

"Troubled—? Yes, ma'am, *I am.*"

Dr. Obama looked at her hands. They were folded politely on the desk in front of her, carefully manicured, and dark and wrinkled with age. "Nobody ever said it would be easy."

"You didn't say anything about *shooting children* either."

"I'd hoped we wouldn't have to."

"Dr. Obama, I don't know what the explanation is, but I can't condone—"

"It's not for you to condone!" Her face was suddenly hard. "Duke passed you the binoculars, didn't he?"

"Yes, ma'am. Several times."

"And what did you see?"

"The first time, I saw only the shelter and the enclosure. The second time I saw the little girl."

"And what did Duke do then?"

"Well, it looked like he was going to rescue her, but then he changed his mind and asked for the rifle instead."

"Do you know why he asked for the rifle?"

"Louis said he saw something."

"Mmm. Did you look through the binoculars again to check him?"

"Yes, ma'am—but I looked because I was curious. I'd never seen worms—"

She cut me off. "But when you looked, you saw them, didn't you?"

"I saw something . . ." I hesitated. "I couldn't be sure what it was."

"What did it look like?"

"It was big, and it was purple or red, it was hard to tell."

"The Chtorr have purple skin and varicolored fur. Depending on the light, it can look red, pink, magenta or orange. Was that what you saw?"

"I saw something purple. It was in the shadows, and it kept moving back and forth."

"Was it moving fast?"

I tried to remember. What was fast for a worm? "Kind of," I hedged.

"Then what you saw was a fully grown Chtorr in the active—*and most dangerous*—phase. Duke recognized it, so did Larry, Louis and Shorty. They signed the report."

"I wouldn't know—I've never seen a Chtorr before. That's why I'm here."

"If they said it was a Chtorr, you can be sure it was—but that's why they passed the binoculars, just to be sure; if Duke had been wrong, one of the others would have been sure to spot it."

"I'm not arguing about the identification—"

"Well, you should be," Dr. Obama said. "That's the *only* reason you could possibly have for not signing this report." She tapped the paper on her desk.

I eyed it warily. Dad had warned me about signing things I wasn't sure of—that's how he had married Mother. Or so he'd always claimed.

I said, "It's that little girl we shot—I keep seeing her skipping around that pen. She wasn't in danger; there was no reason to shoot her—"

"Wrong," said Dr. Obama. "Wrong, twice over. You should know that."

"I shouldn't know *anything!*" I said, suddenly angry. "I've never been *told* anything. I was transferred up here from a reclamation unit because somebody found out I had two years of college-level biology. Somebody else gave me a uniform and a rule book—and that's the extent of my training."

Dr. Obama looked startled, resigned and frustrated, all at once. Almost to herself—but loud enough so I could hear it too—she said, "What the hell are they doing anyway? Sending me kids. . . ."

I was still burning. "Duke should have shot at the Chtorr!" I insisted.

"With *what?*" Dr. Obama snapped back. "Were you packing artillery?"

"We had a high-powered rifle—"

"And the range to the Chtorr was more than seven hundred meters on a windy day!"

I mumbled something about hydrostatic shock.

"What was that?"

"Hydrostatic shock. It's what happens when a bullet hits flesh. It makes a shock wave. The cells are like little water balloons. They rupture. That's what kills you, not the hole."

Dr. Obama stopped, took a breath. I could see she was forcing herself to be patient. "I know about hydrostatic shock. It doesn't apply here. You're making the assumption that Chtorran flesh is like human flesh. It isn't. Even if Duke had been firing point blank, it wouldn't have done any good unless he was lucky enough to hit one of their eyes—or unless he had an exploding cartridge, which he didn't. So he had no choice; he had to shoot what he could." Dr. Obama stopped. She lowered her voice. "Look, son, I'm sorry that you had to come up against the harsh realities of this war so quickly, but—" She raised her hands in an apologetic half-shrug, half-sigh, then dropped them again. "—Well, I'm sorry, that's all."

She continued softly, "We don't know what the Chtorr are like inside —that's why we want you here. You're supposed to be a scientist. We're hoping you'll tell us. The Chtorr seem to be pretty well armored or segmented or *something*. Bullets don't have much effect on them—and a lot of good men died finding that out. Either they don't penetrate the same way, or the Chtorrans don't have vital organs that a bullet can disrupt—and don't ask me to explain how that one's possible, because I don't know either. I'm just quoting from the reports.

"We do know, though—from unfortunate experience—that to shoot at a Chtorran is to commit suicide. Whether they're intelligent or not—as some people think—makes no difference. They're very deadly. Even without weapons. They move fast and they kill furiously. The smartest thing to do is not to shoot at them at all.

"Duke *wanted* to rescue that child—probably more than you realize —because he *knew* what the alternative to rescue was. But when Louis saw Chtorr in the woods, Duke had no choice—he didn't dare go after her then. They'd have read him halfway down the hill. He'd have been dead before he moved ten meters. Probably the rest of you too. I don't like it either, but *what he did was a mercy.*

"That's why he passed the binoculars; he wanted to be *sure* he wasn't making a mistake—he wanted you and Shorty and Larry to double-check him. If there was the slightest bit of doubt in any of your minds, he wouldn't have done what he did; he wouldn't have had to—and if I thought Duke had killed that child unnecessarily, I'd have him in front of a firing squad so fast he wouldn't have time to change his under-wear."

I thought about that. For a long moment.

Dr. Obama waited expectantly. Her eyes were patient.

I said, suddenly, "But Shorty never looked at all."

She was surprised. "He didn't?"

"Only the first time," I replied. "He didn't look when we saw the child and he didn't look to confirm it was Chtorr."

Dr. Obama grunted. She was writing something on a note pad. I was relieved to have her eyes off me even for a moment. "Well, that's Shorty's prerogative. He's seen too many of these—" She finished the note and looked at me again. "It was enough that he saw the enclosure. But it's you we're concerned with at the moment. You have no doubt, do you, that what you saw was Chtorr?"

"I've never seen a Chtorran, ma'am. But I don't think this could have been anything else."

"Good. Then let's have no more of this nonsense." She pushed the report across the desk. "I'll take your signature on the bottom line."

"Dr. Obama, *if you please*— I'd like to know why it was necessary to kill that little girl."

Dr Obama looked startled again, the second time since the interview began. "I thought you knew."

I shook my head. "That's what this whole thing is about. I *don't.*"

She stopped. "I'm sorry . . . I really am sorry. I didn't realize—No wonder I couldn't sandbag you. . . ." She got up from her desk and crossed to a filing cabinet. She unlocked it and pulled out a thin folder —it was lettered SECRET in bright red—then returned to her seat. She held the folder thoughtfully in her hands. "Sometimes I forget that most of what we know about the Chtorr is restricted information." She eyed me carefully. "But you're a scientist—"

She was flattering me, and we both knew it. Nobody was anything anymore. To be accurate, I was a student on leave, temporarily contracted to the United States Armed Services, Special Forces Operation, as a full-time exobiologist.

"—so you should be entitled to see these things." But she still didn't pass them over. "Where are you from?" she asked abruptly.

"Santa Cruz, California."

Dr. Obama nodded. "Nice town. I used to have some friends just north of there—but that was a long time ago. Any of your family still alive?"

"Mom is. Dad was in San Francisco when it—when it—"

"I'm sorry. A lot of good people were lost when San Francisco went under. Your mother still in Santa Cruz?"

"I think so. Last I heard, she was helping with the refugees."

"Any other relatives?"

"I have a sister near L.A."

"Married?"

"Yes. She's got a daughter, five." I grinned at the thought of my niece. The last time I had seen her, she had been barely beyond the lap-wetting stage. I went sad then, remembering. "She used to have three. The other two were boys. They would have been six and seven."

Dr. Obama nodded. "Even so, she's very lucky. So are you. Not many people had that many members of their family survive the plagues." I had to agree with her.

Her face went grim now. "Have you ever heard of a town called Show Low?"

"I don't think so."

"It's in Arizona—it *was* in Arizona. There's not much left of it now. It was a nice place; it was named after a poker game—" Dr. Obama cut herself short; she laid the folder on the desk in front of her and opened it. "These pictures—these are just a few of the frames. There's a lot more—half a disk of high-grain video—but these are the best. These pictures were taken in Show Low last year by a Mr. Kato Nokuri. Mr. Nokuri apparently was a video hobbyist. One afternoon he looked out his window—he probably heard the noise from the street—and he saw *this.*" Dr. Obama passed the photographs across.

I took them gingerly. They were color eight-by-tens. They showed a small-town street—a shopping center—as seen from a third-story window. I flipped through the pictures slowly; the first showed a wormlike Chtorran reared up and peering into an automobile; it was large and red with orange markings on its sides. The next had the dark shape of another climbing through a drugstore window; the glass was just shattering around it. In the third, the largest Chtorran of all was doing something to a—it looked like a body—

"It's the last picture in the bunch I want you to see," said Dr. Obama. I flipped to it. "The boy there is only thirteen."

I looked. I almost dropped the picture in horror. I looked at Dr. Obama, aghast, then at the photograph again. I couldn't help myself; my stomach churned with sudden nausea.

"The quality of the photography is pretty good," she remarked. "Especially when you consider the subject matter. How that man retained the presence of mind to take these pictures I'll never know, but that telephoto shot is the best one we have of a Chtorran feeding."

Feeding! It was rending the child limb from limb! Its gaping mouth was frozen in the act of slashing and tearing at his struggling body. The Chtorran's arms were long and double-jointed. Bristly black and insect-like, they held the boy in a metal grip and pushed him toward that hideous gnashing hole. The camera caught the spurt of blood from his chest frozen in midair like a crimson splash.

I barely managed to gasp, "They eat their—their prey *alive?*"

Dr. Obama nodded. "Now, I want you to imagine that's your mother. Or your sister. Or your niece."

Oh, you monster—I tried not to, but the images flashed across my mind. Mom. Maggie. Annie—and Tim and Mark too, even though they were seven months dead. I could still see the boy's paralyzed expression, the mouth a silent shriek of *why me?* startlement. I could see that expression superimposed on my sister's face and I shuddered.

I looked up at Dr. Obama. It hurt my throat to swallow. "I—I didn't know."

"Few people do," she said.

I was shaking and upset—I must have been white as a scream. I pushed the pictures away. Dr. Obama slid them back into the folder without looking at them; her eyes were studying me. She leaned forward across her desk and said, "Now, about that little girl—do you have to ask why Duke did what he did?"

I shook my head.

"Pray that you never find yourself in the same situation—but if you do, will you hesitate to do the same thing? If you think you will, take another look at the pictures. Don't be afraid to ask; any time you need to remember, come to my office and look."

"Yes, ma'am." I hoped I wouldn't need to. I rubbed my nose. "Uh, ma'am—what happened to Mr. Nokuri, the photographer?"

"The same thing that happened to the boy in the picture—we think. All we found was the camera—"

"You were there—?"

"—the rest of the place was a mess." Dr. Obama focused on something else for a moment, something very far away. ". . . There was a lot of blood. All over everything. A lot of blood. . . ." She shook her head sadly. "These pictures—" She straightened the folder on her desk meaningfully. "—an incredible legacy. This was our first real proof. The man was a hero." Dr. Obama looked at me again and suddenly snapped back to the present. "Now you'd better get out of here. I have work to do—oh, the report. Take it with you and read it again. Bring it back when you've signed it."

I left. Gratefully.

THREE

I WAS lying on my bunk when Ted, the other fellow up from the university, came gangling in. He was a lanky smart-aleck with a New England twang. "Hey, Jim boy, chow's on."

"Uh, no thanks, Ted. I'm not hungry."

"So? You want me to call the doc?"

"I'm okay—I'm just not in the mood to eat."

Ted's eyes narrowed. "You still brooding about what happened yesterday?"

I shrugged where I lay. "I dunno."

"You talk to Obie about this yet?"

"Yeah."

"Ah, that explains it—she gave you the shock treatment."

"Well, it worked." I turned on my side and faced the wall.

Ted sat down on the bunk facing mine; I could hear the springs creak. "She showed you the Arizona pictures, didn't she?"

I didn't answer.

"You'll get over it. Everybody does."

I decided I didn't like Ted. He always had *almost* the right thing to say—as if he took his lines from a movie. He was always being just a little *too* wonderful. Nobody could be that cheerful all the time. I pulled the blanket over my head.

He must have gotten tired of waiting for a response, because he stood up again. "Anyway, Duke wants to see you." He added, *"Now."*

I turned around, but Ted was already out the door.

So I sat up and ran a hand through my hair. After a moment, I slipped on my shoes and went looking for Duke.

I found him in the recreation room talking to Shorty; they were sitting on one of the couches going over some maps together. There was a pot of coffee on the table before them. They looked up as I approached. "Be with you in a minute," said Duke.

I hung back politely, keeping my attention focused on the opposite wall. There was an old photograph on it, a faded magazine shot of President Randolph Hudson McGee; I studied it with no interest at all, the square jaw, the shiny gray hair, and the campaign-convincing blue eyes. Finally, Duke mumbled something to Shorty and dismissed him. To me he said, "Sit down."

I did so, nervously.

"Want some coffee?"

"No, thanks."

"Have some anyway—be polite." Duke poured out a cup and set it before me. "You've been here a week, right?"

I nodded.

"You've talked to Obie?"

"Yes."

"Seen the pictures?"

"Yes."

"Well, what do you think?"

I said, "I don't know. What am I supposed to think?"

"Never answer a question with a question, for one thing."

"My father used to tell me that's the only way to answer a rhetorical question."

Duke slurped his coffee and grimaced. "Ugh. It gets worse every day. But don't tell Sergeant Kelly I said so." He looked at me speculatively. "Can you operate a flamethrower?"

"Huh?"

"I'll assume that's a 'no.' How fast can you learn? By the end of the week?"

"I don't know. I guess so. Why?"

"I need a backup man. I thought you might want the job." I started to protest—Duke ignored it. "This time it's not just a scouting foray; it's a search and destroy. We're going back to do what we should have done yesterday. Burn some worms." He waited for my answer.

"I don't know," I said at last.

His eyes were steady. "What's the problem?"

"I don't think I'm much of a military type; that's all."

"No, that isn't all." He fixed me with his steely gray eyes and waited. I felt transparent before him. I tried to glance away, but I felt drawn back to his face. Duke was grim, but not angry—just patient.

I said slowly, "I came out here to *study* the worms. This . . . doesn't exactly fit my expectations. Nobody told me I'd have to be a soldier."

Duke said, "You're getting military credit for it, aren't you?"

"Service credit," I corrected. I'd been lucky. My biology background had qualified as a "needed skill"—but just barely.

Duke made a face. "So? Out here we don't draw lines that thin. There's no difference."

"I beg your pardon, Duke, but there's a lot of difference."

"Eh? How so?"

"It's in my contract. I'm attached as a scientist. Nowhere does it say I have to be a soldier."

Duke leaned back in his chair. "Better take another look at that contract, boy—the 'special duties' clause."

I quoted from memory—we had studied it in school; Duke raised his eyebrows, but let me continue. " 'In addition, the employee may be required by the employer, as represented by his/her immediate, or otherwise, superiors, to perform any special or unique duties for which he is properly and duly equipped, whether by training, nature or other; and which relate or pertain to the basic obligation as herein detailed—' " Duke smiled. I continued, " '—*except* where those duties are in direct conflict with the intent of this contract.' "

Duke was still smiling. "That's right, McCarthy—and the duties I'm asking of you are not in direct conflict. You're not under a 'peaceful intention' clause, are you?"

"Uh, I don't know."

"You're not. If you were, you'd have never been sent up. Every man here has two jobs—his own and killing worms. Do I have to say which one takes priority?"

I said slowly, "What does that mean?"

"That means," said Duke, "that if the mission is military, *everyone* is a soldier. We can't afford to watch out for deadheads. I need a backup man. You want to study worms, learn how to operate a flamethrower."

"That's what you mean by 'special duties,' huh?"

He said calmly, "That's right. You know I can't order you, McCarthy. Any operation requiring a risk to life has to be entirely voluntary.

And not the old-fashioned 'I'll take you, you, and you' kind of volunteering either." Duke put down his coffee cup. "But I'll make it easy on you. You have till tomorrow to choose. When you do, go see Shorty. Otherwise, you're shipping out on Thursday's chopper. Got that?"

I didn't answer.

"Did you get it?"

"I got it!" I snapped.

"Good." Duke stood up. "You already know what you're going to choose, Jim—there's no question about that. So quit obsessing over it and get on with the job. We don't have the time."

He was right, and I knew it, but it wasn't fair, his pressuring me.

He caught the meaning of my silence and shook his head. "Get off it, Jim. You're never going to be any readier than you are now."

"But I'm *not* ready at all!"

"That's what I meant. If you were, we wouldn't need to have this conversation. So . . . what is it?"

I looked up at him.

"Yes . . . ?"

"Uh—I'm scared," I admitted. "What if I screw up?"

Duke grinned. "There's a very simple test to know if you've screwed up. If you have, you've been eaten. Everything else is success. Remember that."

He picked up his coffee cup to carry it back to the kitchen. "I'll tell Shorty to expect you. Wear clean underwear." Then he turned and left, leaving me staring after him.

FOUR

LEGALLY, I was already in the army.

Had been for three years. Sort of.

You were automatically enlisted when you showed up for your first session of Global Ethics, the only mandatory course in high school. You couldn't graduate without completing the course. And—you found this out only afterward—you hadn't completed the course until you'd earned your honorable discharge. It was all part of the Universal Service Obligation. Rah.

The instructor was somebody named Whitlaw. Nobody knew much about him. It was his first semester here. We'd heard some rumors though—that he'd once punched a kid for mouthing off and broken his jaw. That he couldn't be fired. That he'd seen active duty in Pakistan—and still had the ears of the men and women he'd killed. That he was still involved in some super-secret operation and this teaching job was just a cover. And so on.

The first time I saw him, I believed it all.

He stumped into the room and slammed his clipboard down onto the desk and confronted us. "All right! I don't want to be here any more than you do! But this is a required course—for *all* of us—so let's make the best of a bad situation!"

He was a squat bear of a man, gruff-looking and impatient. He had startling white hair and gun-metal gray eyes that could drill you like a laser. His nose was thick; it looked like it had been broken a few times. He looked like a tank, and when he moved, he moved with a peculiar rolling gait. He rocked from step to step, but he was surprisingly graceful.

He stood there at the front of the classroom like an undetonated bomb and looked us over with obvious distaste. He glowered at us—an expression we were soon to recognize as an all-purpose glower of intimidation, directed not at any of us individually, but at the class as a unit.

"My name is Whitlaw!" he barked. "And I am not a nice man!"

Huh—?

"—So if you think you're going to pass this class by making friends with me, *forget it!*" He glared at us, as if daring us to glare back. "I don't want to be your friend. So don't waste your time. It's this simple: I have a job to do! It's going to get done. You have a job to do too. You can make it easy on yourself and own the responsibility—or you can fight it and, I promise you, this class will be worse than Hell! Understand?"

He strode to the back of the room then, plucked a comic book out of Joe Bangs's hands and ripped it up. He tossed the pieces in the trash can. "Those of you who think I'm kidding—let me disabuse you of that now. We can save ourselves two weeks of dancing around, testing each other, if you will just assume the worst. I am a dragon. I am a shark. I am a monster. I will chew you up and spit out your bones."

He was in motion constantly, gliding from one side of the room to the other, pointing, gesturing, stabbing the air with his hand as he talked. "For the next two semesters, you belong to me. This is *not* a pass-or-fail course. *Everybody* passes when I teach. Because I don't give you any choice in the matter. Most of you, when you're given a choice, you don't choose to win. That guarantees your failure. Well, guess what. In here, you don't have a choice. And the sooner you get that, the sooner you can get out." He stopped. He looked around the room at all of us. His eyes were hard and small. He said, "I am a very ugly man. I know it. I have no investment in proving otherwise. So don't expect me to be anything else. If there's any adapting to be done in this classroom, I expect *you* to do it! Any questions?"

"Uh, yeah—" One of the clowns in the back of the room. "How do I get out?"

"You don't. Any other questions?"

There were none. Most of us were too stunned.

"Good." Whitlaw returned to the front of the room. "I expect a hundred percent attendance, one hundred percent of the time. There are no excuses. This class is about results. Most of you use your circumstances as reasons to not have results." He looked into our eyes as if he were looking into our souls. "That's over, starting now! From now on, your circumstances are merely the things you have to handle so you can have results."

One of the girls raised her hand. "What if we get sick?"

"Are you planning to?"

"No."

"Then you don't have to worry about it."

Another girl. "What if we—"

"Stop!" Whitlaw held up a hand. "Do you see? You're already trying to negotiate a loophole for yourselves. It's called, 'What if—?' 'What if I get sick?' The answer is, make sure you *don't*. 'What if my car breaks down?' Make sure it doesn't—or make sure you have alternate transportation. Forget the loopholes. There aren't any! The universe doesn't give second chances. Neither do I. Just be here. You don't have a choice. That's how this class works. Assume that I'm holding a gun to your head. Because I am—you don't know what kind of a gun it is yet, but the fact is, I *am* holding a gun to your head. Either you're here and on time, or I pull the trigger and splatter your worthless brains on the back wall." He pointed. Somebody shuddered. I actually turned to look. I could imagine a red and gray splash of gore across the paneling.

"Do you get that?" He took our silence as assent. "Good. We might just get along."

Whitlaw leaned back casually against the front edge of his desk. He folded his arms across his chest and looked out over the room.

He smiled. The effect was terrifying.

"So now," he said calmly, "I'm going to tell you about the one choice you do have. The *only* choice. All the rest are illusions—or, at best, reflections of this one. You ready? All right—here's the options: you can be free, or you can be cattle. That's it."

He waited for our reactions. There were a lot of puzzled expressions in the room.

"You're waiting for the rest of it, aren't you? You think there has to be more. Well, there isn't any rest of it. That's all there is. What you think of as the rest is just definitions—or applications. That's what we're going to spend the rest of this course talking about. Sounds easy, right? But it won't be—because you'll insist on making it hard; because this course is not just about the definitions of that choice—it's about the *experience* of it. Most of you aren't going to like it. Too bad. But this

isn't about what you like. What you like or don't like is not a valid basis
for choice in the world. You're going to learn that in here."

That's how he started out.

It went downhill from there—or uphill, depending on your perspective.

Whitlaw never entered the room until everybody was seated and settled. He said it was our responsibility to run the class—after all, he already knew the material; this class was for us.

He always began the same way. When he judged we were ready, he entered—and he always entered speaking: "All right, who wants to start? Who wants to define freedom?" And we were off—

One of the girls offered, "It's the right to do what you want, isn't it?"

"Too simple," he countered. "I want to rip off all your clothes and have mad passionate intercourse with you, right here on the floor." He said it deadpan, staring her right in the face. The girl gasped; the class laughed embarrassedly; she blushed. "What keeps me from doing it?" Whitlaw asked. "Anyone?"

"The law," someone called. "You'd be arrested." More laughter.

"Then I'm not completely free, am I?"

"Uh, well . . . freedom is the right to do whatever you want as long as you don't infringe on the rights of others."

"Sounds good to me—but how do I determine what those rights are? I want to practice building atomic bombs in my back yard. Why can't I?"

"You'd be endangering others."

"Who says?"

"Well, if I were your neighbor, I wouldn't like it."

"Why are you so touchy? I haven't had one go off yet."

"But there's always the chance. We have to protect ourselves."

"Aha!" said Whitlaw, pushing back his white hair and advancing on the unfortunate student. "But now *you're* infringing on *my* rights when you say I can't build my own A-bombs."

"Sir, you're being ridiculous now. Everybody knows you can't build an A-bomb in your back yard."

"Oh? I don't know that. In fact, I *could* build one if I had access to the materials and enough time and money. The principles are well known. You're just betting that I don't have the determination to carry it through."

"Uh—all right. But even if you did, the rights of the individual still have to be weighed against the safety of the general public."

"How's that again? Are you telling me that one person's rights are more important than another's?"

"No, I—"

"Sure sounded like it to me. You said my rights have to be weighed against everyone else's. I want to know how you're going to determine them. Remember, all of us are supposed to be equal before the law. And what are you going to do if I don't think your method is fair? How are you going to enforce your decision?" Whitlaw eyed the boy carefully. "Try this one—it's more likely: I'm a plague victim. I want to get to a hospital for treatment, but if I even approach your city, you're going to start shooting at me. I claim that my right to medical care guarantees me entrance to that hospital, but you claim that your right to be free of contamination gives you license to kill. Whose rights are being infringed upon the most?"

"That's not a fair example!"

"Huh? Why not? It's happening in South Africa right now—and I don't care what the South African government says about it, we're talking about rights. Why isn't this a fair example? It's your definition. Sounds to me like there's something wrong with your definition of freedom." Whitlaw eyed the uncomfortable boy. "Hm?"

The boy shook his head. He gave up.

"So, let me give you a hint." Whitlaw turned to the rest of us again. "Freedom is *not* about what you *want.* That doesn't mean you can't have what you want—you probably can. But I want you to recognize that going for the goodies is just going for the goodies, nothing else. It has very little to do with freedom." He sat down on the edge of the desk again and looked around. "Anyone have another?"

Silence. Embarrassed silence.

Then, a voice: "Responsibility."

"Eh? Who said that?"

"I did." A Chinese boy in the back of the room.

"Who's that? Stand up there. Let the rest of the class see what a genius looks like. What's your name, son?"

"Chen. Louis Chen."

"All right, Louis. Repeat your definition of freedom for the rest of these louts."

"Freedom means being responsible for your own actions."

"Right. You have your A for the day. You can relax—no, you can't; tell me what it means."

"It means you can build your A-bombs, sir, but if you aren't taking proper precautions, then the government, acting on behalf of the people, has the right to take action to guarantee that you do, or shut you down if you don't."

"Yes—and no. Now we have something else to define. *Rights.* Sit down, Louis. Give someone else a turn. Let's see some hands."

Another boy in the back. " 'Rights: that which is due a party by just claim, legal guarantee, or moral principle.' "

"Hm," said Whitlaw. "You surprise me—that's correct. Now close the book and tell me what it *means.* In your own words."

"Uh . . ." The fellow faltered. "That which is rightfully yours. The right of . . . the right to . . . I mean, it's what you're entitled to. . . ." He became flustered and trailed off.

Whitlaw looked at him with a jaundiced expression. "First of all, you can't use a concept to define itself. And secondly, nothing is *rightfully* anyone's. We've already covered that one, remember? There's no such thing as ownership; there's only *control.* Ownership is just a temporary illusion, so how can there be any such thing as rights? You might as well insist that the universe owes you a living." Whitlaw grinned abruptly. "As a matter of fact, it does—but it's a lifetime job to collect."

He resumed his machine-gun attack. "Look, I'm going to make this easy for you. All that stuff that we call rights—that's just a lot of stuff that politicians say because it sounds good, so people will vote for them. They're actually ripping you off because they're confusing the issue, putting a lot of stuff in the way between you and the source of it all. So I want you to forget for a moment all of that stuff that you believe about rights. Because the truth is, it doesn't work. In fact, you can even forget about rights in the plural sense. There's only one right—and it isn't even a right in the traditional meaning of the word at all."

He was in the center of the room. He turned slowly around, meeting the eyes of all of us as he spoke. "The *defining* condition of adulthood is responsibility. So what's the one thing you need to experience that responsibility? It's so simple you won't get it—it's the *opportunity.*" He paused a moment to let it sink in, then repeated, "The *opportunity* to be responsible for your*self.* That's it. If you're denied that one, then you're not free, and all of the other so-called rights are redundant. Rights are opportunities—that's the definition. And opportunity demands responsibility."

A hand went up. "What about people who can't take care of themselves?"

"You're talking about the insane and the immature. That's why we have keepers and parents—to watch out for them, to clean up their messes and paddle their behinds and teach them not to make any more messes—and not turn them loose upon the world *until* they learn. Part of the responsibility of adulthood is seeing that others *also* have the opportunity to reach adulthood and be responsible for themselves too. Mentally as well as physically."

"But that's the government's job—"

"*What?* Somebody call the asylum—one of the lunatics is loose. Surely you don't mean that, son."

The boy looked stubborn. "Yes, I do."

"Mm, okay," said Whitlaw. "Justify yourself."

"It's the government's responsibility," he said. "By your definition."

"Eh? No, I said it's the people's responsibility."

"The government *is* the people."

"It is? Not the last time I looked—according to the book, the government is the *representative* of the people."

"That's not fair, sir—you wrote the book."

"I did?" Whitlaw looked at the text in his hand. "Hm, so I did. All right, point for your side. You caught me begging the question."

The boy looked smug.

"—But you're still wrong. No, you're only half wrong. The purpose of a government—the *only* justifiable reason for its existence—is to act on behalf of the member population in a delegated area of specific responsibility. Now, what's a 'delegated area of specific responsibility'?" Whitlaw didn't wait for someone to guess at it—he bulldozed on. "It works out to be anything that enough people are committed to— *whether it's right or wrong.* Get this! A government, acting on behalf of the member population—*and in their name*—will do *whatever* it is delegated to do, regardless of any defined morality in the matter. If you want proof, read a good history book." He plucked one off his desk. "A good history book is one that tells you what happened. Period. Forget the ones that explain history to you—they're ripping you off of the opportunity to see the *whole* picture."

He sat down on the edge of his desk again. "Listen, the government does what *you* want it to. If you say that you don't make a difference, you're guaranteeing that you won't. The fact of the matter is that anyone who is committed enough to enroll other people into the same commitment *will* make a difference. I want you to know that it does *not* take a majority. Some of the games that specific segments of this nation's population have enrolled the rest of us into include an extensive military organization, a space exploration agency, an interstate highway system, a postal service, a pollution control agency, an economic management bureau, a national education standard, a medical insurance service, a national pension plan, a labor management bureau and even a vast and complicated system of taxation so that each of us can pay for his or her fair share of those services—whether we wanted them or not in the first place." Whitlaw stabbed at us with one long bony finger, making his points in the air like a shrike impaling its prey on a thornbush. "So the conclusion is inescapable. *You* are responsible for the actions of your government. It acts in your name. It is your *employee.* If you don't properly supervise the actions of your employee, you're not *owning* your responsibility. You'll deserve what you get. Do you know why the government is in the shape it is today? Because you aren't doing your job. After all, who *else's* responsibility *could* it be? I mean, can you imagine anyone in his right mind *deliberately* designing such a system? No—no one in his right mind would! The system is continually falling into the hands of those who are willing to manipulate it for short-term gain—because *we* let them."

Someone raised his hand. Whitlaw waved it down. "No, not now." He grinned. "I'm not through 'brainwashing' you. I know that's what some of you think this is—I've seen the editorials in the newspapers too, the ones calling for the end of 'political indoctrination classes.' Let me just say this about that: you'll notice I'm not telling you what you *should* be doing. Because I don't know what that is. It's *your* responsibility to determine it for yourselves—you get to create your own form of participation. Because that's the only real choice you ever get in your whole life—whether or not you're going to participate. You might want to notice that *not* participating is also a decision—it's a decision to be a victim of the consequences. Refuse to handle your own responsibilities and you will get the consequences. *Every time!* You can count on it.

"So here's the punch line—pay attention. 'Let George do it' is not just the slogan of a lazy man—it's the credo of the slave. If you want to be taken care of and not have to worry, that's fine; you can join the rest of the cattle. Cattle are *comfortable*—that's how you recognize them. Just don't complain when they ship you off to the packing plant. They've bought and paid for the privilege. You sold it to them. Now if you want to be free, then get this: freedom is *not* about being comfortable. It's about seizing and using opportunities—and using them *responsibly.* Freedom is not comfort. It's *commitment.* Commitment is the willingness to be *un* comfortable. The two aren't incompatible, but there are damn few free men on welfare.

"The free man, class, doesn't just *survive*—he *challenges!*"

Whitlaw was right, of course. He usually was. If he'd ever been wrong, none of us had ever caught him at it. And after a while, we'd gotten pretty good.

I knew what he would say. The choice was mine. Even if I could have asked him for advice, he would have only said, "I can't answer that question for you, son. You already know the answer. You're just looking for agreement."

Right.

I couldn't depend on the good will of the universe any more. Five big plagues and a score of little ones had seen to that.

My coffee had gone cold.

So I went looking for Shorty.

FIVE

SHORTY TOWERED over me like a wall.

"Here," he said and thrust a flamethrower into my arms. "Don't flinch," he grinned. "There's nothing to be afraid of. It's not charged."

"Oh," I said, not at all reassured. I tried to figure out how to hold it.

"Watch it," he warned. "That'd be a good way to burn off your— here, hold it like this. One hand on the flame control there, the other on the stock—see that handle? That's right. Now, hold still while I fix your straps. We'll work without the tanks until you get the feel of it. You know, you're lucky—"

"Oh?"

"That torch is a Remington. Almost new. Designed for the war in Pakistan, but never used. Didn't need to—but it's perfect for us now because it'll take anything that burns and flows. See, the trick is this: you can shoot a stream of pure fuel alone—jellied gasoline is best—or you can shoot a barrage of exploding pellets, soaked in the fuel. Or you can shoot both at once. The pellets are pressure-loaded in this chamber here. Because they're pellets, you have a greater range, and because they explode on impact, you get a larger splash. The effect is terrific— don't point that at the ground, or you'll take off."

"Uh, Shorty . . ."

"Something wrong?"

"Napalm was outlawed almost ten years before the Pakistan conflict. What was the government doing with flamethrowers?"

He let go of the straps he was adjusting. "You're gonna need shoulder pads." He turned away. I thought he wasn't going to answer the question, but as he came back from the Jeep, carrying the pads, he said, "Same thing they were doing with A-bombs, nerve bombs, bacteriological weapons, hallucinogenic gases, nerve gases and poison vectors. Stockpiling them." He stopped my next question before I could ask it. "I know, they're illegal. That's why we had to have them—because the other side had them too. Letting them know was the guarantee. That's why the treaty worked."

"But—I thought the purpose of the whole thing was to outlaw inhumane weapons."

"Nope. Just to keep 'em from bein' used. There's always a difference between what you say and what you really want. If you're sharp enough to know what you really want, then it's easy to figure out what to say to get it. That's what that whole conference was about." He paused sourly. "I oughta know. I was there."

"Huh?"

Shorty looked like he wanted to say something, but he stopped himself. "Never mind. Some other time. Let me ask you this: what is it that makes a weapon inhumane?"

"Uh . . ." I thought about it.

"Let me make it easier for you. Tell me a *humane* weapon."

"Um—I see your point."

"Right. There's no such thing. It's like Christmas—it's not the gift, it's the thought that counts." He came around behind me and started fitting the pads under the straps. "A weapon, Jim—never forget this, lift your arms—is a tool for stopping the other fellow. That's the purpose—*stopping* him. The so-called humane weapons merely stop a man without permanently injuring him. The best weapons—you can put your arms down now—are the ones that work by implication, by threat, and never have to be used at all. The enemy stops himself.

"It's when they don't stop"—he turned me around to adjust the fittings in front—"that the weapons become inhumane, because that's when you have to use them. And so far, the most effective ones are the ones that kill—because they stop the guy permanently." He had to drop to his knees to cinch the waist strap. "Although . . . there's a lot to be said for maiming—"

"Huh?" I couldn't see his eyes, so I didn't know if he was joking or not.

"—but that's asking too much of both the weapon and its user." He straightened again and rapped the buckle in the center of my chest.

"Okay, that's the quick-release latch. Flip that up and the whole thing falls apart. That's in case you have a sudden need to run like hell. And if you do, you'd better. Five seconds after you drop that, it blows itself to bits. All right, I'm gonna hang the tanks on you now."

"You were going to say something about the Moscow Treaties before, weren't you?" I prompted.

"Nope." He headed for the Jeep.

I flexed my arms. The harness was stiff, but it wasn't uncomfortable. I guess Shorty knew what he was doing.

He came back with the tanks. They sloshed lightly. "They're only half full. I don't want you starting any forest fires. Turn around."

As he hung the tanks on my shoulders, he said, "You want to know about the treaties? They were dishonorable. To make false rules about 'I won't use this if you won't use that' may seem civilized because it lessens the brutality—but it isn't. It just makes the brutality tolerable for a longer time. And that's not civilized at all. If we're in a situation where we have to stop the other fellow, then let's just *stop* him. It's more efficient. There, how does that feel?"

I tested my balance. "Uh, fine—"

He scowled. "No, it isn't. You're off balance. They're too low. Hold still." He lifted the tanks off my back and began readjusting the straps of the harness. "This torch—" he said, "—this torch is a truly beautiful weapon. It has a maximum range of sixty meters. Eighty with a supercharger. It makes you a totally independent fighting unit. You carry your own fuel, you choose your own targets, point and squeeze. *Vrr-o-oomm!* It'll stop a man instantly—or a worm. It'll stop a tank. It'll burn out a pillbox. There isn't anything that can resist a torch—except very thick armor or a lot of distance. It is not"—he gave a hard yank—"humane. You pull that trigger and that's not a man in front of you anymore; it's a private piece of hell. You can watch him turn black and shrivel as his blood boils out of his skin. You can feel his flesh roasting. Sometimes you can even hear the scream of the air exploding out of his lungs." He gave another sharp pull at the straps. "And that's good, Jim, that's very good. You *should* be right down there next to what you're doing. If you're going to be a killer, you should do it personally, so you *experience* what you're doing. That's the civilized way." He poked me. "That torch is *not* humane, but it is civilized."

My mouth was very dry. I managed to say, "Civilized—?"

"It stops them, doesn't it? Hold still, here come the tanks again. A weapon should let you sleep well at night. If it doesn't, there's something wrong with the war."

He caught me unprepared. I almost staggered. I stiffened against the weight. But he was right. The balance was better this way.

He must have seen the look on my face. "Jim—war isn't polite. Especially not this one. We don't have the time to be fair. That torch will burn a Chtorran like fluff, and that's all that matters—you don't get a second chance with worms. They come at you at a good sixty-five kilometers an hour—two hundred and twenty-five kilograms of angry worm. And they're all teeth at the business end. If it's purple, burn it. That's a standing order. You don't have to wait for permission."

"I won't."

He locked eyes with me and nodded sharply; his expression was hard. "There's one more thing. Don't ever balk because you might hit a man. Don't hesitate because you think you might be able to save him—you can't. Once a Chtorran starts eating, there's no way to stop it. It *can't* stop. Not even if it wanted to. Burn them both, Jim. And burn them fast. He'd thank you for it if he could." He studied my face. "Can you remember that?"

"I'll try."

"It's like that little girl. It's the kindest thing you can do."

I nodded and shouldered the flamethrower. I didn't like it—I probably never would. Too bad. "Okay," my mouth was saying. "Show me how to work it."

SIX

RECONNAISSANCE CONFIRMED that there were only three worms in the valley, as Duke had guessed, but also that they were very busy with something. When Larry reported that, Duke frowned. He didn't like worms being so active—that made them hungry.

Dr. Obama ordered satellite pictures and the USAF ROCKY MOUNTAIN EYEBALL sent us a full-spectrum series, a twelve-hour surveillance of the valley and surrounding regions. The frames started arriving within an hour of Dr. Obama's request.

We all studied them, particularly the infra-red ones, but they told us little we didn't already know.

"Look here," said Larry, "the igloo." It was a bright red blotch; the frame was pseudo-color enhanced to show heat sources. "Something very hot in there. They must be large."

"And very active," grunted Duke. "That's almost too much heat." He poked Shorty. "What do you think? How much mass are we looking at?"

Shorty shrugged. "Hard to say. Three tons at least. Probably more. The resolution on the infra-red is lousy. The wavelength's too long."

"Yeah," said Duke. "I guess that settles it. We'll take three teams."

We left just before dawn. Chtorrans don't like direct sunlight, so we figured to drive all morning and catch them in the hottest part of the day, when they were most likely to be torpid. We hoped.

There were twelve of us. Four men with torches, three with grenades and two with rocket launchers. And the three Jeep drivers would be carrying laser-sighted AM-280s. The 280 was recoilless and could fire twenty-three hundred rounds per minute. A mere touch on the trigger would put fifty rounds inside a seven-centimeter circle—whatever the target beam touched. You could shoot from the hip and aim it like a flashlight. The 280 could chew holes in a brick wall—it was the high volume of fire that did it. If any gun could stop a Chtorran, it would have to be the 280.

I'd heard only a single complaint about the guns—from Shorty, of course. Denver had sent up some specially loaded magazines for them. Every hundredth round was a needle dart packed with a variety of particularly nasty germs. The reasoning was that if we failed to kill the Chtorrans right away, the bugs might get them later. Shorty had snorted contemptuously. "It's in case we don't come back. That's how much faith they have in us." He looked at me. "Listen, boy—that's not the way we do it here. We plan on coming back. Got that?"

"Uh . . . yes, sir."

The Remington hadn't been that hard to master. I'd spent the first couple of days starting forest fires—clearing brush and widening the scorched area around the camp; then had switched to target practice— trying to burn an asbestoid-and-wire framework dragged behind a Jeep.

"Now, be careful," Shorty had warned. "If you fire too soon, the Chtorran will veer off—but you won't be able to see that until the smoke clears. By then it's too late. Wait as long as you can before firing."

"Until I see the whites of his eyes, huh?"

Shorty grinned as he got back into the Jeep. "Sonny, if you get close enough to a worm to see the whites of his eyes—you're lunch." He drove off and began his run.

I missed, of course. I waited too long and nearly got knocked down by the cage.

Shorty braked to a stop, stood up in the Jeep and rang a big triangular dinner bell. "Come and get it, Chtorrans! Dinner is served! Nice fresh human—not dangerous at all! Come and get it!"

I waited till he was through. "I assume that means I was too slow."

"Too slow—? Of course not. You just move too long in the same place."

We tried again. This time he drove straight at me. The Jeep bounced across the field, the asbestoid worm in hot pursuit but never quite catching up. I planted my feet solidly and counted slowly. Not too soon, now—

I missed again.

This time Shorty got out of the Jeep and strode back to the target. He pulled a fifty-casey note out of his pocket and stapled it to the cage. "There," he said. "I'm betting fifty C's that you can't hit it." He started back to the Jeep. "You know, you really ought to learn how to run faster. Make the worms earn their lunch. We don't want any fat Chtorrans on this planet, do we?"

"We don't want any at all," I said.

"That's the idea," he grinned. "I thought you forgot. Want to try it again?"

"Yeah. This time I'll get it."

He hooked a thumb at the target. "I've got fifty caseys says you won't —prove me wrong." He gunned the engine and jolted off.

While he circled, I tried to figure out what I was doing wrong. Obviously I was waiting too long to fire—but Shorty had said not to fire too soon or the Chtorran would have time to veer off.

On the other hand, if I held off too long I might not get the chance to fire at all.

Hmm. The best time to shoot had to be at just that moment when it was too late for the Chtorran to change course. But when was that? How close did a Chtorran get before the bloodlust took over? Fifty meters? Twenty-five? Hmm, think of a stampeding elephant. Call it fifteen meters. . . .

Hey, wait a minute—! This torch had a range of almost seventy. What was Shorty trying to pull? I could burn worms long before they got close enough to chomp me!

I waved at him and tried to attract his attention, but he only grinned and waved back. He started heading toward me. Fast. He was beginning another run.

Well, I'd show him. I reset the range of the flamer to maximum. This time I'd fire as soon as the target got close enough. I wouldn't wait one second longer than necessary.

I focused on the wire-mesh worm, estimated its range, waited till it bounced across an invisible line and squeezed the release. The flame whooshed out with a roar, startling me with its intensity. The asbestoid worm disappeared in a ball of orange fire. Oily black smoke rose from it.

Shorty leapt from the jeep, howling. I cut off the torch hastily. But he wasn't mad at all about his fifty caseys—not even angry about his singed eyebrows. He just ran over and pulled the plug on my battery pack.

"Now you're thinking like a worm-burner," he said. "Fire as soon as they get within range."

I glowered at him. "Why didn't you tell me that in the first place?"

"What—? And let you miss the excitement of learning how to out-think a Chtorran? That's what the lesson was all about."

"Oh," I said. Then, "Can we try it again?"

"Uh, I think not." He was feeling the damage to his eyebrows. "At least not until I get a longer towline for that target."

We never did get the longer towline, what with preparations for the big burn and all, but it worked out all right anyway. A couple more days of shooting at the target—Shorty wore his asbestoid pajamas—and I was ready for the real thing. At least Shorty and Duke were willing to take the chance. I wasn't as sure. I'd heard that worms could be as long as four meters and weigh as much as nine hundred kilos. Or more. Maybe those were exaggerations—I'd find out for myself soon enough —but I'd been brought up to worry.

It's a family tradition. Good worrying is never wasted.

Well, I'd certainly done enough this time—and just in case I hadn't, I was doing a little extra in the Jeep. Just to be on the safe side.

Duke noticed it, of course. We were both in the second car. "Relax, Jim. It's not white-knuckle time yet."

"Sorry," I said, trying to grin.

"We won't be there for hours." He leaned back against the seat and stretched his arms. "Enjoy the morning. Look at the scenery."

"Uh, shouldn't we be on the lookout for worms?"

"We are."

"Huh?"

"Shorty's in the first Jeep. Louis and Larry are in the last one. You don't know what to look for—that's why you're in the second. And I have more important things to think about." He folded his arms behind his head and appeared to go to sleep.

"Oh," I said.

I was beginning to get it. In this man's army, you don't worry unless you're ordered to—and if I want you to have an opinion, I'll give you one.

In other words, this was not the army I had thought I was joining— the Teamwork Army. That was dead and gone. I don't know why I hadn't realized. This was something else altogether.

SEVEN

WHITLAW TALKED about the army once.

One of the girls—one of the older ones; her name was Patricia—had been complaining about how her draft board had rejected her choice of "needed skill." (Well, Creative Anarchist had been pretty far out. I couldn't blame them.) "I might as well join the army and be a whore," she said.

"Mmm," said Whitlaw. "With an attitude like that, you probably wouldn't be a very good one."

The class laughed, but she looked miffed. Insulted, even. "What do you mean by that?"

"I mean, you might not be acceptable to them. Morale is very important in the army these days."

"Morale—?" The girl seemed astonished. "They're only a bunch of sweat-pushers—! What about *my* morale? I'm a political scientist!"

"Not in here, you're not." Whitlaw sat down on the edge of his desk, folded his arms and grinned. "And, obviously, not to your draft board either. Maybe a little honest sweat is exactly what you need to appreciate its value."

She sniffed proudly. "But my work with my brain is much more valuable than their work with their bodies."

"Wrong," said Whitlaw. "Your work is valuable only when it's needed. And *you're* only valuable when your particular skill is scarce. It takes time to train a biological engineer or a quantum mechanic or even a competent AI hacker—but if we had a hundred thousand of them, how much do you think a single one would be worth?"

She didn't answer.

"The only reason we haven't trained that many is that we don't need them. If we did, our society could produce them in two to four years. We've proven that time and again. Your grandfathers proved it when they needed computer programmers and engineers and aerospace technicians and a thousand other specialties to put the first man on the moon—and most of those specialties had to be invented as the needs arose. By the end of the decade, it seemed as if they were as plentiful as sweat-pushers; in fact, some of them actually *had* to start pushing sweat to survive when the space program was cut back."

"But that was . . . just economics," she insisted. "It's the education that makes a person valuable, isn't it?"

"Is it?" Whitlaw looked at her blandly. "How do you define value? Can you fell a tree? Or milk a cow? Do you know how to operate a bulldozer? Can you lay bricks?"

"Of course not—"

"Then by some standards, you're not valuable at all. You're not a survivor type."

"But—that's manual labor! Anybody can do that."

Whitlaw blinked. "But *you* can't?"

She looked surprised. "Why should I have to?"

Whitlaw stopped. He eyed her curiously. "Haven't you read any of the assignments?"

"Of course I have, but I'm talking about the *real* world now."

Whitlaw stopped in mid-turn toward his podium. He looked back at her, a startled expression on his face. "I beg your pardon."

The class groaned—*uh oh*—we knew what was coming.

He waited until her mouth ran out of momentum. "Let me explain something to you. In the whole history of the human race, in all the time since we first climbed down out of the trees and stopped being monkeys and started learning how to be people, in all those years, we have managed to maintain what passes for modern civilization for only a very short period. I mark the beginning of modern times with the first industrialization of electricity. That makes the—ah, you should pardon the expression—*current* era less than two centuries long. That's not a long enough test. So it still isn't proven that civilization isn't a fad. I'm betting on history—it's got the track record. Do you understand what I'm trying to tell you? What you think of as the *real* world is actually a very *unreal* world, an artificial environment that has come into existence only by the determination of a lot of sweat-pushers looking for a way to make their lives easier, and by the good will of the universe—and the latter condition is subject to change without notice. That alone guarantees that this "—he lifted his hands wide to take in the room, the building, the city, the world—"is just a temporary condition. Certainly on a cosmic scale it is." He brushed his white hair back with one hand. There was fire in his voice as he added, "Listen, you're capable—that's not the question. You just refuse to acknowledge your own capability—and that's your problem. Did you know that in the Soviet Union today there are more women bricklayers than men? And it's been that way for at least fifty years. No, your only excuse is that you're not *trained* for it. And that's also the reason why you wouldn't be a good whore—you don't know how to be. But you could be, if you had the training. The fact is, you can be anything you choose if you have the training—and you would if it meant the difference between eating or starving."

"I'm sure I could," she said. "I could learn to milk a cow, if I had to—"

"I'm sure you could too. It'd only take a few minutes." He eyed her. "Or longer."

"—but then what?"

"Then you'd milk cows, of course!"

"But I don't want to milk cows!"

"Neither do I—but if the cow has to be milked, someone has to do it! That's what makes it a *needed* skill. Listen—" He turned to the rest of us now. "Too many of you sitting in this classroom have been separated from those very necessary skills for too many generations. It's given you some very peculiar ideas of your own importance. Let me relieve you of that foolishness right now—most of you have to depend on too many others for your survival, and that makes you vulnerable. It wouldn't be a bad idea to learn a few of those basic skills, because as far as the society you live in is concerned, it's the training that's valuable, not the individual.

"Right now, most of our laborers in the army take a lot of pride in what they're doing—believe it or not. So what does it matter that some of them were sixth-generation welfare recipients? They're not anymore! Now they're taxpayers, just like the rest of us. And the skills they learn in the army may be enough so that they'll never have to go back on welfare again. And at least *they* can see the physical fact of what they're accomplishing—most of *us* never do. I don't. I doubt you'll remember a tenth of what I tell you a year from now—and you don't know how frustrating that is for me to realize—but *they* can point to a new park or a reclaimed building and say, 'I did *that.*' And that's quite a feeling. I know! This country benefits from their labor, you and I benefit—and most of all *they* benefit, because their lives are enriched. They gain skills, they gain pride and they regain their self-respect, because they're doing a job that makes a difference!"

Whitlaw stopped and took a breath. I found myself wondering again about his limp, where he had gotten it. He covered it well. I hadn't noticed it until someone else pointed it out to me. He looked at the girl whose comment had sparked this discussion as if to say, "Do you get it?"

She made a mistake. A little one, but it was enough. She sniffed.

Whitlaw's expression froze. I'd never seen him looking so angry. He said quietly, "You know something? If you were a whore, you'd probably starve to death."

Nobody laughed. Nobody dared to.

Whitlaw leaned in close to her, his face only inches away from hers. In a stage whisper, he said, "You've been ripped off. You've been allowed to turn yourself into an egocentric, selfish, spoiled brat—a self-centered, empty-headed, painted little cock-tease. You think the sanctity of your genitals is important? You're *already* a whore and you don't even know it!"

"You can't talk to me that way—" She started to rise—

—but Whitlaw didn't back away. He leaned in even closer. There was no room for her to rise, and she fell back in her seat. "Listen, I've seen you. You shake your tits and simper and expect the football team to fight for the privilege of sitting next to you in the cafeteria. You pout at Daddy and he hands you his credit cards. Someday you'll make a deal to screw twice a week and some poor sucker will give you a house and a car and a gold ring to wear. If that isn't whoring, I don't know what is. The only difference between you and a licensed courtesan is that he or she gives honest service."

"Hold on there—!" One of the fellows in the back of the room stood up suddenly. He was red in the face. He looked ready to punch Whitlaw. I didn't know whether to be scared for him or Whitlaw.

"Sit down, son!"

"No! You can't badger her like that!"

"How would you like me to badger her? *Sit down!*" Whitlaw turned to the rest of us, not bothering to look and see if the fellow had followed instructions or not. "How many of you think I'm out of line here?"

Most of the class raised their hands. Some didn't. Not me. I didn't know what to think.

"So get this! I don't care what you think! I've got a job to do! And if that means hitting some of you broadside with a shovel, I'll do it—because it seems to be the only way to get your attention! Listen, dammit! I am not a babysitter! Maybe in some of your other classes they can pour the stuff over you like syrup and hope some of it will stick; but in this class, we do it *my* way—because my way produces *results!* This class comes under the authority of the Universal Service Act—and it's about growing up!" He poked the girl harshly. "You can go home and complain to your daddy if you want—I know who you are—and he can go and complain to the draft board. Mean old Mr. Whitlaw is picking on Daddy's little girl! They'll just laugh in his face. They hear three or four of those a week. And they love them—it proves I'm doing my job." He leaned in close to her again. "When things get uncomfortable, do you always run to Daddy? Are you going to spend the rest of your life looking for daddies to defend you against the mean old Mr. Whitlaws of the world? Listen, here's the bad news—you're going to be a grownup soon! You don't get to do that anymore!" He reached out and took her chin in his hand and pointed her face back toward him. "Look at me, Patricia—don't hide from it! There are tigers outside—and you are fat and plump and tender. My job is to toughen you up, so you have a chance against them. If I let you get away with this bullshit that you run on everybody else, I'd be ripping you off of the opportunity to learn that you don't need it. That you're bigger than all of that 'sweet little Daddy's girl' garbage. So leave it at the door from now on. You got that?"

She started to cry. Whitlaw pulled a tissue from his pocket and dropped it on the desk in front of her. "That racket won't work in here either." She glared at him, then took it and wiped at her eyes quickly. For the rest of the session she was very quiet and very thoughtful.

Whitlaw straightened and said to the rest of us, "That applies to the rest of you too. Listen, this is about *service.* Most of you are operating in the context that the obligation is some kind of *chore,* something to be avoided. Do you know you're cheating yourself? The opportunity here is for you to use the resources of the United States government to make a profound difference for yourselves and the people you share this planet with. And we'll be talking about specifics later in the course. You just need to get one thing—this isn't about you serving others as much as it's about you serving yourselves." He stumped to the back of the room and faced the entire class. We had to turn in our seats to see him. His face was flushed, his eyes were piercing.

"Listen," he said. "You know about the Millennium Treaties—the final act of the Apocalypse. I know what you've been taught so far. In order to guarantee world peace, the United States gave up its right to have an international military force. We lost a war—and this time, we had to take the responsibility for it. Never again would an American president have the tools of reckless adventurism at such casual disposal —it's too dangerous a risk. The Apocalypse proved that.

"So what we have instead is the Teamwork Army—and what that means to you is that your service obligation is no longer a commitment to war, but a commitment to peace. It's an opportunity to work not just here, but anywhere in the world, if you so choose, attacking the causes of war, not the symptoms."

Abruptly, Whitlaw stopped there. He shoved both his hands into his jacket pockets and returned to the front of the room. He stood there with his back to us, peering at his notes on the podium. He stood like that long enough for the classroom to become uncomfortable. Some of us traded nervous glances. Without looking up from his clipboard, Whitlaw said quietly, "Paul, you have a question?"

It was Paul Jastrow, in the back of the room. How had Whitlaw known that? "Yeah," said Paul, standing up. "I've been reading here"— he held up one of the texts—"our situation is like that of Germany at the end of World War One, right?"

Whitlaw turned around. "In what way?"

"Well, we're being punished for starting a war. So we're not allowed to have the kind of military that could be used for starting another war, right?"

Whitlaw nodded. "One thing—in our case, it isn't a punishment. It's a commitment."

"Yeah," said Paul. "I hear you—but the terms of it are the same, no matter what you call it. We don't have a real army—not one that carries guns." He looked angry.

"Only the domestic service, of course," Whitlaw noted. "But essentially, you're right. So what's the question?"

"I'm getting to it. It's this 'Teamwork Army'—" He said it with disdain. "It sounds an awful lot like what the Germans had after World War One. They had all these work camps and youth groups and they drilled with shovels instead of rifles and they did public works and all that kind of thing. And all that was really just a fake, because when the time came, these guys put down their shovels and picked up rifles and turned into a real army again. And we know how that turned out."

"Yeah," said Whitlaw. "So?"

"So—what about our so-called Teamwork Army? I mean, couldn't they be turned back into a military force?"

Whitlaw smiled. For some reason, it made him look dangerous. "Yep," he said, looking straight at Paul.

"Well—?" asked Paul.

"Well what?"

"Was that intentional?"

"I don't know." Whitlaw's tone was casual. Perhaps he really didn't know.

"Well, doesn't that mean the Teamwork Army's a fake?"

"Is it?" Whitlaw asked. "You tell me."

Paul looked uncertain. "I don't know," he said.

Whitlaw stood there for a moment, waiting. He looked at Paul, he glanced around the room at the rest of us, then looked back to Paul. "Is that an observation, Paul, or is there a question in there somewhere?"

"Uh, yeah. There's a question in there, but I don't know what it is. It's just—I don't get it."

"I see that. And thanks for being honest about it—that's good. So let me work with that for a second. Let's start with the facts about the Teamwork Army. These are men who are building things. People who build things tend to be very defensive about the things they build. It's called territoriality. It turns out they make very good soldiers. Yes, the possibility is there. The Teamwork Army could be converted to a regular military force in . . . oh, let me see, now—what did that report say?" He made a show of returning to his clipboard and calling up a specific page of notes. "Ah—twelve to sixteen weeks."

He paused. He let it sink in. He looked around the classroom, meeting the gaze of everyone who dared to look at him. I think we were horror-struck; I know I was. It wasn't the answer I wanted to hear. After a long, uncomfortable silence, Whitlaw said quietly, *"So what?"* He stepped out into the middle of the room again. "The question is not *why* is that possibility there—because there is *always* that possibility of military adventurism—the question is *what,* if anything, do we do about it?"

Nobody answered.

Whitlaw grinned at us. "That's what this course is about. *That responsibility.* Eventually it's going to be yours. So your assignment is to look at how you'd like to handle it. What would *you* do with the army? It's *your* tool. How do you want to use it? We'll talk about that tomorrow. Thank you, that'll be it for today." He returned to the podium, picked up his clipboard and left the room.

Huh—? We sat and looked at each other. Was that it?

Patricia looked unhappy. "I don't like it," she said. "And I still don't know what to do about my draft board."

Somebody poked her. "Don't worry about it," he said. "You'll think of something. You've got time."

But he was wrong.

She didn't have time—and neither did any of the rest of us. She was dead within six months. And so were most of the rest of my classmates.

EIGHT

WHEN THE plagues first appeared, the medical community assumed they were of natural origin, simple mutations of already familiar diseases. Hence the names: Black Peritonitis, African Measles, Botuloid Virus, Comatosis and Enzyme Reaction 42—that last one was particularly vicious. They were so virulent and they spread so fast that it wasn't until afterward that all of them were identified.

I remember Dad frowning as he read the newspaper each night. "Idiots," he muttered. "I'm only surprised it didn't happen sooner. Of course you're going to get plague if you put that many people into a place like Calcutta."

Within a couple of weeks, the frown gave way to puzzlement. "Rome?" he said. "I thought the Italians were more careful than that."

When it hit New York, Dad said, " 'Nita, I think we should move up to the cabin for a few weeks. Jim, you'll come with us, of course."

"But, I've got school—"

"You can afford to miss it. I think I'll call your sister too."

At first, the doctors thought they were dealing with only one disease —but one with a dozen contradictory symptoms. They thought that it took different forms, like bubonic and pneumonic plague. Then they thought that it was so unstable it kept mutating. Everyone had a theory: the super-jumbos were the vectors; we should ground all air travel at once and isolate the disease. Or the bacterio-ecology had finally developed a widespread tolerance for our antibiotics; we shouldn't have used them so freely in the past. Or it was all those experiments with fourth-dimensional physics; they were changing the atmosphere and causing weird new mutations. Things like giant centipedes and purple caterpillars.

The first wave swept across the country in a week. A lot of it was carried by the refugees themselves as they fled the East Coast, but just as much was spread by seemingly impossible leapfrog jumps. Airplanes? Or something else? There was no direct air service at all to Klamath, California, yet that city died before Sacramento.

I remember one broadcast; this scientist—I don't remember his name —was claiming that it was biological warfare. He said there were two kinds of agents: the Y-agents for which there were vaccines and antitoxins, and the X-agents for which there were no defenses at all. Apparently, he said, some of these X-agents must have been released, either accidentally or perhaps by terrorists. There was no other way to explain this sudden outbreak of worldwide uncontrollable death.

That idea caught on real fast. It made sense. Within days the country was in an uproar. Screaming for revenge. If you couldn't kill the germ, at least you could strike back at the enemy responsible for releasing it.

Except—who was that? There was no way of knowing. Besides—and this was the horrible thought—what if the bugs were *ours?* There were just as many people willing to believe that too.

After that, things fell apart real fast. We heard some of it on the short wave radio. It wasn't pretty.

We were fairly well isolated where we were, even more so after somebody went down to the junction one night and set the bridge on fire. It was an old wooden one and it burned for hours, until it finally collapsed into the stream below. Most of us who lived on the hill knew about the shallow place two miles upstream. If necessary you could drive a vehicle across there, but Dad had figured that the burned-out bridge would stop most refugees from trying to come up the mountain. He was almost right. One of our neighbors down the hill radioed us once to warn of a caravan of three land-rovers heading our way, but not to worry. A while later we heard some shooting, then nothing. We never heard anything more about it.

After that, however, Dad kept a loaded rifle near the door, and he taught all of us how to use it—even the kids. He was very specific in his instructions. If we did shoot someone, we were to burn the bodies, *all* their belongings, their cars, their animals and everything they had touched. *No exceptions.*

We stayed on the mountain all summer. Dad phoned in his programs

until the phones stopped working; then he just kept working without
sending them in. I started to ask him once why he kept on, but Mother
stopped me. Later, she said to me, "Jim, it doesn't matter if there's ever
going to be anyone again who'll want to play one of his games—he's
doing them for himself. He has to believe—we all do—that there *will* be
a future."

That stopped me. I hadn't thought about the future—because I
hadn't comprehended the awesome scale of the pestilence. I had
stopped listening to the radio early on. I didn't want to know how bad it
was. I didn't want to hear about the dead dying faster than the living
could bury them—whole households going to bed healthy and all of
them dying before they awoke. I didn't want to hear about the bodies in
the streets, the panic, the looting, the burnings—there had been a firestorm in Los Angeles. Was anybody left alive?

We stayed on the mountain all winter too. It was rough, but we
managed. We had a windmill, so we had electricity—not a lot, but
enough. We had a solar roof and a Trombe wall, we wore sweaters and
we stayed warm. We'd used the summer to build a greenhouse, so we
had vegetables, and when Dad brought down the deer, I understood
why he had spent so much time practicing with the crossbow. We survived.

I asked him, "Did you know that something like this would happen?"

He looked up at me across the body of the deer. "Something like
what?"

"The plagues. The breakdown."

"Nope," he said, wiping his forehead. The insides of that animal were
hot. He bent back to his task. "Why do you ask?"

"Um, the crossbow, the cabin—and everything. Why this particular
mountain? I always thought you were a little bit . . . well, wobbly for
making such a thing about being self-sufficient. Now it seems like awfully good planning."

He stopped and laid down his knife. He wiped the blood off his
gloves. "It is impossible to work in weather like this." His breath was
frosty in the air. "And I can't get a grip through these gloves. No, I
didn't know—and yes, it was good planning. But it wasn't my idea. It
was your grandfather's. I wish you could have known him better. He
used to tell me that a man should be prepared to move suddenly at least
three times in his life. That is, if you're planning to live a long life. You
know why, of course. Pick any period of history, any place. It's hard to
find seventy years of unbroken peace and quiet. Somebody's tree is

always too crowded." He sighed. "When the screeching starts, it's time to go someplace quieter." He picked up the knife and went back to his evisceration of the buck. "Our family has a history of narrow escapes— wait a minute. Hold that—ah, there! One of your great-grandfathers left Nazi Germany in 1935. He kept heading west until he got to Dublin— that's why your name is McCarthy today. He forgot to marry your great-grandmother in a church."

"Oh," I said.

"Your grandfather bought this land in 1986. When land was still cheap. He put a prefab on it. Came up here every summer after that and built a little more. Never saw the sense of it myself until—let's see, it was before you were born—it would have had to have been the summer of '97. Right, we thought that was going to be the year of the Apocalypse."

"I know," I said. "We studied it in school."

He shook his head. "It's not the same, Jim. It was a terrifying time. The world was paralyzed, waiting to see if they would drop any more bombs. We were all sure that this was it—the big one. The panics were pretty bad, but we came through it all right, up here. We spent the whole year on this mountain—didn't come down till Christmas. The world was lucky that time. Anyway, that's what convinced me."

We began pulling the buck around and onto the sled. I said, "How long do you think we'll have to stay up here this time?"

"Dunno. Could be a while—maybe even a couple years. In the fourteenth century, the Black Death took its time about dying out. I don't expect these plagues to be any different."

I thought about that. "What do you think we'll find when we do go back?"

"Depends."

"On?"

"On how many people have . . . survived. And who." He looked at me speculatively. "I think you'd better start listening to the radio with me again."

"Yes, sir."

About a month after that, we caught a broadcast out of Denver, the provisional capital of the United States. Martial law was still in effect. The thirty-six surviving members of Congress had reconvened and postponed the presidential election for at least six months. And the second-generation vaccines were proving nearly sixty percent effective. Supplies were still limited though.

Dad and I looked at each other and we were both thinking the same thing. *The worst is over.*

Within a month, Denver was on the air twenty-four hours a day. Gradually, the government was putting its pieces back together. And a lot of information was finally coming to light.

The first of the plagues—they knew now there had been several—had appeared as isolated disturbances in the heart of Africa. Within a few weeks, it had spread to Asia and India and was beginning its westward sweep across the world. The second plague came so hard on its heels that it seemed like part of the same wave, but it had started somewhere in Brazil, I think, and swept north through Central America—so fast, in fact, that many cities succumbed before they even had a chance to identify it. By the time of the third plague, governments were toppling and almost every major city was in a state of martial law. Almost all travel worldwide was at a standstill. You could be shot for trying to get to a hospital. The fourth and fifth plagues hit us like tidal waves, decimating the survivors of the first three. There was a sixth plague too— but by then the population density was so low, it *couldn't* spread.

Some areas had been lucky and had remained completely unaffected, mostly isolated out-of-the-way places. A lot of ships just stayed at sea, particularly Navy vessels, once the admiralty recognized the need to preserve at least one military arm relatively intact. Then there were remote islands and mountaintop settlements, religious retreats, survival communities, our entire Nuclear Deterrent Brigade (wherever they were), the two lunar colonies, the L5 construction project (but they lost the ground base), the submarine communities of Atlantis and Nemo and quite a few places where someone had the foresight to go down and blow up the bridge.

But even after the vaccines were in mass production and the plagues had abated (somewhat), there were still problems. In fact, that was when the *real* problems began. In many parts of the world, there was no food, the distribution systems having broken down completely. And typhus and cholera attacked the weakened survivors. There was little hospital care available anywhere in the world; the hospitals had been the first institutions to go under. (Any doctor who had survived was automatically suspect of dereliction of duty.) Many large cities had become uninhabitable because of fires and mass breakdown of services. Moscow, for instance, was lost to a nuclear meltdown.

It was the end of the world—and it just kept on happening. So many people were dying of exposure, starvation, anomie, suicide, shock and a thousand other things that people didn't usually die of but which had suddenly become fatal, that it seemed we were caught up in a larger plague with no name at all—except its name was despair. The waves of it rolled around the world and kept on rolling and rolling and rolling. . . .

Before the plagues had broken out, there had been almost six billion human beings on the Earth. By the end of it, nobody knew how many were left. The United States government didn't even try to take the next national census. If anybody in authority had any idea how many people had survived, they weren't saying. It was almost as if they were afraid to make it real. But we heard on the short wave one night that there had to be at least a hundred million dead in this country alone. Whole cities had simply ceased to exist.

We couldn't comprehend that, but there were all those reports on the radio and pictures on the TV. Large areas of the countryside were returning to wilderness. There were ruins everywhere. Burned-out houses were commonplace—frightened neighbors had tried to halt the spread of the disease by burning the homes of the dying, sometimes not even waiting until the dying were dead. Everywhere there were abandoned cars, broken windows, faded billboards, uncut lawns and more than a few mummified corpses. "If you come upon one," said the voice from Denver, "exhale quickly, don't inhale, hold your breath, don't touch anything and back away—practice it till it becomes a reflex. Then place yourself in quarantine—there may be a chance for you, *maybe*— and call a decontamination squad. If you're in a place where there are no decontamination units, set a fire. And pray you've been fast enough."

We stayed up in the mountains through spring. And listened to the radio.

Denver reported that it looked like the plagues were beginning to die out. There were less than a thousand outbreaks a week worldwide, but people were still dying. There were famines now—there were crops that hadn't been planted—and mass suicides too. If the plague without a name had been despair before, then now it was madness. People slipped into and out of it so easily it was recognized as a fact of life—a complaint so common that no one was untouched, so universal it became transparent. Like air, we couldn't see it anymore, but nonetheless we were enveloped in it every moment of existence.

The news reported only the most shocking or disturbing cases, the ones too big to ignore. We listened, wondered and sometimes cried. But there was just too much hurt to handle. Most of it we buried. And some of it we didn't—we just avoided it the best we could. Somehow we managed not to care too much. Somehow we managed to survive.

I was afraid that we would never be able to come down from the mountain—but we did, eventually. In April, Dad and I took the station wagon and ventured slowly down the hill and across the stream. If anyone was watching us, we didn't see them. We paused once to wave a white flag, but there was no answering "Halloooh."

It was as if we'd been traveling to another star for a hundred years and had only just returned. We felt like alien explorers—we felt as if we didn't belong here anymore. Everything was both familiar and different. The world looked deserted and empty. And it was uncannily quiet. But there were burned-out buildings everywhere—scorched monuments to the dead. Each one was testimony—a body had been found here.

We had to wend our way carefully around abandoned vehicles and fallen trees. I began to get uneasy. We saw nothing for miles until we came to a pack of dogs trotting down the highway. They started barking when they saw us. They chased the car for almost a kilometer. My unease gave way to fear.

Later we saw cattle wandering free; they looked thin and sickly. We saw a dazed young woman walking up the road. We tried to stop her, warn her about the dogs, but she just kept on walking past us as if we weren't there. After that we saw a naked boy hiding in the trees, but he turned and ran when we called to him.

"Too soon?" I asked.

Dad shook his head. "Not soon enough. There's work to be done, Jim." And his face tightened in pain.

We stopped to fill our gas tank—there was an official-looking sign on the station, proclaiming that it had been nationalized for the duration of the emergency and whatever fuel and supplies still remained were freely available to all registered survivors.

"But aren't they afraid someone will steal it?"

"Why bother?" Dad said. "There's more than enough for everyone now."

I thought about that. The plagues had been fast. A thousand frightened people had scrambled aboard a super-jumbo in New York, and by the time the plane was over St. Louis, half of them were dead and the other half were dying. Only the flight crew, in their locked cabin, survived—but they were dead too, because there was no airport in the country that would let them land. And even if they could have landed, there was no way to get that flight crew out of the plane except through the passenger cabin. That happened three times. The one plane that did land was burned immediately as it rolled to a stop. The other two flight crews took the faster way out. After that *all* the airports were shut down.

Dad was saying, "It's all still here, Jim—almost everything. There wasn't time for a panic. That's how fast it happened." He shook his head sadly. "It's as if the human race has gone away and isn't coming back. There isn't any reason to steal anymore, no need to hoard—only to *preserve.*" He smiled sourly. "For the first time in the history of the human race, there's more than enough of everything for everybody. We've all been made suddenly wealthy." He sounded very sad.

Eventually, we came to a town. Two men with rifles met us at a roadblock. They were very polite about it, but we would not be allowed to pass until we had been cleared through decontamination. Their guns were very convincing.

It was an uncomfortable fifteen minutes. We stood by the car, our hands held away from our sides, until the decontamination team arrived. They pulled up in a white van with a large red cross on each side. We stripped naked and two helmeted figures in white safety-suits sprayed us with foam—our station wagon too, inside and out. I was glad it was a warm day. They took blood samples from each of us and disappeared back into their truck; they were gone for a long time. I began to shiver, even in the afternoon sun.

Finally the door opened and they came out again, still masked. Dad and I looked at each other worriedly. They came up to us, each one carrying a pressure injector. The shorter one grabbed my arm and held the nozzle against the skin. Something went *pssst* and my arm felt suddenly cold and wet. I flexed my fingers experimentally. "Relax, you'll be all right," she said, pulling off her hood—they were women! And they were grinning.

"They're clean!" shouted the gray-haired one; she turned to Dad. "Congratulations." Dad handled it with remarkable aplomb. He bowed.

I was already reaching for my jeans. The guards laid their guns aside and ran up to shake our hands. "Welcome to Redfield. Is either one of you a teacher? Or a sewage engineer? Do you know anything about fusion systems? We're trying to get the northwest power-net up again. Can you handle a stereo cam?"

I rubbed my arm; it was starting to sting. "Hey—what's this mark?"

"Coded tattoo," said the one who had vaccinated me. She was very pretty. "Proves you're clean—and immune. Stay away from anyone who doesn't have one. You might pick up spores and not know it."

"But we've got family!"

"How many? I'll give you extra vac-pacs to take with you—and coveralls. And foam! Oh, damn! I don't have enough! You'll have to stop at the med-station. Listen to me—you can't come in direct contact with your own people again until they've been vaccinated too. Even though *you're* immune, you can still carry spores—you could be very dangerous to anyone who isn't inoculated. Do you understand?"

I nodded. Dad looked worried, but he nodded too.

"Good."

We went first to the med-station, formerly a drugstore across the street from the two-story city hall. The teenager in charge gave us complete decontamination and vaccination kits, and very thorough instructions on how to use them. She gave us extra vac-pacs for our neighbors on the mountain too.

Then she sent us to the Reclamation Office to register. "First floor, city hall," she pointed. "It's not exactly mandatory," she said, "but it'll be better for you if you do."

I asked Dad about that as we crossed the street. He shook his head. "Later, Jim—right now, we play by the rules."

The "office" was a desk with a terminal on it. It asked you questions, you answered. When you were through, it spat out a registration card at you. Dad thought for a moment, then registered only himself and me. No mention of Mom or Maggie or the boys. "There'll be time enough later, if it's necessary," he said. "Let's see if we can pick up some supplies. I really miscalculated on the toilet paper."

That was the strangest shopping trip I'd ever been on. Money wasn't any good anymore. Neither was barter. There was a wizened little old man at the checkout counter of the mall, a few other people moving in and out of the shops. He was shaking his head in slow rhythmic beats, and he couldn't focus his eyes on anything for long. He told us that the mall was under the authority of the local Reclamation Office—Dad and I exchanged a look—and we were free to claim what we needed. "When you leave, stop by here and show me your card. I punch it in. That's all."

"But how do we pay for it?"

"If you're lucky, you won't have to." He giggled.

Dad pulled me away. "Come on, Jim. Get a cart. I think I understand."

"Well, I don't! It sounds like legalized looting!"

"Shh, keep your voice down. Now, think about it. What good is money if you can walk into any empty house or store and walk out with handfuls of it—or whatever else you find? A year ago, there were enough goods in this country for three hundred and fifty million Americans—not to mention goods produced for export. Look around, Jim— how many people are left? Do you want to take a guess at the percentage that survived? I don't—I don't want to scare myself. But it's fairly obvious, isn't it, that in circumstances like this even barter is unnecessary. These people here have worked out an answer to the immediate problem of survival. The goods are here. The people need them. We can worry about the bookkeeping later. If there is a later. For many of them there may not be—at least not without this kind of help. It all makes sense—sort of."

"But if they're giving things away, then why the registration cards?"

"To give a semblance of control, maybe. To give us the feeling there's still some authority in the world. You notice how industrious some of these people seem? Maybe it's to keep themselves going—because if they stop for even a moment and realize—" He caught himself. "Come on, get that cart."

We picked up toilet paper, a couple of radiophones, some cartons of canned goods and freeze-dried foods, a new first-aid kit, some vitamins, some candy for the kids, *a newspaper,* rifle shells and so on. The only things we couldn't afford were the fresh meats and vegetables. Those had to be paid for—in United Nations Federal Kilo-Calorie notes, caseys for short.

"Aha—yes. The nickel drops."

"What?"

"What's the only thing in short supply today, Jim?"

"People."

"Trained skills. That's what they're trading here. Ability. Labor. That's the new money-standard. Or it will be." He looked almost happy. "Jim"—he grabbed my shoulders abruptly—"it's over. These people are organizing for survival, for a future. There's work to do and they're doing it. They have hope." His grip was tight. "We can come down from the mountain now. We're *needed.* All of us. Your mom's a nurse. Maggie can teach. . . ." His eyes were suddenly wet. "We made it, Jimmy. We made it through to the other side!"

But he was wrong. We hadn't even seen the worst of it yet.

NINE

THE PLAGUES weren't over.

But this time we were better prepared. We had vaccines, and the lower population density and all the precautions still in effect from the first calamitous waves slowed the spread of the new plagues to a containable crawl.

The one that hit us was supposed to be one that you could recover from, although it might leave you blind or sterile—or permanently deranged. It had been around since the beginning—it just hadn't been noticed until the others were contained. Not controlled, just contained.

We lost the boys to it—Tim and Mark—and we almost lost Dad too. Afterward, he was a different man. He never fully recovered. Haggard and gray, he was almost a zombie. He didn't smile anymore. He'd lost a lot of weight and most of his hair, and suddenly he looked old. It was as if the mere act of surviving had taken all of his strength; he didn't have any left for living. A lot of people were like that.

And I don't think Maggie ever forgave him for the death of her sons. It had been his decision to bring us down from the mountain by July, but he couldn't have known. No one did. We all thought it was over.

The last time I saw him was when he left for San Francisco. They'd "drafted" him—well, not quite drafted, but the effect was the same. Someone was needed to manage the reorganization of the Western Region Data Banks, and Dad was one of the few free programmers left. Most of those who'd survived had already nested themselves into security positions; programmers were *valuable*—without them, the machines would stop. But Dad was still a free agent, and therefore subject to the control of the Labor Requisition Board. He'd been right to be cautious about registering. When we came down from the mountain, his orders were waiting for him. He appealed, but it was rejected. The national welfare came first.

I drove Dad down to the train station that last day. Mom couldn't get away from the clinic—she'd made her goodbyes the night before. Maggie wouldn't come. Dad looked very thin. He carried only a single small suitcase. He didn't say much while we waited for the train to arrive. We were the only ones on the platform.

"Dad? Are you all right? You know, if you're ill—"

He didn't look at me. "I'm all right," he snapped. And then he said it again in a quieter tone. "I'm all right." He still wasn't looking at me, he was still staring down the track, but he reached over and put his hand on my shoulder.

"Do you need to sit down?"

He shook his head. "I'm afraid I might not be able to get back up." He said, "I'm tired of this, Jim. I'm so tired. . . ."

"Dad, you don't have to go. You have rights. You can claim the shock of—"

"Yes, I do," he said. And the way he said it left no room for argument. He dropped his hand from my shoulder. "You know about the guilt, Jim—survivor's guilt? I can't help it. There were people who *deserved* to live. Why didn't I die instead?"

"You did what you had to!"

"Just the same," he spoke haltingly, "I feel . . . a responsibility now . . . to do something, to make amends. If not to the rest of the world, then to . . . the babies. Tim and Mark."

"Dad"—this time I put my hand on his shoulder—"listen to me."

He turned to me. "And I can't stand the look in her eyes anymore!"

"Maggie?"

"Your mother."

"She doesn't blame you!"

"No, I don't think she does. And she has every good reason to. But it's not the blame, Jim—it's the pity. I can't stand that." He faltered, then said, "Maybe it'll be better this way." He stooped to lower his suitcase to the ground. Very slowly, he put his hands on my shoulders and pulled me close for a last hug. He felt even thinner in my arms than he looked.

"Take care of them," he said. "And yourself."

He pulled back and looked at me, searching my face for one last sign of hope—and that was when I saw how old he had become. Thin and gray and old. I couldn't help it. I felt sorry for him too. He saw it. He had been looking for my love, and instead he saw my pity. I knew he could tell, because he smiled with a false heartiness that felt like a wall slamming into place. He clapped me on the shoulder and then turned quickly away.

The train took him south to San Francisco and we never saw him again.

It took the Bureau of Labor Management a lot longer to catch up to me, almost a year.

I had gone back to school. They had reorganized the State University system and you could get study credits for working on a campus reclamation team, saving and preserving the state of human knowledge as it existed before the plagues. It seemed in those first hectic months that everyone was an official of some kind or other. *I* even held a title or two. For a while, I was Western Regional Director of the Fantasy Programmers' Association—I only did it because the president of the organization insisted. She said I owed it to my father's memory as an author. I said, "That's hitting below the belt, Mom," but I took the job. My sole responsibility was to sit down with a lawyer and witness a stack of documents. We were claiming the copyrights of those authors who had not survived and for whom no surviving kin could be located. The organization was becoming the collective executor of a lost art form, because no one had the time for large-scale fantasy games anymore.

Halfway through the spring semester, I was drafted—really drafted, not labor-requisitioned.

The army was one of the few institutions that was structured to cope with massive losses of manpower without loss of structure; its skills were basic, widespread and nonspecialized. Therefore, it was the army that managed the process of survival. The army reestablished communications and maintained them. The army took charge of resources and utilities, protecting and allocating them until local governments were again able to assume the responsibilities of control. The army distributed food and clothing and medical aid. The army contained the plague districts until decontamination teams could be sent in—and as ugly as that latter task was, they handled it with as much compassion as was possible under the circumstances. It was the army that carried the country through the worst of it.

But that wasn't the army that I was drafted into.

Let me say this: I hadn't believed in Chtorrans any more than anybody else.

Nobody I knew had ever seen a Chtorran. No reputable authority had ever come forward with any proof more solid than a blurred photo, and the whole thing sounded like another Loch Ness monster or Bigfoot or Yeti. If anyone in the government knew anything, they weren't saying—only that the reports were "under investigation."

"Actually, the truth should be obvious," one of the coordinators—they didn't call them instructors if they didn't have a degree—at the university had said. "It's the technique of the 'big lie' all over again. By creating the threat of an enemy from outer space, we get to be territorial. We'll be so busy defending our turf, we won't have time to feel despair. That kind of thing is the perfect distraction with which to rebuild the morale of the country."

That was *his* theory. Everybody had an opinion—everybody always does.

And then my draft notice arrived. Almost two years late, but still just as binding. Congress had amended the draft act just for us survivors.

I appealed, of course. So they gave me a special classification. "Civilian Personnel, Attached." They were doing that a lot.

I was still in the army—

—and then Duke shot a little girl.

And I knew the Chtorrans were real.

The human race, what there was left of us, was at war with invaders from space. And I was one of the few people who knew it. The rest of them didn't believe it—and they wouldn't believe it until the day the Chtorrans moved into their towns and started eating.

Like Show Low, Arizona.

TEN

WE LEFT the Jeeps at an abandoned Texaco station and hiked across the hills—and that flamethrower was *heavy.* According to the specifications in the manual, fully loaded and charged, tanks and all, it should have weighed no more than 19.64 kilos—but somewhere along the way we lost the decimal point, and Duke wouldn't let me go back and look for it.

So I shut up and climbed.

Eventually—even with Tillie the Ten-Ton Torch on my back—we reached the valley where we had spotted the worms less than a week before. Duke's timing was just right; we arrived at the hottest part of the day, about two in the afternoon. The sweat had turned the inside of my clothing clammy, and the harness for the torch was already chafing.

The sun was a yellow glare in a glassy sky, but the valley seemed dark and still. The grass was brown and desiccated and there was a light piney haze hanging over the woods; it looked like smog, but there hadn't been any smog since the plagues. This grayish-blue haze was only natural hydrocarbons, a byproduct of the trees' own breathing. Just looking at it I could feel the pressure in my lungs.

The plan was simple: Shorty and his team would go down on the right flank, Larry and his would take the left, Duke would take the center. I was with Duke's squad.

We waited on the crest of the ridge while Shorty and Larry moved to their positions with their men. Meanwhile, Duke studied the Chtorran igloo. There was no sign of life; but then we hadn't expected any, didn't *want* any. If we had guessed correctly, all three of the worms would be lying torpid within.

When the binoculars were passed to me, I studied the corral in particular. There weren't any humans in it, but there was *something*—no, there were a lot of somethings. They were black and shiny, and covered the ground like a lumpy carpet. They were heaving and shifting restlessly, but what they were I couldn't make out at this distance.

Shorty signaled then that he was ready, and a moment later so did Larry.

"Okay," said Duke. "Let's go."

My stomach lurched in response. *This was it.* I switched on my helmet camera, hefted the torch and moved. From this moment on, everything I saw and everything I heard would be recorded for the log. "Remember," Duke had said, "don't look down if you have to take a leak—or you'll never hear the end of it."

We topped the ridge without any attempt to conceal ourselves and started moving down the slope. I suddenly felt very naked and alone. My heart was thudding in my chest. "Oh boy . . ." I said. It came out a croak.

And then *remembered the recorder!* I caught myself, took three deep breaths and followed Duke. Was anybody else this scared? They didn't show it. They looked grim.

This side of the valley was rocky and treeless; it was the other side that was dangerous. Duke signaled and I stopped. We waited for the others to take the lead. Count to ten. Another signal and we advanced. We were going leapfrog fashion; two men would move while the other two kept lookout, then the first two would watch while the second two advanced. All three groups moved forward this way. I kept my torch charged and ready; so did Duke, but the climb down the hill was slow and uneventful. And painful.

Nothing moved in the woods opposite. Nothing moved in the valley. And certainly nothing moved near the igloo—we watched that the hardest. Everything was still. We approached cautiously, three groups of four men each, spaced about a hundred meters apart.

Where the ground leveled off, we paused. Duke sniffed the air and studied the forest beyond the chunky dome. Nothing. Still, he looked worried.

He motioned Larry's team forward. They had the Mobe IV with them—they called it "Shlep." The dry grass crunched under its treads. We waited till they were about a hundred meters forward, then followed. After a bit, Shorty and his men took up their position to the rear.

It seemed to me that the three groups were spread too far apart. Maybe Duke thought he was being careful by having us stretched across more territory; it'd be harder for the worms to overpower or surprise us. On the other hand, though, maybe he was being a little reckless too. Our combined torch ranges overlapped, but not by very much; we couldn't come to each other's aid as fast.

I was about to point this out to him when Larry's team stopped ahead of us. We approached to about thirty meters and then waited till Shorty's group was an equal distance behind. Then we all started moving again. Duke looked a little less grim and I started to breathe easier myself—but not much; this was still worm country.

We were close enough now to see the construction of the igloo in detail. I estimated it was four meters at its highest point and fifteen in diameter. It was made of layered rows of light-colored wood paste and chips; it looked fairly strong. All around the base was a jumble of dark vegetation so purple it was almost black. The scent was faint, but cloying nonetheless—like honeysuckle, but tasting of something fruitier.

I would have expected the dome to be more cone-shaped, like a beehive because of the way it must have been built, one layer at a time; but no, it was more of a mound—a spherical section with a flattened top. The door was a large arched opening, wider than it was high, and shielded by an interior baffle—like the "spirit wall" the Chinese used to put behind their front gates to keep ghosts out. We couldn't see into the hut. There was no telling if there were worms inside or not.

Larry paused at a safe distance and unlocked the Mobe. The rest of us stopped too, all keeping our same relative positions. Larry stood up again and sent two of his men to circle the igloo; he and the remaining man, Hank, moved around the opposite way. Shlep waited alone, its radar turning back and forth in patient unquestioning rhythm. The rest of us watched the front door.

In front of the dome was something I hadn't noticed before—had it been there last time? It was a kind of . . . totem pole. Only it looked like—I don't know, a piece of blast art perhaps. Like something half-melted, a liquid shape frozen in the act of puddling. What the hell was it? A signpost? A mailbox? It was made out of the same stuff as the dome and the corral. There was one large hole in the base of it, then three more of decreasing sizes placed almost casually above, oddly off center, and a score of ragged tiny holes all around. The thing stood more than two meters high, half the height of the dome, and directly in front of it.

After a bit, Larry and his men reappeared, each having circled the dome completely. Larry signaled that it was all clear. There was no back door; we couldn't be taken by surprise that way.

"All right," Duke signaled back. "Send in the Mobe."

Larry waved and turned to Hank. He unfolded the remote panel on the man's back and armed Shlep. The Mobe's bright red warning lights began to blink; it was now unsafe to approach. If its sensory apparatus detected a large heat-radiating body close by, the EMP-charge on its back would flash, instantly roasting everything in the dome and probably a good way beyond—like a microwave oven, but faster.

EMP stands for Electro-Magnetic Pulse; it's a burst of widespectrum high-energy radio noise.* *Very wide* spectrum. From radio to gamma. *Very high* energy. Linearly amplified.

It probably would have been simpler to just toss a grenade into the hut and duck, but Duke wanted to capture this shelter intact. We needed to learn everything we could about the Chtorrans. The EMP-flash would kill them without destroying them or the dome.

Larry waved again and Duke snapped, "All right, everybody down." This was probably the most dangerous part of the mission—we had to lie down in the grass to minimize the effects of stray radiation from the flash, but the position left us vulnerable because we couldn't use the flamethrowers if we were surprised.

Hank lay down with the remote panel and sent the Mobe rolling forward. He had his eyes pressed into the stereo sight and was looking solely through the eyes of the Mobe now. Beside him, Larry kept uneasy watch. The other two men had stretched a protective flash-foil in front of all four of them—the remote antenna stuck up beyond it—but the Mylar struts were refusing to stay anchored and the men were having to hold them up by hand. The rest of us were far enough back not to need foil, but we stayed down anyway.

The Mobe was in the dome now. Again we waited. The minutes ticked off with deliberate hesitation. The only motion was Hank's hands on the Mobe controls. He was murmuring as he worked and Duke was

---

* An EMP-grenade will cook or curdle any living matter within a radius of *(CLASSIFIED)*. A single charge will yield as many as *(CLASSIFIED)* usable pulses. There is also the tendency of the flash to destroy all unshielded electronic gear within the larger radius of *(CLASSIFIED)*.

listening to his comments on a disposable (it would have to be) ear-phone. I couldn't hear what he was saying.

Hank stopped disgustedly and said something to Larry. Larry stood up, swearing softly. Hank turned back to his panel and did something, then sat up. The others let the flash-foil collapse. The Mobe was coming out of the hut now, operating on its own guidance. Had it flashed? No, the red warning blinker was still going. Hank hit the remote and dis-armed it; the light went out. The rest of us stood then, brushing our-selves off and checking our weapons.

The Mobe said there were no worms in the hut—but Duke never took a machine's word for anything. Mobes had been fooled before. Maybe the worms were cold-blooded, or perhaps they didn't give off much heat while they were torpid. Larry was going in to see.

The supposition was that at this time of day the worms should be slow and Larry should be able to burn them before they came fully awake and active. We wanted that shelter, and any piece of worm we could get. So he was going to try to scorch them lightly—enough to kill, not enough to destroy. It was tricky and dangerous and not recom-mended for those who wanted to die in bed. But if they were in there, Larry would get them. If not . . .

Well, that was why the rest of us were waiting outside with torches.

Larry put on his O-mask then, stooped and entered, the man with the grenades right behind him. Insurance. The grenades had suicide fuses. I didn't envy either of them. They bent low inside the "foyer" and disap-peared to the right of the spirit wall.

Silence. And again we waited. A bee—or something—buzzed around my right ear and I brushed at it in annoyance. A drop of sweat trickled from my armpit down my side. The insect buzzed again.

I studied the plants around the base of the dome through the binocu-lars. They were scraggly clumps of something that looked like midnight ivy, mixed with something else that looked like sweet basil—or black marijuana. Both were a deep, intense shade of purple, almost black and almost impossible to see clearly. The coloring of the ivy must have shaded off into the ultraviolet because it seemed oddly out of focus in the bright sunlight—as if each curling leaf were outlined with hazy red neon. The ivy was streaked with fine veins of white, the basil stuff was spattered with red. We were close enough for the cloying scent to be annoyingly pungent. I assumed it was a product of the basil stuff. At closer range it would be overpowering.

At last Larry and the other man reappeared, angrily pulling off their masks. Larry's face was white. "It's empty!" he shouted. "There's nothing here!"

Duke said, "Damn," and kicked at a rock. "Shorty, keep an eye out. McCarthy, come with me." Then, abandoning his carefully staked-out position, he stalked toward the dome. I followed, struggling to keep up.

"How long has it been empty?" Duke asked.

Larry shrugged. "Beats the hell out of me. You know as much about their nesting habits as I do. But it smells *warm.* . . ."

Duke shoved past him and ducked into the doorway. I started to follow, despite myself, then stopped—my mouth was dry. I stared at that dark hole of an entrance as if it were death. I couldn't take another step. And yet—I wanted to, more than anything. I peered cautiously, but couldn't see beyond the foyer. The interior was unlit. I took a step forward, tried to convince myself to make it two—

Abruptly, Duke exited, straightening and almost bumping into me. He shot me an absentminded look of annoyance, then turned to Larry. "Check the enclosure. See what's in it. Post lookouts on the other side —but keep in sight of each other." He turned back to me. "You. You're supposed to be a scientist. I'll give you ten minutes to inspect the inside of that nest. Then I'm going to burn it."

"Huh? But we're supposed to—"

"Never mind what we're supposed to. *That thing is full of eggs!* You think I'm going to leave them here to hatch?"

I didn't bother to answer. The question was rhetorical. I bent and entered the worm hut.

The spirit wall was more than just a baffle behind the door. It joined the roof low enough to force me into a crouch, forming a circular cross section and becoming two inward-curving passageways, one to either side, that followed the wall of the dome—how far around, I couldn't see; the ends were lost beyond the curve. The passages were ramped upward; the floors were made of the same material as the walls and the roof, only the floors seemed spongier.

I crouch-crawled into the branch on the right; that was the way Duke had gone. The passage led up and around through ninety degrees of arc and opened onto a circular room eight or nine meters in diameter and just tall enough to stand in. The leftward passage opened up in the wall opposite.

I had a flashbeam, but it wasn't necessary here. There was an opening two meters across in the center of the roof. Light streamed in through this, as well as fresh air, but the temperature wasn't as cool as I had thought it would be inside. In fact, it was almost stuffy. There was a strong, stifling smell about the nest, somehow familiar; a sickly sweetish odor, but I couldn't place it easily. . . .

The room seemed smaller than I'd expected and the ceiling was lower than it had appeared from outside—of course, those upward-sloping ramps—this was the *top* part of the dome.

Was there a bottom section? There had to be. Or was it all foundation? There were several openings in the floor, all of them ominously dark. I stood there, hesitating. I was a scientist—*supposed* to be a scientist; at least that's what it said on my pay vouchers—but that didn't keep me from being afraid. I stood there indecisively and sniffed—that odd-flavored smell. . . .

As my eyes adjusted to the dim light, I noticed something about the walls; they had a peculiar way of reflecting the light. I forgot the holes in the floor for the moment and turned off my flashbeam; the walls seemed almost—no, they *were*—translucent. The glare from outside was forcing its way through the material of the dome.

I inspected closer—and found that it wasn't a hardened wood paste at all, but some kind of dried wood-foam—a much lighter substance, but no less sturdy. Wood chips were suspended in it like raisins. I poked it with my knife and it was like carving hard paperboard. The walls of this dome were actually tiny bubbles of cellulose-based glue. That explained their peculiar light-transmitting properties, and they were probably excellent insulators as well. I sliced off as large a chunk of the wall as I could and dropped it into my sample pouch.

The rest of the room was featureless, except for those holes. There was an absolute lack of artifacts, excepting some chunks of chewed-up *something,* globs of grayish material like masticated asbestos. Some of the globs were almost a meter in diameter. They were stuck casually to the walls like pieces of chewing gum. I shrugged and cut off a sample and bagged it. If these Chtorrans were truly intelligent creatures, you couldn't prove it by this dwelling.

I wondered—where were the eggs that Duke had seen? Probably down one of the openings. There were three of them spaced equidistantly around the sides of the dome. The largest was against the inner side of the spirit wall. The other two holes were against the outer walls of the dome.

I inspected the largest hole first. I shone the flashbeam down it, but it was only another room like this one, and apparently just as empty. The overripe stench was particularly strong here; I decided not to climb down. Besides, there didn't look to be an easy way to climb back up.

The next hole was some kind of a well. It just went straight down and disappeared in blackness. A toilet, perhaps? Could have been; it smelled like it. I didn't know—what kind of droppings did Chtorrans leave? I was beginning to realize all the things I should have known, but didn't.

The last hole was the one with the eggs.

The hole was against the back wall and it was full of them. They were shiny things, each about the size of a tennis ball, deep red but bathed in a milky white ooze that made them look pearlescent. There must have been hundreds of them—*how deep was the hole?* It was almost perfectly circular and about two meters wide; it seemed to be as deep as the others, but the level of eggs was almost close enough to touch.

So I did something stupid.

I laid down the torch. I unbuckled the tanks and took them off. Then I sat down on the floor and lowered my feet into the hole and started to climb down.

I miscalculated though, and slipped. I dropped—*squish!*—into the eggs; it was like tumbling into oyster-flavored Jell-O. For an instant, I thought I was going to lose my footing and topple face first into them, but I caught myself against one wall. Then I thought I was going to be sick. My throat went tight, and I had to swallow quickly—and painfully —to keep from retching.

I was standing in a red and slimy-white mess up to my knees.

Thankfully, these eggs were fairly recent. I don't think I could have stood it if I had found myself in embryonic Chtorrans. Carefully—I couldn't move too fast because of my unsure footing—I gathered up as many of the still intact eggs as I could reach, bagged them and stuffed them into my pouch. I tried to lean against the wall as much as possible. The feel of those eggs was . . . uneasy.

I was shuddering when I finally braced my hands against each side and levered myself out of that hole. Those eggs were sticky, and they smelled like raw fish left out in the sun too long. If I never saw another one, it would still be too soon.

I was trembling violently as I shrugged back into the tank harness and picked up my torch again. Even if it had been only for a minute, that was still sixty seconds too long to be unarmed in a worm nest.

I looked around then for something else to take samples of. There was nothing. Just the walls and the globs of Chtorran chewing gum, and I already had samples of those. I inspected the other two holes again. The pungent smell from the center one seemed stronger, which surprised me—I should have been used to it by now—but otherwise there was nothing I hadn't seen.

I went out through the left-side passage. It was identical to the right.

Duke was standing there, waiting for me. He glanced at the mess on my legs, but didn't say anything. Instead, he gestured over his shoulder. "Go take a look in the corral. Larry's found something interesting."

I wasn't sure I wanted to. I remembered what had been in that enclosure a week ago. I nodded and kept moving.

The enclosure resembled a large frontier-type stockade about ten meters across, only circular. Its walls were nearly three meters high and slanted inward as if the whole were an incomplete dome. The material was the same as the nest, but thicker and darker. There were the same dark plants around the base—the ivy and the basil stuff. I bagged a couple of smaller ones as specimens; the basil was the one with the cloyingly sweet smell. The leaves of the ivy were waxy and had a sticky feeling to them.

There was no opening in the corral wall. Instead, a steep ramp leaned against the side and up beyond by an equal length; it was rough-hinged to seesaw down into the center. Larry was perched at the top. He waved when he saw me. "Come on up."

The ramp was steep, but ribbed horizontally. It was not quite a ladder and not quite stairs, but something of both. Even though I had to use my hands, the climb was easier than I expected.

"What do you make of that?" said Larry, pointing down inside.

I straightened carefully, making sure I had my balance before I looked. Even so, I was startled, and Larry had to grab my arm to steady me.

The interior of that stockade was a swarming mass of—*insects.* Or, if not insects, then something very much like them. They were large, most of them almost a half-meter long—although some were longer—and black and shiny. Their bodies were slender and jointed like metal-covered wire. Each was fringed with hundreds of flashing legs. They moved across the shadowed floor, twisting and whirling like an explosion of metal pieces.

"Centipedes," said Larry. "Giant centipedes."

"Millipedes," I corrected. *"Thousand*-leggers."

He shrugged; it was all the same to him. "You ever seen anything like that before?"

I shook my head. The floor of the corral was seething. The creatures were oblivious to each other. They raced back and forth across the dirt or curled into balls. They climbed over each other's bodies or just stood and twitched nervously. Or they explored the periphery—several of them were chewing methodically at the walls.

"Look, they're escaping," I said.

Larry shook his head. "Watch."

I did so. One of the largest of the millipedes, nearly a meter long, seemed just on the verge of breaking through. He was almost directly under me and chewing with a vengeance; the sound was a sticky, vicious kind of crunching, like sizzling fat or grinding light bulbs. Abruptly he stopped and backed away. He waved his feelers about in confusion, then began to wander aimlessly—until he came to another section of wall. He tested it cautiously. After a moment, he began chewing again, though not as industriously as before.

"What happened?" I asked.

Larry pointed. "He broke through."

I looked closer. Where the millipede had been chewing was a tiny black hole. A dark, pitchy substance was oozing out of it. "This is a double wall," said Larry. "The inside is filled with something they don't like."

I nodded silently. Elsewhere around the edges, other millipedes were repeating the performance of the first one, and there were numerous other holes with hardened plugs of the same dried, pitchy substance to testify to the millipedes' persistence.

"I didn't know centipedes grew so big," said Larry.

"They don't," I answered, suddenly remembering something from my plague-aborted course in entomology. "And they don't have four antennae either. Their mouths aren't shaped like miniature garbage disposals, their eyes aren't so large and they aren't herbivorous—they shouldn't be eating those walls at all. These aren't millipedes."

Larry shrugged. "Well, if they're not, they'll do until the real thing comes along."

"I don't know *what* these are," I said. "I've never seen anything that even resembles them before. Real millipedes don't have as many legs or body sections. Look how they're segmented—and what are those humps behind the eyes? And what are they doing *here?*" I indicated the enclosure.

"Isn't it obvious? This is the Chtorran larder. They like their food fresh. They keep it in this corral until they're hungry. Look." He pointed again. "See that? Somebody was having a snack earlier."

I saw a pile of discarded shells and disjointed body sections. I repressed a shudder—these millipedes were nothing more than food for Chtorrans. They were live lunch from the planet Chtorr! "Hey! These things are extraterrestrial too! The Chtorrans brought them! I've got to catch one!"

He stared at me. "Are you crazy—? Those things might be man-eaters."

"I doubt it," I said. "If they were, they wouldn't be chewing on wood." It sounded good to me.

"They might be poisonous—"

I shook my head again. "Herbivorous creatures never are; they don't need it."

"How do you know they're *only* herbivorous? They might have a taste for meat as well."

That made me pause—but not for long. "There's only one way to find out. Help me down."

He set his jaw stubbornly. "No."

"Larry," I said, "this is every bit as important as burning worms. Anything we can find out about them will help us destroy them."

"I'm not going to help you get killed."

"Then I'll do it myself—" I took a step upward on the ramp; another one and I was beyond the wall; a third and it began to teeter precariously. Larry took a step back down to stop it.

"Look," I said to him, "somebody's got to do it."

He didn't answer, just took another step downward to counterbalance my weight. I stared at him until he looked away. I took another step up. One more and the ramp began to lower slowly on my side. I took another step and the rate of swing increased.

Larry started to move—too slowly. He said a word and gave up. He adjusted his position to keep the ramp from moving too fast. "Okay," he growled, "but if you get your legs chewed off, don't come running to me."

I grinned. "Thanks,"—then had to grab suddenly to keep from toppling off. The ramp kept swinging—Larry rose above me unhappily—till my end touched ground near the center of the corral with a *thump*. I found myself balanced in an awkward position and had to scramble around in order to climb down more easily—or *up*, if I had to. I looked down warily. A couple of the millipedes had already begun inspecting the foot of the ladder, and one of them had even begun to chew on it. But so far, none of them had made any attempt to climb out. If anything, most were moving *away* from it. Had they learned already to associate the lowering of the ramp with predatory Chtorrans? It seemed likely.

I swallowed and began climbing down. About a foot above the ground, I paused. I held my leg out carefully to see if they would jump or snap at it. One of them rose halfway up as if to sniff, but almost immediately lost interest. I waved my foot above another. He rose up too, and even grabbed hold; I flinched, but held still and waited as he flicked his antennae back and forth across the toe of my boot. After a second, he lost interest too and dropped away. I managed a weak grin and lowered my foot to the ground. "Well, that's one more giant step for mankind." I was breathing a little easier.

The millipedes showed no alarm at my presence. If one did come in contact with my shoes, he either turned away or climbed over them as if I were just one more bump in the landscape. Mostly, they ignored me.

I wondered if it would be safe to pick one of them up with my bare hands, or even with my gloves on. I poked one of the creatures with the tip of the torch and immediately it curled into a ball, showing only its shiny black shell. Okay, so maybe that established they were cowards, but they still had mouths like miniature scrap-metal processors—you know, the kind that can reduce a new Cadillac cruiser into assorted pellets of steel and plastic, none larger than an inch across. I decided to play it safe.

That was when I found out how ill-equipped my sample pouch really was. I didn't have anything to carry them in. A plastic bag? Uh uh, they could go through that in seconds; a creature that can chew its way through wood foam and wood chips isn't going to be stopped by anything less. I wished I'd had the foresight to bring some wire-based netting. Should I risk my canvas pouch? It didn't seem a good idea. I had no guarantee that a captured millipede would stay politely curled up all the way back to base or until I could find a proper cage for it.

I wondered—I was wearing a polymer-asbestoid liner between myself and the torch harness, also a shock vest. The vest alone should be enough—at least I hoped it would—so I began shrugging out of the tanks again.

"Hey!" called Larry. "What the hell are you doing?"

"Taking a shower," I called back. Then, "Relax. I know what I'm doing."

He scowled doubtfully, but shut up and looked unhappy. I took off the liner and dropped it to the ground, then I pulled the tanks back on.

Two of the millipedes explored the plastic-looking shirt without much curiosity, then wandered away. Good. I hoped that meant they'd found it inedible.

Quickly, I poked the three nearest specimens with the nozzle of the torch. They curled up obediently. I rolled them onto the asbestoid cloth, made a sack out of it and tied it at the top by looping the sleeves around and tying them in a hasty knot. My pouch was beginning to bulge like the belly of a pregnant hippo—and I must have looked every bit as proud. As a sample-collecting trip, this was turning into quite a bonanza. First the eggs; now the millipedes. For good measure, I added a piece of the enclosure wall and some of the pitchy substance that filled it, also a few of the discarded shells and body sections from the recent Chtorran snack.

Larry was visibly relieved when I began climbing out. I think the idea of a man going willingly into a Chtorran larder—even if only to look around—was too much for him. He waited until I was almost to the top and then shifted his weight to seesaw the ramp up from the center and down on the outside.

We climbed down together; it was wide enough for that. At the bottom, Larry looked at me with grudging respect. "I gotta admit," he said, "that took guts. I wouldn'ta done it. I don't like bugs of any kind."

I shrugged. "I was only doing my job."

"Well, I wouldn't trade with you," he said. This from the man who had gone into the dome first to see if there were worms inside. "Come on, let's go see if Duke has figured out where the worms are hiding—"

And then all hell broke loose.

There was a purple *chirruping* sound and a sudden cry. Larry went white and grabbed for his grenade belt. We heard the roar of a torch and from the other side of the nest puffed a gout of black smoke. I dropped my sample pouch and went charging after Larry.

I saw Shorty first. He had his legs braced firmly apart and was stabbing a finger of flame at something large and black and writhing. It was totally enveloped by the fire and smoke—the burning carcass of a worm!

I kept running—now I could see beyond the curve of the nest. There was another Chtorran there. I skidded and stopped in sheer horror—I had seen the pictures, yes, but they hadn't prepared me for the incredible size of the creature! It was huge! Nearly twice the length of a man, bright red and more than a meter thick at the head! Its eyes were black and lidless. It reared up into the air and waved its arms and made that chirruping sound again; its mouth was a flashing maw. *"Chtorr!"* it cried. *"Chtorrrr! Chtorrrrrr!"*

I was fumbling with the safety on my torch; the damn thing seemed frozen. I jerked at it unmercifully.

I glanced up, half expecting to see that crimson fright charging down on me—but no, it was still reared up in the air, half its length. Its fur was standing stiffly out from its body, revealing its skin of deep purple. Abruptly, it came back to ground and lowered its head; its eyes were like black searchlights fixed directly on me. I braced my legs as Shorty had shown me and steadied my flamer—damn! Larry was blocking my shot! He was just pulling the pin on a grenade—

The worm moved then. So did I, sliding sideways to catch it before it could bear down on Larry; he was closest. It turned toward him and streaked across the ground like hot lava, a flowing red silkiness. Stiff-armed he flung the grenade. It arced high—simultaneously, Shorty's flame flicked across that purple and red horror. It exploded in a tongue of orange—and then exploded again as the grenade shattered its writhing form.

There was another explosion in the distance, and then it was all over. Shorty cut off his flamer and its roar became a sigh, then faded out altogether, leaving only the sizzle of burning worm, the insistent crackle of its blackening flesh, and a smell like burning rubber.

Duke came stumbling through the smoke. "Anybody hurt over here?" He gave a wide berth to the still burning carcasses.

Shorty called back. "We're okay. I got 'em both easy." He grinned. "And Larry wasted a grenade."

Larry mock-scowled. "Well, I couldn't wait all day for you." To Duke: "Everybody all right on the other side?"

Duke nodded. "No problem. That worm never had a chance, but I was worried when I saw the other two headed this way."

"Hell, boss, you oughta know better than that," Shorty boomed jovially. "Fact is, Jim here saw how well me and Larry were doing; he decided to take a nap."

Duke's eyes flickered over me. "He better not have," he muttered.

Shorty ignored it. "How big was the one you got?"

Duke shrugged. "About the same as these. Maybe a little bigger."

"How about that," Shorty said, directing it toward me. "We just burned two and a half tons of worm."

Duke said sourly, "We were almost caught by surprise." He turned to Larry. "I thought you said that dome was empty."

"Huh? It was—!" His face looked confused. "You saw that yourself!"

"I didn't inspect it all, Larry—I took your word for it. I only checked for eggs. It was your responsibility to check the other holes."

"I did!" Larry repeated. "They were empty! The Mobe tapes will confirm it!"

Duke narrowed his eyes. "Larry, those worms came charging out of that dome. I saw it myself."

"And I tell you that dome was empty—if it wasn't, you think I'd be standing here now?"

"I can confirm that," I said. They both looked at me. "Remember? I went into the dome too, and I poked my nose into everything. I didn't see any worms."

Duke closed his mouth. He studied his boots for a moment. "All right," he said. "Let's drop it for now." He turned and walked off.

Larry looked at me. "Thanks, kid."

"For what?" I said. "That dome *was* empty. Duke's gotta be wrong. The worms must have come from the woods."

"Uh uh," said Larry. "If Duke says he saw them come from the dome, then that's where they came from. There was something we missed, Jim—both of us. We haven't heard the end of this."

I shrugged and followed him. We passed between the two crackling worm carcasses toward where Duke and the others were gathering. Larry looked unhappy, so much so that I wanted to say something more to him, but Shorty caught my arm. "Leave him be, Jim. Let him work it out for himself. Larry's that way."

"But it's not his fault—and nobody got hurt."

"But somebody *could* have been," said Shorty. "It was his responsibility to check out that nest and he thinks he failed. In Larry's eyes, a reprimand from Duke is pretty serious." He added, "If it were me, I'd be feeling that way too."

"Oh," I said. I thought about it. "Okay." Then I remembered. "Oh, I forgot my sample pouch. I dropped it when the excitement started. Wait a minute—" I broke away and started back toward the enclosure.

Shorty nodded. "I'll wait here."

It took only a moment. I dashed around the smoking worms and up to the foot of the ramp. The pack was where I had left it. I scooped it up and hung it on one shoulder, checking the contents as I walked back.

I came around the nest in time to see the biggest worm of all attacking Shorty.

Shorty was just turning toward me, grinning—then there was that

chirruping sound, *"Chtorrrr! Chtorr!"* and a section of the nest wall
next to him fell away. A thick, purple-red body streamed out, all mouth
and grabbing arms. *I couldn't reach my torch!* The goddamn pack was
in the way! *"SHORTY!"* Shorty was already turning toward the worm,
sudden realization appearing on his face—and then it was on him. He
didn't even have time to yell.

I found my hands and I burned them both. I held the torch on them
and *burned.* Bright gouts of flame. Searing tongues of flame. Red and
black and orange! Roaring, cleansing fire! I held that trigger firm and
squeezed, *squeezed* and screamed. The flamethrower screamed too. I
played it back and forth across the worm long after the thing had
ceased to writhe. Then I turned it on the nest and burned that too. I
didn't stop until it was completely aflame and the roof had collapsed.

But by then the torch was out of fuel anyway and they had to pry it
out of my hands.

ELEVEN

WE RODE back in silence. I sat and stared at the sample pouch in my lap and tried not to think of the price Shorty had paid for my stupidity. It was my stupidity, wasn't it? I mean, to carry the pouch like that.

Duke was in the front seat, conferring softly with Hank. I tried not to listen, but the wind kept whipping their words back to me. They were battering at the facts, replaying them over and over again. "That fourth Chtorran—" Duke insisted, "—it shouldn't have been there."

Hank was making noises in response, quacking duck-billed platitudes. "Aww, Duke—we don't know enough about them yet—"

Duke ignored him. "—I thought that shelter looked a little too big— damn Reconnaisance! They're going to hear about this. I should have flashed that damned Mobe, and to hell with the cost."

"Hey, how about the kid—?"

"Huh?"

"He's taking it pretty hard."

"We all are."

"But he's the one who pulled the trigger."

"It's a risk we all have to take," Duke said. "You know that."

Hank glanced back at me. "Still . . ." he said quietly, "it wouldn't hurt to have a word with him . . . or something."

Duke didn't answer for a moment. When he did, his voice was strained. "Damn you, Hank. Just once I want to lick my own wounds first—Shorty was my friend too." He fell silent, then turned away in his seat and stared at the passing hills; they were shadowed in dusk. The clouds were shiny pink against a pale gray horizon.

I pulled my jacket tighter around me. The wind kept slapping at my hair and eyes; it was cold and dusty, and I was miserable, both inside and out. Occasionally, the millipedes would start to move; the bag would squirm uneasily, but a gentle rap with my hand was enough to make them curl up again; three hard little knots the size of cantaloupes.

It was past nine when we got back to base. It had been a boys' camp once, but now it was a makeshift Special Forces base. As the Jeeps pulled up in front of the mess hall, men began pouring from its doors. "How was it? How many worms did you get?" Their voices were loud and excited.

Almost immediately, though, they caught our mood, and when Duke said, "Shorty's dead," an uncomfortable silence fell over the group. They followed us into the mess hall where Sergeant Kelly was pouring out coffee in her usual don't-bother-me manner and distributing platters of hot biscuits with businesslike dispatch. I snagged a couple of the biscuits—I could live without Sergeant Kelly's coffee—and faded into a corner. Nobody paid me any attention, for which I was more than grateful.

Duke also stood alone. Holding his mug by the bowl, not the handle, he sipped his coffee steadily, grimacing at its taste and ignoring the occasional question. The other men from the mission were tumbling out their stories as fast as they could talk. When they came to the part about Shorty some of the men glanced toward me and lowered their voices, but an excited murmur rose from the rest of the group. "A *fourth* worm—? Impossible!" But incredulity was met with insistence and the discussions splintered into speculations.

Dr. Obama came in then and took Duke off to one side where they conferred for a few moments; once they looked over in my direction, but when they saw me looking back at them they turned away; then Duke put down his coffee cup and the two of them left.

Abruptly, Ted was standing in front of me. He was hunched over, with his hands thrust deep into the pockets of his jeans. He had a peculiar expression on his face, like someone looking at an auto accident.

"Are you all right?"

"I'm fine."

He sat down opposite me, folded his arms and leaned across the table on his elbows. "Quit trying to be brave. You look like hell."

"You don't look so hot yourself," I muttered. His sandy hair was rumpled, his face was puffy. He looked like he'd just gotten out of bed. Was it that late?

He ignored it. "I hear you had a pretty rough time."

I didn't answer.

He eyed my sample pouch. "Did you find anything interesting?— Hey, it's moving!"

I rapped the bag quickly and it stopped.

Ted gaped. "What've you got in there?"

"Some of the bugs from the corral. That's what you can do. Go find a cage."

"A cage—? How big? Would a chicken coop do?"

"As long as there isn't any wood in it."

"Uh uh. Aluminum and wire." He scooted out the door.

Some of the men were trickling out now, headed for the rec room, probably. Others refilled their mugs, slurped noisily, and followed them —that was probably the loudest sound in the room. I thought Sergeant Kelly was in the kitchen flashing more biscuits, but she wasn't. "Here," she said, putting a chicken sandwich and a glass of milk in front of me. "Eat." Her expression was difficult to read, as if her face had been detached from her emotions.

I looked back down into my lap. "I'm not hungry."

"So?" she snapped. "When did that ever stop you from eating?"

"Sergeant," I said, lowering my voice, "I had to kill Shor—"

"I know," she said, cutting me off. "I heard." She placed her hand gently on my shoulder. When I didn't look up, she reached over and cradled my head into her hands—they were *huge*—and pulled me to her. I couldn't help myself. I started crying, bawling like a baby into her lap. Sergeant Kelly is the only person in the world who has a lap standing up. I buried my face in it and sobbed. It was the first time I had cried all day. "That's my boy," she said. "That's my good boy. Let it out. Let it all out. Mamma's here now. Mamma's here."

After a while, I stopped. "Sergeant," I said, wiping my nose on her apron, "thank you." I looked blearily up at her; her eyes were bright. "I love you!"

"Uh . . ." For a moment, her composure seemed uncertain. She looked startled. She said, "I left something in the kitchen," and bustled quickly off. I thought I saw her wiping her eyes as she ducked through the door.

When I turned back to the table, Ted was standing there with the chicken coop. How long he had been there, I didn't know—and didn't want to ask. He didn't say anything about my red eyes; he just set the coop down on the table and waited.

I covered my embarrassment by fumbling with the pouch. Ted opened the top of the coop and I put the asbestoid shirt with the millipedes into it. I loosened the knot and tumbled them out, three hard, black nuggets. Then I latched the cage securely.

"That's it?" asked Ted. He sounded disappointed. "Those are actual Chtorran animals?"

I nodded. The millipedes were still rolled up in balls; their shells seemed almost metallic. If they were still alive, they hadn't shown it yet.

"They're not much to look at, are they?"

"Wait'll they open up," I said. "They're cute as baby spiders."

Ted made a face.

Meanwhile, Sam, the camp mascot—a large gray and white tabby cat who had adopted us—hopped up onto the table to inspect. *"Mrowrrt?"* he asked.

"No, Sam, that's not to eat." That was Ted.

Sam sniffed in annoyance. He turned his attention instead to my chicken sandwich and milk, an unexpected bonanza. Neither Ted nor I pushed him away. He ate noisily. Dainty bites, but noisy ones. He was purring appreciatively while he ate.

Louis sauntered over next. He'd stripped down to his T-shirt. He was beginning to show a layer of fat on his middle-age spread. I guess the army couldn't afford to be too choosy any more. "Is that the bugs from the worm camp?" He peered close. "How come they're all rolled up?"

I shrugged.

"Have you tried feeding them yet? Maybe that's the trouble. Maybe they're hungry."

"Or scared," I suggested.

He ignored it. "What do they eat?"

I shrugged again.

"Don't you know?"

"How could I? Could be anything. When I caught them, they were chewing on the walls of their enclosure."

"Well, you gotta feed them something," he insisted. Two or three other men had wandered over. A small crowd was forming. One or two of them muttered agreement.

"I'll have to make some tests," I mumbled. "To see what they like."

"Aah, you don't know anything about animals. I grew up on a

farm—" He put his finger up to the mesh and clucked. "I'll bet they're just like chickens. Chtorran chickens. Come on, little bugs, come on— see what Daddy's got for you—" He shoved a little piece of biscuit through the wire. "Come on—"

I was hoping the millipedes would ignore him, but one of them chose that moment to uncurl. No longer restrained, and finding no reason to keep hiding, it began exploring its surroundings; its antennae waved tentatively, first forward, then back, then randomly in all directions. After a moment, it slithered across the floor and even part way up the walls of the cage, giving me a good look at its soft underside. Soft? It was a deep disturbing purple with dark bands separating the—what?— they looked like segments. I could see how all the shells were jointed; the creature's body was a train of tiny armored cars on legs.

The millipede tested the aluminum frame with its feelers and tried to poke its head through the wire mesh. For a moment, it seemed to be staring right at me; its eyes were black discs the size of quarters. They made me think of Chtorran eyes. They weren't faceted like normal insect eyes.

It pulled back then and continued exploring, coming at last to the sliver of biscuit. The millipede touched it lightly with its probing antennae, then ate it. It simply moved forward, chewing as it went, until there was no more left. "Hey," said Louis, grinning. "He likes it. Here, have some more." He shoved the rest of the biscuit into the cage.

The millipede made short work of this piece too. One of the others uncurled then and also began exploring the coop.

"Hey, Louis," said one of the men. "Now you gotta feed the other one."

Louis glanced around. His eye fell on the chicken sandwich that Sam was still working on. " 'Scuse me, kitty, but I need this."

"Maoww—" Sam protested loudly, but to no avail. Louis tore the bread into pieces and pushed it through the mesh. Sam licked his chops deliberately, hoping the chicken wouldn't follow.

He was wrong. "Let's see what else they like," said Louis, and the chicken was pushed through the wire as well. Also the lettuce and tomato.

"Looks like we have to apologize for hurt felines," remarked Ted. "Here, Sam, drown your sorrows in some milk."

"Mrowwt," said Sam. But he drank the milk.

Meanwhile, the third millipede had uncurled and joined its fellows in consuming the feast before them. "Look, they like chicken too."

"And lettuce. *And* tomato." Ted looked at me. "I wonder if there's anything they *don't* like."

"The stuff inside the enclosure wall," I said. "They don't like that. I brought back a sample for you to analyze." I pulled the plastic bag from my pouch.

Ted opened it and sniffed. "I hate to tell you what it smells like." He wrinkled his nose and closed it up again.

Louis was still at the cage. He poked his finger through the mesh and clucked. "Pretty baby, come to Poppa. . . ." I could understand his fascination with them. They seemed somehow more *intelligent* than mere insects. It was their eyes; they were large and round and dark, they were almost soft—like puppy eyes; they were all pupil. And it was the way they looked at you through those eyes—peering and turning toward every sound, studying each object with dispassionate curiosity. They seemed *knowing*. These creatures were to ordinary bugs as an owl is to other birds—clearly the same type of creature, but definitely something *more*. One of the millipedes rose up into the air to sniff Louis's finger—

—and suddenly bit it.

"Aaii—*Hey!!*" He jerked his finger back, but the millipede had a firm grip. For a moment, Louis was caught there while the creature thrashed about within the cage—then he broke free, blood streaming from the missing joint. "Aaah! Son of a bitch!" he gasped.

Someone wrapped a paper napkin around his hand; it quickly stained red. "Get him to the doctor!" said someone else. Two men hustled Louis out the door. He was making little gasping sounds.

In the cage, the millipedes were unperturbed. Their black eyes were suddenly baleful.

"I should have warned him," I said.

Ted looked at me. "Did you know they would do that?"

I shook my head.

"Then shut up. It was his own fault for putting his finger in the cage. Sometimes Louis can be a real fool. Tonight he outdid himself. The bugs must have thought it was still feeding time." He put on a thoughtful expression. "These things do have an appetite, don't they?"

"So do Chtorrans," I said, remembering. "Here. These were in the enclosure too." I passed him the empty shells and body sections.

Ted raised an eyebrow.

"Lunch," I explained. I pointed at the cage. "The Chtorrans eat them."

"Sounds risky," he quipped. "But it makes sense. And better them than us." Then he thought of something. "Say, how did you catch them without getting attacked yourself?"

"I don't know—they just didn't seem interested in me. I thought I was safe and I was."

"Hm." Ted frowned. "There must have been a reason."

"Maybe I'm just inedible."

"So? Stick your finger in the cage and prove it."

"On the other hand," I said quickly, "maybe there's some other reason."

Ted looked disappointed. "Spoilsport—it would have been a valid test."

"If you're so eager, you stick *your* finger in."

"Ah, but it's not my inedibility we're testing. No, you're right; there must be some other reason. You're probably edible, just not very tasty. How did you go into the enclosure? Just hold your nose and jump?"

"No, I tested with my foot first. I waved it above their heads to see if they'd attack."

"Well, so you're smarter than I thought. I would have guessed you crossed your fingers and hollered 'King's X!' Maybe they just don't like shoe leather—let's find out." He pulled off a boot and pressed one side of it against the mesh. All three of the millipedes attacked it. "Well, that settles that."

Then he tried to pull his boot away. But their combined grip was too strong. "Aww, come on, now—" Not wanting to hurt them by pulling harder, he let go of the boot. It hung there while the insectoids chewed at it and the men around us snickered. The millipedes ate until they could chew no further and the boot clunked to the floor.

Ted picked it up sadly and fingered the holes in it. "My best pair of boots," he mourned. He sighed and pulled it back on, all the while shaking his head. He looked at me. "Okay, let's have one of yours—"

"Huh? Are you crazy? You just got through proving that they *like* shoe leather—why do you want to ruin my boots too?"

"Dummy," he said patiently, "this is a scientific experiment to determine why you're still walking around. Now, let me have one of your boots before I break off your leg and beat you to death with it."

He was right. I'd seen the way the millipedes had attacked his footgear. It was identical to mine and the millipedes had ignored me. I pulled off my boot and handed it across.

He held it up to the mesh. The millipedes tested it with their antennae, then lost interest in it and wandered away. Ted tried it again on the other side. The millipedes did the same thing.

Ted frowned and held the boot close to his face. He sniffed. Once, twice, a third time, curiously. "Smells fishy. What'd you step in?"

"Nothing," I said. Then remembered. "Uh—eggs."

"Eggs—? You mean like in chicken, cluck-cluck-cluck?"

"No. I mean like in Chtorran."

His expression was incredulous. "You stepped on Chtorran eggs—?"

"It was inside the nest—"

"Inside the nest—? Yipe! I take it all back, Jimmy boy. You're not smart at all. There's a safer way to kill Chtorrans than by walking into their nests and stomping on their eggs. What do you think flamethrowers are for?"

"I didn't *mean* to step on the eggs. It was an accident."

"I hope you told that to Mamma Chtorran."

"Besides, Duke was going to burn them anyway, so I climbed down and saved a few."

For a moment there was silence.

Then Ted said, "Do you have them with you?"

I upended the pouch and tumbled them out onto the table. There must have been a dozen, at least.

Ted stared; so did the two other men who still remained. I didn't know their names. The eggs were blood-red and smooth, still moist-looking and slightly translucent. There was something dark inside. Gingerly, Ted picked one up and sniffed it. "Raw fish, all right." He held it against the side of the millipede cage. They tested it incuriously, then lost interest. "Well, that's what saved your life, Jimbo—the fact that you're such a clumsy retard. You must have had egg all over you."

I thought back. "You're right. I know I had it up to my knees and all over my arms." I shuddered at the thought of what might have happened if I hadn't. And that was probably why my three specimens hadn't tried to chew their way out of the sample pouch—the smell of the eggs around them.

"Uh huh—" Ted was holding the egg up to the light.

"See anything?" I asked.

"It says, 'Disregard previous egg.' " He replaced it on the table. "I can't tell."

"You know what these remind me of?" I said. "Ant eggs."

"Ant eggs?"

"Uh huh. They have that same kind of almost-translucency. And their shells are soft too. Look, see how they bounce? What does that suggest?"

"Handball?"

I ignored it. "It means we can begin to learn something about how they evolved. Birds and reptiles have hard-shelled eggs—it's for extra strength and water retention. This might indicate a lower level of development. Insects or amphibians."

"Worms are a little bit of each?"

"Maybe." I picked up the egg again. "On the other hand, maybe the Chtorran atmosphere is humid enough so that moisture retention is not a very important survival factor. And this shell seems to be awfully thick, almost cartilaginous. That might provide the protection the embryo needs, particularly if Chtorr *does* have a higher gravity than Earth. That's what some of the fellows around here think. It would explain the Chtorrans' extreme strength and mobility." I frowned and held the egg up to the light. "I don't know. The shape of an egg and the texture of its shell should tell you things about the conditions it's meant to hatch under—and that should give you clues about the nature of the parent and the offspring. But I don't know how to begin to figure this one out. My brain hurts—there are too many questions. Like, for instance, how come if these millipede things are so incredibly voracious they aren't interested in the eggs?" I pressed the egg to the mesh again. "It doesn't make sense."

"Maybe they can tell it's a Chtorran, and they're afraid of it even before it hatches."

"Sorry, I can't imagine these creatures passing up a free meal. There must be something about these eggs that's distasteful."

Ted blinked. "Wow! An egg with its own defense mechanism." He looked up. "What are you planning to do with them?"

"I was thinking of rigging up an incubator."

Ted whistled softly. "Jimmy, I've got to admire your . . . bravado. Or something. You're either the smartest damn fool around here—or the dumbest. It's not enough you have to rescue Chtorran eggs from the incinerator; now you want to hatch them. When Duke hears about this, he's going to have a fit."

I hadn't thought about Duke. "Why? What's wrong with the idea?"

"Oh, nothing; it's just that the purpose of this Special Forces operation is to kill worms, not breed them."

"Not entirely," I insisted. "You and I were sent up here to study the Chtorrans."

"That doesn't mean we have to make pets of them."

"And how else are we going to get close enough to study them? Do you know a better way to observe one long enough to learn anything? On a hunt, as soon as you see a worm, you burn it. No, the only way we're going to be the scientists we were sent up here to be is to put some worms in a cage and watch to see what makes them tick—and if we can't capture a live one, then we'll have to grow our own."

"Simmer down, I'm on your side. I think. It's just that I don't think the idea is going to be very popular around here; this isn't a P.O.W. camp—and that's another thing; even if you do hatch a few worms, where are you going to keep them?"

"We'll think of something," I mumbled. I was trying to think of something.

"We?" He raised an eyebrow.

"Yes. We. Remember, you're an exobiologist too."

"Oh, yeah—I forgot." Ted looked unhappy. "But I think this is one of those times when I'd rather be a botulinus tester." He said, "I mean, raising the worms is going to be the easy part—"

"Huh?"

He clapped me on the shoulder. "Jimbo, put the bugs to bed. I'm going to talk to Duke."

"Want me to come along?"

"Uh, better not. Duke's had a . . . rough day. I think I can be more tactful. You just tuck 'em in for the night and leave the rest to me."

"Well . . . okay."

I left the millipedes in the mess hall for the night, with a canvas draped over the coop and a sign that said DANGER! on it. The eggs were slightly more difficult, but I borrowed Ted's electric blanket and put them in a cardboard box with it draped across the top as a makeshift incubator. To keep the eggs from drying out, I lined the box with a layer of plastic, then a layer of towels, and then sprayed it all with warm water—enough to keep the towels damp, but not soggy. It was just a guess. I'd have to work out something more permanent in the morning.

I had trouble falling asleep. I couldn't help it. Someone was screaming in my head, *Shorty's dead!*

I kept telling myself that I had barely known him; I shouldn't be feeling it this hard. But I hurt all over, and—oh, hell, I couldn't help it; I started crying again.

I was still awake, just lying there, aching, when Ted came in. He didn't turn on the light, just undressed in the dark and slipped into his bed as quietly as he could.

"What did Duke say?" I asked.

"Huh? Oh, I didn't know you were awake."

"I'm not. Not really. What did Duke say?"

"Nothing. I didn't talk to him."

"You were gone an awfully long time."

"Yeah," he said. "I'll tell you in the morning. Maybe." He rolled over and faced the wall.

"Ted," I said, "Shorty died because I wasn't fast enough, didn't he?"

"I don't know," he mumbled. "I wasn't there."

"It's *my* fault, isn't it?"

"Shut up, will you?"

"But—"

"It'll all be settled tomorrow. There's going to be a hearing."

"A what?"

"An inquest, stupid! An inquest. Now, go to sleep, damn you!"

TWELVE

THE INQUEST was held in the mess hall. Duke, Hank, Larry, two of the other men from the mission (whose names I still didn't know) and myself. Dr. Obama, doubling as medical officer, sat at the head of the table. She had a yellow, legal-sized pad of paper in front of her, covered with precise little notes. Ted sat just to her left with a transcriber terminal; his job was to answer the machine's questions about sound-alike or mumbled words. I was at the opposite end—with sweaty palms. Dr. Obama was looking very quiet and when she finally did speak, I had to strain to hear her. "All right, Duke," she said. "What happened?"

Duke told her, quickly and efficiently. He left out nothing, but neither did he waste time on elaborate descriptions. Dr. Obama showed no reaction throughout, other than an occasional nod, as if she were ticking off each of Duke's facts on a mental checklist.

"We followed procedure all the way," concluded Duke. "That's the annoying thing. If there were only something I could identify as a mistake—some error in judgment, even my own, that I could find—at least we might learn something; but I've been over this thing a hundred times, and I just don't know. We did everything by the book. . . ." He hesitated. "Maybe the book is wrong." He fell silent, spreading his battered hands out on the table before him; they had been scrubbed unnaturally clean for this hearing. "I have no explanation how we missed those worms."

Dr. Obama was thoughtful. She didn't look at Duke at all. At last, she cleared her throat slightly and murmured, "It seems we have several areas of investigation here." She shifted the pad of paper in front of her and read from it: "First, where were the Chtorrans hiding that they were undetectable to the Mobe sensors, as well as to Duke, Larry—"

Ted murmured something, his fingers suddenly moving on the terminal keyboard.

"Eh? What's that?" Dr. Obama looked annoyed.

"Last names," whispered Ted. "The record requires it."

"Oh." Dr. Obama went blank for a moment, trying to backtrack her train of thought. "Uh—" She looked at her yellow pad again. "Where were the Chtorrans hiding that they were undetectable to Captain Archibald 'Duke' Anderson, Lieutenant Lawrence Milburn, Corporal Carlos Ruez and Observer James McCarthy—who else was inside the hut?"

"No one," said Duke. "Just the four you listed."

Dr. Obama seemed not to hear him; she continued on to her second point, "Next. *Why*—and this is a very important point to consider— why did *all* of them miss detecting the Chtorrans? That the Mobe also missed the Chtorrans is very important. . . ." She glanced at Ted. "This part is off the record, Jackson." Ted stopped, hit a button and rested his hands by the sides of the terminal. To the rest of us, Dr. Obama continued, "While I may know each of you personally and am willing to vouch for your integrity, there are those who prefer to look for scapegoats when something like this happens. In most cases, they would sooner take the word of a machine and suspect the human beings of carelessness. Machines rarely have ulterior motives. Count it as a blessing that the machine agrees with you here." She nodded at Ted, then continued with a touch more formality. "That the Mobe was unable to detect the Chtorrans confirms your story that the dome was to all appearances empty. The Mobe is supposed to be able to detect things beyond the range of normal human senses—and, vice versa, a human observer also has capabilities that the machine lacks, not the least of which is a sense of *judgment.* Wherever the Chtorrans were, both kinds of observation failed to detect them, indicating—as do certain other facts which we will consider—that the standard procedures do not allow for every contingency."

She referred again to her notes. "Third, the assumption was made that the Chtorrans would be torpid within their shelter. This has been the pattern in the past, but now we must ask, were they in fact within the shelter the whole time? And were they in fact in their most inactive state? It has been a general experience, not just in this area, but in other locations as well, that when worms—excuse me, Chtorrans—go inactive they do so as a group, and generally they go to the coolest part of their shelter; that is, the second level, the underground half. If they were there, the Mobe should have detected them, as should have any of the aforementioned individuals. Which brings up two more questions: What range were the Mobe's sensors set for? How were these parameters determined? On what basis? Perhaps we will have to reexamine that particular aspect of our procedure. Yes, Hank?" To Ted, "Henry Lannikin."

Hank cleared his throat uncomfortably. "Well, Dr. Obama, there *is* a window in the sensing matrices—but it shouldn't have been big enough to let a Chtorran slip through, let alone three—I mean, four—of them. A hot Chtorran within ten meters will trigger the flash, but with a cold one—that is, one that's inactive—the Mobe has to be within four meters. Sorry, but they work so far in the infrared, they can't help but be nearsighted. The point is, if those worms were in the hut, whether hot or cold, the Mobe should have flashed. The only way it could have missed cold ones, they'd have had to have been too far away—like *out* of the hut. And we know that wasn't the case, because we didn't see them."

"Maybe those domes are getting bigger on the inside," Larry offered.

Dr. Obama looked at him coldly. "Do you think that's possible?"

"Hell, I don't know," said Larry. "Every other one I've been into has only had two levels, top and bottom. If the worms started digging deeper than that, I didn't see 'em."

Dr. Obama considered the thought. "It isn't impossible that the wor —*Chtorrans* have changed their life style, but we have several other discrepancies to consider as well." She looked annoyed. "This has been a very atypical affair all around." She resumed her professional manner. "Sixth question, *why* was there a *fourth* Chtorran in the nest? Where did it come from? And why did it delay its attack? What was there different about this one that caused it to hang back for several moments? Also notice that it was the largest of the four Chtorrans encountered—*significantly* larger. What is the importance of that? Finally, is such an event likely to be encountered again in the future? Obviously we will have to modify our existing procedures to allow for that possibility.

"Seventh and eighth questions. What, if any, is the significance of the plant life surrounding the Chtorran shelter? We have not found such plants around the shelters in the past. Why here? Why now? Are these, in fact, specimens of native Chtorran vegetation?"

I'd transplanted all of my samples, each into its own pot. I had no idea how to handle them. Were they dangerous—or what? I wasn't even sure how to test them. Dr. Obama's questions barely scratched the surface.

She continued, "And what about the creatures observed in the Chtorran corral—those were burned as well? Ah, good. What is *their* place in the Chtorran ecology?" She stopped, looked around the table. "Are there any other questions that we want to consider? Yes, Duke?"

"What about Shorty?"

Abruptly, my stomach dropped.

"Yes." Dr. Obama looked to her notes, but she'd already turned to a blank page. There was no answer there. "We all feel bad about that."

"That's not what I meant," said Duke, very quietly.

I wondered if I was going to be sick.

"I know what you meant, Duke." Dr. Obama was every bit as quiet. "All right," she said. "Let's get it over with. Could you have saved him?"

"No," said Duke.

"Is there anyone here who could have saved Sergeant Harris?" asked Dr. Obama. She looked around the room. Larry was studying his fists; they were buried in his lap. He almost looked like he was praying. Carlos and Hank didn't say anything either; even Ted's hands were motionless on his keyboard.

"I should have been faster," I said. The words seemed unnaturally loud in the mess hall. Everyone but Dr. Obama looked at me, but having said it, I felt relieved. There, it was out. "I should have been faster, but the specimen pack was in the way. I couldn't get at my torch quick enough. If I'd been faster, maybe I could have saved him; maybe I could have gotten the worm before it—"

Dr. Obama said, "I doubt it. Sergeant Harris himself checked you out on that torch." She was still looking at her notepad. "And I approved his certification of you. Under the circumstances, that makes me equally responsible. As well as Duke."

"Thank you, ma'am. I recognize what you're trying to do—but I know that I was carrying the pack wrong."

Dr. Obama shook her head. "There's no one else who saw that. Despite your good intentions, McCarthy, I can't accept your statement as evidence."

"Excuse me," I said.

"Something else?"

"Yes," I insisted. "There is." I was suddenly aware that everyone in the room was looking at me. "I was wearing the helmet. I made a sound and video record. I—I think that there's some question here about what I did, and whether or not I—uh, acted properly. And I think that the video could clear that up. I'd like to have it shown. Please."

"I'm sorry. That's not possible."

"Huh—?"

"Duke and I tried to look at it last night. Unfortunately . . . um . . . the memory clip was defective."

"What?"

"The write-protect tab was out—"

"That was a brand new clip! I loaded it myself."

"—so the camera and microphone signals were not recorded. The clip was *blank.*" She said it firmly and looked at me, as if daring me to argue with her.

"But—" I'd tested that clip myself! I—saw the look on Ted's face and—stopped. "Yes, ma'am."

She gestured to Ted and Ted switched off the transcriber again. She said, "Look, it's irrelevant. No matter what we decide here, it won't bring back Shorty. I promise you, he's going to stay dead. So if you're trying to justify your guilt feelings, please stop wasting our time. It doesn't produce much result."

"I'm sorry, ma'am," I protested. "I understand what you're saying—but I should have done better—I mean, if only—"

"Stop!" She glared down the table at me. "Jackson, is that thing off?" He checked and nodded. "Thank you," she said. "You're not getting it. So let me give it to you another way. Listen, McCarthy, the responsibility for putting that weapon in your hands was *mine*—do you get that?"

I nodded.

"So if there was an error there, it's *my* error too. Do you get *that?"*

I nodded again.

"And I don't make errors. Not of this kind. You were handed that weapon because you were judged to be capable of handling the responsibility. Shorty thought so. Duke thought so. I thought so. Are you telling us now that all three of us were wrong?"

"Uh—no, but—"

"No buts about it. Either we were wrong or we were right. This thought you have that you screwed up is nothing more than an attempt to avoid the responsibility, and pass the error back up the line to the people who authorized the weapon for you. I'm sorry, but we're not accepting delivery. You took the job. You knew what was involved. You accepted the responsibility. So I don't care how *you think* you handled it. You handled it appropriately." She glared at me with eyes like fire. *"Can you get that?"*

"Y-yes, ma'am." I shoved my fists into my lap and stared at them. She didn't want to hear me.

Dr. Obama stopped and cleared her throat, coughing into her clenched fist. She took a drink of water, then looked up again without focusing on anyone in particular. She nodded to Ted. He switched the transcriber back on. "Does anyone else have anything to add?" She waited without expression. "Then I take it that all of you here are convinced that Shorty Harris's death was unavoidable. Is there anyone who disagrees? Is there anyone who disputes the validity of McCarthy's response? No one?" She looked at Duke. Duke did not meet her gaze. He seemed troubled and for a moment I thought he was going to speak; then, instead, he just shook his head.

Dr. Obama waited a moment longer, then exhaled softly. She seemed relieved. "All right, let the record show that this hearing has determined that James McCarthy acted with dispatch and fortitude. Those present at the scene confirm that McCarthy's actions were appropriate and above reproach. Furthermore, it is the opinion of this body that McCarthy's professed clumsiness is an expression only of his feeling of inexperience in combat, not negligence."

She looked around the table. Duke nodded his reluctant approval. Everyone else seemed . . . deliberately nonchalant.

"All right, before we adjourn is there anyone who has any information which would cast any light on any of these questions we've brought up?" She waited only a second. "I thought not. It is hereby determined that this board of inquiry is unable to reach a conclusion about the circumstances of yesterday's operation, and for all the usual reasons: we simply do not have the knowledge of the Chtorran species that we need. It is the sense of this session and the conclusion of this panel that we have only the questions and none of the answers. We therefore make no recommendations of any kind. This meeting is adjourned. File that, Jackson, and put a copy on the wire—no, let me see it before you send it out." She stood up, gathered her notepad, and nodded. "Good day, gentlemen."

THIRTEEN

DUKE AND I were left alone in the room.

He looked haggard and very old. He was leaning on his elbows and staring into yesterday. His bony hands were clenched, two knotted fists pressed hard together, pressed against his jaw.

"Uh, Duke . . ."

He looked up, startled. When he saw it was me, his face tightened. "What is it?"

"Um—I have some specimens."

Duke blinked. For a moment, he wasn't there; then he remembered. "Right. You'll find a set of handling cases in the storeroom. Do you know where it is? It's bungalow six. We'll send them out on Thursday. Try and keep those eggs and millipedes alive."

"I think the bigger problem would be killing them—" I saw that he had disappeared inside himself again. He had dismissed me. "Uh—Duke?"

He came back impatiently. His eyes were red. "Yeah?"

"Uh, did Ted talk to you yet?"

"No, he hasn't. About what?"

"He said he was going to. We thought that maybe—I mean, I am supposed to be an exobiologist—"

Duke held up one hand. "Spare me the story. What do you want?"

"A lab," I said quickly. "So I can do some of my own observations on the millipedes and eggs and that purple stuff from around the dome."

He looked annoyed. "I don't want you damaging those specimens before they get to Denver! I've got enough problems—"

"I'm not gonna *'damage'* anything!"

Duke snorted.

I said, "Duke, if you're pissed at me, then say so."

"I am not pissed at you—"

"I don't believe you." I walked around and sat down in Dr. Obama's chair and faced him. "What's going on here, Duke? This was the stupidest inquest I've ever been to—" He looked up at that, a question in his eyes. "Three," I answered before he could ask, "—not counting this one. Nothing was established here. Nothing at all. I grant that there aren't a lot of answers yet to most of our questions—but the questions that could have been answered *weren't*. They were whitewashed. So excuse me for being suspicious, but what was all this about?"

Duke shook his head. He stared at his hands. "You don't want to know."

"Yes, I do!"

Duke let that sink in. Then he said quietly, "You were only doing what Shorty told you to do. You were following orders."

I sniffed. I quoted from somewhere, " ' "I was only following orders" is not an excuse—it's an indictment.' "

"Who said that?"

"I just did."

Duke's expression was scornful. "Don't give me slogans, son. I've got a low threshold of bullshit. Especially today."

"I heard it in Global Ethics. And it's no slogan. It's true for me. Look—there's something I want you to know."

"I don't really want to hear it," he said. "In fact, I don't want to talk at all right now."

"Neither do I," I said. I could feel my voice starting to quaver. "But I have to! Until someone just *listens* to me!" My throat was tightening and I was terrified I was going to start crying. It was all bubbling up. I didn't even know what it was. I said, "I'm the guy who pulled the trigger, Duke. I'm the guy responsible. You and Dr. Obama can say whatever you want in an inquest, but I'm still the guy who did the job."

He looked like he was going to say something else, but he stopped himself. "All right, say what you have to then, and get it over with." His voice was very quiet.

"I didn't sleep last night. I couldn't. I needed someone to talk to. I wanted to talk to you. I even got up once and went looking for you. I got as far as your door. I almost knocked. And I didn't—I don't know why. Yes, I do—I was scared. See, I didn't know if I did wrong yesterday or not. I wanted some . . . help. But all I could hear was Shorty's voice saying, 'Figure it out yourself.' Like he did with the manuals. So I didn't knock. And besides, I saw the light was on under your door. And I thought I heard voices. And I didn't want to interrupt anything—"

Duke started to say something, but I cut him off. "No, I want to finish this. Then you can talk. I didn't go right back to my room. You know the hill behind the camp? I went up there and sat by myself for a while. And—I let myself cry. At first I thought I was crying for Shorty, only after a while, I found out I wasn't. I was crying for myself, because of what I was realizing. And it has nothing at all to do with Shorty being dead."

I realized I was trembling. My hands were trembling on the table. I thrust them between my legs and held them there with my knees pressed together. I felt very small and very cold. I looked at Duke and said, "What I realized was that—even if Shorty hadn't told me to do what I did—I still would have done it, done the same thing."

Duke was genuinely surprised. "You would?"

I swallowed hard. It wasn't easy to speak. "Duke, it was the only thing to do. That's why I've been so . . . crazy. I'd been trying real hard to convince myself that I did it because Shorty told me to—only *I knew I hadn't.* There wasn't time to think about it—it just happened. I didn't remember what to do or what I'd been told. I just did it—*without thinking.*" I was looking down into my lap now. "Duke, I've never killed anyone before. I never thought I'd ever have to. All I knew was that it was something I never wanted to do—and then, yesterday afternoon, I found out that I *could* do it—and do it *easily.* And I've been going crazy ever since trying to explain it to myself. I keep looking for a way to make it *all right.* I keep saying that it was the circumstances, except that I know it *wasn't* the circumstances at all. It was me! And now—after this inquest—I can't even have it be a mistake! It was me. I did it. Nobody else. And I have to live with that now—that I can kill people." I added, "It's not really something that I want to know."

Duke was silent a moment, just studying me. I studied back. His face was craggy and weathered, his skin was sun-darkened and crinkled with use. His eyes were sharp and alive again and boring straight into mine. I stared right back.

Abruptly, he said, "All right, you've got your lab."

"Uh—*thank you!*"

"Yeah, I'll see how you feel in a week. Where did you want to set up this zoo?"

"The new bath house."

Duke looked at me sharply. "Why?"

"It's obvious. It's the only building in camp that's suitable. It's got concrete walls and very high small windows. Nothing could escape. At least, not easily. Nobody's using it because the plumbing was never completed; we could bring in portable heaters and fix up the interior any way we need."

Duke nodded. "That's exactly where I would have chosen. But I would have chosen it for you because it's a good safe distance from the rest of the camp. You'll have to clear out the stuff that's already in there. Tell Larry what you'll need in the way of special equipment, or if you need anything built. He'll find some men to help you."

"Yes, sir—and thank you."

He lifted his hand the barest distance from the table, a wait-a-minute gesture. "Jim?"

"Sir?"

"This is no party. Make your results count. Those specimens were awfully expensive." When he looked at me, his eyes were shinier than I'd ever seen. He looked haunted.

"I know," I said. It was suddenly very hard to speak. "I—I'll try."

I left quickly.

FOURTEEN

AN HOUR after I started cleaning out the bathhouse, Ted showed up with a sour look on his face. I told him what I wanted to do and he pitched in, but without his usual repartee of puns, wisecracks and pontifical observations. Usually, Ted radiated a sense of self-importance, as if he were coming straight from some very important meeting. He always seemed to know what everyone else was involved in. But this morning he seemed chastened, as if he'd been caught with his ear to the keyhole.

After a while, Larry and Carl and Hank joined us and the work moved a lot faster. They didn't speak much either. There was a Shorty-shaped hole in all our lives now and it hurt too much to talk about it.

There was a lot of work to be done. It took us half the afternoon just to clear out the lumber and other supplies that had been stored in the concrete-brick bunker, and the rest of the day to make the place millipede-proof. There were vents to be covered with mesh and windows to be sealed, and we had to install doors too; the latter had to be wrapped with wire mesh, and we had to mount metal plates on the bottoms too, just in case.

The final touch was provided by Ted, a brightly painted sign which stated in no uncertain terms:

THE BENEDICT ARNOLD HOME FOR WAYWARD WORMS
TRESPASSERS WILL BE EATEN!!
No bugs, lice, snakes, snails, toads, spiders, rats, roaches, lizards, trolls, orcs, ghouls, politicians, lifers, lawyers, New Christians, Reve-

lationists or other unsavory forms of life allowed. Yes, this means you!

       Visitors allowed only at feeding time.
       Please count your fingers when leaving.
                 —Ted Jackson,
                 Jim McCarthy,
                 Proprietors.

The interior of the bath house was divided into two rooms. One had been intended as a shower room; the other would have been for changing clothes and drying off, a locker room without lockers. We decided to use the locker room for the millipedes and the shower room for the eggs —if we had to choose one or the other to put in a tile-lined room behind two solid doors, it had to be the eggs because of the *potential* danger they represented. An escaped millipede would be far less serious than an escaped Chtorran.

We installed two large work tables in each room, connected the electric lighting and heaters, built a special incubator for the eggs and a large metal and glass cage for the millipedes. Sergeant Kelly was happy —she had her mess hall back—and so were we; we had a lab.

By suppertime, we were seeing our first results. We determined that the millipedes were omnivorous to a degree that made all other omnivores look like fussy eaters. Primarily, they preferred roots, tubers, shoots, stems, flowers, grasses, leaves, bark, branches, blossoms, fruit, grain, nuts, berries, lichens, moss, ferns, fungi and assorted algae; they also liked insects, frogs, mice, bugs, lice, snakes, snails, toads, spiders, rats, roaches, lizards, squirrels, birds, rabbits, chickens and any other form of meat we put before them. If none of the above were available, they'd eat whatever was handy. That included raw sugar, peanut butter, old newsprint, leather shoes, rubber soles, wooden pencils, canned sardines, cardboard cartons, old socks, cellulose-based film and anything else even remotely organic in origin. They even ate the waste products of other organisms. They did not eat their *own* droppings, a viscous, oily-looking goo; that was one of the few exceptions.

After three days of this, Ted was beginning to look a little dazed. "I'm beginning to wonder if there's anything they *won't* eat." He was holding one end of a typewriter ribbon and watching the other end disappear down a millipede maw.

I said, "Their stomachs must be the chemical equivalent of a blast furnace; there doesn't seem to be anything they can't break down."

"All those teeth in the front end must have something to do with it," Ted pointed out.

"Sure," I agreed. "They cut the food into usable pieces, particles small enough to be dissolved—but in order to make use of that food, the stomach has to produce enzymes to break the complex molecules down into smaller, digestible ones. I'd like to know what kind of enzymes can handle such things as fingernail clippings, toothbrush bristles, canvas knapsacks and old videodisks. And I'd like to know what kind of stomach can produce such acids regularly without destroying itself in the process."

Ted looked at me, one eyebrow raised. "Are you going to dissect one and find out?"

I shook my head. "I tried it. They're almost impossible to kill. Chloroform hardly slows them down. All I wanted to do was put one to sleep for a while so I could examine it more closely and take some skin samples and scrapings—no such luck. He ate the cotton pad with the chloroform on it."

Ted leaned forward; he put his elbows on the table and his face into his hands. He peered into the millipede cage with a bored, almost weary expression. He was even too tired to joke. The best he could manage was sarcasm. He said, "I dunno. Maybe they're all hypoglycemic. . . ."

I turned to look at him. "That's not bad. . . ."

"What is?"

"What you just said."

"Huh?"

"About the blood sugar. Maybe something keeps their blood sugar permanently low, so they're constantly hungry. We may make a scientist out of you yet."

He didn't look up; he just grunted, "Don't be insulting."

I didn't bother to respond. I was still considering his offhand suggestion. "Two questions. How? And why? What's the purpose? What's the survival advantage?"

"Um," he said, guessing. "It's fuel. For growth?"

"Yeah . . . and then that raises another question. How old are these things? And how big are they going to get? And does their appetite keep pace? And what *is* their full size? Or is this it?" I sat down on the edge of one of the tables, facing the glass wall of the millipede cage. I began chewing on the end of my pencil. "Too *many* questions—" Hanging around the millipedes was affecting *my* eating habits. I folded my arms across my chest. "And what if we're not asking the right questions in the first place? I mean, what if it's something so simple and obvious that we're overlooking it?"

"Hm," said Ted; then, "Maybe they're not getting the right kind of food—and that's why they stay so hungry. . . ."

"Hey!"

Ted looked up. "What?"

I pounced on the thought. "Try this: maybe they're *dextro*- and we're *levo*—they're made out of right-handed DNA! And they need right-handed proteins to survive! And this is a left-handed world!"

"Um," said Ted. He scratched his nose and thought about it. "Yes and no. Maybe. I have trouble with the right- and left-handed idea. I don't think it's possible. It's certainly improbable."

"The worms themselves are improbable," I pointed out.

He scratched his nose again. "I think the fact that they can safely eat any Earth-based organic matter without immediately falling down, frothing at the mouth in deadly convulsions, is a pretty good sign that our respective biologies are uncomfortably close. If I didn't know better, I'd say almost related."

Another idea bobbed to the surface. "Well, then—try it this way. Earth isn't their native planet, so maybe they have to eat a lot of different things to get all of their daily requirements. I mean, their metabolisms *must* be different because they've evolved for a different set of conditions, so they have to be unable to make the best use of Earth-type foods—it follows, doesn't it?—so they'd have to increase their intake just to survive."

"Um, but look, if that were true of the millipedes, then it would have to be true for the worms. They'd have to be even more ravenous than they already are. They'd be eating everything in sight."

"Well, they do, don't they?"

He shrugged. "Who knows what's normal for a worm?"

"Another worm?" I suggested.

"Mm," he said. And then added, "—Except, there are no normal worms on this planet."

"Huh?" I looked at him suddenly.

"It was a joke!" he said.

"No—say it again!"

"There are no normal worms on this planet."

"What did you mean by that?"

He shrugged. "I don't know; it just seemed . . . obvious. You know?

I mean, we don't know what the worms are like in their own ecology; we only know them in ours—and we don't even know how they got here. So if there's something—*anything*—that's making them or their behavior atypical, we wouldn't know, would we? And neither would any other worm on this planet, because they'd all be experiencing the same effects."

"That's great!" I said, "It really is—I wonder if anyone else has realized that yet."

"Oh, I'm sure they have—"

"But I'll bet that's part of the answer. We're dealing with crazy Chtorrans! And I like your other idea too—about something keeping their blood sugar permanently low. I just wish I had a good biological justification for it." I scribbled it into my notebook. "But it fits in with something else. Here, look at these—" I went rummaging through the mess on the desk behind me and came up with a folder marked UGH. I pulled out a sheaf of color eight-by-tens and passed them across. He stood up to take them. He leaned against the table and began to leaf through them.

"When did you take these?"

"This morning, while you were on the terminal. I finally found my close-up lenses. There's some real high-power stuff there. Look at the structure of their mouths."

He grimaced. "They look like worm mouths."

I shrugged. "Similar evolutionary lines, I guess. What else do you see?"

"The teeth are like little knives."

"You notice anything else? The teeth are slanted inward. Here, look —compare these two pictures where he's eating the cigar. When the mouth is at its widest, the teeth are pointing straight up and down and just a little bit outward; but as the mouth closes, they curve inward. Here, see how they mesh? Once a millipede bites something, the teeth not only cut it, they push it down the throat. A millipede *can't* stop eating—not until the object is finished—*because he can't let go.* Every time he opens his mouth, he automatically takes another bite; every time he closes, he pushes it down his throat. That's why his teeth have to grind and cut and slash—otherwise, he'd choke to death."

"Um, I doubt that last," he said. "I don't think they're capable of choking. With a mouth arrangement like that, they wouldn't have a swallowing mechanism that could so easily kill them. It would be self-defeating. I'd guess that the arrangement of the teeth is so they can get

a good hold on their prey and, if nothing else, get one good bite out of it
—like Louis."

"Have it your own way, Perfessor—but I watched him eat the cigar,
and that's the way he used those teeth."

"But, Jimbo—that doesn't make sense. What happens to the little
bastard who gets stuck to a tree?"

"He eats or dies," I offered. "Remember what you learned in school:
'Mother Nature doesn't give a shit.' "

"Um," Ted said, shaking his head. He continued paging through the
photographs. "How did you shoot this one?" He was staring down the
wide-open mouth of one of the millipedes.

"Which one? Oh, that. I shot that through a pane of glass. There's a
spot of grease smeared on it; he's trying to bite it off. The focus isn't so
good because of the grease, but it was the only way I could look down
his mouth. They learned real quick that they couldn't get through the
glass, so they stopped lunging at it when I held up a finger. That's why
the grease. Here, this one's sharper—this was before he scratched the
glass."

Ted peered close. "Hand me that magnifying glass, will you? Here,
look—what do you make of this?"

"Hey! I didn't notice that before—a second row of teeth!"

"Mm," said Ted. "I wonder if he ever bites his tongue."

"Those are molars!" I said. "See? They're not as sharp. The first row
is for cutting; these are for grinding. And look—do you see anything
farther back?"

"Uh, I'm not sure. It's awfully dark down there."

"We can digitize this and bring up the resolution, but doesn't that
look like a third row?"

"I can't tell. It could be."

I looked at him. "Ted, maybe these things have teeth all the way
down their throats. That's why they can eat so much, and so many
different things. By the time the food reaches the stomach, it's been
ground to pulp. They'll still need strong stomach acids, but now the
food has a lot more surface area exposed to the action of the enzymes."

"Well, this makes them a little more . . . believable." Ted grinned.
"I find it very hard to trust any kind of creature that eats tennis shoes,
wallpaper and baseballs, not to mention bicycle seats, clotheslines and
Sergeant Kelly's coffee."

"Ted, give me a break. Please."

"All right—they wouldn't drink the coffee. That's probably what the

Chtorrans use in that corral fence to keep them from getting out—Sergeant Kelly's coffee grounds."

"Oh, no," I said. "Didn't I tell you?"

He looked up. "What?"

"You should have guessed. What's the one thing the millipedes won't eat—the one *organic* thing?"

He opened his mouth. He closed it.

"That's right," I said. "Used food. No creature can live in its own excrement—those are the things its metabolism *can't* use. And that's what the worms put between the double walls of their corral. As soon as the millipedes sense it, they back away."

"Wait a minute, boy—are you telling me the worms are going around gathering up millipede droppings for fence insulation?"

"Not at all. I didn't say anything about millipede waste. I just said it was waste"—he opened his mouth to interrupt; I didn't let him—"and it's not terrestrial waste either. Remember we were wondering why we never found any worm droppings? This is why. Evidently, the worms have been using it to keep their 'chickens' from escaping. The worms and the millipedes must be similar enough so that it doesn't make any difference. What a worm can't use, neither can a millipede. The tests on the droppings from the enclosure and the specimens we've got here show a lot of similarities. Mostly the differences are dietary, although a lot of the special enzymes don't match up. If I had more sophisticated equipment, I'd be able to spot the subtler differences."

Abruptly, Ted's expression was thoughtful. "Have you written any of this down?"

"I've made some notes. Why?"

"Because I heard Duke talking to Dr. Obama about you—about us. He wants Obie to send us to Denver."

"Huh?"

Ted repeated it. "Duke wants Obie to send us to Denver. With the specimens. On Thursday."

I shook my head. "That doesn't make sense. Why should Duke do any favors for us?"

Ted perched himself on the edge of the table. The three millipedes looked at him with patient black eyes. I wondered if the mesh of their cage was strong enough. Ted said, "Duke's not doing us any favors. He's doing it for himself. We don't belong up here and he doesn't want to be a babysitter. And after what happened with Shorty—well, you know."

I sat down again. I felt betrayed. "I thought . . . I mean . . ." I shut up and tried to remember.

"What?" asked Ted.

I held up a hand. "Wait a minute. I'm trying to remember what Duke said." I shook my head. "Uh uh—he didn't say anything. Not about this. I guess I just thought I heard—" I stopped.

"Heard what?"

"I don't know." I felt frustrated. "I just thought that we were going to be part of the Special Forces Team."

Ted dropped off the table, pulled the other chair around and sat down opposite me. "Jim boy, sometimes you can be awfully dumb. Listen to your Uncle Ted now. Do you know where these Special Forces Teams came from? I thought not. These are—or *were*—top-secret crack-trained units. So secret even our own intelligence agencies didn't know they existed. They were created after the Moscow Treaties. Yes, illegally —I know—and you used a flamethrower last week, remember? It saved your life. Guess what the Special Forces were for—and a lot of other innocuous-looking institutions. Too bad you slept through history, Jim, or you'd understand. Anyway, the point is, these men have lived together and trained together for years. And they're all weapons experts. Have you ever seen Sergeant Kelly on the practice range?"

"Huh? No—"

"Well, you should—or maybe you shouldn't. You'd be too terrified to complain about her coffee. These people think and act as a family. Do you know what that makes us? Just a couple of local yokels. We're outsiders—and there's nothing we can do that will change that. Why do you think Duke gave us this lab—practically shoved it on us? Because he wants an excuse to send us packing. And this is it. He'll be able to say we're too valuable as scientists to be risked out here in the field."

"Oh," I said. "And I was just beginning to like it here."

"Better than Denver?" Ted asked.

"I've never been to Denver."

"Trust me. You'll love it. It'll be just like civilization. Jim, do you really want to stay here, where the odds are seven to one that you'll end up in a Chtorran stewpot? Or didn't you know that?"

I didn't answer right away. At least now I knew why Ted had been so cooperative these past few days. But I still felt as if a rug had been yanked out from under me. I looked across at Ted. He was peering into my face, still waiting for my reaction.

"Damn," I said. "I wish you weren't always so . . . ubiquitous."

He shrugged. "So what? You'll thank me for it in Denver."

"I know. *That's* the annoying part!"

FIFTEEN

THE THURSDAY chopper was pushed back till Saturday, so we had four days left—if we were going. They still hadn't told us. Ted said that was the army way. If they told us, we'd only worry about it. This way, we didn't have anything to worry about.

I worried anyway—and made the best use I could of the time.

I borrowed the helmet camera and set it up in front of the millipede cage. I digitized the image, fed it into one of the computers—and I had an activity monitor. The program counted the number of pixel changes per second, noted the scale of change, the time and the temperature. As it built up information, it correlated trends, fit them into curves and made them available for display on continually updating graphs.

The bugs did not like heat. Temperatures above twenty-five degrees Centigrade made them lethargic, and higher than thirty-five degrees they refused to move at all. Generally they seemed to prefer a ten-degree environment, although they remained active at temperatures as low as freezing. Lower than that, they would curl up.

I repeated the tests under different lighting conditions. The bath house had been rigged with two bare twelve-hundred-lumen plates; when I replaced them with outdoor lamps, some of the vari-temp, night-into-day lights for hydro- and aeroponics, the millipedes curled up as if to shield themselves, regardless of the temperature. Clearly, they did not like bright light.

But I wanted to measure their activity levels through a full range of lighting conditions, charting the curve all the way from pitch dark to bright sunlight—and through a complete range of temperatures too.

We borrowed the air conditioner from Dr. Obama's office—we didn't dare try to take the one from the mess hall—and Larry found a spare heater for us somewhere. Between the two I was able to achieve most of the test temperatures I wanted. I rewrote the program, put the lights on a rheostat with a photodiode to measure the lumens and connected everything to the computer.

The result was a two-dimensional data-base demonstrating the milli-pedes' reactions to a variety of environments.

But it was inconclusive. The bugs liked low temperatures and dim lights. They tolerated high temperatures. They didn't like bright lights at any temperature. That didn't make sense. It was too simple. Did they come from a dark planet? There wasn't enough data.

So I repeated the whole series of tests another dozen times, but now with the lights tweaked to a different color each time.

This left me with a *three*-dimensional graph—now I was nine times as certain that I didn't trust the results. There was a funny anomaly at the low end of the spectrum. I knew it meant something, but I was more confused than ever.

I was still sitting in front of the terminal, leaning back in my chair, arms folded across my chest, staring at the screen and waiting for inspi-ration to strike me, when Ted bounced in. "Okay, Jimmy boy! Pack your comic books! It's time to go."

I didn't even look up. "Later. Not now—"

He grabbed my chair from behind and pulled me back away from the terminal. "Come on—Obie wants to see us."

"About what?"

"Huh? Have you forgotten? Denver, remember? It's a large city in Colorado . . . next to a mountain?"

"Oh, yeah." I said, "I can't go."

"Huh?"

"I'm not done." I leaned over to the terminal and touched a button. The screen started cycling through the pages of my report and over a hundred different three-dimensional graphs. There were cross sections too. I pointed. "Look at that activity curve, Ted! It doesn't make sense. These things look like they should be nocturnal—but their behavior pattern with light and temperature variations says they're not. And look at the way it spikes on the spectrum tests—what does that mean?"

Ted pulled me to my feet. "What it means is congratulations!" He pumped my hand heartily. "You've just won a free trip to Denver!"

"—But the job is incomplete!"

"It's good enough! You don't have to interpret it! They have *real* brains in Denver. They'll take one look at what you've done and have the answer for you in no time. You'll probably get a nice footnote in somebody's report." He placed one hand in the middle of my back and *shoved.* "Now, move! The chopper's already on its way—yes, it's a day early; Larry's bringing packing crates—is your data disked? Here, take it. Let's go!" We were out the door and on our way before I even had a chance to punch him.

We tumbled into Dr. Obama's office like a small stampede. We were both out of breath and flushed. Dr. Obama barely glanced up as Ted snapped a precision salute. I realized what he had done and hastily followed suit, only not as precise.

Dr. Obama almost smiled. She said, "I see you've heard." She handed across two envelopes. "Well, we might as well make it official— here are your orders."

We read them together. I finished first and looked up. "Thank you, ma'am." And then I added, "I think—?"

She nodded. "You're right. I'm *not* doing you a favor. Denver isn't going to be any more pleasant, but you'll find that out for yourselves. You'll both want to be real careful."

"Ma'am?" I asked.

"I mean, don't screw it up—you're going to be playing in a much bigger game. There are worse things than being eaten." She looked unhappy. She said, "I suppose I should wish you luck and tell you I'm proud of you. But I won't. I'm not proud of you, and you're going to need a lot more than luck. Let's have no illusions. I didn't want you up here, either of you, and I'm going to be glad to have you out. This is no place for untrained replacements. But I'll give you this much. You did your jobs—and you were appreciated. You're both intelligent. Wherever you end up, you should do fine"—she looked at Ted, she looked at me —"each in your own inimitable style." She glanced at her watch. "The chopper's already on its way. You have less than an hour. Pack your specimens and be in front of the mess hall at twelve-thirty. Duke is driving you to the helipad. There are metal cages for the bugs and an insulated box for the eggs right outside. Try not to get sent back."

"Yes, ma'am. Thank you." I started to rise.

"Don't be so quick—there's one more thing. Jackson, would you excuse us a moment? Wait outside. And, ah—this time, would you please *not* eavesdrop?"

"Huh? Who, me?" Ted looked puzzled as he stood. "I don't know what you're talking about, ma'am."

"Yes, I'm sure you don't," Dr. Obama said quietly as the door closed after him. She opened her desk drawer and pulled out a small flat lockbox the size of a paperback book. "I have a . . . personal favor." She lowered her voice, "There's a Lieutenant Colonel Ira Wallachstein attached to Project Jefferson. Would you please deliver this to him?"

"Certainly, ma'am—"

"I want you to *personally* place it in his hands."

"Yes, ma'am."

"If for any reason that's not possible, take this out to an open field and punch the date into the lock. Then walk away quickly. Thirty seconds later, it'll self-destruct. Any questions?"

"No, ma'am."

"Repeat it back to me."

I did so and she nodded in satisfaction. "Good," she said. "Thank you. That'll be all."

The helipad was a kilometer down the mountain. It took five minutes to drive there. Duke was tight-lipped all the way. What was it about the Special Forces anyway that they didn't let you in unless you were terminally nasty?

Ted was stretched across the back. I was sitting in the front, half-turned toward Duke. "Uh—Duke?"

"Don't talk." He said it very flatly.

I shut up. And wondered what was eating him now—

Abruptly, Duke said, "Listen, both of you—you've both taken the oath and you're both entitled to wear the Special Forces insignia. I would prefer that you didn't."

"Sir?"

Did Duke look annoyed? The expression flashed so quickly, I wasn't sure. He said, "What you need to know is this: if you wear your insignia, you will attract the attention of people who will ask you questions that you are not prepared to answer. That could be very embarrassing for you. Or worse. Got that?"

I started to say, "I don't understand—" but Ted poked me in the ribs. *Hard.* "We got it," he said.

I looked at him. He looked back at me. I remembered what we had talked about the day before. "Oh," I said.

We pulled up at the helipad then—actually just a large clear space next to the road, bulldozed flat and surrounded by automatic lights and plastic markers. The chopper was nowhere in sight yet. Duke glanced at his watch. "Looks like we're a little early."

"Or they're a little late." That was Ted. He hopped out of the Jeep and walked off a way to admire the view.

"Duke," I said. "I want to thank you."

He looked at me skeptically. "For what?"

"For lying to me."

"Eh?"

"I went and reread my contract. I'm 'scientific personnel attached to the military, specifically exempt from military duties and functions.' I'm not in the army at all."

"I never said you were. I didn't lie to you, McCarthy. You told me your contract requires you to obey your immediate superiors and I agreed with you." He grinned. "I just didn't tell you that neither Dr. Obama nor myself are in that chain of command. Except by courtesy. Legally, you're an independent agent."

"Um," I said. "Well, thank you for fooling me."

"I didn't fool you. You fooled yourself. What I said was this: 'If the mission is military, *every* man is a soldier.' That has nothing at all to do with your contract. You could have stood your ground as a 'scientist,' and there wouldn't have been a thing I could have done about it— except, you would have never seen a worm. That's all. Either way, you still get sent to Denver—but this way, I'll shake your hand and mean it." He held out his hand.

His grip was firm. I looked at him and his eyes were bright. Almost smiling? No, it must have been a trick of the sun. I looked away, embarrassed.

The chopper appeared in the distance then and Duke sat up in his seat to see it better. "By the way," I asked, "if neither you nor Dr. Obama has the authority to give me orders, who does?"

Still peering into the distance, he said, "That's in your contract too."

"No, it isn't," I said. "There's not a word about where I fit into the chain of command."

He looked at me then and grinned. "That's what I meant. You're your own man—all civilian attached personnel are. But we try to keep you from finding out, else you're hard to put up with. I can't give you orders, only recommendations. Same for Dr. Obama and every other officer. Take a look at your papers on the way up. You're carrying pinks, not yellows; you're a free agent, responsible only to the team or task you're assigned. But, ah—don't get cocky. You still have to earn the right to talk to a Special Forces man."

We could hear the chopper now, a distant blurring in the air. Duke was already getting out of the Jeep. "Come on, I'll help you with your gear."

By the time we had unloaded the last of it, the chopper was already overhead, engines screaming and stirring up clouds of choking dust with their downdraft. It was one of the new Huey Valkyrie 111s; with jet-assisted flight, its range was more than two thousand miles—at least, that's all the army would admit. Privately, it was said to be a lot more. The landing gear flexed and gave as the copter settled its weight to the ground, but its rotors continued to strop the air. The thunderous roar of the jets muted temporarily to an impatient whine. We picked up our bags and ran for it.

Ted was up the ladder first. I bumped into him as he did a sudden stop in the door. The pilot was an impeccable-looking redhead in jump-suit and major's insignia, Army Air Corps. I wondered if she was friendly. She looked through us as we climbed aboard with the speci-men cases. "Secure those boxes in the back, then get out. I'm in a hurry." No, she wasn't.

"Uh—" I said, "—we're coming with."

"Forget it—I don't carry passengers." She booted my duffel casually out the door.

"Hey!" I yelped, but she was already turning to Ted.

He was unbuttoning his pocket. He handed her our orders. She didn't even bother to look, just snapped, "I said, 'Forget it.' "

Ted and I exchanged a glance—

Duke called up, "What's the matter? What's going on?"

—and I shouted back, "No problem. We're just going to have to find some other transportation, that's all. Come on, Ted—I'll get the eggs, you unstrap the cages."

"Hold it, Charlie!" she barked.

"Just hold it yourself!" I barked right back. "We have a job to do too!" It worked. She stopped—but only for a moment. "You'd better read our orders," I said, very calmly.

She took them from Ted and scanned them quickly. "Pinks!" she snorted, handing them to me. "Doesn't mean a thing. Those are just advisories."

"Right," I said. I kept my voice innocent as I carefully refolded and pocketed our papers. "We're advised to deliver these specimens. And you're advised to take us."

"Uh uh." She shook her head. "Nobody told me about it. I'm only taking those." She pointed at the cages.

"No way." I cleared my throat and prayed that my voice wouldn't crack. "If we don't go, they don't go. Duke, hand me that duffel?"

She looked at me, then really looked. I glared right back. She had very bright blue eyes—and a very dark expression. She flicked her glance briefly over Ted, then back to me again. I was already stowing my bag. She said a word, a not-very-ladylike word, then, "The hell with it—I don't care! Fight it out with Denver. How much do you turkeys weigh?"

"Seventy-three kilos," grunted Ted. He didn't look happy.

"Sixty-four," I said.

"Right." She jerked her thumb at me. "You sit on the left." To Ted: "Secure that box on the other side. Both of them. Then belt up." She didn't even wait to see; she pulled the door shut behind us with a slam, secured it and climbed forward again. She checked to see that Duke was clear—I just had time to wave; he nodded back—and punched us up into the air.

The mountain dropped quickly, then angled off and slid sideways as we described a sharp sweeping turn. The acceleration pressed me against the wall of the cabin. We had hardly leveled off—I had to trust my eyes for that; my stomach was no longer speaking to me—when the jets cut in and a second press of acceleration forced me deep into my seat. The cabin tilted steeply and my ears popped as we climbed for height.

There was nothing to see out the window except clouds; the stubby wing of the copter blocked my view of the ground and the bulge of the jet engine was not enough to hold my interest. The scenery in the distance, what little of it I could see, was too far away to be impressive.

I realized the pilot was speaking to us: "—be in the air a couple hours. If you're hungry, there's a ration box plugged into the wall. Don't eat all the chocolate ice cream."

Ted was already rooting around in it. He came up with a couple of sandwiches and a container of milk. Grinning hungrily, he went forward and plopped into the copilot's seat.

The redhead eyed him. "You got a certificate?"

"Well, no—but I am licensed." He gave her what he probably hoped was a friendly smile; it came out as a leer.

"*Jeezus!* What is it with you guys? Go sit in the back with the rest of the passengers."

"Hey, I'm only trying to be friendly."

"That's what stewardesses are for. Next time, take a commercial flight."

"And, uh—I wanted to see how this thing flew," he added lamely.

She did something to the control panel, set a switch and locked it in place. "Okay," she shrugged. "Look all you want. Just don't touch." Then she unstrapped herself and came aft. The tag on her jumpsuit said L. TIRELLI.

"What's in the boxes?" she asked. She nudged the insulated one with her foot.

"Eggs," I grunted.

"And in here?"

"Bugs," I said. "Big ones."

She looked disgusted. "Right. Bugs and eggs. For that they cancel my leave. Oh, yeah. I always get the good ones." Still muttering, she turned her attention to the ration box. "Damn! Clot-head took all the chicken." She pawed through the remaining sandwiches sourly.

"Uh—I'm sorry," I offered.

"Forget it. Everybody's an asshole. Here, have a sandwich." She picked one at random and tossed it at me before I could say no. She took another one for herself and dropped into the seat opposite. "What's so special about *your* bugs and eggs?"

"Uh—I don't know if I'm allowed to—" I looked to Ted. "Are we top secret?"

"What've you got—more Chtorrans?" To my startled look she said, "Don't worry about it. It's no secret. I carried a live one into Denver a month ago."

"A live *Chtorran?*"

"Uh huh. Just a small one. They found it in Nevada, dehydrated and weak. I don't know how they caught it. I guess it was too sick to fight back. Poor little thing, I felt sorry for it. They didn't expect it to live, but I haven't heard if it died."

Ted and I looked at each other. "Some scientists we are," I said. "They don't tell us anything."

"Well, there goes our big claim to fame," he added. "We thought we had the only live specimens around."

"That's a pity," she said, around a mouthful of sandwich. "But don't worry about it. They wouldn't have let you take the credit anyway."

"Thanks for the encouragement."

She wiped at her mouth with a napkin. "Don't thank me. It was free. Worth exactly what you paid for it. I'd have done the same for anyone."

She started to go forward again, but I stopped her. "What's the *L* for?"

"Huh?"

I pointed at her name tag.

"Oh—it's Liz. Short for Lizard."

"Lizard?" I raised an eyebrow.

"I come by it honestly. You'll find out."

"I think I already have."

"Just eat your sandwich," she said. "You're getting skinny." And then she climbed forward and back into her pilot's seat. Ted smiled hopefully, but she just jerked her thumb rearward and paid him no further attention.

He sighed and came back, and strapped himself into the chair where she had been sitting. "Whew!" he whispered. "I remember her. She bumped into the *Titanic* once and sank it."

"Oh, I don't know. I think she's terrific!" I didn't think she had heard me, but the tips of her ears turned pink. At least, I think they did.

Ted merely grunted, curled up sideways in his seat and went to sleep.

I finished my sandwich and spent the rest of the trip thinking about a tall spiky anomaly at fifty-nine hundred angstroms. I wished I had a terminal so I could study the data first hand instead of in my memory. Something about the millipedes' behavior—something so obvious I couldn't see it—was staring me right in the face. It was frustrating as hell—because I couldn't *not* think about it! It was a bright red vision, a blood-colored room with a table in the middle, and sitting on the table, a cage full of skittering active millipedes. Why? I leaned my head against the window and studied the clouds and thought about rose-colored glasses.

The chopper banked then and the sun flashed in my eyes, leaving a brilliant afterimage. I put my hand over my eyes, closed them and watched the pulsating blob of chemical activity on my retinas. It was white and yellow for a while, then it was crimson and it looked like a star—I decided it was Chtorr, and wanted to blow it up. After a while, it started turning blue and faded away, leaving me with only its memory and another dozen questions about the possible origin of the Chtorran invasion. I also had a niggling suspicion about something. More than ever, I wanted to get back to a terminal.

The chopper banked again and I realized we were coming in toward Denver. And Major Tirelli was about to demonstrate a "stop and drop."

She'd brought us straight over the Rockies without bothering with a descending glide path—and now that we were over the city there wasn't room for one, at least not without a long swing over eastern Colorado to shake off ten kilometers of altitude. So instead, she cut in the rotors, baffled the jets down and let us fall. The technique had been developed eight years earlier, but never used; the army had wanted a way to boost men and supplies quickly over enemy territory, never coming low enough to be in range of their portable ground-to-air missiles. It was one more thing to be grateful to the Pakistan war for. Even if your nerves forgave you for such a landing, your stomach never would.

"Wow," gasped Ted when he realized what she was doing; we'd been dropping for several decades, even though my watch insisted it was only two and a half minutes. "Either she's a real hot shot, or somebody wants to see us in an awful hurry."

"Both," she called from up front. She was downchecking the auto-monitor.

Ted looked embarrassed; he hadn't realized she could hear us.

She got on the radio then to warn them we were dropping in. "Stapleton, this is Tirelli. Clear the dime—I've got that high-pri cargo and I'm putting it right where I said I would."

A male voice answered immediately. "Negative, Tirelli. Your priority's been double-upped. They need the chopper for some brass. Veer off and drop it next door on Lowry. There's a truck waiting for you on north zero-six."

"Oh, hell," she said. But she began cutting in the jets, firing short bursts to bring us around and slow our descent. The deceleration was sideways. And bumpy.

"By the way," added the radio. "Tag your auto-monitor for inspection. We lost some of our remote metering just before you voiced in."

"Naw, that was me. I was downchecking."

"Damn it, Liz! You're not supposed to do that in the air."

"Relax, Jackie. You had me on your scopes. I saw the beeper. You didn't need the telemetry or the inertial probe anymore. And I'm in a hurry."

"Liz, those systems are for your safety—"

"Right. And worth every penny of it." She grinned. "I can't talk anymore, Jackie. I'm gonna drop this thing." She switched off the voice circuit. The auto-monitor continued to flash.

"Uh," I said, "maybe I don't understand—"

"You're right," she cut me off. "You don't." Without taking her eyes off her controls, she explained, "The excuse I gave him was a blind. What I'm really doing is cutting the control monitors. I don't want him knowing I'm not using noise abatement—it takes too much power from the engines."

"Oh," I said. "But what about the people below?"

"I try not to think about them," she said. And then added, "Would you rather be a considerate spot of red jelly on the runway—or rude and in one piece?"

"I see your point." I shut up.

"Besides," she continued, "anyone who lives that close to an airport deserves it—especially now, when half the city is empty." The copter was caught by a crossdraft then and we slid sideways. For a moment I thought she'd miscalculated and we were going to miss the runway, but she did nothing to correct our descent. Then I caught sight of the truck and realized that she'd even outthought the wind. We were being blown *toward* our landing spot.

A moment later we touched ground easily. It was the last easy thing in Denver. Even before the jets whined down to a stop, a ramp was slammed into place and the door was being pulled open.

It popped outward with a whoosh of pressurized air and slid sideways. Almost immediately, a hawk-nosed major with red face and beady eyes was barking into the cabin, "All right, Liz, where are the—"

And then he caught sight of me and Ted. "Who're you?" he demanded. He didn't wait for an answer, but snapped at Major Tirelli, "Dammit, Liz, there wasn't supposed to be any deadheading on this flight!" He was wearing a Sony Hear-Muff with wire mike attached. "Hold a minute," he said into it.

"We're not deadheading," Ted said.

He blinked at us, annoyed.

Ted poked me. "Show him the orders."

"Orders? What orders?" To the mike: "Stand by. I think we got a foul-up."

I pulled the papers out of my jacket pocket and passed them over. He took them impatiently and scanned them with a growing frown. Behind him, two middle-aged privates, obviously tapped for the job of carrying the specimen cases, peered at us with the usual mixture of curiosity and boredom.

"What the hell," he muttered. "This is a bloody nuisance. Which one are you?"

"I'm McCarthy, that's Jackson."

"Right. McCarthy. I'll remember you." He handed our orders back. "Okay, grab your cases and lug them down to that cruiser." He turned and ducked out. "You two are dismissed. They sent their own flunkies." He had all the charm of a drill press.

Ted and I exchanged a glance, shrugged and reached for the boxes. Major Tirelli finished her power-down, locked the console, and squeezed past us toward the door.

As we stumbled down the ramp after her, I noticed that the two privates had parked themselves in the V.I.P. seats of the wagon, leaving the service seats for us. The major—already I disliked him—was standing by the hood, talking to an unseen someone. "Yeah, that must be it. . . . Well, find someplace to bed them down until we can figure out what to do with them—I don't care where. . . . What? . . . I don't know. They look like it. Wait, I'll find out for sure." He glowered over at us. "Are you boys fairies?"

"Oh, honey!" Ted gushed at him. "When are you going to learn? The word is *faggot!* Don't they teach you anything at those fancy eastern schools?" Before I could react or step away, Ted had hooked his arm through mine. "Jimmy, we've got a lot of consciousness-raising to do here."

"*Ted!*" I jerked away and stared at him angrily.

"Yeah, they are," the major was saying. "Put them somewhere out of the way. Let's not give our Fourth World friends any *more* ammunition. . . . Right. Out." He looked at the two privates. "Move it! Make room there for Major Tirelli!" To us, he just growled, "Stash those in the back! You'll have to crawl in with them; there's not enough room up front." He planted himself beside a weary-looking driver.

I scrambled in behind Ted and tried to make myself comfortable— Hah! That bus hadn't been designed for comfort. There must have been an army regulation against it. We bounced across the field toward a distant building.

"What was *that* all about?" I hissed at Ted.

Ted half-shrugged, half-grinned. "I don't know. Seemed like a good idea at the time."

"Not to me!"

Ted reached over and patted my arm affectionately. I glared at him. He said, "Jimbo, take a look around you. It's a *beautiful* day. And we are back in civilization! Not even the army can spoil that!"

"I'm not a fairy!"

"I know, dear—but the major was looking for a reason to dislike you and I didn't want to disappoint him. Wow! Look at that sky! Welcome to Denver!"

SIXTEEN

OUR FIRST stop was Specimen Section, ET-3. Ted and I pushed the cart down the long disinfectant-smelling hall of the section, while Major Bright-Eyes and his honor guard followed us—glowering.

At one point we passed a heavy steel door with a very tantalizing sign:

LIVE CHTORRAN OBSERVATION
AUTHORIZED PERSONNEL ONLY

I craned my neck as we passed, hoping to peer in through the windows in the doors, but there was nothing to see. And Major Shithead gave me a dirty look for my trouble.

We went all the way to the end of the hall through a pair of double doors marked SUPERVISION. The person in charge of the section was a surprisingly unmilitary little old lady, who peered at us over the tops of her half-frame spectacles. "Well, hello!" She gave us a twinkly-sweet smile. "What did you bring me today?" She took the clipboard from the major and peered at it, smiling and blinking as she did so. "Uh huh, yes . . . yes, very good. . . ." She had rosy pink cheeks and shiny white hair piled and curled on top of her head. She was wearing a white lab coat, but where it was open at the neck I could see the collar of a green and blue flowered dress. Her nametag said M. PARTRIDGE, Ph.D.

"Millipedes, yes . . . uh huh, eggs . . . uh huh, wall scrapings . . ." She thumbed through the rest of the specimen list, squinting carefully as each page flashed up on the clipboard. "What's this? *Purple Coleus?* Whose classification is that?"

"Mine." I raised my hand.

"Oh, yes." She blinked at me. "And you are—?"

"McCarthy, James. Special Forces."

"Ah, yes," she said. "Well, James, please don't classify specimens anymore. Leave that to those who are better qualified for the task. I know you were only trying to be helpful—"

"Excuse me," I interrupted. "But I am qualified."

"Eh?" She looked up at me. And blinked.

"I'm Special Forces, ma'am. Extraterrestrial Section. I gathered those specimens myself. *At some risk.* And I've had several days in which to observe them. I've also had access to the entire Scientific Catalog of the Library of Congress. 'Purple Coleus' is an accurate description of that plant, regardless of the qualifications of the person pointing to it and saying, 'That's a purple coleus.' " I looked at Ted, but he was busy admiring the ceiling. It was very well plastered.

The major was glaring at me. Dr. Partridge shushed him and turned to me. "James, we receive many, many specimens every week. I have no way of knowing whether this is the first time we've seen samples of this particular species or not. This may not even be a Chtorran species at all—"

"It was growing in a carefully cultivated ring all around the Chtorran igloo—" I started to explain.

"Yes, yes, I know." She held up a hand. "But please let *us* make that confirmation. If we accepted the classifications of every person who brought in specimens, we'd have fifty different descriptions of every single plant and animal." She patted my hand like a forgiving grandmother. "I know you'll remember that with the next batch of specimens you bring us."

"Uh, ma'am—" I fumbled my orders out of my pocket. "We've been reassigned here. We're detached from the Rocky Mountain Control District to function as independent observers in the National Science Center, Extraterrestrial Division."

She blinked. And blinked again. "Goodness," she said. "Well, it wasn't cleared with me. How do they expect me to run a section if they don't keep me informed?" She took the pink copy of my orders, adjusted her glasses on her nose and looked down at it. She held it almost at arm's length. When she finished scanning, she said, "Hm," very quietly. She passed the paper back almost absentmindedly. "Yes. Well,

I'm sure we can find something for you boys to do. Come and see me on, ah . . . Tuesday. No, wait a minute—where did I leave my calendar?—oh, here it is. Let's see, now. No, Thursday will be better—"

"Uh, ma'am?" She stopped and blinked and gave me that wide-eyed look again. "We'd like to get to work *immediately*. If you could assign us a terminal . . . ?"

"My goodness, are you Special Forces boys always in such a hurry?"

"Yes, ma'am, we are. There's a war on." I remembered something Shorty had said and added, "It's the first invasion ever fought on American territory." I held up my disk meaningfully. "A terminal? And can we get our live specimens settled in?"

Major Bombast interrupted then. "Dr. Partridge—it's already Friday afternoon, and you have a reception and a plenary session—"

"Yes, I know." There was an impatient edge to her voice. She caught herself and smiled sweetly at him. "I'll finish up here, and you can pick me up for the briefing in—ah, forty-five minutes." The major hrumphed and disappeared. Dr. Partridge stepped to a desk and hit a buzzer. "Jerry!" she called.

Jerry was a dumpy-looking potato of a human being hiding a rubbery face behind thick glasses and a frazzle of dirty blond hair. He appeared in a smudged lab coat and was carrying a disemboweled modulator. He didn't seem to be aware that he still had it in his hands. His nametag said J. LARSON, and he wore a slightly confused frown, as if he were perpetually preoccupied in some minor befuddlement.

Dr. Partridge gave him a cloying smile. "Oh, there you are. Will you handle James and—what is your name? Ted? Will you help them out? They're here as observers."

"Oh," said Jerry. He stared at us as if we were intruders. He looked to be somewhere in his mid-thirties, but he could have been any age from twenty-five to fifty. "Do you have orders?" he asked.

I passed them over. As he glanced through them, Dr. Partridge chirped, "I know that Jerry will take good care of you. If there's anything you need, just see him. He represents me. Now, if you'll excuse me—" And she disappeared into an office.

Jerry finished reading our orders and passed them back. "Special Forces, I see." He coughed. "My uncle's in the Special Forces. My Uncle Ira."

I nodded politely. "Sorry. I don't know him. Look, can we get on with this? I need a terminal. And I want these millipedes installed under special conditions."

Jerry rubbed his nose, then looked at me with a flat expression. "I'll have to have you cleared before I can assign you a terminal and work space. It'll take two weeks."

"Oh, terrific," I said. "Look—I'm in the middle of a process here. I can't wait two weeks." I pointed to the cases on the cart. "Those eggs and millipedes have to be installed under special conditions—"

"What kind of conditions?" Jerry had stepped over to the cart and was opening the metal handling cases and peering in.

"A cool, dry place for the eggs. The millipedes too—a cool room with dim light. I can give you specific recommendations."

"That won't be necessary."

"Ahh—I strongly suggest it."

Jerry opened another case. "Why?"

"Because that's what they like." I stepped over to the cart next to him. "Use a little common sense. Look at the size of their eyes. They're all pupil. Of course they're not going to like bright light."

Jerry hmphed.

I said, "Hazy sunshine blinds them. Indoor light blinds them. Even dim light blinds them. They can maneuver in twilight or dusk, but they can only see well in the dark."

Jerry looked skeptical. "Even *absolute* dark?"

I nodded. "I think their eyes are heat sensitive. I wasn't able to test it, but it looks as if they can see pretty far into the infra-red."

Ted spoke up then, for the first time. "Tell him what that means, Jim."

"Uh . . ." I wished he hadn't done that. I said, "They're not noctur-nal—"

Jerry looked up from the case, frowning. He shoved his hands into the pockets of his lab coat. "I don't get that."

"—on their home planet. On Earth, they have to be."

"Huh?"

"Well," I said, "it's the size of their eyes. That really suggests that they've evolved under much poorer lighting conditions than we have here. It's compensation. Either their home planet is farther from its primary, or the primary doesn't put out as much light in the visible spectrum as Sol. Or both. That makes the planet noticeably cooler than Earth; probably its temperatures range between five and twenty degrees Centigrade. Maybe it's in a long glaciation. The millipedes seem most comfortable between ten and thirteen degrees, but that depends on the amount of light hitting them."

Jerry began to look interested.

"Earth daylight is too bright," I continued. "It slows them down, even makes them curl up. At a light level approximating dusk, they're at their most active across the widest possible temperature range—that's when they really *move*. When we found them, they were torpid—but only by comparison. I take it to be a pretty good indication of the general level of brightness to be found on Chtorr. Hence, the big eyes."

Jerry said, "Hm," and looked back into the millipede case with studied thoughtfulness.

"If I had access to a terminal," I hinted, "I could tell a lot more. It's very interesting how sensitive to light and temperature differences these creatures are. That suggests to me that the climate on Chtorr is incredibly stable. The nights must be fairly warm in relation to the days. I'd guess that the planet has a fairly hazy atmosphere with a lot of carbon dioxide in it; that would create a greenhouse effect and keep the nights from cooling too much. I also think the planet may not have any moons —or maybe only very small ones. Nothing that can exert strong tidal effects. That would make the planet stormy, not hazy."

"Hazy, huh?" Jerry pursed his lips as he thought. His whole rubbery face deformed. "I do know a little bit of theoretical ecology," he said. "You might be right—" Then he added, "—but I doubt it."

"Oh, thanks." I folded my arms across my chest. "Listen, if you know a little bit, then you know a little bit isn't enough."

He nodded his agreement. "I know. I took my degree in T.E."

"B.S.?"

"Ph.D."

"Oh." Suddenly, I felt stupid.

"Listen, I applaud your industriousness—as well as your imagination —but your theory has holes in it big enough to drive a worm through."

"Name six."

"Just one will do." He closed the lid on the case again. "If Chtorr has a hazy atmosphere, then that means they can't see the stars. If the atmosphere is hazy enough, they won't see any moons either, especially not if they're small. That means no celestial objects in the sky to attract their interest—and that means no incentive for an intelligent race to discover space travel. If your theory is correct, these bugs shouldn't be here, and neither should the worms who brought them."

"Their eyes are much more sensitive than ours," I replied. "They should be able to see celestial objects under far worse viewing conditions. Look—" I took a deep breath. "To an exobiologist, the species filling the bottom rungs of the ladder are very efficient little monitors of the physical conditions of the planet—its rotation, its temperature cycles, its light levels, its weather patterns and a thousand and six other variables. You can extrapolate the context of the ecology out of the content, if you know what to look for. Based on this evidence, Chtorr is a perpetually smoke-filled room. Or haze, or smog, or something. The point is, the atmosphere is thick and the primary is dim, but how much of each, I don't know—oh, but I can tell you what color it is."

"Huh?" Jerry's jaw dropped. "How?"

"That's what I've been working on." I tapped my disk. "It's all on here."

He blinked. "What is it?"

"It's a three-dimensional graph—the variables are temperature, light intensity and light frequency, demonstrated by millipede reactivity."

"Oh," said Jerry. He looked impressed.

"Well, hey—!" put in Ted, "What color *is* it?"

"It's red," I grinned. "The star is dark red. What else?"

Jerry considered that. His face was thoughtful. "That's fairly well advanced along the sequence. I can see why the Chtorrans might be looking for a new home; the old one's wearing out." He looked at me. "How do you know?"

"Serendipity," I admitted. "I thought I could approximate darkness with a two-hundred-lumen output in the red band—well, it works in a dark room; why not here? I got tired of stumbling into things. But then the new measurements didn't fit the curve I'd already established. The bugs were way too active. So I started thinking about the wavelengths of their visual spectrum. All last night I had the computer varying the color temperature of the plates at regular intervals. I gave the bugs eighteen different colors. Most of them provoked no response at all. The yellow gave some, the orange a bit more, but it was the red that made them sit up twice. A little more testing this morning showed they like it best no brighter than a terrestrial twilight—and then it correlates almost perfectly with the other set of tests."

"It sounds like a good piece of work," said Jerry. Suddenly, he grinned. On his face, the effect was grotesque. "It reminds me of a project I did once. We were given three disparate life forms and we had to extrapolate the native ecology. It was a two-year project. I used over twenty thousand hours of parallel processing." He grew more serious. "So please don't be upset when I tell you that your conclusions might be premature. I've been through this exercise once. I know some of the pitfalls. You can't judge a planet by a single life form. There's a lot of difference between rattlesnakes and penguins. You don't know if these millipedes are representative or just a special case. We don't know what part of the planet they're from, or what kind of region—are they from the poles or the equator? Are they representative of mountainous fauna on Chtorr, or swampland creatures? Or desert, or grasslands, or *what?* And what would that identification imply about conditions on the rest of the planet? What kind of seasons are these bugs geared to—how long are they? What kind of biological cycles? How long are the days, months, years? If they have no moons, or more than one, do they even have cyclical equivalents of months? The real question about these specimens is, where do these millipedes *fit* in the Chtorran ecology? All you have here are indicators: the worms like to eat bugs, and the bugs like to eat anything—is that a general or arbitrary condition? What can we imply about the shape of their food chain? And what about their breeding—what is their reproductive cycle like? What are their growth patterns? Their psychology—*if* they even have one? Diseases? And I haven't even *begun* to ask questions."

"That's what we're here for," I said. "To help ask questions—and to help find answers."

Jerry accepted that. "Good." He said, "I'll see that your information gets passed along to those who can make the best use of it. You've probably opened up a valuable area of inquiry." He held his hand out for the disk.

"Sorry." I shook my head. "No terminal, no disk."

"Uh—" Jerry looked annoyed. "If you have information about any extraterrestrial or suspected extraterrestrial life forms, you know you're required by law to report it to the federal authorities. This is the agency." He held out his hand again.

"No way," I said. "A man died for this information. I owe it to him to see it delivered. I don't want it disappearing down some rabbit hole."

"It's against regulations to let you on a terminal before you're cleared." He looked unhappy. "What branch of Special Forces did you say you were with?"

"Alpha Bravo."

"And what do you do?"

"We burn worms."

"I wouldn't phrase it like that, if I were you. At least, not around here." He thought for a moment, then made a face. "Phooey on regulations. You've got a green card, haven't you? All right, I know how to do it. Come on." He led us to a nexus of four terminals, powered up two of them, logged himself in on one and slaved the second one to his control. "Go ahead," he said. "Create a password for yourself. You too—Jackson, is it? You'll be operating on a special department account for V.I.P.s—oh, and don't tell anyone I did this. Now, first thing—I want you to *dupe* that disk—"

SEVENTEEN

THE BUS station was next to the PX. There were fifteen or twenty people standing around and waiting, most of them dressed in evening clothes or uniforms.

Hardly anybody looked up as we approached. "What's up?" I whispered.

Ted said, "I'll find out," and disappeared into the crowd. He left me standing there looking after him.

Our intention had been to ride into town and take in a show or a tribe-dance. Now I just stood in front of the bus terminal, staring at the big wall-screen. It was flashing: NEXT BUS—22 MINUTES. There was a blinking dot on the map, showing its present location.

I shoved my hands into my pockets and turned around. Almost immediately, I found myself staring into the face of a thin, pale little girl who couldn't have been more than sixteen at most, probably younger; she was hanging on the arm of a large, bombastic-looking man. He was puffy and florid-faced, and obviously drunk. He was old enough to be her father. He wore a plaid kilt and a rumpled military jacket. I didn't recognize the nationality; he could have been anything from Australian to Scot. I pegged him as a colonel. Or a buffoon. I was just about to give the girl a smile when he noticed me studying them. He glared and I turned away embarrassed.

I looked at the two WACs instead—at least, I assumed they were WACs. They could just as easily have been whores. Dad always said the way to tell the difference was that "whores dress like ladies, and ladies dress like whores." But I never understood what he meant by that. I always thought a whore *was* a lady. By definition. These two were murmuring quietly to each other, obviously about something neither of them cared about. They were swathed in elegance and indifference. They should have been waiting for a limousine, not a bus; but—well, the whole crowd was an odd conglomeration. Maybe they were with the three Japanese businessmen in Sony-suits who were arguing so heatedly over something, while a fourth—obviously a secretary—kept referring to the readouts on a pocket terminal.

There were four black delegates speaking some unidentifiable African language; I would have guessed Swahili, but I had no way of being sure. Three men and a tall, striking woman with her hair in painful-looking corn rows. All were in bright red and gold costumes. The woman caught me looking at her, smiled and turned away. She whispered something to one of the men and he turned and glanced at me; then he turned back to his companion and the two of them laughed softly together. I felt myself getting hot.

I was embarrassed. I turned and stared into the PX window. I stayed that way, staring at faded packages of men's makeup kits until Ted came up grinning and punched my arm. "You're gonna love this!" he said.

I turned away from the dusty window. "What did you find?"

"Oh . . . something." He said it smugly.

"For instance?"

"An orientation reception. You know what's going on here?"

"Chtorran studies, I hope."

"Better than that. The First Worldwide Conference on Extraterrestrial Life, with special emphasis on the Chtorran species, and particular objectives of contact, negotiation and coexistence."

"What about control?"

"I guess that's implied. There is a subsection on defensive procedures and policies, but it seems to be downplayed. In any case, this is a major effort. There are five hundred of the best scientists—"

"Best *remaining*," I corrected.

Ted ignored me. "—in the world. Not just biologists, Jim boy, but psychologists, ecologists, anthropologists, space scientists—they've even got the head of the Asenion Foundation coming in."

"Who's he?"

"It's a group of speculative thinkers. Writers, artists, filmists, programmers—like your dad—and so on. People with a high level of ideational fluency. People who can extrapolate—like futurists and science fiction writers."

"Oh," I said. "Crackpots. I'm whelmed."

"You gonna come?"

"Huh? We're not officially invited, are we?"

"So? It's about Chtorrans, isn't it? And we're Chtorran experts, aren't we? We have as much right as anybody to be there. Come on, the bus is here." It was a big Chrysler hydro-turbine, one of the regular shuttles between the base and downtown. The driver had all her lights on and the big beast gleamed like a dragon.

I didn't get a chance to object. Ted just grabbed my arm and pulled me aboard after him. The bus was moving even before we found seats; I wanted to head for the back, but Ted pulled me down next to him near a cluster of several young and elegantly dressed couples; we rumbled out the front gate and onto the main highway and I thought of a brilliantly lit cruise ship full of revelers in the middle of a dark and lonely ocean.

Someone up front started passing a flask around and the party unofficially began. Most of the people on the bus seemed to know each other already and were joking back and forth. Somehow, Ted fit himself into the group and within minutes was laughing and joking along with them. When they moved to the lounge at the front of the bus, he waved for me to come up and join them, but I shook my head.

Instead I retreated to the back of the bus—almost bumping into the thin, pale little girl as she came out of the lavatory. "Oops, sorry!"

She flashed a quick angry look at me, then started to step past.

"I said I'm sorry."

"Yeah—they all are."

"Hey!" I caught her arm.

"What?!"

I looked into her face. "Who hurt you?"

She had the darkest eyes. "Nobody!" she said. She pulled her arm free and went forward to rejoin her friend, the fat florid colonel.

The Marriott-Regency was a glimmering fairy castle, floating like a cloud above a pool of silvery light. It was a huge white pyramid of a building, all dressed up in terraces and minarets, and poised in the center of a vast sparkling lake. It towered above Denver like a bright complacent giant—a *glowing* giant. Starbursts and reflections twinkled and blazed across the water—there were lights below as well as above— and all around, shimmering laser beams played back and forth across the sky like swords of dancing color; the tower was enveloped in a dazzling halo.

High above it all, flashing bursts of fireworks threw themselves against the night, sparkling in the sky, popping and exploding in a never-ending shower of light. The stars were dimmed behind the glare.

By comparison, the rest of the city seemed dark and deserted. It was as if there were nothing else in Denver but this colossal spire, blazing with defiant life—a celebration for the sheer joy of celebration.

A gasp of awe went up from some of the revelers. I heard one lady exclaim, "It's beautiful! But what are they celebrating?"

"Nothing," laughed her companion. "Everything. Just being alive!"

"They do it every night?"

"Yep."

The bus rolled down a ramp, through a tunnel and up into the building itself, finally stopping on an interior terrace overlooking a frosty garden.

It was like stepping into a fairy tale. The inside of this gaudy diamond was a courtyard thirty stories tall, bathed in light, divided by improbable fountains and exuberant forests, spotted with unexpected plateaus and overhung with wide terraces and balconies. There were banners hanging everywhere. I got off the bus and just stared—until Ted grabbed my arm and pulled me along.

To one side was a lobby containing the hotel's registration desk and elevators, on the other was a ramp leading down into the heart of the courtyard. A Marine Corps band in shining silver uniforms occupied one of the nearby balconies and strains of Tchaikovsky's *Sleeping Beauty March* filled the air. (It used to be a waltz, until the Marines got ahold of it.) Everywhere I looked, I saw uniforms—from every branch of the service, and quite a few foreign ones as well. Had the military taken over the hotel?

There was a young lieutenant—good grief! When had they started commissioning them that young?—at the head of the ramp. He was seated behind a porta-console, checking off each person against the list in the computer. Although we didn't see him prevent anyone from going down the ramp, his authority to do so was obvious. I wondered how Ted was going to get us past.

It turned out to be no problem at all. Ted had attached himself to the buffoon with the sixteen-year-old girl, showing interest only in the buffoon and none at all in the girl. He looked like a hustler in his gaudy flash-pants; now he was acting like one. We approached the console in a group; Ted hooked one arm through the buffoon's, the other through mine. "Now, come on, Jimmy-boy," he said. "Don't be a party-poop." The looey looked up at all four of us, tried unsuccessfully to conceal his reaction and nodded us past without comment.

Turned out the buffoon was one of the better known buffoons in Denver. As well as his predilections for—well, never mind. The girl was not his daughter. But she *was* hungry.

I shook off Ted's arm and pulled angrily away. I stopped on the ramp and let them keep going without me. Ted just nattered along, barely noticing my departure.

I stood there watching them, Ted gushing on one arm of the buffoon, the girl on the other, and hated all three of them. This wasn't what I'd come to Denver for. I felt hot and embarrassed, a damn fool.

Screw them. I went looking for a phone.

Found one, inserted my card and dialed home.

Got a recorded message. "Not here now, back tomorrow." *Beep.*

Sigh. "Mom, this is Jim—"

Click. "Jim, I'm sorry I missed you. I'm not in Santa Cruz anymore. I've moved down the coast to a place called Family. It's on the New Peninsula. We take care of orphans. I've met a wonderful man here—I want you to meet him. We're thinking of getting married. His name is Alan Plaskow; I know you'll like him. Maggie does. Maggie and Annie send their love—and we all want to know when we'll be seeing you again. Your Uncle Ernie will be in town next month, something to do with the Reclamation Hearings. Please let me know where I can get in touch with you, okay?" *Beep.*

"Hi, Mom. I got your message okay. I don't know when I'll be able to get away, but as soon as I can I'll come home for a few days. I hope you're well. I hope everyone else is okay too. I'm in Denver right now at the National Science Center and—"

A metallic voice interrupted: "It is required by law to inform you that this conversation is being monitored for possible censorship under the National Security Act."

"Terrific. Anyway, Mom, I'll be in touch with you as soon as I can. Don't try to call me here; I don't think you'll have much luck. Give my love to everyone." I hung up. I tried calling Maggie, but the lines to Seattle were out, or busy, or something. I left a delayed message, pocketed my card and walked away.

I found myself in front of a newsstand, studying headlines. It was the same old stuff. The President was calling for unity and cooperation.

Again. Congress was in a wrangle over the economy. Again. The value
of the casey had jumped another klick. Bad news for the working man.
Again.

On an impulse, I picked up a pack of Highmasters, opening them as I
headed back.

I stopped to light up at the top of a ramp.

"Who's that?" said someone behind me.

"Who's who?" someone answered.

"The preacher."

"Oh, that's Fromkin. Ego-tripping again. He loves to play teacher.
Whenever he comes to these things, he holds court."

"Looks like a full house."

"Oh, he's a good speaker, never dull—but I've heard him before, and
it's always the same sermon: 'Let's be unreasonable.' Let's go somewhere else."

"Okay."

They wandered off. I studied the man they were talking about for a
moment, then headed down the ramp for a closer listen. He did look
like a preacher. The effect was accomplished by a ruffled silk shirt and a
black frock coat—he looked like he'd just stepped out of the nineteenth
century. He was lean and spare and had a halo of frosty-white hair that
floated around his pink skull like a cloud.

His eyes sparkled as he spoke; he was very much enjoying himself. I
edged into the crowd and found a place to stand. One of the women at
his feet was saying, "But I don't see how it's possible to inflate a labor
economy, Professor. . . . I mean, I thought that everything was
fixed."

"It's really quite simple," Fromkin said. "Just devalue your counters."

"But that's what I mean. I thought the point of the whole thing was
to create an economy that *couldn't* be devalued."

"Sure. But—oh, hell, it requires too much explanation. Wait a minute, let me see if I can boil it down. Look, the theory of money is that
it's a tool to allow a social organism to manipulate its energy—that is,
money units are the corpuscles of the cultural bloodstream; it has to
flow for the system to be able to feed itself. You like that, huh? What we
think of as money is really only counters, a way of keeping score which
organ in the social body—that means you—is presently using or controlling this piece of energy. It's when we start thinking that the counter
is valuable that we confuse ourselves. It's not—it's only the symbol."

"I could use a few of those symbols," one wag remarked.

Fromkin looked at him with withering gentleness. "So create some," he said. Suddenly, I knew who he reminded me of—Whitlaw!

"I'd love to. How?" said the wag.

"Easy. Create value—for others. The truth is that you can only measure your wealth by the amount of difference you make in the world. That is, how much do you contribute to the people around you? And to how many people do you contribute?"

"Huh?" The wag had stopped being funny. Now he was honestly curious.

"All right, stick with me. The physical universe uses heat to keep score. Actually, it's motion, but on the molecular level we experience it as heat. Just know that it's the only way one object ever affects another, so it's the only way to measure how big a difference an object *really* makes. We measure heat in BTUs. British Thermal Units. Calories. We want our money to be an accurate measure, so we use the same system as the physical universe: ergo, we have the KC standard, the kilocalorie."

A chubby woman in a bright-flowered dress giggled nervously. "I used to think we were spending pieces of fat. I thought I'd be rich." Fromkin acknowledged her attempt at humor with a noncommittal smile, and she gushed happily.

The man next to her asked, "How much *is* a pound of flesh these days?"

"Um, let's see—a pound is two-point-two kilograms. . . ."

"It'd be three caseys," I said. "A pound of flesh is three thousand calories." I looked back to Fromkin.

He was ignoring the interruption. He took a final sip from his drink and put it down. Someone immediately moved to refill it, a thin, bony-looking woman with basset-hound eyes.

Fromkin returned his attention to the brunette who had asked the original question. "Still with me? Good. Okay, this is what the casey teaches us about the law of supply and demand. The purchase price of an object is determined by how much of your labor you're willing to trade for it. The difference between the purchase price and its actual value is called *profit*. Stop wrinkling your nose, my dear; profit is not a dirty word. Profit is a resource. It is a necessary part of the economic process; it's what we call the energy that the organism uses for reinvestment if it is to continue to thrive and produce. This apple, for instance, is the apple tree's profit—the meat of it is used to feed the seeds inside,

and that's how an apple tree manufactures another apple tree. So you
cannot charge less than an item costs in energy, but you can charge
more; in fact, you *must.*"

"So why does a kilo of Beluga cost more than a kilo of soya?" someone asked. "The soya has more protein."

Fromkin smiled. "Isn't it obvious? As soon as you have one unit less
than the number of willing buyers, you have an auction going. The price
will rise until enough people drop out and you have only as many
buyers as units to sell; it's called 'whatever the market will bear.' "

He stood up then and stepped to a nearby buffet table and started
loading a plate. But he kept talking. The man was incredible. "Under
the labor standard, a nation's wealth is determined by its ability to
produce—its gross national product. Cut the population and you cut
the wealth of a country. Automatically. But the amount of counters still
in circulation remains high. And there's no easy way to cut back the
coinage; it can't help but inflate—and even if you *could* cut back all the
excess cash in circulation, it wouldn't be enough. The system is still
pegged to its history. Bonds, for instance—a government sells bonds on
the promise of paying interest on them. Interest can only be paid when
the system is in a growth situation. If there's no growth, then interest is
only a promise by the government to continue inflating the economy
and further reduce the value of the counters—the money. That's why I
oppose letting the government borrow money—under *any* circumstances. Because it sets a bad precedent. If it can't pay it back, then it
has to borrow more, and the inflationary spiral is endless. Let the government go into debt and we're mortgaging our own future incomes.
This country—the whole world, in fact—is in an extreme no-growth
situation, yet the interest will still be paid on all outstanding bonds. It
has to be; it's the law. So . . . the more cash in circulation, the less
each bill is worth. Thank God we still have the dollar—that's at least
backed by paper, and it can't inflate as fast as the casey can under these
circumstances—and it'll continue that way for a long time. It *was* a
commodity; someday soon it'll be money again. We're at the beginning
of a long recede—"

"Beginning—?" said the brunette. "I thought—"

"Nope." Fromkin was sitting again, eating. He paused to chew and
swallow. "You're wrong. That was a population crash. When four and a
half billion people die in two years, that's a crash. The U.N. definition
of a recede specifies seven percent or more over an eight-month period
—but when it's seventy percent, that's a crash. We're just coming out of

the crash now; the curve is finally starting to level off. Now we're going into the recede. The *real* recede. It's the aftershock of the crash. But it's a lot more than that too. Believe it or not, the human race may have been knocked below the threshold of viability. There may not be enough of us left to survive."

"Huh?" That was a newcomer to the group. His posture was military even though he was wearing a dress jacket. He was standing with a plate in one hand and a drink in the other. "Are you serious? Fromkin, I think you're ignoring the fact that the human race has survived a long time—and we've only been above one billion individuals for a little more than a century."

Fromkin looked up. He recognized the man and grinned. "You'd better stick to your spaceships, Colonel Ferris. Someone make room for the colonel here, thank you. You're right about your figures, of course— I saw the same report—but the figures alone don't tell the whole story. You need to know the demographic cross section. Right now, we are not functioning from a stable population of family or tribal groups. The human network is mostly disjointed—we're all individual atoms, swirling in chaos. We haven't reformed into molecules—although that process has begun—let alone crystals and lattices. We're still a very long way from the creation and operation of the necessary social organisms that a self-generating society needs to survive—and I'm still only talking about survival; I haven't even touched upon anything beyond that— like celebration."

Ferris looked unhappy. Some of Fromkin's other listeners looked puzzled.

"Okay, let me put that in English for you. We are not a population yet. We are just a mish-mash of people who've been lucky enough—or perhaps I should say *unlucky* enough—to survive." He looked at Ferris as he said it. "Each of us has his own horror story."

Now I knew him. Jarles "Free Fall" Ferris. The Lunar Colony. One of the seventeen who made it back. We never heard how they chose who stayed and who returned. I wondered if we'd ever find out.

Fromkin was saying, "The fact is, we're still getting after-effects of the plagues. We'll be getting them for another year or three—but we're nowhere better equipped to handle them for a small, spread-out, disorganized population than we were able to handle them for a large, dense, organized one. If anything, an individual's chances are worse now for survival. There are still ripples of those plagues circulating. Slowly, but surely, we're going to lose another half-billion people—that's the guess of the Rand-Tanks. Then, of the survivors, we're going to lose ten percent who will have lost the will to live. Anomie. Shock. The walking wounded—and just because you don't see them wandering around in herds anymore doesn't mean they're not there. Then we'll lose the very old and the very young who won't be able to take care of themselves. And the very ill too. Anyone on any kind of maintenance is in danger, even if it's something as easily controllable as diabetes. There simply won't be either the medical care or the supplies. We lost nearly eighty percent of the world's supply of doctors, nurses and support technicians. We'll lose a lot of children because there won't be anyone around to parent them. Some will die, some will go feral. The birth rate will be down for a long time. We're going to lose all the babies who won't be born because those who could have been parents are no longer capable or willing. We'll lose even more babies who are born to parents who can't or won't maintain them. Should I go on? No? Okay—but we're real close to the edge. It'll look like positive feedback on the cultural level: psychoses creating more psychoses, distrust and suspicion leading to more distrust and suspicion. And if enough people start to perceive that there isn't enough of anything to go around—food, fuel, whatever —they'll start fighting over what's left. And by then we'll be into serious problems with population density; the survivors—a rag-taggle conglomeration of misfits by any definition—may be too spread out to meet and mate. Those few left who are capable and willing to be responsible parents may not be able to find each other. I expect the recede to take us right down to the level where it will be questionable if we can come back. Which means, by the way, that the casey was a noble experiment, but I'm afraid it's going to be overinflated and worthless for a long time to come. I wish I were wrong, but I've already converted most of my holdings to property or dollars. I'd advise the rest of you to do the same. With a shrinking tax base, the government is going to have to take drastic steps soon, and you're going to have to protect your wealth, or you might find yourself turned into a pauper overnight by a paper revaluation. That's happened a couple times in the past two decades, but this next one ought to be a wowzer."

He paused to take another bite of food and wash it down with a drink.

Maybe it was my high-school reflexes—I had to say something. He was talking about the fact that the dying hadn't ended yet, that we were going to lose one-third, maybe even one-half, of the remaining human beings left on the planet. He wasn't talking about how to save them; he was talking dispassionately about how to avoid economic discomfort. No—he was talking about how to profit from it. I couldn't help myself. "Sir—"

He looked up. His eyes were shaded. "Yes?"

"What about the people?"

"Say again?"

"The people. Aren't we going to try to save them?"

"Save whom? From what?"

"You said at least another half-billion people are going to die. Can't we do something about that?"

"What would you have us do?"

"Well—save them!"

"How?"

"Um, well—"

"Excuse me—I should have asked, 'With *what?*' Most of us are spending most of our energies just staying alive. Most governments are having too much trouble just maintaining internal order to mount a rescue effort even for their own populations, let alone others. And how *do* you rescue people from the crisscrossing wave fronts of five different plagues, each wave front more than a thousand kilometers wide? We may have identified the plagues, but we haven't finished identifying the mutations. By the way, are you vaccinated?"

"Sure, isn't everybody?"

He snorted. "You're vaccinated because you're in the army, or the Civil Service, or something like that—someone considers you valuable enough to justify keeping you alive; but that vaccine costs time, money —and, most valuable of all, human effort. And there isn't enough of the latter to go around. Not *everybody* is vaccinated—only the ones that the government *needs* to survive. We don't have the technicians to program even the automated laboratories. We don't even have the personnel to *teach* new technicians. We don't have the people to maintain the equipment. We don't have—"

"I get the point—but still, isn't there something—?"

"Young man, if there were something, we would be doing it. We *are* doing it. Whatever we can. The point is, that even with our best efforts we are still going to lose that half-billion people. It's as unavoidable as sunrise. We might as well acknowledge it because, like it or not, that's what's so."

"I don't like it," I said.

"You don't have to." Fromkin shrugged. "The universe doesn't care.

God doesn't take public opinion polls. The fact is, what you like, what I like, what anyone likes—it's all irrelevant." His expression was deceptively cordial. He seemed almost deliberately hostile. "If you really want to make a difference, then you need to ask yourself this question about *everything* you do: will this contribute to the survival of the species?" He looked around the gathering. "Most of us here are breeders. Would you have us compromise that breeding potential in favor of some altruistic gesture of ultimately questionable value? Or let me put that another way: you can spend the rest of your life raising and teaching the next generation of human beings, or you can spend it nursing a few dozen of the walking wounded, catatonics, autistics and retards who will never be able to contribute, who will only continue to use up resources—not the least of which is your valuable time."

"I hear you, sir. But to sit calmly and eat caviar and strawberries and bagels and lox while talking about global death and benevolent genocide—"

He put down his plate. "Would it be more moral if I starved while I talked about global death and benevolent genocide? Would starving make me care more? Would it increase my ability to do something—other than *hurt?*"

"You shouldn't be talking about it so dispassionately at all," I said. "It's unthinkable."

A flicker of annoyance crossed his face, but his voice remained steady. "It is *not* unthinkable." He said it very deliberately—was he *angry?* "In fact, if we do *not* think about it, we will be risking the consequences of being caught by surprise. One of the basic fallacies of sophomoric intelligence—don't take it personal, son; I insult everybody equally—is moral self-righteousness. Merely being able to perceive the difference between right and wrong does not make you a moral person; it only gives you some guidelines in which to operate." He leaned forward in his chair. "Now, here's the bad news. Most of the time those guidelines are irrelevant—because the pictures we hold in our heads about the way things *should* be usually have very little relation to the way things actually *are.* And holding the position that things should be some way other than what they are will only keep you stuck. You'll spend so much time arguing with the physical universe that you won't produce any result at all. You'll have some great excuses, but you won't have a result. The fact that we can do nothing about the circumstances that are sending us into a long recede is unpleasant, yes—now let's stop arguing about the situation and start handling it. There is still much we can do to minimize the unpleasantness—"

"One half billion human deaths is more than just an unpleasantness—"

"Four and a half billion human deaths is more than just an unpleasantness too." He looked at me calmly. "And please, lower your voice— I'm sitting right here."

"Sorry. My point is, this whole discussion seems inhumane."

He nodded. "Yes, I have to grant that. It does *seem* inhumane." He changed his tone suddenly. "You know any crazy people?"

"Damaged," I corrected. "Crazy is a negative connotation."

"Sorry," he amended. "I grew up in a different time. Old habits are hard to break. I still hadn't gotten used to women having the vote when the next thing even lawyers wanted to ride in the front of the streetcars. Do you know any *mentally dysfunctional* human beings? Any *damaged* people?"

"A few."

"Did you ever stop to consider why they were that way?"

"They were irrational, I suppose."

"Were they? Sometimes irrationality is the only *rational* response to an irrational situation. It's a very human thing—and it's not limited to humans alone." He said softly, "That's what we're doing here—the only rational response to an irrational and very frightening situation. Quite possibly—no, quite *probably*—of the people in this room"—and he gestured to include the whole reception, spread out across several acres of hotel—"less than half of us may be alive next year at this time. Or even next week." He shrugged. "Who knows?"

The sweet young thing, whose knee he was resting his hand on, went pale at that. He patted her gently, but otherwise ignored her. He continued looking at me. "All of a sudden, there are a lot of things out there that can kill human beings. And there isn't a lot left to stop them. You know, we've had our way on this planet far too long. Nature is always willing to take advantage of our weaknesses. Remember, Mom's a bitch. We've spent centuries building a technology to isolate us from the real world. That isolation has left most of us survival-illiterate and vulnerable. But the machine has stopped—is stopping *now*—and most people are going to be at the mercy of the contents of their stomachs. Nature doesn't care; she'll finish the job the plagues started and never miss us. Humans weren't always the hunter at the top of the food chain—we were just a passing fad. Now we're going to be prey again, like in the old days. Ever seen a wolf pack?"

"No. . . ."

"We've got them running loose in the streets of Denver. They're called poodles, terriers, retrievers, Dobermans, shepherds, collies, St. Bernards and mutts—but they're still wolf packs. They're hungry and they can kill. We could lose another thirty million people to animals, formerly domestic and otherwise, right there. Probably more. I'm talking about worldwide, of course. And I'm including people packs in that estimate too—those are animals of another sort. We'll probably lose a hundred million people who would not have died otherwise, but there's no longer the medical care to take care of the injuries and illnesses that they'll incur in the next twelve months. Did you know that appendicitis can be fatal? And so on—" He stopped, looked at me and smiled. I was beginning to understand his charm. He never intended anything personally. "So, my young friend—much as I respect your indignation and the emotions on which it is based—what we are doing here tonight is quite probably the most rational thing we can be doing. I notice you haven't tried to excuse *your* presence here; perhaps you're quite rational too. In fact, there is only one thing more rational for a person to do that I can think of."

"What's that?"

He went soft for a moment, *gentle.* "Make love to someone you care about. You're not immortal, you know. If you don't take the opportunity to tell someone you love them tonight, you may never get another chance."

He was right. I thought about a whole bunch of someones.

Fromkin stood up and offered his arm to the girl. She and another woman both tried to take it. Fromkin smiled and offered his other arm. He smiled at me again, knowingly, and then the three of them moved off and away.

Yes, just like Whitlaw. He got the last word too.

EIGHTEEN

I TURNED to go and almost bumped into a dream. "Oops, excuse me—" I caught her to keep from stumbling, then forgot to let go.

"Hello!" she said, laughing.

"Uh—" I flustered, unable to speak. I was mesmerized—her eyes were soft and shiny gray, and I was lost in them. Her skin was fair, with just the faintest hint of freckling. Her face was framed by auburn curls that fell in silk cascades down to her shoulders. Her mouth was moist and red.

I wanted to kiss her. Who wouldn't?

She laughed again. "Before you ask," she said, "the answer is *yes.*"

"Huh?"

"You *are* going to proposition me, aren't you?" Her voice was dusky velvet, with just the slightest hint of Alabama in it.

"Uhh . . ." I took a step back. My feet stayed where they were, but I took a step back.

"Are you shy?" Yes, Alabama. Definitely. She spoke each word so slowly I could taste it. And she smelled of honeysuckle and lilac—and musk.

I found my voice. "Um, I used to be. . . ."

"I'm glad to see you got over it," she said, laughing. She put her arm through mine and started walking me toward the elevators to the garage levels. "What's your name?"

"Jim. Uh, what's yours?"

"Jillanna. Everyone calls me Jilly."

I felt suddenly embarrassed. I started to speak—"Um . . ."—and then shut up.

She looked at me, her head slightly tilted. "Yes?"

"Nothing."

"No, tell me."

"Well, I . . . uh, I guess I'm just a little startled."

"Why?"

"I've never been picked up like this before."

"Oh. How do you usually get picked up?"

"Um. I don't," I admitted.

"Goodness. You *are* shy!"

"Um. Only around women."

"Oh, I see," she said. "Are you gay?"

"I don't think so. I mean, I never tried."

She patted my arm. Did she mean that as reassurance? I didn't ask.

"Uh, I'm here on research," I offered. "I mean, I'm with the army. That is, I'm doing research for them."

"Everyone is," she said. "Everyone in Denver is working on Chtor-rans."

"Yeah," I thought about it. "I guess so."

"Have you ever seen one?" She said it casually.

"I . . . burned one . . . once."

"Burned?"

"With a flamethrower."

She looked at me with new respect. "Were you scared?"

"No, not at the time. It just happened so fast. . . . I don't know—it was kind of sad, in a way. I mean, if the Chtorrans weren't so hostile, they could be beautiful. . . ."

"You're sorry you burned it?"

"It was awfully big. And dangerous."

"Go on," she said. Her hand tightened around mine.

I shrugged. "There isn't much to tell. It came out of the hut and I burned it." I didn't want to tell her about Shorty, I don't know why. I said, "It all happened so fast. I wish I'd seen it better. It was just a big pink blur."

"They have one here, you know." Her grip was very intense.

"I know. I heard from the Lizard."

"You. Know. *Her?*"

"No, not really. She was just the pilot who flew us in. Me and Ted."

"Oh." Her grip relaxed.

"She told us about the Chtorran they have. She flew it in too."

We took the elevator down to the third level of the garage where she had a custom floater waiting in one of the private pads. I was impressed, but I didn't say anything. I climbed in silently beside her.

The drive whined to life, cycled up into the inaudible range, and we eased out onto the road. The light bar on the front spread a yellow-pink swath ahead. The bars of the incoming traffic were dim behind the polarized windshield.

"I didn't know any of these had actually hit the market," I said.

"Oh, none of them did. Not really. But several hundred of them did come off the assembly line before Detroit folded up."

"How did you get this one?"

"I pulled strings. Well, Daddy did."

"Daddy?"

"Well . . . he's like a daddy."

"Oh."

Abruptly she said, "Do you want to see the Chtorran?"

I sputtered. "Huh? Yes!" Then, "—But it's locked up. Isn't it?"

"I have a key." She said it without taking her eyes off the road. As if she were telling me what time it was. "It's in a special lab. One that used to be a sterile room. If we hurry, we can watch them feeding it."

"Feeding? It?"

She didn't notice the way I'd said it. "Oh, yes. Sometimes it's pigs or lambs. Mostly it's heifers. Once they fed it a pony, but I didn't see that."

"Oh."

She went on babbling. "They're trying to duplicate what it eats in the wild. They're hunters, you know."

"I'd . . . heard something like that."

"They don't kill their prey—that's what I find interesting. They just bring it down and start eating. Dr. Mm'bele thinks there's a kill reflex involved. This one won't eat dead meat unless it's very, very hungry, and even then only when it's being moved around so he can attack it."

"That's interesting."

"They say that sometimes they eat human beings. Do you think that's true? I mean, doesn't that seem atypical to you?"

"Well—"

She wasn't waiting to hear. "Dr. Mm'bele doesn't believe it. There aren't any reported cases. At least, none that have been verified. That's what the U.N. Bureau says. Did you know that?"

"No, I didn't." Show Low, Arizona. "Um—"

"There was supposed to be one once," she said, "but—well, it turned out to be just another hoax. They even had pictures, I heard."

"A hoax, huh?"

"Yep. You didn't know that, did you?"

"Uh, how did you hear about it?" I don't think she noticed, but I was riding at least three lanes away from her.

"I work here. I'm permanently stationed. Didn't you know?"

"Oh. What do you do, exactly?"

"Executive Vice-Chairperson, Extraterrestrial Genetic Research Coordination Center."

"Oh," I said. Then, "Oh!" Then I shut up.

We turned off the main highway onto the approach road. There had been very little traffic going either way.

"Is there anything interesting about the Chtorrans? I mean, genetically?"

"Oh, lots. Most of it is beyond the lay person, but there is a lot to know. They have fifty-six chromosomes. Isn't that odd? Why so many? I mean, what is all that genetic information for? Most of the genes we've analyzed seem to be inactive anyway. So far, we've been unable to synthesize a computer model of the way the whole system works, but we're working on it. It's just a matter of time, but it would help if we had some of their eggs."

"I—uh, never mind. I'm just amazed that they have chromosomes and genes."

"Oh, well, that's universal. Dr. Hackley proved it almost twenty years ago—carbon-based life will always be built on DNA. Something about the basic molecular structure. DNA is the most likely form of organic chain—almost to the point of inevitability. Because it's so efficient. DNA is almost always there first—and if other types of organic chains are possible, DNA will not only outgrow them, it'll use them as food. It's really quite voracious."

"Um," I said. "How appropriate."

She burbled on. "It's really amazing, isn't it? How much we have in common with the Chtorrans?"

"Um, yeah. Amazing."

"I mean sociobiologically. We both represent different answers to the same question—how can life know itself? What forms give rise to intelligence? And what . . . structures do these forms have in common?

That would tell us what intelligence is a response to, or a product of. That's what Dr. Mm'bele says."

"I've, uh, heard good things about him."

"Anyway, we're trying to put together a program to extrapolate the physiology of the Chtorran animal from its genes, but we don't have anyone who can write a program for it yet. You're not a programmer, are you? The lack of a good hacker will probably add anywhere from two to three years to our research schedule. And it's a very important problem—and a double-edged one. We don't know what the genes are supposed to do because we don't know the creature, at least not very well. And we can't figure out the creature because we don't understand the genes. Some really peculiar things." She took a breath. "Like, for instance, half the chromosomes seem to be duplicates of each other. Like a premitosis condition. Why is that? We have more questions than answers."

"I'm sure," I said, trying to assimilate what she was telling me. "What about the millipedes? Didn't they give you any clues?"

"You mean the insectoids? They're another whole puzzle. For one thing, they all seem to be the same sex—did you know that? No sex at all."

"Huh?"

"We haven't found any evidence—nobody has—that there's any sexuality in them at all. Not physically, not genetically; no sex organs, no sexual differentiation, no secondary sex characteristics, no markings and not even any way to reproduce."

"Well, they must—"

"Of course they must, but the best we've found are some immature structures that might—just *might*, mind you—be undeveloped ovaries or testes—we're not sure which—and a vestigial reproductive tract, but they've been inoperative in every specimen we've dissected. Maybe they're just growth glands. But even if they were sexual structures, why are they buried so high up in the abdomen with no apparent connection to any outlet?"

She stopped at the main gate just long enough to flash her clearance at the scanner, then zoomed forward, turning sharply right and cutting across a lot toward a distant L-shaped building.

"The Chtorrans have some sexuality, don't they?"

"Oh, yes. Quite a bit. We're just not sure how it works. The one we have—we thought it was a female. Now we're not sure. Now we're guessing it's a male. At least, I think it is, but . . . we don't have

anything to compare it with. We've been able to dissect some dead ones
in the past couple months—two we think were females, one pretty definite male and two we're still not sure of. The big one was definitely
male," she repeated. Her voice went funny then. "I wish I could have
seen that one alive. He must have been magnificent. Two and a half
meters thick, maybe five meters long. We only got the front half. The
back half was . . . lost. But he must have been magnificent. What a
warrior he must have been. I'll bet he ate full-sized cattle."

"Um," I said. I didn't know what else to say. I was beginning to
wonder—was this part of getting laid? Or what? I wasn't sure I wanted
to any more.

The floater slid to a stop before the building. It wasn't L-shaped, but
X-shaped. We had parked in one of the corners. Bright lights illuminated the whole area. As I got out, I paused to look up at the poles. Just
as I thought, there were snoops on every tower; that's what the lights
were for. Security. Nothing was going to get in—or out—without being
recorded.

I wondered if anyone was looking at the recordings.

And then I wondered if it mattered.

There were eleven other people already in the room. It was long and
narrow and dimly lit. Two rows of chairs ran the length of the room,
facing a wall of glass. I could make out five women, six men. The men
all seemed to be civilian types, but I couldn't be sure. I didn't know if
the women were their colleagues or their companions for the evening. If
the latter, I couldn't help but wonder at their choice of entertainment.
The men waved to Jillanna and looked curiously at me. I waved back,
halfheartedly.

Jillanna's eyes were wide with excitement. "Hi, guys. Have we started
yet?"

"Smitty's just getting ready."

"What's on for tonight?"

"Coupla dogs they picked up from the shelter."

One of the women, the redheaded one, said, "Oh, that's awful."

"It's in the interest of science," someone answered. I wasn't convinced.

Jillanna shouldered her way up to the glass. "Okay, make room,
make room." She squeezed a place for me.

The glass slanted diagonally out over a deep room below us; we
overlooked it as if on a balcony. The light was dim below, hardly much
brighter than the viewing room. There was a distinct orange cast to the

illumination. I felt pleased at that—so someone else had discovered the same thing!

Deep, slow-paced sounds were coming from two wall speakers. Something breathing.

I stepped forward to look. There was an inclined notebook rack at the bottom of the glass; I had to lean out over it to see.

A layer of straw—it looked orange in this light—was spread across the floor. The room was high and square, a cube, but the bottom half was circular. The corners had been filled in to make a round enclosure four meters high; the top of it came right up to the window. There were cameras and other monitoring devices on the resulting shelves formed in the corners.

The Chtorran was directly below me. It took a second for my eyes to adjust.

It was a meter thick, maybe a bit more; two and a half, maybe three meters, long. Its fur was long and silky and looked to be deep red, the color of blood-engorged skin. As I watched, it humped forward once, twice, a third time, then stopped. It was circling against the wall, as if exploring. It was cooing softly to itself. Why did that unnerve me? As I watched, ripples—like waves moving through sluggish oil—swept back across its body.

"That means he's excited," breathed Jillanna. "He knows it's dinner time."

It slid forward into the middle of the room then, began scratching at the straw on the floor. From this angle, I could see its cranial hump quite clearly—underneath that fur, it was helmeted across the shoulders. A bony carapace to protect the brain? Probably. Its long black arms were folded now and held against its sides like wings, but I could see where they were anchored to the forward sides of the helmet. The brain bulge was directly behind the creature's two thick eyestalks. From this angle, the Chtorran looked more like a slug or a snail than a worm.

"Does he have a name?" one of the women asked. She was tall and blond.

Her date shook his head. "It's just *it.*"

Sput-phwut went the speaker. *Sput-phwut.*

"What was that?"

Jillanna whispered, "Look at his eyes."

"It's facing the wrong way."

"Well, wait. He'll turn."

"Be a good show tonight," the guy at the end said as he lit a cigarette.

"Saint Bernard and a Great Dane. I'm betting the Bernard puts up a better fight."

"Aah, you'd bet on your grandmother."

"If she still had her own teeth, I would."

Jillanna leaned over to me. "He needs fifty kilos of fresh meat a day. They have a real problem getting a steady supply. Also, they're not sure that terrestrial animals provide all the nutritional elements he needs, so they keep varying the diet. Sometimes they pump the animals up with vitamins and stuff. Sometimes he rejects the food; I guess it smells bad to him."

Sput-phwut.

The Chtorran humped around and looked at us with eyes like black disks. Like dead searchlights. It humped up, lifting the front third of its body into the air, trembling slightly, but focusing its face—like the front end of a subway, flat and emotionless—toward us. I stepped back involuntarily, but Jillanna pulled me forward again. "Isn't he beautiful?" Her hand was tight on my sleeve.

Sput-phwut.

It had blinked. The sound was made by its sphincter-like eyelids, irising closed and open again. *Sput-phwut.* It was looking right at me. Studying dispassionately.

I didn't answer her. I couldn't speak. It was like looking into the eyes of death.

"Don't worry. He can't see you. I think. I mean, we're pretty sure he can't."

"It seems awfully interested." The Chtorran was still reared up and peering. Its tiny antennae were waving back and forth curiously. They were set just behind the eyes. Its body rocked slightly too. I wished I had a closer view—something about the eyes; they weren't mounted *in* a head, but seemed instead to be on swiveled stalks inside the skin. They were held high above the body and gimbaled independently of each other. Occasionally one eye would angle backward for a moment, then click forward again. The creature was constantly *alert.*

The Chtorran lowered suddenly and slid across the floor, right up to the wall below us and halfway up it, bringing its face within a meter of the glass. I got my wish—a closer look. It angled its eyes upward, bringing them even closer. Its mandibles—sinuous like an underwater plant—waved and clicked around its mouth. Its eyes opened as wide as they could. *Sput-phwut.* "Too interested. You sure it can't see us?"

"Oh, he tries that almost every night," called the guy on the end with the funny-smelling cigarette. Laced with dream dust? Probably. "It's our voices he hears. Through the glass. He's trying to find out where the sound is coming from. Don't worry, he can't reach up here. He has to keep at least half his length on the ground to support himself when he rears up. Of course, if he keeps growing—as we think he will—we'll have to move him to a bigger lab. There might come a day when he won't wait for Smitty. He'll just come right up here and help himself."

The women shuddered. Not Jillanna, just the women. They moved instinctively closer to their dates. "You're kidding," the redheaded one said plaintively. "Aren't you?"

"Nope. It could happen. Not tonight, though—but eventually, if we don't get him into a bigger tank."

The Chtorran unfolded its arms then, like a bird flapping its wings once to settle them, but instead of refolding, the arms began to open slowly. They came away from the hump on the back and now I could see exactly how the shoulders were anchored, and the curve of that bony structure beneath the fur, how the skin slid over it as the muscles stretched, how the arms were mounted in their sockets like two incredible gimbaled cranes. The arms were covered with leathery black skin and bristly black fur. They were long and insect-like. How long and thin they were, and so peculiarly double-jointed. There were *two* elbows at the joint! And now the arms came reaching upward slowly toward us. The hands—they were claws, three-pronged and almost ebony—came tapping on the glass, sliding and skittering up and down it, seeking purchase, leaving faint smudges where they touched. There were soft fingers within those claws. I could see them pressing gently against the glass.

The eyes stared emotionlessly, swiveling this way and that—and then both of them locked on me. *Sput-phwut.* It blinked. And kept on staring.

I was terrified before it. I couldn't move! Its face—*it didn't have a face!*—was searching mine! If I had stretched, I could have touched it. I could see how narrow its neck was—a shaft of corded muscle terminating in those two huge, frightening eyes. I couldn't look away! I was caught like a bird before a snake—its eyes were dark and dispassionate and deadly. What kind of god could make a thing like this?

And then the moment broke. I realized that Jillanna was beside me, breathing heavily.

One more *sput-phwut* and the Chtorran began sinking back down to the floor. It slid away from the wall and began roving around the room again, sometimes humping like a worm, other times seeming to flow. It left a swept trail through the scattered straw and sawdust. There were several bales of it against one wall. It stopped to pull at one of them, did something with its mandibles and mouth, then left behind a small mound of weak-looking foam.

"Building instinct," Jillanna said.

"It doesn't seem very intelligent," the redhead whispered to her date.

"It isn't. None of them are," the man whispered back. "Whatever kind of invaders these Chtorrans are, they don't seem to be very smart. They don't respond to any kind of language—or any attempts at communication. Then again, maybe these are just the infantry. Infantry doesn't have to be very smart, just strong."

I realized then that we were all whispering. As if it could hear us.

Well, it could, couldn't it?

"Look at the way his arms fold up when he's not using them," Jillanna pointed. "It's like they're retractable. They're not bones, you know, just muscle and some kind of cartilage. Very flexible—and almost impossible to break. You'll see them in action when he's fed—oh, here we go now."

A slit of light appeared at the base of the left wall; it slid upward to become a door, revealing a closet-shaped cubicle. The Chtorran arced around quickly—amazing, how fast the thing could move. Its eyes rotated forward, up and down, in an eerie disjointed way. The sliding door was completely open now. A Great Dane stood uneasily in the lit cubicle before the Chtorran. I thought of horses—Great Danes, with their lumbering huge paws, long legs and heavy bodies, always made me think of horses. I could just barely hear a low rumbling growl coming from the dog.

For a moment, everything was still: the Chtorran, the dog, the watchers at the glass. Below, in the glow of light reflected from the cubicle, I could see a dark window just across from us. It looked as if there were someone behind the glass, watching.

The moment stretched—and broke. The Chtorran's arms came slightly out from its body. I thought of a bird getting ready to fly. It was a gesture of readiness, the way they were poised—the claws open, ready to grab.

The Chtorran slid forward.

The dog jumped sideways—

—and was caught. One of the arms reached out at an impossible angle and snatched the dog in mid-leap, knocked it to the ground on its back. The Chtorran *bent* sideways in mid-flow—as if the dog in its claw was a pivot and it was pulling itself around. The other arm came around. The Chtorran flowed. Its great black jaw was a vertical open hole that split the front of its crimson body. The dog was pinned by both arms now—I could see how the claws dug into its flesh like pincers. It thrashed and kicked and snapped and bit. The red beast raised and stretched and arced—and came down upon the hapless Dane almost too fast to follow. There was a thrash and slash and flurry—and then stillness. The back half of the Dane protruded from the Chtorran maw.

Was that it? The Chtorran was holding the dog like a snake with a mouse, frozen in lidless contemplation before commencing the long process of swallowing. Its mandibles were barely moving, just a slight ready trembling barely visible against the Dane's side. The Chtorran held the dog between its claws; its mouth was stretched impossibly around it. Its eyes stared impassively off, as if thinking—or savoring.

Then something awful happened. One of the dog's hind legs kicked.

It must have been a reflex reaction—the poor animal couldn't have been still alive—

It kicked again.

As if it had been waiting for just that thing, the Chtorran came to life and began to chew its way forward. Its mandibles flashed shiny and red, slashing and cutting and grinding. The kicking leg and tail were the last parts of the dog to disappear.

Blood poured onto the floor from the Chtorran mouth. The mandibles continued to work with a dreadful wet crunching. Something that looked like long sausages drooled out, dripped on the floor. The Chtorran sucked it back in. Casually. A child with a strand of spaghetti.

"Wow!" said someone. It was one of the women, an unafraid one. The blonde. The redhead had hidden her eyes the moment the door slid open to reveal the dog.

"He'll take a moment to digest," said the guy at the end, the one who would bet his grandmother. His name, I found out later, was Vinnie. "He could eat another one without waiting, but it's better to give him a moment or two. Once he ate too fast and threw up everything. Jee-zus, what a mess that was. It would have been hell to clean up, but he ate it again almost immediately."

The cubicle door dropped closed and the dim figure in the window across from us disappeared into the deepness behind it. Two more people came in silently behind us, both men, both smelling of alcohol. They nodded at Jillanna; they obviously knew her. "Hi, Vinnie. Did we start yet?"

"Only a Great Dane, but it wasn't much. The Saint Bernard will be better."

"You hope," said his friend, the man he'd made the bet with.

Vinnie won the bet. The St. Bernard did put up a better fight than the Dane. At least, that's what the sounds coming from the speaker suggested. I was looking at my shoes.

"Well, that's it," said Vinnie. "Let's go pay the man and finish getting drunk."

"Hold it," said the speaker. Smitty? Probably. "I've got one more. Dessert."

"I thought you only got two from the pound."

"I did—but we caught this one digging in the garbage, been turning over cans for weeks. Finally trapped him this evening. We were gonna send him down to the shelter. But why bother? Let them save the gas."

When the door slid open this time, there was a hound-sized mutt standing there, his nose working unhappily. He was shaggy with matted pinkish-looking fur, stringy and dirty—as if he'd been hand-knit by a beginner. He was all the beat-up old mutts in the world rolled into one. I didn't want to look, but I couldn't stop—he was too much the kind of dog I would have cared about, if . . . the kind of dog that goes with summer and skinny-dipping.

The Chtorran was lying flat in the center of the room. Engorged and uninterested. His eyes opened and closed lazily. *Sput . . . phwut.*

The dog edged out of the cubicle—he hadn't seen the Chtorran yet. Sniffing intensely, he took a step forward—

—and then every hair on his back stood up. With a *yowp* of surprise, the dog leaped backward into the nearest wall. Something about the Chtorran lying there in a pool of dark red blood smelled very bad to this poor creature. He cowered along the wall, slunk toward the space behind a bale of hay—but it smelled even worse there; he froze indecisively, then began backing away uncertainly.

The Chtorran half-turned to watch him move. Twitched. One arm scratched lazily.

The dog nearly left his skin behind. He scrambled toward the only escape he knew, the tiny lit cubicle. But Smitty had closed it. The dog sniffed at it and scratched. And scratched. Frantically, with both front legs working like pedals, he clawed at the unyielding door. He whined, he whimpered, he pleaded with terrible urgency for impossible escape.

"Get him out of there!" It wasn't me who said it—I wish it had been
—it was the redhead.

"How?" said Vinnie.

"I don't know—but do something. *Please!*"

No one answered her.

The dog was wild. He turned and bared his teeth at the Chtorran,
growling, warning it to keep back; then almost immediately he was
working at the door again, trying to get one foot under it, trying to lift it
up again—

The Chtorran moved. Almost casually. The front half of it curled up
into the air, then came down again, making an arch; the back half
barely moved forward. It looked like a toppled red question mark, the
mouth flush against the floor where the dog had been.

The Chtorran stayed in that position, its face directly against the
straw-matted concrete. Blood seeped outward across the dirty stained
surface.

There hadn't even been time for a yelp.

"That's it?" asked Vinnie.

"Yep. That's it till tomorrow," replied the loudspeaker. "Don't forget
to tell your friends about us. A new show every night." Smitty's voice
had a strange quality to it. But then, so did Vinnie's. And Jillanna's.

The Chtorran stretched out again. It looked like it was asleep. No,
not yet. It rolled slightly to one side and directed a stream of dark
viscous fluid against a stained wall, where it flowed into a trough of
running water.

"That's all that's left of last night's heifer," snickered Vinnie. I didn't
like him.

Jillanna led me downstairs and introduced me to Smitty. He looked
like an ice-cream man. Clean-scrubbed. The kind who was a compulsive
masturbator in private. Very fair skin. Wisps of sandy hair. Thick
glasses. An eager expression, but haunted. I did not shake hands with
him.

"Jillanna, did you tell him?"

"Oh, I'm sorry. Jim?" She turned to me and went all coquettish,
twisting two fingers into the material of my shirt. She twinkled up at me
—a grotesque imitation of a woman, this creature who was sexually
aroused by the death of three dogs to a giant day-glow caterpillar. She
lowered her voice. "Uh, Jim . . . will you give Smitty fifty caseys?"

"Huh?"

"It's for . . . you know." She cocked her head toward the other side of the wall where something pink was trilling softly to itself.

I was so startled that I was already reaching for my wallet. "Fifty caseys?"

Smitty seemed apologetic. "It's for . . . well, protection. I mean, you know, we're not supposed to let unauthorized personnel in here— and especially not when we're feeding it. I'm doing you a favor letting you be here."

Jillanna solved it by plucking my wallet out of my hand and peeling a crisp blue note from it. "Here, Smitty—buy yourself a new rubber doll."

"You should talk," he said, but not very strongly. He pocketed the bill.

I took my wallet back from Jillanna and we left. There was a dark pressure at the back of my skull. Jillanna squeezed my hand and the pressure grew darker and heavier. I felt like a man walking toward the gallows.

I stopped her before we reached the floater. I didn't want to say it, but I didn't want to continue with this horror one moment more.

I tried to be polite. "Uh, well—thanks for showing me," I said. "I uh, think I'll call it a night."

It didn't work.

"What about *us?*" she asked. She *demanded.* She started to reach for me.

I held her back. I said, "I guess I'm . . . too tired."

She toyed with the hairs on my arm. "I have some dream dust. . . ." she said. Her fingers tiptoed toward my elbow.

"Uh—I don't think so. That just makes me sleepy. Listen, I can walk back to my barracks from here—"

"Jimmy? Please stay with me—?" For just a moment, she looked like a lost puppy, and I hesitated. "Please . . . ? I *need* someone."

It was the word *need* that got me. It felt like a knife in my gut. "I—I can't, Jillanna. Really. I can't. It's not you. It's me. I'm sorry."

She looked at me curiously, one beautiful eyebrow curling upward like a question mark.

"It's, uh—that Chtorran," I said. "I wouldn't be able to concentrate."

"You mean you didn't find him *sexy?*"

"Sexy—? My God, it was horrible! That poor dog was frantic!"

"It was just an old mutt, Jim—the Chtorrans are something magnificent. They really are. You have to look at them with new eyes. I used to think it was awful too, but then I stopped anthropomorphizing—stopped identifying with the dogs and started looking at the Chtorrans objectively. The strength, the independence—I wish humans had that kind of power. I want to do it like that. Please, Jim, stay with me tonight. Do it to me!" She was plucking at my jacket, at my shirt, at my neck.

"Thanks—" I said, remembering something my father used to say. Something about knowing what you're getting into. I disengaged myself from her hands. "—But, no thanks." I wanted to say something else, but a vestigial sense of tact prevented me from telling Jillanna what I really thought of her. Perhaps the Chtorran had no choice in being what it was. She did. I began to pull away—

"You *are* some kind of queer, aren't you?"

To hell with tact. "Are *you* the alternative?" And then I turned and walked away from her.

She didn't say a thing until I was halfway across the lot. Then she hollered, "Faggot!" I turned around to look, but she was already roaring off in the floater.

Shit.

By the time I found my way back to my barracks, I was chilled. But I wasn't trembling anymore, and I wasn't angry anymore. I was only . . . sick. And tired. I wanted to be young again, so I could cry into my father's lap. I was feeling very, very much alone.

My bed was like an empty grave and I lay in it shivering, trying to feel compassionate, trying to understand—trying to be *mature*. But I couldn't be mature—not when I was surrounded by idiots and assholes, blind and selfish and wallowing in their own sick games and fetishes and power ploys. What I really wanted to do was hit and kick and burn and smash and destroy. I wanted to pound and pound and pound. I wanted to grab these people and shake them up and down so hard their eyes would rattle in their heads.

I wanted to feel safe. I wanted to feel that someone, somewhere—*anywhere*—knew what he was doing. But right now, I didn't think that anyone in the world knew what he was doing, not even me.

Were they *all* that blind or sick—or stupid?

Why couldn't they see the truth in front of them?

Sput-phwut.

Why couldn't they see it?

Show Low, Arizona, was no hoax!

NINETEEN

TED STAGGERED in at six in the morning, slamming into the room, switching on the lights and banging and clattering his way from wall to wall to bathroom. *"Hooboy!"* he shouted. "I am going to be limp for a week—and walk funny for two." The rest of it was lost under the sound of running water.

An axe would be too messy, I decided. It would have to be a gun.

"Hey, Jim! You awake?"

"I am now," I grunted. No, the gun would be too quick. I wanted it to be painful. I'd use my bare hands.

He lurched into the room, grinning. "Hey—you getting up?" What was left of his makeup was smeared.

"Yeah. I've got something I want to do."

"Well, let it wait. This is more important. You're lucky I had to come back for clean clothes. You can ride back with me—but hurry up!"

I sat up on the edge of the bed. "Ride back where?"

"Back to the hotel. The first session isn't until ten, but I've got a breakfast meeting—"

"Breakfast meeting?"

"Yeah—you got any sober-ups?"

"I dunno. I'll have to look—"

"Never mind, I can get some at the hotel. Come on, get dressed—"

"Just a minute—" I sat there, rubbing my eyes. My head hurt. I granted him a temporary stay of execution while I reviewed the evidence. "What's this all about? Where were you all night?"

"Painting the town black and blue. Come on—" He pulled me to my feet. "—Into the shower with you. I did a party-walk—"

"Party-walk?"

"Is there an echo in here? Yeah, a party-walk." He was punching up a cycle on the shower panel. "Come on, get out of those—unless you're going to shower in your underwear."

"Wait a minute—!" I started to sit down on the commode.

"We haven't got a minute." And suddenly, he was lifting me up bodily, stepping into the shower and holding me under the running water. "Goddammit!" Not even a phone call from the governor would save him now. All I needed was a jar of honey, an anthill and four stakes.

My paper underwear was already shedding off. He handed me the soap, then shredded off his own sopping shirt. He peeled off his kilt—it was real—and tossed it out of the shower onto the bathroom floor.

I had to ask. "Did you leave them somewhere?"

"Leave what?"

"Your underwear?"

"Never wear any. It's traditional. Nothing's worn under a kilt." He grinned foolishly. "Well, it's a little worn this morning, but give me a couple days—I'll be all right."

I turned away from him, stuck my head under one of the shower heads and just stood there. *Aahhh.*

"Anyway—" he continued, "—I went for a party-walk." Maybe if I let the water run into my ears, I wouldn't be able to hear him. "Only this time, I did it with a purpose. I started out on the main floor of the reception with Colonel Bustworth—remember him? The one with the girl? He's a very important man to know—he's in charge of requisitions, supplies and transportation for the whole Denver area. He's the perfect bureaucrat—he makes the paper run on time. Anyway—Jim, stand a little closer to the soap! We're in a hurry! Anyway, I stuck with him long enough to get into a private party in the penthouse. The Conference Committee. Sat in the corner near three of the armpieces and listened to them gossip. In fifteen minutes I knew who was important in that room and who wasn't. Another fifteen minutes and they knew who I was—Senator Jackson's nephew from Mormon University!"

"Huh—?"

"Shut up and scrub—I haven't finished my story."

"Ted, you can't tell lies like that—"

"How should I tell them?"

"You know what I mean. Not to congressmen and generals and God knows who else!"

"Jim, it didn't matter. No two of them were paying any attention to anything except what was coming out of their own mouths—or going in. And when they were ready to drift on to the next party, I drifted with them. And met another roomful of people and did it again. I listened to the gossip and picked out the most important—it's easy to tell, the gossip gets particularly nasty—and got as close to them as I could. I went through seven parties that way, each one better than the last. There was a United Nations reception, just for the diplomatic corps—did you know half the world is here? Your Uncle Sam rented a ballroom—I met a senator over the guacamole dip—but it was the Communists who had the most lavish spread. They were in the Imperial Suite. And I even got into the Society for Wholesale Aggression; now, there's a weird bunch. But useful. Do you know how important mercenaries are to the balance of world power?"

"No, and I don't care." On second thought: "Do they do assassinations? And how much do they charge?"

"Only character—and if you have to ask, you can't afford it."

I started getting out of the shower, but Ted grabbed me. "Wait a minute—you haven't heard the best part."

"Yes, I have!"

He pulled me back into an affectionate hug. "You're beautiful when you're angry—"

"Knock it off, Ted!"

"—and I love it when you play hard to get." But he let me go. I stepped away hotly. The only thing keeping Theodore Andrew Nathaniel Jackson alive now was my inability to think of a convenient way to dispose of the body.

I stood under the shower again—he'd gotten soap all over my back. The spray was alternating between warm rain and hot needle-jets. "I want you to cut that out, Ted."

"You don't have to worry—everybody knows it's all over between us now, anyway. I met this girl last night, and let her 'cure' me. Oh, I didn't want to, Jim. I tried to be faithful—I told her I had made a solemn commitment—but she convinced me to try it once the *other* way —and she was right. That was all I needed."

"Terrific. I'm very happy for you. You've not only convinced everybody I'm a fag—now I'm a jilted fag. And I don't even know how the whole thing started." I turned around under the shower, lifting my arms to rinse underneath them. At the exact same moment, the water spray went icy—a sudden pummeling jackhammer of very cold water, the run-off from the local glacier. *"Aahhh!"* said Ted. "Doesn't that feel great? Doesn't that just wake you up?"

I couldn't answer. I was too busy swearing—I was out of the shower and shivering into a towel before the walls stopped echoing. I was now completely awake, and it didn't matter anymore whether I had a way to dispose of the body or not.

"Answer the door, Jim!"

"Huh?"

"The door—can't you hear the knocking?"

I grouched out of the bathroom and puddled over to the door. "Yeah—?" I snarled.

It was a bony-looking woman with bassett-hound eyes. Why did she look familiar? Oh, yeah—the one who'd refilled Fromkin's drink. She'd been waiting on him all evening, now that I thought about it. "Hi, Jim," she said. "We haven't been formally introduced—" She grabbed my hand and pumped it. "—I'm Dinnie. Are you guys ready yet?" She had bad teeth.

"Uh—no."

"Okay, I'll wait." She swept past me and parked herself in the room's one chair.

"Uh—right. You do that." I grabbed some clothes and retreated to the bathroom.

"God," said Ted, stepping out of the shower bay. "Isn't morning wonderful?" He poked me in the ribs as he passed.

"Yeah." I was thinking that no jury in the country would convict me. I pulled my clothes on quickly.

When I came out of the bathroom, Dinnie was just handing Ted a light brown T-shirt that said: NOT JUST ANOTHER LOVE STORY . . . "Here," she was saying, "This will drive the women crazy. It shows off your muscles."

"Especially the one between his ears," I muttered. They ignored me.

Ted grinned and pulled on the shirt and a maroon windbreaker. He picked up his carryall and started for the door. "Come on, everybody ready? Let's go."

I grabbed my jacket and followed them. I squinted back sudden tears as we came out into the morning sun. I hadn't realized how bright

Colorado could be in the daytime. Ted was already falling into the driver's seat of a long silver—

"Ted! Where did you get *this?*"

"I told you. Colonel Bustworth is an important man to know. You like it?"

"Isn't it a little . . . ah . . . extravagant?"

"There is no such thing as a *little* extravagance," Ted replied. "Are you getting in?" He turned the key and the engine roared to life with a guttural rumble that rattled windows for a kilometer around.

I climbed into the back. Ted didn't even wait for me to close the door, just hit the acceleration and climbed into the air at an angle steep enough to scare the nickels out of my jeans.

"Wheee-oww!" hollered Dinnie, with elaborate enthusiasm. She applauded the takeoff, and bowed in her seat to the pilot. Maybe it should be a double murder.

Ted leveled off into an easier climb. Dinnie turned around to look at me. "So wasn't Uncle Daniel terrific, Jim?"

"Who?"

"Dr. Fromkin."

"He's your uncle?"

"Well, not legally." She pointed her nose upward. "He's my *spiritual* uncle. Ideationists are all one big family, you know."

"Oh," I said.

"You met Fromkin?" That was Ted. "You didn't tell me."

"You didn't ask. He's um—interesting." I said to Dinnie, "Do you work for him?"

"Oh, no—but we're very good friends. I probably know him better than anybody. The man's a genius."

"If you say so." I didn't know. He had seemed like just another pompous ass to me.

She said, "Plowboys should never pull on number-one guns. You're lucky he was in a good mood." She explained to Ted. "Jim challenged him."

"Jim?" Ted was quietly incredulous. *"Our Jimmy?"*

"I just asked him about—oh, never mind." My face was burning.

Dinnie turned to me. "So how was Jillanna?"

"Huh?" said Ted. "Who's Jillanna?"

"Jim went off with her last night. Everybody noticed."

"I hadn't realized I was so . . . popular," I mumbled.

"Oh, it wasn't you. It's Jillanna. She's got quite a reputation. There was this Air Force colonel who died in the saddle—a 'massive coronary event'—but Jillanna didn't stop; not until she finished her own ride. You've got to respect a woman with that kind of control. And let's face it—how many can fuck you till your ears bleed?" Dinnie looked at me with wide-eyed frankness. "So, punkin? Was she good enough to stop your heart?"

"Mmfle," I mmfled. "I didn't do anything with her." Maybe I should just throw myself from the car.

"That's our Jimmy," said Ted. I could see the grin even on the back of his head.

"What a waste," said Dinnie, turning forward again. "Jillanna is so beautiful. She even put the make on me once, but I had to turn her down. Now I wish I hadn't, but I had taken a vow of celibacy for a year. Just to prove I could. There were just too many people trying to climb into my panties. Mother! I was wearing myself out."

Something in the back of my head went *twang*. Ted had gone social climbing last night—*deliberately*—and come up with this?

She continued on, candidly. "It was a good thing I did, though. It made me appreciate things all the more. I mean, I must have come at least *eleven* times last night. I know *you* did," she said to Ted. "Then I lost count."

Good lord! I folded my arms across my chest and turned to the window. Did I really need to hear all this? Below, I could see huge burned-out areas—swaths of blackened rubble that marred the even march of avenues to the horizon.

Hardly anything moved. No cars, no buses, no pedestrians, no bicyclists—there was nothing. I saw three dogs trotting down the middle of a street and that was all. The stillness of that silent landscape was unnerving.

Someone had inscribed a giant graffito along a block-long wall. The letters must have been three meters high; it was readable even from the air. It said: WHERE HAVE ALL THE PEOPLE GONE?"

There was dust, sweeping down in yellow gusts, piling up against a wall or curb or house. Would there be desert here—or what? Or would the prairie just reclaim the land, preserving almost perfectly a record of the last days of our civilization for some distant unseen archaeologists?

What would they make of us, those prying future eyes? I found myself resenting them. How dare they dig into our tragedy!

Dinnie broke the mood.

She was patting her hair into place with one hand; it was a peculiar orange color. "So many people just don't understand how sensitive he is; I do. The man is too talented. If he ever learns to control his tools, he'll be dangerous."

I looked at Ted, wondering—what had he been thinking of?—but he was expressionless now. Occasionally he would nod or grunt, but his reactions were only noncommittal acknowledgments. Dinnie didn't seem to notice, or if she did, she didn't seem to mind. Good lord! Didn't her tongue ever get sunburned?!

"What's your meeting about?" I asked Ted.

He opened his mouth to answer—and Dinnie said, "It's the Spiralist Free World Association."

"Spiralism? You're going in for Spiralism now? I—" Stopped myself. "Never mind—" I held up both my hands. "—It's not my business. Everybody gets to go to hell in their own handbasket."

"It's only a breakfast, Jim—" he started to say.

Dinnie plowed right over him. "They're *really* charming people. And it's at Ragamuffin's, which is one of the *few* places that knows how to serve a *decent* continental breakfast—although I have to say, I *don't* think their wine list is very good, so I wouldn't recommend them for anything past brunch. Did I tell you how I once sent back the *sommelier?*"

Suddenly, I was no longer angry at Ted. He'd found a far more appropriate fate than anything I could plan for him. "Well, it certainly sounds . . . uh, interesting. Um—will they be drinking the blood of any gentile babies this morning?"

I saw Ted's quick glance to the rearview mirror—he caught the expression on my face, how far my tongue was in my cheek. At least it was in my *own* cheek.

"Listen, Jim," he said, seriously. "I'm going to leave you off outside the hotel. But it's not really a hotel anymore. Uncle Sam's taken it over, using it as a temporary conference center. For the duration. So that makes it permanent. Anyway, I've gotten us both C-clearances—don't ask—so you'll have access to just about every formal session and most of the informal ones. I don't know if that includes the red-lined ones. You'll have to scout that out yourself—but carefully. Listen, you don't want your credentials examined too closely; you're valid, but just barely, so try to be inconspicuous, okay?"

"Sure—sounds good to me. But how *did* you do it?"

"I come from a long line of dog-robbers. Now, listen—you'll have to check in, first thing. Dial CORDCOM-REG; any of the terminals can rewrite your card. Oh, and by the way, your clearance also entitles you to use the vehicle pool. Unlimited access. It's very convenient. You don't have to bother with Rec-Rec's paperwork. You can have almost anything except the President's limousine or a Patton charger."

"Now, why would I want a laser-equipped tank?"

Ted shrugged. "For the fun of it?" The car bumped as it hit the road, bounced once and settled heavily. Ted touched the brakes lightly to bring the cruising speed down.

"You *could* get it, you know, if you really wanted it. Because you're —um, military. *Special,* you know? That's where the clearances came from too. All you have to do is take a couple hours training. And prove you have a real need for it."

"I'll pass, thanks."

"Well, keep it in mind. Could you imagine the look on Duke's face— *or Obie's*—if you drove up in one of those?"

I thought about it. No, I couldn't imagine it.

Ted turned onto a ramp and pulled up at a convenient side entrance. "I'll see you later, okay?"

"Sure. Uh, nice meeting you, Dinnie." I stepped back as they rolled away. *Spiralism?*

I shoved my hands into my jacket pockets and headed into the hotel —huh? What was *this?* Oh, Dr. Obama's lockbox. I'd almost forgotten I was carrying it.

I found a row of terminals and slid into a booth. It took only a moment to REGister with CORDCOM. My card disappeared into the slot, then rolled out again, overprinted with a yellow stripe. A large C in a red box had also been printed in the upper right corner. Was that it?

I cleared and punched for DIRectory, Lieutenant Colonel Ira Wallachstein.

The screen flashed: SORRY, NOT FOUND.

Huh?

Maybe I had miskeyed. I typed it again.

SORRY, NOT FOUND.

Well, that was . . . weird. I called up PROJECT JEFFERSON next, tried to list its personnel.

SORRY, NOT AVAILABLE.

Tried the Denver Area Military Directory. He wasn't listed there either.

I sat puzzled for a moment, wondering what to do next. I scratched my head. Why would Dr. Obama give me a package for somebody who wasn't here? Or maybe this Colonel Wallachstein had moved on and hadn't let Obama know? Maybe I should call Dr. Obama and ask. No, something told me not to.

I took the box out of my pocket and looked at it. There was nothing extraordinary about it, just a one-piece lightweight unit. Rounded corners. No markings, other than the printed keyboard and the lock. Not much rattle to it either. I had to think about this. I didn't want to destroy it. Not yet. That would feel like failure.

I slid it back into my pocket. Maybe tonight, back at the barracks. Maybe I'd missed something obvious.

I cleared the board and called up the day's conference schedule. The general session on Chtorran biology and behavior began at ten o'clock. Apparently it was a weekly session. I scanned the rest of the calendar, hard-copied it, logged off and went in search of breakfast.

I had bagels and lox and strawberries and cream. I ate alone, and I was still in better company than Ted.

TWENTY

THE MAN at the podium looked unhappy.

There were too many empty seats. The auditorium was only a third full.

I hesitated at the back of the room. The audience had already begun to segregate themselves into sections.

The military attendees were seated up close, but on the sides. I hadn't realized it was possible to sit at attention. The funny-looking types were all in the first five rows. Of course, I'd never been to a convention where it hadn't been so. The serious types scattered themselves in the center of the room. The turbans and the burnooses—and there were an awful lot of them—were milling in the aisles, chattering away at each other as fast as they could, ignoring the frowning man on the dais.

The room roared with the noise of a thousand separate conversations —a babbling torrent of words. Didn't they realize how loud they all were? Each one was shouting to be heard above all the rest, and as each one raised his or her voice, all the rest became correspondingly louder too. It wasn't hard to see why the man at the podium was so unhappy.

I found an empty row halfway to the front and took a seat near the center. I put a fresh clip into my recorder and slipped it back into my pocket.

The unhappy man stepped to the edge of the stage and whispered something to an aide, the aide shrugged, the man looked unhappier. He checked his watch, I checked mine—the session was already fifteen minutes late. He stepped back to the podium and tapped the microphone. "Gentlemen? Ladies?" He cleared his throat. "If you would please find seats, we can begin—?"

It didn't work. The noise of the conversations only increased as each speaker shouted to make himself heard over the public address system. I could see that this was going to take a while.

"Delegates? *If you please—?*" He tried again. "I'd like to call this session to order."

No one paid attention. Each and every one of them had something so important to say that it superseded every other event in the auditorium.

The unhappy man tried one more time, then picked up a tiny mallet and started striking an old-style ship's bell that was perched on top of the podium. He hit it four quick times, then four times more, then again and again. He kept on striking it, over and over, a steady rhythmic dinging that could not be ignored. I saw him looking at his watch while he did it. Apparently he'd been through this before.

The groups began to break up. The various conversations splintered and broke off—they couldn't compete any longer—and the participants began drifting into their separate seats. The only conversation still going full bore was one between three deaf women—or maybe they were interpreters—in Ameslan.

"Thank you!" the unhappy man said at last. He touched some buttons on the podium in front of him and the screen behind him lit up with an official-looking announcement. It repeated itself every fifteen seconds, each time shifting to a different language: French, Russian, Italian, Chinese, Japanese, Swahili, Arabic—I couldn't identify the rest. The English version said: "English interpretations of foreign language speakers may be heard on channel fifteen. Thank you."

He waited while the various delegates inserted earpieces or put on headphones. They rustled and gobbled among themselves, each one taking an impossibly long time.

Something on the right caught my eye—Lizard! Major Tirelli! She was on the arm of a tall black colonel; they were laughing and chatting together as they found seats three rows forward. I wondered if I should call hello, then decided against it. It would probably only annoy her, and besides the auditorium was filling up now and it would be conspicuous, and probably embarrassing. I wondered if I should save a couple of seats for Ted and Dinnie—except I didn't want to—until finally the question was answered for me when a dark, handsome woman sat down on my right, and a second later, a pair of lieutenants took two of the three seats on my left. The handsome woman was in a lab coat and was carrying a clipboard. She switched it on while she waited and began reading through some notes.

I took my recorder out of my pocket to turn it on, and she touched my arm. "Not a good idea," she said. "Some of this may be classified."

"Oh," I said. "Thanks." And dropped it back into my pocket, thumbing it on anyway as I did so. I don't think she saw.

The unhappy man began banging his bell again. "I think we can begin now. For those of you who don't know, I'm Dr. Olmstead, Dr. Edward K. Olmstead, and I am the acting director of the Extraterrestrial Studies Group of the National Science Center here in Denver. I'd like to take this opportunity to welcome all of you to this special session of the Continuing International Conference on Extraterrestrial Affairs.

"I am required by the rules of this conference to remind you that much of the material that we will be presenting here is generally classified on a need-to-know basis. While that includes all of our registered attendees and their respective staffs, we still want to stress that the material is for your use only and should be treated as confidential. We are not yet prepared to release some of this information to the general public. The reasons for this will be discussed in tomorrow's session on culture shock. Your cooperation is greatly appreciated. Thank you.

"This special Saturday session is being held for the convenience of those delegates who will not be here for the full conference schedule. As always, this session is going out live on channel two. If you need more information on any specific subject, that access is available through the project network, of course. Please feel free to tap in. If you don't already have a clearance number, check with the desk.

"As you can see by your schedules, we're going to try to present all of the scientific material in the first two and a half hours, and follow up with the more important questions of contact and containment procedures this afternoon—after a reasonable break for lunch, of course. As I'm sure most of you have already discovered, the hotel here has an excellent buffet. Tomorrow we will spend the morning session on the cultural and psychological questions, and the afternoon meeting will deal with the economic sphere. We do apologize for presuming on so much of your time, and we thank you in advance for your cooperation. This is, of course, a working weekend, so at this time I'd like to turn the microphone over to our conference chairperson, Dr. Moyra Zymph."

There was a spattering of polite applause as Dr. Zymph came up to the dais. She was a stout woman, slightly disheveled, and she moved like a truck driver. When she spoke, it was with a gravelly, I-mean-business voice. "All right, let's get to it." She slapped her clipboard down onto the podium. "I know that most of you are more interested in finding out the answers than in listening to the questions. Unfortunately, all we have right now are questions. We have *lots* of questions . . ." She paused for effect. ". . . and a few educated guesses, which I will share with you.

"I want you to think of a jigsaw puzzle—with most of the pieces missing and no picture on the cover of the box to guide you. Now think of a warehouse full of similar incomplete jigsaw puzzles. Now mix them all up. Now find someone who's never seen a jigsaw puzzle before in his life, and put him in the middle of this pile of mixed-up pieces and ask him to figure out what's going on here. At the point he realizes what a jigsaw puzzle is, he's won the game. He's solved the hardest part of the problem.

"I want you to hold that picture in mind, because that's what we're up to here. We've got a warehouse full of pieces. We know what individual pieces look like, but we don't know what the pictures look like—we do know for sure that this is a warehouse full of incomplete puzzles. We've solved the *hard* part. And we'll tell you about that.

"Now, some of you are not going to like what you hear. You are especially not going to like the implications. Some of you may be so disturbed by the material presented that you'll want to question its validity. You'll want to dismiss our conclusions because you can't accept the facts. Please do not make that mistake.

"I want you to know that it's *all right* to be uncomfortable with the material. We certainly are . . . and we've been living with it for a while. Just don't use that discomfort as an excuse to hide from the urgency of the situation." She paused long enough to let that sink in, looking around the auditorium as if daring anyone to object.

No one did. Not yet. Dr. Zymph nodded and continued. "Good. So what we're going to do here today is show you some of the pieces that we are certain about and then go from there to the larger pattern. I will not be showing you all of our puzzle pieces—we don't have the time—but I will be showing you those items which you most need to know about."

She switched her clipboard on and began referring to it. "First off, we can tell you this. The Earth, this planet that we live on, is experiencing an ecological infestation. The source of the infestation is presumed to be extraterrestrial." She touched a hidden control on the podium and the screen behind her came back to life, showing two views of the Earth, front and back. There were red splotches blinking across the larger land areas. It looked like a case of measles. She continued: "The infestation has appeared on all five major continents: Asia, Africa, both of the Americas and to a lesser extent—although we don't know why yet— Europe. We have not yet confirmed any signs of infestation in Australia or Antarctica. So far, the evidence suggests that it is generally limited to the temperate zones of the planet, the same areas in which the bulk of our human population is established. That is, the *remaining* human population." She stopped and looked out at the room. "The—uh, population crisis will be discussed at tomorrow's session. I urge all of you to be there. We do have some specific recommendations, but they have to be implemented immediately. And I want to point out that our primary concern is not *just* saving our human resources, but putting them to work in ways that contribute to the larger effort." She looked uncomfortable. She bent back to the security of the notes on her clipboard.

"The infestation has manifested itself in several distinct forms that we are aware of—and probably quite a few more that we have not yet discovered." She stopped, touched a control, looked behind her to see that the screen was showing the appropriate slide—some kind of red sludge floating on a lake—and continued. "While most of the attention has been focused on the more, ah, dramatic aspects of this infestation, I want to make you aware that there is considerable ecological impact in other areas as well. We are experiencing events in the microbial and botanical spheres, for instance, that are every bit as serious, though perhaps not as noticeable.

"I'm going to give you only a few examples to demonstrate the scope of the problem. Please be assured that it is far worse than these examples suggest. This first one is a kind of algae. It breeds fast, it floats on the surface of the ocean and it's moderately toxic. It tends to occur primarily in the offshore regions, but it can also be found on still lakes and backwaters. Once it establishes itself, it tends to choke out most other plant life. It does not use chlorophyll for photosynthesis, which explains its red to red-purple color." Behind her, the screen showed muddy crimson breakers crashing on a long stretch of shore. The pink sand was stained with dirty streaks that looked like clotted blood.

"As I said, it is moderately toxic, and I want to take a moment to expand on this. The sludge exudes a particularly nasty set of byproducts, including some interesting long-chain molecules that seem intended for use by the next creature in line in the ecology; but whatever that creature is, it hasn't manifested itself yet. And I don't know whether to be thankful or not.

"Sludge-infested water usually feels oily—and the oil is particularly difficult to clean off. But if you do get the oil on you, it's essential to get it off as quickly as you can, because it very effectively clogs human pores and reduces the skin's ability to breathe. For the record, it also smells bad—so at least you have that much warning.

"If you are unlucky enough to *swallow* sludge-infested water, you will definitely regret it. You'll experience nausea, diarrhea, vomiting and fever. If you're strong, you'll survive. If not, you won't.

"Now, I want you to think about the fish and the plants in that same water—unlike you, they can't get out to go lie down for a while. Prolonged exposure to the sludge is *always* fatal to them. The smaller the creature, the quicker it dies.

"Wherever the red sludge appears, the plankton disappears—followed by the fish that feed on the plankton and the predators that feed on them, all the way up the food chain. The red sludge turns ocean into desert. This is going to have a disastrous effect on the global food chain if it is not controlled. If the seas die, *we* die. And already the red sludge has infected three-tenths of a percent of the world's farmable waters, and that figure is climbing at an alarming rate. Now, I know that three-tenths of a percent doesn't sound like a lot, but when you consider that two-thirds of the Earth is covered by water, then you have to realize that we are already talking about several hundred thousand square miles—and it may be in the millions already; we don't know for sure. But you can extrapolate from that." The screen showed the map of the world again. There were red streaks off the coast of China, California, Brazil and parts of Africa. "These are the areas of primary infestation," she said. "At the present rate of spread, within two to five years most of the world's richest sea farms will be lost.

"I *do* wish to alarm you about this—because this may be the single most threatening aspect of the infestation. So far, the sludge has resisted most of our attempts to control it. It does not seem to be temperature sensitive, and it can survive a wide range of water conditions. We've had some success at inhibiting the growth of the sludge with tailored bacteria, but it is a limited success. To date, our best results have been obtained by pouring crude oil on the water and setting it on fire. I'm sure I don't have to say much about the unacceptability of *that* solution."

She stopped to take a drink of water, checked her notes, then brought up another series of pictures on the screen—some kind of insect-looking bug; but it stood on two legs. Its front four legs were very short, they looked atrophied, except that each terminated in a very strong-looking claw. The grasshopper in its mandibles established a sense of scale. The bug was the size of a sparrow. "This is not an insect," Dr. Zymph said. "Do not fall into the trap of thinking that it *is* an insect, because to do that is to wear blinders to the possibilities that the creature has some very un-insectlike capabilities."

The next picture showed the creature standing—almost *lurking*—in a dark corner. It stood erect, and its long black shell-casing enveloped it like a cape. The shape of its head as well as its posture made me think of Jack the Ripper. "We call this fellow the nightwalker," Dr. Zymph said. "He's a comparatively recent discovery, so we can't tell you too much about him. He eats most kinds of terrestrial insects, and is not averse to the occasional mouse, bird or frog. This is a small one. We've found them as big as twenty centimeters. We hope that's as big as they get. We're not sure. They are not poisonous, but the bite is painful. An interesting thing about that bite—most predatory insects liquify their food to eat it; this fellow is large enough, he doesn't have to bother. He uses his mandibles like teeth. We believe that his digestion is something like a bird's in that he may have to swallow small pebbles to help grind the food in his stomach. This is a good place to note that he is a serious competitor for the birds' place in the ecology. He has a voracious appetite and will undoubtedly provide some very powerful competition to all of our smaller predators."

Another set of pictures—this time, it was a pink puffball thing. "We're still not sure if this one is plant or animal. We call it the cotton candy bug. It's as light as a dandelion, and it's as easily spread. It is nontoxic, it is edible and, as far as we have been able to determine, it does not appear to endanger its surroundings. What that means is that we still haven't determined what kind of a danger it is—and I'll touch on that point in a minute too.

"First, I want to show you this cute little fellow—" There was polite laughter as the slide came up on the screen. "We call him the pipe cleaner bug, because he looks like he's made out of pipe cleaners. Again, do not be misled by the fact that he looks like an insect. That's just the ecological niche he lives in. He does not have a segmented body, and his exoskeleton is covered with a thick skin and that soft white fur that you see. That fur is actually a very sensitive olfactory organ. The creature smells the air with his whole body. Now note the bunny feet: those pads are also sensory organs, even more sensitive. He's not just standing on that leaf, he's tasting it as well. The creature's eyes are on the tip of those two antennae, and they *are* regenerative. This fellow eats the cotton candy bugs; he is eaten by the nightwalker. I can't tell you much more than that. We know nothing about his breeding habits. We can tell you that he moves very fast and can eat twice his own weight in leaves every day. We expect to be seeing a lot more of him next summer. Or even sooner."

The next picture was of a scarlet-leafed field of ivy. "We call this one red kudzu for obvious reasons. The leaves are bright red and veined with white. It likes marshes and shallow water, and it breeds like madness, advancing at the rate of two meters per week. So far, we've only found it in the Louisiana bayous, but we expect to see it spread throughout the entire Gulf Coast if it isn't controlled."

The audience was beginning to get uneasy. There were too many of these creatures.

"Now this one—looks like an Earth millipede, except for the hump across its, ah, shoulders—we're not even sure it belongs here in this catalog. There's some evidence to suggest that it may be a terrestrial creature; we know that there were several of them under study at the African Ecology Center in Nairobi more than twenty years ago, but they were lost in the firestorm that destroyed the city. These creatures are omnivorous, and they're capable of short bursts of speed across open territory. We think they serve primarily as scavengers in the Chtorran ecology. We've not seen a lot of them. Now, this next one—"

Huh? Was that it? She hadn't said *anything* about the millipedes! And why did the Chtorrans have a corral full of them?

"—looks like the *anopheles* mosquito, but again, please do not be fooled by the resemblance. It's only superficial. There are significant internal differences. We call this a stingfly. It feeds on blood—human blood is fine, but it's just as happy with cats, dogs, cattle, horses— anything else it can find. It's not choosy, and for that reason we suspect it to be a primary vector for disease. . . ." She had to pause here; there was an excited hubbub in the audience. After a moment, she raised her voice and continued over it. "We *suspect* it; we are not yet certain. There are too many questions still unanswered. But"—and she leaned forward on the podium now, steepling her hands in front of her—"we *are* looking at it as the most likely mechanism for introducing the plagues into the human population." She was well aware of the ramifications of that statement. And so was her audience.

She said loudly, "I want you to get this—it's still only a theory! We do know that two of the plagues appeared in more than one form—like the bubonic and pneumonic forms of the Black Death. And most of them can be spread by a sneeze, or by touching a contaminated cup or blanket. So what we're looking at here—this stingfly—is not a primary vector, merely a method of introduction. If that. But this does lead right into the next point . . . the plagues themselves.

"We are now operating on the theory that the seven major infections and nine minor ones that have decimated the human species must also be considered as part of the overall pattern of ecological infestation. I want you to know that we came to this realization slowly. When you look at the overlapping patterns of disease and infestation, the relationship is obvious; but even as recently as several months ago, when most of us were still reeling from the initial impact of the disaster, we simply did not have enough reliable information to establish the correlation.

"Um, I'm not going to go into the political and psychological arenas here, but I do want to point out the reasons why conclusive identification of the diseases as extraterrestrial was delayed until the early part of this year. Convincing our respective governments—and I do not mean this as criticism—that there was a very real *presence* on this planet was, under the circumstances, the hardest part of the job. We had very little hard evidence, and it was difficult to have our voices heard during the, ah, worst of the hysteria. We *cannot* afford to let confusion like that happen again!" She stopped herself. Apparently, she realized she was getting angry. She took a sip of water and looked at her notes. She seemed to do that a lot when she was dealing with an uncomfortable subject. Was that for herself or her audience? I wasn't sure. When she was ready, she looked out over the room again.

"I want to say something here. I want to deal with certain avenues of speculation. During the early days of the plagues, there were a number of accusations—on all sides—that they were a weapon of war. At that time, it was assumed that there was a human agency responsible. We know that not to be the case now. The devastation has touched all of us equally, and no nation on this planet has profited by the plagues. And, of course, now the biological evidence is also falling into place—so we must put our distrust and our suspicion behind us. *Now!* The situation is too urgent for us to have our energies divided."

She placed her hands on both sides of the podium. She looked around the room, as if she were looking into the eyes of each and every one of us in the auditorium. She said, "The accusation that the plagues are a weapon of war is not entirely accurate—because *it's too shortsighted!* They are actually a tool of ecological engineering. We as humans may be somewhat biased about the application of such a devastating tool, but as scientists we cannot help but admire the skill with which this particular tool was applied. Almost eighty percent of the members of the dominant species of this planet have been excised as neatly as a surgeon cutting out a cancer with a laser. If that is how they see us, then they should have no problem with the subsequent applications of —continuing with the same metaphor—chemotherapy. We shall see. But if that was their goal, then they have accomplished most of their objective in a very short time. Less than two years." She stopped and wiped her forehead with her handkerchief. She took another drink of water.

When she spoke again, her voice was lower, slower and steadier. The gravelly quality was muted somehow, and she seemed suddenly very serious. "We have been speaking of this as an ecological infestation, because we can't prove that it's anything more. We have specifically *not* called this an invasion, because *we have not been able to find an invading force.* We have no evidence of extraterrestrial landings, no sightings of ships, no evidence of advanced technology of any kind. If we are being invaded, then *where* are the invaders?

"For a while, we suspected that the large purple and red creatures that we have been calling Chtorrans were our alien visitors, but this theory is rapidly falling into disrepute, because we have not been able to prove that these creatures even have the *potential* for intelligence—let alone the *capabilities* necessary to mount such an invasion across the vast distances of space. We are assuming, of course, that this ecological infestation has as its source a planet in another star system—it could not possibly have originated on any of the planets in our own solar system. I refer you to Dr. Swale's analysis for the reasons why we have come to that position. So the question remains: *where* are the invaders?

"I'm actually going to answer that—in a way. But it's a circuitous route. You'll have to bear with me a bit, because in order to find out who the culprit is, we have to take a good long look at the evidence.

"When we look at the overall pattern—the stingflies, the nightwalkers, the red kudzu, the sea sludge, the bacteria that caused the plagues, even the, ah, Chtorrans themselves—we find that there is a pronounced tendency toward voraciousness, as if all of these life forms have evolved in a much more competitive ecology, not only surviving, but succeeding in that environment. Here on Earth, without their natural predators—

all the checks and balances of a stable ecology—these life forms cannot help but run wild. We're seeing it happen all over the planet.

"We expect to find that *none* of these creatures are harmless to the Terran ecology—*especially* not the ones that *look* harmless. They're the ones that represent the biggest danger, because they're the ones we're *most* likely to underestimate. We have one hundred and fifty-four new species identified, and there are probably a lot more that we haven't yet discovered. And that's because we don't have the people. For all practical purposes, most of the world's ecological maintenance agencies have ceased to exist. And that leaves us particularly vulnerable to this kind of ecological infestation—twice over. Once because we don't know all of what's happening out there, and twice because even where we do have monitors in the field, we do not have the resources to respond. We need to rebuild those agencies—without delay! If we mobilize now, there is still the chance that we can create a strong response to the threat. If not, then the pressure on our ecology of those hundred and fifty-four various and voracious new species will surely shatter what remains of life as we know it on this planet.

"It is this simple: *our ecology is under attack by a far more successful ecology.* The home planet may be half a billion—I said *billion*—years older than the Earth—with all the corresponding advantages of extended evolution that implies for the member species of that planet's ecology. The implied age of the ecology and its host planet may also be a clue to *why* this infestation is occurring at all. The host planet may be wearing out. Or its sun may be going cold. What we are seeing may very well be an attempt by an intelligent species to outlive the death of its home system.

"And—if we are correct about the age of the Chtorran ecology, that is also why we will not be able to use terrestrial microorganisms against the Chtorran life forms. If the Chtorran life forms that we have seen are the products of an extra umpteen million years of evolution, then that implies that they would also have the cumulative immunities against every mutation of every germ that has evolved on their home planet. And that suggests that they would therefore have a greater spectrum of resistance to unknown microorganisms. Our germs are going to be no threat to them, because to them, our ecology is simpler—much simpler. We are the great reptiles looking at the appearance of grass and blossoming flowers and therapsids in our ecology and wondering what the hell is happening to our world. We have no *natural* defenses here."

She leaned out across the podium as if to look into the face of every one of us in that auditorium. "If we accept this hypothesis—and I do not see how we can avoid it—then the motive of the initiating agency is no longer in question. There is only one possible interpretation of the situation: *we are at war!* A war unlike anything ever experienced or even conceived in the history of this planet!" She stopped herself, as if she were embarrassed at her own intensity. She covered it with a drink of water, just a sip, then continued. "The problem is that we have no evidence of the agency behind this invasion. It has to be there, but where is it? Again we come back to the question: where are the *real* Chtorrans?" Dr. Zymph let the question hang there in the air for a moment. She looked over her notes and rubbed the bridge of her thick nose between thumb and forefinger.

She looked up again, and when she spoke, it was like a burst of gunfire. "Actually, we might be asking the *wrong* question. We have to look at the situation from an invader's point of view. I refer you now to the Skotak-Alderson studies on how to colonize a planet. In those papers, of course, the authors were talking about Venus and Mars, but the general principles they laid down are extensible to any world.

"Briefly, Skotak and Alderson broke the colonization process down into sections. Part I is Terraforming and Phase I involves producing an atmosphere that Terran organisms can survive in. Phase II begins with the introduction of selected life forms to create a favorable protoecology on the world to be colonized.

"Now, applying that to our own situation, obviously some intelligence somewhere is working its own Phase II here on Earth. They are *Chtorraforming* the planet, if you will.

"Just as we would need to establish grasslands to feed our cattle, cornfields to feed our chickens, forests to provide our paper and lumber and plastics, bees to pollinate the blossoms of our plants so we can have fruits and vegetables, so must our unknown Chtorran planners need to establish the equivalent support species necessary to the survival of their civilization. That is precisely what is happening now. And will continue to happen.

"Based on a weighted Skotak-Alderson simulation, the infestation of the Earth will occur in three, perhaps four, distinct stages. Each stage will see a specific level of species support established before the next level appears. In other words, they won't bring in the Chtorran equivalent of coyotes until the Chtorran rabbits are fat, and they won't bring in the Chtorran rabbits until the Chtorran pastures are green—or in this case, purple—and they won't plant the pastures until the Chtorran earthworms have softened the ground. That puts us at a disadvantage, because we'll be seeing each species out of context, not knowing where each one fits in the larger pattern. It'll be as difficult as trying to extrapolate the rest of the symphony, when all you have is the sheet music for the tympanist and the third trombone.

"That's why we can't give you the hard answers yet. What facts we do have are still unconnected. We can only give you the larger pattern that all the facts point to. This infestation of the Earth is their way of clearing the land. It's the easiest way to deal with the local residents—clear them out before you move in. We're supposed to be long gone before the new tenants arrive. If you'll pardon an unpleasant metaphor, what we are experiencing is the Chtorran version of a slum clearance. A neighborhood improvement project—"

She pointed to the screen behind her. It lit up with slides of the nightwalker, the millipedes, the sea sludge, the red kudzu, the stingfly, the puffball creature, the pipe cleaner bug and a whole bunch of other things I didn't recognize. Dr. Zymph said, "—and these are the *shock troops*—the advance men for a highly competitive ecology; these are the bugs and beasties that are intended to soften up this planet for the rest of the ecology to follow. Let me say it again: the present infestation is only the first wave of a much larger and *meaner* infestation still to come. What comes next are *the creatures that eat these!*"

She bent to her notes for a moment, frowning, then looked up at us again. Her expression was grim. "Don't be misled by those who would minimize the situation. We are not going to find any *easy* controls for this or later infestations. We do not have the necessary competition on this planet. We human beings may not even be competitive enough, *ruthless and vicious enough,* to muster the necessary effort. I hope I'm wrong. But I don't think I am." She paused a moment to let that sink in.

"We must recognize from the very beginning that our natural defenses are not going to work. Our only possible countermeasures will be developed by finding the weaknesses within the Chtorran ecology. We must discover the interrelationships of these creatures and sabotage them in any way we can. We must use this invading ecology *against itself!* We must start today! It will not be an easy task! It will require a massive mobilization—the complete and total mobilization of every human being on this planet! And we must begin it *immediately!*"

She stopped to wipe her forehead. She was beginning to show the strain of what must have been for her a very difficult task. I was beginning to suspect something from the audience reactions around me. These delegates hadn't come here to be frightened out of their wits, but that was exactly what she was trying to do. From their continual disturbed murmuring, I guessed that they had come with the idea that they were going to be reassured that everything was under control—we just need an increase in next year's appropriations, no problem, and then we can all go home, back to our newly claimed wealth. Only it wasn't working out that way.

Dr. Zymph was talking about the end of the world. And I could see the hostility on some of the faces of her listeners.

She was saying, "—I will not try to soften this for you, because I do not think the dangers can be understated. We are facing *extinction.*

"We are *not* being invaded," she said. *"Not yet.*

"But—we are *going to be invaded.*

"How soon it will happen, we don't know. How long this phase will last, we don't know. What kind of creatures have initiated it, we don't know. What kind of creatures will appear next, we don't know. But I promise you—we *will* find out. If we live.

"It is inevitable. *We are going to be invaded.* By something. By the next level of this ecology. By the life forms that feed on these. And whatever comes, whatever form it takes, will be umpteen times more competitive—meaner, nastier and more vicious—than the things we're seeing now. What you see up there"—and she pointed toward the screen again, her arm stretched up and back, her finger stabbing like a pistol at the last of her slides, the gaping maw of a full-sized crimson Chtorran—"is just a candle before the firestorm!"

And with that she was through. She did not say, "Thank you," but it was clear that she was finished. She switched off her clipboard and strode from the stage.

There was no applause.

TWENTY-ONE

DR. ZYMPH'S remarks had not gone over well. You could feel the resentment. The audience boiled out of the auditorium like a nest of hornets. Their voices rising shrilly, they clustered into angry knots. Small arguments were breaking out all over, some erupting into shouting matches.

"—outrageous!" fumed one little man, shoving rudely past me. He was dark-skinned, he wore an expensive suit and he had a thick Middle-East accent. "Lies and propaganda! Next we're going to be told that the only answer is a military one! But my government isn't going to buy their horror stories! They're using this as an excuse for their own rearmament—" The rest was lost in the hubbub.

"I'm telling you she did not!" A tall, bald man with glasses was surrounded by a score of other scientists. "If anything, this was the toned-down version! If there's been *any* misstatement in the facts, it's been on the side of caution!"

The roar and buzz of a thousand separate voices swirled in the air above the lobby. A large crowd surrounded a huge fat man and a small loud one who were alternately booming and sniping at one another—a duel between a foghorn and a magpie. I couldn't get close enough to hear what they were saying, and the spirited reactions of their listeners were drowning out the meaning, leaving only the shredded sounds of their voices.

Behind me, someone else was preaching; I turned to see a bulldozer-shaped woman backing a nervous-looking man up against a corner. "—

and we have the papers to prove it! Have you read them yet? No? I'll
send you copies. Marsha got a letter from the man himself, saying how
impressed he was by her volume—"

I faded sideways, almost into the center of another conversation, a
very quiet one. The speaker was a well-mannered black man, very soft-
spoken. His listeners were a group of reporter types, each one holding
his or her recorder out like a shield. ". . . The people have had enough
bad news. They want to hear something good for a change. Of course,
Dr. Zymph's remarks are not going to be popular—I expect to see a lot
of resistance. But now let me add this. If the threat *is* real, you can be
sure that the American people will shoulder their fair share of the
responsibility. We'll handle it."

I'd heard enough. I headed out toward the lounge area. I was confused at the reaction of the delegates—didn't they realize?—and angry
at them as well. I stood in the middle of them and fumed. I would have
liked to have stuffed a few of them into the nearest Chtorran in full view
of their colleagues. That would change some minds, all right!

I was still hesitating, standing in the middle of the crowd and wondering what to do next, when I heard my name called. A hand was
waving at me from halfway across the lobby. Ted's. I began working my
way over to him. He was standing with a short, barrel-shaped man who
was wearing a dark suit and a frown; he looked constipated, perpetually
glaring out at the world through thick-lensed horn-rimmed glasses.
"This is Martin Miller," Ted said, "managing director of the Erewhon
Project."

"Oh," I said. I looked around. "Um, what happened to Dinnie?"

Ted shrugged. "I dunno. We got separated. No problem."

"I thought you two were, ah . . ."

"Huh? You've gotta be kidding!"

"Then what was that business about eleven orgasms?"

Ted put his hands on my shoulders and looked me straight in the eye.
"Jim, trust me. Someday, you'll know this for yourself—when you finally manage to lose that legendary virginity of yours—but until then,
take my word for it: *it is impossible even for a normal healthy male in
the peak of physical condition to come eleven times in one night.*" And
then he added, "I know—I've tried. But the most I've ever managed
was seven. And it wasn't with Dinnie."

"She seemed to think so."

"Jim, I am telling you the truth. I only came once. And I had to
think of raw liver to do even that. Let her believe what she wants."

"Then why the hell did you—"

"Shh! Keep your voice down! I'm gonna teach you one of the secrets of success. If you need to get to know a great number of people in a hurry—especially important people—find yourself the most ambitious social climber you can, and flatter her. Or him. You can get into a lot of otherwise closed doors that way. Look, you don't mind, do you?" He had slipped one arm around my shoulder and turned me sideways away from Miller. "This could be very big. For *both* of us. He's not even twenty-five yet and he's making multimillion-casey decisions. I'll talk to you later, all right?"

"Huh—? But you called me!" But Ted had already turned back to his conversation. Something about flash-doming urban tracts for future re-development. Miller was explaining how preservation grants would allow them to claim large areas of already developed but abandoned property, and Ted was babbling about getting the Reclamation Office to foot most of the bill. I didn't think either one was hearing a word the other was saying.

"Listen, you've got to stop seeing it as a set of political moves," the woman behind me was saying. She was speaking to a small cluster of Fourth-World delegates. She looked deceptively friendly. Her face was framed with dark curls and her mouth looked like a kiss looking for a place to happen. Her nametag said s. DORR. "I understand your concerns, I really do. Your governments are justifiably afraid that the United States is using this ecological infestation as an excuse for rebuilding its military strength. And certainly, that would be a legitimate concern under any ordinary circumstances. But these are *not* ordinary circumstances. You heard Dr. Zymph's presentation." Her badge identified her as a deputy ambassador to the United Nations. She spoke calmly and with authority. "Perhaps you've seen the reports, perhaps not, but the United States is the only nation left on this planet that can still muster the human resources necessary to meet this challenge. If you don't allow the passage of the Allowance Act, you're hurting yourself as much as us. These are the hard, cold facts—Europe is in ruins, barely surviving; Africa is at war with itself; most of South America is out of communication—all we know about are a few major cities; Russia's in turmoil; and we have no idea how bad the situation is in China. At least the United States still has a workable military organization. That's because this country did *not* mobilize its military for civilian population control during the plagues. We were forbidden to mobilize, so we kept our units isolated and as a result most of them survived. We now represent a reservoir of ability that the international community of nations desperately needs to draw upon—*must* draw upon—*despite the fact* that it would require the one thing that a majority of nations in the U.N. are most opposed to: an extraordinary American military reconstruction! But that's what's needed if we are to mount realistic opposition to this invasion." She held up a hand to forestall an interruption. "Please—I need to make the point understood. What we intend is *not* a military campaign in the traditional sense of armament and mobilization—there simply isn't the manpower for that—but rather a worldwide call to purpose with the same sense of discipline and urgency that are the hallmarks of a successful military operation. We would use the existing structure of the United States Civilian Operations Corps as a foundation on which to build our proposed worldwide ecological defense—because it's there and it's ready to go to work, and we don't have the time to spare making everything politically satisfactory for all concerned parties.

"We know that several members of your delegation were upset by Dr. Zymph's remarks, but my government is prepared to stand behind them. We are also prepared to share our knowledge freely. Your scientists are welcome to verify our facts; we're sure that they'll come to the same conclusions."

Her audience listened politely and patiently, but when she finished, the leader of the group spoke up. His English was thickly accented, but his words were blunt. "And if we don't do as you wish—what then? You go ahead and do it anyway, right? Who is to stop you now? Who has the power to stop anybody anymore? So what you're asking is not permission, not even cooperation—but approval. I cannot see my government granting that, Ms. Ambassador. I cannot see *any* government going out on that limb."

The woman flushed. Was it anger or embarrassment? Her tone of voice was too deliberately calm. "Dr. T!Kai, you disappoint me. If the United States were able to do this alone, we would already be in the process of doing it—that is how serious we consider this situation. But we are not able to do this alone; that is the purpose of this special conference, to demonstrate the scale of the problem and to call for worldwide cooperation—"

He interrupted her. "I find a flaw in that reasoning, Comrade Deputy Ambassador. First you tell us that we are not capable, that only the United States is capable. Now you tell us that you cannot do this without us. Which is it, please? You cannot have it both ways?"

This time, it *was* obvious. She was angry. "Dr. T!Kai, you are supposed to be a man of science, a visionary among your own people. You have even been called the mastermind of the African social revolution. We have been putting facts before you for three days now. We have many more facts to put before you. Please listen to them. *Realize what they mean.* If you have any questions at all, the entire staff of the National Science Center is at your disposal. You've seen the live specimens—if you need to see them again, it can be arranged. But *please* hear what we are trying to tell you!"

He looked at her calmly and said, "I am hearing. I am hearing all too well." He shook his head. "What I hear are excuses and justifications. I do not want to hear any more. Excuse me, please." He gestured to his retinue, and the group of them turned away and moved off down the hall.

Deputy Ambassador Dorr looked after them, tears welling up in her eyes. She mouthed a phrase that looked like *Damn fools!* Then she caught me looking at her and she smiled with embarrassment. She said, "You weren't supposed to hear that."

I said, "I've seen the Chtorrans. You're right."

"Yes," she said. She didn't look happy about it. "But this isn't about being right."

TWENTY-TWO

WHEN THE conference resumed, there were some conspicuously empty places in the auditorium. I wasn't the only one who noticed; behind me, I heard someone say, "Good. Now maybe we can get something accomplished."

I found a seat closer to the front this time. Almost immediately, two MP-types dropped into the empty places on my left and a narrow-looking scientist type with curly black hair, glasses and a big nose plopped himself down on my right. He was carrying a clipboard. Funny —there were a lot of people carrying clipboards today; most of them looked like they were part of the cadre that was running this operation. Professional, determined and grim. The foreign delegates had a more casual air, and they had secretaries and aides with them instead of clipboards—an almost ostentatious display of wasted labor.

Dr. Olmstead called the conference back to order then and introduced the next speaker, Dr. Indri Kwong from the Asian Control Center. Dr. Kwong was very thin and very old. He wore one of those quasi-military suits that all those Asian officials like to wear. And he was tiny; they had to lower the podium for him. There was something wrong with his right arm—he kept his hand tucked into his pocket and used only his left.

He fumbled around with his notes for a moment, then began. "Is that screen working? Ah, yes—good. Thank you." His English was almost too good—he spoke in precisely clipped phrases. "Thank you. Thank you for inviting me to address this conference. But if you will forgive the presumption of an old man, it is entirely appropriate that this section be the responsibility of the Asian Control Center. We were not only the first to isolate and identify specimens of the Chtorran gastropedes, but we have also compiled the greatest record of experience with these creatures. I wish to point out, however, that the term 'gastropede' is a misnomer. The creatures are only superficially sluglike under their fur. They actually have many small pairs of legs—so, if anything, they are giant, pink, fur-covered caterpillars."

He stopped then and paged slowly through his notes. I thought it was strange that he was using hard copies instead of a clipboard or a terminal, particularly because of the extra burden of having only one hand to manipulate the pages with.

"May I have the first slide, please? Ah, thank you. This is the first public presentation of these photographs, and we believe them to be the best set of photos yet obtained. Perhaps I should take a moment to present the background here. It has been only recently discovered that the mountainous regions of Manchuria are the site of a rather heavy infestation of gastropedes and associated ecology. On somewhat short notice we organized a small caravan of armored vehicles and airlifted them into the area. They were able to send out the following pictures before contact was lost. I wish to point out that the loss of the caravan does not necessarily imply that the gastropedes reacted with hostility to the human presence. The area is also known to be a staging site for several well-organized bandit gangs—"

"Hmp," muttered one of the MPs on my left. "They won't let him admit they've got a rebellion on their hands. Those are probably guerrillas."

"—and it's equally possible the caravan may have been attacked by one or more of these gangs."

I looked at the MP, and whispered, "How come everybody is so reluctant to admit that the worms are dangerous?"

"Eh?" He looked annoyed at me, but before he could answer, the curly-haired fellow on my right shushed us both.

Dr. Kwong was saying, "The evidence of these pictures should effectively dispel several of the more pernicious rumors that the creatures feed on human flesh. As you can see here—ah, yes, here's the shot—this particular individual is stripping the bark off a tree. During this entire sequence of photos—until the creature realized it was being observed—it felled several small saplings and ate most of the smaller branches and leaves. Later on, other individuals were seen to duplicate this behavior."

Huh? But what about—

I shut my mouth and listened.

Dr. Kwong adjusted his glasses on his nose and looked out over the audience. "We do not dispute that there have been attacks on humans, but we do believe now that such incidents are atypical. Not all tigers are maneaters either. A tiger has to learn that a man is easy to kill. Um . . . let me digress here. A tiger perceives that a human being is larger than he actually is because a man stands erect and seems to tower over the tiger. The tiger's perception of the man's height overrules his perception of the size of the man's body. So there is probably the element of, say, surprise for the tiger that a human being is easier to kill than he might have thought. But even that is not enough to turn a tiger into a man-eater. Human flesh does not taste good to the average predator—particularly the big cats. No, the tiger has to have a susceptibility, a *need*, before it can turn into a man-eater. Salt is one of its primary needs. A lack of it is usually enough to turn the tiger into an enemy. We suspect that the gastropedes that have attacked human beings may be suffering from a similar kind of dietary deficiency and human flesh may inadvertently be one of the sources for whatever the element is that they need."

Another picture came up on the screen. Obviously a telephoto shot. A small Chtorran carrying a sapling across the ground.

"We suspect that the natural behavior of the creatures is closer to that of the North American beaver. This colony was observed for quite some time performing a very pastoral set of behaviors. As you can see here, they are in the process of damming a small stream.

"This is one of the larger Chtorran settlements that the team discovered. Notice that there are three domes here, and an equal number of domes still under construction—"

"Those are corrals," I said. I folded my arms across my chest. Dr. Kwong didn't see that the Chtorrans were predatory, so he obviously couldn't recognize their corrals for what they were.

The curly-haired man on my right gave me a look. "You know something?"

"Damn right I do."

"Better keep it to yourself. This isn't the place." He didn't intend it angrily, but I didn't want to hear it.

Dr. Kwong was saying, "—we do find it interesting that the Chtorran gastropedes come three to a nest. Never more than that—"

"Excuse me, sir," somebody said, standing up. It was me.

Heads swiveled to look at me. Dr. Kwong stopped in midphrase, unable to ignore me. He blinked twice and said, "I beg your pardon?"

"Have you ever found *four* Chtorrans in a nest?"

Dr. Kwong looked mildly annoyed. "Young man, I just finished saying that there were *never* more than three."

"Are you *sure* about that?"

"Young man, what is the purpose?"

"I'm sorry, sir. But they do come four to a nest. I've seen it."

Beside me, the curly-haired man was tugging at my sleeve. *"Sit down!"* he hissed. I ignored him.

Dr. Kwong wasn't angry—just surprised that someone would display the incredibly bad manners to interrupt him. "Are you arguing with me, young man?"

"No, sir. I'm correcting you. I've seen it. Four worms—Chtorrans—in a nest. I was there."

"I see. Young man, I am the Director of the Asian Control Center. We have a network of observers that spans the largest continent on this planet. This is the first time I have ever heard of a fourth Chtorran in a nest. So perhaps you can understand my reluctance to accept this information. Particularly in *these* circumstances. I'm sure your story merits investigation. Perhaps some anomaly has occurred, but this is neither the time nor the place, so if you would resume your seat, I might continue—"

Something brittle snapped. "If *this* isn't the place, then *where the hell is?* I have information! I saw this myself." I said it loudly, and there was anger in my voice. "There was a hut and a corral and the corral was full of millipedes and the hut was full of eggs. And when the Chtorrans came out of the hut, *there were four of them.*"

By now, the people around me were calling for me to sit down, but I ignored them. Curly-hair was slumped in his seat, one hand over his eyes.

Dr. Kwong motioned away a concerned aide. "No, no, let him be—I can handle him." Everything he said was amplified by the PA system, whether he faced the microphone or not. He said to me, "Young man, may I ask, on what do you base your knowledge? What is your credential?"

"United States Army. Sir. My name is James Edward McCarthy, and I hold the rank of corporal."

Somebody behind me snorted. Somebody else called, "That's as low as they have left. They can't find anyone willing to be a private anymore."

My mouth opened again and said, "United States Army, Special Forces Operation. I was assigned as an exobiologist and an observer."

"Special Forces?" There was something odd about the way he repeated it.

"Yes, sir."

"And your duties involved . . . ?"

"I was on a reconnaissance mission and on a Chtorran-hunting mission."

"A *what—?*"

"Uh—to say it in plain English—which is something nobody else around here has done yet—we went out to burn some worms. And we killed three of them. And then the fourth one came out and killed my friend. And I had to burn them both."

"I beg your pardon? Did you say *burn?*"

"Yes, I did."

He was leaning forward intently. "What do you mean, 'burn'?"

"Burn! Flamethrowers, sir. Napalm. Jellied gasoline. It's the only thing that'll stop a worm fast." There was a startled reaction from the audience, loud gasps and cries.

Dr. Kwong was holding up his hand. "Please, please—may we have some order? Napalm? Are you sure?"

"Yes, sir. I had to kill one of the best men I've ever known. It was the only way. I wouldn't lie about a thing like that."

"You used *napalm?* Napalm is an illegal weapon!"

"Yes, sir. I know that. I raised the same objection myself. But you missed the point, sir. There were *four* worms in that hut!"

"Young man, there are some very good reasons why napalm was outlawed as a weapon of war. If you'll wait a moment, I'll show you one of them—" He was fumbling with his jacket. One of his aides stepped up to help him, but Dr. Kwong brushed him peevishly aside. He unzipped the tunic and dropped it to the floor, then he opened his shirt to reveal a withered right arm and a mass of white scar tissue that stretched from his neck to his waist, and probably a good way down his leg as well. He walked with a slight limp as he stepped around the podium. "Take a good look—this is what napalm can do to a human being. I was seven years old. United States soldiers came to my village, looking for the enemy. The enemy was long gone, but they burned the village anyway. And most of the villagers too. I have lived all of my life carrying the scars of your country's crime against mine.

"Many other nations had to suffer the same ravages to discover sanity in the ashes—and it took a long time for it to happen—but the peace-loving nations of this world finally enforced a lasting peace against the imperialistic savageries of the United States. Napalm was the most pernicious of the American weapons to be restricted. There are too many thousands of crippled men and women who can tell you why. Look and see what it does to the human body, young man. There is no easy healing here—there is no healing at all, only scars. And now—you stand there in your ignorance, your bare-faced naïveté, and dare to tell me that the United States is using such weaponry again? In disregard of all the treaties and United Nations mandates?"

"That's not the issue!" I was screaming now. "You grandstanding son of a bitch! You think the worms are so goddamned friendly, why don't you go in and see for yourself? They have one here at the center! He's in a glass-walled room—why don't you go in and try hand-feeding him! Then you'll find out if they're man-eaters!"

"Sit down!" That was Dr. Olmstead, pointing at me and shouting through a bullhorn—where the hell had he gotten that?

Dr. Kwong was shouting back at me, "I've seen the specimen—and that's a feral animal. It has no inhibitions and only animal intelligence. It may be that the other creatures we've observed *do* have some intelligence. Had you let me finish, I would have discussed that point. We have been making attempts to establish contact with them, but since you and your cohorts have been burning every one of them you come in contact with, you've made it impossible for us. You're the ones who've made them into an enemy—you and your execrable military mind-set!"

Off to my right, one of the African delegates was standing and shouting now. "Don't be sidetracked! Let's deal with this napalm issue! The United States is in violation of—"

"What about the fourth Chtorran?"

"You can't bomb your way to peace," called someone else, and still another voice responded, "It's a helluva start!"

"Come on," the curly-haired man said, grabbing my arm. "You're getting out of here!" He gestured to the MPs. "That way—"

"Huh? What is this? You can't—"

"Shut up, stupid! You want to get out of here in one piece?" He pushed me roughly forward.

"Wait a minute! What about the fourth Chtorran—? Wait a minute!"

TWENTY-THREE

THE TWO MPs moved through the crowd like destroyers. One of them had my arm in a steel grip and was pulling me after him—I caught quick glimpses of roaring faces turning toward me, but I couldn't even shout. Curly-hair, holding my other arm in an equally painful vise, brought up the rear. We were out the side door of the auditorium so fast we could have been on rails.

"This way—" the MP said, jerking me sideways into a hallway. Behind us, I could hear the angry outcry rising. "Damn!" said curly-hair bitterly. "You just started a riot."

"Uh, sorry about that."

"Be smart for a moment. Shut up." To the MPs he said, "Tailor shop."

"Right." They grabbed me between them, one on each side—one hand under the armpit, the other under the elbow—and we *moved*. They held me like I was furniture; it didn't matter if I moved my feet or not to keep up—we *moved*. Curly took the lead, angling right into a dark service corridor, then left into a broom closet, opening up a door where no door should be.

We stepped through and there was silence. We were in darkness.

"Wait a minute." Curly was punching something into a wall terminal. Dim red ceiling lights came up and I could see we were in another corridor, only this one was featureless. To the MPs he said, "You can let go of him now. You, come with me."

I followed him into a small room. There were a desk and two chairs.

He slapped his clipboard down onto the desk and sat down behind it. He pointed at the other chair and I sat down too. He opened a drawer and pulled out a pack of cigarettes, shook one out and lit it. He did not offer one to me.

So—this was to be an interrogation.

I remembered something I had seen in a movie. I leaned forward and shook a cigarette out of the pack for myself.

"I didn't say you could smoke."

"You didn't say I couldn't." I glared back at him.

He grinned abruptly. "It won't work. I saw the same movie."

I shrugged and stubbed the cigarette out. "I don't smoke anyway."

He didn't laugh. He let the grin fade and studied me for a moment, thoughtfully. At last he said, "You have something for me?"

"Huh?"

"You were trying to find me this morning, weren't you?" He tapped his chest.

"Huh?" And then I saw it. His name badge. WALLACHSTEIN. "*Oh!*" I said, realizing. "But the directory said you don't exist."

"You better believe it." His chair creaked alarmingly when he leaned back. "I'm not even here now. This is all a hallucination you're having. Now, I believe you have something for me?" He held out his hand.

I was still smarting. I folded my arms. "I want some answers first."

His hand was still outstretched. "Listen, stupid, you're in big trouble, so be a good boy for a while and maybe I can get you out of here quietly. Maybe." The air had gotten noticeably chillier.

"I didn't ask to be rescued from anything. You dragged me in here against my will—"

"You want to go back? That can be arranged too. Just give me the package that Obie gave you, and Sergeants Kong and Godzilla will put you right back in the center of what you started. Although I think you'd be a lot better off with us. We did you a favor and you might want to say thank you."

"Yeah—and I might want to say 'fuck you' too! I'm getting really tired of all the 'oughts' and 'shoulds' and 'musts' that are being dropped on me. And all without explanations. Nobody ever explains anything. And then you get pissed off because I'm not following the rules! So fuck you! I was told that if I couldn't find you I should destroy the package. Well, I couldn't find you. You don't exist. Now, which way is out—?"

"Sit down, Jim," he said. "You made your point. Besides, the door's locked until I'm ready to unlock it."

It was his use of my name that stopped me.

He'd been expecting me. And something else—he'd purposely sat down next to me in the auditorium! And the MPs too! They'd had me bracketed since . . .

"How long?" I asked.

"How long till I unlock the door?"

"No. How long have you—whoever you are—been watching me?"

"Oh, that. Since about three minutes after you checked my name in the directory. You've been under surveillance ever since."

"The woman on my right—the one during Dr. Zymph's presentation?"

"Uh huh, and the two lieutenants on your left as well. I don't know what you're carrying, but Obie says it's important." He added, "I don't mind telling you that I'm curious to see what Obie thinks is too dangerous to send over a wire—even a secure and coded one." He leaned forward to drop his cigarette into an ashtray. "May I have it, please?"

I took a breath. I exhaled. "Yeah, I guess so."

He raised an eyebrow at me. "No more argument?"

"You called her Obie."

Wallachstein grinned. "You know something? You're not so stupid."

I pulled out the lockbox and passed it over to him. He turned it over and laid it face down on the desk. I didn't see exactly what he did with his fingers, but the back of it slid off, revealing a thin false bottom. There was a single memory clip inside. Wallachstein picked it out and dropped it into his jacket pocket as casually as if it were something he did every day; then he looked up and noticed my expression. "Something the matter?"

"Uh, I've never seen one like that."

"And you'll probably never see another one either."

"Can I ask why? The false bottom, I mean."

"Sure. These things aren't too difficult to break into, not for a skilled laboratory." He turned it over and slid it across. "Here. What's your birthday? Punch it in."

"My birthday?"

He nodded. I tapped it out on the keyboard and the box popped open. Inside was a package of fifty thousand-casey notes.

"Happy birthday," he said.

"Huh?"

"Courier fee. You got your message through without being killed. The money's unimportant. It's just a decoy, in case you lose the box.

The wrong person opens it; he thinks that's what's being transported. Burn the paper wrapper—just in case they're not fooled by the money, there's a microdot on the wrapper. It's nothing but a very long random-number sequence. You could go crazy trying to decode it, because it won't. It's just hash. Another decoy. A practical joke, even—but the idea is to distract the enemy, draw him away from the real trick. We're all so marvelously subtle these days—on both sides—that no one stops to think there might be an easier way."

"Uh . . . sir . . . *the enemy?*"

"You've already met them. Out there." He pointed at the door. He dropped the money out of the box onto the table before me and slid the box into a desk drawer. "Go ahead, take it. Better spend it before it goes *completely* worthless."

"Uh, shouldn't I be discreet? I mean, won't people wonder where it came from?"

"Don't bother. Nobody else does. We're all stealing from the dead one way or another anyway. Nobody's going to question you." He picked up his clipboard and stood up, all in one motion. "I'm going to ask you to wait here while I go and see what's on this." He tapped his jacket pocket meaningfully. "You want coffee?"

"Yeah, thanks."

"Right." He was already out the door.

He'd given me a lot to think about. Just what was going on here? What had I stumbled into? And how was I going to get *out?*

I tried the door. He'd locked it behind him. I sat down again.

Then I got up and tried the drawers on the desk. They were locked too. I shrugged and went back to my chair. Then I wondered if I'd done something stupid. Did the walls of this room have eyes as well as ears? I hoped I hadn't picked my nose in front of one of their cameras.

The door to the room slid open and one of the two MPs came in carrying a tray. He closed the door behind him, crossed to the desk and set the tray down. He pushed it toward me: a pot of coffee, one cup, a cream pitcher, a sugar bowl and a spoon. He sat down in the chair behind the desk, folded his arms casually and leaned back in the chair. It complained loudly. He stared at me.

I poured myself a cup of coffee and tasted it carefully. *Ugh!* Had they sent all the way back to Sergeant Kelly's kitchen for this?

"Well. Here we are," I said. "Uh, are you Sergeant Kong or Sergeant Godzilla?"

He opened his mouth and said, "Shut up."

I shut.

It was a very uncomfortable half-hour. At least, it felt like a half-hour. We sat and glowered at each other the whole time.

At last Colonel Wallachstein came back. He motioned Sergeant Kong —or maybe it was Godzilla—out of the room with a jerk of his head and sat down at the desk again. He pushed the coffee tray to one side without even looking at it. He waited until the door was closed before he said, "I believe you. About the fourth Chtorran. You've had a rough time of it, haven't you?"

I shrugged. "Who hasn't?"

"You'd be surprised. The world's full of opportunists. Never mind. Obie says you're okay. She also asked me to honor the obligation. If I thought it appropriate."

"Obligation?"

"I think she may have mentioned it already. Every member of the Special Forces not only has the right, but the obligation, to understand the responsibilities of his orders—"

"You mean I have the right to ask questions after all?"

He nodded. "And I have the responsibility to answer them."

"Well, it's about time. Yeah, I have a lot of questions. First of all, just what the hell is going on? Not just here, but out there? Why won't any of those bozos take the Chtorrans seriously? And—"

He held up a hand to slow me down. He waited until my questions petered out on their own. He looked unhappy. "I said, 'if I thought it appropriate.' I'm sorry, but I don't. Not yet. Maybe not at all. You're a real pain in the ass, you know that? Unfortunately . . ."

"Unfortunately *what?*"

He glanced at me wryly. "Unfortunately, you're a *smart* pain in the ass." He looked unhappy. He looked at his watch and looked even unhappier. "I don't know what to do with you. And I have to get back. I have to monitor something this afternoon. I hate to leave you hanging, but I don't have any choice—and I'm sorry, but it wouldn't be a good idea for you to go back to the conference. Not today, at least. There're a few people looking for you, and not too many of them are friendly. We still have to figure out how to handle this—what you started. Um, listen, I'll arrange for you to monitor the rest of the conference by remote, and we'll cover your disappearance for a couple of days too. At least until Tuesday when most of the foreign delegates are on their way out. I owe you that much at least. And maybe by then I'll have figured out what to do with you."

"Uh, don't I get any say in the matter?"

"Haven't you said enough today?"

"All I did was stand up and ask a question. I still haven't gotten any answers."

"Did it ever occur to you that there may not be any to give?" He stood up. "You wait here." And he exited again.

This time I didn't have to wait as long. The door slid open and Major Lizard Tirelli stuck her head in. "McCarthy?"

"Huh? Yeah—hi!"

She looked annoyed. "Come on," she said. I followed her out into the darkened hall and to the right. Now where were we going? The door was back the other way.

We stopped in front of an elevator alcove. The door slid open at our approach. I followed her in. There was only a single button on the control panel. She pressed it and the door closed. The elevator slid upward.

"Where are we going?"

"Thirteenth floor," she said.

"Huh? Hotels don't have thirteenth floors."

"This one does," she said. Her voice was brittle. Obviously, she didn't want to talk. At least, not to me.

I shut up and we rode the rest of the way in silence.

TWENTY-FOUR

THE THIRTEENTH floor looked like any other floor of the hotel—except it only had *one* elevator door.

My dad had told me about controlled-access architecture a long time ago. I'd just never seen any firsthand. Apparently, the builders of this hotel had intended the architectural camouflage for business purposes, probably to provide a floor of private suites and offices for visiting dignitaries and other celebrities who needed tight security.

If someone were to notice that there was a physical gap between twelve and fourteen, and were to ask about it—and he'd probably have to walk the fire stairs to figure it out—he'd probably be told it was a "service area." Which it was, sort of. He just wouldn't be told what service. The purloined letter again. Like a lockbox with a false bottom.

I would bet, however, that the present occupants of the thirteenth floor were not the ones for which it had been originally intended. Or were they?

We stopped before a featureless gray metal door. Room 1313.

"Am I going to be locked in?" I asked.

Lizard ignored me as she slid the room card into the slot. She punched a number and the door slid open. She handed me the card. "You can change the combination if you want. You can leave if you want."

"But I thought—"

"What?"

"—that Colonel Wallachstein wanted me to wait."

"Who?"

"Colonel Wallachstein—the man who pulled me out of the auditorium and interrogated me and—"

She stepped close to me. "Listen, stupid. The man you're talking about doesn't exist. There's nobody in Denver by that name. Do you understand?"

No, I didn't. "Uh, I guess so. Can I ask something?"

She looked annoyed and impatient. "What is it?"

"What the hell is going on?"

"I can't answer that."

"Am I under arrest?"

"You're free to go any time you want. It just wouldn't be a good idea. There are people looking for you—some of them you wouldn't like very much."

"Oh. Then I'm being held in protective custody?"

"You're not being held at all."

"Then why am I here?"

"I don't know. It's not my job to answer your questions."

"Is *anyone* going to answer my questions? Or am I just going to be shoved from place to place until I'm out of everyone's way?"

"That sounds like a good idea. Oh, you can't phone out from here without clearance, but you can get room service."

"Which is the way out?"

"For you? Take the fire stairs up to fourteen or down to twelve and catch an elevator from there. But you won't be able to get back. My advice is for you to do exactly what you're told and wait here." She turned to go.

"Um—Major?"

She stopped and looked at me.

"Am I in trouble? I mean, should I be worried?"

I guess I was scared. I guess it showed in my voice, because she caught herself. A flicker of annoyance had started to cross her face, a reflex reaction to another stupid question, but then she realized the concern behind the question and softened. She said, "You didn't do anything that at least half a dozen other people didn't want to do. You just didn't know why you shouldn't have."

I felt the pain of embarrassment flooding into my face—of being identified as the guy who'd screwed things up. "Is anyone ever going to tell me?" I asked.

She wanted to go, I could see that, but instead she took my arm and dragged me into the room, closing the door behind us. "Sit down." She looked at her watch. "All right, I have time. You want coffee? No? Well, I do." She stepped over to the apartment's kitchenette and opened a cupboard. "You'd better enjoy your coffee today, Jim—there won't be much of it tomorrow."

"Huh?"

"Never mind. Listen—what did you major in?"

"Biology. Software. Humanity Skills. Problemantics. The usual."

"Right. Did you take any history?"

"Only the basic requirements."

"Damn." She was silent a moment. I didn't know if her outburst was because I hadn't taken any history or because she'd spilled some water. She turned back to me.

"Did you have a Global Ethics course?"

"Yeah. Everybody did. It was required study."

"Uh huh. Do you know why?"

"To prevent another Apocalypse."

"Right. What do you know about the Apocalypse?"

"Um, not a lot, I guess. Just what we were taught in class."

"Go on," she encouraged.

"Well—you sure you want to hear this?"

"I said, go on."

"Well—um, there was a war. In the Middle East. There are always wars in the Middle East, but this one got out of control. It was between Israel and I forget who, but there were a lot of other countries lined up against Israel. And there were African and Chinese mercenaries involved. And finally it got so bad that Israel had no choice but to threaten to use nuclear weapons. And finally they did."

"And then what happened?"

"The United States withdrew its support for Israel and Israel had to surrender."

"And?"

"Everybody was so scared at what had almost happened that they all went to Russia and signed the Moscow Treaties."

"Yeah." She looked skeptical and turned back to the coffee. "You want milk or sugar?" she asked as she poured. I shook my head. As she handed me the cup, she said, "That version is the one they teach in the schools—but it's so simplified, it's almost a fairy tale. Israel didn't drop those bombs. We did."

"Huh? But that's not—"

"Of course that's not. But the truth is a little less palatable. That was *our* war and we told Israel to drop those bombs, because we thought it would bring an end to the war. Well, it did—but not the way we thought it would. What they didn't tell you is that the President lost his nerve."

"Huh?"

"What did they teach you in class?"

I shrugged. "The way we heard it, there was a midnight Cabinet session and all of his advisors were arguing loudly back and forth about how many people would die in each exchange and whether or not our third-strike capability would survive, and the President was just sitting quietly at the end through all of this, puffing on his pipe like he always did. And finally, after several long hours, one of the Joint Chiefs of Staff summed it up by saying, 'The moral arguments are irrelevant here. The war is *inevitable.*' And that's when the President said, '*Like hell it is!*' "

"Yeah, that's the story. But it's not true. That is, it's only half true. The part you don't hear is about the ultimatum that the Soviet ambassador had handed him just that afternoon. If Israel launched any more nuclear weapons against Soviet allies, the Soviet Union would view those attacks as originating in the United States, and would respond accordingly. It was the same ultimatum that John F. Kennedy handed Nikita Khrushchev in October of 1962, when Russian missiles were discovered in Cuba—and the Russians were aware of the irony of the situation. They used the exact same phrasing in their note."

"I never heard about this," I said.

"You weren't meant to—but that's what was on his mind during that meeting. That the other side had decided that all-out nuclear war was inevitable too."

"But, I always thought he was a hero."

Major Tirelli looked wistful. "So did I—I still do. And maybe he was —maybe it takes more guts to stay *out* of a war. But either way, we inherited the consequences of that decision."

I sipped at the coffee. It was hot. And bitter. I said, "What we were taught was that he made a speech, an extraordinary speech, in which he said that the responsibility had been handed to him whether or not the world should be plunged into Armageddon. And regardless of the morality of any other issue, this one fact remained uppermost in his mind: if it could be stopped, it had to be stopped, and he would do whatever was required of him to prevent the deaths of millions and millions of human beings. He said that by the act of using nuclear weapons, a nation disqualifies itself from the community of rational thought."

"I heard the speech," she said. "My parents made me stay up to hear it. But I didn't understand what it meant until later. That man went to Moscow, hoping that it would be seen as a gesture of sanity. Instead, they saw it as capitulation and forced him to accept a crippling peace, a debilitating compromise. The tragedy is he knew exactly what they had done to him. Oh, he looked like a hero—he was being hailed as a courageous man all over the world—but he knew what he had given away: America's right to protect her foreign interests. What do you think Pakistan was about? It was an attempt to reestablish the old prerogative. And it failed. This time it was the Chinese who handed us the ultimatum. And this time, the treaties were even more crippling. Do you know what the allies did to Germany after the First World War? They took away that nation's right to an army. That was what was done to us. The United States was told that our existence as a nation would continue only so long as we maintained no direct threat to any other nation on this planet. And the cooperation with that agreement would be monitored by an international committee."

"We never heard this," I said.

"I told you, you weren't meant to. It's a part of our history that we aren't very proud of, so officially, it doesn't exist—like all the other pieces of history we don't acknowledge."

I hid my reaction behind the coffee cup again. When I lowered it, I said, "Is that why the foreign delegates are so paranoid about the way we want to fight the Chtorrans?"

"Right. Very few foreign governments see the Chtorrans as the threat we do. The reasons are varied. Some of them don't see science as anything more than a way to make the crops grow bigger. Others don't think the Chtorrans will be a threat next year because they aren't a threat this year. Most of the people we're dealing with don't even comprehend the scale of death produced by the plagues—so how can they comprehend that the plagues are only a small part of a much larger infestation?"

"Then Dr. Zymph was right?"

"If anything, she was understating the case. You've had enough direct experience with the Chtorr to know what they're like. But try to tell that to someone who's never seen one in action. They won't comprehend it. They don't want to."

"Doesn't that get frustrating?"

Lizard nodded wearily, and grinned. "Incredibly so!" She sipped at her coffee, then said, "Dr. Zymph knew that was how the delegates would react. She was willing to have it. We have to keep putting the facts out, but it happens every time the subject is raised in the international community. The delegates go crazy. They see the Chtorrans only as America's latest rationalization for rearmament. Listen, we're already rearming ourselves. We don't *need* a rationalization." She shook her head sadly. "But they're frightened; that's what it really is. Just about every nation on this planet is in trouble of one sort or another—there isn't one of them that isn't vulnerable to the first serious military threat that occurs. They're not concerned about the Chtorrans because they've never been bitten by one—but they're sure as hell scared of American military power, because they're still carrying scars. At least we're a threat they can comprehend, so they're displacing their fear and their anger onto us." Lizard looked at me. "Now do you see what kind of cow pasture you stepped into?"

"Ugh," I said.

She glanced at her watch. "I gotta go—but look, you can use the terminal here to tap into the History section of the Library of Congress. You might find it interesting. You probably don't know it, but as a member of the Special Forces, your security clearance is high enough to get you access to most of what you need to know."

"I didn't know that."

"Then you've got an interesting afternoon ahead of you. It'll be a while before anyone can get back to you. Be patient, okay? There are some decisions that have to be made first—"

TWENTY-FIVE

I HADN'T thought about Whitlaw in a while.

I wondered if he was still alive. I'd never given it any thought before; I couldn't imagine him dead. I'd always just assumed he would be one of the survivors.

But then again, I couldn't imagine Shorty being dead either. Or my dad. And they were—so what did it matter whether I could imagine it or not? The universe was going to do what it damn well wanted regardless how I or anyone else felt about it.

Whitlaw ran his class the same way. He didn't care how we felt either. "You don't get to vote," he used to say. "You already did when you put yourself in this class. You belong to me, body and mind, until I'm ready to turn you loose upon the world."

The class was a two-semester unit. Toward the end of the first semester, Whitlaw abruptly asked, "Does anyone here know *why* this is a required course?"

"If we don't take it, we don't graduate." That was one of the mindless lurches who usually roosted in the last row of seats. A couple of his buddies laughed.

Whitlaw eagle-eyed the hulk over the heads of the rest of us. He gave him a thorough half-second of examination and then said, "That isn't the answer I was looking for, but considering the source, I guess it's the best I could have expected. Anyone else?"

No. No one else.

"It'll be the first question on your final exam," he prompted. Someone groaned.

Whitlaw stumped back to his desk. I wondered if his limp were bothering him. He didn't look happy. He opened the loose-leaf binder he used as his source book and paged through it silently, until he found the page he was looking for. He studied it with a thoughtful frown. After a moment, he looked up again. "No takers?"

No. We'd gotten too smart for that.

"Too bad. All right—we'll try it this way then. How many of you think it's appropriate for a population to rebel against tyranny?"

A few hands went up immediately. Then a few more, tentatively, as if terrified that they were volunteering to be on the front lines. Then a few more. I raised my hand. Pretty soon almost everyone had. Whitlaw didn't wait to see if it would be unanimous. He pointed at one of the abstainers. "How about you? Don't you think so?"

"I think you have to define your terms. You're being too general. What tyranny? Which one?"

Whitlaw straightened and eyed the fellow with narrowed eyes. "Are you on the debate team? No? Well, you ought to consider it. You're doing everything but confronting the issue. So all right, I'll make it easy on you—" He closed his book.

"—Let's say this room is the nation of Myopia. I'm the government. You're the citizens. Now, you know governments are not free. So the first thing I'm going to do is collect taxes. I want one casey from each of you." He started striding down the aisles. "Give me a casey. No, I'm not joking. These are your taxes. Give me a casey. You too. Sorry, I don't accept checks or paper money. What? That's your lunch money? Gee, that's tough, but your government's needs come first."

"But that's not fair!"

Whitlaw stopped, his hand full of coins. "Who said that? Take him out and execute him for sedition!"

"Wait a minute! Don't I get a fair trial?"

"You just had one. Now shut up. You've been executed." Whitlaw kept collecting. "Sorry, I want exact change. You don't have it? Don't worry about it. In your case, I'll levy a four-casey surcharge. Consider it a penalty for paying your taxes with paper money. Thank you. Thank you—fifty, seventy-five, a casey, thank you. All right, I've got forty-eight caseys here. This'll buy me a good lunch. Everybody be sure to bring another casey tomorrow. I'll be collecting taxes every day from now on."

We looked at each other nervously. Who was going to be first to complain? Wasn't this illegal—a teacher taking money from his class?

A tentative hand. "Uh, sir . . . your majesty?"

"Yes?"

"Uh, can I ask a question?"

"Mm, depends on the question."

"Can we ask what you're going to do with our money?"

"It's not your money anymore. It's mine."

"But it was ours to start with—"

"—and now it's mine. I'm the government." He slid open his desk drawer and dropped the coins loudly into it. "Eh? Your hand is still up?"

"Well, it just seems to me—to all of us—"

"To *all* of you?" Whitlaw looked at us with raised eyebrows. "Is this an insurrection that I see before me? I guess I'd better hire an army." He stumped to the back of the room, pointing at the huskiest boys in the class. "You, you and, ah, yes, you too. And you. Come up front. You're now in the army." He opened the drawer and scooped up coins. "Here are two caseys for each of you. Now, don't let any of this rabble near the royal palace."

The four boys looked uncertain. Whitlaw shoved them into position between himself and the class. "Now then—you were saying?"

"Mr. Whitlaw!" Janice MacNeil, a tall black girl, stood up. "All right! You've made your point. Now give everybody back their money—" Janice was in student government.

Whitlaw peered between the shoulders of two of his tallest "soldiers." He grinned. "Uh uh," he said. "This game is being played for keeps. Now, what are you going to do about it?"

Janice didn't fluster. She said, "I'll go to a higher authority."

Whitlaw was still grinning. "There aren't any. This class is autonomous. See that plaque on the wall? That's the charter of the Federal Education System. You've been in this classroom nearly every day for eighteen weeks, and I'll bet you still haven't read it, have you? Too bad —because that's the contract you agreed to when you entered this classroom. I have total authority over you."

"Well, of course, I *understand* that!" she snapped. "But I'm talking about the *real world* now. You have to give us back our money!"

"You *don't* understand." Whitlaw grinned at her. "This *is* the real world. Right here. And I *don't* have to. I am empowered by the federal

government to do whatever is necessary to fulfill the course requirements. And that *includes* taxes—if I so deem it necessary."

She folded her arms. "Well, we don't have to cooperate."

Whitlaw shrugged. "Fine. I'll have you arrested."

"What? You'll send me to the principal's office?"

"No, I mean arrested, as in read you your rights and throw you in the
slammer, the lockup, the hoosegow, durance vile, the Bastille, the
Tombs, the Tower of London, Devil's Island and Alcatraz—do I make
myself clear?"

"You're kidding."

"No, I'm not. Look it up."

"But that's not fair!"

"So what? You already agreed to it, so what are you complaining
about?" He tapped two of his troops. "Throw her out of here—and that
other fellow too, the one we executed earlier. They're automatically
flunked." Whitlaw's army didn't look happy about it, but they started
down the aisle.

Janice looked genuinely scared, but she scooped up her books and
clipboard and went.

"You'll wait next door until the period is over," Whitlaw said. "Anyone else want to question the authority of this government?"

No. Nobody else did.

"Good." Whitlaw sat down and put his feet up on his desk. "I'm
flunking everyone who opens his mouth out of turn." He picked up a
book and an apple, opened the book and started reading. Periodically,
he would take a loud bite from his apple, audibly reminding us of his
presence.

The army looked uncertain. "Should we sit down, sir?"

"Of course not. You're on duty."

The rest of us exchanged glances. What was the point of this? The
fellow to whom Whitlaw had recommended joining the debate team
leaned over and whispered to a friend, "He's daring us to try something."

"Well, you try. I don't want to get thrown out."

"But don't you see, if we all organize—"

Whitlaw stood up suddenly, glowering. "What's that? Sounds like
subversion to me!" He stepped forward and grabbed the debater by his
shirt, pulling him out of his seat. "I won't have that!" He dragged the
boy out of the room.

In the brief moment that he was gone, there was bedlam.

"The man's a loonie—"

"—This is crazy—"

"—Can't we do something?"

I stood up. "Listen! We outnumber him! We don't have to let him get away with this."

"Shut up, Jim! You're just gonna get us all in worse trouble!"

"Let him talk—"

"You got an idea, Jim?"

"Well, no . . . but . . ."

Whitlaw came back in then, and I slid back into my seat fast enough to feel the heat.

Whitlaw turned to his troops. "What kind of army are you? I leave the room for less than a minute, and I come back to find rabble-rousers preaching sedition in the aisles! I want you to arrest and expel every one who complained—or you'll get thrown out too!"

There were five of us.

"Is that all?" Whitlaw bellowed. "If you missed anyone, I'll have your heads!"

The army looked scared. After a moment's whispered conference, they picked three more people and all eight of us trooped out. "But I didn't even say anything!" Joey Hubre looked close to tears. "Tell him!" he appealed to his twin.

"You do," shouted Whitlaw, "and you go too. In fact, you'd better go anyway—you're probably both trouble!"

There were twelve of us in the next-door classroom. We sat glumly looking at each other. Confused, puzzled and very hurt. We could hear Whitlaw bellowing. And then, abruptly, there was silence. A moment after that, three more exiles joined us.

"What'd he do? Execute the class?"

"Naw—he declared a national silence," said Paul Jastrow. "That's why he threw us out. I passed a note. He said I was publishing treason."

"What's he trying to prove?" complained Janice.

"Tyranny, I guess. That's what started this, remember?"

"Well, what are *we* supposed to do about it?"

"Isn't it obvious? We're supposed to rebel!"

"Oh, sure! We can't even open our mouths to complain! How are we going to organize?"

"*We* can organize," I said. "In here. We'll form an army of liberation. The other class members will support us."

"You sure of that? He's got them so terrified they're pissing in their pants."

"Well, we've got to try," said Hank Chelsea, standing up. "I'm for it."

"Count me out," said Jastrow.

I stood up. "I think it's the only way."

Janice stood up. "I—I don't like this, but I'll go along with it because we've got to show him he can't do this to us."

Two of the other boys stood up, and one of the girls. "Come on, John. Joey?"

"Uh uh. I don't want to get yelled at anymore."

"Aren't you angry?"

"I just want my money back."

"Paul?"

"He'll just throw us out again."

"Wait a minute, Jim." That was Mariette. "Just what is it you want us to do anyway? What's your plan?"

"We go in there and declare the dictatorship over."

"Oh, sure, and then he yells at us some more and his army throws us out again. He's hired two more thugs."

"They're not thugs, they just look like it."

"All football players are thugs to me. Anyway, there's six of 'em now. So what are you gonna do about that?"

Six people started to answer her at once, but Hank Chelsea held up his hand and said, "No, wait—she's right! We need a plan! Look, try this. We open all three doors of the room at once—that startles everybody. Then, before he can say anything, the girls have got to go for the army—no, listen to me. I'm betting that they won't hit the girls. What you do is put one girl on each soldier. She gives him a big hug and a kiss and tells him to join us—"

"Yeah, and then what?"

"—and that we'll pay them *double* what he's paying them!"

"He's paying them three caseys each now."

"No, they'll join us. But only if each girl takes one boy. Grab his arm and start talking to him. Say whatever you have to, and don't let go until he agrees to join us."

"Yeah, right, Mr. Big Shot. So you get the women to do the dirty work. What are the men going to do?"

"We're going after the honcho and reclaiming the national treasury."

We debated the plan for a few more minutes, during which time two more exiles joined us. They agreed to join the revolution almost immediately and suggested some refinements to the attack. We were almost ready when Joey Hubre sniffled and said, "What if someone gets hurt? What about that?"

That stopped us for a moment, and we had to rethink our plan again. But Paul Jastrow said, "Well, what of it? This is war, isn't it?"

"No, he's right," said Hank. "Maybe Whitlaw wouldn't care if he hurt anyone, but we're supposed to be an army of liberation. We're not going to hurt anyone."

"Unless they ask for it," muttered Jastrow.

"No, not even then," snapped Hank.

"Who appointed you general? I didn't!"

"All right—" Hank put up his hands. "We'll take a vote—"

"No!" I said. "We have a plan. We're ready to go! Armies don't vote!"

"They do now!" said Jastrow.

"But not in times of war! Is there anyone who needs to vote?"

"Yeah, I want to go over this war plan again—"

"Oh, terrific! There goes the revolution! Let's have a parliamentary battle instead. Wait a minute, I've got a copy of *Robert's Rules of Order* here—"

"McCarthy, shut up! You're an asshole!"

"Yeah? Then why are you the one who's giving us shit?"

"Hey, wait a minute—we're being distracted from our goal by this! We're forgetting who the real enemy is." Hank Chelsea stepped between us. "Now, look, we've got a plan. Let's do it! All right?"

Jastrow looked at Chelsea's proffered hand skeptically. "I don't like this—"

"Aw, come on, Paul," said Mariette and Janice, and then everybody else said it too, and Paul looked embarrassed and shrugged and said, "All right," and we went and invaded Mr. Whitlaw's Global Ethics course.

He was ready for us.

All the desks had been piled up to form a barricade across half the room. The kingdom of Myopia had built a Maginot Line.

We stopped and looked at each other.

"I've heard of paranoia, but this is crazy!" said Janice.

"Yeah. Well, I told you it wouldn't work," growled Paul.

"Now what do we do?" said Mariette.

We stood there exchanging glances. "Can we pull it down?"

"We could try," I said. "But I don't think that's the way we're supposed to solve this problem."

"Okay, Mr. Megabyte," said Paul Jastrow. "What's your solution?"

"I don't have one. I just said, I didn't think the physical way is the answer. I think we're supposed to use our brains here." I shut up then. I realized I was looking straight through the barrier at Whitlaw. He was making notes on a clipboard, but he had paused and was looking at me with a slight smile. "Um . . ." I tried to continue, but my train of thought had disappeared. "Let's have a conference. In the hallway. I think I have an idea."

We trooped out to the hall. I said, "I think we should go in and try to negotiate a peace treaty."

"He's not going to negotiate with us."

"Yes, he is," I said.

"What makes you so sure?"

"Because they can't get out of there unless they do. We have the side of the room with the doors. I don't think they're going to want to climb out of a third-story window."

There was a moment of appreciative silence. You could almost hear the smiles spreading.

"Yeah, let's go. Who's got a handkerchief? We need a white flag—"

We trooped back in and announced, "We come in peace. We want to negotiate a settlement."

"Why should I? You're a bunch of radicals and subversives who were thrown out of the system because you wouldn't cooperate with it."

"The system doesn't work," said Janice. "We want a better one."

"Yeah," said Mariette. "One we can be a part of."

"You're already part of the system. You're the rebels. We have to have rebels to punish as examples."

"Well, we don't want to be rebels anymore!"

"Too bad," said Whitlaw from behind his barrier. "You're troublemakers. The only role for you is rebels. That's what you're good at." We could see him grinning.

"You gotta take us back, Whitlaw—" That was Paul Jastrow.

"Eh? I don't *gotta* anything!"

"Yes, you do," I said. "You can't get out of the room until we let you."

"Ahh," he said. "You found something to bargain with. All right, what is it you want?"

"We want our money back!" screamed Joey Hubre. Joey?

"We want to come back to class," said Janice.

"—amnesty!" said Paul.

"—a fair deal!" I said.

"—respect!" said Mariette.

"—the rights of Englishmen," said Hank quietly, and we all turned to look at him. "Huh?"

But Whitlaw was grinning. "You—your name? Chelsea? Right." He made a note on his clipboard. "A for the day. Now let's see if you can keep it. What are those rights?"

Hank was standing before the barrier of desks, his arms folded. "No more taxes, Mr. Whitlaw, unless we get some say in how the money is to be spent. No more expulsions from the class unless there's a fair hearing. No more unfair use of force. We want the right to disagree with you, and the right to express our disagreements freely without you throwing us out."

"It's my classroom and the law says I can run it any way I want."

"Well, then we want that law changed."

"Sorry, that's one law I didn't make. I can't change that."

"It doesn't matter. You can change the way you run your class. You said you have autonomy. Let's negotiate some changes that'll make this class acceptable to all of us."

"Since when do students have the right to tell teachers how to teach?"

"Since we have all the doors!" cried Paul.

"Shh!" said Hank.

"Who appointed you president?"

"Will you shut up? One person is supposed to talk for all of us!"

"I didn't agree to that!"

"It doesn't matter what you agreed to—it's the way things are!"

"You're just as bad as he is! Well, the hell with you, then!" Paul marched to the end of the room and sat down, glowering.

Hank looked around at the rest of us, a little panicky. "Listen, people —if we don't cooperate with each other, this isn't going to work. We can't show any weakness."

"Yeah," said Janice. "Hank's right. We can't bog down in arguments among ourselves."

"Yeah, but that's no license for you to take over," said Mariette. "Paul's right. We didn't have an election."

"Wait a minute," I said. "I don't want to argue—and I agree with you that we've all gotta pull together or we'll certainly be pulled apart

—but I think we have to recognize that each of us is in this rebellion for a different reason and each of us wants to have a say in the negotiations. I want the same thing Paul wants—to be heard."

"May I say something?" John Hubre stepped forward, the silent twin. "Let's draft a list of our demands, and vote on the ones that we want to make Whitlaw adhere to."

Hank looked defeated. "All right. Who's got some paper? I'll write 'em down."

"No," said John. "We'll put them on the screen, where everyone can see them. And I think the entire class should discuss them and vote on them. Is that okay by you, Mr. Whitlaw?"

"Do I have any choice?"

John looked startled. "Uh . . . no. Of course not."

"May I offer a suggestion?" asked Whitlaw.

"Uh . . . all right."

"Let's dismantle this mountain of furniture so we can operate in a more civilized situation. The rest of this war is cancelled until further notice."

In short order, we looked like a classroom again, except that instead of tyrannizing us, Whitlaw was standing quietly to one side, observing —and only occasionally offering suggestions.

The list of demands grew to thirty in less than five minutes.

Whitlaw looked them over, snorted and said, "Don't be silly."

The class reactions ranged from, "Huh? What's wrong with these demands?" to "You don't have any choice!"

He held up a hand. "Please—I want you all to take another look at this list. Most of your grievances appear to be legitimate, but take another look and see if you notice something about your demands."

"Well, some of these are kind of petty," said Paul Jastrow. "I mean, like number six. No more ripping shirts. Maybe that one's important to Doug—but how important is it to the rest of us?"

Janice said, "And some of them are redundant—like the right to express ourselves freely encompasses the right to assemble and the right to speak and the right to publish—so we don't have to list all three, do we?"

And then other voices chimed in with their opinions. Whitlaw had to hold up a hand for silence. He said, "You're all right, of course. It's important to have protection for every situation, whether we specify it or not. I suggest that what you're looking for is an umbrella under which you can operate—an all-purpose rule."

He let us argue for only a few moments, then brought us back to the issue again. "Your demands are valid. Look at your rules again, and see if you can boil them down to one or two sentences."

We did as he suggested. With a little help, eventually we came up with "The government shall be accountable to the people for its actions. The people shall have the right to express their differences freely."

"Congratulations," smiled Whitlaw. "Now what happens if I refuse to accept it?"

"You don't have any choice," said Mariette.

"Why not?"

"Because if you don't, we'll just rebel again."

"Uh huh. What if I hire some more football players?"

"You can't afford to hire as many as you'll need."

"I'll raise taxes."

That prompted some groans and an immediate response from one of the boys who had not been expelled. "Where do I sign up to join the rebellion?"

"That's why you don't have any choice," Hank said. "You don't have the tax base."

"You're right," Whitlaw said. He went back to the front of the room. "All right, then—are we in agreement on this point? That if a government is not accountable to its citizenry, that citizenry is justified in removing that government from power—by whatever means necessary?"

There was general assent.

"I see. The kicker in there is the last line. 'By whatever means necessary.' Obviously it includes open rebellion. How about terrorism? How about assassination? And at what point do you decide that those actions are necessary?"

Paul Jastrow was still sullen. He said, "When there's no other course of action left to us."

"All right, let's consider that. Was your rebellion justified?"

General assent.

"Because I didn't want to listen to what you wanted to say, right?"

Again agreement.

Whitlaw said, "Suppose I had set up a complaint box. Would the rebellion still have been justified?"

There was a thoughtful pause while each of us considered it. I raised my hand. "What would you do with the complaints put into the box?"

Whitlaw grinned. "I'd throw them away at the end of each day without reading them."

"Then, yes," I said. "The rebellion would have been justified."

"What if I read the complaints?"

"What would you do about them?"

"Nothing."

"It's still justified."

"What if I acted on those I agreed with? All the ones that didn't inconvenience me personally."

I thought about it. "No, that's still not good enough."

Whitlaw looked exasperated. "What is it you people want?"

"A fair system of handling our grievances."

"Ahh, now we're getting somewhere. Do you begin to understand now? Your credo up there is very pretty, but it's worthless without the legal guarantees to back it up. What kind of system are you asking for— uh, McCarthy, is it?"

"Yes, sir. How about an arbitration panel of three students? You pick one, we pick one and they pick the third. My father's union uses that system to handle disagreements."

"All right, suppose I decreed that's the kind of system we'll have?"

"No, sir, it has to be voted on. We all have to agree to it. Otherwise, it's still a case of you dictating to us."

Whitlaw nodded and looked at his watch. "Congratulations. In just a little more than an hour, you've recreated more than a thousand years of human history. You've overthrown a government, established a charter for a new system and created a court system with which to enforce it. That's a fair day's work."

The bell rang then. We'd used an entire ninety-minute class period. As we started to gather our books, Whitlaw held up a hand. "Hold it. Stay in your seats. You're not going to your next class today. Don't worry, your other instructors have been informed. They know not to expect you. Does anyone need to pee? Okay, take ten minutes. Be back here and ready to go at eleven-forty."

When we resumed, Joey Hubre was the first to raise his hand. "When do we get our money back?"

Whitlaw looked at him severely. "Don't you understand? You *don't.* The government always plays for keeps."

"But . . . but . . . but we thought this was—"

"What? A game?" Whitlaw looked a little angry. "Weren't you paying attention? This was a tyranny! Would you have overthrown the government if you thought I wasn't playing for keeps? Of course not!"

"All I want is my money back—"

"It's part of the national treasury now. And even if I wanted to give it back, I couldn't. I've been overthrown. It's up to the new government to decide what to do with the money."

The classroom was getting tense again. Janice stood up and said, "Mr. Whitlaw! You were wrong to take our money!"

"No, I wasn't—as soon as I declared myself a government, I was within my rights. You were wrong for letting me get away with it. Every single one of you. You!" He pointed at the first student who had handed over a casey. "—you were wrong for handing me that first coin. Why did you do it?"

"You told me to."

"Did I tell you I was going to give you anything in return for it?"

"No."

"Did I tell you I was going to give it back to you when we were through?"

"No."

"Then why did you give it to me?"

"Uh . . ."

"Right. You gave it to me. I didn't take it. So why are you telling me I'm the one who did wrong?"

"You had an army!"

"Not until after you gave me the money to pay for it." He said to the whole class, "Your only mistake was your timing. You should have rebelled when I declared myself your government. I had no right to do so, but you let me get away with it. You should have demanded accountability then—before I had enough money to hire an army."

He was right. He had us there. We all looked a little embarrassed.

"Well, what do we do now?" wailed Mariette.

"I don't know. I'm not the government anymore. You overthrew me. You took away my power. All I'm doing now is following orders. Your orders. I'll do anything with this money that a majority of you can agree on."

It took less than thirty seconds to pass a resolution requiring the disbursement of all funds collected in the recent taxation.

Whitlaw nodded and opened his desk drawer. He started counting coins. "Uh, we have a problem—there are forty-four of you in this class. But there are only thirty caseys here. If you'll remember, the former government spent eighteen caseys on an army."

Four people stood up to author the next resolution, requiring the return of funds paid to former members of the Imperial Guard. Whitlaw vetoed that. "Sorry. Doesn't that fall into the realm of confiscation? Remember the five-casey note I took unfairly? You just had a rebellion because you didn't want a government able to do that. Now you're setting up a new government to do exactly the same thing."

"But this is different—"

"No it isn't! Confiscation is confiscation! It doesn't matter who does the confiscating—the person still loses something!"

"But . . . then how do we redress previous wrongs?"

"I don't know either. You're the government now. You tell me."

"So why can't we just take the money back?"

"Because the army was fairly paid. They did their job and they were paid a fair wage for what they did. You can't take that money away from them now because it's theirs."

"But you had no right to give it to them!"

"Yes, I did! I was the government!"

Hank Chelsea was standing then. "Wait a minute, sir! I think we all understand what you're trying to teach us. We have to find a fair way to do this, don't we?"

"If you can, you'll be a better man than I am. In the eleven years that I've been teaching this class, not one session has ever found a way that was both *fair* and *legal* to take money out of one person's pocket and put it into another's." He motioned for Hank to sit down. "Let me give you this to think about: a government—*any* government—is nothing more than a system for reapportioning wealth. It takes money from one group of people and gives it to another group of people. And when it happens that enough people decide that they don't like the way the wealth is being reapportioned, that's when that government will be replaced by another one more to the people's liking. As has happened here! But you cannot use the new government to redress all of the wrongs of the previous government—not without creating far more problems than you'll ever clean up. You'll end up with a government entirely concerned with past events and not present ones. That's a sure way to set yourself up to fail. If you're going to win at this game, you have to deal with circumstances the way they are, not the way they used to be or the way you'd like them to be. In other words, only operate on those events you *have* control over. That's the only way to produce results. The real question, then, is, what *do* you have control over? We'll probably spend the rest of the semester tackling that one. Right now, let's handle the immediate problem." He opened his desk drawer. "There are forty-four of you and only thirty caseys here. If you don't reimburse the six members of the Imperial Guard, you're still going to be eight caseys short. And one of you is going to be at least four caseys short because I took a fiver off him."

It was moved, seconded and approved to return four caseys to Geoff Miller to bring his loss into line with the rest of ours. This left the national treasury at twenty-six caseys. We were now short twelve caseys if we wanted to return the money equally.

One of the former members of the Imperial Guard stood up. "Here, I'll give back the extra two caseys that Whitlaw paid me. I don't think it's fair for me to keep it." He poked his buddy, who also stood up. "Yeah, me too." Two more former soldiers also chipped in then, but the last two just sat in the back of the room with their arms folded.

"We earned it fairly. We're entitled to it."

"Well," said Whitlaw, "that brings the national debt down to two caseys. Not bad. Now all you have to do is decide who gets the short straws."

"This isn't fair!" said Mariette again.

Whitlaw agreed with her. "You're beginning to see it. No matter how hard we try, the government *cannot* be fair to everybody. *Cannot.* The very best that it can do is treat everybody equally *un*fairly."

The immediate classroom problem was finally resolved when John Hubre realized that the casey isn't indivisible. Thirty-eight students, each of whom had paid one casey in taxation, were repaid ninety-four cents each. There was twenty-eight cents left over. Whitlaw started to pocket it, but Hank Chelsea said quickly, "Sorry—that's the national treasury. We'll have one of our own hold it, if you don't mind."

Whitlaw passed it over with a grin. "You're learning," he said.

TWENTY-SIX

"ALL RIGHT," said Whitlaw. "Obviously, there was a point to that little exercise. No, put your hands down. I'm just going to give you this straight out. There's no such thing as a government."

He looked around the room. "Point to it. Show me the government. Show me *any* government." He waved our hands down again. "Forget it. You can't. You can show me some buildings, and some people and some rules written down on paper, but you can't show me a government. Because there's no such thing in the physical universe. It's just something we made up. It exists only by our agreement that it does. You just proved that here. We agreed that we wanted some stuff managed and we agreed on some rules for how it should be managed. The agreements are the government. Nothing else.

"How big the government gets depends on how many agreements you make. If enough people agree, we'll build some buildings and hire some people to work in them and manage the agreements for us. Now, here's the question—how do you know if something is the business of the government or not?—that is, the business of the people we've hired to work in our buildings and manage our agreements for us. How do they know what to manage? What's the test?

"No—put your hand down. It's too simple. A person, place, or thing is in the jurisdiction of a government if it *tests* that government's agreements. If it doesn't, it isn't.

"The government doesn't have to manage the people who *keep* the agreements. They don't need managing. They're being responsible. It *is* the business of the government to manage those people who *test* the agreements. This is it. The *whole* of government consists of the art of managing people to keep the agreements—*especially* those who do the managing."

Whitlaw moved thoughtfully to the back of the room. He sounded as if he were speculating idly aloud. "Now . . . management is decision-making, right? Anyone not see that? So, the question is—what are the guidelines by which the managers make their decisions? What is the meter-stick?" He looked around at us.

Marcie something-or-other: "The agreements, of course. The rules."

Whitlaw snorted. "Not bloody likely. The rules are just the context—the *authorization* for the decisions. In fact, the history of this nation is about men and women *not* following the rules. History is a list of who tested what agreements.

"Every time an agreement is tested, the person whose responsibility that agreement is, is also being tested. So, what does that person use for guidelines?—particularly when there are no guidelines! What is the *source* of that person's choice?" Whitlaw shoved his hands into his jacket pockets and turned slowly around, making sure we were all paying attention. When he spoke, his voice was low and quiet. "The truth is that ultimately every single choice . . . is a reflection of the integrity of the individual making it."

"You might want to notice that—that everything we've done in this country, *everything* that we've accomplished—good or bad—in nearly two and a half centuries, has been done out of the integrity—or lack of integrity—of people *like ourselves* who are willing to make decisions and be responsible for them, especially when they know those decisions will be unpopular."

I wondered what he was working toward. He wandered back to the front of the room and sat down on his desk, facing us with an anticipatory expression on his face.

"Do you think the Moscow Treaties were fair?" he asked abruptly.

The class was divided. Some thought yes, some thought no. Most weren't sure.

Whitlaw said, "Well, let's look at it from the rest of the world's point of view. How do you think we looked to them?"

"We're the home of the free, the land of the brave—all the refugees come here." That was Richard Kham Tuong. He had almond eyes, brown skin and curly blond hair. He said it proudly. "People come here looking for freedom. We're a source of hope."

"Uh huh," said Whitlaw, unconvinced. He stood up and strode casually back to stand directly in front of Richard Kham Tuong. "Let me run some statistics by you. One half of the world's population goes to bed hungry every night. There are nearly six billion people on this planet—but the three hundred million who are lucky enough to live in the United States consume one-third of the planet's resources every year. For most of the last century, it was closer to one-half, by the way. Do you think that's fair?"

"Uh . . ." Richard recognized that as a loaded question and did the only thing he could. He stalled.

"Or let me try it another way," Whitlaw went on. He was sandbagging Richard now; we all knew it. "Suppose we order a couple of pizzas for this class. There are twenty-two very thin slices in a pizza, so there should be just enough for everybody to have a little bit. But when they arrive, I take fifteen of the slices for myself and leave the rest of you to fight over what's left. Is that fair?"

"You're loading the question, sir. Obviously, the way you say it, it's *not* fair."

"Well, what do you think we should do about it?"

"Everything we can, I guess."

"All right. Let's see. Are you willing to give up all of your clothes except what you're wearing now? Are you willing to survive on one meal of rice and beans per day? Are you willing to give up your automobile? And all use of electricity? Because that's the kind of sacrifice it would take—every single American would have to give up that much before we would be able to start paying back our debt to other nations. Are you ready to agree to that?"

There was silence in the classroom. Nobody wanted to be the first to admit it.

"It's all right," encouraged Whitlaw. "You'll notice I'm not ready to go hungry either."

"Okay, so we're selfish—what's the point?"

"That is the point. That's how we look to the rest of the world. Like pigs. Rich and fat and selfish. Let's go back to the pizza analogy. Here I am sitting with my fifteen slices. Are you going to let me get away with it?"

"Of course not."

"Then you think you're justified in restricting me?"

"Of course."

"All right, now you understand part of what the Moscow Treaties were about. Yes, there was a war—and the Moscow Treaties were aimed at the causes of it. A very large part of it was the perception that the United States had been selfish with the world's resources."

"Wait a minute!" Paul Jastrow said. "That's only in the eyes of the other nations. There's another side to that argument, isn't there?"

"I don't know," Whitlaw said innocently, his blue eyes twinkling. "Is there? You tell me."

Paul Jastrow sat down, frowning. He had to think about this.

Joey Hubre raised his hand. "Sir, I read somewhere that the problems that the United States has been experiencing for most of our history have been the problems of success, not failure."

"So?"

"Well . . . I mean, um, I hope I get this right. The article said that the size of a success is proportional to the amount of energy invested, and that all of the technological advances that have occurred in this country could have only occurred because of the huge amount of resources available to apply to the problems."

"And—?"

"Well, the point was that this justified our prodigious energy appetite. You have to put fuel in the jet if you want it to go. The other nations in the world have benefited from our advances. They can buy the fruits of the technology without having to invest in all the research. Um, the article used energy satellites as the example. A poor nation—a landbound one—doesn't have to develop a whole space program to have an energy station in space. They can buy one from us for only two million caseys. It was the United States that spent billions of caseys developing the industrial use of space, but everybody benefits."

"I see—and that justifies it?"

"Would it have been better for us to have spent that money on food for the poor? We'd still have lots of poor people today, but we wouldn't have energy stations in space. And those energy stations may eventually make it possible for poor nations to feed all their people."

Whitlaw kept his face blank. "If you were one of those poor people, Joey, how would you feel about that? No, let me be even more graphic. If you were a poor farmer, and your wife and three children were so malnourished that together the five of you weighed less than a hundred kilos, how would you feel about that?"

"Uh . . ." Joey sat down too.

Where was Whitlaw going with this? A lot of people were starting to get angry. Were we wrong for enjoying what we had?

Paul Jastrow spoke up for all of us. He was slouched low in his chair and had his arms folded angrily across his chest. "It's our money," he said. "Don't we have the right to say how we want to spend it?"

"Sounds good to me—except what if it isn't all your money? Remember, we've been consuming nearly one-half the world's resources for most of a century. What if it's *their* money too?"

"But it wasn't their money—it was their resources. And they *sold* them to us on a free market."

"A free market which they claim we manipulated to our advantage."

"And they haven't manipulated back?"

"Ah, I didn't say that." Whitlaw was trying to keep a careful neutrality. He held up a hand. "I don't want to repeat the whole argument—that's not what we're going for today—but are you beginning to understand the *nature* of the disagreement? Do you see the validity of *both* points of view?"

A general murmur of assent swept the room.

"Now," said Whitlaw, "we've seen how a group of people can make a decision that affects all of them, and that decision can still be unfair. Most of the nations on this planet think the Moscow Treaties were fair. Do you?"

We thought about it. Some of us shook our heads.

"Why not?" Whitlaw pointed.

"Our economy was almost destroyed. It took us over a decade to recover."

"Then why did we agree to those treaties?"

"Because the alternative was war—"

"They had us outnumbered—"

"We didn't have a choice—"

"All right, all right—" He held up his hand again. "All of that is all very well and good—but I want you all to consider something else now. Isn't it possible that your perception of the treaties' unfairness is a *biased* perception, a product of your own subjective points of view?"

"Uh . . ."

"Well . . ."

"Sure, but . . ."

"No." That was Paul Jastrow. Everybody turned to look at him. He said, "It doesn't matter how many people say it's right if it isn't. We just spent a whole session learning that everything a government does is going to be unfair to somebody, but a good government tries to minimize the unfairness."

"Uh huh. . . ." Whitlaw nodded. He was wearing his devil's-advocate expression and using a pleasant, noncommittal tone of voice. "But isn't that what the Moscow Treaties were supposed to do? Establish a more equitable distribution of the world's resources?"

"Yes, but they did it wrong—they were confiscatory. And you just demonstrated to us that you can't redress old wrongs that way without creating new wrongs."

Whitlaw picked up his clipboard and made a note. "You're right." He sat down on the edge of his desk and did something very unusual—for Whitlaw. He *lowered* his voice. He said, "A large part of this course is supposed to be about the Moscow Treaties, so you'll understand why they were necessary. And I think now you understand why many Americans resented them. It felt like we were being unfairly punished for being successful. And it didn't matter to the other nations that all of our studies and data models and simulations showed that most of their starving populations were beyond saving—they still felt that they had to make that commitment to try—"

"But not with *our* resources—"

"Hush a moment, Paul," said Whitlaw, uncharacteristically polite. "Let me finish this. It didn't matter what we felt. We were outvoted. The other nations of this world were going to see that we cooperated whether we wanted to or not—because data simulations or no, they still *had to try* to save their starving populations. And yes, it was unfair the way it was done—and that's a large part of what I wanted you to realize —but that was the best solution they could come up with. And yes, it was a punitive one—"

He stopped to catch his breath. He looked a little gray. Janice Mac-Neil said, "How come it was never explained this way before? I mean, all the news ever said was that it was our own noble sacrifice to help the rest of the world. I never heard before that they were holding a gun to our heads."

"Well, which would you rather believe? That you're doing something because you're being charitable or because you're being forced to? If you were President, which would be easier to sell to the electorate?"

"Oh," she said. "But didn't anybody notice?"

"Sure, lots of people did. And they said so, very loudly—but nobody wanted to believe them. Remember, most people were so relieved at having avoided a nuclear war they were willing to believe that its nonoccurrence was proof of the nobility of both sides. They were *eager* to believe it, rather than that someone had blackmailed someone else under the table. People who complained were called extremists; after all, you don't have to listen to extremists. It's easier than you think to devalue a truth that you don't want to hear. And remember this: *any* unpopular idea is going to look extreme, so you want to be responsible in how you present it. It is almost always dangerous to be right—and it is *certainly* dangerous to be right too soon."

"Well—um, does the government know now? I mean, what did we do about it? Or what *are* we going to do about it?"

Whitlaw said, "The process of making that decision has been going on for almost twenty years now. We are doing it every day. We are surviving. We are continuing—and we're *contributing*.

"You see, this is the hard part to accept. In retrospect—now that we have had the benefit of twenty years of hindsight—we can see that what was done was perhaps the very *best* thing to do under the circumstances. If you want to look at it from a nationalistic point of view, those treaties were only temporary setbacks, because they did not cripple us permanently. And furthermore, they made it possible for us to deal with the rest of the world in an atmosphere of reduced hostility because they finally felt they had evened the score.

"Now, you need to know just *how* we paid our reparations. We only shipped food and farm machinery; instead of cash, we gave them energy satellites and receiving stations. That way, they all had a vested interest in keeping our space program going. We shipped teachers and technicians. We exported ourselves—"

And suddenly, three years later and a thousand miles away, the coin dropped. Whitlaw had never come out and said so, but he had made it pretty clear that we had lost that war. And that we knew we had lost the war—and it seemed as if we had actively cooperated in the process of our own punishment. Or had we?

There were a lot of government programs that only made sense in retrospect—like the Teamwork Army, for instance. That was only supposed to be a peacetime solution for massive unemployment—the regimen was exactly like that of the regular army, except they didn't drill with guns; but then, how long does it take to learn how to use a gun? Six weeks?

And the space program—as long as we had mass-drivers on the moon, there wasn't a city on Earth that was safe. We didn't need atom bombs—we could drop asteroids.

And all those shipments of food and farm machinery—that helped our economy more than theirs, because we got to retool our assembly lines to build a new generation of technology.

And all those energy satellites—every nation that accepted one would be dependent on us for its maintenance.

And our export of more than half a million teachers to the underprivileged nations—the next generation of world leaders would be taught with American values.

It made a crazy kind of sense. I could almost imagine the President saying, "What if we only *pretended* to lose?"

I thought of a lockbox with a false bottom and a suite of rooms on the thirteenth floor. You can't hide anything forever—you can only misdirect the attention of the searcher.

The rest of the world would be looking for evidence of military buildup—and we were hiding it as economic recovery and reparations and civilian solutions to unemployment! And the best part of it was that those things were always exactly what they *seemed* to be, even when they weren't.

And something else—

Even Whitlaw's class had been a sham.

I'd always wondered why there was a Federal Education Authority. Now it made sense. Under the guise of teaching us history—how we had lost a war—Whitlaw was teaching us how to win the next one without ever fighting it. He'd taught us to outthink our enemies, because it was easier than outfighting them.

I felt like a grenade had gone off in my belly. A grenade that Whitlaw had shoved down my throat three years before and had taken this long to explode.

I'd never thought about the Special Forces before—they were just another military unit, one specifically trained for crisis deployment. I guess I'd thought that meant natural disasters and riots—I hadn't realized there was a second Special Forces hidden in the one place nobody would think to look: inside the regular Special Forces.

I realized that and my heart popped. What was the Special Forces *really* for? What had I been a part of?

TWENTY-SEVEN

THERE WERE four of them. Colonel Wallachstein, Lizard, a tiny, friendly-looking Japanese lady with graying hair, and a dark fellow in a black suit. They seated themselves around the small table facing me.

Wallachstein said, "No introductions, McCarthy. Understand something. This meeting didn't happen. And these people don't exist. Neither do I. Got that?"

"Uh, yes, sir."

"Good. I hope so. Because this comes under the jurisdiction of the National Security Act. If you commit any further violations you're likely to disappear. Permanently."

"Yes, sir."

"Now, before we begin, there are some things I have to say. I'm required by law to do this." He looked at a sheet of notes before him, and read, " 'A fair trial presupposes that the defendant is a responsible human being, capable of understanding the difference between right and wrong and able to gauge his actions and their consequences on that basis. Therefore, the outcome of this hearing is dependent on your ability to deal with the information available to you.' " He looked up at me. "Do you understand this?"

I nodded. My throat had gone dry again. Was I on trial? For what?

Wallachstein was frowning. "Is something the matter?"

"Sir," I managed to croak, "what kind of hearing is this? I mean, under what authority—?"

He held up a hand. "Let me finish first." He resumed reading. " 'Under such operating conditions, we cannot judge "guilt" or "innocence" as absolute moral value—nor should we attempt to. Instead, we are determining an organism's ability to deal rationally with its environment. Instead of seeking punishment, revenge or even rehabilitation, it is the purpose of this tribunal to determine the *value* of the individual's contribution to the social environment versus the cost of his continued existence in that environment.' " He pushed the sheet of paper aside and looked directly at me. "Do you understand that?"

I nodded.

"Right. Now, one other thing. What I just read you is in compliance with the Revised Legal Code of 2001. In this hearing, in any area where there is conflict between the Revised Legal Code and the standards of the National Security Act, the standards of the National Security Act shall have precedence. Do you understand that?"

"Uh, I think so. But . . . ?"

"Yes?"

"May I ask questions?"

He said, "You have the right to establish for yourself the authority of this tribunal and its jurisdiction over you. Your question?"

"I have several," I began.

"Let's hear them."

"What's going on here? Who are you? What is your authority? And what am I charged with?"

Wallachstein exchanged glances with the Japanese lady. She smiled sweetly and spoke in a lightly accented voice, but she slurred some of her consonants and I had to concentrate to be sure I understood all of her words. "As a member of the Special Forces Warrant Agency, you are under the direct command of the National Security Office, Military Branch, and therefore you are under the multilevel jurisdiction of the National Security Code, the United States Military Code and the United States Civilian Code, in that order. The purpose of this hearing is to determine the circumstances that resulted in a breach of security that occurred this morning in front of some two thousand witnesses, among whom were individuals known to be agents of hostile foreign governments. The members of this tribunal are authorized to act on behalf of the National Security Office. For reasons of national security, no other identification of the officers of this court will be made. Do you understand?"

"Yes, ma'am."

She smiled sweetly back at me.

"Um," I said, "I have some other questions."

They waited expectantly.

"First, I'd like to know how long the Special Forces has been the cover for a secret military operation. I want to know what the nature of that operation is and whatever else you can tell me about it. I understand that as a member of the Special Forces, I'm entitled to be fully briefed."

Wallachstein exchanged a glance with the dark fellow. He looked at me and said, "Who told you that?"

"Nobody. I put the pieces together myself. It wasn't hard."

Wallachstein said, "There is no secret military operation within the Special Forces. At least, not on paper. However, the internal nucleus of the organization has stood ready to handle necessary but nasty security operations for over a hundred years. The current operation is almost exclusively targeted at controlling the Chtorran infestation. It is a secret operation because we are using weaponry that has been proscribed by international agreement—as you are well aware. What else do you want to know?"

"I want to know what the Chtorrans are. Are they really from another world or are they a biological weapon developed here?"

The Japanese lady said, "Dr. Zymph's report on the infestation, which you heard, is our best assessment of the situation to date."

"How do I know you're telling the truth?"

"You don't." She added, "I will tell you that Dr. Zymph is too proud a lady to lie for anyone, if that helps."

"That may be, but the Chtorrans are too well adapted to this ecology. And the United States is taking too much advantage of the situation."

"Yes," she said. "I see." She didn't say anything else. She just blinked at me.

"Well, aren't you going to answer those points?"

She shook her head. "Unfortunately, there are no satisfactory answers—at least none that will satisfy you right now."

"Well, give me the unsatisfactory answers then."

She said, "I can't tell you anything about the Chtorrans that you don't already know. Yes, they are terribly well adapted to our ecology. We've noticed it too. Someday we hope to find out why. I will tell you that if any nation on this planet had the ability to create—in absolute secrecy—several hundred new species of virulent life forms, totally unrecognizable to state-of-the-art genetic tailoring, it would have to be the United States. We know that we didn't do it. What we're seeing is beyond our ability to construct. And we know that no one else has the capability to do it either.

"Now, as to the second part of your concern: yes, the United States *is* exploiting the situation—but we did not create the situation, nor would we have if we did have the ability. But it does exist and we will use it. We would use any situation that occurred. We have a responsibility to the remaining member population of this nation to manage the affairs of state in a way that best serves their interests. If we didn't, they would have the right to replace us with individuals who would."

"I can't say I like that very much," I said.

She nodded. "I told you that the answers were unsatisfactory. I'm afraid that you will have to resolve your conflict with them for yourself."

She looked to Wallachstein. He looked at me. "Is that it? Or is there something else?"

"Just one thing more, sir. How did *I* end up in the Special Forces?"

For the first time, he smiled—it was a grim smile, but it still qualified: the corners of his mouth twitched. He said, "By mistake. The . . . ah . . . plagues destroyed several key lines of communication. We lost some of our most valuably placed people. The individuals who replaced them were not aware of the unique status of the Special Forces. We've been very successful in establishing ourselves as our own cover organization, but even we were not untouched by the plagues, and it took a while to reestablish all of our necessary controls. Unfortunately, during that time, a number of individuals—like yourself—were assigned to Special Forces units that they should not have been. For the most part, we've been able to locate and isolate those individuals who were unable to meet our special . . . criteria. You, unfortunately, have proven to be something of a difficult case. Had you made the attempt to contact me immediately upon arrival, I might have been able to prevent the scene in the conference hall this morning." He cleared his throat, then allowed himself another grim smile. "On the other hand, in all fairness, there are a number of people who feel exactly as you do and who would have liked to have done the same thing you did—except that they knew the reasons why they shouldn't."

"Oh."

Wallachstein and the Japanese lady whispered together for a moment, Lizard and the dark fellow listening in. Dark fellow shook his head about something, but Lizard shook her head harder, disagreeing with him. I caught the phrase "—can't afford to waste personnel—" and then they shut up when they realized they were getting too loud.

Wallachstein said, "I think I have to agree with Major Tirelli's assessment." He turned to me. "McCarthy, let me be honest with you. I don't give a damn what happened this morning. I'm not so sure that you did any serious damage to us, and you may even have done some good by drawing off some of the heat from Dr. Zhymph's presentation. We expected there to be fireworks over that, because there were individuals in attendance whose sole purpose in attending was to create fireworks and embarrass the United States. We knew about them in advance. You seem to have stolen their thunder and embarrassed one of their most respected spokesmen."

"*I* embarrassed *him?*"

"You dealt with the issues. He didn't. More importantly, you kept him from making his presentation. He was going to minimize the Chtorran problem in favor of a global reconstruction plan—it would have been a very attractive plan too, because the United States would have ended up paying for most of it. Essentially, we would be shipping out every unclaimed machine in the country, every vehicle, computer, airplane, TV set and toaster. And if we couldn't do it fast enough, they'd send in volunteer troops to help us. To be honest, McCarthy, I couldn't have staged a better diversion if I'd wanted to. And believe me, I wanted to. I didn't because I thought it would be too obvious. And that's the problem here. You called attention to yourself as a member of the Special Forces Warrant Agency, and even though you didn't know what you were doing, you have given the United Nations Inspection Authority additional reason to suspect the Special Forces as an undercover operation. Our enemies are already claiming that this morning's events were carefully planned to discredit their position. They're right and wrong at the same time. If we had thought we could have gotten away with something like what you did, we would have done it—but we didn't think we could have. And you proved that our estimation of the situation was correct. In your ignorance, you did the right thing—that's why it was wrong, because it was so right. Do you understand?"

"Uh, sort of, but not really."

Wallachstein was grim. "I'm not sure what I should do with you, McCarthy. I can't give you a medal and I don't have time to hang you. Do you have any suggestions?"

I thought about it for a moment. They waited patiently. When I finally spoke, it was with carefully chosen words. "I'm interested in

Chtorrans, sir. I'm not interested in playing spy games. Up in the mountains, we knew who the enemy was. He was big and red and always screamed before he leaped, and there wasn't anybody to say how we should or shouldn't fight back. We just did what we had to."

Wallachstein said, "In that, I envy you. There have been occasions when I wished for the application of a flamethrower to solve some of my problems down here." He opened a notebook in front of him and scribbled something on a page. He ripped the page out and shoved it toward me. "Here. I want you to go someplace this afternoon."

I took the paper and looked at it. "A doctor?"

"A psychiatrist."

"I don't understand."

"Have you ever heard of survivor's syndrome?"

I shook my head.

He said quietly, "When you wipe out three-quarters of the human race, all you have left are orphans. There isn't a human being on this planet who hasn't been affected in some deep way. The dying has touched us all. I'm sure you've seen some of the reactions, the herds of walking wounded, the manics, the zombies, the suicides, the sexual obsessives, the ones who are so desperate for stability that they've become drones, and so on. I don't know if you've seen much of the opposite side of that coin though. Like any ordeal, the plagues destroyed the weak and tempered the strong. There are a lot of people who are just coming alive now because they have something *worthwhile* to do. Before you can become a *real* member of this Special Forces, we have to know which kind of survivor you are."

I blurted, "I don't know. I never thought about it. I mean, I just picked myself up and kept on going. It seemed the only logical thing to do—"

Wallachstein held up a hand. "Don't tell me. Tell the doctor. We'll recess this hearing until . . ." He glanced at his watch, scowled. ". . . until further notice. Take a scooter from the car pool, McCarthy. Major Tirelli will show you where to go. Don't talk to anyone else. Go directly back to base and plug into Dr. Davidson. Get something to eat at the base commissary. Better get a change of clothes too, and then come back here immediately."

"Uh, sir?"

He looked up. "Eh?"

"I thought I was . . . under arrest. I mean, what's to keep me from getting on the scooter and heading west?"

"Nothing," he said. "In fact, it'd probably solve a lot of problems if you did. It's not something many people know, but not a lot of traffic is getting over the Rockies these days. Something keeps stopping the cars and peeling them open like sardine cans. Besides"—he looked me straight in the eye and his expression was taut—"you're not the kind who bolts. You'll come back. By then we'll have Dr. Davidson's report and we'll know what to do with you. Major Tirelli, will you escort McCarthy to the car pool? We have some talking to do here."

TWENTY-EIGHT

THE ROOM was empty.

A rug. A chair. A table with a pitcher of water and a glass on it. Nothing else. No other doors except the one behind me.

"Please sit down," said a disembodied female voice. I looked, but I couldn't see a speaker system. I sat down. The chair creaked, but it was comfortable. It was a swivel-rocker, upholstered in dark brown leather. It felt reassuring.

"Your name, please?"

"McCarthy, James Edward."

"Ah, yes. We've been expecting you. Dr. Davidson will be with you shortly. While you wait, I'll play a short film for you."

"Um—" But the room was already darkening. The wall in front of me began to glow and images began to solidify in the air. I shut up, decided to relax and enjoy it.

The film was . . . a montage. What they call a tone poem. Music and images wrapping around each other, some sexual, some violent, some funny, some happy—two naked children splashing in a rocky stream dissolved into a tiny jeweled spider weaving a diamond tapestry against a blue and velvet background—that shimmered into an eagle soaring high above a desolate landscape as if looking for a haven—the eagle became a silver sailship hanging effortlessly in space below an emerald-shiny Earth, and then a pair of male dancers, clad only in briefs, whirled around each other, their bodies glistening with sweat—

resolving now into a cheetah racing hard across the veldt and bringing down a zebra, terrified, in a cloud of stinging dust—

It went on like that for ten or fifteen minutes, a tumble of pictures, one after the other, faster than I could assimilate. A couple of times I felt frightened; I didn't know why. Once I felt angry. I didn't like the film. I wondered why they were showing it to me. This was boring. And then, just when I started to get interested again, it ended.

When the lights came back up, a quiet voice said, "Good afternoon." The voice was male. Quiet. Very mature. Grandfatherly.

I cleared my throat again, and I found my voice. "Where are you?" I asked.

"Atlanta."

"Who are you?"

"You may call me Dr. Davidson, if you wish. That's not my real name, but that's the name I use for these sessions."

"Why is that?"

He ignored the question. "If you'd like to smoke, please feel free," said Dr. Davidson. "I won't mind."

"I don't smoke," I said.

"I meant dope."

I shrugged. "I don't do much of that either."

"Why not?" he asked. "Do you have strong feelings about it?"

"No. I just don't like it much." Something was making me uncomfortable. I said, "Can you see me?"

"Yes, I can."

"Is there any way I can see you?"

"If you mean, is there a screen for two-way video, I'm sorry, there isn't. If you mean you'd like to see me face to face, you'll have to come to Atlanta. I'm something of an invalid. That's one of the reasons why we don't have two-way hookups. Sometimes my . . . ah, condition can be disconcerting."

"Oh." I felt embarrassed. I didn't know what to say.

Dr. Davidson said, "Please tell me about yourself."

"What do you want to know?"

"Why do you think you're here?"

"I was told to come here."

"Why?"

"They want to know if I'm too crazy to be trusted."

"What do you think?"

"I don't know. The way I always heard it, the crazy person is the worst one to judge."

"Just the same, what do you think?" Dr. Davidson's voice was mild —and incredibly patient. I began to like him. A little.

I said, "I think I'm doing okay. I'm surviving."

"Is that your gauge of success? That you're surviving?"

I thought about it. "I guess not."

"Are you happy?"

"I don't know. I don't know what happiness feels like anymore. I used to. I don't think anyone's happy since the plagues."

"Are you unhappy? Do you feel depressed?"

"Sometimes. Not a lot."

"Hurt? Confused?"

"Yeah. A little."

"Angry?"

I hesitated. "No."

There was silence for a moment. Then Dr. Davidson asked, "Do you *ever* feel angry?"

"Yeah. Doesn't everybody?"

"It's a normal response to frustrating situations," Dr. Davidson admitted. "So what makes *you* angry?"

"Stupidity," I said. Even talking about it, I could feel my muscles tightening.

Dr. Davidson sounded puzzled. "I'm not sure I understand that, Jim. Could you give me some examples?"

"I don't know. People lying to each other. Not being honest. . . ."

"Specifically?" he urged.

"Um—well, like the people I met at the reception last night. And the scientists this morning. And even Colonel Wa—the people who sent me here. Everybody's talking to me. But so far, nobody wants to listen."

"I'm listening, Jim."

"You're a shrink. You have to listen. That's your job."

"Did you ever wonder what kind of person becomes a psychiatrist, Jim?"

"No."

"I'll tell you. Somebody who is interested in other people enough to *want* to listen to them."

"Well . . . but it's not the same. I want to talk to the people who can answer my questions about the Chtorrans. I want to tell them what I saw. I want to ask them what it meant—but it doesn't seem like *anyone* wants to listen. Or, if they listen, they don't want to believe. And I *know* I saw a fourth Chtorran come out of that nest!"

"It's difficult to prove, isn't it?"

"Yeah," I grumbled. "It is."

"Why don't you sit down again."

"Huh?" I realized I was standing. I hadn't remembered getting out of the chair. "Sorry. When I get angry, I pace."

"No need to apologize. How else do you deal with your anger, Jim?"

"Okay, I guess."

"I didn't ask you how well you thought you dealt with it. I asked you specifically what you *do* to deal with it."

I shrugged. "I get mad."

"Do you tell people when you're angry?"

"Yeah. Sometimes."

Dr. Davidson waited. Patiently.

"Well, most of the time."

"Really?"

"No. Hardly ever. I mean, I blow up sometimes, but most of the time, I don't. I mean . . ."

"What?"

"Well—um, I don't really like to tell people that I'm pissed at them."

"Why not?"

"Because, people don't want to hear it. They only get mad back at you for getting mad at them in the first place. So when I get mad at someone, I—try not to let it get in the way, so I can deal rationally with the other person."

"I see. Would it be fair to say that you suppress your anger, then?"

"Yeah, I guess so."

There was a longer pause this time. "So you're still carrying a lot of it with you, aren't you?"

"I don't know." And then I looked up. "What do you think?"

"I don't think yet," said Dr. Davidson. "I'm looking for patterns."

"Oh," I said.

"Let me ask you something, Jim. Who are you angry at?"

"I don't know. People talk to me, tell me what to do—no, they tell me who I am and I know that's not who I am. They talk to me, but they don't want to listen. My dad—whenever he would say, 'I want to talk to you,' he really meant, 'I'm going to talk and you're going to listen.' Nobody wants to hear what I have to say."

"Tell me more about your dad," said Dr. Davidson.

I rocked back and forth in the chair for a moment. Finally I said, "Well, see, it wasn't that my dad and I couldn't communicate. We could —but we *didn't*. Not very often, that is. Oh, once in a while he tried— and once in a while I tried—but most of the time both of us were too involved with our own concerns to be involved with each other."

I said, "You know, my dad was famous. He was one of the best fantasists in the country. Not the most popular—he didn't go in for a lot of flash and dazzle—but still he was one of the most respected, because his simulations were intelligent. When I was a kid, a lot of people used to tell me how lucky I was—even my own friends—because I got to play all his programs before anybody else. They couldn't understand my matter-of-fact attitude about his work, and I couldn't understand their awe."

"How *did* you feel about his work?"

I didn't answer that immediately. I wanted to interrupt and give Dr. Davidson a compliment—he was asking the right questions. He was very astute. But I realized I was sidetracking myself. And I realized why. I didn't want to answer that last question.

Dr. Davidson was very patient. The chair arms were warm. I let go of them and rubbed my hands together. Finally, I admitted it. I said, "Um . . . I guess I didn't realize it at the time, but I think—no, I *know*—I resented my dad's work. Not the games themselves, but his total involvement with them. I was jealous, I guess. My dad would get an idea —say, like *Inferno* or *Starship* or *Brainstorm*—and he'd turn into a zombie. He would disappear into his office for weeks at a time. That closed door was a threat. Do not disturb under penalty of immediate and painful death. Or possibly something worse. (Beware of Yang the Nauseating.) When he was writing, it was like living with a ghost. You heard sounds, you knew there was someone in the house with you, but you never saw him in person. And if by chance you did, it was like meeting a stranger in your living room. He'd mumble an acknowledgment, but he'd never lose his million-light-year stare.

"I don't know how Mom learned to live with it, but she did. Somehow. Dad would be up before seven, fix his own breakfast and then disappear for the day—only coming out of his office to help himself to something from the refrigerator. Mom made a point of leaving plates of food for him, so all he had to do was grab the plate and a fork and he could vanish back into his study. Usually we wouldn't see him again until after midnight. This could go on for weeks at a time.

"But we always knew when he had reached a halfway point—he took three days off to recharge his battery. It wasn't for us that he took the break; it was for himself. He'd take us out to dinner and a show, or we'd take a couple of days and go to an amusement park, but it was always strained. Maggie and I didn't know how to react around him because we'd been tiptoeing past his office for so many days in a row. Now, suddenly, he wasn't a monster anymore; he wanted to be our friend— but we didn't know how to be friends with him. He'd never taken the time to give us a chance to learn.

"For a long time I was jealous of his computer, but then I learned how to survive without a real dad and then it didn't matter anymore. Pretty soon, the hard parts were only when he was trying to make up for lost time. We all felt so uncomfortable, it was always a relief when he'd finally stretch his arms out and say, 'Well, I guess I'd better get back to work. Somebody's got to pay the bills around here.'

"Mom had her own work, of course—but she was able to switch off the terminal and walk away from it without looking back. Dad never was—when he had a problem to solve, he gnawed at it like a puppy with the legbone of a steer. Later, when I was old enough, I was able to appreciate the elegance of Dad's work. His programs not only played well, but they were so beautifully structured they were a joy to read. But no matter how much I respected the products of his labors, I still resented the fact that so much of his emotional energy went into his creations that there was only a little left for me. For the family.

"When Dad was finally finished with a program, he would be *completely* done. He wouldn't go near the machine for . . . I don't know— it seemed like months. He wouldn't even play other authors' games. Those were almost okay times, because he'd try to make the effort to learn how to be a real human being again—a real father. But by then, we'd learned to recognize the signs—that he couldn't really do it. Whenever he got too close, he'd get just so close and then he'd retreat again. He'd suddenly—*conveniently*—get another idea and he'd be gone again.

"So Maggie and I—well, I don't know about Maggie, but it *seemed* that she felt the same way—had that gap in our lives, and we either had to look somewhere else for something to fill it or learn to live with the lack. Which is mostly what I did—lived with the lack—because I didn't know that a family *wasn't* supposed to be that way. Maggie—well, she found her own answer. We weren't that close.

"Anyway, that was before the plagues. When we went up to the cabin, something in Dad changed—not better, just different. At first I didn't notice, because I didn't have enough experience with him to know, and then when I did, I didn't know what to make of it. I guess it scared me. As if I didn't know who he was after all.

"Several times a week, he and I would make the rounds of our security sensors—no one could have approached within a mile of the cabin without our knowing about it, not even a deer. We never had any people come near, but the system kept us in fresh meat and I learned how to skin a carcass and hang it. At first, Dad and I each kept mostly to ourselves, but after a while, he began talking to me. As if I were a real person. As if he'd just been waiting for me to grow up first.

"It confused me. I mean—hell, how can you expect someone to suddenly be a *real* son when you've spent twenty years ignoring him?

"And yet, even as I resented the goddamned presumption of the man, I still wanted him to finally be my father. So I stopped hating him for a while and began to discover what an interesting person he really was. I'd never known some of the things he'd done when he was my age— you know, he once met Neil Armstrong!

"I guess that was when Dad and I finally got to know each other. And I know this sounds strange, but those days up at the cabin were probably the happiest time of my life. It was a vacation from reality, and for a little while, we were a real family. It was nice. For a while. . . ."

After a while, Dr. Davidson prompted, "Go on, Jim."

"Huh?"

"What happened?"

I shrugged. "We came down from the mountains too soon. And we got caught in the last wave of the plagues. And the boys died. And— um, Dad never forgave himself. My sister never forgave him. And my mother—well, she never stopped pitying him because she knew what private hell he was living with. I guess he couldn't take that."

"Jim—"

"Huh?"

"You didn't say how you felt."

"Yes, I did. I said I loved him."

"How did you feel about coming down from the mountain too soon?"

"Uh . . . it was a mistake, but it was an honest one. I mean, anyone could have . . . I mean, it wasn't his fault—"

"Jim," Dr. Davidson said very quietly, "you're not being honest with me."

I jerked my hands back from the arms of the chair—

"Yes," he admitted. "There are sensors in the chair—but that isn't how I know you're lying. I can hear the stress in your voice."

I felt suddenly flustered—and angry. I jumped up out of the chair— "How *did* you feel, Jim?"

"None of your damn business! I'm tired of people telling me who I am, who I have to be. I'm tired of people lying to me! Everybody lies. Obama lied. Duke lied. You're lying now, I'll bet. I'm tired of it—tired of being used and manipulated. It isn't fair! It wasn't fair when my father did it!" The words were tumbling out now. I knew what I was saying, but I couldn't stop myself—I didn't even know if I meant any of it. "He didn't listen to me either! I wanted to stay up in the mountains longer! We were happy there!" The words caught in my throat and I choked. I started coughing.

After a polite pause, Dr. Davidson said, "There's water on the table."

I stepped over to it and poured myself a glass. I drank it, then poured another and downed half of it too. My throat still felt dry. I carried it back to the chair with me. I sat down again. I tried to perch on the edge of the seat, but the chair wasn't designed for it; I had to lean back.

"You said you were happy there, in the mountains," Dr. Davidson prompted.

"Yes," I admitted, glad to finally have it out. "I was. I wasn't competing with the computer anymore. We were involved with living. Surviving. I mean, it wasn't easy; we had to chop our own wood and do a lot of maintenance on the solar panels, but we were *involved* with what we were doing—and with each other. We talked to each other about what we had to do. We shared our experiences. We *cooperated.* Oh, there were fights, a lot of arguments—especially at first—but we were a family finally. And it wasn't fair to end it. We could have stayed up there longer. We should have waited. I didn't want to come back. I wanted us to stay up there—"

"So it wasn't the boys at all?" asked Dr. Davidson.

"No," I admitted. "Not for me. It was . . . I was afraid I was going to lose him again."

"So you were angry at your father?"

"Yeah, I guess so. Yeah, I was."

"Did you tell him how you felt?"

"No, I never did. I mean, there wasn't any point. Once he'd made up his mind, that was it. Oh, I tried—I did tell him. I said we shouldn't go down yet, but he said we had to. I didn't want to, but you couldn't argue with him, so I didn't. I just figured he was going to have his way, so I started putting up the walls again. You know, I'd let them down for a while, but now that he was making plans to come back, I had to protect myself again and—" I stopped to take a sip of water.

"Did he notice it? Did he see a change in your behavior?"

"I don't see how he could have missed it. I was a real asshole there for a while."

"I see."

There was silence. While I realized. It wasn't just Maggie's anger. Or Mom's pity. It was me too. My resentment. Was that what he'd been trying to tell me that last day at the depot? Did I drive him away too?

"What are you thinking about now?"

"Nothing," I said. "I'm just wondering who I should be angry at. My dad? Or me? He was there when I needed him. But I wasn't there when he needed me. I abandoned him because . . . because . . ." My face was getting hot. This was the hard part to admit. I could feel my throat tightening up. ". . . I thought he was going to shut me out again and I wanted to shut him out first—to show him what it felt like, to show him he couldn't jerk me around like that! I mean, everybody else does it, but not my dad! It wasn't fair!" I started coughing then, and my eyes were blurry. I rubbed my palms against them, realized I was starting to cry—and then broke down and bawled like a baby.

Dr. Davidson waited patiently. Finally he said, "Are you all right?"

"No," I said, but I was. I was *relieved* to have finally spoken it aloud. It was as if I had released a great pressure that I hadn't even known was there until the words had given it form. "Yes," I said. "I'm all right. Well—a little better, anyway. I hadn't realized I was living with such . . . guilt."

"Not just guilt, Jim. Anger too. You've been carrying your anger for such a long time, Jim, it's become a habit. It's part of you. My job is to assist you in giving it up. If that's what you want."

I thought about that. "I don't know. Sometimes I think my anger is all that keeps me going."

"Maybe that's because you haven't experienced anything else as intense. Have you ever been in love?"

I shook my head.

"Perhaps you ought to think about that—consider what it is you expect a lover to be. We could talk about that next time."

"Next time?"

"If you wish. You can call on me any time you want. That's what I'm here for."

"Oh. I thought this was only a one-time interview."

"It doesn't have to be."

"Oh," I said. Then, "Thank you."

TWENTY-NINE

DINNER WAS a thick steak (medium rare), real mashed potatoes, green peas (with melted butter on them), fresh salad (bleu cheese dressing) and a chocolate soda. All of my favorite foods. Even an army commissary couldn't do too much damage to a T-bone steak. Although they tried.

I wondered about Ted. I wondered where he was and what he was up to now. Or who.

I'd never been able to keep up with him. And I knew why.

Paul Jastrow said it to me once—I didn't remember the argument, but I did remember the insult: "Hey, McCarthy—there are human beings and there are ducks. You're a duck. Stop pretending to be a human being. You're not fooling anyone." Some of the people around him laughed, so after that, whenever Paul wanted to get a laugh, he'd turn to me and start quacking, then he'd turn to his friends and explain, "You have to talk to them in their own language if you want them to understand anything."

I never understood why he'd picked me out for the honor of that particular humiliation—not until much later when I saw some comedian on TV do the exact same routine to an unsuspecting member of the audience. It wasn't personal; he was just using the fellow—he was someone to hit with the rubber chicken. That's when the nickel dropped. Paul had been imitating this comic. Maybe he hadn't even meant it personally—it was just a cheap way to get a laugh. But nobody had let me in on the joke. So I didn't get to laugh too. And even though

I understood it now, in retrospect, it still didn't lessen the hurt. I could still feel it, could still hear the laughter.

I think it hurt the most because I was afraid it might be true.

I was looking at my half-finished steak. I was wishing I had someone to share the meal with. It's no fun eating alone.

I pushed myself away from the table. I wasn't hungry anymore. I hated to waste food, but—

—and then I had to stop myself, or I would have laughed out loud. There weren't any children starving in Africa anymore—or India, or Pakistan, or anywhere else! Nobody was starving anymore. If there was one good thing the plagues had accomplished, they had ended world hunger. It didn't matter if I wasted this steak or not. There was steak enough for everybody now. There was steak to waste! It was an eerie realization.

But I still felt guilty about not finishing. Old habits die hard. If you train yourself to think a certain way, will you keep on thinking that way, even after it's no longer a valid way to think?

Hm.

Did I think like a duck? Was that it? Did I keep on doing ducklike things because I didn't know how to do anything else? Was it that obvious to the people around me?

Maybe I should stop being me for a while and start being someone else—someone who didn't have so much trouble being me.

I wasn't hungry anymore. I got up, took my tray to the bus window and left the commissary.

I wondered if I walked funny. I mean, I was short and a little pudgy around the bottom. Did I look like a duck? Maybe I could learn to walk differently—if I stood a little taller and carried my weight in my chest instead of in my gut—*"Oof!* I'm sorry." I had been so busy walking, I hadn't been looking, and had plowed straight into a young woman. Quack. Old synapses never die, they just fire away. "I'm really sorry—oh!"

It was Marcie. The thin girl with the large dark eyes. From the bus. Colonel Buffoon.

"Hi—" I flustered for words. "Uh, what are you doing here?"

"Feeding my dog—they give me the scraps." She showed me the package she was carrying.

I held the door for her. She stepped through, but didn't say thanks. I followed after.

She stopped on the sidewalk. "Are you following me?"

I shook my head. "No."

"Well, then, go away."

"You're very rude, you know."

She stared at me blankly.

"You don't even give people a chance."

She blinked. "I'm sorry. Am I supposed to know you?"

"Uh—we were on the bus together, remember? Last night?"

She shook her head. "I don't remember anything from last night. Were you one of the boys I screwed?"

"Huh? No . . . I mean . . . *what?*"

"He doesn't use me at all. I know that's what people think, but he's never touched me. But he likes to watch me do it with the young men he picks out. And then he likes to—well, you know."

"Why do you stay with him?"

She shrugged. "I don't know. I don't have anywhere else to go." And then she added, "I really am sorry. I don't remember you at all. I was stoned last night. He had some Atlanta Blue. I don't think I did it with anyone, but I'm not always sure. Were you there?"

"I told you. We were on the bus together. Remember? The bus into town?"

"Oh, yeah. I'm sorry. Sometimes I don't remember things at all. If you say so." She turned away from me then, bent to the ground and unwrapped her package to reveal a large pile of meat scraps and bones. "He's going to love this. Rangle!" she called. "C'mon, boy. Here, Rangle, come and get it or I'll give it to the dog!" She turned back to me. "I don't like to do dust, but—well, it helps sometimes. You know. Sometimes I get . . . lonely. You know?"

"Yeah. I know."

"That's funny, isn't it? There are still lots of people, if you know where to go, but it's all crowds of strangers. I don't know anybody anymore."

"I know what you mean. And everybody always seems so *agitated.* It's like—you know, the social Brownian movement has been speeded up—"

Her expression was blank. She didn't know.

I said, "It's because there are less people now—we all have to move faster to make up for the difference."

She was staring at me. Had I just said something stupid? Or had she not gotten it? She said, "I used to be smart. Like you. Only it stopped being useful to be smart. So I stopped being smart." She looked sad.

"The dust helps a lot. You can get real stupid real fast with dust." She caught herself then, as if she'd said something she shouldn't have. She lifted her voice again. "Hey, Rangle! Come on! Where are you, boy?" There was an edge of impatience in her tone. She turned back to me. "You'll like him. He's really a very friendly dog—I just don't know where he is now."

"Oh, well . . . maybe he got caught up in traffic, or something."

She didn't react to the joke. She turned her wide-eyed stare on me again. "Do you think so?"

"Are you still dusted?" I asked.

"Oh, no. I haven't sniffed since yesterday. I don't like it. Why do you ask?" Before I could answer, she clutched my arm. "Am I being weird? I'm sorry. Sometimes I get weird. It happens. But nobody ever tells me if I'm weird or not. That scares me sometimes—that I might be so weird that no one will tell if I am or not. One time, everybody else got dusted and I had to stay squeaky—because it was my period and I didn't want to risk hemorrhaging—and I was really bored. They didn't understand why I wasn't giggly like them—"

"Yes," I said. "You're being weird."

She looked into my face. Her eyes were very large and very dark. She looked almost like a little girl right then. She said, "Thank you. Thank you for telling me that." She blinked and I saw the tears welling up in her eyes. "I don't know anything anymore, except what other people tell me. So thank you for telling me the truth.

"Do you hate me?"

I shook my head.

"Do you feel sorry for me?"

"No, I don't." I thought about my father for an instant. "No, I don't feel sorry for anyone anymore. It only kills them."

She kept on looking at me, but she didn't say anything for a long moment. We stood there in the Colorado dusk, while overhead the stars began to come out. To the west, the mountains were outlined in a faint glow of orange. The breeze was warm and smelled of honey and pine.

The silence stretched until it was uncomfortable. I began to wonder if I should apologize for being honest with her. Finally she said, "I wish I knew where that damn dog went to. It's not like him to miss his dinner! Rangle!" She looked annoyed, then as if embarrassed to have been angry, she said, "I don't know why I'm getting so upset—he's not my *real* dog. I mean, he's just a stray. I sort of adopted him—" And then she admitted, "—but he's the only person I know who . . . well, he doesn't care if I'm weird. Rangle doesn't care. You know?"

"Yeah, I do. We all need someone these days." I smiled at her. "Because we're all we've got."

She didn't answer immediately. She was staring at the paper with the meat scraps on it. Overhead, the street lights came on, filling the twilight with a warm glow. When Marcie finally spoke, her voice was very soft. "You know, I used to know what was important in life and what wasn't. Being beautiful was important. I had my nose fixed—my whole face—because I wanted to be beautiful. Like, you could have that bump on your nose fixed—"

"It was a motorcycle accident," I said.

"—only you'd still be you inside, wouldn't you? Well, that's what happened to me. I had my face remodeled—only afterwards, I was still me. I think that's what's happened to the world. We're all still who we were last year—only our outsides have changed and we don't know it yet. We don't know who we're supposed to be anymore. I'm nervous and I'm scared—all the time," she said. "I mean, what if I do find out who I am, and then someone comes up and tells me no, that's not who I am after all? Do you know what I mean?"

I said, "Ducks. We want to feel like swans, and they keep telling us we're ducks—and not even very good ducks at that."

"Yeah," she said. "That's good. You do understand. Sometimes I wonder if there's anyone else in the world who feels what I do—and sometimes I find someone who does; but it's always a surprise to find out that I'm not completely alone."

She shivered and I put my arm around her. "I know."

Petulantly, she said, "I just wish I knew where Rangle was. He'll probably show up tomorrow, grinning and wagging. He's a real practical joker, but I don't like worrying. You've seen him around, haven't you? Sort of halfway between brown and white, almost pink—real shaggy, with big floppy paws like bunny-feet slippers. Big brown eyes and a black gumdrop nose."

Yes, I had seen him.

From a glass booth above a circular room.

Last night. With Jillanna.

He had been—dessert.

I could feel my stomach tightening. Oh, shit. How should I handle this one?

Marcie looked at me. "Did you say something?"

"Uh—Marcie, I—uh, don't know how to tell you this, but—" *Just tell the truth,* the voice in my head said. "—uh, Rangle is dead. He was —uh, hit by a car. It happened late last night. I saw it happen. He was killed instantly. I didn't realize that was Rangle until you described him."

She was shaking her head. "Oh, no—he couldn't be! Are you sure, Jim?" She searched my face for some sign that I was mistaken.

I swallowed hard. My throat hurt. I remembered something I'd heard in the booth, about how this dog had been scrounging around the commissary for a while. "Marcie," I said. "I'm sure. He was about so high, right?"

She nodded slowly. She gulped for a moment, as if she couldn't get air. And then she put her hands to her face and held them there. It was as if she were shattering into a thousand screaming pieces all at once, and only the sheer pressure of her hands was keeping all those pieces from flying off into space.

And then, abruptly, she straightened up and her face was like a mask. When she spoke, her voice was flat and dead. "I'll be all right." She shrugged. "He was only a dog." She was a zombie again.

I stared at her as she bent and picked up the package of meat scraps that Rangle would never eat. She folded the paper up neatly and walked over to a nearby garbage can and dumped it in. "Now I can stop caring."

"Marcie, it's all right to care. We all have to have someone to care about."

"I don't," she said. She pulled her coat around her, as if to shield herself against the cold—but it was a warm night and it wasn't the cold she was shutting out. She brushed past me and started walking away.

"Marcie!" She kept on walking and I felt powerless to stop her. It made me angry—the feeling of helplessness; it was the same feeling as when my father walked away from me for the last time. "No, goddammit! I'm tired of people walking out on me!" Something flickered like a frame in a movie and then I was moving across the space between us and grabbing her arm. I pulled her around to face me. "Knock it off!" I snapped at her. "This is really stupid. I've seen other people do it. You start retreating from life because it hurts. You do it one step at a time, but pretty soon it becomes such a habit that you do it automatically— you run from everything. Of course it hurts! How much it hurts shows how much you care! And that proves just how much alive you are!"

"Let go of me! I don't need a sermon!"

"You're right! You don't! You need a year in a rubber room!"

She broke free of my grip, her eyes wild. "Don't say that!" she shrieked. Her hands were like claws.

"Why? Because it might be true? You said you were terrified of being weird, that you might be one of those ladies with the fried eggs on their foreheads, but nobody would tell you. Well, I'm telling you. If you run away from me now, that's the first step toward the fried egg."

She looked as if I'd slapped her, blinking at me in the glow of the street lights. Her expression seemed to dissolve as the meaning of the words sank in. I could almost see them penetrating, layer after layer. "I've been there," she said. "I don't want to go back."

"So *don't.* You don't have to. It's all this running from stuff that keeps you crazy. You think you're the only one who's crazy? The rest of us are just as wacko! All you have to do is look. The only difference is we don't let it stop us." I added, "Too much."

"But it hurts!"

"So what? Let it hurt! At least that way you get it over with! What you're doing now sure isn't producing results, is it?"

She nodded and gulped, and then her eyes welled up and she clutched my shirt and she grabbed me and started bawling. I pulled her close and held onto her, as if I could shield her from the pain—only it wasn't pain from the outside anymore, it was pain that bubbled up from the inside and burst out through her eyes and nose and mouth. "It isn't fair! It isn't fair! Why does there have to be so much dying?!! I want my dog!! Oh, Rangle, Rangle! I want my Rangle back!" She sobbed and screamed into my jacket. She gulped for air and sobbed again. The tears were streaming down her cheeks now. "It isn't fair! Everything I've ever loved—I don't want to love anything anymore! I'm tired of losing! It hurts too much to care! I want an end to it! I want my dog!"

I thought about the men who'd captured Rangle and thought about what I'd like to do to them. Marcie was right—it wasn't fair. They killed the dog, but I had to deal with the guilt and the grief! Why did I have to clean up their mess?! All of their messes?!! I could feel my fists tightening against Marcie's back. Her shoulders heaved. She began coughing and I unclenched my fists and started thumping her gently. "It's all right, baby," I said. "It's all right. Let it out, that's the way, it's good to cry. It shows how much you cared. Just scream it out, that's the girl—" I just kept babbling, trying to comfort her and slowly ease her back. It was amazing how much she cared about that dog. She just kept on crying—or was she crying for more than just the dog right now? I held her and let her weep. Two soldiers walked past us without stopping. They took us for granted. Such scenes were common nowadays.

Marcie sniffed and looked up at me. "Jim?"

"Huh?"

"I'm all right now. You can let go."

"Oh. I'm sorry."

"No. Don't. Thank you."

"Come on. I'll walk you back to your room."

"Okay."

We walked in silence. She had a small apartment in the second building past the commissary, one of the co-ops we'd seen on the way in. It was austere, but homey.

Once inside, she put her arms around me again and held me close. "Thank you," she said. I put my arms around her and we stood that way for a while.

"Jim," she said softly, "will you make love to me?"

I could smell the perfume in her hair; it made me dizzy. I didn't speak; I just nodded, then brought my face around to hers. Her eyes were wide—she looked like a frightened little girl, afraid I'd say yes.

I said, "Yes," and her eyes closed gently. She laid her head against my chest and I could feel her body beginning to relax. She was all right. At last she knew she was all right. Because I was all right, and I said so.

I stroked her hair with my hand. She was . . . so tiny, so pale, so thin. So fragile. So warm.

There were a thousand things to say.

I didn't say any of them.

After a while, we moved to the bed.

"Turn off the light?" I said.

"I'd rather leave it on."

"Oh. Well . . . okay."

THIRTY

I FLOATED in the land of Afterward, drifting toward the land of Nod—until suddenly, I jerked awake and sat up in a cold sweat. "Holy buffalo shit!"

Next to me, Marcie rolled over, alarmed. "Huh? What is it?"

"I have to go—I have to be back at the hotel! What time is it? Oh, sweet Jesus—it's almost midnight! They're gonna hang me for sure!"

"Jim, are you all right?"

"No—I'm not!" I was already pulling on my pants. "Where are my shoes?"

"Don't go—"

"I have to!" And then I saw the look on her face—that hurt, used expression—and I sat down next to her and pulled her into my arms. "Marcie, I'm sorry. I wish I could stay here with you, but I can't. I—I'm under orders. I know this looks like I'm running out on you, but I'm not. Please believe me."

"I believe you," she said, but I could feel her stiffening in my arms. She rubbed at her eyes. "I'm not angry. I'm used to it."

I tilted her face toward mine and kissed her. "I'm not like that, Marcie."

"Yeah, I know. Nobody's like anybody else anymore—only everybody's still running from everybody else."

I started searching for my shirt. "I'm not running *from*, I'm running *to*. If you knew—"

"Uh huh. You've even got a secret mission. Like everybody else." She threw herself back in the bed, rolling up in the blankets, pulling a pillow over her head. "Just go away, Jim—quietly! Okay?"

I sat down on the bed next to her while I pulled on my shoes. "Listen, I'll come back, all right? If it's not too late. I want to."

"Don't bother," she mmfled from under the pillow.

"Marcie, please don't be angry with me. I wish I could tell you, but I can't." I bent to kiss her, but she wouldn't let me pull the pillow away from her head. "All right, have it your own way."

I drove back to the hotel, feeling like something that had crawled out from under a rock and not knowing why. Dammit—the harder I tried to be honorable the worse I felt. Why couldn't I just be a shit like Ted and have everybody falling all over me?

The only answer I could think of to that was that I didn't know how to be a shit. I was doomed to go through life always trying to be nice. Always trying to rationalize. Always trying to understand.

I switched on the auto-terminal angrily, and punched for channel fifteen. It was a replay of one of the Free Forum sessions at the conference, but listening to it only made me angrier. Why were they broadcasting this bullshit anyway? If these people wanted to be stupid, that was their business—but how many innocent people were going to be endangered because they believed what they heard on the network? I was almost trembling with anger when I finally pulled into the hotel's underground parking.

I circled down into the concrete bowels of the building. There was a ramp marked SERVICE and I pulled into that. The robot guard scanned my card, looked at my face and cleared me without question. The elevator also checked my identity before delivering me to the thirteenth floor.

There were no armed guards waiting for me when the elevator doors slid open. I let out the breath I had been holding all the way up.

I went back to the room they had assigned me and checked in at the terminal. "Request instructions."

The screen cleared, then flashed: "Please wait at this location until further notice."

What did that mean?

I sat in front of the terminal and waited, staring at the screen. How long?

Had Wallachstein and the others already met and decided my fate? While I hadn't been there to speak for myself?

I went into the kitchen and got myself some tomato juice, then I came back to the keyboard and sat down again. Still nothing. I thought

of Marcie. I could still smell the honey-warmth of her hair. It made me
feel warm and toasty inside—until I remembered the bitterness of my
abrupt exit. I wondered if she'd forgive me.

Well, maybe I could do something while I waited. I cleared the screen
and punched for Library Service. The screen flashed: "Sorry. This terminal is locked."

Huh?

I tried again. Same answer.

I pulled my card out of the reader-slot and went to the door.

It wouldn't open. "Invalid code."

I came back into the room, stood in the center of it and looked
around for another way out. The balcony?

I opened the sliding door and stepped out, leaning out over the railing to see how high I was. Too high. Thirteen stories. It wasn't the fall
that was dangerous, it was the abrupt stop at the end.

What about climbing over the railing to an adjacent balcony? Not
possible. The balconies were isolated for privacy. Another service of
your security-conscious Marriott.

I looked down again, then went back into the room and took inventory. Two sheets, king size. Two blankets, king size. Not enough. Even
with the drapes, I'd probably be four stories short.

I sat down in front of the terminal again and began to drink my
tomato juice. It was tart. It made the salivary glands at the back of my
mouth hurt. Did I have any other options?

I couldn't think of any.

Why did I want to escape anyway?

Because they had locked me in.

And why had they locked me in?

Because they were afraid I might try to escape.

And what did that imply? That they had made a decision? That they
had something planned for me that I might not like?

And I had rushed from Marcie's bed to come here? No wonder so
many people thought me a fool.

I downed the rest of the juice in a few quick swallows, then sank back
in the chair and glowered at the implacable screen of the terminal.

It was totally disconnected. Before it would respond again, it would
have to be cleared by someone with a priority code.

I thought about Marcie and my promise to call her. I wouldn't even
be able to do that.

I thought about Wallachstein and his barely veiled threats. Had I failed the psychiatric examination?

What if they did decide to make me disappear? Wasn't I entitled to a fair trial—or had I already had it? How would they do it? Would I get any warning? How did they make people disappear anyway?

I realized I was sweating. I couldn't sit still. I got up and searched the room again, the balcony, the door—

The door beeped.

I started to call, "Who is it?" and then stopped. What if it were a firing squad? Would they do it here in the room? Or would they take me somewhere else to do it?

I stood there, debating whether to holler for help or try to hide.

Before I could make up my mind, the door slid open. "May I come in?"

"Huh? Who—?" And then I placed him. Fromkin. The man who ate strawberries and lox while talking about global starvation. The pompous asshole.

"I said, 'May I come in?' I'm not interrupting anything, am I?"

"Uh, no—I—uh, how did you open the door?"

He held up a card with a gold stripe on it for me to see.

"Oh," I said.

I made room, he stepped inside and the door slid closed. I looked at it, wanting to see if it would open for me now, but I resisted. I followed him into the room and we sat down. He sank into his chair with easy grace. How old *was* he, I wondered?

He studied me for a moment with sharp dark eyes, then he said, "I'm here because a *mutual friend* of ours suggested that I talk to you. Do you understand?"

"No names, huh?"

"That's right." He repeated, "Do you understand?"

Wallachstein had asked the same question several times. A phrase floated into my mind: *the comprehension of the defendant.* It was an important legal consideration. There had been a Supreme Court decision about it once. I wondered, was this part of my trial too?

"Is this official?" I asked.

He looked annoyed. "Unless you answer my question, I have to leave. Do you understand?"

"Yes," I said quickly. "I do. I understand. Now answer my question. Is this an official visit, or what?"

"If you want to look at it that way, yes. Our *mutual friend* thought we ought to have a little chat. It's to your benefit."

"Is it? Really?"

Fromkin looked annoyed, but otherwise he ignored the question. He said, "In case you're wondering, yes, I did see your performance this morning—and yes, I also remember you from last night. For someone who only got in town yesterday, you've certainly let people know you're here." I must have looked embarrassed, for he added, "To be fair, it's not *all* your doing. This city is just another small town these days. The number-two indoor sport is gossiping about the number-one indoor sport—and who's playing which position. You and your boyfriend just got caught in the middle, that's all."

"We're not boyfriends. The middle of what?"

Fromkin scratched his head. "Uh, let me explain it this way. There's a certain group of people; rumor has it that they're very important. Although nobody knows who's in the group, or even who does what, or even what the group is supposed to be doing, everybody suspects that anybody who knows anything must be in that group. It just so happens that some of those suspicions are very accurate. So when one of those supposed-to-be-important individuals is suddenly called away from her —ah, personal affairs—to bring in a Very Important Delivery, well, then, naturally there's going to be a great deal of interest in that delivery."

It took me a moment to translate that, and then it took another moment for it to sink in. Right. It was worse than I thought. I said, "Ted and I are not boyfriends. Or any other kind of friends. And I don't know how important our delivery was or wasn't—we were told it wasn't."

"I don't know about that." Fromkin spread his hands wide in a gesture of innocence. "That's not what I want to talk about anyway. Do you mind if I record this?" He held up his unit. I shook my head and he switched it on. "Did you see any of the playbacks of the conference sessions?"

"Only a little. I heard some of it while I was driving back here this evening."

"What did you hear?"

"A lot of uproar. About how to deal with the worms. Apparently there's a faction that wants to try to establish peaceful contact."

"Do you believe that's possible?"

"No."

"Why not?"

I blinked. "Uh, you don't know much about the Chtorrans, do you?"

"That's not germane. I'm asking *your* opinion."

"I never saw a Chtorran who wanted to stop and chat first. We never had any choice but to kill them."

"How many Chtorrans have you seen?"

"Live or pictures?"

"Total."

"Um, well—I've seen the Show Low photographs—"

Fromkin nodded knowingly. "Go on."

"—and I've seen the nest I mentioned this morning. The one with the fourth Chtorran. The one I burned."

He waited expectantly. "Is that all?"

"Um—no, there was one more. The one here at the Science Center."

His eyes narrowed. "Tell me about that," he said slowly.

I shook my head. "It was just . . . there."

He looked into my eyes and said, "I know about those sessions, son. Is that what you saw, one of them?"

I nodded. "There were some dogs. They fed them to the Chtorran. Live. Do you know about that?"

Fromkin said, "They say that Chtorrans won't eat dead meat—they have to eat their prey live."

"That's true. At least, as far as I know it is."

"Mm hm. And those are all the Chtorrans you've seen?"

"Yes."

"Are you an expert on Chtorrans?"

"No, of course not. But I've had more experience than most other people have had—at least those who've lived to tell about it. Some of those assholes this afternoon were talking about making friends with Chtorrans. And that's no more possible than a steak making friends with a dog—except from the inside."

"Couldn't it be that your experience with Chtorrans is limited, and that's colored your perceptions of them . . . ?"

"You mean, maybe there are peaceful ones, but I don't know about it?"

He nodded.

I weighed the possibility. "Well, yeah—maybe there *are* peaceful ones. I've never heard of any. And I don't think anybody else has either —or else we'd have heard about it by now. Somebody would have said something this afternoon. Somebody would know about it, wouldn't they?"

Fromkin didn't answer.

"What's this all about, anyway?" I asked.

He shook his head. "Just for information. Raw material. You know. The truth can only be seen when looked at from many points of view at once."

I shook my head. "You're not asking for information. You're digging for something specific."

"You're too suspicious. I'm a civilian, son. Can we go on?"

"There's more?"

"Just a little. This afternoon, you stood up in front of a crowd of people and said you had to burn a man because he was being attacked by a worm."

"Yes, I did." Part of me was insisting that I put up a defensive barrier against this man's probing, but another part was insisting on telling the truth, no matter who heard it. The only way we would defeat the Chtorrans would be by telling the truth. I added, "It was the kindest thing I could do."

"Kindest—?" He raised an eyebrow at me. "How do you know that?"

"I beg your pardon?"

His expression had turned hard. "Have you ever been on the receiving end of a flamethrower?"

"No, I haven't."

"Then where do you get your information?"

"That's what I was told by Shorty."

"Who's Shorty?"

"The man I had to burn. *Sir.*" I said that last deliberately.

Fromkin was silent for a moment at that, turning the information over to see if it was mined. Finally he said, "I'm told—by someone who *knows*—that death by fire has to be the most horrible thing imaginable. When you're hit by napalm, you can feel your flesh turning into flame."

"Sir," I said stiffly, "with all due respect, when a wave of fire from a flamethrower hits you, there isn't time to feel either the heat or the pain. It's a sudden descent into unconsciousness."

Fromkin looked skeptical.

"I was there, sir. I saw how quickly it happened. There wasn't any time for pain."

He studied that thought for a long moment. "How about guilt?" he asked finally. "Was there time for that?"

"Huh?"

"Do you feel guilty about what you did?"

"Guilt? I did what I had to do! What I was told to do! I never questioned it! *Hell, yes,* I feel guilty! And ashamed and shitty and a thousand other things that don't have names!" Something popped for me. "What's this all about anyway? Are you judging me too? Listen, I have enough trouble living up to my own standards—don't ask me to live up to yours! I'm sure your answers are better than mine—after all, your integrity is still unsullied by the brutal facts of practicality! You've been sitting around eating strawberries and lox! I'm the guy who had to pull the trigger! If there is a better answer, don't you think I want to know? Don't you think I have the first right to know? Come up to the hills and show me! I'd be glad to find you're right. But if you don't mind, I'll keep my torch all charged and ready—just in case you're wrong!"

He waited patiently until I ran down. And even then, he didn't answer immediately. He got up, went to the kitchen and got a bottle of water from the refrigerator. He took a glass, filled it with ice and came back into the living room, slowly pouring the water over the cubes. He eased himself back down into his chair, took a drink and studied me over the glass. When he spoke, his voice was quiet and calm. "Are you through?"

"Yeah. For now."

"Good. I want to ask you some questions now. I want you to consider a couple of things. All right?"

I nodded. I folded my arms across my chest.

"Thank you. Now, tell me this. What difference does it make? Maybe it's a kindness to burn a man, maybe it isn't. Maybe he doesn't feel a thing—and maybe it's the purest form of pain, a moment of exquisite hell. What difference does it make, Jim, if a man dies crushed in the mouth of a Chtorran or burned by napalm? He's still dead. *Where* does it make a difference?"

"You want me to answer?"

Fromkin said, "Go ahead. Take a crack at it."

I said, "It doesn't make a difference—not the way you ask it."

"Wrong," he said. "It does. It makes a lot of difference to the person who has to pull the trigger."

I looked at that. "I'm sorry. I don't see how."

"Good. So look at it this way. What's more important? Killing Chtorrans or saving lives?"

"I don't know."

"So? Who do I have to ask to find out?"

Huh? Whitlaw used to ask the same question. If I didn't know what I thought, who did? I said, "Saving lives."

"Good. So what do we have to do to save lives?"

I grinned. "Kill Chtorrans."

"Good. So what happens if a human being gets in the way? No, let me rephrase that. What would have happened if you had tried to save—what was his name, Shorty?"

"We'd have both bought the farm."

Fromkin nodded. "Good. So what's more important? Killing Chtorrans or saving lives?"

"In this case, killing Chtorrans."

"Uh huh. So does it matter what justification you use?"

"Huh?"

"Does it matter whether you believe that a man dies painlessly under the flame or not?"

"Well, no, I guess not."

He nodded. "So how do you feel about it now?"

I shook my head. "I don't know." I felt torn up inside. I opened my mouth to speak, then closed it again.

He gave me another raised eyebrow.

"I don't know," I repeated.

"All right," he said. "Let me ask it this way. Would you do it again?"

"Yes." I said it without hesitation.

"You're sure of that?"

"Yes."

"Thank you. And how would you feel about it?"

I met his gaze unashamedly. "Shitty. About like I feel now. But I'd still do it. It doesn't matter what the policy is." I added, "The important thing is killing Chtorrans."

"You're really adamant about that, aren't you?"

"Yeah, I guess so."

He took a long breath, then switched off his recorder. "Okay, I'm through."

"Did I pass?"

"Say again?"

"Your test—this was no interview. This was an attitude check. Did I pass?"

He looked up from his recorder, straight into my eyes. "If it were an attitude check, what you just asked would probably have flunked you."

"Yeah, well." My arms were still folded across my chest. "If my attitude leaves something to be desired, so does the way I've been treated. So we're even."

He stood up and I stood with him. "Answer me something. Are there peaceful Chtorrans?"

He looked at me blankly. "I don't know. What do you think?"

I didn't answer, just followed him to the door. He slid his card into the lock-slot and the door slid open for him. I started to follow him out, but there were two armed guards waiting in the hall.

"Sorry," said Fromkin. For the first time, he looked embarrassed.

"Yeah," I said, and stepped back. The door slid shut in front of me.

THIRTY-ONE

I STOOD there staring at that goddamned door for thirty seconds without saying a word.

I put my hands on it and pressed. The metal was cold.

I rested my head against the solid wallness of it. My hands clenched into fists.

"Shit!"

And then I said a whole bunch of other words too.

I swore as long as I could without repeating myself, then switched to Spanish and kept on going.

And when I finally wound down, I felt no better than when I had started.

I felt used. Betrayed. And stupid.

I began to pace around the apartment again. I kicked the terminal every time I passed it. Useless hunk of junk. I couldn't even use it to call room service.

I wandered into the kitchen and opened the fridge—it was surprisingly well stocked. But I wasn't hungry. I was angry. I started opening drawers. Someone had thoughtfully removed all of the carving and steak knives.

And swearing didn't do any good anymore. It only left my throat dry. And me feeling foolish. The minute you stop, you start to realize how silly it looks.

What I really wanted to do was get even.

I walked back into the living room of the suite and gave the terminal another kick. A good one—it nearly toppled off the stand, but I caught it in time. And then I found myself wondering *why.* The damn thing wouldn't communicate with me—I didn't owe it any favors.

I shoved it off the stand and onto the floor.

It hit with a dull thud.

I picked it up and shook it. It didn't even sound broken.

"I know—" I carried it out to the balcony and threw it over the side.

It bounced and scraped down the sloping side of the building and shattered on the concrete below with a terrifically satisfying smash.

I threw the stand after it.

And then a chair.

And a lamp.

And a small table.

The TV screen was bolted to the wall. I hit it with the second chair—it took three tries to smash it—and then threw the chair after its companion.

Bounce, bounce, scrape, slide, crash, smash. Great.

What else?

The microwave oven.

The nightstand from the bedroom.

Three more chairs.

Two more lamps.

The dining-nook table.

A hassock.

All the hangers from the closet.

Most of the towels and sheets.

A king-size mattress and box spring. Those last were particularly difficult.

It was while I was struggling with the box spring that I realized a crowd had gathered below—at a safe distance, of course. They were applauding each new act of destruction. The more outrageous it was, the louder the cheers.

The bedframe and headboard drew a standing ovation.

I wondered what I could do to top it. I began to clean out the kitchen.

All the dishes—they sounded great as they clattered and crashed on the street below—and all the pots and pans.

All the flatware.

The contents of the refrigerator—and the shelves as well.

Almost all the bottled water. I opened one for myself and took a long drink. I stood there on the balcony, catching my breath and wondering why nobody had come up to stop this rain of terror. I finished the bottle and it too sailed out into the night to shatter somewhere in the darkness below.

I looked back into the apartment. What else? What had I missed?

The bar!

I decided to start with the beer. There was a nearly full keg in a half-fridge under the counter. It clanged and bonged all the way down, exploding in a sudsy fountain when it hit. There were screams from the ones who got drenched.

The half-fridge followed the keg. Shit! Wasn't anything built in anymore? What kind of lousy workmanship was this anyway?

I stopped, arm cocked in the act of defenestrating a bottle of scotch.

No. Some things are sacred.

What was it Uncle Moe used to say? Never kill a bottle without saluting it first? Right.

I took a swig and sent it to its death.

There were three bottles of the scotch. I toasted every one. Then I murdered the bourbon. I began to realize that I was going to have to take smaller swigs. This was a very well-stocked bar.

I assaulted the rums, both light and dark.

Exterminated the vodka.

Executed the gin.

Raped the *vin rosé.*

There were fewer shouts coming from below now. Apparently, once I had stopped dropping the big exciting stuff I had lost most of my audience. Well, just as well. Spectacle may be impressive to the unsophisticated, but the real artist works for elegance.

I staggered back and finished off the liqueurs and the brandies. I saved the sherry for last—after all, it was an after-dinner drink.

There was a selection of different glasses on a crystal shelf. They followed the bottles. And so did the shelf.

I prowled around the room, looking for things I'd missed. There wasn't much. I wondered if I could roll up the rug.

No—I couldn't. I was having too much trouble standing.

Besides, I had to pee first. I stumbled into the bathroom and threw up. Then I peed.

"How about a shower?" I hiccuped. "Okay," I agreed with myself, and turned the water on. I found a towel that I'd forgotten to throw and some soap. I also found a box of Sober-Ups in the medicine cabinet. No —I wasn't ready to sober up yet. I put them aside.

The shower had terrific acoustics. The resonance was perfect for singing. It was all the encouragement I needed. *"When I was a lad in Venusport, I took up the local indoor sport—"* I went through the complete librettos of *A Double Dose of Love* and *A Bisexual Built for Two* before I ran out of soap.

The nice thing about hotels, though—you never run out of hot water. But you can't sing without soap. It just doesn't feel right.

I turned off the water, found the forgotten towel and began to dry my hair. Still singing, still toweling, I walked back into the living room—

Wallachstein, Lizard and the other two were standing there, waiting for me.

"Uh—" I said. "Hi." And lowered the towel to my waist. "Can I, uh, offer you a . . . seat?" Only Lizard smiled; she turned her head to hide it. The others just looked grim.

"Thank you," said Colonel Wallachstein. "I think we prefer to stand."

"Well—" I said. "It's nice of you to drop in like this. I wish you would have phoned ahead, though, so I could have tidied up a little—"

If Wallachstein was angry, he hid it well. He kept his voice flat and emotionless. His dark eyes were unreadable. He indicated the empty room. I'd pretty well stripped it bare. "Is there some explanation for all this—?"

I shifted my weight to what I hoped was an assured stance. "Yes. I was bored."

"I beg your pardon?"

"Someone locked me in. Disconnected the terminal. I didn't have anything else to do. I began to experiment with the psychoacoustic properties of falling objects, trying to determine which common household items made the most satisfying crashes."

"I see . . . and what did you determine?"

"Ceramic lamps are very nice. So are beer kegs. And almost any liquid-filled bottle. Chairs and mattresses are impressive, but dull."

Wallachstein nodded thoughtfully. "I'll remember that for future reference. In case I'm ever in a situation where I need to use those facts." He looked at me curiously. "Is there anything else you want to add?"

"Yes, I think there is," I said. I started off slowly. "I'd like to know why I was locked in here, for one thing! You asked me to cooperate with you. Is this how you guarantee it? Or is there something else going on that I don't know about? Have you and your disappearing committee that doesn't exist already decided my fate? Do I still exist? I suppose you don't want my opinion in the matter, do you? And while I'm at it, I want to know what ever happened to fair trials. I still don't even know what I'm charged with! I think I want an attorney present before we go any further." I folded my arms across my chest—then had to grab my towel to keep it from falling. I resumed the pose, but the effect had been spoiled.

Wallachstein took a moment before answering. He glanced around the room as if looking again for a place to sit, then looked back at me. "Well, yes—I suppose we do owe you an apology for that. It was a mistake."

"Was it?" I demanded. "How come everything is always a mistake? Doesn't anybody around here do anything on purpose anymore?"

"Like the furniture?" he prompted.

"Yeah, like the furniture! That was on purpose." I shoved my chin out in what I hoped was a pugnacious expression. "You want me to pay for it? I have fifty thousand caseys."

He shook his head, held up a hand. "Don't bother. This room doesn't exist. Neither does the furniture. Neither do I. And, perhaps—neither do you. If you'll shut up and listen for a moment. . . ."

That brought me down. I shut up.

"The fact that you were detained against your will is unfortunate. I assume full responsibility. I gave an order and it was misinterpreted. I apologize. I can understand—and sympathize—with your reaction. In fact, it's something of a healthy sign. It indicates you have a side that is not only independent, but occasionally downright antisocial. For our purposes, those are valuable traits." He rubbed his chin thoughtfully and went on. "Now, as to your other questions: there was no hearing. You were never on trial. You were never charged. Do you understand?"

"Uh . . ." There was that question again. "Yes, sir. I do."

"Good. The paperwork has been destroyed. There's nothing on record to indicate that you committed a breach of security. Furthermore, I've placed on record a copy of your orders, which you received yesterday morning *in writing,* instructing you to report the information about the fourth Chtorran to the members of this conference, in whatever forum available. Do you understand?"

"Uh, yes, sir."

"Good. Now go get dressed. There's something else we have to talk about, and I'd prefer to do it a little more formally."

"Yes, sir." I retreated to the bathroom, downed a handful of Sober-Ups and pulled on my clothes. It was while I was running a brush through my hair that I overheard raised voices. One of them was Lizard's.

She was saying, "—still disagree. It isn't fair."

"It's a fact of life, Major! We're all expendable." I didn't recognize the voice. Mr. Darkfellow?

"That's not the point! It's this particular operation! It's slimy!"

"It's *necessary!* We've been forced by circumstance. The decision has already been made—"

And then, suddenly, there was silence—as if someone had realized how loud they were all getting and had hushed them. I frowned at myself in the mirror. What the hell was going on now? What kind of rabbit hole was I falling into this time?

I clipped my hair in the back, splashed some more water on my face, toweled carefully, counted to ten and came back into the room.

Only Wallachstein was left. The others were gone. Lizard. The Japanese lady. Mr. Darkfellow.

Wallachstein said, "I asked them to leave. It was getting a little loud."

"Something you didn't want me to hear?"

"Perhaps. I have a job to offer you. It's rather dangerous. But I think you're qualified for it."

"Why?" I asked.

"Because you're one of the few personnel around who has both a scientific background and first-hand experience with Chtorrans in the field."

"What's the job?"

"I want to put you into the Chtorran Control Section of the Agency."

"I thought that's where I was already."

He shook his head. "That's not a permanent operation. It's only a temporary holding of the line while we try to figure out what we're really up against. We're putting together something a little more *responsible*. You'll do pretty much what you were doing up at Alpha Bravo—searching out and destroying pockets of infestation. The only difference is that we'll be using the team to develop methods of capturing Chtorrans alive—if we can. The only live specimen we have to date may be an atypical example. You've seen it, I've heard."

I nodded.

"So how does that sound to you, McCarthy?"

I shrugged. "It's not exactly what I had in mind. I want to be attached to the Science Center here. I want to finish what I started with those specimens."

Wallachstein shrugged it away. "Don't bother. Let one of Molly's button-pushers play with that stuff. We find those things every time we find a hut. The only reason we still collect them is to keep Dr. Partridge's section so busy they can't get into trouble anywhere else. So far, it works. We keep a man in her section to keep us posted if anything interesting comes in. I believe you met him. By the way, that was a nice piece of work, figuring out that the Chtorrans live under a red sun."

"Thank you. But the job isn't finished."

He shook his head. "It's unimportant. Those specimens are unimportant."

"Huh? Then why were we flown in on a priority flight?"

"You figure it out. What did you deliver?"

"Millipedes. Plants. Scrapings—"

"Worthless. We've got specimens."

"—Chtorran eggs!"

"Mm hm. Maybe. We'll know when they hatch." Wallachstein was unimpressed. "What else? What did you bring in worth fifty thousand caseys?"

"Oh!" The lockbox. "The memory clip."

Wallachstein nodded. "All that other stuff was just a cover. To tell the truth, I wish you'd left it behind."

"Huh? Why?"

"Look around—you see this city? It looks like it survived, right? Wrong. It's too big. It's not supportable. We don't have the people. It's just a matter of time until it breaks down."

"I thought the government wanted to bring the people back into the cities."

"It does. But militarily, it's not a good idea. What if we have another plague? We lose everything all over again. We can't risk it. No, we're more convinced than ever of our need to decentralize, especially our labs. I want every unit in the country to be studying the Chtorrans independently. We'll have the network fully reestablished by the end of next month, so you'll be in full communication with everyone else's work at the same time. I can offer you that. You'll be in communication with some of our best brains."

"I don't understand this," I said. "This afternoon I was nothing but a pain in the ass to you. An embarrassment. What changed?"

"We figured out how to make an asset of a liability, that's all."

"Oh?"

He smiled gently. "You're not stupid, McCarthy. Not when you sit down with a terminal. But sometimes you don't see what's in front of your own face. I'd have thought you'd have figured it out by now."

"Well, I haven't."

"It's like this. You are uniquely valuable. You know something that nobody else does. You know that there are sometimes four Chtorrans in a nest."

"But nobody believes me."

"I do," he said. "And so do a lot of other people. Some very important people."

"Huh?"

"That memory clip. You were wearing a helmet, remember?"

It took a second for me to realize what he was talking about. "But— Obama said the clip glitched."

"She was protecting you. She didn't know if it was important or not. She couldn't assess the impact by herself. So she passed it by a nonstandard channel. You carried it yourself."

"You've seen it—?"

He nodded. "All of us. And the inquest. It's pretty scary stuff."

For a moment, I couldn't catch my breath.

"Are you all right?"

"No," I said. I looked at him. I could feel my heart pounding. "I need to know. What did that clip show? Did I . . . screw up? I mean —could I have saved Shorty?"

He said it quietly. "Yes."

I felt as if I'd been slammed by a wall of guilt. I sank to the floor, to my knees. I was hurting too hard to cry. I put my hands on the rug to hold myself up. I felt like I was falling. My head was burning and I was trapped inside it. I wanted to puke. My stomach jerked and heaved. I wanted to die—

I came to with my head in Wallachstein's lap, crying. He was patting my face gently with a cool, damp towel. When he saw my eyes were open, he put the towel down. He stroked my hair gently. "How are you feeling, son?"

"Shitty." The tears were still rolling down my cheeks.

"Good. That's what you should be feeling." He kept stroking my hair. I was willing to lie there and let him. It didn't seem odd at all.

"I want to go home," I said. "I want this thing over! I don't want it this way!" I was crying again. "I want my mommy to tell me everything is going to be all right again!"

"Yeah," said Wallachstein. "Me too."

And then I started laughing. It hurt too much to cry anymore. All I could do was laugh.

And cry.

And then laugh some more.

Wallachstein mopped my face with the wet towel again. "How are you feeling now?"

"Better. Thank you." I realized how odd this scene must look and I felt uncomfortable. I tried to get up. He pushed me back down into his lap. "Stay. I want to talk to you."

"Yes, sir." I let myself stay.

"We've known that there's been something happening with the Chtorrans for seven or eight weeks now. We started losing teams and we had no idea why—just that they'd go out to handle a nest and they wouldn't come back.

"We had some guesses but no proof, so we sent out teams with cameras and radios. We lost two of them and still didn't know any more. Your team is the first one that returned. Your clip is the answer we needed. We've already found two more huts with four Chtorrans in them. Both have been neutralized. We're already changing our procedures. You saved a lot of lives."

"I wish somebody had told me some of this before."

Wallachstein patted my forehead with the towel again. "I think you'd better review your actions since you arrived and answer that one yourself. We weren't sure what kind of bozos you and your friend were. We're still not sure about your friend, but he's keeping himself busy and out of the way, and I suppose I should be thankful for that much at least. Eventually I'll find something for him, something where he can't get into too much trouble."

I let it all sink in. It didn't change anything. "I still didn't save Shorty."

"That's right. He's still dead." Wallachstein added, "And likely to remain that way."

I sat up and looked at him. "That's pretty callous."

"I suppose it looks like that. Jim, whether you could have saved him or not, does it make a difference anymore?"

"No, I suppose not."

"Good. Real good," he said. "Fromkin was right about you."

"Fromkin?"

"What do you think that interview was about? I wanted to know what your feelings were about killing Chtorrans, and how candid I could be with you."

"What did he say?"

"He said I should tell you the whole truth and nothing but. He said you'd be difficult about it too."

"Am I?"

"Yep." He grinned. "Now, do you want the job?"

"I don't know. I'll still be on the front lines, won't I?"

"There's a commission involved."

"How high?"

"Second lieutenant."

"You're kidding."

"I wish I were. But only officers can be cleared for Chtorran security. So if we want to add a member to the team, we have to make him an officer."

"Can't I stay 'Civilian Personnel, Attached'?"

He shook his head. "No nonmilitary personnel are going to be allowed access to the Control Arm's operations. So what's your choice?"

"Can I have some time to think it over?"

"I need your answer tonight. That's why we were late getting back to you. We had some decisions to make. Some of them were triggered by the events this afternoon. And you're a part of those decisions too. I had to twist some arms to bring you aboard. Now, either take it or leave it."

"What if I leave it? Then what?"

"I don't know. We'll find something to do with you. I promise, you won't like it."

"So I don't really have a choice, do I?"

He looked annoyed and apologetic, both at once. "Son, I don't have time to play games. There's a war on. Do you want to be a part of it or not?"

I looked into his face. "Yes, I do—it's just that I'm not used to straight answers, so you'll understand if I'm a little skeptical."

He didn't answer that. He said, "You'll take the job?"

"Will you make me a first lieutenant?"

He blinked. Then he laughed. "Don't push too hard. I'll go for first. I won't go as high as captain." He looked around. "Did you throw the Bible out too? No—there it is. Stand up. Raise your right hand. Repeat after me—"

THIRTY-TWO

I ENDED up with a rifle in my hands and a feeling of *déjà vu*.

The rifle was an AM-280 with tunable laser sight. The output was set high in the UV and I had to wear an EV-helmet with retinal-focused eyepieces to see the beam. It spat high-velocity bursts of eighteen-grain needles, as many as three thousand per second. You pointed the beam at your target and pulled the trigger. The needle bursts would tear holes in a steel door. They said you could slice a man in half with a 280. I didn't want to try.

I hefted the rifle and looked at it. I had a sour feeling in my stomach. I'd trusted Duke and Obama and ended up with a torch in my hands and Shorty on the receiving end. It'd left me with a bad feeling about weapons. I could admire the technology here. It was the use which bothered me.

The lieutenant slid two boxes across the counter toward me. "Sign here that you've received the rifle and ammo."

I held up a finger. "Wait a minute. Who's supposed to check me out on this?"

"I don't know anything about that."

"Then I'm not signing for it."

"Have it your own way." He shrugged and started to turn away.

"Hold it. Is that phone secure?"

"You can't use it."

"Slide it over here. This is company business."

He started to say something else, then thought better of it. He pushed the phone at me. I slid my card into it and punched the number Wallachstein had given me.

The line beeped as it switched to code mode and Wallachstein came on the line, "Joe's Deli. Joe ain't here."

"Uncle Ira?"

"Speaking."

"I've got a problem."

"Tell me about it."

"I'm not taking this weapon."

"Why not?"

"Nobody seems to know who's responsible for checking me out on it."

"Don't worry about it—"

"I am worried about it."

"—you're not going to have to use it. It's for show."

"I'm sorry, sir, but that's not good enough."

"Look, son, I don't have anyone free to check you out on that piece before this afternoon. All I want you to do is stand there and look like a soldier. I'll see that you have a thorough course of instruction in it before the week is out."

I started to protest. Instead, I said, "May I have that in writing, sir?"

There was silence from the other end of the line. Then he said slowly, "What's the matter, son?"

"Nothing, sir. But it's like I told you last night. I'm not taking anybody's word for anything anymore."

He sighed. I could almost see the expression on his face. I wondered if I'd overstepped myself. He said, "I'll put it in your file. You can check it yourself this afternoon."

"Thank you."

"Right." He signed off.

I hung up the phone and turned back to the lieutenant. "Have you got a manual for this thing?"

He looked sour. "Yeah. Somewhere. Wait a minute." He disappeared into the back and came back with a thin booklet which he tossed onto the counter. "Anything else?"

"No, thanks." I put the book in the rifle case along with the two boxes of clips, and closed it. I signed the receipt and picked up the helmet.

As I turned to leave, the lieutenant said, "You know something? I don't believe you're a lieutenant any more than I believe any of the other stories I've heard about you."

I met his gaze. "I really don't care. What you believe is none of my business."

I went outside and tossed the rifle and helmet into the trunk of the car and locked it. Instead of going back to my barracks, I pulled the base map out of the glove compartment and looked for the practice range. There it was, on the far north end of the camp. It took ten minutes to get there—I had to take the long way around.

There was no one there when I arrived. Good. I wanted privacy. I unpacked the rifle and sat down in the car with it across my lap while I read the manual. I locked both safeties, and practiced loading and unloading it. An empty magazine would be automatically ejected. A full one could be snapped into place as easily as inserting a memory clip into a recorder. Good.

Now, how did the laser sight work?

According to the manual, the laser randomly retuned itself every ten-thousandth of a second to a different point in the spectrum, but always beyond the range of visible light. The laser would fire its microsecond bursts at randomly computed intervals. There was no regularity either in the frequency of the beam output or in its frame rate. Only an EV-helmet, when it was plugged into the rifle, could track the myriad infinitesimal packets of coherent light. The wearer would see the laser as a steady beam. No one else—goggled or otherwise—would see anything at all, except perhaps an occasional subliminal flash. The idea was to prevent enemy snipers from homing in on the human end of the beam. Without sophisticated equipment, tracking it was impossible.

Next I tried on the helmet.

It was like looking into hell. I was staring into a *glowy*, ethereal-looking world, colored all in shades of red and gray. The helmet sensors scanned the spectrum from beyond ultraviolet to below infra-red, then the image was digitized and new color values were assigned; the resynthesized image was projected directly onto the retina. Clever. But it hurt my eyes. It would take some getting used to.

I retuned the color spectrum and lowered the brightness of the image. Now the scene was multichromed, but individual objects were not. Every building, tree, car, or whatever, was painted only in shades of one dominant color—pink or green or blue. The horizon and distant landscape appeared as layers of purple and gray while closer objects stood out in translucent, almost glowing pastels. They seemed to float against the dingy background. There were no shadows.

It was an eerie and compelling kind of imagery. The world was both familiar and surreal. I could identify objects, I could see them in better detail than I could with the unaided eye, but at the same time, everything had a shimmering aura in this ghostly twilight landscape.

I looked at my hands; they were pale, shading almost to green. In fact, my whole body looked green. Would all human beings look this color?

I got out of the car and turned around slowly, examining the world around me as if I'd never seen it before. And in this sense, I never had. Finally, and with a definite sense of regret, I went back to the car for the rifle.

I connected the helmet-control wire to the stock of the weapon and switched the laser on.

Nothing.

No beam.

I switched it off. I took off the helmet. I reset the laser for standard operation. I switched it on. A bright red beam stabbed across the practice field.

Great. The laser worked.

I reset it for coded operation and put the helmet back on.

Nothing.

I took off the helmet and double-checked its batteries and all connections. They appeared to be in order. I double-checked the connection to the rifle. Again correct. Hm. I put the helmet back on, waited for the image to solidify and turned on the beam again. If it was working, you couldn't prove it by this helmet.

I switched everything off and went back to the manual. It took only a few minutes to find the appropriate section. In large block letters, it said: "IMPORTANT: BE SURE THAT THE SETTING OF THE CODE KEYS IN YOUR HELMET IS IDENTICAL TO THE SETTING OF THE CODE KEYS IN YOUR WEAPON."

It took a few minutes to find the section on the code keys—there were matching panels on both the helmet and the rifle. The laser sent a control pulse to the helmet every time it fired. Both the rifle and the helmet had identical random-number generators, but if they weren't starting from the same seed—the setting of the code keys—the helmet wouldn't track with the laser as it continually retuned itself every ten-thousandth of a second.

You could use the weapon without its laser sight, but with nowhere near the same kind of accuracy.

I reset the code keys on both helmet and rifle and put the helmet on again. Once again, I stood at the center of a surreal world: a landscape of gray, populated with glowing pastel trees and buildings. But this time, when I switched on the laser, the beam appeared as a luminescent bar that seemed to be all colors at once: pink, green, white, blue, yellow, red—it flickered through the spectrum faster than the eye could identify individual hues. I saw only the afterimages as they blurred into each other, and the effect was the perception of colors that I'd never seen before. They were intense and glorious. The beam sliced across the nacreous landscape like a razor. I wrote my name across the sky with it, and I could see the afterimage as a shimmering blur. Was that my eyes or the sensors or something in the digitizing process? No matter, it was eerily beautiful.

You could easily become addicted to this other-worldly sense of perception. It was very distracting.

Finally, I stopped. I couldn't stall any longer. I loaded a clip into the rifle and switched off both the safeties. I touched the beam to one of the haystacks on the other side of the field. I pulled the trigger.

Someone kicked my arm and the haystack exploded.

I locked both the safeties on and flipped the goggles of the helmet up.

Yes, the haystack had exploded.

The AM-280 was supposed to be recoilless, but it wasn't. No gun is ever completely recoilless. You have to be careful with repeating weapons because they'll "walk up" on you. That's what had happened to me here. Instead of punching a hole in the haystack, I had sliced it vertically upwards.

I flipped the goggles back down, switched off the safeties and blew up another haystack. It took three more tries before I could control the weapon well enough to just punch holes in them. The trick was to focus on the end of the beam and lean into the action of the rifle to steer it. I sliced up the last two haystacks, just to see if the rifle could be used as an axe. It could. Good.

Maybe I could even cut a Chtorran in half with it.

Except I didn't know if I was looking forward to that opportunity or not.

I went back to the car and put the gun back into the case and locked it in the trunk, the helmet too. I drove back to the barracks feeling curiously happy. As if I'd proven something to myself, although I wasn't sure what.

THIRTY-THREE

THERE WAS a box on the bed when I came in. Inside was a uniform, with appropriate insignia. Only one. There were supposed to be two. Typical army efficiency—half the job is always done on time. I took it out and looked at it. Something was giving me a vaguely uneasy feeling—and it wasn't just the aftereffects of last night's booze. I'd thrown up most of that before it had gotten into my bloodstream, and the Sober-Ups had neutralized the rest before it could do any real damage. No, this was something else, but I couldn't put my finger on it. I just knew that I wouldn't feel quite right wearing this uniform. It had come . . . too easily.

Still pondering, I hung it up in the closet.

I was in the shower when Ted staggered in. He didn't even take off his clothes; he just stepped into the shower with me and held his head under the spray.

"Good morning," I said.

"Oh," he said. "Is it morning?"

"For a little while longer anyway." I pulled him away from the shower head so I could rinse off. He sagged against the wall.

"What day is it?" he asked.

"Sunday."

"Of what year?"

"Same one." I got out of the shower and grabbed a towel. I didn't particularly want to talk to Ted right now.

I was half-dressed when he sloshed out of the bathroom after me. "Hey, Jim—" he began.

"Eh?"

"I'm sorry I wasn't here yesterday. Or last night. Or this morning. Things just got away from me, that's all."

"Oh?"

He must have sensed my coolness. "Look, you've got to understand —I was doing it for us, trying to make some connections! And I did! I didn't even see any of the sessions yesterday."

"Oh?" Then he must have missed the scene in the conference hall. I didn't ask.

"No. I was scouting."

"I'm sure."

"Listen, it paid off! I've been offered a commission in the Telepathy Corps. I go in for my operation on Wednesday. I'll be getting one of the new multiband implants."

"Oh, terrific."

"It is, Jim!" He grabbed my shoulders. "Before the plagues, it would have taken an Act of God—or at least an Act of Congress—to get into the corps. Now they're so desperate, they're even willing to waive the psychological requirements."

"I can see that."

"No, you know what I mean."

Yes, I did. "What else did you do for *us?*"

"I'm sorry, Jim. I did speak up for you, but you weren't qualified. I've got the electronic-language background. And I can travel."

I pulled away from him and went to the closet.

"But listen to me—that's not all. Remember that Chtorran that we heard about, the live one that they captured?"

"Yeah . . . ?"

"Well, I got to see him last night. He's amazing!"

"Oh . . . ?"

"Yeah—I met that girl you were talking about, Jillanna! You were right. She's really something! That's why I wasn't here last night. I spent the night with her. She's with the project, and she got me in to see him. Really extraordinary. It was feeding time, and—"

"Ted! *Stop!*"

"Huh?"

"I don't want to hear about it, okay?"

He looked at me confusedly. "You're sure?"

"I'm sure."

He peered at me. "Are you all right?"

"I'm fine."

"Are you upset because I didn't come looking for you so you could see it too?"

"No, I'm not."

"—because if that's what it is, Jimbo, I'm sorry, but this was an invitation only for one. If you know what I mean."

I pulled away from him and started getting dressed.

He said, "Hey—you'll get your chance. They're going to show it to the conference this afternoon! They're trucking it over to the hotel right now."

I ignored him. I opened the closet door.

"Hey!" said Ted. "Terrific! They've already delivered my uniform! Great!" I stepped back and he pulled it off its hanger. "How do I look? Lieutenant Theodore Andrew Nathaniel Jackson?"

"Uh—" I didn't say it. I closed my mouth and went back into the bathroom to get a hairbrush instead.

"Oh, come on, Jim—don't be a spoilsport! Say congratulations!"

"Congratulations."

"Like you *mean* it!" he wailed.

"Sorry, I can't do that. I am not going to sleep better tonight, knowing that you are helping to defend America."

"Well, then that's your problem."

"Don't slam the door on your way out," I said.

He didn't.

"Shit," I said.

THIRTY-FOUR

"IS THAT thing armed?"

I looked up. The speaker was another one of those cranky-looking officers I had been running into ever since getting off the chopper.

"Yes, sir. It is."

"By whose authority?"

"Special Forces."

He shook his head. "Sorry, soldier. Not here. This operation is regular army." Somehow, the way he said it, he meant the *real* army.

I looked at his bars. "Major," I said, "I was given orders to stand right here and wear this helmet and carry this rifle. I was told to do this because there is a large, purple and red, man-eating caterpillar in the cage under that curtain. The theory is that if that creature should somehow break loose, I'm supposed to stop it."

The major put his arm around my shoulder and led me off to a corner of the stage. The curtain was still closed. "Son—" he started to say warmly.

"Don't call me 'son.' I'm an officer."

"Lieutenant," he said stiffly, "don't be an asshole. I want you off this stage—and the other jerk-off too." He pointed to the rifleman on the other side of the stage. I hadn't exchanged more than two words with him. All I knew about him was that his name was Scott and he stuttered.

"I'm sorry, sir. I can't do that."

"Listen to me, stupid. Under the terms of the conference charter, this is supposed to be an entirely civilian operation. The military is only to provide supplementary aid and keep a very low profile. I am *ordering* you off this stage."

"Yes, sir. Would you put that in writing, sir?"

He hesitated. Then he said, "Listen to me—the glass walls of that cage are laced with doped silicon monofibers. Do you honestly think that creature is likely to break through those panels?"

"It doesn't matter whether I think it's likely or not, sir. Would you put those orders in writing?"

"Who's your commanding officer?" he scowled.

I could have kissed him for asking. "Uncle Ira," I said.

"I see. . . ." He said it slowly. I could almost see the wheels turning in his head. "Those are his orders, then?"

"Yes, sir."

"Well"—he had to say something—"lock those safeties on. I don't want any accidents."

"Yes, sir."

"All right. Thank you. Resume your post."

I went back to the side of the cage. As soon as the major left the stage, I flicked the safeties off again.

A few minutes later, Dr. Zymph walked through. She took one look at me and another at the other lieutenant on the other side and frowned. She disappeared into the wings of the stage for a moment, and when she came back, she came straight toward me.

"Lieutenant?"

I flipped the goggles up. "Ma'am?"

Apparently she didn't recognize me from yesterday, not with the helmet on. Just as well. She said, "Would you mind standing in the wings where the audience can't see you?"

"I thought you said these things were dangerous."

"I did and they are. But I want you out of sight. Please?"

I thought about it. "Sure. No problem." I moved off. She went and spoke to Scott on the other side and he did likewise.

Dr. Zymph waved to an aide—it was Jerry Larson from Molly Partridge's office. I wondered what he was doing here. He gestured to someone else offstage and the stage lights shifted to a dimmer, redder color, and after a few tests with some sophisticated light sensors, Dr. Zymph was satisfied. She nodded to Larson and he and another aide began undraping the glass case with the Chtorran in it.

Without thinking, I flipped my goggles down over my eyes and switched the laser beam on. The red light of the stage turned gray. The beam appeared as an eerie bar of flickering luminescent color.

They were undraping the other side first, so I didn't see the Chtorran —only the reactions of those who were looking toward it. Their faces were pearly green. Their expressions were stiff. They looked like zombies. I wondered how the rest of the conference would react when the main curtain went up. And then the last of the drape came off the glass case on my side and I could see the Chtorran too. It was a bright silvery worm. Its color was *beautiful* in the adjusted image of the goggles. It *glowed*.

Almost instinctively, I brought the rifle barrel up. The flickery beam played across the Chtorran's soft fur. Immediately—as if it could *sense* the beam, somehow—it turned to look at me. Its great lidless eyes focused on me with dispassionate interest. The same look it had given the dogs.

Was this the last thing Shorty had seen?

I lowered the beam. I didn't know if the creature could sense it or not, but I didn't want to irritate it. The Chtorran continued to study me. It unfolded its arms and pressed them against the glass. Then it moved forward and pressed its face—if you could call it a face—against the cold surface. Was it tasting?

It slid even further forward then, lifting a third of its bulk up the side of the cage. It leaned on the glass. The frame creaked ominously.

"Don't worry, it'll hold," someone behind me said. I didn't turn to look. I just brought the beam back up and held it on the Chtorran's belly until it slid back down again.

"Trrlll . . ." it said.

Dr. Zymph walked up to the cage then, ignoring the Chtorran, and bent to inspect the front of the platform supporting it. She looked worried. She lifted the edge of the dust ruffle and peered at the supports. She called Larson over and the two of them bent together to look. "I thought I heard it creak," she said. "Does that look correct to you?"

He nodded. "We're okay." He looked at his watch. "You'd better get started."

"Right." She stood up then. "Everybody please clear the stage." She raised her voice and repeated the command. "If you're not wearing a red badge, you're not authorized to be here." She came over to my side of the stage and peeked out through the edge of the curtain. She nodded, satisfied.

"Counting the house?" I asked.

"Eh?" She looked at me, as if surprised I could speak. "Just checking the seating arrangements." She picked up her clipboard from the stand where she'd left it, gave a thumbs-up signal to Larson on the opposite side of the stage and stepped out in front of the curtain.

They must have hit her with a spotlight then, because I could see it from this side as a bright spot shimmering in the folds of cloth. Her shadow was a silhouette in the center. She switched on her microphone and began to speak. We could hear her clearly backstage. "I don't suppose I have to make much of an introduction this afternoon, even though this is something of an unscheduled event. But after the, ah, heated discussions of yesterday as to just how *dangerous* the gastropedes may be, we thought it best to bring our one live specimen out for display and let you judge for yourselves."

The Chtorran was looking at me again. I wished it would turn around and look at the fellow on the other side. He was meatier than I.

"Now, before we open the curtain, I want to caution all of you against taking any flash pictures—and we also request that you please try to be as quiet as possible. We're going to bring the lights all the way down and put a spotlight on the gastropede. We're not sure how it will react to a large audience, so we're going to keep it dazzled by the light. For this reason, it's imperative that you not make any unnecessary sounds."

The Chtorran was fascinated by Dr. Zymph's voice. It kept cocking its eyes back and forth, trying to locate the source of the sound. If it had any external ears, I couldn't see them. I wondered if that suggested a higher-density atmosphere. That would certainly go with a heavier gravity. Sound waves would be more intense—experientially louder. The creature's ears could be a lot smaller. But would its hearing be better or worse on Earth? Or maybe it didn't need ears. Maybe it could hear with its whole body. Maybe it could even *see* with its whole body.

"All right, now—" Dr. Zymph was saying, "—remember to keep very very quiet. Can I have the curtain opened, please?"

It slid open like the doorway to a hangar. A single pink shaft of light streamed directly in, widening as the curtain opened. The Chtorran turned to look at it. I could hear gasps from the darkness beyond.

Dr. Zymph didn't say anything. The Chtorran's presence was statement enough. It unfolded its arms and began exploring the front surface of the cage, as if trying to reach the light.

I touched the contrast knob on my helmet and the shaft of the spotlight faded. The audience appeared beyond it in a dim green gloom. I

turned the knob another klick and the bright parts of the image faded
further; the darker areas brightened again. I could see the whole auditorium now. The audience was very upset and restless. I could see them
whispering excitedly to one another. I could hear them rustling in their
seats.

The Chtorran slid forward, lifting the forward third of its body up
against the glass. I heard sudden gasps. The creature must have heard
them too—it hesitated and stared, trying to focus on the space beyond
the light. It remained poised in that position. This was the third time I
had seen a Chtorran reared up like that; what did the position mean in
Chtorran body language? Was it a challenge? Or a prelude to attack?

I looked at the audience again. I could pick out faces in the first few
rows. There was Lizard, sitting at the far end of the front row. I didn't
recognize the fellow with her; he looked like the same colonel I had seen
her with the day before. Next to him was Fromkin, wearing another of
those silly-looking, old-fashioned frilly shirts. All of them looked odd,
painted in shades of pale green. While I watched, an aide came up to
Lizard and bent to whisper something to her. She nodded and got up.
The colonel got up with her. Fromkin waited a moment longer, then
followed them off to the side of the auditorium. I knew that exit. That
was the door Wallachstein had hustled me through.

The Chtorran slid down from the glass then. It turned around in its
cage, exploring the length and breadth with its oddly delicate hands. It
looked at me, and then it turned and looked at the guard on the other
side. Did it understand why we were here? It must have. It brought its
gaze back to me again. I was afraid to look it in the eye. It turned to
study the audience. It peered out through the spotlight, blinking. It
blinked and blinked again. I couldn't hear the *sput-phwut* through the
glass. It kept blinking and I wondered what it was doing. It looked as if
its eyes were shrinking. It peered out at the audience again and this time
it acted as if it could see them through the spotlight.

There were other empty seats in the auditorium now, most of them
near the ends of rows. I didn't see anyone else I knew, only a couple
that I recognized. There was that constipated fellow Ted had been talking to. And Jillanna. Was it my imagination, or was her face shining a
little brighter than those of the people around her?

The Chtorran slid forward again, this time with a more deliberate
motion. It slid forward and forward, lifting more than half its length up
against the front of the glass. I held my beam directed against its side.

In the audience, a couple of people were standing nervously, pointing. A few were even backing up the aisles. I wondered how close we were to panic. Dr. Zymph's silent presentation was more effectively terrifying the members of the conference than anything else she could have done. A movement caught my eye. Dr. Zymph was picking up her clipboard and stepping back away from her podium. Was she pointing to someone on the opposite side of the stage—?

I heard the *cra-a-ack* of the glass before I knew what it was.

I turned in time to see the Chtorran falling forward through a shower of glass fragments. They glittered around it like tiny sparkling stars. In one smooth movement, it poured through the glass and flowed down off the stage and into the shrieking audience. It hit the front rows like an avalanche.

I sliced my beam across to follow—hesitated half a second as I realized I'd be shooting into a crowded auditorium—then pulled the trigger anyway.

The Chtorran reared up, a struggling woman in its mouth. It dropped her and whirled around—I could see that there were several other people pinned beneath it. I fired again. Where the beam touched its side, I was digging out great gouts of flesh—but I wasn't even slowing it down! I couldn't tell if the other rifleman's beam was working or not—I didn't think so. I could see that he was firing too—there was a line of bloody black divots across the Chtorran's silver back, but it was ragged and uneven. He was having no more effect than I was. The Chtorran whirled and swung and pounced. It rose and fell and rose again, its eyes swiveling this way and that, its maw working like a machine. Even from this distance, I could see the blood spurting. The creature raised up high again, another victim in its mouth. The other rifleman dropped his gun and ran.

The auditorium was a screaming madhouse now. The green-lit mannequins streamed toward the exits. The crowds were piling up at the doors in great knots of struggling bodies, jamming and trampling. The Chtorran noticed them; its eyes angled first one way and then the other. It dropped the body it was holding in its maw and *moved.* The Chtorran leaped across the rows to land among the screaming people, flattening them to the floor or pinning them against their seats. It *flowed* up the aisle. It picked the people up and threw them, or pounced upon them as it had the dogs—but it wasn't eating! It was in a killing frenzy!

I didn't know what I was doing. I ran forward, dropping off the edge of the stage—almost losing my balance—catching myself and racing toward that silver horror. I angled the blue-white-crimson beam at it and pulled the trigger, pulled the trigger—trying to slash a line across the Chtorran's flesh, trying to carve the beast in half. There were people lying all around it. Most were motionless. A few were trying to crawl. I stopped worrying if they were in my line of fire. It didn't matter. Their only hope was if I could stop this creature quickly.

I skidded on something wet and sprawled sideways. I could see my beam slicing sideways across the wall—*Oh, God! This is it!* But the Chtorran wasn't even turned toward me. Yet.

I scrambled back to my feet. The Chtorran was terrifyingly close. It had swung around and was working its way back down the aisle again. I saw now, in dreadful clarity, exactly how it killed. It raised the forward part of its body high and brought it directly down upon its victim —this time, a member of the Chinese delegation, a slender young man —no, a girl! She couldn't have been more than sixteen. The creature pinned the screaming girl to the floor with its gnashing maw; then, holding her down with its black, peculiarly double-jointed arms, it tried to pull away—but its mouth was like a millipede's, with rows and rows of inward curving teeth. It couldn't stop eating! It couldn't stop chewing something once it started—not unless the object was deliberately pulled out of its mouth! That's why the creature held the bodies down when it backed away—so it could pull free.

The effect was to rend the body as thoroughly as if it had been pulled apart by a threshing machine. The Chinese girl screamed and jerked and twitched and then was still. The Chtorran lifted up then and began to turn—and I could see that there were human entrails hanging from its mouth. There were bodies on the floor around it—they were badly ripped and mauled. They had died horribly.

I touched my beam to the creature's shoulder. The arms were anchored against a hump on its back. If I could keep it from holding the people down, it wouldn't have the leverage to pull back and free. It would be stuck with the one victim! I squeezed the trigger hard and dug gobbets out of the Chtorran's silver body. But the hideous arms kept moving! And the creature started swiveling toward me—

I kept firing! The Chtorran's side was an exploding mass of flesh. Suddenly the arm collapsed—the limb fell useless, hanging and waving. It jerked and twitched erratically and black blood spurted from the wound. In the hellish view of the helmet, I could see the steam as pinkish vapor rising from its silver body. The rest of the world was a gray and green and orange backdrop to this horror.

I couldn't see the other arm to shoot at it; the Chtorran's body blocked my shot. I touched the beam to its eyes and squeezed the trigger! Again and again! The rifle dug against my shoulder as it shrieked, as it roared. One of the Chtorran's eyes disappeared, replaced by a bloody hole. The whole mound of flesh burst like jelly.

The Chtorran raised up then, up and up and up, revealing its darker mottled belly—was it going to throw itself at me?—and then it screamed! An agonizing, high-pitched howl of rage! *"Chtorrrrr! Chtorr-rrrr!"* Without thinking, I skittered back, my feet slipping on the bloody carpeting of the auditorium. A row of seats had been broken from their anchors by the weight of the creature and there were people from the row behind pinned under them. The monster didn't notice. It broke its scream and focused. It looked at me and *knew.* For one single terrifying instant the two of us—human and Chtorran—shared a communication that transcended words! I knew it like a shout of rage and pain: *Kill!*

The moment broke.

And then it came toward me. It arched its body forward and poured itself across the seats, flowing toward me like a river of teeth.

I stabbed the beam into its other eye and fired—tried to fire. Nothing happened—out of ammo—the empty clip popped up and out and clattered on the floor. I fumbled with a second magazine, sliding it into place even as I kept moving backward. When I squeezed again, the creature's other eye exploded in a vaporous cloud.

It didn't slow the creature down! Even blind, the Chtorran could still sense its prey! Did it smell my terror? I was screaming now, a wordless rage of profanity, a wall of obscene fury that I flung against the horror! I had moved beyond my terror, was in a state where every action happened in slow motion, so slowly I could see the spurt of every droplet, the flex of every muscle, but even so could not move fast enough to escape the charging death.

The Chtorran reared again, and this time it was close enough to strike. I stabbed the beam into its mouth and carved it into bloody jelly. I squeezed the trigger hard and dug a screaming gory line straight down the monster's front and up again. The silver fur was streaked with red and black.

The Chtorran towered over me, shuddering with each punch of needles from the rifle, one arm hanging useless, the other grabbing, clutching frantically—its eyes were scarlet pudding, its mouth was twitching teeth—

Somewhere in that jerking mass of flesh, there was a brain, a control center—something! I squeezed again and the second empty clip popped up. I grabbed my belt for another magazine—

—and then the Chtorran toppled forward onto me and I went out.

THIRTY-FIVE

SOMEBODY WAS calling me.

Uh uh. Go away.

"Come on, Jim. Time to wake up."

No, leave me alone.

She was shaking my shoulder. "Come on, Jim."

"Leemea lone—"

"Come on, Jim."

"What're you want—?"

She kept shaking mc. "Come on, Jim."

I went to brush her hand away. I couldn't move my hand. "What do you want, goddammit?"

"Come on, Jim."

I couldn't move my arm! "I can't move my arm!"

"You're connected to an IV. If you promise not to pull it loose, I'll untie your arm."

"I can't move my arm—!"

"Do you promise not to pull the IV out?"

"Untie me!"

"I can't do that, Jim. Not until you promise."

"Yes, yes, I promise!" I knew that voice. Who was she? "Just untie me!"

Somebody was doing something to my arm. And then it was free. I could move it around. "Why did you wake me up?"

"Because you have to wake up."

"No, I don't. Leave me alone."

"Uh uh. I have to stay with you."

"No, I want to be dead again. The Chtorran killed me—"

"No, he didn't. You killed him."

"No. I want to be dead. Like everybody else."

"No, you don't, Jim. Ted wouldn't like it."

"Ted's an asshole. He isn't even here." I wondered where here was. I wondered who I was talking to. She was holding my hand. "I want to be dead too. Everybody else gets to be dead—why can't I?"

"Because once you're dead, you can't change your mind about it."

"I don't want to change my mind. Being dead can't be all that bad. Nobody who was dead ever complained about it, did they? Like Shorty. Shorty's dead. He was my best friend—and I didn't even know him. And my dad. And Marcie's dog. And the little girl. Oh, God"—I started to cry then—"we shot a little girl! I was there, I saw it! And Dr. Obama—she told me it was all right! But it wasn't! That's all bullshit! She's still dead! We didn't even try to save her! And I didn't see any Chtorrans! Everybody else said there were Chtorrans, but I didn't see any Chtorrans!" I wiped at my face, wiped the snot away from my nose. "I didn't believe in the Chtorrans. I never even saw the pictures. How was I to know?" The words bubbled up in my throat, tumbling out one after another. "I saw the Chtorran kill Shorty. I burned it. And I saw them feeding dogs to the Chtorran. Marcie's dog. I saw them bring the Chtorran onto the stage. Dr. Zymph checked the glass—oh, God—I saw it break. The Chtorran just boiled out into the auditorium. I saw the people running—I saw it—" I was choking on my own sobs now. She was holding my hand tight—

I wiped at my face again, but she was there with a tissue. I took it and mopped at my nose and eyes. Why was I crying, I wondered. And why was I saying all of this? "Don't go away!!" I said suddenly.

"I'm right here."

"Stay with me."

"It's all right, I'm right here."

"Who are you?"

"It's Dinnie."

"Dinnie? I don't know any Dinnie." Or did I? Why did the name sound familiar? "What's wrong with me?"

She patted my hand. "Nothing's wrong with you that won't get better. Are you through crying?"

I thought about it. "Yeah, I guess so."

"You going to open your eyes?"

"No."

"Okay. Don't."

I opened my eyes. Green. The ceiling was green. The room was small and dimly lit. A hospital? I blinked in confusion. "Where am I?"

"Reagan Memorial."

I turned my head to look at her. She wasn't as weird-looking as I remembered. She was still holding my hand. "Hi," I said.

"Hi," she said. "Feeling better?"

I nodded. "Why did you wake me up?"

"House rules. Anyone on pentothal has to be awakened when they come out of surgery, so we're sure they can handle their own breathing."

"Oh," I said. I was covered with blankets. I couldn't feel anything. "What happened?"

She looked unhappy. "The Chtorran killed twenty-three people. Fourteen more died in the panic. Thirty-four were injured, five of them critically. Two of those are not expected to live." She eyed me critically. "In case you're wondering, you will."

I started to ask, "Who—" But my voice cracked and I didn't finish the sentence.

" 'Who' what?"

"Who was killed?"

"They haven't released any names yet."

"Oh. So you don't know."

I couldn't fathom her expression. She looked oddly satisfied. "Well, I can tell you this—some of the Fourth World delegations are going to have to be restaffed. We've filled up two wings and the morgue with them. They were all sitting in the first five rows. And the worm threw himself across that whole section."

Something occurred to me then, but I didn't say it. Instead, I asked, "How did it get out?"

"They had the wrong kind of glass in the cage. They thought they had hundred-strength. It was only ten. There's going to be an investigation, but it looks like there was some kind of foul-up in supply. Nobody knew."

I tried to sit up and couldn't. I was strapped to the bed.

"Uh, don't," Dinnie said, putting her hand on my chest gently. "You've got five broken ribs and a punctured lung. You're lucky you didn't hit a major blood vessel. You were under that Chtorran for fifteen minutes before we got you out. You were on CPR maintenance for at least thirteen of those minutes."

"Who—?"

"Me. And you're lucky, buster, because I'm damned good at it. It's a good thing you took a step back before he fell on you, else I wouldn't have been able to reach your face with the mask—or your chest with the thumper. It took seven men to roll that Chtorran off. They wanted to flame it, but I wouldn't get out of the way. You can thank me later. They *weren't* too happy about it. Who have you got mad at you anyway? I never saw so many angry men with torches. But I don't abandon my patients. By the way, I think one of those broken ribs is mine. Don't ask. I couldn't be gentle. Oh, and you've also got a fractured kneecap. You were on the table five hours." She hesitated and then mouthed the words, "On purpose."

"Huh?"

She leaned over me to fluff my pillow, and as she did her mouth came very close to my ear. "Somebody didn't want me to save you," she whispered.

"Huh?"

"Sorry," she said out loud. "Here, let me fluff that better." Again, she whispered, "And they wanted to let you die on the table. But you're under medical protection here, and nobody's going to be allowed to see you without a nurse present. Me."

"Uh . . ." I shut my mouth.

Sitting back again, she said, "By the way, you may be a hero. Some of the doors in that room were jammed. No telling how many people that thing might have killed if you hadn't stopped it before the rest of the cavalry arrived."

"Oh." I remembered the Chtorran swinging around and starting toward me, and suddenly, I was nauseous—

Dinnie saw the look of alarm on my face, and was there with a basin almost immediately. My stomach lurched and my throat convulsed—and there were cold iron claws digging into my chest—

"Here!" She shoved a pillow into my arms, wrapped me around it so it splinted my abdomen and chest. "Hang onto that."

—nothing came up. I retched again, and then once more. Each time the pain dug into me again.

"Don't worry about your incision—you're well-glued. I did it myself. You won't splatter."

But the feeling had passed. The pain had blotted out the need to vomit.

I looked at Dinnie. She grinned back. And in that moment, I resented her all over again. For her presumption of such familiarity. And then I felt guilty for resenting her when I owed her so much. And then I resented her for making me feel guilty.

"How are you feeling now?"

I took inventory. "I feel like shit."

"Right. You look like it too." She got up then and went to the door and whistled. "Hey, Fido—!"

A ROVER unit trundled in then and wheeled up to the bed. She plucked a handful of sensors out of the basket on top—they looked like poker chips—and started sticking them to various points on my chest and forehead, neck and arms. "Three for EKG, three for EEG, two for pressure and pulse, two for the pathologist, one for accounting and an extra one for luck," she said, reciting the nurse's mnemonic.

"Accounting?" I asked.

"Sure. It automatically checks your credit rating while you're lying there, so we know how much to charge."

"Uh, yeah."

She turned to the ROVER unit and studied its screen. "Well, bad news for your enemies. You'll live. But a word of advice: next time you try to make love to a Chtorran, you be the boy. You're a lot safer on top."

She peeled off the sensors then and dropped them back into the basket. "I'll leave you now. Can you fall asleep by yourself, or do you want a buzz-box?"

I shook my head.

"Terrif. I'll be back with your breakfast."

And then I was alone again. With my thoughts. I had a lot to think about. But I fell asleep before I could sort things out.

THIRTY-SIX

I WAS back in Whitlaw's classroom.

I felt panicky. I hadn't studied for the test—I didn't even know there was to be one. And this was the final exam!

I looked around. There were people here I didn't know, but as I looked at them, their faces solidified into familiarity. Shorty, Duke, Ted, Lizard, Marcie, Colonel Wallachstein, the Japanese lady, the dark fellow, Dinnie, Dr. Fromkin, Paul Jastrow, Maggie, Tim, Mark—and Dad. And then a lot of other people I didn't recognize. A little too many.

Whitlaw was in front of the room, making sounds. They didn't make sense. I stood up and said so. He looked at me. They all looked at me. I was in the front of the classroom and Whitlaw was in my seat.

A little girl in a brown dress was sitting in the front row. Next to her, just sliding up, a gigantic orange and red Chtorran. He turned his blackeyed gaze to me and seemed to settle down to listen.

"C'mon, Jim!" Whitlaw hollered. "We're waiting!"

I was angry. I didn't know why. "All right," I said. "Listen, I know I'm a screwup and an asshole. That part is obvious. But, see, what I've been doing is assuming that the rest of you *aren't.* I mean, here I am listening to you people making noises like you know what you're doing, and I've been believing you! What an asshole I am! The truth is, you people don't know what you're doing either—not any more than I do— so what I'm telling you is that my experience is just as valid, or just as *in* valid, as yours. But whatever it is, it's my experience, and I'm the one who's going to be responsible for it."

They applauded. Whitlaw raised his hand. I pointed at him. He stood up. "It's about time," he said. He sat down.

"You're the worst, Whitlaw!" I said. "You're so good at pouring your bullshit into other people's heads that it keeps floating to the top for years afterward. I mean, you gave us all these great belief systems about how to live our lives and then when we tried to plug into them, they didn't work. All they did was create inappropriate behavior."

Whitlaw said, "You know better than that. I never gave you a belief system. What I gave you was the ability to be independent of a belief system, so you could deal with the facts as they happened to you."

"Yeah? So how come every time I try to do that, you come in and give me another lecture?"

Whitlaw said, "If you've been inviting me into your head and letting me run my lectures on you, that's *your* fault. It isn't me who's doing that. It's you. You're the one running those lectures. I'm dead, Jim. I've been dead for two years. You know that. So quit asking me for advice. You're living in a world I know nothing about. Quit asking me for advice and you'll be a helluva lot better off. Or ask me for advice, if it's advice you want—and if it isn't appropriate, then ignore it. Get this, asshole: advice isn't the same as orders; it's only another option for a person to consider. All it's supposed to do is widen your perspective on the thing you're looking at. Use it that way. But don't blame me if you don't know how to listen."

"Must you *always* be right?" I asked. "Sometimes it gets *awfully* annoying."

Whitlaw shrugged. "Sorry, son. But that's the way you keep creating me."

He was right. Again. He always would be. Because that was how I would always create him.

There were no other hands. "Then we're clear? I'm running this life from now on? Right."

I looked at the little girl in the brown dress. She didn't have a face. And then she did. It was Marcie's face . . . and Jillanna's face . . . and Lizard's face. . . .

I turned to the Chtorran. "I have some questions for you," I said.

It nodded its eyes, and then looked into my face again.

"Who are you?" I asked.

The Chtorran spoke in a voice like a whisper. "I don't know," it said. "Yet."

"What are you? Are you intelligent? Or what? Are you the invaders? Or the shock troops?"

Again the Chtorran said, "I don't know."

"What about the dome? Why was there a fourth Chtorran inside?"

The Chtorran waved its eyes from side to side, the Chtorran equivalent of a headshake. "I don't know," it said, and its voice was louder. Like the wind.

"How did you get here? Where are your spaceships?"

"I don't know!" it said. And it was roaring now.

"How can we talk to you—?"

"I DON'T KNOW!" And it was raising up in front of me as if to attack—

"I AM IN CHARGE HERE!" I bellowed right back at him. "AND I WANT SOME ANSWERS!"

"I DON'T KNOW!!" the Chtorran shrieked—and exploded into a thousand flaming pieces, destroying himself, destroying me, destroying the little girl sitting next to him, the classroom, Whitlaw, Shorty, all the people, everything—dropping it all into darkness. . . .

THIRTY-SEVEN

TED WAS sitting in the chair, looking at me. His head was bandaged.

"Did it get you too?" I asked.

"Did what get me?"

"The Chtorran. Your head is bandaged—did the Chtorran get you too?"

He grinned. "Jim, it's Wednesday. I just had my surgery this morning. They wouldn't let me in to see you before this."

"What surgery?" And then I remembered—"Oh!"—and came awake. "Wednesday?" I started to sit up, found I couldn't, and fell back into the bed. "Wednesday? Really?"

"Yup."

"Have I been unconscious for three days?"

"No more than usual," Ted said. "You know, with you it's hard to tell sometimes." Then, seeing my expression, he added, "You've been floating in and out. You've also been heavily drugged. So's most everybody else. They've had so many casualties to treat that they just plugged everybody into their beds and kept them on maintenance. You're one of the first to wake up. I had to pull a few strings to do that. I wanted to have a chance to see you—to say goodbye."

"Goodbye?"

He touched the bandage around his head. "See? I had my surgery. They did the implant. I'm in the Telepathy Corps now. My transfer became official when the implant went in."

"Is it working? Are you receiving?"

Ted shook his head. "Not yet. Not for a while. First I have to go through a two-week training to learn how to experience myself more intensely. But I'm already sending. They're continually recording me, calibrating my connections and storing my sense of self so I won't lose touch with who I really am, all that kind of stuff. It gets very complex. The training is designed to rehabilitate your ability to experience. Do you know we spend most of our lives being unconscious, Jim? Before you can be a telepath, you have to wake up—it's like having a bucket of ice water thrown in your face. But it's incredible!"

"I can see," I said guardedly. His eyes were bright. His face was shining. He looked like a man possessed with a vision.

He laughed then—at himself. "I know—it sounds *weird*. To be a telepath is a daring adventure, Jim—you have to surrender yourself to the network. But it opens up a whole new world!"

"Have you done any receiving yet?"

"Just a little. Just enough so they would know that the connections were in. Jim, I know this sounds stupid, but I've been doing the most *wonderful* things! I tasted vanilla ice cream! That is, somebody else tasted it, but I tasted it with her! And I kissed a redhead. And I smelled a flower. And I touched a kitten. And an ice cube! Have you ever really felt what *cold* is?"

I shook my head. I was startled by the change in Ted. What had they done to him? "Uh, why? What was the purpose?"

"To see if I could *experience* things," he explained. He said it quietly. "You know—like pressure, heat, cold, taste, smell, vision—all that stuff. Once it's certain that the incoming linkage is working properly, then we test the broadcasting connections. Only first I have to train my natural ability to experience living. So I don't send spurious messages—like if I'm feeling cranky one day, it would color my perceptions. So I have to give that up. God, it's terrific! I love it!" He stopped and looked at me. "So, Jim. What's new with you?"

I couldn't help it. I started giggling.

"Well, I killed a Chtorran. Another one."

"Yeah. I heard about that. I saw the tapes. It's been on all the news channels. You can't believe what's going on! It's the greatest game of uproar I've ever seen."

"Really?"

"It's the best! It's the funniest political circus since the vice-president was found in bed with the attorney general. Everybody's running

around and screaming that the sky is falling, and why isn't somebody
doing something about it? The Africans are the most upset. They lost
some of their loudest mouthpieces."

"Wow," I said. "Who?"

"Well, Drs. T!Kung and T!kai—and Dr. Kwong, the one you had the
argument with."

I snorted, remembering. "It's poetic justice. Who else? I saw Lizard
in the audience. Was she hurt?"

"Who?"

"Major Tirelli. The chopper pilot."

"Oh, her. No, I saw her at the funeral. They had a mass service for
the victims. Cremated the remains in case the Chtorran bite had bugs in
it."

"Oh. Good."

Neither of us said anything for a moment. We just looked at each
other. His face was glowing. He looked like a very shy schoolboy, eager
and excited. He did not look like the same person.

In that moment, I found myself actually *liking* him.

"So," he said. "How do you feel?"

"Fine, I guess. Numb." I smiled. "How about yourself?"

"Pretty good. A little scared."

I studied his face. He looked back at me unashamedly. I said, "You
know, we haven't had much time to talk since we got here."

He nodded.

"This may be the last time I get to talk to you."

"Yeah, it may be."

"Yeah," I said. "I wanted to tell you how pissed I was at you. That I
thought you were acting like a real asshole."

"S'funny. I was thinking the same about you."

"Yeah. But I guess—I just want you to know that I—uh, I appreciate
you. A lot."

He looked embarrassed. "Yeah. Me too." And then he did something
uncharacteristic for him. He came over to the bed, sat down on it,
leaned over me and hugged me gently. He looked into my eyes, leaned
down and kissed me once, very lightly on the lips. He brushed my cheek
with his hand.

"If I never see you again—" he said, "—and there is that possibility

—if I never see you again, I want you to know this. I do love you. You're an asshole most of the time, and I love you in spite of yourself." He kissed me again, and this time I didn't resist it. There were tears in my eyes and I didn't know why.

THIRTY-EIGHT

THIS TIME, when I awoke, it was daylight.

And the Very Reverend Honorable Dr. Daniel Joseph Fromkin was sitting quietly in a chair studying me.

I raised my head and looked at him. He nodded. I looked around the room. The blinds were drawn, and afternoon sunlight filtered through the narrow vertical slats. Dust motes danced in the beams.

"What day is it?"

"Thursday," he said. He was wearing a muted coppery-gold suit— almost, but not quite, a uniform. Where had I seen—oh, I got it. Mode. He was a Modie.

"I didn't know that," I said.

He saw that my glance was on his tunic. He nodded an acknowledgment and asked, "How are you feeling?"

I looked. I wasn't feeling anything. "Empty," I said. I wondered if I was still under the influence of the drug. Or its aftereffects.

"Anything else?" asked Fromkin.

"Naked. As if I've been stripped and held up for display. I have memories that I'm not sure actually happened or if I just dreamed them."

"Uh huh," he said. "Anything else?"

"Angry. I think."

"Good. Anything else?"

"No, I don't think so."

"Great." He said, "I'm here to debrief you. Are you up to it?" He looked at me expectantly.

"No."

"Fine." He rose to leave.

"Wait a minute."

"Yes?"

"I'll talk. I have some questions of my own."

He raised an eyebrow at me. "Oh?"

"Will you answer them?"

He said, "Yes. As a matter of fact, I am authorized to answer your questions."

"Honestly?"

He nodded his head slowly. "If I can."

"What does that mean?"

"It means I'll tell you the truth as I know it. Is that all right?"

"It'll have to do."

He looked impatient. "What's the question?"

"All right. Why was I set up to be killed?"

Fromkin sat down again. He looked at me. "Were you?"

"You know I was! That Chtorran was supposed to get me too. That's why I was assigned there—so when the glass broke, I'd be the first. I wasn't supposed to have a working weapon, was I? Except I took the manual and went out to the range and familiarized myself with the gun. So it didn't work, did it?"

Fromkin looked unhappy—not pained, just sad. He said, "Yes. That was the expectation."

"You didn't answer the question."

"I will. Let's hear the rest."

"All right. Why was the Chtorran supposed to break out? I saw Dr. Zymph check the case with an aide. They weren't checking to see if it was safe. They were checking to make sure it would break at the right moment. When the Chtorran put its weight on it. Right?"

Fromkin said, "That's what you saw?"

I nodded. "All those people were *supposed* to die, weren't they?"

Fromkin looked at the ceiling for a moment. Composing his answer? He looked back at me. "Yes, I'm afraid so."

"Why?"

"You already know the answer, Jim."

"No, I don't."

"Go over it again. Why do you think the attack was set up?"

"After the fact, it's pretty obvious. Most of those people disagreed with the United States position on the Chtorran threat, so you invited them to a first-hand look at how one *feeds*. That's the guaranteed shock treatment. It always works. It worked on me, and all I had seen were the Show Low pictures. These people got the special live performance. It was set up so that none of our people were killed or injured, only those who opposed us." I studied his face. His eyes were shaded. "That's it, isn't it?"

"Pretty much," Fromkin said. "You're only missing the context."

"The *context*? Or the *justification*?"

Fromkin ignored my jibe. "You saw how the convention was progressing. Can you give me a *better* alternative?"

"Have you tried education?"

"Yes! Do you know how long it takes to teach a politician something? *Three elections!* We don't have the time! We have to make our point *today*."

I must have been frowning, for he said, "You heard those delegates. They were running everything they saw and heard through the filter that the United States was using the Chtorran menace as an excuse to exploit the rest of the world again."

"Well? Isn't that true?"

Fromkin shrugged. "Frankly, it's irrelevant. The war against the Chtorr is going to last anywhere from fifty to three hundred years—if we win. That's our window for a *best-case* approximation."

"And? What's the worst case?"

"We could all be dead within ten years." He said it dispassionately, but the words came out like bullets. "The situation calls for extraordinary crisis-management skills. It demands the kind of unified effort that this planet has *never* seen. We need a controlling body that can function free of the usual inertia common to an accountable government."

"You're advocating a dictatorship?"

"Not hardly. I'm advocating universal military service for every man, woman, child, robot, dog and computer on the planet. That's all." He allowed himself a wry smile. "That's hardly a dictatorship, now, is it?"

I didn't answer. He stood up and went to the window and looked out. "The irony of the situation," he said, "is that the only surviving institutions who have the resources to handle the situation are the very ones least able to apply those resources—the world's great technological nations. The conference is dominated by Fourth Worlders who are still in a pre-Chtorran consciousness—you know the one: 'They've got theirs,

now I'm going to get mine.' And they're not going to let us play any
other game while they still see themselves as not being equal partners.
And the fact of the matter is, they're already equal partners. The Chtorrans find them just as tasty—they don't care!"

Fromkin turned to face me. He came back to the chair, but didn't sit
down. "Jim, every day that passes without a program of unified resistance to the Chtorran invasion pushes the window of possible victory
two weeks farther away. We're rapidly approaching the point where the
window becomes totally unattainable. We don't have any time. They've
taken the position that the United States is their enemy, one who will
use any devious means to exploit them. They don't dare give up that
position, because giving it up looks exactly like admitting they've been
wrong. And that's the hardest thing in the world for a human being to
do—be wrong. Do you know that people would rather die than be
wrong?"

I saw the Chtorran pouring itself off the stage again. I heard the
screams of terror. I smelled the blood. Those people died because they
were wrong? I looked into Fromkin's face. His expression was intense.
His eyes were hurting.

I knew it wasn't true even as I said it, but I had to say it. "So they're
wrong—and you're right?"

Fromkin shook his head. "We did what we had to do, Jim, and the
only way to explain it is so unsatisfactory that I don't even want to try."

I thought about it. "Try me anyway," I said.

He looked unhappy about it. "All right, but you won't like it. This is
a different game—with different rules, one of the most important of
them being 'All previous games are no longer valid.' And anyone who
keeps trying to play the old game in the middle of the new is in the way.
Got that? So we put all of our biggest problems in the front rows. We
didn't like it, but it was *necessary.*"

"You're right. I don't like it."

He nodded. "I told you that you wouldn't." He continued, "But, Jim
—every single one of those survivors has now *experienced* the war at
close range. It is no longer just another political position. It's a bloody
scar on the soul. The people who came out of that auditorium know
who their enemy is now. What you saw—what you participated in—
was a very necessary piece of shock treatment to the community of
world governments."

He sat down again, leaned forward and put his hand on my arm. "We
didn't want to do this, Jim. In fact, as of last week, we had decided not

to. We were hoping then that the facts alone would be enough to convince the delegates. We were wrong. The facts aren't enough. You demonstrated that when you stood up in front of the entire conference. You demonstrated to us just how completely crystalized the Fourth World position was."

"Oh, sure—that's right," I said. "Blame it on me now!"

Fromkin leaned forward and said intensely, "Jim, shut up and listen. Stop showing off your stupidity. Do you know what you've given us? The lever with which to engineer a massive realignment of political intention. The tapes of the conference have been released to the public channels. The whole world has seen that Chtorran attacking a roomful of their highest leaders. The whole world has seen you bring that Chtorran down. Do you know you're a hero?"

"Oh, shit."

Fromkin nodded, "I agree. You're not the one we would have chosen at all, but you're the one we got, so we just have to make the best of you. Listen, the public is alarmed now—we *need* that. We didn't have it before. It makes a difference. We're seeing some very powerful people suddenly declaring their intentions to martial every resource necessary to resist the Chtorran invasion."

I leaned back in the bed and folded my arms across my chest. "So the United States wins after all, right?"

Fromkin shook his head. "That's the joke, son. There may not even be a United States when this war is over—even if we win. Whatever is necessary for the human species to defeat the Chtorrans is of such overriding importance that the survival of any nation, as a nation, becomes a minor matter. Every single one of us committed to this war knows that the survival of *anything* is of secondary importance when weighed against the survival of the species. Period."

He leaned back in his chair again. I didn't say anything. There wasn't anything to say. And then I thought of something. "I can see that's *your* position. Now, what was the justification for including me? Remember, I was supposed to get killed there too—not be a hero."

Fromkin did not look embarrassed. He said, "That's right. And you weren't supposed to be rescued either. That nurse, Dinnie—she can be a perfect pain in the ass sometimes—she saved your life. She disabled two of our marines when they tried to pull her away."

"They were going to kill me?"

"Uh, not exactly. It just seemed, ah, politic not to rush to your aid. But nobody told her that. When they tried to pull her away, she crip-

pled them. Broke one fellow's kneecap, the other one's collarbone, arm
and sternum. She stayed with you the whole time, wouldn't let anybody
near you unless she knew them personally."

"And what happened in the operating room?"

Fromkin looked startled. "You know about that too?"

I nodded.

"A senior officer suggested that your treatment be . . . postponed.
She invited him to leave the operating theater. He refused. She gave him
a choice. Under his own power or otherwise. If otherwise, she guaranteed he wouldn't like it. She was right. He didn't like it. She's under
arrest now—"

"Huh?"

"Protective custody. Until some things get sorted out. I promise you,
she'll be all right. But you and I need to have this little chat first."

Something occurred to me then. "Why you and I? Where's Uncle
Ira? Shouldn't he and I be having this conversation?"

Fromkin hesitated. "I'm sorry. Colonel Wallachstein is dead. He
didn't get out of the auditorium in time." There was pain in his face.

"No—!" I cried. "I can't believe that!" I felt like I'd been slammed in
the chest with a brick—

"He pushed three people out ahead of him," said Fromkin. "I was
one of them. He went back for someone else. I waited for him at the
door. He never came out."

"I—I don't know what to say. I hardly knew him. I don't know if I
liked him—but I respected him."

Fromkin waved it away. "He respected you for killing that fourth
Chtorran. He told me so. In fact, he authorized your bounty check
Sunday morning, just before the session."

"Bounty check?"

"Don't you know? There's a one-million-casey bounty for every
Chtorran you kill. Ten million if you capture one alive. You're a mil-
lionaire now. Twice over. I'll authorize your second check. I'm taking
over certain responsibilities for the Agency. That's why you and I are
having this chat."

"Oh. Are you my superior officer now?"

"Let's just say I'm your, ah, liaison."

"With who?"

"You don't need to know their names. They're the people who
worked with Uncle Ira."

"The same people who decided I should be killed?"

Fromkin exhaled in quiet annoyance. He folded his hands into his lap and collected himself. He looked me in the eye and said, "You need to understand something about that. Yes, you were supposed to die. The people you work for made that decision."

"Nice people," I said.

"You'd be surprised."

"I'm sorry, they don't sound like the kind of people I *want* to work for. I may be an asshole, but I'm not a stupid one."

"That remains to be seen." Fromkin went on quietly, "Until Sunday afternoon, as far as anyone could tell, you were a liability. Nobody figured on you bringing that Chtorran down. I admit it, I'm *still* surprised—but when you did that, you stopped being a liability and started being a hero. You're an asset now, son. Sunday's pictures demonstrate that a human being *can* stop a Chtorran. The world needs to know that. You've become a very useful tool. We want to use you—if you're willing to be used. The earlier decision is inoperative now. You can thank Dinnie for that. She bought you enough time so we could come to that realization. Hm," he added. "We may have to recruit her."

I didn't know whether to feel relieved or angry. I said, "That's all I am? A tool? You can tell them I'm grateful. I hope I can do the same for them sometime."

Fromkin caught my sarcasm. He nodded in annoyance. "Right. You'd rather be right. You'd rather exercise your righteousness."

"*I'm angry!*" I shouted. "It's my *life* we're talking about! That may not mean much to you, but being eaten by a Chtorran could ruin my whole day!"

"You have every right to be angry," Fromkin said calmly. "In fact, I'd worry about you if you weren't, but the thing you need to get is that it's irrelevant. Your anger is *your* business. It means nothing to me. So handle it so you can get on with your job."

"I'm not sure I want the job."

"You want to kill Chtorrans?"

"Yes! I want to kill Chtorrans!"

"Good! We want you to kill Chtorrans too!"

"But I want to trust the people behind me!"

"Jim, *stop taking it personally!* Any of us—*all* of us—are expendable, if it will bring the rest of us closer to the goal of stopping the infestation. Right now, our problem is the resistance of every person who doesn't see that the Chtorran problem is the overriding one—especially those who are *entrusted* with the responsibility for *handling* this circum-

stance. They're in the way. If they're in the way, they have to be moved
out of the way. So don't get in the way. And if you do, don't take it
personally."

"I think that makes it even *more* horrifying," I said. "The sheer
callousness of it."

Fromkin was unimpressed. "Oh, I see—your ideals are more important than winning the war. That's too bad. Do you know what a Chtorran calls an idealist? Lunch."

I glanced at his uniform. "Is that an *enlightened* position?"

"Yes," he said. *"It is."* He didn't expand on it.

I said, "You still haven't answered my question."

"Sorry. Which one?"

"What was the justification for wanting me dead too?"

Fromkin shrugged. "It seemed like a good idea at the time."

"I beg your pardon?"

"You looked like a liability, that's all. I told you, don't take it personally."

"Is that it?"

"Uh huh." He nodded.

"You mean it was just calmly decided—just like *that?*"

"Yep."

I couldn't believe it. I began to splutter at him. "You mean to tell me
that you—and Colonel Wallachstein—and Major Tirelli—just calmly
sat around and decided my death?"

He waited till I ran down. It was a long wait. Then he said, "Yes—
that's *exactly* how it happened. Calmly and unemotionally." He met my
furious stare with an unashamed expression. "In the same way that we
calmly and unemotionally decided to turn the Chtorran loose on a
roomful of our colleagues. In the same way that Duke calmly and
unemotionally decided to handle that little girl in the brown dress. Yes,
I know about that too." He added, "And in the same way that you
calmly and unemotionally decided to handle Shorty and that fourth
Chtorran. There's no difference, Jim. We just left out some of the hysteria and drama. But otherwise, there's no difference, Jim, in what we did
and what you did.

"You accepted the responsibility when you accepted that flamethrower in the first place. The truth is, the things we did that you don't
like are really the things *you* did that you don't like. Right?"

I had to admit it.

I nodded. Reluctantly.

"Right. So give the people around you a break. It isn't any easier over here. We just don't have to be drama queens about it. So you can spare me your goddamned self-righteousness! If I want to be beaten up, I can do it far better than you can! In fact, I already have. I know the arguments—better than you, probably! You think I haven't gone around this bush myself a few times?"

"I hear you," I said. "It's just—I hate the way I've been treated."

"I got it," Fromkin said. "And that's understandable. The fact of the matter is, the agency owes you several dozen apologies—we owe you more than we can ever repay. But would it make a bit of difference? Or would it use up time we need for more immediate problems?"

I stopped the anger I was building up long enough to look at his question. No, it wouldn't make a bit of difference. I looked at him again. "No, it wouldn't."

"Right. What we did was wrong. You know it. We know it. We thought it was necessary—and the fact of the matter is that we never expected to have this conversation. But now we've got it and it's my responsibility to clean up the mess—so consider it an acknowledgment of the contribution that you've made that I'm taking the time. So pay attention. I have a job for you."

"Huh?" I sat up straighter in bed. "That's it? That's how you say thank you?"

"That's right. That's how we say thank you. We give you another job."

"Most people at least say, 'Attaboy. You done good.' "

"Oh," said Fromkin. "You want me to pat your fanny and blow in your ear first, is that it?"

"Well, no, but—"

"—But, *yes*. Listen, I don't have time to waste telling you how wonderful you are—because you won't believe it anyway. If you need to be reminded, then you've got a question about it, don't you? So I'm going to give you the short cut to wonderfulness, so you'll never have to worry about that one again. Ready? What are you doing that makes a difference on the planet? That's your meter stick by which to measure your worth. Got that?"

I nodded.

"Good. Now we have a job for you. The Agency wants to put you to work. Does that tell you anything?"

"Uh, yes. It does," I said. I held up a hand for time. I needed a moment to think this through. I wanted to say it clearly. "Look, I think one of us has got to be a fool—and I know *you're* not. And I'm not sure *I* want the nomination."

"I beg your pardon?" Fromkin looked puzzled.

"How do I know you won't find me . . . ah, what's the word, *expendable* again some time in the future?"

"You don't."

"So there's no guarantee, is there?"

"Right. There's no guarantee. You want the job?"

"No." I didn't even have to think about it.

"Right." He stood up to go—

"Wait a minute!"

"You've changed your mind?"

"No! But—"

"Then we have nothing further to talk about." He started for the door.

"Aren't you going to try to . . ."

"What? Convince you?" He looked genuinely puzzled. "Why should I? You're a big boy now. At least that's what you've been telling us for the past three days. You can choose it or not. You don't need the sales pitch. And I don't have anything to sell."

"Aren't you at least going to tell me what it is?"

"No. Not until I know what your agreement is."

"Agreement?"

He looked annoyed. "Your commitment. What is it we can count on you for?"

"To kill Chtorrans. You can count on me for that."

"Good," he said. He returned to his chair. "Now, quit being an asshole about it. We're on the same side. I want the same thing you do. Dead Chtorrans. I want to put you to work. Do you want to work? Or do you want to screw around with politics—like our Fourth World friends?"

I glared at him. I didn't like this at all. But I said, "I want to work."

"Good. So get this—the time is *over* for games. And that *includes* self-righteousness. I'm telling you the truth now and you can count on me to keep on telling you the truth." His eyes were fierce. His expression was intense, but unashamed. I felt naked before him. Again.

I said, "This is very hard."

He nodded.

"I don't know if I can believe you or not."

"So don't believe me," Fromkin said. "Your belief is irrelevant. The truth is what's so, whether you believe it or not. The question is, what do you want to do about it?"

"Well—" I began. I felt myself smiling. "Revenge would be silly—"

"It's also out of the question." He smiled back.

"—so I might as well be useful."

"Good idea," Fromkin agreed. He leaned back in his chair. "You know, you may have forgotten, but you're an officer now. You fooled us. Nobody expected you to live long enough to use your commission. But you have, so now we've had to create an appropriate job for you."

"I've got one."

"Eh?"

"I've already got a job," I repeated. "I'm working on the Chtorran ecology. There are too many people making guesses without enough information. There aren't very many people out there actually gathering it. I had an instructor once who said that if you offered him the choice between a dozen geniuses for his lab or a couple of idiots who could handle field work, he'd take the idiots. He said it was more important to observe the facts accurately than to be able to interpret them, because if you observed enough of them accurately, you wouldn't have to interpret them—they'd explain themselves."

"Makes sense. Go on."

"Right. Well, you've got almost nobody out in the field. This war against the Chtorr doesn't exist yet because you—*we* don't have any intelligence on them!" I thumped my chest meaningfully. "*That's* my job! I'm an intelligence agent! That's where you need me the most. Because we don't even know yet who or what we're fighting—"

He was holding up one hand to stop me. "Hold it! You're preaching to the choir, son. I got it." He grinned broadly. It was the cheeriest expression I'd ever seen on him. "You know, it's a funny thing. That's *exactly* the same job we had picked out for you."

"Really?"

"Really." He nodded as he said it. "I'm making the assumption that we *are* on the same side, then?"

I looked at him. "I guess we are."

He said, "I know. It doesn't feel like it, does it?"

"No, not really. Not yet."

"So I'll tell you this. You don't get to choose your friends *or* your enemies. They're always thrust on you. All you get to choose is which category you're going to put them in." He grinned. "Wanna be my friend?" He held out a hand.

"Yeah." I took it.

"Thank you," he said, looking into my eyes. His gaze was intense. "We need you." He held onto my hand for a long moment, and I could feel his gratitude, almost like energy, flowing into me. I realized I didn't want to let go.

He smiled at me then, a warm expression like sunrise coming up over a cold gray beach. "You'll do fine. Major Tirelli will be by later to get you started. Do you have any other questions for me now?"

I shook my head. And then I said, "Just one—but it's irrelevant. Does the Mode training really work?"

He grinned. "Yes, it does. It did; I'm sorry it's such a low priority these days." His expression went wistful. "Someday, when there's more time, I'd like to tell you about it."

I said, "I'd like that."

That made him smile proudly. "I think you would." He stood up to go. "Oh, one more thing." He glanced at my meal tray. "Don't drink the orange juice."

"Huh?"

"I said, don't drink the orange juice."

I looked at his face. "I passed another test?"

"Right." He grinned again. "Don't worry, it's the last one."

"Is it?" I asked.

"I sure hope so, don't you?" He was laughing as he left.

I looked at the meal tray. There was a glass of orange juice on it. I poured it into the potted palm.

THIRTY-NINE

THE MORNING sun was very bright, and I felt terrific. My knee hardly hurt at all. The doctors had replaced my kneecap with one grown in a tank and shaved to fit my bones; they told me to minimize my walking for a week—and to guarantee that I did, they put my leg in a case so tight I couldn't bend it. But I could limp—with crutches or a cane—and as soon as I could I was out of the hospital.

I found Ted at the bus station.

He was sitting quietly and waiting. He looked *subdued,* which surprised me. I guess I didn't know what I was expecting. Silver antennae sticking out of his head? But, no—he was just sitting patiently in a corner, a detached look on his face.

I hobbled over to him, but he didn't see me—not even when I stood in front of him. "Ted?" I asked.

He blinked twice.

"Ted?" I waved a hand in front of his face. He didn't see me. His expression remained unchanged. Not just detached—absent. Blank. Nobody home.

"Ted? It's Jim."

He was a zombie.

I sat down next to him and shook his leg. He brushed my hand away. I shook his shoulder and shouted in his ear. "Ted?"

Abruptly, he blinked—and then a confused expression came over his features. He looked like a sleeper awakening suddenly in a strange place. He turned his head slowly and looked at me. Recognition finally came to him. "Jim . . . ?"

"Ted, are you all right? I had to knock three times."

"Yeah," he said quietly. "I'm fine. I was just . . . plugged in."

"Oh. Well, uh, I'm sorry if I interrupted you. But I just got out of the hospital, and this was my only chance to say goodbye before you shipped out."

"Oh," he said. His voice was flat. Distracted. "Well, thank you."

He started to go emotionless again, but I caught his arm. "Ted, are you all right?"

He looked at me, a flicker of annoyance in his eyes. "Yes, Jim, I'm *fine.* But there's a transmission coming in from Capetown that I want to return to."

"I got it," I said. "But I want you to take a moment to be with me. Okay?"

He blinked at me. I knew the expression. Bored patience. "What is it, Jim?"

"Well, I thought . . . just that . . . we might have some things to say to each other. . . ."

His voice went distant. "I saw your Chtorran again. We had a transmitter in the front row. He died. I experienced his death."

"Oh," I said. "Uh—that must have been very hard for you."

"It wasn't the first death I've experienced. I've been playing a lot of tapes." Suddenly, he looked very old.

I put my hand on his arm. "Ted, is it hard?"

He looked at me, but didn't answer. Was he listening to another voice again?

"Ted," I said, "what's it like?"

He blinked, and for just a moment he was the old Ted looking out at me from inside his body, and for just that moment I thought I saw stark terror. "Jim," he said intensely, "it's wonderful! And it's . . . terrible! It's the most intense and exhilarating experience a human being can have. I've been a thousand different people—I can't explain it. It's all still so confusing. I'm being bombarded with experiences, Jim! Constantly. And I don't know which of them are mine—if any! I don't even know if it's me sitting here talking to you. You could be talking to *any* telesend on the circuit. I can remote-access anybody else's experience and, if necessary, even take over control. And they can use my body too!"

I opened my mouth to say something, but he stopped me with a desperate hand on my arm.

"No—listen to me. I'm out of the circuit now, but only for a moment. The trainees have to take the dirtiest jobs—it's that way in all the services. I'm on call sixteen hours a day. Yesterday, I was . . ." He stopped, as if he were trying to form the words and finding it difficult. His eyes looked red. "Yesterday, I was . . . ridden. By a Russian government official. I don't know if it was a woman or a homosexual or—I don't know, but whoever it was used my body to make love to another man. And all I could do was do it. I had no control of my own."

"Did you file a grievance?"

"Jim, you don't understand! It was *wonderful!* It was complete and absolute *service!* Whoever it was gave me the opportunity to confront a different experience! That's what this is about—the expansion that comes from confronting the totality of human experience!"

"Ted, can't you get out?"

"Get out?" Ted looked incredulous. "Get out? Jim, don't you understand? I don't want out. Even while I was hating it, I was loving it— good *and* bad. The Telepathy Corps is a chance to share the experiences of a million other human beings. How else could a person ever get to live a million other lives?" His eyes were feverish now, intense. "Jim, I've played the tapes! I know what it feels like to die—in a hundred different ways. I've gone down in plane crashes, I've drowned, I've fallen off buildings, I've burned to death and I've even been eaten by a Chtorran! I've been afraid in more different ways than I ever dreamed possible—and I've been exhilarated in as many different ways too! I've climbed mountains and gone into space. I've lived in free fall and at the bottom of the ocean as a gillman. I've done so much, Jim—it's like making love to the universe! And I've made love a thousand different ways as well! It's all on the tapes. I've been a naked child in Micronesia and a fifteen-year-old courtesan somewhere in Osaka. I've been an old man dying of cancer in Morocco, and—Jim, I know what it is to be a woman, a girl! Can you comprehend what it is to leave your own sex behind, like a fish discovering air—discovering how to fly? I've made love as a girl! And I've carried the child that resulted and given birth to it!! I've nursed it and raised it! And I died with it when the plagues came! Jim, I've experienced more of life in just the past few days than I'd ever known in all the years before. And I'm terrified and excited because it's all coming down so fast I can't assimilate it. Jim"—he clenched my arm so tight it hurt—"Jim, *I'm disappearing!* Me—Ted!

My identity is dissolving under the assault of a thousand other lives! I can feel it happening! And I know what it will feel like to stop existing as me, because that experience is recorded too! And, Jim, I want it even as I'm afraid of it. It's a kind of death. And it's a kind of *orgasm* too! This is incredible stuff! Jim, my life is over! Now, I'm a part of something else, something larger and—Jim, I want to say this to you while there's time—"

Abruptly, his grip on my arm loosened. His face relaxed, the tension disappeared and he became detached again.

"Ted?"

"I'm sorry, I'm on call now, Jim. I have to go."

He started to rise, but I pulled him back down. "Wait—you started to say something?"

"Perdóneme?" A strange voice came from his mouth.

"Uh, nothing." I let go in horror.

Ted's body nodded. *"Bueno."* It got up and walked away. The last I saw of Ted, his body was just getting on a helibus. The chopper clattered up into the air and disappeared into the east.

I wondered where Ted was in the circuit now. I knew it didn't matter. The half-life of even a strong identity was less than nine months. I'd probably never see Ted again. His body, maybe, but the thing that animated it—where would that be? Experiencing what? Or whom? Within a few months, it wouldn't even be a personality anymore. Ted had known what he was getting into when he'd made the decision to receive the implant. He'd known what it meant. At least, that was what I wanted to believe.

I turned and hobbled back to the Jeep I'd requisitioned. I didn't feel so terrific anymore. I had a lot to think about. I levered myself in and said, "Science Section, please."

The Jeep replied "Acknowledged," and whined itself to life. It waited till its whirring stabilized, then backed smoothly out of the parking slot. As it eased forward, it announced, "Incoming message."

I said, "I'll take it."

Marcie's voice: "Jim, I want you to stop calling me. And stop leaving messages for me to call you. I have nothing to say to you. And you have nothing to say that I want to hear. I don't want to see you and I don't want to talk to you. I hope I'm making myself clear. I want you to leave me alone, because if you don't, I promise you, I'll file a postal grievance."

The message ended abruptly, and the Jeep trundled across the tarmac. I thought about Marcie, tried to figure out what was going on. I remembered something Dinnie had said. "We're all crazy these days. *All of us.* We were crazy before the plagues too, but now we're *really* crazy." Or was that just a convenient justification? I didn't know.

Dinnie had said, "The thing is, none of us can see our own craziness, because it's the filter we look through. All we can see is what we project on the people around us. And then we blame it on them." She'd smiled and said, "Do you know how to tell if you're crazy? See if the people around you are."

I looked—and *everybody* around me was crazy.

That was the joke. You know you need help when the people around you are crazy.

The hell with her. I didn't have time to be crazy anymore.

The Jeep said, "Will there be a reply?"

I said, "No. And post this. Refuse all future messages from the same source."

"Acknowledged."

I still felt lousy.

FORTY

THE JEEP lurched to a stop in front of the Science Section, and I climbed out carefully. There were no guards here. None were necessary anymore. Since the reorganization, no doors would open for you unless you had a red card or higher. I had a gold card.

Once past the fourth set of security doors, I pointed at two lounging aides and said, "You're temporarily requisitioned. I have some things I want loaded."

They grumbled and fell into line behind me. "I don't want to hear it," I said.

We went directly to the extraterrestrial specimen section. A woman in a lab coat looked up as I came in.

"Where's Dr. Partridge?" I asked.

"She doesn't work here anymore. She's been transferred to Administration."

"What about Larson?"

"Who?"

"Jerry Larson?"

"Never heard of him." She put her clipboard down and looked at me. "What can I do for you?"

"I'm McCarthy," I said.

"So?"

"I requisitioned some specimens." I pointed to the wall of cages. "Three millipedes and an incubator of eggs. They were supposed to be ready for me."

She shook her head. "The orders didn't come through here."

"Fine," I said. "I'll give them to you now—" I pulled my copy of the flimsies out of my pocket.

She blinked at me. Her face hardened. "Whose authority are you operating under, *Lieutenant?*"

"Special Forces Warrant Agency," I snapped. My leg hurt. I was tired of standing. I tapped the card pinned to my chest. *"This* is my authority. I can requisition any goddamned thing I want. If I want to, I can requisition you to Nome, Alaska. Now, I want those three bugs and that box of eggs." I gestured to the aides. "There's a Jeep out front. Load 'em in the back."

"Just a minute," she said, reaching for a phone. "I want confirmation—"

I hobbled over to her, leaning heavily on my cane. "One," I said, "I gathered those specimens. Two, I killed a Chtorran to get them here. Three, I haven't seen one piece of research out of this lab, so as far as I'm concerned, the effort in bringing them here was wasted. Four"—I was unfolding the orders that had been handed me that morning by Major Tirelli—"I have all the confirmation you need right here. And five, if you don't get out of my way, I'm going to place this cane in a most uncomfortable place. And if you don't believe I can do it, I'm the fellow who killed the Denver Chtorran."

She read the orders, then handed them back without comment. She sniffed. "No, you're not."

"I beg your pardon?"

"You didn't kill it."

"Say again?"

She raised an eyebrow at me. "Do all lieutenants have lousy hearing? I said, 'You didn't kill it.' "

I turned to the aides. "Load that stuff on the Jeep. I'll be right out."

"Hold it!" She barked. "You touch those cages, I'll have you shot." The aides stopped where they were. She poked my chest. "Let's you and me settle some things first."

I looked at the woman in the lab coat. She wasn't wearing a name badge. She had green eyes. "What's your name?" I demanded.

"Lucrezia Borgia."

"Is there a rank in front of that?"

"Just Doctor."

"Right. Well, Dr. Borgia, do you want to start making some explanations?"

She pointed to a set of double doors at the end of the room. "Two rooms down," she said.

I hobbled through the double doors. She followed after me. I was in a wide hallway with another set of double doors at the end. I pushed through those and—

—there was the Chtorran, almost motionless in the center of a large room. The room was brightly lit. The Chtorran's flanks heaved regularly as if its breathing were labored. There were men attaching probes to its sides. There were ladders and scaffolds all around the creature.

"I . . . uh . . ."

"Didn't kill it." She finished for me.

"But I—never mind. What're they doing to it?"

"Studying it. This is the first time we've ever been able to get close enough to a live one to poke it and prod it and see what makes it tick. You crippled it. It can't see, it can't hear, it can't move. At least we don't think it can see or hear. We're sure it can't move. It certainly can't eat. Your gun pretty well destroyed its mouth. We're pumping liquids into it."

I didn't ask what kind of liquids. "Is it safe to approach?"

"You're the expert." She said it acidly.

There were men and women all over the animal. I hobbled forward myself. Only one or two of them looked up at me. Dr. Borgia paced me quietly. She took my cane and poked at the creature's mouth. "Look here," she said. "See that?"

I looked. I saw a clotted mass of flesh. "What am I looking for?"

"See that row of bumps? New teeth. And if you could climb the ladder, I'd show you the creature's arm stumps. And its eyes. If we could get underneath, I'd show you its feet. The thing is regenerating."

I looked at her. "How long?" I asked.

She shrugged. "Three months. Six. We're not sure. Some of the gobbets we've carved off it show signs of trying to grow into a complete creature too. Like starfish. Or holograms. Each piece has all the information necessary to reconstruct the original. You know what this means, don't you?"

"Yeah. They're almost unkillable. We *have* to burn them."

She nodded. "As far as the rest of the world is concerned, you killed this thing. They even paid you for it. But the truth is, you only stopped it. So don't you ever come into my lab again, throwing your weight around and acting like an expert! You got that?"

I didn't answer. I was looking at the Chtorran. I took a step toward it and reached out and touched its skin. The creature was warm. Its fur was silky. Oddly alive. It felt electric! My hand tingled as I stroked it.

"Static electricity?" I asked.

"No," she said.

I took another step forward, almost leaning on the warm side of the Chtorran, almost pressing my face into it. Some of the strands of fur brushed softly against my cheek. They felt like feathers. I sniffed deeply. The creature smelled warm and minty. It was oddly inviting. Like a big friendly fur rug you wanted to curl up in. I continued stroking it.

"That isn't fur," she said.

I kept petting. "It isn't? What is it?"

"Those are nerve endings," she said. "Each individual strand is a living nerve—appropriately sheathed and protected, of course—and each one has its own particular sensory function. Some can sense heat and cold, others light and darkness, or pressure. Some can smell. Most —well, while you're busy petting it, it's quietly tasting you."

I stopped petting it.

I pulled my hand back. I looked at her. She nodded yes. I looked at the Chtorran fur again. Every strand was a different color. Some were thick and black. Others were fine and silvery. Most were various shades of red—a whole spectrum of red, shading all the way from deep purple to bright gold, and touching all the bases in between: magenta, pink, violet, crimson, orange, scarlet, salmon and even a few flashes of bright yellow. The effect was dazzling.

I brushed my hand against the fur again, parting it gently. Beneath, the Chtorran skin was dark and purple, almost black. It was hot. I thought of the skin on a dog's soft underbelly.

I realized the Chtorran was trembling. Every time I touched it, the intensity of the shivers increased. Huh—?

"You're making it nervous," Lucrezia said.

Nervous—? A Chtorran? Without thinking, I slapped the creature's flank. It twitched as if stung.

"Don't," she said. "Look—"

A shudder of reaction was rippling up and down the Chtorran's body. There were two technicians on a platform hanging just above the Chtorran's back. They were trying to secure a set of monitor probes. They had to pull back and wait until the Chtorran stopped shuddering. One of the technicians glared at me. When the creature's flesh stopped rippling, she bent back to her work.

"Sorry," I said.

"The creature is incredibly sensitive. It can hear everything that goes on in here. It reacts to the tone of your voice. See? It's trembling. It knows you're hostile. And it's afraid of you. It's probably more afraid of you than you are of it."

I looked at the Chtorran with new eyes. It was afraid of me—!

"Remember, it's just a baby."

It took a moment for me to grasp the implications of that—not just for here in the lab, but for outside as well, out there, where the wild ones were.

If this was a baby—if all of those *out there* were babies—then *where were the adults?* The fourth Chtorran—?

"Wait a minute—this can't be a baby!"

"Oh?"

"It's too big—I brought in eggs! A baby Chtorran should only be . . ." I spread my hands as if to hold a puppy. ". . . oh, about yay big. . . ."

"Have you ever seen one?"

"Uh—"

"What's the smallest Chtorran you've *ever* seen?"

"Uh—" I pointed. "This one."

"Right. Have you ever heard of heavy metal accumulation?"

"What about it?"

"It's a way of measuring the age of an animal. The body doesn't pass heavy metals, like lead or mercury; they accumulate in the cells. No matter how clean a life you live, it's inevitable that you'll pick up traces just from the atmosphere. We've tested this creature extensively. Its cells are remarkably earthlike. Did you know that? It could almost have evolved on this planet. Maybe someday it will. But here's the thing: it doesn't have enough trace metals in its system to be more than three years old. And my guess is that it's actually a lot less. Maybe eighteen months." She held up a hand to forestall my objection. "Trust me— we've tested it. We've deliberately introduced trace metals into its system to see if perhaps it doesn't have some way of passing them. And yes, it does—our estimate of its age is based on *that* equation. And that's no anomaly, buster. All of our supplementary evidence supports the hypothesis. Eighteen months. Maybe two years at the most. It's got an incredible growth rate."

I was shaking my head. "But what about my eggs—?"

"Oh, that's right. Your eggs. Your *Chtorran* eggs. Come with me." I followed her back to the room we had just left. She brought me up to the row of cages. "Here are your eggs," she pointed. "See all the baby Chtorrans?"

I stepped close to the cage and peered.

Inside were two small millipedes. They were sleek and wet-looking. They were busily chewing on some pieces of shredded wood. A third baby millipede was just now chewing a hole in the shell of its egg. It paused abruptly and looked straight out at me. I felt a cold chill.

"The only thing interesting about these babies," she said, "is the color of their bellies. See? Bright red."

"What does that mean?"

She shrugged. "Means they're from Rhode Island. I don't know. Probably it doesn't mean anything. We've found all kinds of color bandings on these creatures' bellies."

"When did they hatch?" I asked.

"Early this morning. Cute, don't you think?"

"I don't get it," I said. "Why would the Chtorrans keep millipede eggs in their dome?"

"Why do you keep chicken eggs in your refrigerator?" Dr. Borgia asked. "What you've found is the ubiquitous Chtorran version of the chicken, that's all. These things eat the stuff that's too low on the food chain for the worms to bother with. They're convenient little mechanisms to gather up food and store it till the worms are hungry."

"I'm confused. Those eggs looked too big to have been laid by a millipede."

"Do you know how big millipedes get?"

I shook my head.

"Look down here."

"*Jesus!*" I yelped. The thing in the cage was as big around as a large python. It was over a meter long. "Wow!" I said, "I didn't know that."

"Now you do." She looked at me, and her green eyes flashed smugly. "Any *more* questions?"

I stepped back and turned to her. I said, "I apologize. I've been a jerk. Please forgive me."

"We're used to dealing with unpleasant creatures." She smiled innocently. "You were no problem at all."

"Ouch. I deserved that. Listen, it's obvious that you know what you're doing here. And that just hasn't been my experience elsewhere in the Center. I didn't even know this section existed until this morning."

"Neither did anybody else until we took custody of Junior in there—" She jerked a thumb over her shoulder at the other room.

"I'm really sorry," I said.

She swung to face me. "I got that. Now listen up and listen good. I don't give a damn how sorry you are. I really don't. It's over. Now, let it be something you can learn from."

"Uh, yeah."

"You're an officer now. So I'll give you the bad news. Every damn schmuck who sees those bars on your arm wants you to succeed, you know that? He wants to know that he can trust you *totally* when his life is on the line. That's how you want to feel about your superiors, don't you? Well, that's how your men want to feel about you. You act like a jerk and you blow it—not just for yourself, but for every other person who wears the same bars. So get yourself tuned in to what this is about. Those stripes are not a privilege! They're a responsibility."

I was feeling a little sick.

I guess it showed. She took me by the elbow and turned me to the wall. She lowered her voice. "Listen, I know this hurts. And here's what you need to know about that: criticism is an acknowledgment of your ability to produce results. I wouldn't be giving you correction if I didn't think you could take it. I know who you are. I know how you got those stripes. That's fine; you deserve 'em. I've heard a lot of good things about you. Believe it or not, I don't want to see you screwing up. You got that?"

"Uh, yeah. I got it."

"Is there anything you want to say to me?"

"Uh . . . thanks—I think." I added, "I'll know when the bleeding stops. Uh, I'm awfully embarrassed."

"Listen, all new officers make the same mistake. You're lucky you made it here instead of someplace serious. You think the bars change you somehow. They don't. So don't let them get in the way. You're not your rank—you're just a person being trusted with that amount of responsibility. So I'll let you in on the secret. Your job isn't to order people—it's to *inspire* them. Remember that and you'll be very successful."

"Thank you," I said again. There was something about the way she spoke. "Are you related to Fromkin?"

She grinned. "I trained with him. Nine years ago." She stuck out her hand. "My name's Fletcher. Call me Fletch."

I shook hands gently. My wrist was still sore.

She said, "If you still want the bugs, take them."

I glanced back at the cage. The third baby millipede had finally gotten out of its shell. It was trying to crawl up the surface of the glass. Its belly was bright red. It stopped and stared at me. Its eyes were large and black and unnerving.

I shrugged. "I don't know now. I only wanted them back because I thought nobody around here *cared.* Now, I see that's not so. If you can do a better job . . ."

Fletcher grinned again. "Yes, we can."

I made a decision. "Well, then—keep 'em here. I just want to know what there is to know about them."

"I'll put your name in the computer," she said. "You can plug into the files any time you want. Our job here is to disseminate information, not hide it." Then her eyes twinkled and she added, "Visiting hours are every day from noon to five. Next time, bring flowers."

"I will," I said. I dropped my gaze away from her eyes. For some reason, they were suddenly too beautiful to look at. I made a show of looking at my watch. I was embarrassed again, but this time for a totally different reason. "Well—" I said "—I guess I'd better get going. I have a plane to catch. Thanks again. For *everything.*"

I turned awkwardly toward the door. She stepped in front of me. "Just one thing. That *was* a pretty fair piece of shooting. I was there. My compliments." And she stretched upward and kissed me warmly on the lips.

I could feel myself blushing all the way to the Jeep.

FORTY-ONE

WE WERE on a high hill overlooking a shadowed valley, almost a canyon. At the bottom, a glittering stream sluiced down between the two sheer slopes, zig-zagging from north to south and forming a wide, shallow pond where the canyon opened up. The surface of the water reflected back the sky; it looked like blue glass. At the far end of the pond, the water poured gently over the edge of a low earth-and-wood dam.

A long shelf of land bordered the little lake. Near the dam was a rounded dome, almost unnoticeable against the black earth of the hill behind it. I studied it through the binoculars for a long time. The dome seemed darker than usual. It looked as if mud had been smeared all over its surface. Not a bad camouflage, but still not good enough to fool the computers. Satellite reconnaissance was monitored, processed and analyzed on a twenty-four-hour basis for telltale changes in local terrain. The particular rounded bump of the worm hut, the dam, the local harvesting of trees—any of these things alone could have triggered an investigation; all of them together had put this valley on the Immediate-Attention list. It had taken us three weeks to get to it.

I passed the binoculars over to Duke. He peered through and grunted.

"They're getting smarter," I said.

He nodded. "Yeah. This one is just plain inaccessible. There's no way we can get down there unnoticed."

Larry was studying the canyon upstream. "Can't raft in," he said.

Duke nodded in agreement. "Didn't think we could." He turned to Larry. "Call the blimp. We're dropping the team in." Larry nodded and thumbed his radio to life. Duke looked toward me. "What are you thinking?"

I said, "It puts it all on the shoulders of the first man. He's got to hold the position until the others are safely down." I closed my eyes for a second and visualized what it might be like. "I'll do it," I said.

"You don't have to," Duke said.

"Yes, I do."

"All right," said Duke. "Fine. Do you have any problems with the plan?"

"No," I said. And then I shrugged and grinned. "I hate it—but I have no problems with it."

Duke eyed me steadily. "What's that about?"

"I hate blimps. I have this thought the worms will hear us coming. Or see the shadow."

"Anything else?"

"Yeah. I hate heights."

"Is that it?"

"Yeah."

Duke looked at Larry. "You?"

"I'm fine."

"I don't get that from you—what's going on?"

Larry shook his head.

"You still obsessing about Louis' death?"

Larry shook his head. Louis had died two weeks after his finger had been bitten. He'd started shivering one afternoon, then collapsed. He sank into a coma that evening and was dead the following morning. The autopsy showed that almost every red blood cell in his body had been exploded—from the inside. The killer was a virus that behaved like malaria. There were now thirty-four viral or bacteriological agents that had been identified as active agents in the Chtorran infestation. Louis had been lucky. His death had been quick, and relatively painless.

Duke said, "Larry, are you going for revenge?"

Larry didn't answer.

"—Because if you are, you'll stay behind. It'll get in the way."

"*I'll be fine!*"

Duke looked at Larry. "You fuck up, I'll put a stake through your heart. I promise you."

Larry grinned, "I got it, boss."

"All right." Duke included me again. "Let's get moving. Be sure your teams are clear. We'll have a final briefing just before we go." Duke looked at me. "Jim, you and I will go over the attack plan with the pilot. You're right about the shadow—we have to keep it off the dome—and the engine noise, so let's see what the wind is doing. If it's light enough, we'll *float* across the valley."

We slid back down the hill. We'd left our Jeep a quarter-mile away, on a fire road. It took us another half-hour to get to the landing site where the blimp was waiting. Our three attack teams were going through a last check of their equipment as we pulled up. Larry hopped out even before the Jeep had finished rolling to a stop. "Only three torches—" he called. "There's too much fire danger. We'll use the ba-zookas—"

Duke poked me. "Let's talk to Ginny."

I followed him to the command tent, where a 3-D map of the valley was displayed across the situation table. He nodded perfunctory greetings to the watch officers and tossed his pack to one side. "All right, let's get to work." He stepped up to the table and picked up a light pen. He drew a red target circle in the large clearing next to the dome. "That's where I want to put the team."

Captain MacDonald stepped up to the table opposite Duke and frowned. Her white hair was pulled back into a crisp military bun. She wore a tight jacket, trousers, a sidearm and a stern expression. She pointed. "I've got fifteen knots of wind coming from the southeast. It's going to be tight."

Duke dialed down the magnification. The image shrank as if it were dropping away. The tabletop now included several square miles of surrounding mountains. "I got that. And we need thirty seconds over the landing site." He pointed at the now reduced red target circle. "Can we do it with the engines off?"

Ginny closed her eyes and thought a moment. She said, "Tricky . . ." She typed something into the keyboard and studied the monitor. "Looks like a split-second drop. Your men are going to have to take their cues from the box—"

She stopped and looked at us. "I can't promise to do it with the engines off. I *can* promise to give you forty-five seconds over the target site—and I'll keep the engines off as long as possible."

Duke didn't look happy. "There's a real potential for disaster here." He turned to me. "Jim, I don't want anyone dropping in the water. And

I don't want anyone dropping too near the dome. Can we trust your team?"

"We'll hit our marks."

"Can I count on it?"

"I'm the one taking the biggest risk." I met his eyes. "You can count on me."

"All right." Duke turned back to the display. He dialed the image up to maximum and centered it on the dome. "What does that look like to you?"

I checked the scale indicator at the edge of the table. "It's too big. How old is this picture?"

Ginny looked at the monitor on her side of the table. "Eighteen hours. This is yesterday afternoon."

"Thank you." I picked up the light pen. "Here—this is where to look. Around the perimeter of the dome. Look for purple coleus or wormberry plants. Every time we find evidence of cultivation, we also find a fourth Chtorran. There's none of that here yet. Nor is there a totem pole in front—that would also be evidence. But" —I shook my head—"this dome is too big. I want an extra watch at the back of it."

Duke looked at me sharply. "Reason?"

"I don't have one. Just a feeling something's weird here. Maybe it's the location of the dome, maybe it's the mud camouflage. But I get a sense there's some intelligence here."

Duke nodded. He studied the terrain again. "I'll buy it. Ginny?"

Captain MacDonald nodded too. She touched the keyboard in front of her and wind lines appeared across the map. She studied the monitor screen for a second, then said, "There's your course, the red line. If the wind holds, you'll have fifty seconds over the target area. I'll come across the valley from the southeast." She pointed with the light pen. "Now, look, we're coming down a very narrow track. I've got mountains on one side and water on the other. The shadow will be north and west of us. And so will the dome. I can't promise I'll miss it, not without the risk of dropping men in the water, unless you want to wait till later in the day."

Duke shook his head.

"All right. I'll do my best, but your first man will have to start down the rope even before we clear the dome. And he'll be hitting the ground awfully close—"

Duke looked at me. I shook my head. "No problem."

"—otherwise, the last of the team will be falling in the water."

"They had their baths this month," I said. "Don't worry about it."

"Anybody have anything else to add?" asked Duke. "No? Good. Let's go. Load 'em up." As we stepped out of the tent, he clapped my shoulder. "How are you feeling?"

I said, "Who's good idea was this anyway?"

He grinned back. "Right."

My team was to jump first, so that meant we boarded last. While we waited beneath the curve of the huge sky-blue blimp, I briefed them quickly. The job is routine, the jump's a little tight. Any questions? None. Good. Any problems or considerations? Larry had handled them already. Fine.

I moved among them quietly, double-checking the charges on their weapons and the expressions on their faces.

"How's it look, Cap'n?" That was Gottlieb. He had apple cheeks, a frizz of curly hair, and a perpetually eager smile. Right now he looked worried. I could tell because his smile was uncertain.

"Piece of cake."

"I heard the valley's awful narrow—"

"Yep. It is. That's just to make it interesting. These things are turning into turkey shoots. We don't want you falling asleep." I looked into his face. There was still too much tension there. I wondered if I should pull him. I put my hands on his shoulders and leaned over and whispered in his ear. "Listen, asshole—I promise you, you're going to do fine. You know how I know? Because if you don't, I'm going to rip your arms off."

He knew I meant it. He grinned. "Yes, sir!"

He'd be okay now. He was more afraid of me than he was of the worms. The worms didn't stand a chance.

"Two minutes!" called Larry.

I turned and found myself looking at Amy Burrell. Eighteen years old, tiny frame, large eyes, dark hair. Trembling in her boots. She was wearing the helmet camera and carrying an AM-280. "Sir—?"

I knew what she was about to say. I didn't give her a chance to say it. "Ah, Burrell—good. Once you hit the ground, I want you to stay close. I'll be moving around to the back side of the dome. Keep fifty feet behind me and you'll do just fine. Keep your camera running, and if anything comes out of the dome, just keep looking at it. We need the pictures. Oop—the line's moving. Get going!" I turned her and pushed. I slapped her on the backside. From here on, she wasn't going to have time to be scared.

The blimp took us up quickly. Captain MacDonald was sharp. She turned into the wind immediately and headed south. She was going to give herself lots of maneuvering room before heading for the target.

The engines thrummed with quiet power. We could feel their high-pitched whine in our butts and our backbones. Beneath us, the ground tumbled away like a rumpled brown sheet. The wind whistled coldly past us. I licked my lips and wondered if they were going to get chapped.

We were on two platforms mounted on the sides of the gondola. Each one of us had his or her own rope. On the signal, all the ropes would be dropped simultaneously. On the count, we would drop as our numbers were called. I tugged experimentally at my pulley. It was fine. I realized I was fingering the double-breakaway punch on my chest and stopped.

Captain MacDonald swung the blimp around then, heading us back toward the target. I watched our shadow as it moved across the treetops below. When she cut the engines, we were plunged into an eerie silence. Burrell looked at me nervously. The absence of sound was deafening.

I was about to thumb my microphone to life, to say something to fill the moment—when abruptly, music filled my earphones. Williamson's *Angry Red Symphony.* A perfect choice! Ginny was more than a pilot—she was an artist. I shut up and listened.

Too quickly, the approach to the target appeared before us. I recognized the escarpment at the top that looked like a dragon's backbone. And there was the fire road, and the place we had parked the Jeep. And now, as we came closer, there was the canyon and the valley beneath it. The blimp shadow was sliding down the slope—*and suddenly turned sideways.* Were we heading in at an angle? Had the wind changed? Abruptly the engines came whining back to life—*damn!*

The computer interrupted the music then. "Team One: stand by to drop."

There was the dome. And the blimp shadow was moving uncomfortably toward it—

"Five seconds!" said the computer. Something clicked, and all the ropes began dropping away, snaking to the ground like yellow spaghetti. "Three seconds!" I stood up. The blimp shadow moved across the dome. *Goddammit!* "Two!" I released the safety on my pulley. And —"Drop Alpha!" I lifted my knees and fell forward into nothingness. The pulley shrieked and screamed as it careened down the rope. "Drop Beta!" Above me, I could hear an echoing shriek, and then another and another.

The ground rushed up toward me. The ropes below were crackling and undulating like live wires. And two of the largest Chtorrans I'd ever seen came streaming purple out of the hut—*"Chtorrrrr! Chtorrrr-rrr!"*

"Shit!"

I yanked a grenade off my belt, pulled the pin, and sighted below. There wasn't time, I was falling too fast. I dropped the grenade—

It fell short. The blossom of fire went off in front of the first charging worm, deflecting it but not slowing it down. The roar of the blast kicked upward like a hammer-blow. I grabbed for another grenade, knowing it was already too late—and then the worm was hit by two more sudden explosions, one right after the other. The shock of them kicked me momentarily upward. Somebody above me must have dropped grenades —I hoped they hadn't dropped any more.

The Chtorran was writhing on the ground. It had been cut in half by one of the blasts. The second Chtorran was almost directly beneath me now, and the third and largest one was just coming out of the dome. I released the safety on my torch and pointed it straight down. I hoped Shorty had been right about this. The second Chtorran was reared up and reaching for me and I was dropping right into his churning maw—I could see straight down his throat. I pulled the trigger. The air beneath me exploded into flame. I couldn't see the Chtorran through it. The burning ground rushed up to meet me. I didn't even know if there was still rope for my pulley anymore. I pointed the torch sideways and fired again and the jet kicked me away from the burning worm. I released the trigger and hit the ground hard. I fell on my ass—*"Oof!"*—and had the breath knocked out of me—

The third worm was charging straight toward me. *"Chtorrrr! Chtorr-rrrrr!"* I didn't even have time to stand. I just pointed the torch and fired—

When I finally let go of the trigger, there was nothing left of the worm but a snaky dark mass of writhing, burning, rubbery flesh. It smelled terrible.

And then Duke was there, standing over me, offering me a hand. I thanked him as I pulled myself to my feet. He glanced around at the three burning worms. "You want to remember you're a guest here and leave something for the rest of us?" And then he was away, pointing and directing the rest of his team to fan out.

I looked at the three worms myself. "Babies, huh?" And shook my head. I didn't know if I wanted to meet Mama or not.

Larry's team was already moving to the far side of the dome. My team was moving into position, but uncertainly; several of them were staring at me and the still-burning carcasses. They looked stunned. I clicked on my microphone. "Goddammit! Move out! Haven't you ever seen a man burn a worm before?" I started striding toward the back of the hut. "Burrell! Get your ass in gear!" I wondered how badly mine would hurt tomorrow from that hard landing. I wasn't going to worry about it now. I hit the breakaways on my chest, kicked out of the drop harness and kept going.

I planted myself directly in front of the back wall of the dome. I gave it a lot of room. I checked the charges on my tanks. Still half full. Good. More than enough.

I glanced around behind me. Amy Burrell, white as a sheet, was fifty feet away. She held her rifle in a death grip. But she was ready. I looked at the wall again. Nothing. I checked the rest of my team. They were ready too.

My mike was still on. I switched channels and said quietly, "Apple."

"Baker," said Larry.

"Charlie," said Duke. "Hold your positions."

I looked at the rear wall of the dome. It was blank and featureless.

"All right," I barked. "Bring me a freeze machine. *On the double.*"

The freeze machine was a large plastic crate filled with styrofoam doodles. Inside the doodles were two tanks of liquid nitrogen and a spray nozzle. They'd been dropped after everyone else was down safely. We had two of them.

If we hadn't wakened the Chtorrans with our arrival, we would have used the liquid nitrogen instead of the torches. Gottlieb and Galindo wheeled up one of the kits. Riley and Jein were just unloading the other. They touched the release and the crate popped open with a *thump*.

"I'll take the kit. Michael, you cover me with the torch." Gottlieb grinned as I passed it over to him. He loved the excitement.

The nozzle for the freeze machine was lighter than the torch, and I didn't wear the tanks on my back. It was Galindo's job to move them— if we had to move. I wore a pair of insulated gloves so thick they could have been used in a boxing match. I closed the faceplate on my helmet again and I was ready.

The back wall of the dome remained unchanged.

Duke's voice whispered in my earphones. "You okay, McCarthy?"

"I'm fine. But when this is over, my ass is going to hurt."

"You did good."

"I know," I said. And then I added, "Thanks."

There was silence for a bit, so I asked, "What happened with the blimp?"

"I don't know. I didn't have time to ask. We came over the edge and the wind shifted. But Ginny did her job. Nobody hit the water."

"When we get back, I'm going to buy her flowers."

"Do that. Better yet, buy her a bottle. It looked like a quick save." He was silent a moment, then asked, "Jim, how long do you want to wait?"

"At least a half-hour. Remember what happened to that team in Idaho."

"Right." Duke said, "There was a lot in that report to worry about."

"You mean the tunnel they found?"

"Yeah. If the worms are changing their nesting behavior . . ." He didn't finish the sentence; he didn't need to. The job was already difficult enough.

I studied the wall some more. There was no evidence of a hidden exit.

"Do you want to send in the Robe?" asked Larry. The blimp had also dropped a meter-high mechanical walker—a more sophisticated version of Shlep, the Mobe, only it didn't have Shlep's good looks or personality.

"No," said Duke.

Larry argued for it half-heartedly for a few moments, then trailed off. Duke didn't reply. I couldn't see either of them. There was just me and the wall.

"Jim?"

"Yeah, Duke?"

"You want to switch positions?"

"Naw, I'm fine."

"You sure?"

"I'm sure."

"All right."

The wall was unchanged. Something very small and loud buzzed around me. A stingfly? It was too fast to see. I waved it away with one gloved hand.

"Burrell? Time check."

"Twelve minutes, thirty seconds."

"Thank you."

I could feel myself sweating. I was starting to feel clammy inside the insulated battle-suit. I wished the fourth goddamn worm would quit waiting and come on out already. "Come on, worm! I've got a nice cold bath for you! Just the thing for a hot summer afternoon!"

There was silence.

Something hooted.

I found myself growing drowsy. I shook myself back awake; I stamped my feet, jumping back and forth from leg to leg for a moment.

I squeezed the trigger, just a touch, and let loose a cold cloud of freezing steam. It put a chill into the summer air and a cold pain into the eyes. Water droplets crystalized and pattered on the ground. That would keep me awake for a bit.

We'd been freezing worms for a month now. It was still a new technique. I didn't like it. It was more dangerous. And you still needed a backup man standing by with a torch, just in case.

But Denver had this idea that if you could freeze a Chtorran, then you could map it internally, so we'd been freezing them and sending them to the photo-isotomography lab in San Jose. I'd seen the process once. It was impressive.

You take a frozen Chtorran, you put it up on a big frame and you point a camera at one end. Then you start taking thin slices off of it, taking a picture of the cross section after each slice. You do this with the entire worm. Then you give the pictures to the computer.

The computer gives you back a three-dimensional map of the internal structures of the Chtorran body. Using a joystick and a screen you can move around inside the map and examine specific organs and their relationships to each other. We still didn't know half of what we were looking at, but at least we had something to look at now.

The process had been successfully completed with four gastropedes of varying sizes. We didn't know why, but they seemed to be from four different species. Denver was going to keep freezing and mapping worms until the discrepancies were resolved.

"Duke," I said.

"Yeah?"

"Why do you think the fourth worm always waits so long to attack?"

"Beats the hell out of me."

"Yeah. Well, thanks anyway."

"No trouble at all, son. If you don't ask questions, how will you ever learn anything?"

The wall in front of me began to bulge.

I studied it offhandedly. Odd. I'd never seen a wall do that.

It bulged a little more. Yes, the dome was definitely being pushed out of shape. I raised the nozzle and pointed it directly at the center of the bulge.

"Duke, I think we got something. Burrell, pay careful attention now. I'll show you how this is done."

The dome began to crack ominously. The crack suddenly stitched up from the ground and across and then down again, and then the outlined piece began to topple outward—

"CHTORRRRRRR!! CHTORRRRRRRRR!!" This worm was the largest of them all! Was there no limit to their growth? Or was *this* the adult form?

It came sliding toward me like a freight train. I pulled the trigger and screamed and released a cloud of icy steam and a deadly spray of freezing liquid nitrogen. It spread out in sheets, enveloping the Chtorran. For a moment, it was hidden by the clouds and spray, and then it came plunging through, its fur streaked with white and icicles.

"Hold your torches!" I shouted, but it kept coming! And then, in a single startling instant of terror, the Chtorran raised itself up and up and up! The worm was three tons huge! It towered above me, crackling, wreathed in shining ice and silvery burning steam! And in that moment of deadly cold confrontation, I thought for sure that this was finally it— this brilliant beast of hell was about to topple down across me! This final frozen fury would be its last revenge! And then, instead, the momentum of its upward thrust continued and it began to slowly teeter sideways, farther and farther, until at last it toppled and came crackling and crashing down across the ground like a mountain of collapsing, shattering ice.

I could smell the cold like a knife within my brain, across my eyes. The pain of it was exquisite! The Chtorran was a fallen chimney. It lay shattered on the ground. Its fur was crystalizing in the sun, the ice was streaked along its sides in sheets and sprays and icicles. Something inside the creature exploded softly with a muffled *thump*—and as if in answer, one of its arms broke quietly off and slid and clattered to the ground.

How many more?

I turned away from the shining carcass and looked to the mountains climbing away to the north and west. How many more were out there? This was the twentieth I'd killed. But I didn't feel joyous—I felt only frustration. The job was taking too long!

The noise of the choppers pulled me back to the present. The first of the landing craft were already dropping down over the hill. They'd be bringing the rest of my science team and our equipment.

The security squad was just following the Robe unit into the hut. Not until they'd searched every room and tunnel would anybody else be allowed to enter. It was fine by me. I'd seen my share of worm huts. They were starting to look all alike to me.

For just a moment I felt tired. I didn't feel my usual exhilaration. I didn't even feel satisfied.

"Jim?" That was Duke, an ever-present voice in my ears, in the middle of my head.

"I'm fine," I responded.

"Good. Check out the corral, will you?"

"Right." I secured the freeze machine and headed around the dome. It didn't matter how I felt. That was irrelevant—I still had a job to do. I looked up at the corral and I remembered a little girl in a torn brown dress—

—and suddenly the feeling passed. And I knew why I was here. Because there was no place else that I would rather be. There was nothing else for me to do but *this!* It was perfect. The job was going to be done, and suddenly it was a beautiful day! I started toward the landing site to pick up the rest of my team.

Just one thought remained—

There has to be a better way!

A DAY FOR DAMNATION

THANK YOU

Dennis Ahrens
Morrie Bennett
Seth Breidbart
Jack Cohen
Diane Duane
Richard Fontana
Bill Glass
Harvey and Johanna Glass
David Hartwell
Robert and Ginny Heinlein
Don Hetsko
Karen Malcor
Henry Morrison
Jerry Pournelle
Rich Sternbach
Tom Swale
Linda Wright
Chelsea Quinn Yarbro
Howard Zimmerman

FOR THE MCCAFFREYS,
ANNE,
GIGI,
TODD,
AND ALEC,
WITH LOVE

ONE

THE CHOPPER looked like a boxcar with wings, only larger. It squatted in the middle of the pasture like a pregnant sow. Its twin rotors stropped the air in great slow whirls. I could see the tall grass flattening even from here.

I turned away from the window and said to Duke, "Where the hell did *that* come from?"

Duke didn't even look up from his terminal. He just grinned and said, "Pakistan." He didn't even stop typing.

"Right," I said. There wasn't any Pakistan any more, hadn't been a Pakistan for over ten years. I turned back to the window. The huge machine was a demonic presence. It glowered with malevolence. And I'd thought the worms were nasty to look at. This machine had jet engines large enough to park a car in. Its stubby wings looked like a wrestler's shoulders.

"You mean it was built for the Pakistan conflict?" I asked.

"Nope. It was built last year," corrected Duke. "But it was *designed* after Pakistan. Wait one minute—" He finished what he was doing at the terminal, hit the last key with a flourish, and looked up at me. "Remember the treaty?"

"Sure. We couldn't build any new weapons."

"Right," he said. He stood up and slid his chair in. He turned around and began picking up pages as they slid quietly, one after the other, out of the printer. He added, "We couldn't even replace old weapons. But the treaty didn't say anything about research or development, did it?"

He picked up the last page, evened the stack of papers on a desk top, and joined me at the window. "Yep. That is one beautiful warship," he said.

"Impressive," I admitted.

"Here—initial these," he said, handing me the pages.

I sat down at a desk and began working my way through them. Duke watched over my shoulder, occasionally pointing to a place I missed. I said, "Yeah, but—where did it come from? Somebody still had to build it."

Duke said, "Are your clothes custom made?"

"Sure," I said, still initialing. "Aren't everybody's?"

"Uh huh. You take it for granted now. A computer looks at you, measures you by sight, and appropriately proportions the patterns. Another computer controls a laser and cuts the cloth, and then a half-dozen robots sew the pieces together. If the plant is on the premises, you can have a new suit in three hours maximum."

"So?" I signed the last page and handed the stack back to him.

He put the papers in an envelope, sealed it, signed it, and handed it back to me to sign. "So," he said, "if we can do it with a suit of clothes, why can't we do it with a car or a house—or a chopper? That's what we got out of Pakistan. We were forced to redesign our production technology." He nodded toward the window. "The factory that built that Huey was turning out buses before the plagues. And I'll bet you the designs and the implementation plans and the retooling procedures were kept in the same state of readiness as our Nuclear Deterrent Brigade for all those years—just in case they might someday be *needed.*"

I signed the envelope and handed it back.

"Lieutenant," Duke grinned at me, "you should sit down and write a thank-you note to our friends in the Fourth World Alliance. Their so-called 'Victory of Righteousness' ten years ago made it possible for the United States to be the best-prepared nation on this planet for responding to the Chtorran infestation."

"I'm not sure they'd see it that way," I remarked.

"Probably not," he agreed. "There's a tendency toward paranoia in the Fourth World." He tossed the envelope into the safe and shut the door.

"All right—" he said, suddenly serious. "The paperwork is done." He glanced at his watch. "We've got ten minutes. Sit down and clear." He pulled two chairs into position, facing each other. I took one and he took the other. He took a moment to rub his face, then he looked at me as if I were the only person left on the planet. The rest of the world, the rest of the day, all of it ceased to exist. Taking care of the soul, Duke called it. Teams had gone out that hadn't and they hadn't come back.

Duke waited until he saw that I was ready to begin, then he asked simply, "How are you feeling?"

I looked inside. I wasn't certain.

"You don't have to hit the bull's-eye," Duke said. "You can sneak up on it. How are you feeling?" he asked again.

"Edgy," I admitted. "That chopper out there—it's intimidating. I mean, I just don't believe a thing that big can get off the ground."

"Mm hm," said Duke. "That's very interesting, but tell me about James McCarthy."

"I am—" I said, feeling a little annoyed. I knew how to clear. You dump your mind of everything that might get in the way of the mission.

"There—" pointed Duke. "What was that?"

I saw what he meant. I couldn't hide it. "Impatience," I said. "And annoyance. I'm getting tired of all the changes in procedures. And frustrated—that it doesn't seem to make a difference—"

"And . . . ?" he prompted.

"And . . ." I admitted, ". . . sometimes I'm afraid of all the responsibility. Sometimes I just want to run away from it. And sometimes I want to kill everything in sight." I added, "Sometimes I think I'm going crazy."

Duke looked up sharply at that, but his phone beeped before he could speak. He pulled it off his belt, thumbed it to life, and snapped, "Five minutes." He put it down on the table and looked at me. "What do you mean?"

"Well . . . I'm not sure if it's even real or not . . ." I weaseled.

Duke glanced at his watch. "Come on, Jim—there's a chopper waiting for us. I need to know if you're going on it or not. What's this 'crazy' stuff about?"

"I've been having . . . episodes. . . ." I said.

"What kind of 'episodes'?"

"Well, dreams. Sort of. I don't know if I should even be telling you this. Maybe I should plug into Dr. Davidson—"

"Yes, you should be telling me this!" Duke looked annoyed and impatient now. " 'Cause if you don't, I'm going without you." He started to rise.

I said quickly, "I've been—hearing things."

Duke sat back down.

"And," I continued, "—I've been remembering things. Mostly when I'm asleep or dozing. But it's things I've never heard or seen before. And—this one is the most confusing; you know how most people dream in pictures? Well, last night, I dreamed in sound. A symphony. It was cold and ghostly. It sounded like it was coming from another world, or another plane of existence. I thought I was dying. I woke up in a sweat, it scared me so."

Duke studied me like a father. His eyes were sharp. "Dreams, huh? That's what's been bothering you?"

I nodded.

He didn't say anything immediately. He looked away, out the window, then looked back to me. "I have dreams all the time," he admitted. "Nightmares actually. I keep seeing all the faces of all the people—" He stopped in the middle of the sentence. He dropped his gaze and looked at his hands. His huge old battered hands. I wondered if I should say something. Abruptly he looked back up at me, and he was Duke again—and he'd left several volumes unsaid. "But I don't let it stop me. Jim, do you hear what I'm saying?"

"Uh huh. It's just—"

"What?"

I was embarrassed to admit it. "It's just that I'm afraid of going out of control," I said. "It's almost like there are voices—I think if I could just make out what they're saying, I'd know the answer and everything would be all right. But I can never quite make it out. It feels like distant whispering." There. It was out. I waited for his reaction.

Duke looked troubled. He looked as if he couldn't find the answer he was looking for. He looked out the window at the chopper again. When he came back at me, his expression was unhappy.

"By all rights," he said, "I should ground you pending a medical exam. Except, I can't. I need you for this mission. That's the way this whole damn war is being run. There's not a one of us that doesn't deserve a couple of years of R and R. But we'll never see it. Instead, we'll just keep getting kicked from one crisis to the next and we'll have to take care of our sanity at the stoplights." He studied me sharply. "Do *you* think you're crazy?"

I shrugged, "I don't know. I certainly don't think I'm normal."

Abruptly, he grinned. "Now—*that's* normal! Nobody's normal on this planet, Jim. If you're aware of that, you're not crazy. It's only when you start insisting that you're sane that we're going to lock you up."

I blinked and hesitated—and then I got the joke. Sanity. If you thought you had it, you probably didn't. The evidence that you have it is that you wonder if you do. You can go crazy thinking about that one too long.

"Jim—" Duke said, "put all that aside for the moment. What are you here for? What's the job?"

"I'm here to kill worms. The job is to stop the Chtorran infestation of the Earth. By whatever means possible."

"Good," Duke said. "Now, let me ask you another question. Do you have to be sane or fit some standard of 'normality' to do that job?"

I thought about it. I looked at the answer inside my head. Obviously not. "No," I said.

"Good. So you see, it doesn't matter if you're crazy or not. There's only one thing I need to know. Can I count on you today?"

Now it was my turn to grin. "Yes, you can count on me."

"Absolutely."

"*Absolutely.*" And I meant it.

"Good," he said. "Grab your kit and let's go."

I didn't move. There was one more thing. "Uh—"

"Something else?" He looked concerned.

"Um, not really. Just a question—"

"Yes, what?"

"Um . . . Duke—who do *you* clear with?"

He looked startled. He turned away from me while he picked up his phone and his traveling kit. Then he turned back to me and said, "I check in with the boss from time to time." He jerked a thumb toward the ceiling—and beyond. "The man upstairs." And then he was out the door.

I followed him, shaking my head in wonderment. The universe was full of surprises.

TWO

I WAS wrong.

A machine that big *could* get off the ground.

It lumbered through the air like a drunken cow, but it flew—and it carried enough troops and gear to overthrow a small government. We had three of the best-trained teams in the Special Forces—Duke and I had trained them ourselves—a complete scientific squad, and enough firepower to barbecue Texas (well, a large part of Texas anyway).

I hoped we wouldn't need to use it.

I climbed into the back and sat down with the "enlisted men." Draftees, all of them. Except they weren't called draftees any more. The Universal Service Obligation had been rewritten—twice—by the New Military Congress of the United States. Four years of uniformed service. No exceptions. No deferments. No "needed skill" civilian classifications. And this means *you.* You were eligible on the day you turned sixteen. You had to be in uniform before your eighteenth birthday. Very simple.

To get into the Special Forces, though, you had to *ask.* In fact, you almost had to *demand* the opportunity. You couldn't end up in the Special Forces any more unless you *wanted* to be here.

And then, you have to prove you could handle the job.

I didn't know how rigorous the training was—I'd fallen into the Special Forces by accident, before the standards were tightened, and I'd been spending most of my career playing catch-up—but I could tell by looking at this team that it produced the result. I'd also heard that three-quarters of those who started the training dropped out before it was halfway over.

These were the survivors. The winners.

There wasn't one of them old enough to vote. And two of the girls didn't even look old enough to be wearing brassieres. But they weren't kids. They were combat-hardened troops. That these soldiers still counted their ages in the teens was incidental; they were as dangerous a bunch as the United States Army could put together. And it showed on their faces. They all had that same coiled look behind their eyes.

They were passing a cigarette back and forth between them. When it came to me, I took a puff—not because I wanted one, but because I wanted to make sure it wasn't "dusted" before I passed it on. I didn't think any of my troops would be that stupid, but it had been known to happen—on other teams, not mine. The army had a technical term for officers who let their troops go into combat situations stoned; we called them *statistics.*

The team wasn't talking much, and I knew why. It was my presence. I wasn't much more than three years older than the oldest of them, but I was the Lieutenant and that made me "the old man." Besides—they were afraid of me. Rumor had it I'd once burned a man alive on a worm hunt.

I felt old looking at them. And a little wistful too. These kids would be the last ones on the planet for a long time who would be able to remember what a "normal" childhood was like.

They should have been in high school or their first year in college. They should have been putting up balloons in the gymnasium for some school dance, or worrying about their Global Ethics reports, or even just hanging out down at the mall.

They knew this was not the way the world was supposed to work. And this was definitely not the future they had planned on. But this was the way it had turned out; there was a job that had to be done and they were the ones who had to do it.

I respected their commitment.

"Sir?" That was Beckman, tall and gangly and dark. I remembered, his family was from Guam. I glanced over toward him. "Are we gonna be back in time for *Derby?*" he asked.

I thought about it. We were headed into Southern Wyoming. Two hours in the air each way. Four hours on the ground, maximum. *Derby* was on at 9:00 P.M. T.J. had found out that Stephanie was coming back from Hong Kong. Now for sure, he had to locate the missing robot before Grant did. "Should be," I said. "If we're off the ground by six. No later." I glanced around at the others. "Can you guys target on that?"

They nodded agreement.

"Sure."

"Fine by me."

"Let's do it."

I gave them a grin. A trick I learned from Duke. Spend your smiles as if each one cost you a year off your life. Then your troops will bust their buns to earn them.

They looked so thrilled, I had to get up and go quickly forward—before I burst out laughing.

Duke glanced at me as I climbed up beside him. "They okay?"

"They're worried about the missing robot."

"Huh?"

"Derby. It's a TV program."

"Never touch the stuff myself," he said. He checked his watch. He leaned forward and tapped the pilot's shoulder. "You can call Denver now. Tell them we've passed Go-NoGo Lambda. They can launch the follow-chopper." To me, Duke said, "You can start warming up the Jeeps now. I want to drop the hatch and roll as soon as we hit dirt. I want this ship empty in thirty seconds."

"You got it," I said.

The target was nearly fifty klicks south of Wheatland.

It had been spotted, almost accidentally, by a Reclamation Scout. Fortunately, he knew what he was looking at. He called it in, then turned his Jeep north and drove like hell. He nearly made it too.

A response team spotted the overturned Jeep from the air a day later. A drop squad pulled the Jeep's log-disk, and the video record confirmed the infestation site. Four worms. Three "children" and an "adult." The nest would have been burned or frozen within forty-eight hours—except this time, Denver had a *better* idea.

This time we were going to capture a whole Chtorran family *alive.*

Duke and I always got the *good* jobs.

THREE

WE BANGED down onto the ground with a thump hard enough to rattle the teeth out of our skulls. Almost instantly, the rear door of the chopper blew open and the exit ramp popped out and down with a metal clang. It felt like the whole ship was coming apart at once. The lead Jeep was already bouncing down the ramp and onto the hard Wisconsin clay. The rollagons rumbled right down after it. And then the rest of the convoy.

The lead Jeep wheeled north immediately; its wheels stirred up the loose dirt on the ground and it left a thick cloud of dust in its wake. The dust tailed out quickly—the wind was strong today, not the best of conditions.

The other seven vehicles turned north also, forming a ragged diagonal line on the prairie. I was riding in the command vehicle with Duke, the largest of the rollagons—it looked like a landing barge with centipede legs and balloon tires, but it was steady and it was almost comfortable. In addition to our driver, we also had two auxiliary technicians, and a drop squad. For the moment, it was their mission. Duke and I were just cargo. Our job was to sit quietly and be delivered on-site.

We had a huge bank of tactical displays at our command. We could see our approach on a representational map, or as a color-coded radar scan of the surrounding terrain. We also had a dead-reckoning inertial guidance display and continuous confirmation by satellite Earthwatch. When we were two kilometers away, Duke halted the rollagon and sent the attack vehicles scurrying off to their positions for Go-NoGo Point

Kappa, and I launched a skyball—an aerial drone—for one last look-see before we went in.

The image on the screen tilted and swooped dizzily as the skyball skidded and slid across the sky. It was having trouble navigating in the wind. After a moment, though, it figured out what it was doing and the image steadied into a long glide.

The nest came up on the screen suddenly. It was a squat brown dome with a bulging circular entrance.

"A textbook case," I said. "See the purple stuff around the outside?"

Duke grunted. "You can spare me the narration."

I nodded and tapped at the keyboard, bringing the drone lower. The image turned slowly as the skyball circled the nest. I punched for scanning. The image shifted colors then: blue for cold, red for hot, yellow for in between. Most of the screen was orange. I had to turn down the range.

The corrected scan was mostly green and yellow. A faint orange track led to the dome. Or away from it. The track was at least an hour old.

I glanced at Duke; his expression was unreadable. "Scan the dome," he said.

We knew that the worms were hot when they were active. But we also knew that when they went torpid—which was usually during the hottest part of the day—their body temperatures could drop as much as thirty degrees. That was why the earliest mobile probes had failed to register their presence. The worms had been too cool.

We knew better now.

The worms went *deep* and they went *cold.* Men had died to find that out.

The skyball came in low and close now. The dome filled the screen. I punched in a sonic-scan overlay. There was something there, all right— a dark blue mass, mottled with quickly shifting colors. It was large and deep below the surface.

The screen said it massed four tons.

"That's a good-sized family," said Duke. "Can we take 'em?"

I was wondering the same thing. "Denver says the gas is good. This is at the upper end of the range, but it's within the limit."

"How do you feel about it?"

"I say go."

"Good," said Duke. "So do I." He thumbed his mike. "All units. It's a go. I repeat, it is a *go.* Proceed to your final positions. This is it."

We were committed now. There were no more Go-NoGo points.

Duke leaned forward and rapped our driver. "Come on—let's move!" The big rollagon trundled forward, up a small ridge and then down the long slope on the opposite side.

I pulled the skyball up and directed it to circle the dome on a continual scan. If there was any change in heat level, it would sound an immediate alarm. We would have between ten and ninety seconds' warning—depending on the worms. I checked my earphones and mike. This was the most dangerous part of the mission. We were too vulnerable to ambush on the approach.

I had to read this dome quickly and say if it was safe to proceed. If not—if I thought it appropriate—I had the authority to abort the entire mission. This was the last Go-NoGo and I was the worm expert.

The troops liked to believe that I had some kind of uncanny "worm sense." I didn't, of course—and the rumor made me nervous. But they wanted to believe it—I was as close to a lucky charm as they had—so I didn't try to squelch the story.

And besides, I sort of halfway wished it was true. It would have made me feel a lot better about how little I really knew.

The rollagon bounced onto level ground then and I stood up in my seat to peer ahead. There was the dome. It looked deceptively small in person. Most of the nest was underground. We really didn't know how deep the worms would tunnel. We weren't willing to let a family establish itself long enough to find out.

I tapped the driver's shoulder. "This is close enough," I said. "It's spider time. I'll walk the rest of the way."

The rollagon slid to an uneven halt. I sat down again at my keyboard, and activated United States Military Spider ARAC-5714.

Beside me, I could hear Duke acknowledging each of the other vehicles as they slid into position around the dome. I didn't bother to look up. I knew that the teams were already dropping out of their vehicles, torches at the ready. We were eight tight little islands of death. Priority one: *survive.* Dead heroes do not win wars.

The green ready light came up. I slid the console back and pulled the spider control board up and into position. I slipped the goggles over my head, waited for my vision to clear, and slipped my hands into the control gloves.

There was the usual moment of discontinuity, and then I was *in* the spider. I was looking through its eyes, hearing through its ears, feeling through its hands. "Forward," I said, and the point of view moved down, out of the forward ramp of the rollagon, and forward toward the quiet-looking dome.

My point of view was closer to the ground than I was used to, and my eyes were farther apart, so everything looked smaller—and the perspective was deeper. I needed this walk to slip into my "spider-consciousness mode." I had to get into the *feeling* of it.

The military spiders were hasty adaptations of the industrial models. This one had a black metal body, eight skinny legs—each ending in a large black hoof—and an observation turret. The spider could function with half its legs disabled; any two of its legs could also function as arms. There was a waldo inside each hoof, complete with tactile sensors.

During the plagues, the spiders had been used extensively in situations where human beings could not—or would not—go themselves. The spiders had been very useful in hospitals. And in crematoriums. The spiders had gathered most of the dead.

"Slower," I commanded. We were approaching the entrance to the dome. "Scan. . . ."

The image before me shifted down the spectrum. The colors of objects changed, then changed again. Green and yellow again. Some orange, but very very faint.

"Sonic scan . . ." I said, and turned my attention into the dome. The large blue mass was clearer here. I could almost make out the shape of four huge worms. They were intertwined in a circular formation, if I was reading the image correctly. And they were still cold.

"Well?" asked Duke at my shoulder.

"They're an awfully pretty shade of blue," I replied. "It's go." I gave the command, "Forward."

The spider entered the dome.

Turn right, go up and around and enter the central chamber. Go to the center hole. Squat over the hole. Look down.

Nothing in the lower chamber?

Look again.

I made that mistake once. I won't make it again.

The worms are huge. It's hard to see them as worms. They look like a huge furry carpet.

Scan. . . .

Still blue.

I wonder what it looks like when they wake up—but I'm not going to wait to find out.

Lower the nozzle.

And . . . give the command, "Gas."

There is a hissing noise.

The color of the worms goes darker—

I slipped my hands out of the gloves and pulled the goggles off my eyes. I looked at Duke. "Done," I said.

Duke grinned and clapped me on the shoulder. "Good job." He turned to the communications technician. "All right, bring the chopper down. We'll be ready to start loading in thirty minutes. Move the 'dozer unit into position and tell them to fix grapples and stand by for detox. Have everybody else move in to the primary perimeter."

The rollagon lurched forward again and Duke gave me a cheerful thumbs-up signal. He started to say something, but I didn't hear it. A second huge cargo chopper was just clattering in overhead. It sounded like a cosmic jackhammer—the one God uses for starting earthquakes.

This was the machine that would carry the worms back to Denver.

I wondered if it would be big enough.

FOUR

AS SOON as we pulled into position, I took a second reading on the mass of the worms. They were too big. I couldn't shake the feeling that I was making a mistake here. Perhaps I should have said no at the last Go-NoGo point.

I almost turned to Duke then, but I stopped myself. I did this every time. As soon as it was too late, I started second-guessing. It didn't matter any more what I thought. We were committed.

I took a second reading on the mass of the worms, recalculated the gas dosage according to Denver's mass-ratio equations, and detonated another pellet. I wondered if it should have been two. I'd rather kill the worms than have them wake up while we were loading them.

We gave the gas a full ten minutes. I took a final reading—the worms were the most wonderful shade of dark purple I'd ever seen—then brought the spider out.

Then we pulled the dome off its foundations. We anchored grapples in its base, attached tow ropes to a Jeep and backed up slowly. The hut ripped off like so much Styrofoam. The worms didn't build for strength. They didn't have to.

We had to do it twice; the dome shredded too easily. I felt like an intruder, a vandal. We had to pull it off in pieces. Then we had to rip off the top floor too.

That job was harder. We had to plant small charges in the floor to break it up. It was made out of the same material as the dome walls, but it was denser and had the strength of industrial Kevlar. It would have to be strong to hold the weight of a healthy worm family.

The worms built their nests by chewing up trees and spitting out foam. Apparently they could vary the mix enough to produce lightweight translucent walls and heavyweight hardwood floors all from the same basic ingredients. A neat trick.

When the lower half of the nest was finally revealed, there was a moment of . . . hesitation. The teams—men and women alike—gathered in silence around the edge to stare down at the exposed worms.

They were huge. Just knowing they were huge from the readings on the screen was not the same as actually seeing them in the flesh. Even the smallest of them was a meter thick and three meters long. The "adult" was two meters high at its brain case and twice as long as the baby. I wished I'd given them that third pellet.

The worms were coiled around each other like lovers, head to tail, head to tail, in a circular formation. They were shadowed in the lower half of the nest, but even so their fur still shone a brilliant red. It was almost alluring.

Duke came up beside me to look. His expression tightened, but he didn't speak.

"Looks like we interrupted a Chtorran orgy," I said.

Duke grunted.

"The baby's about three hundred kilos," I offered. "Papa bear is probably a thousand."

"At least," said Duke. He didn't like it, I could tell. He was too silent.

"Too big?" I asked.

"Too expensive," he grumbled. "You're looking at fifteen cows a week. That's a lot of hamburger." He clicked his tongue and turned away. "All right," he bawled, "let's get down in there and get to work." He pointed to a man with a headset. "Tell that chopper to drop the slings. Now!"

We had one bad moment with the loading.

We started with the baby. One squad dropped into the pit while the other two teams stood above them with flame throwers, bazookas and incendiary bullets. The worm was too big to lift or roll onto a sling—it had to be lifted so the canvas could be pulled beneath it.

The squad in the pit quickly slid a series of stainless-steel rods underneath the smallest worm to form a lattice of crossbars. These were then connected at their ends to two longer bars placed lengthwise against the worm. The baby was now lying on a ladder-shaped bed.

The chopper was already clattering into place overhead, whipping us with wind and noise. Its cables were already lowering. The team didn't try to grab the free-swinging ends—instead they waited until the lines touched ground and there was enough slack. They grabbed the cables and ran to attach them to the ladder under the worm. Beckman gave a thumbs-up signal and the chopper began to raise the cables. They tightened visibly. The ladder shuddered and began to lift—

For a moment, the worm resisted—it was just a large limp bag of scarlet pudding—and then the connection with the other worms was broken and it pulled up into the air.

Immediately, every worm in the pit began to stir.

Papa worm grunted uneasily. The other two actually chirruped and rumbled. But baby worm was the worst. It writhed as if in pain, and let loose a plaintive wail of anguish. It curled and looped like an earthworm cut in half. The ladder swung recklessly. The cables groaned—and then its eyes popped open. They were huge and black and round—they slid this way and that, unfocused and unseeing.

The team jumped backwards, flattening themselves against the nest wall—

"Hold your fire—!" I was screaming. "Hold your fire, goddammit!" Somehow I made myself heard above the terror. "It's still unconscious! Those are automatic reactions!"

Indeed, the baby was already calming down again. Its eyes slid shut and it curled—tried to curl—into a swollen red ball, still hanging above the floor of the nest.

"Oh, Jesus—" gasped someone. "I don't need this—" He started scrambling out. The two men on either side of him looked uncertain—

Duke didn't give the team a chance to be scared. He jumped down into the pit with them and started snapping orders. "Come on—let's get that bastard onto the mat. Come on, move it!" He grabbed the soldier who'd started to panic and pushed him straight at the worm. "You're riding up with it, Gomez. Thanks for volunteering." Gomez kept moving in the direction of Duke's shove. It was safer.

"Come on! Move that mat! Pull it under! Under—goddammit! *Under!* Good! All right—" Duke pointed up at the communications tech, still bellowing, and waving his arm like a semaphore. "Down—! Bring it down!" And then back to the squad again. "All right! Let's get those bars out! Let's get those cables attached! Now! Goddammit! Now! Let's move!"

The pit squad moved like demons then, detaching the cables from the bars and reattaching them to the canvas faster than Duke could swear. They pulled the bars out from under the worm and backed quickly out of the way. The chopper lifted then—just a bit, to bring the edges of the canvas up—and the worm was strapped into its sling. Two of the bars were slid through the straps then to seal the worm into a steel and canvas cocoon and four more cables were attached to the ends of these. It was for *its* protection as much as ours. We didn't want the creatures banging loose around the inside of the chopper. The worms would be kept strapped and hanging the whole trip.

"All right! Take it up!" Duke hollered and waved. The clatter of the chopper drowned his words and the wind whipped at his face. He didn't even watch, he was already turning to the next worm. "What are you slobs waiting for? Let's get those bars under—"

The other three worms were easier—but not much.

At least now we knew that when we separated them, they'd react—but they wouldn't wake up. We could handle that. The team worked faster now—

The chopper hovered overhead, growling and rumbling, and we lifted the worms one by one into its massive cargo bay. The big creatures sagged ominously in the creaking slings.

It was a terrifying job.

The wind was rising and the chopper began to pitch and slide sideways in the air. I wondered if we were going to have to return without all four—but the pilot turned the ship into the wind and told us to keep going. Whoever she was, she was good.

Once—the worm in the sling was banged against the side of the nest; it moaned in its sleep, a dark purple rumble of despair. The pit squad turned and looked with wild expressions on their faces. The monster chirruped like a crying woman. The sound of it was *devastating*. Suddenly, this creature was an object of *pity*. Then the worm cleared the nest wall and rose swiftly into the air—and Duke was pointing and waving again.

Papa worm was last. As the big creature came rising up out of the ground, the afternoon sun struck highlights off its bright red fur. It shimmered with a thousand flickering colors—it looked like a heavenly pink aura. I couldn't help but marvel—it was the most beautiful color I'd ever seen. . . .

The creature lifted into the sky like a big pink blimp. I followed it all the way up. It disappeared into the belly of the chopper and the giant black doors of the machine slid shut with a *whump*.

Duke signaled the tech, the tech said something into his microphone, and the chopper whirred noisily off southward.

"All right," he said. "Let's go home and watch TV. Is T.J. going to tell Stephanie about the missing robot or not?"

FIVE

STEPHANIE STAYED in Hong Kong for an emergency meeting with the Chinese ambassador, so T.J. didn't tell her about the robot. Grant found out who the baby's father *really* was, and confronted Karen with the lie. The robot remained missing.

Obviously, we made it back in time.

Toward the end of the show, an orderly came in and tapped Duke on the shoulder. He got up and left quietly. I noticed, but didn't follow. If Duke needed me, he'd let me know.

A few minutes later, the orderly came back and tapped me on the shoulder. "Duke wants to see you."

I thanked her and went up to the office. Duke looked unhappy. He was sitting at his terminal, staring glumly at the screen. His hands were hesitating above the keyboard.

"What's up?" I asked.

He didn't answer; he just punched up another display and studied it sourly.

I walked around behind him and looked over his shoulder. He was sorting through the list of targets for the mission we'd just completed.

"Those are the alternate targets, Duke. Are you planning another mission?"

He shook his head. "Just looking." He lifted his hands away from the keyboard and stopped. "I don't see what we could have done different. We made the best choice we could." He swiveled to look at me. "Or do you disagree?"

"No," I said. "We chose the right nest." I stood there before him, waiting.

He said, "What do you think about the Lake Hattie site? Would you recommend going in there?"

"You *are* planning another mission. What happened? Our worms died from the gas?"

"I wish," Duke said bitterly. He leaned back in his chair and folded his arms. "No. The gas wore off early. They woke up in the chopper. Thirty minutes short of Denver."

"Oh no—" I felt suddenly weak. I wanted to sit down. I had a sick feeling in my gut. Live worms aboard a chopper—?

"The chopper went down in the mountains," Duke said. "There were no survivors." He studied me for a moment—as if he knew what I was thinking—then he swiveled to face the window and the dark night outside.

I wanted to say something, but I didn't know what. I felt like I'd been opened up with a machete and my guts were spilling out on the floor.

Duke said, "If it makes it any easier, they think it had something to do with the altitude."

"No," I said. "It doesn't make it any easier."

I went to the water cooler and filled a plastic cup. I wasn't thirsty, but it was something to do.

Behind me, Duke said, "There's a bottle of Scotch in the bottom drawer of the filing cabinet. Pour two."

I handed Duke his drink, found a chair, and sat down across from him.

"I screwed up," I said. "I should have followed my instincts. I looked at those worms and I wanted to detonate every pellet in the spider. I wish I had. Instead, I followed orders."

"That's right," said Duke. "Make it Denver's fault. To err is human. To blame the other guy is even more so. I'm glad to see you're taking it so well."

I ignored his comment. I was still putting the pieces back together. I said slowly, ". . . I follow Denver's orders because I like to think they know what they're doing. But they don't—they really don't. And we both know that!" I was being careless, I knew it, but Duke didn't react or try to stop me, so I plunged on. I wanted to get it all said before I ran out of steam. "It's crazy, Duke. They're so insulated from the front lines of this war that all they've got left are their theories and speculations—and they're making policy based on those theories. When that filters down here, to our level, we have to make life and death decisions based on those policies and hope that it's appropriate! And sometimes it is! They get it right just often enough to keep us trusting them."

Duke said, "I've heard this all before, you know. None of it is original. Every lieutenant goes through it." He glanced at his watch. "You're right on schedule."

He was being flip about it, but he was right. Of course. Again.

I felt embarrassed. I didn't know what to say. I flustered.

I looked at my drink. I took a belt of it. "Duke—" My voice cracked. I was out of anger—I felt drained. I said, "Duke—I'm losing it. Really. It's *all* meaningless voices now. I mean, I don't know that I can follow *anyone's* orders any more. I mean—if nobody else knows what they're doing either, Duke—and *I'm* the guy who ends up being responsible, then I'm the guy who *really* has to be sure. And I know that I'm not. So I follow orders—not because it's the safest thing to do, but because I can't think of anything *better!* And that still doesn't work. People still die—and it's *still* my fault. I didn't even know that chopper crew! I didn't even know their names—"

"Wolfman. Wein."

"—whatever. They're still dead and it's my fault. No matter how you slice it, it still stinks!"

"And—" prompted Duke.

"And I don't like it!" I finished lamely. I wished it had been a little more *profound,* but at least this was the truth.

Duke had listened to my outpouring in silence; he had remained carefully blank the whole time. Now he looked up at me with a peculiar expression on his face. "I'll tell you something, Jim." He took a breath. "What you like is unimportant. I know you don't even like hearing that, but it's true. Whether you like it or not is ultimately irrelevant. The job still has to be done. And mistakes are always going to be made—again, like it or not."

He hesitated for a beat, as if considering his next sentence. He looked into his cup thoughtfully; his eyes were shaded. When he spoke again, his voice was lower. "I know it's frustrating. It's *always* frustrating. It's always going to *be* frustrating. You think I haven't been there? This is Pakistan all over again—only this time I know how deep the brown sauce is. You want to know what's really crazy? Almost all of our procedures are derived from a war that was *lost* twelve years ago. That's crazy. But—" he shrugged, "—it always comes back to this. The job still has to be done."

"I don't know—" I said. "I mean, I don't know if I can do this job any more." I didn't look at him when I said it.

"Jim, don't be stupid." Suddenly, there was a hint of metal in his voice. "Don't you think we've *all* gone through this? I have. Shorty did. It's part of the responsibility. You get to make mistakes. You can't help it. It's part of being human. Now, I'm going to tell you the other part. You don't get to use your mistakes as an excuse to quit."

"I'm sorry. I don't see it that way."

"Then you're missing the obvious. If we discharged every man or woman who ever made a mistake, we wouldn't have an officer left in the United States Army. Myself included."

"Yeah, but my mistakes kill people—"

"So do mine," he said quietly. His eyes were hard. "You think you have a monopoly on that one?"

I didn't answer. I'd already proven myself a fool. Why compound it?

Duke put his cup down on the desk next to him. "Listen, Jim—the truth is, a mistake is just one more opportunity to put in the correction. It's not a club to beat yourself with. It's just something to learn from. The only *real* failure is quitting. That's where you waste lives. Those pilots—Wein and Wolfman—they knew the risk. They were willing to take it."

"They trusted my judgment—"

"So—? So do I. So what?"

"But what if next time, it's you—?"

Duke shrugged. "It could just as easily be you too, Jim. I have to trust you. You have to trust me. It's part of the job. So what? I mean, so what about it? Do you want to feel sorry for yourself, or do you want to get on with the job? You do want to kill worms, don't you?"

"Don't be silly—"

"Well, then—this is where you learn to pick up the pieces and keep going. Consider it part of your training to be a captain. This is the part where you accept the responsibility for the decisions that *hurt.*"

"But, it hurts—" I knew it was stupid even as I said it, but I said it anyway, "—and I don't know what to *do.*"

"Nothing," he said. "There's nothing *to* do, Jim. Just hurt. Until you stop hurting. You don't even have to dramatize it. You can spare me the weeping and wailing. I've seen weeping and wailing. And better than yours."

Then he added quietly, "I know you're hurting, Jim. I'd worry about

you if you weren't. What you need to know is that it's all right to hurt."
His eyes were surprisingly compassionate.

I felt—grateful. But I was too embarrassed to meet his gaze. I said,
"Thanks," and looked away quickly.

Duke asked, "Is that it? Or is there anything else you want me to
know?"

I shook my head. "I think that just about covers it." I finished my
drink and wondered if I should get myself another. I deserved to get
drunk tonight. Except—I knew it really wouldn't help. This was something I was just going to have to work through by myself. One day at a
time. Damn. I was getting too rational for my own good.

"All right—" I sighed and slid my chair over to another terminal. "I
guess I'd better start mapping another operation. At least, we've proven
we can get them out of the ground alive—"

Duke said, "Hold it, Jim. I haven't given you the *bad* news yet."

I lifted my fingers from the keyboard and looked over at him. "It gets
worse?"

He nodded. "We're being pulled out."

"The whole team?"

"No. Just you and I. There's a chopper on the way. It'll be here in an
hour."

"Where are we going? Denver?"

"Oakland."

"Oakland?!! What the hell is in Oakland?"

"The Gertrude Stein memorial plaque—" Duke said. He levered
himself to his feet. "—Among other things. You've got an hour to pack.
Be on the field at 23:30. We'll be briefed in the air."

I looked at the terminal display again. "But—" I said, hopelessly,
"—I wanted to go to Lake Hattie!"

"If it's any consolation, Jim, so did I." He crumpled his cup and
tossed it at the wastebasket as he left the room. The cup missed the
basket and bounced into a corner.

I scooped it up and popped it in.

Damn.

SIX

THE CHOPPER was an hour late, and it was another hour before we got off the ground. Then there was a spring storm over most of Utah, so the pilot chose to detour south. It would be daylight before we touched down in California.

And the only reading matter aboard was the briefing book. It was incomplete and took only twenty minutes to finish. It was all background, nothing about our assignment, and it didn't tell me anything I didn't already know. The infestations were spreading faster than our ability to burn them out.

There was one interesting footnote, however. Oakland had two worms now, but they didn't really know what to do with them because they didn't know how to interpret their behavior. The note said they needed a worm expert, someone who knew the creatures in their normal habitat.

I pointed out the use of the word "normal" to Duke. He snorted too when he saw it.

"Not if I have anything to say about it," he added. He closed his eyes again and appeared to go back to sleep.

I envied him. I can't sleep on airplanes. I can doze, but I keep waking up suddenly. Any little noise, any little bump or bounce, any change in engine sound and I'm instantly alert, wondering if everything is all right. I get off airplanes exhausted.

I stared out the window at the distant flashes of lightning. The storm was a nasty one. The cloud banks towered like the walls of a canyon—a gigantic one. The moonlight gave them an eerie blue sheen. Every few seconds, one or another of the towering masses would crackle and flare and light up the whole sky. Beautiful—and terrifying.

I wondered about the people below.

Did anyone still live out there?

We were a planet of scattered survivors, all scrambling like mad to stay alive long enough to get the crops in. Somewhere between seventy and ninety percent—there was no way to know for sure—of the human race had died in the first three years. There was no way to know how many had been lost to the plagues and how many to associated disasters and aftereffects. I'd heard a rumor, unconfirmed, that the suicide rate was still climbing.

I wondered about that too. When you've lost everything and have nothing left to live for—I wondered how close I was—

It was a long flight. . . .

Eventually, the sun tinged the horizon behind us and we began dropping toward Oakland. I was on the wrong side of the ship to see San Francisco. I was disappointed in that—I wanted to see how bad it looked from the air. They said the city was still in pretty grim shape. I'd seen pictures, of course, but it wasn't the same. Besides, my dad had died in San Francisco—

Well, disappeared anyway. . . .

There was a car waiting for us on the ground, but we were delayed by the inevitable decontamination baths—no telling what bugs were still floating around—and then had to wait again until our vaccinations could be updated.

It was another hour before we were in the Jeep and on our way south. We didn't have a driver—the car knew the way without one. There was the standard taped welcome on the screen, which Duke and I both ignored, and a thermos of tea and a box of breakfast rolls in the flashbox. The tea was already lukewarm; the rolls were stale.

The Jeep delivered us to the Special Forces officers' billet—formerly the downtown Oakland Holiday Inn. "Probably because they couldn't find worse," Duke explained. There were no humans on duty here either—just a couple of terminals, a bell-cart and a mindless robot, noisily polishing the lobby floor. We had to step around it to get to the desk.

The terminal beeped and clucked, checked our ID, issued us keycards and wished us a nice stay. It also called us "Mr. and Mrs. Anderson."

Duke wasn't amused.

"It must have heard what you said—" I pointed out. We were following the bell-cart down the hall. "You know, all these machines talk to each other. They compare notes."

Duke gave me a withering sideways glance. I shut up. One day I would learn—Duke did not appreciate whimsy. "Clean up quickly," he said.

"No sleep—?"

"You'll sleep in October. There's a war on, remember?"

Right.

A hot shower and a shave later—the second-best substitute for six hours sleep, (the first-best being *eight* hours sleep)—Duke handed me hardcopy orders. "There's a colloquium at ten hundred about the worms. You're already cleared through. I want you to specifically see if anyone knows anything about nesting habits. They've already got the disks of yesterday's mission. Find out if they've seen them. I think we're seeing another shift in behavior. Oh yeah—and be polite. The science boys are starting to chafe at the presence of the military."

"Right."

As interested as I was in the Chtorran ecology, I still would have preferred the sleep. With luck, I could sleep in the session—as long as they didn't put me in the front row.

The Oakland Control Section of the United States Ecological Agency was hidden behind a long range of rolling hills. The Jeep whined as it rolled up the winding slope. As it came over the top, I saw that most of the buildings below were hardened inflatables. They were large and roomy and blandly amorphous. A platoon of twenty shining robots was mowing the lawns around the buildings. Lawns! I didn't know whether to laugh at the extravagance—or be annoyed at the waste of energy. But the grass was green and lush looking.

I showed my credentials to the gort at the entrance—it scanned them with an evil-looking eye; these machines weren't designed for friendliness—and then passed me through. I still hadn't seen another human being yet.

The Jeep headed toward the largest of the domes. It rolled right into the building and delivered me to a tall set of double-steel doors and an armed sergeant in a glass booth. The glass looked thick and the sergeant wore a grim expression.

The Jeep beeped. Something clicked. The red lights went on above the doors. Surveillance cameras swiveled to look at me—and so did other devices that weren't cameras.

Maybe this wasn't going to be as easy as I thought.

The sergeant looked up, saw I was an officer and saluted perfunctorily. Then he directed me to approach the booth and stand on the white platform in front of it.

After he finished scanning me, the sergeant let me take two steps forward to state my business. He studied his screens for a moment, nodded and hit a button. The red lights went off, the surveillance cameras swiveled back into their housings—so did the other devices—and I relaxed. Somewhat.

The sergeant touched another button and the steel doors groaned and slid apart, revealing a bright-lit maze of doors, passageways, stairs, halls, catwalks and elevators. There were conduits and pipes everywhere, all brightly colored and labeled with large stenciled letters and numbers. It looked like they'd forgotten the interior walls of the building.

I looked to the sergeant with what I hoped was a questioning expression.

The sergeant nodded—obviously he'd seen the expression before—and pointed to a door. He directed me down a long featureless corridor —follow the red stripe on the floor—and into an anteroom, through the double doors and—

A lady in a white coat looked up from her desk and greeted me with a frown. "You're—?"

"McCarthy, James Edward, Lieutenant, Special Forces."

She looked back to her terminal. "You're not on *my* list—"

"I just arrived in Oakland two hours ago—"

"I'll have to double-check this—" She was already reaching for the phone.

I said the magic words: "—and I'm in the Uncle Ira Group."

She replaced the phone neatly on the hook. "Right." She slid her chair back and stood up. I saw that she needed a cane to walk. "Follow me, please—"

Through another set of double doors, and down another corridor— why bother with security, I wondered; just paint out all the stripes and nobody will be able to find anything—and into a small angular theater, already darkened. The seats were stacked in steep rows overlooking a curtained wall. A young-looking woman in a lab coat stood at the podium. I saw a lot of uniforms and lab coats and grim faces. I looked for a place in the rear of the room, preferably a comfortable one—

"There's one down here, Lieutenant—" the woman at the podium said. She looked familiar.

I threaded my way down toward the front row. Damn.

"Oh—it's McCarthy. I thought I recognized the Special Forces."

Now I knew her. I smiled back—weakly. Her name was Fletcher—but she'd once introduced herself as Lucrezia Borgia. I didn't know her first name. As I took my seat, she said, "Good to see you again, Lieutenant."

The man sitting in the next chair glanced at me curiously. I flushed with embarrassment.

"All right," said Dr. Fletcher. "Let's get back to work. Dr. Abbato at the Cairo Institute has raised an interesting question about the gastropedes—and their place in their own ecology—and that's opened up a very interesting, and perhaps very fruitful, line of research. I think you'll find today's demonstration very—" she allowed herself a smile, "—enlightening."

I propped my elbow on the chair arm and my chin on my knuckles, and tried to look awake.

Dr. Fletcher had close-cropped dark hair. She had high cheekbones and wore thin-rimmed glasses—and she had that *professional* look, neither plain nor pretty. She looked competent. I guessed it was the crisp way she handled herself.

"Dr. Abbato has posed the question—what kind of ecology could produce creatures like the Chtorran worm? What is the home planet like? That's where he began.

"All right—these are *today's* answers:

"Heavier gravity, we know that. The musculature of Chtorran creatures, the strength of their shells and skeletons, the rigidity of Chtorran plant stems—we are assuming that Chtorr had a minimum gravity of 1.1 Earth normal and a maximum of 1.5. That latter figure is probably a little high, but we're giving ourselves a margin for error.

"A thicker atmosphere, of course, but we have no way of really knowing its makeup. Chtorran plants and animals are extraordinarily good at extracting oxygen from this atmosphere, so we are allowing the assumption that the Chtorran air has somewhat less free oxygen.

"We do think that the Chtorran primary is a red star. Very old. Perhaps very close to final collapse. Chtorran plants seem to prefer red light, the redder the better, and Chtorran eyes seem to work best in the red end of the spectrum.

"And finally, we think that the Chtorran ecology is at least a half-billion years older than ours. That means—if Chtorr evolved anything like Earth—that there were the equivalent of mammals, or even more advanced life-forms, walking the surface of Chtorr when the best this planet had to offer was slime not even distinctive enough to make an interesting fossil. That means that the Chtorran ecology has at least a half-billion-year head start in the evolution race."

I tried to stifle a yawn. I knew all this—

Dr. Fletcher looked over at me. "We'll get to the good parts in a minute, Lieutenant. Try to stay awake until then, if you can."

I blushed embarrassedly and straightened in my seat.

Dr. Fletcher continued, "If the same processes of evolution have held true on Chtorr, then the planet should have evolved a particularly nasty and competitive food chain—and so far, that's exactly what we've seen.

"Using our own ecology as a model—the only ecology we have to base a model on—we know that the process of evolution is a process of continually adding links to the food chain. Reptiles evolved out of fish to eat fish—and then each other. Mammals evolved out of reptiles to eat reptiles *and* fish—and each other.

"What comes after mammals? And what comes after that? And after that? And whatever comes after that—presumably, that's what rules Chtorr. Whatever it is, it *has* to be at the top of its food chain.

"That was the *initial* hypothesis. I'll give you a minute to think about that. The implications are interesting. Dr. Abbato did his homework on this one."

Dr. Fletcher studied her notes for a moment, then looked back up with a smile. "The first one is that a sentient species has to be at the top of its food chain. It can't be otherwise. Think about it. New forms *always* arise to feed on the old. What else can they feed on? The high levels have to be predatory. And predators are the life-forms most likely to develop intelligence. You're probably all familiar with Dr. Cohen's famous remark, 'Intelligence develops first in predators. After all, how much brains does it take to sneak up on a blade of grass?'"

There were polite chuckles. It was an old joke.

But Dr. Fletcher wasn't interested in laughs. She pushed on. "It's pretty clear that the higher level the predator, the higher its capacity for intelligence. Carrying that one step further, we think that sentience is most likely to develop in a top-level omnivore." Dr. Fletcher allowed herself an impish smile. "We recognize, of course, that we may be biased in that assumption—because we are the only proof of it we have.

"But, we think it is also what we will find with the Chtorran sentient

Chtorran species—when we meet it. We expect that they will be nothing less than the most cunning and sophisticated predator of all Chtorran life-forms. And, of course, that implies—given the half-billion-year evolutionary advantage of the Chtorr—that the primary perception that sentience can have of us, specifically our ecology, will be as *prey*. Food. Another kind of snack. At best, lunch.

"In fact, given that half-billion-year advantage, the rest of the Chtorran ecology can be expected to operate the same way. We are nothing more than fuel for them—and probably not even very efficient fuel, at least not as efficient as they're probably used to, which is probably why they need to burn so much of it—us. As a matter of fact, the Chtorran ecology has demonstrated a voraciousness that is nothing less than stunning. Of course, that also suggests that the Chtorran ecology has to generate a prodigious supply of life-support to fuel its primary species.

"So, given all of that, we have been making the assumption—and so did Dr. Abbato—that the Chtorran species we've seen so far are just the advance guard of a much greater invasion still to come. The assumption is that whatever agency or sentience is responsible for the infestation depends on these creatures for life-support—*and* that we are not going to see the arrival of the next level of infestation until such time as this life-support level is safely and solidly established. As a matter of fact, our whole war effort has been geared not toward eradication—because we don't yet have the resources or the knowledge necessary for that, perhaps someday—but toward destabilizing the interrelationships of the infestation. Finally, that brings us back to Dr. Abbato. And the questions he was left with.

"Dr. Abbato wondered, 'If all of these assumptions are indeed true, then what is the purpose of the gastropedes in the Chtorran food chain? What *function* do they serve?' "

I wondered if she had an answer—and if we'd get to it today. I snuck a glance at my watch.

"This is one of those questions that seems very innocuous, until you get into it—then you find out it's actually a major paradigm-shifter. It's forcing us to rethink everything we know, so pay attention here. You too, Lieutenant—"

She didn't miss a thing! No more front row seats.

"We've been assuming that the worms are at the top of the Chtorran food chain—that is, this particular subset of it. We've not yet found a worm predator. Considering the voraciousness of the worms, I'm not sure we want to see a next step. We still don't know how to cope with this one. But, if the worms actually are at the top of the food chain, then they would also have to be the sentient species—and so far there's no evidence of that. In fact, there's quite a bit of evidence to the contrary. So, we're pretty sure that the worm predator has not yet shown up or established itself. Which brings us back to Dr. Abbato's question. What *are* the worms?

"As a matter of fact, the worms seem to be something of an anomaly even in their own ecology. For instance, what do the worms feed on?"

They eat people, I answered. But I didn't say it aloud.

"We can't identify a prey species," Dr. Fletcher said. "Yes, we've seen the worms eating millipedes and other Chtorran life-forms—that's to be expected—but for the most part, the worms have been feeding on the host planet ecology: cattle, sheep, horses, dogs—and humans, unfortunately.

"We've analyzed the protein requirements of an average-size worm and measured it against the amount of millipedes and other Chtorran life-forms it would have to consume to generate that amount of protein, and the ratio is simply unworkable. The worms can't eat enough millipedes and shambler bushes and libbits to survive. These Chtorran life-forms are simply not high enough on the chain to be the primary food source for the worms. The worms are not the predators for these Chtorran species, and these species are not the prey for the worms. If this is a food chain as we understand it, then there are links *missing* from this food chain!

"And that brings us to this very important question: if the worms are supposed to be predators, then where—or *what*—are the creatures they are supposed to prey on?

"Dr. Abbato has advanced a very interesting hypothesis—albeit an unpleasant one—that *we* are the intended prey."

Huh? I sat up straight.

Dr. Fletcher had paused to let the murmurs of her audience to die down. She looked out over the room. Abruptly, she pointed at someone behind me. "Yes, you have a question?"

I turned around in my seat to look. It was a tall man in an army uniform. A grim-looking colonel. He had a tight mouth. I wondered, do colonels get special training to master that expression? He asked, "Can you prove that?"

Dr. Fletcher nodded and rubbed the side of her neck thoughtfully. She looked as if she were debating whether to give the long answer or the short one. She glanced up at the rest of us. "The question is, how do we know that the purpose of the worms is to eat people? The answer is, because that's exactly what they're doing."

"That's not the kind of answer I was expecting—" the colonel said.

Dr. Fletcher nodded in agreement. "I know it sounds flip," she said. "I'm sorry, but Dr. Kinsey summed up all animal behavior a long time ago: the only unnatural act is the one you can't do. If the worms couldn't eat Terran life-forms, they wouldn't."

I held my tongue—it made sense. Too much sense. The realization was a pain in the gut.

"Dr. Abbato has based a very interesting argument on this fact. He is postulating that this circumstance is *not* accidental. He is suggesting that the *real* purpose of the worms is a cleanup of the top level of the Terran ecology. The worms are *specifically* targeted to eat those humans who have survived the plagues."

My stomach felt like it was contracting into a pinhole. I almost missed what she said next.

"Dr. Abbato thinks that it is unlikely that the worms are food for the next step in the invasion. The worms are *too* efficient a predator. Too specialized for sentience? Rather, he thinks that the worms are a partner species and that ultimately, they will serve some kind of support function for the real invaders." She paused and looked carefully around the room. "Do you get it? *The worms are domestic animals!* Dr. Abbato guesses that they're the equivalent of sheep dogs; they function as guardians of the host species' property."

Urk. I squirmed uncomfortably in my seat. I didn't want to know this. My belly hurt.

"If this is so—" Dr. Fletcher was pointing out, "then it means that the worms can be *tamed.*" She stopped and looked out over us. "Think about it. Think about the possibilities. If we can tame them—perhaps we can turn them into an ally. Perhaps we can even use them as the first line of defense against the sentients who put them here."

I doubted that, but she had my attention. You couldn't have dynamited me out of my chair. Stomach pain and all.

"The question is—how do you tame a worm?

"But let's get even more basic than that. How do you communicate with a worm? Or even—*can* we communicate with the worms? In fact, even more basic than that, the question is this: how *intelligent* are the worms? That's what we need to know first—and that is the point of today's demonstration."

Huh? Demonstration? Had I slept through something?

She lifted her podium and carried it over to the right side of the stage. "I'll open the curtain in a minute and you can see the specimen we're currently working with. We call it 'Tiny'—you'll see that it's anything but. I think you'll also see that the question of intelligence is very clearly answered by this demonstration.

"Tiny was captured near Mendocino late last year. At that time, the specimen massed four hundred and fifty kilos. It is now twice that weight. Tiny is living proof that the gastropedes have an incredible rate of growth. By the way, you'll notice that we try to be very careful not to use 'he' or 'she' when talking about the worms. We're still not certain of their sexuality and we don't want to accidentally prejudice our own perceptions."

She touched a button on her podium and the curtains behind her slid open to reveal a pink-lit chamber. The theater overlooked a deep-walled room, large and almost featureless; we were staring down into it. "The color of the light is halfway between Earth-normal and what we believe to be Chtorr-normal."

Dr. Fletcher touched another button and a panel on the opposite wall of the chamber slid open. There was darkness beyond. "This is Tiny," she said. A medium-sized worm slid out of the darkness, sniffing the air as it moved. It was thick and red. The brain case hump on its back was very pronounced and it held its eyes high and alert. They swiveled back and forth, up and down, scanning the entire space. The worm hesitated, blinked and paused and looked up toward us.

I'd seen worms in viewing theaters before. I always had the impression that they could somehow see through the glass—that they knew we were out here. This time was no different. Tiny looked *curious*. Its long dark arms were still folded against the brain case, but the claws were twitching gently. At a guess, I'd say the creature was a little impatient.

"Now," said Fletcher, "—you need to know that Tiny is essentially a child, a youngster, and like all youngsters Tiny likes an occasional treat. With dolphins you use fish, with chimps you use grapes—with Tiny, we use rabbits."

She touched another button and another panel on the wall slid open. There was a fat brown rabbit in a glass case at Tiny's eye-level. Below the case was a complicated assembly of rods and gears and latches. In front of that was a panel of assorted knobs and switches; all were thick and heavy-looking. "That's our test setup," said Fletcher. "It's a puzzle. Each one of those knobs and levers controls a different part of the lock. If Tiny operates them all in the right order, the glass case will open and it can have the treat."

Tiny cocked its eyes sideways and looked at the rabbit. The rabbit was huddling in the corner of the case. Tiny cocked its eyes the opposite way and studied the rabbit from a different angle. The gesture gave the worm a floppy, hand-puppet expression. It would have been funny if I didn't know how dangerous a worm could be.

Tiny hunched around to examine the case and the lock and the panel of switches closer. Through the speakers we could hear the thoughtful clicking of its mandibles. It made a grunting noise and then moved up to the panel of knobs and switches.

The worm unfolded its arms and arched them over its eyes and down to the puzzle. It let its claws drift thoughtfully over the controls of the locks before it selected one.

"For your information," Fletcher said, "Tiny has never seen this puzzle before. It is not the most complicated one we've assembled, but for the purposes of this demonstration we thought we'd keep it short. All of our puzzles are rigged to keep a record of Tiny's moves—and once Tiny goes to work the life-expectancy of the rabbit can be measured in minutes. The longest Tiny has ever taken was half an hour."

Tiny was already hard at work, turning the knobs and observing what effect they had on the machinery, sliding the levers back and forth and peering cockeyed at the lock.

"As you can see," Fletcher said, "Tiny has a high degree of manipulative curiosity. We think this indicates a pretty good spatial sense for all worms—but again, that's only an extrapolation and not to be treated as hard fact."

"A question—" It was the same grim-looking colonel.

"Yes?" Fletcher asked.

"How does a human being compare on these same puzzles?" he asked.

"A good question," Fletcher acknowledged. "We haven't been running direct comparisons, but I can tell you that humans usually take at least forty-five minutes—even on the easy ones."

"So you're saying that these worms are smarter than men?"

"Not at all, Colonel. They just have a highly advanced manipulative sense. They should be very good with tools, but—" she added, "—so far, we haven't found much evidence that they use tools. At least, not naturally."

"Mm hm," said the colonel. He wasn't impressed.

A chime sounded then—

"That means Tiny's solved the puzzle," said Fletcher.

—the glass case popped open.

Tiny grabbed the rabbit with one dark claw, lifted it up high—it *squealed,* I didn't know that rabbits could scream—and shoved the creature into its gaping maw. There was a wet slobbery crunching sound, and then Tiny uttered a soft trill of pleasure, and looked around for more.

Behind me, I could feel the room stiffening. It was not pleasant to watch a worm eat. I didn't like being reminded.

Dr. Fletcher touched a control and the panel with the puzzle slid closed. She said, "Tiny took eleven minutes to solve this problem. We are now going to reset the puzzle. It'll take about two minutes. Does anyone have any questions, so far? Yes—"

A dark man with an Indian accent. "Your work is remarkably advanced, Dr. Fletcher. I am most impressed. May I ask you, how do the worms reproduce?"

"We don't know. I'm sorry, I can't even give you a good guess. There aren't any. Next? Yes—" She pointed.

"Dr. Fletcher, why do they call these things worms?" asked a broad ruddy-faced man. "It looks more like a big pink caterpillar to me. Hell, I've picked bigger caterpillars off my rosebushes back home in Amarillo." There was good-natured laughter in the room.

Even Dr. Fletcher smiled. She replied, "The first reliable sighting of a worm actually occurred about a year before the outbreak of the first plagues. Some of you may even remember. It happened in Northern Canada. A troop of scouts was on a three-day outing. They were on horseback. One of the girls was momentarily separated from the rest of the troop. She had stopped to readjust her saddle straps. Something attacked her horse. The rest of the troop heard her screams and started back for her. They met her halfway. She was so hysterical they almost couldn't catch her to calm her down. The most they could get out of her was that it was big, it was dark, it looked like a giant worm, and it kept saying, 'Chtorrrr! Chtorrrrrr!' "

Dr. Fletcher added, "The troop leader and two of the boys went back to investigate. They found the horse had been half-eaten. They did not see a worm. They did not hear it cry, 'Chtorrrr!' The Royal Canadian Mounted Police later searched the surrounding area as thoroughly as it could—it was near the Canadian Rockies—but they found nothing.

"Naturally, the news media played it for laughs. It was a dull summer, so The Giant Canadian Rocky Mountain Worm filled a lot of space on otherwise slow news days. Of course, once the plagues broke out it was forgotten. It wasn't until much later that we realized that this event, and several others like it, were actually harbingers.

"We know now that the worms have a fairly thick coat of fur, and that the name 'worm' is something of a misnomer. We think that what we've seen is another Chtorran adaptation to the planet. The first worms to appear did have very little fur, and they really did look like worms. But over the last three years, we've seen the worms developing thicker and thicker coats. But what it means, I can't tell you. Actually, it's not even fur—it's sensory antennae. The creature is coated with nerve fibers. So, probably what we're seeing is a more—you should pardon the expression—*sensitive* worm. And yes, you're right; they do look like caterpillars."

She glanced down at her podium display. "I see the puzzle has been reset—"

I looked down into the chamber again. Tiny was still positioned eagerly in front of the panel. Apparently the worm had learned to anticipate its second chances at the puzzles.

The panel slid open before it. There was a new rabbit in the cage. The puzzle machinery had been reset. Tiny slid quickly forward and began to operate the levers and knobs. Its claws moved with a certainty that hadn't been present before.

The chime sounded. The cage popped open.

There were gasps in the room.

"Forty-three seconds," Dr. Fletcher said dryly. Tiny was already eating the rabbit. The sound was hideous. I remembered the feeding room in Denver. And the dogs. And the people who liked to watch.

Dr. Fletcher waited in silence until Tiny was finished, then touched another button on her podium and opened the passage back to its cell. The worm slid obediently into it. She remarked, "We've found Tiny to be surprisingly cooperative. It seems to appreciate the discipline." She checked that the passage was clear, then closed the panel—and then the curtain.

She looked calmly out over the room. "I think that pretty well answers the question: how intelligent is a worm? The answer is very. And they learn fast. As you have seen, incredibly so. Our tests with the second specimen confirm that Tiny's responses are *not* atypical. The other worm is even faster than Tiny—and as other specimens become available for testing, we expect to see the same facility in them as well.

"We're beginning another set of tests next Monday, this time with a completely different type of problem. We're going to further explore the worms' ability to conceptualize. Conceptualization is the key to communication. We're clear that if the worms can conceptualize, they can communicate. But let me caution you, don't confuse conceptualization with sentience. Even a dog can conceptualize; Pavlov proved that. And I think most of you will grant that a dog is capable of a certain rudimentary level of communication. When I talk about communication with the worms, I'm talking about that dog-level of communication. I'm talking about *taming*.

"And in fact, that's the very next question that has to be answered. How can we create a relationship with a worm so that it's *willing* to communicate? In other words, how do we *domesticate* a worm? Your consideration of this particular problem will be much appreciated." She glanced at her watch. "The discussion part of this session will take place this afternoon at fifteen hundred hours. Dr. Larson will be mediating. I thank you for your time and your attention."

I went straight to the men's room and threw up.

SEVEN

I FOUND Dr. Fletcher in her office. She looked up as I came in. "Oh, McCarthy—how are you? Thanks for staying awake this morning." She studied me curiously. "Are you all right?"

"I'm fine." I waved her off. "Just an upset stomach."

"Mm hm," she said. "A lot of people have that problem after they see a worm eat."

I let it pass. "I have a question for you."

"The answer is, 'I don't know.' What's the question?" She glanced at her watch.

"We gassed a nest of worms yesterday afternoon. Four of them. They were all tied together in a knot."

She nodded. "Your videos came in last night."

"Then you saw? Each time we pulled one off, they reacted as if we were breaking a connection."

She frowned, she pressed her lips together. Finally, she pushed back from her terminal and swiveled to face me. She leaned forward intently. "Exactly what did it look like to you?"

"It looked like—they were writhing in pain. They cried. It was an . . . eerie sound. And two of them actually opened their eyes and looked at us. It was very disturbing," I admitted.

"I'll bet. What do you think was happening?"

"That's what I wanted to ask you."

"I want your observations first," she said.

"Well . . . ," I said. "It looked like—I mean, the way they twisted and turned—it made me think of earthworms. Cut in half. Only this was a giant one, cut into four screaming pieces."

"Mm," said Fletcher, noncommittally. "Interesting."

"What do you think it was?"

She shook her head. "I don't. The best thought anyone around here has had is that it was something sexual. Some kind of mating behavior perhaps. And that's why they reacted so strongly. How would you react if somebody interrupted you?"

I blinked. "The worms have four sexes?"

She laughed, a short sharp bark. "Hardly. At least you can't prove it by their chromosomes. So far, all the tissue samples we've examined are genetic nightmares—we have no idea what they're modeling—but we can identify the chromosome structures, and they seem to be pretty much identical from one specimen to the next. No X or Y chromosomes —or equivalents. By that evidence, the worms have only one sex. It's convenient, I guess; it doubles the chances of finding a date for Saturday night, but—it sounds boring. Unless of course you're another worm."

"But—then that brings up another question—"

She glanced at her watch again. "It'd better be a short one."

"I'm interrupting something?"

"Mm, sort of. I need to go into San Francisco—"

"Huh? I thought the city was closed."

"It is. To most people."

"Oh."

"But I'm on the Advisory," she explained.

"Oh," I said again, disappointedly.

Fletcher studied me speculatively. "Family member? Your mother? No—your father, right?"

"My father," I nodded. "We never heard one way or the other. And, uh—I know this is silly—"

"No, it isn't," she said.

"—but my father was always such a . . . survivor. I just can't imagine him dead."

"You think he's still alive somewhere?"

"I . . . just wish I knew for certain. That's all."

"Uh huh," she said. "The truth is, you want to go there and see for yourself. You think you can find him. Right?" She fixed me with a green-eyed gaze. Her manner was startlingly direct. It put me off-balance.

I shrugged. "Yeah," I admitted.

"Mm hm. You're not the first one, Lieutenant. I see it all the time. People don't believe until they see for themselves. Well, all right—"

"Huh?"

"You want to see San Francisco?" She rolled back to her terminal and started typing. "Let me get you a pass. McCarthy . . . James Edward, Lieutenant—" She frowned at the screen. "When'd you get a purple heart?"

"Denver. Remember?"

"Oh, that."

"Hey!" I protested. "I've still got scars. And a bad knee! And besides, it happened the day *after* I was commissioned. It's legal."

"Hmp," she sniffed. "You ruined a perfectly good specimen."

"It lived, didn't it—?"

"Just barely," she said. "Have you ever seen a deranged worm?"

"Lots of times—"

"No. Those were *normal.* This one was deranged." Her fingers tapped at the keys—"Huh?" She stopped abruptly. "That's interesting."

"What is?"

"Uh—nothing really. I've seen it before. Part of your file is locked." She resumed typing.

"Uh—that's right." I had a hunch what that was. Something to do with Uncle Ira. Colonel Ira Wallachstein. The *late* Colonel Ira Wallachstein. But I didn't explain.

"All right," she said. "You're cleared—under *my* authority. So you have to behave yourself—and do what I tell you, all right?"

"Right"

"Good. We'll make a human being out of you yet." She shrugged out of her lab coat and tossed it at a laundry bin. Underneath, she was wearing a dark brown jumpsuit. It matched the shade of her hair; it was good planning on either her part or the government's.

I followed her to an elevator. She flashed a key-card at the scanner. The door chimed and slid open. The elevator dropped us downward; I couldn't tell how many floors though, there were no numbers to watch.

Fletcher had to flash her card before two more doors, and then we were on a ramp leading down to the garage. "That one's mine," she said, pointing toward a Jeep. How could she tell? They all looked alike to me. She walked around the front of the car while I climbed in the passenger side.

"Why all this security?" I asked.

She shook her head. "It's political, I think. Something to do with the Fourth World Alliance. We won't trade information until they open their borders to inspection teams. I think it's a mistake. In the long run, we're only hurting ourselves." She eased the Jeep forward, and pointed it toward the exit. As we rolled out past the final security booth, she added in a quieter tone, "Things are very . . . *cautious* around here. Especially right now." She glanced over at me. "Mm, let me say it this way. The agency does appreciate the cooperation of the military—especially the Special Forces—but, ah . . . there is still a certain amount of individual chafing. The military has everything tied up a little too tight. We're all of us in a great big bag marked TOP SECRET."

I considered what she said. She was being remarkably candid. It was a compliment to me. I replied carefully, "It certainly doesn't make sense from a scientific point of view. We should be sharing information, not hiding it."

Fletcher looked like she wanted to agree. "It's Dr. Zymph's idea. She started out in Bio-War, you know; so her whole career has been about secrecy. I guess she still thinks it's necessary. But it makes it awfully hard to work." Abruptly, she added, "Sometimes I don't know what that woman is up to. She scares me."

Dr. Zymph was the chairman of the Ecological Agency. I looked at Fletcher, surprised. "I thought you admired her."

"I used to. But that was before she became a politician. I liked her better as a scientist."

I didn't reply to that. Fletcher's comments bothered me. I'd first seen Dr. Zymph in action in Denver—and I'd been impressed by her. It was . . . disconcerting to hear this.

The road turned west and then northward. To our left was the metallic wash of San Francisco Bay. The sun was glinting oddly off the surface. The light struck colored sparks.

"The water's a funny color," I said.

"We had an episode of sea sludge," Fletcher said matter-of-factly. "We had to oil and burn it. The bay's still recovering."

"Oh."

"We're waiting to see if it comes back. We think we may have licked it, but it's only a small victory."

"Um—you said something before. About the worm in Denver. You said it was . . . deranged. What did you mean by that?"

"Well—wouldn't you be deranged if someone carved you up like that? You shot out its eyes, you turned its mouth into jelly, and you

broke both its arms. That does not make for a healthy world-view. And
after its fur fell out, the poor thing went autistic—"

"Its fur fell out?"

"Oh, right. That report got squelched. You couldn't have seen it. As
if its injuries weren't enough, the poor beast started throwing symptoms. We thought it was infected and put it on terramycin. Its fur came
out in patches. It was an ugly sight; it really did look like a big red
bristly worm."

"*All* the fur came off?"

She shook her head. "No, only the lighter-colored strands. You know
that the fur is sensory nerves, don't you? We figured out what happened
afterwards. Terramycin can damage human nervous tissue too. Apparently, the pink strands are extremely sensitive. Anyway—after that, the
gastropede showed as much intelligence as a Terran earthworm. It just
lay where it was and quivered and twitched." She shook her head again,
remembering. "It was a very queasy thing to watch."

"How come we didn't see that report? That could be a weapon!"

Fletcher sighed and quoted, " 'Information on ways to combat or
resist the Chtorran infestation is not to be made available to any non-
allied nations or their representatives.' That's the policy—at least until
the Fourth World Alliance signs the Unification Treaty."

"That doesn't make sense."

"It does politically. When the worms—or whatever else—become too
big a problem for the Fourth World member nations to handle by themselves, a signature on a paper might not seem too high a price for
survival. Right now, they'd rather be right. Are you surprised?"

"And you agree with it—?"

She shook her head. "No, but I understand it. The Unification Pow-
ers are playing politics with the war. Did you expect us *not* to? Read
your history. We have twenty years of grudges to work off. At least. So
now, there are people who are willing to let the worms chew on the
Fourth World Alliance for a while."

"And in the meantime, the infestation gets a more solid foothold—?"

"Right. Some people have their priorities way up their fundaments.
Anyway," she added, "Terramycin would not be an effective weapon."

"Why not?"

"You wouldn't like the aftereffects. Two or three weeks later, the
worm's fur started to come back in—only very dark. Mostly red and
purple and black strands. That's when the worm started getting violent.
The more dark fur came in, the more violent it became. Obviously, its

perception of the world was shifting. We finally had to put it down, it was so badly deranged. We weren't sure we could contain it any longer." She clucked her tongue. "You think the worms are nasty now? Infect a few and see what happens."

I didn't answer. It was too much to think about. I'd known the fur was a kind of nerve. Our gas had been based on that fact. But why should the *type* of nerve cells make a worm peaceful or violent?

"Do you have anyone studying worm fur?" I asked.

She shook her head. "I'd like to—but we're already overextended. There're about fifteen other areas we want to look at first."

"It seems to me that it's important to the question of tamability—"

"Mm hm," she agreed. "That's why we're looking for albinos. . . ."

The Jeep was slowing as it approached the Oakland Bay Bridge. Fletcher flashed her card at a scanner and the barricades slid open for us. There was a huge advisory sign hanging over the empty toll booths: BY ORDER OF THE MILITARY GOVERNOR OF CALIFORNIA, THE CITY OF SAN FRANCISCO IS HEREBY DECLARED A BLACK ZONE RESTRICTED AREA. ENTER AT YOUR OWN RISK.

"That's reassuring," I said as we rolled under it.

"It's safe," she said.

"What makes you so sure?"

"I told you. I'm on the Advisory Board. San Francisco is currently zoned as unfit for anything but politics."

"I beg your pardon?"

"It's another one of the Agency's good ideas. San Francisco could be a very good Safe City. It's surrounded on three sides by water. Unfortunately, there're a lot of ruins that have to be cleared—and we've got militant preservationists second-guessing every lamppost. So, the governor locked them out. They pay me ten K a month to swear that the city's still a plague reservoir."

"Is it?"

"The truth is—yes, it is."

We reached the crest of the bridge then and the city spread out before us—what was left of it. The sight was ghastly. San Francisco was a skeleton. The city had been gutted. The stump of the Transamerica Tower gaped like a broken tooth. Coit Tower still stood, but it was blackened by fire. I didn't recognize many other buildings. Where they should have been there was rubble and ruin. "Oh, my God—" I choked on the words.

"I know," she agreed.

"I've seen the pictures," I gasped. "But—I had no idea—this is *horrible.*"

"It gets everybody that way, the first time. I still get a tight throat when I come across the bridge."

"There's . . . nothing left."

"Firestorm," she said. The single word explained everything.

Fletcher unlocked the steering wheel and pulled it into position before her, putting the Jeep back on manual control. Autopilots were fine on paved roads. They had problems with rubble. We rolled down off the bridge in an eerie silence.

"Do you remember City Hall?" she asked.

"Uh huh. There was a big plaza in front."

"It's still there," she said. "But not much of City Hall."

She steered carefully through the steel and brick canyons of lower Market Street. The fires had burned themselves out here. But even so—there were places where the buildings looked blasted, even *melted* from the heat. I noticed a sign that said, SAN FRANCISCO WARLOCK ADMINISTRATION—and wondered if there were any warlocks left in California at all.

We'd thought the plagues were over. We'd come down from the hills, out of our hiding places. We thought we had vaccines. The government said it was safe. We had all the best excuses to return to the cities.

But the plagues weren't over, and the vaccines only worked sometimes, and the cities still weren't safe. The plagues came back stronger than ever.

There was panic. There were fires.

There was a firestorm.

And when it was over, San Francisco was gone.

It was like driving through a graveyard.

"I thought you said the military was working over here," I said.

"Most of the work is still off the corridor," Fletcher said. "And a lot of it is being done by robots." Suddenly, she pointed. "Look, there—"

"What?" And then I saw. She was pointing at a zombie. She slowed the Jeep.

He was papery and thin—naked, except for a ragged blanket he wore like a poncho. There was almost no flesh at all on his bones. He looked like he was a hundred years old; it was impossible to guess what his real age might have been—he was gray and gaunt; his white hair hung down to his shoulders in a greasy mat.

The zombie's face looked mechanically animated; the expression was curiously empty, but the features were in constant motion. The mouth worked continually. The jaw floated up and down, releasing a thin dribble of spittle. The blackened tongue stuck out absently, like a retarded child's, then pulled in again. The cheeks sucked in and puffed out. The face moved as if no one wore it any more. It looked like a fish sucking at the glass wall of the aquarium.

The zombie turned and looked at us then—and for just an instant it was as if whoever might have once lived inside that body was struggling to animate it once again. The expression became momentarily curious, the eyelids fluttered like trapped moths. And then the gaze went confused again. He seemed to be fading in and out of focus—and he had trouble balancing himself as well. He caught himself on the front of the Jeep and stared through the windshield, shifting back and forth between Fletcher and myself. He blinked and blinked again as he stared at us. His face wrinkled in puzzlement.

"He looks like he's trying to recognize us," I whispered.

Fletcher nodded. "He can't. He's lost his timebinding ability."

"Huh?"

"A zombie exists only in the present. He only knows something exists if he's looking at it."

As if in confirmation, the zombie's puzzlement was turning to pain. He looked like he wanted to cry but didn't remember how. He fluttered his fingers toward Fletcher, then toward me—then abruptly he refocused on his hand, a gray claw-like thing on the end of his arm, as if he'd never seen it before. He forgot about us, blinking in confusion. His hand dropped. He turned and moved away without purpose, a soulless thing again. He shambled off toward the west.

"Is that it?" I said. "I've seen zombies before. That's what happens to the walking wounded when they sink to that place below despair. Once they hit the zombie level, you can't bring them back."

Fletcher looked like she wanted to say something in reply to that. Instead, she eased the car forward again.

As we moved up Market Street, we began to see other shambling zombies. Most were heading westward. All of them were thin and dirty. Most wore rags, or less. Their movements were disorganized, fragmented, and surreal. They looked like they'd wandered out of Auschwitz or Belsen or Buchenwald—except for their expressions. The concentration-camp survivors had at least had *life* in their eyes—an awareness of the horror and hopelessness of their situation. The zombies had nothing.

The zombies were . . . detached. From the world, from everything —from their own bodies. They looked curious, and their eyes moved in quick, jerky glances; but they had no focus of attention. Their faces were empty. They moved like palsy victims.

Fletcher slowed the Jeep then to steer around the rubble. Most of the zombies were ignoring us. A dirty creature—male or female, it was impossible to tell—shambled by us. It trailed one hand across the hood of the car. Its expression was . . . almost happy.

"That one looks stoned," I said.

"Mm hm," Fletcher nodded. She angled the Jeep between two piles of bricks and up a side street. I recognized the remains of Brooks Hall on the left. The ruined marquee said simply, SAINT FRANCIS WRITHES AGAIN. I wondered who'd put that message up.

We pulled up facing a wide dirty field. At the far end of it, what was left of City Hall loomed like a broken castle. You could still make out its broad stone steps. This had once been a great plaza; now it was a gray expanse of dust and broken concrete. Nothing grew here any more.

"Okay," I said. "Now what?"

"Now, we get out and look around."

"Huh?"

"It's safe." She patted my hand and climbed out of the Jeep. I had no choice but to follow.

There were . . . people . . . in the plaza. They were pinker and somewhat healthier-looking than the ones we'd passed on Market Street. Zombies? Not quite. Many of them were fairly young—in their twenties and thirties. There were some teenagers, only a few children. There were very few beyond middle age.

Most of the bodies were haphazardly dressed. Or maybe that should have been haphazardly *un*dressed. They moved without regard for their clothing. It was as if somebody else had hung clothes on them, or they had draped themselves with whatever was handy. What clothing they did have seemed to be for warmth, not modesty.

"So?" I turned to Fletcher. "I've seen this before too. These are walking wounded."

"Are they?" she asked.

"Well, sure—" I started to say. And then stopped. I looked at her. "They're something else?"

"Go find out," she pointed. "Try talking to them."

I looked at her as if she were crazy. Talk to them?

"It's safe," she reassured.

I turned back and studied the milling bodies. They moved without purpose, but they didn't shamble. They just sort of . . . moved.

I picked out a young male. Maybe he was sixteen. Maybe he was twenty-five. I couldn't tell. He had long brown hair that hung past his shoulders. He was wearing an old gray shirt, nothing else. He had large dark eyes. He'd been very attractive once.

I walked up to him and touched his shoulder. He turned toward me with a halfway expectant expression. His eyes were bottomless. He studied my face for a puzzled moment, then—not finding anything—started to turn away.

"Wait," I said.

He turned back.

"What's your name?"

He blinked at me.

"Your name?" I repeated.

His mouth began to work. "Nay-nay-nay . . . ?" he said. He was trying to imitate my sounds. He smiled at the noises he made. "Nay-nay-nay-nay-nay-nay—" he repeated.

I put my hands on his shoulders. I looked into his eyes, trying to create a sense of *relationship* through eye contact. The boy tried to look away—I pulled his face back to mine and stared into his eyes again. "No. Stay with me," I said firmly.

He blinked at me uncertainly.

"Who are you?" I asked him.

"Bub," he said.

"Bub? Bob?"

"Bub-bub-bub—" He smiled happily. "Bub-bub-bub-bub—"

"No," I said. "No." I pulled his face back to mine again.

"No-no-no . . ." he said. "No-no-no. . . ." And then, "Bub-bub-bub . . . bub-bub-bub. . . ."

I let go of his shoulders and let him wander away, still bubbling.

I turned back to Fletcher. "All right. What?"

She shook her head. "Uh uh. Keep going."

This time, I chose a little girl. She was wearing only a pair of panties. What was it about these people and clothing anyway? She was very thin, very underdeveloped. She could have been a boy.

I stopped her and looked into her face. She was as blank as the others.

"Who are you?" I asked. "What's your name?"

"My name . . . ?" she said. "My name?" She blinked. Like the boy, her expression was uncertain and puzzled.

"That's right. What's your name?"

"My name, my name . . . is Auntie Mame. My game is fame, my game, my name, my name—" She babbled happily at me, smiling with delight at the sound of her own words. She'd figured out the game. "The game is name is fame is lame—"

I let go of her and turned her back toward the crowd.

"All right," I said to Fletcher, "I got it. They're not zombies. You can interact with them. But they've lost most of their sense of speech, so they're not walking wounded either. They're an intermediate step. Is that all?"

"Part of it," she said.

"What is it?" I asked. "A plague effect? Brain burn fever?"

"Brain burn fever is fatal," Fletcher said grimly. "If this is a plague effect, it's something we can't identify. See that fellow there?" She pointed at a tall beefy man. "He used to be one of the sharpest biologists at the university. He was at the South Pole when the plagues broke out. He was never exposed. He was fully vaccinated before he returned. If it's a plague effect, it's a mental one."

"How did he . . . end up here?" I asked.

She lowered her voice. "He was studying them—" She waved her hand to indicate the wandering bodies. "He thought he could see patterns of herding—something like the Emperor Penguins. He spent a lot of time living with them, moving among them. One day, he didn't come back. When we finally got worried, we came down here and found him wandering around with the rest of them. He couldn't talk much more than they could. He'd become one of them."

I thought about that. Before I could ask the question, Fletcher said, "We're not in any danger. It takes prolonged exposure."

"Oh," I said. I was not reassured.

There were several hundred bodies in the plaza now. I stood there for a moment, watching them, trying to figure out why they seemed so . . . *interesting.*

"There's something about them," I said. "I can't figure it out, but there's something going on here. The minute you look at them, you know that they're not *normal.* What is it?" I asked Fletcher. "What's the signal I'm picking up?"

"You tell me," she said. "Tell me what you see?"

"I see bodies. Pink bodies. That's part of it, isn't it? They don't wear much clothing."

"By summer, they'll all be naked—but that's not it either. San Francisco Plaza has seen crowds of naked bodies before. The average Freedom Day Festival has less clothing than this."

"I wouldn't know. My dad never let me come."

"Too bad. Anyway, nudity is only part of it. What else?"

"Um—their skin. When I touched them, their skin felt slick. Not quite oily. Kind of smooth. *Different.*"

"Mm hm, but that's not the cue either. You don't go around touching people to see if they're different."

"Right." I studied the milling crowd again.

"I'll give you a hint," she said. "What's *missing?*"

"Missing? Mmmm. Talking. There's not a lot of talking. A few of them are babbling to themselves, but it's not loud and offensive, not like a street lady. They're babbling like babies amused with the sounds they're making—wait a minute." A thought was beginning to form. "What's missing is . . . *intensity.* They have a quality of innocence. They're like children, aren't they? It's as if they've given up all the stuff they've ever learned about how to be a grownup so they could go back to the innocence of children. Right?"

"Go on," she encouraged, but she was smiling. I was on the right track.

"They can feel pain or anger—but they don't carry it around with them. Adults do. We get hurt or angry and we carry it around with us for weeks, handing it out to everybody we meet. Did you ever watch *Aroundabout* on TV? One time they did nothing but photograph faces at random on a city street. Almost every single person they showed looked like they were wearing a mask. Their expressions were all pinchy and tight. But these . . . people—I guess that's what I should call them—these people, their faces are *relaxed.* They've given up the pain—"

I realized something else and shut up suddenly.

"What was that?" Fletcher asked.

"Um, nothing really. I was just realizing how sad it must be to have to give up your intelligence to be free from pain." I looked at her. Her face was hurting with the same realization. Her eyes were moist. "Is this what you wanted me to see?"

"Oh, no," she said. She swallowed and looked uncomfortable. "It hasn't even started yet."

EIGHT

I LOOKED at the bodies again. "This is a herd, isn't it?"

"Mm hm," she said. "Last summer, it numbered over twelve hundred. During the winter, it fell to about three. Now it's building up again. We've got about seven fifty here. This is the largest herd in Northern California."

"What happened to the others?"

"Most of them died," she said noncommittally. "A few wander off every night. The pattern is this: you go from shock to being one of the walking wounded. There's hope for the walking wounded. But only if you get quick treatment. Otherwise, you just keep sinking.

"There's an instinct at work here. People seek out crowds, activity. So, this—" she pointed, "—is inevitable. The walking wounded gather in herds. I guess it's an illusion of safety. Some of them, though, are so far gone they can't even survive in a herd. Dropouts become zombies. The life expectancy of a zombie is six weeks. I'm surprised it's that long."

I looked at her. "You've been studying this, haven't you?"

She nodded. "You may be looking at the future of the human race. At the rate this herd is growing, we could hit twenty-five hundred by July. If that happens, we expect it to split into two herds." She pointed across the plaza. "See those two trucks over there? Those are the—you should pardon the expression—cowboys. They keep the herd under control. We used to keep the herd at Golden Gate Park, but we were losing too many every night, so we moved them down here. We can put them to bed in Brooks Hall."

The noon sun was getting warmer. I noticed that more and more of the herd members were discarding what little clothing they wore.

Fletcher followed my glance. "Yeah," she said. "It happens. We used to have a couple little old ladies who did nothing but follow the herd around putting their clothes back on them. There's one of them now. She finally gave up."

She was pointing at a little wrinkled old lady, wearing nothing but a smile and her varicose veins. She looked like a road map of Pennsylvania. She was carrying a parasol to shield herself from the sun.

"Sometimes, I think Jennie's faking," Fletcher said, "but you'll never get her to admit it. It probably doesn't matter anyway."

"Are any of them faking?" I asked.

She shook her head. "It's not something you can fake for long. Every so often we have civilians sneak in here, thinking they could take advantage of the herd—you know, thinking it would be nothing but a sexual free-for-all. But . . . something happens to them. They don't leave. You can only fake it for so long. Even the faking is part of the process of . . . enrollment." And then she added, "On the other hand, they could *all* be faking—but even if that were true, this would still be a *real* phenomenon. Whatever it is, we really don't understand it yet."

"I'm beginning to see a pattern," I said. "There's something very fascinating going on here. But just standing around watching isn't enough. It's like a—an anthropological black hole. The closer you get the more likely it is you're going to get sucked in."

"Mm hm," Fletcher nodded. "That's part of the problem. This herd started out as just another group of walking wounded. But now, it's even pulling in the observers too. Almost everyone who gets close. The cowboys aren't allowed to work more than one day a week, and even that might be too much exposure."

She added, "This herd is one of the main reasons why we're keeping the city closed. We don't know what else to do. We've even discussed . . . euthanasia."

"You're kidding."

She shook her head. "Nope. I'm not. I've argued against it, of course. There's something here we need to understand." She held out a hand to me. "Come on—"

"Huh? Where are we going?"

"We're going for a walk among them. It's safe."

I stared at her. "You've just told me that people are getting sucked into this herd every day, and now you want me to walk through it?"

"I'll be with you."

"That doesn't reassure me."

She held up her wrist and pointed to her watch. "Set your sleep alarm. If you start to fade, the buzzer will wake you up. I promise you, it takes more than an hour's exposure to enchant you."

"Enchant?"

"Uh huh. That's the word. Enchant. You'll see."

I grumbled something about other people's good ideas and cued my own watch. When I looked up, Fletcher was already heading toward the center of the plaza. I hurried to catch up.

"Shh," she said. "Don't run. It upsets them. We had a stampede once. It was awful. Just stand still for a minute and get the feeling of being in the herd. Don't talk. Just look and listen."

We stood there together, side by side, turning slowly and watching the other bodies circling around us. Their faces were *content.* It was unnerving. I felt uncomfortable. I could feel the sweat trickling down from my armpits.

The sun was hot. It felt good. I loosened the top two buttons of my shirt.

There was a naked girl standing in front of me, studying me. She had red hair and a dirty face. She could have been Peter Pan's little sister. She was smiling, but she looked puzzled too. She stepped toward me cautiously and reached out a hand. She touched my shirt. She fingered the cloth. She sniffed it. She looked up at me and sniffed me. She touched my face, let her fingers trail down past my chin to my neck and my chest. She stopped at my shirt buttons and studied them. It didn't take her long to figure it out. She unbuttoned the next button. She smiled with delight at her own cleverness.

She took one of my hands in hers and studied my fingers. She turned my hand over and over. She sniffed it. She must have liked what she smelled, because she licked my fingers. She took my hand and stroked her breasts with my fingertips. Her bosom was small, her nipples were hard.

She let go of my hand; my fingers stayed where they were. She searched my face again, curiously.

Abruptly, she stepped away from me and dropped to the ground. She got down on her hands and knees and presented her rump to me. She looked back at me and smiled and wriggled her butt.

"Uh—" I looked to Fletcher. I could feel myself flushing with embarrassment.

"Go ahead," Fletcher nodded, "if you've a mind for that sort of thing. It's only the first step toward joining the herd."

"I'll pass for now, thank you," I said.

"Most men do. The first time, anyway."

"What do you mean by that?"

She shrugged. "She's communicating on a very direct level. Much more direct than most of us are used to. *That* is very difficult to ignore. It is almost impossible to forget."

The girl looked back at me again, puzzled. She got up from the ground and looked at me again. She looked hurt. She wandered away sadly. I felt sorry for her, but a moment later, she was presenting herself to a teenage boy. The boy mounted her from the rear and took her quickly. She gasped and laughed, so did he.

"From an anthropological point of view—" I began. My voice cracked suddenly. My throat was dry. I cleared my throat and tried again. "Excuse me—I was going to say that what we're seeing is somewhat atypical behavior."

"At the very least," said Fletcher, tongue firmly in cheek.

"I mean—if you study ape and monkey colonies. Promiscuity isn't very often seen, is it?"

"Not like this. But maybe this isn't atypical for a human-ape colony. We don't know. We don't have enough data on human herds yet. My own theory—" She stopped herself.

"No, go on," I said.

"Well . . ." she said slowly. "I was going to say, my own theory is that what we're seeing here is a . . . distillation, or a reflection, of our own culture, but returned to the ape level."

"Is that why they're all so horny?"

She nodded. "It could be. Our culture tends to be oversexed. These . . . apes . . . have learned the lesson well." And then she said, "I also think . . . that they're still acting out the traumas of culturization —the adaptations that the human animal has had to make for sentience. Even though they seem to have given up sentience, they're still acting the roles, the learned behaviors."

"I'm not sure I understand that."

"All right. Try it this way. Consciousness has goals of its own. Consciousness perverts instinctive behavior to accomplish those goals. On the species level, we're all mad—because we've suppressed our natural tribal behaviors to try to be sentient. Most of us are so busy *pretending* to be sentient that we're deliberately tuning out our own bodies, our own feelings. We're detached from ourselves. Most so-called civilized human beings act as if they're living by remote control. They operate like machines.

"I think what's happening here is a kind of a . . . reaction. The plagues so damaged the world-view of these people that they gave up consciousness. Sentience didn't work any more—so they abandoned it. What we're seeing here is the remaining tribal behavior. The expression of it is no longer covert. It's all out in the open now. These . . . people have become beings of pure sensory experience. They're always operating in the present, in the here and now. They have no past or future, no timebinding. They're just *here,* feeling. When they feel sad, they feel sad —until they're through feeling sad; then they stop and feel something else."

She stopped herself abruptly, and looked at me. "In a way, they're lucky. When we're sad, we carry it around with us forever. Most of us are still dragging around the dead bodies of our past." She looked sad for just the briefest instant, then buried it again under a facade of business-as-usual. "Come on, this way—"

"Huh?"

She pointed.

Three huge trucks were grumbling slowly into the plaza. The herd began shifting toward them. I thought of cattle heading toward a pasture. The trucks came to a halt. The backs of the trucks opened, and out of each fell a dozen huge bales of . . . something yellow.

I glanced at Fletcher again.

"Lunch," she explained. "You want some?"

"Huh?"

"Come on." She took my hand and led me through the crowd. It wasn't difficult to push our way through the bodies. I noticed they had a strong rank smell to them and mentioned it casually.

"Herd odor," said Fletcher. "I think that's one of the ways they keep together. After a while, you get so you can find the herd by its scent alone."

We pushed up near one of the bales. It looked like it was made up of big pieces of yellow farfel. It smelled yeasty and buttery.

"It's impregnated with vitamins and antibiotics and God knows what else," Fletcher said.

As we watched, the herd members gathered around the bale and began to pull chunks away from it like pieces of bread. They carried their food away with them, not eating until they found a quiet place. Then they sat and chewed quietly. Their expressions remained blank. The entire process was orderly and remarkably quiet.

Some of them sat with their mates or their companions and fed each other with their fingers. I saw a mother feeding her child—at least, I assumed it was her own child; but it might not have been. Two teenage girls shared their meal, giggling. An old man squatted alone and chewed thoughtfully.

A big bearlike man was carrying a piece of the loaf big enough to feed at least a dozen people. Another man came up to him and ripped part of it away. The bearlike man did not protest; in fact, he anchored himself to help rip the piece in half.

There was no hostility or greed or impatience anywhere in the herd. They moved like cattle. They chewed like cattle.

"Is that stuff drugged at all?" I asked.

She shook her head. "Not any more. We tried it once. It only made them crazy. Crazier. They don't need drugs."

One of the cowboys on the back of the truck waved to us then. "Hey, Fletch!" he called. "Are you here again?"

Fletcher grinned and waved back. "Howya doin', Jake?"

"I'm fine," he said. "But you better watch yourself, or your tits'll be hanging out in the sun with the rest of 'em."

Fletch grinned and waved back. "Not till the food gets a little better. I'm not ready to give up my steaks yet."

The cowboy pulled a big chunk off a bale. "Well, here—try it. We've changed the recipe again. Maybe you'll like this enough to join us." He tossed the breadlike mass across to us.

I stepped forward and plucked the stuff out of the air. I turned and offered it to Fletcher. She pulled a smaller piece off the mass and tasted it. "Not bad," she called, "—but it's still not sirloin." She held out the rest of the piece for me to eat; she practically pushed it into my mouth. It was soft, warm, fresh and buttery. And it required just enough chewing to be . . . pleasant. I took another bite.

"Be careful, Jim." Fletcher took the rest of the loaf away. "That's one of the ways people get started." She handed it to a sad-looking boy who'd been hanging back from the main mass of the feeders. He brightened immediately and scampered off to a deserted place to begin eating. "That's Weepy Willie," she said. "He prefers to beg. God knows what he was like when he was human."

She shook her head sadly. "There are a lot of ways to get sucked in. Mostly, you just get tired of day-to-day living. Just being responsible for yourself can be exhausting sometimes." She stopped and looked at me. "This whole thing is dangerous. It sucks energy. Even studying it is dangerous. Any attention at all we give to it just feeds it. It's a kind of social cancer. It grows and it eats. It turns healthy cells into sick ones— and then the sick cells have to be tended, so more healthy cells have to be exposed. It's a never-ending process."

"I've seen the reports," I said.

"There's something else though. Something that hasn't been in the reports—because we don't know what to make of it. That's what I want you to see." Fletcher brushed her dark hair back from her eyes. She looked grim.

I asked, "All right, so when do I see this whatever it is?"

"Not too much longer. But come on, I want you away from the center. It can get a little . . . overwhelming." She led me back toward our Jeep. "You're already a little glassy-eyed."

"Huh?"

"I said—Never mind. Stop here. Tell me a joke."

"Huh?"

"Tell me a joke—" she repeated.

"Um, why did the Chtorran cross the road?"

"Because it was shorter than going around. Tell me one I haven't heard."

"Why—?"

"I'm trying to find out if you're still home. Humor is a good test—it requires intellectual ability. Tell me another."

"Right. Uh, what does a Chtorran do when he wakes up in the morning?"

She shrugged, "What?"

"Says grace."

She chuckled once and nodded. "You're okay." She turned me to face the milling herd.

"All right. Now what?"

"We wait."

We didn't have to wait long. Lunch was over. Now, the herdmembers were beginning to play among themselves. Some of the younger members were playing a loose form of tag. They reminded me of puppies. Run and chase, tumble and wrestle. But they played in silence, only occasionally yipping or barking. There were no words.

The herd was beginning to be more active now. There was more pairing occurring—some of it was sexual, some of it was not. I noticed that the coupling was remarkably casual. There was little regard for age or sex. A middle-aged female was playing with a teenage male. A male who looked about twenty-five was holding hands with a girl about thirteen. There were several homosexual pairs too, both male and female.

But there were other gatherings that looked to be specifically nonsexual. A cluster of youngish children were milling together and babbling at each other, "Ba-ba-ba-ba-ba-ba. . . ." Other groups were beginning to form now, clusters of three or five or even more. Several of the bull males were circling the edges of the plaza, herding the straggling members inward.

"It's starting, isn't it?" I said.

"Uh huh."

I watched, fascinated, as the herd began to solidify as a mass. The couples who had been initiating sex play were breaking off now to join the clustering masses. I found it hard to see the herdmembers as people any more. They were . . . pink apes. Animals.

I shuddered. I was getting the eeriest feeling. I touched Fletcher's arm. "This is . . . weird," I said. "I feel like an *alien* here. I feel like they're the human race and I'm the outsider."

Fletcher nodded. "I know the feeling."

I didn't let go of her arm. I needed to be touching her. The herd was clustering thicker now. They were becoming a milling compact mass.

"Listen—"

The sound was formless at first. They were murmuring among themselves. Individual voices floated above the rest. But the murmuring was starting to blend now and all the myriad voices were disappearing into an all-pervasive atonal chorus. There was no pattern to it, no sense of harmony or rhythm. Nor even key. It was just a grand and powerful, all-consuming sound. And it was growing.

It was a fascinating sound—full of hints and meaning. An annoying sound. Reasonless and empty. Steady in its intensity, but uneven in its components. The voices whispered—like the voices in my dreams—if only I could hear what they were saying—

I said, "It sounds and feels like the rumble of the machinery that runs underneath the world. It sounds . . . like . . . ."

"Jim, you should hear your voice," Fletcher said.

"Huh?"

"There's a tremble in it—just like that note out there. You're being affected." She caught herself. "And so am I." I could hear the excitement rising in her voice too.

"But this is—incredible!" I said, turning to her—

"Are you all right?"

I nodded. "I'm fine—it's just . . . I can feel that note resonating throughout my whole body." I was still holding her arm. "I can feel myself rumbling with it. I want to echo it. Do you feel it? It feels like . . . we're included, like . . . we're a part of the herd too. . . ."

"We *are* a part of the herd," she said. "We're the part of the human herd that observes itself. We're the parts of the tribe that broke free so we could look back from the outside."

"But we can't stay out here forever, can we?" But she didn't hear me. I let go of her arm—

"That phenomenon—" she was pointing excitedly, "—just might be the place where we experience *home*. You know, the home that we're always longing to return to, but we can never find? That just might be it." She grabbed my hand and forced me to look at her eyes. "Whatever 'space of consciousness' is being created over there—it *includes* us too! Just watching is being part of the herd! And to the extent that we can recognize ourselves in that mass, we're tuned into it. Do you see now why it's so dangerous?"

"Mm hm. Dangerous. . . ." I wondered why she was shouting. Why was she so intense? She didn't have to be. It was nice out here. The herd seemed pleasant enough.

"It's our sentience—our awareness of self—that allows us to stay separate. That chorus is a—a calling, Jim. It's a communication without symbols. To listen to it, you have to abandon concept and listen instead for . . . experience. It's too powerful! It upsets, it annoys, it fascinates, it *enchants*. It can't help but have an effect on us, the way it washes over us. We just—can't allow ourselves to . . . to . . ." She began to trail off. ". . . let ourselves . . . Jim . . . ?"

I was glad that she had stopped talking. Her words didn't make any sense any more anyway. They were just noises strung together. She was keeping me from concentrating on the sound of the rest of the herd. It was an incredible noise they were making. All of them together were making pattering noises. I'd heard this noise somewhere before—as if from a time before I was born. All the voices in the world, talking about something in words that weren't words because words hadn't been invented yet.

My mouth was moving with them. I made mumbling noises of my own, trying to . . . *understand.* Trying to be a part . . .

What was happening here?

Happening. *It* was happening. Herding. Calling. All the voices singing. Laughing. Boys and boys together. Girls and girls. Boys and boys and girls and girls and all of us. Calling. Someone was holding my hand, I couldn't move forward. Calling. The calling was getting louder. What?

Someone was pulling me backward. My feet moved. Moved. Kept moving.

I stumbled. Someone grabbed me, held me up. Someone was saying something. I knew that sound. All purple. "Shim! *Shim!*"

He was calling me—

—face hurt suddenly. Ringing. A slap.

Not shim. Jim.

Me.

"Who?"

"Jim—!"

"Who . . . ?" I couldn't finish the thought.

"Stay with me," the voice said. "Jim!"

"Um . . . I have to know who . . . ?"

"Who what?"

"There was someone—I was . . . someone was calling me—"

"I was. I've been saying your name to you over and over."

"No, it wasn't you. It was someone else. Someone from another—" I rubbed my head. Hard. I didn't have a word for the other *place.* I just knew it wasn't *here.* "I almost . . . had it. . . ."

"Jim!"

"If I could just . . ."

"Jim, stay with me. Jim, look at me."

I looked at Fletcher. Her face was red and intense.

I said, "I was—fading . . . wasn't I?"

"You were *gone.*"

"I—I'm sorry." I blinked. I looked around. "Where are we?"

"Market Street."

"Market . . . Street . . . ?"

She nodded.

"Oh, my God. . . ." I buried my face in my hands. I was overcome. "I had no idea it was that powerful. Jeez—" I glanced back. "Are they still going?"

"They're just breaking up."

"Oh." There was disappointment in my voice. I could hear it myself.

"Jim, stay here. Stay with me."

"I am. I am."

"What was it—? Describe it." She was forcing me to look at her. Look into her eyes. "Can you describe it?"

"We . . . don't have the words for it, . . ." I said. "Um . . . no, that's not right. We do have the words for it." I pointed in the direction of the herd. "*They* have the words. The words are . . . they . . ."

"Stay with me, Jim!"

"What they're doing . . . it's—" I grabbed her hand. "No, don't slap me again. Let me finish this. There are . . . words beyond words. I know that doesn't make sense, but it does if you've let yourself hear them." I let the thoughts come bubbling up now. They floated clearly in the midst of my . . . fog? No, it wasn't fog.

I swallowed and said, "You're right. They are communicating, but they're not communicating in concept." I stopped to catch my breath, but I had to get the words out quickly, before they lost their meaning, before I lost the sense—"Over here, we talk in words. Words are concepts. Symbols. We communicate symbols. We exchange agreed-upon symbols. They don't do that. They talk in sounds. No—they talk in . . . music. They make music and tune themselves to the music. They —I'm getting it. It doesn't make sense to me, but this is what I felt. They communicate in experience. They're communicating by creating experiences together and . . . somehow . . . tuning themselves to each other . . . somehow becoming the cells of a . . . larger organism, the herd . . . and . . ."

Oh, God. I could see it clearly now.

"They don't have identity any more," I said. "That's what they've given up. They've given up the ability to remember. They have no memory—and without memory, they can't have identity. The only identity they can have is the herd. They stay together for food and for sex, but mostly for identity. Oh, my God, this is a whole new kind of humanity we're looking at, isn't it!"

The realization was terrifying.

I was trembling. A chill swept up my spine and I shuddered. "Is there a place to sit down?" I asked. I wiped my forehead. I glanced around, confused. I felt dizzy.

Fletcher led me to a stone bench that had somehow managed to survive the firestorm and sat me down on it. She parked herself beside me.

"Why didn't you warn me—?" I asked; my voice croaked.

"I didn't know," she apologized. "It affects everybody differently." Her eyes were wet.

I looked away, I looked at the ground. The concrete had bubbled and blistered here. I swallowed hard, and admitted, "I'm feeling . . . very confused right now. And very upset. I feel like I've . . ." I made a frustrated face. "I feel . . . ripped off. Ripped open. Ripped up. I feel like hell. I feel like—I've lost something important—" And then I let the tears come, I sobbed into my hands, and I didn't have any idea at all what the tears were all about. I just couldn't stop crying.

NINE

"FEELING BETTER?" Fletcher asked. She offered me a handkerchief.

I wiped my eyes and looked up at her. "How do you do it?" I asked. "How do you resist the . . . pull?"

She shrugged. "I don't know that I do resist it. I think my way of participating is to watch. To try to understand. Because that's what I do everywhere in my life. I watch. I hold back and watch. Maybe that's why I . . . can move through them the way I can."

I handed back the handkerchief. I still felt empty. Drained. I felt as limp as a wet sweat sock. She offered me her hand and I pulled—tried to pull myself to my feet. She grabbed my elbow and lifted me off the bench. "Come on," she said. "Just walk."

I looked at her as she guided me. The set of her mouth was firm. "Thank you," I said. We started back toward the Jeep.

The herd had lost its cohesiveness. The *gathering* was over and the members were scattering across the plaza. There were couples copulating on the dry grass of the lawn.

I asked Fletcher, "Is it always like this?"

She shrugged. "It varies. Sometimes they're positively frenzied. The intensity can build to such a peak we've even lost a few to heart attacks. Sometimes it's languid. This is about . . . average, I guess."

"Does this happen every day?"

She frowned. "About three or four times a week now. When it started, it was just once or twice a month. Then it began happening more and more often. Now . . . it's almost every other day. I expect within a month, it'll be every day. I think—and this is just a guess—but I think that it's some kind of . . . enrollment phenomenon. Since it started, the herd has been growing much faster than we expected. Something about the phenomenon pulls people into it—as you experienced."

I nodded.

She added, *"And* I think it also supports the members in *staying* in the herd. Last year, we had dropouts. We had people actually *coming back.* They were confused, and they needed a lot of support therapy, but they were conscious again. This year—we haven't had any dropouts. Not since this started."

"Tell me about the dropouts," I said. "How does that happen?"

"Um—usually some kind of shock. We had a young man break his leg. The pain was so bad that he started screaming. And suddenly in the middle of the screaming, he was calling for a doctor. His survival was at stake—he had to do something. None of the herd behavior modes were appropriate, he dredged up something from his memories. Unfortunately, for him, everything attached to that memory came with it. He had to start communicating with us to tell us where it hurt, and so on. So . . . he had to be self-aware again."

"So, that's how you can break the herd," I said. "Break all their legs."

Fletcher laughed. "I don't think it's that easy, James. I wish it were. You can shock some of them back to self-awareness, but most of them you can't. They're aware, but they're not self-aware, and they don't want to be self-aware ever again."

"Mm," I said. There was something about that thought that deserved a second look. My mind was already holding it up to the light, turning it over and over, looking for the implications in it and the extrapolations that could be shaken out of it.

I stopped and looked at the herd speculatively. There was something *else* here—something still beyond my ability to comprehend, let alone communicate. I frowned. . . .

Fletcher followed my gaze. She asked quietly, "Are you thinking about your father? Do you still think he's alive? In the herd?"

Her question brought me back to Earth. I looked at the thought for a long moment. And then I shook my head. "No. I can't imagine my father giving up his power of reason—not for this. It's easier to imagine him dead." I turned to her. I felt remarkably complete. "I can believe it now. Thank you."

Fletcher touched my cheek. "I know it was a shock, Jim. It's good that you're—" She saw something past my shoulder and her face hardened abruptly.

I turned to see a tall, broad-shouldered man approaching us. He was naked, and he had a chest like a wall. He was muscled like a bull. His skin was sun-darkened and the sweat glistened on his body. He was a stallion. A bull. His eyes were bright—he had a very direct look on his face. He also had a startling erection, impossible to ignore.

"Isn't that your missing scientist—?" I started to ask, but Fletcher pushed me aside quickly.

She stepped forward, baring her teeth at the bull, and growled deep in her throat.

He hesitated—

She growled again.

The bull began to lose his bullishness.

Fletcher began to punctuate her growls with angry grunts. The bull backed away before her anger. She bared her teeth and shouted, "Na-na-na-na!" The bull turned and retreated hastily.

I looked at her. I started to say, "That's very effective—" but her expression was ashen. "What's the matter?"

"Nothing," she said.

"Bullshit," I said. "You're a lousy liar."

She tried to wave me away—but I grabbed her arm. "Hey—you're not fooling anybody."

She yanked her arm free and turned away from me. She put her hands to her eyes and her shoulders shook for a moment. She fumbled for her handkerchief. She turned back to me, wiping at her eyes. "We used to be lovers," she admitted. "I uh—still have trouble seeing him like this. Especially . . . when he does *that*. I'm sorry."

I didn't know what to say, so I didn't say anything. I took her hand and led her back to the Jeep. We climbed in, but she didn't start the engine. "That's why you're so interested in the herd, aren't you?"

She nodded. "I want to make sure that he's all right. I—owe him that."

"And . . . ?" I prompted.

She let her breath out. "And . . . I keep hoping that I'll figure it out. The herd. And that . . . I can have him back again." She rubbed her nose. Her eyes were very red.

"He means a lot to you, doesn't he?"

She nodded. "He was—*is*—very special. An incredibly *gentle* man." She looked out across the milling bodies. "Sometimes . . ." she said. She didn't finish the sentence.

I followed her glance.

"It's very tempting," she admitted. "They're at peace. And they have joy." She added, "Perhaps, they're the only ones on the planet who do."

"I wonder . . ." I said. "How long will they last when there's no one left to take care of them?" I looked at her. "Their joy is a very *dangerous* luxury. I don't think we can afford joy any more. At least, not like that."

She didn't answer. She was looking off across the herd. The bull had found a mate for the afternoon. A teenage boy who looked up at him with adoring eyes. Evidently the bull wasn't too picky. I glanced at Fletcher. Her eyes were hard, so I didn't say anything.

She started the Jeep and we headed back toward Oakland.

She didn't say anything until we were halfway across the bridge. "Do me a favor?" she asked.

"Sure."

"Don't say anything about this to anyone."

"I wasn't even here."

"Thanks." She smiled gratefully.

I said, "Besides, I'd just as soon not have Duke know that I was—affected."

She switched the Jeep onto autopilot and pushed the wheel away from her. "He'll never hear it from me."

"Thanks," I said.

She reached over and patted my hand. We'd traded secrets. Everything was okay now.

Fletcher dropped me back at the barracks with a wave and a promise to put me on the permanent pass list for the lab section. I watched her drive off thoughtfully. How many times a week did she cross the bridge into San Francisco?

Well . . . maybe it wasn't really my business.

Duke wasn't in, but he'd left a message: go to bed early, we scramble at six.

There was a new briefing book on my bed. I read it over dinner. A spotting mission? For this we were pulled out of Colorado?

It didn't make sense.

I went to bed still feeling troubled.

My night was restless and full of voices. But they didn't tell me anything either.

TEN

MORNING CAME too soon.

I put the body on automatic and got out of its way. I caught up with it again in the Jeep; the noise woke me up. We were rolling across the cracked and oily tarmac of Oakland International Airport. There was a fully armed Banshee-6 waiting for us at the far end of the runway. Its engines were already screaming.

Duke ran the Jeep right up to the foot of the ramp. Holding my ears, I followed him up the steps at a run. We climbed into the jet-chopper and the door slammed itself shut behind us. The pilot didn't even wait till we were seated; she reached up over her head, released a double-handled lever, and we were rolling. I tossed my bag at the back and scrambled for the seat opposite Duke. The lady punched us up into the air so fast I didn't even have time to finish fastening my safety harness.

She was speaking to her microphone: ". . . Heading three five two. *Enterprise,* you can launch your birds now. We'll pick 'em up over San Pablo Bay."

I knew that voice. Lizard Tirelli! I should have recognized her by that takeoff. I leaned across to Duke. "Remember when Ted and I left Alpha Bravo?" He nodded. I jerked a thumb forward. "That's the same pilot."

She put the ship on autopilot, then swiveled her seat around to face us. She was as pretty as I remembered. I wished she weren't wearing that helmet. I liked looking at redheads. "I'm Colonel Tirelli," she said.

"You're Captain Anderson?" Duke nodded. "And Lieutenant McCarthy, of course."

I nodded. "Congratulations on your promotion, Colonel."

She ignored it. She looked to Duke. "I know you're probably surprised at the suddenness of your transfers. I specifically asked for the two of you to be reassigned to me."

"Eh?" That was Duke.

Colonel Tirelli explained, "I like your statistics. You're effective. The Rocky Mountain District is controllable today because of the way you martialed your resources last year."

"That job isn't even begun," said Duke. I could hear the stiffness in his voice. I didn't know if the Lizard could.

"I know what shape that territory's in. I read your reports. But somebody else is going to have to take it over. You're needed here."

Duke looked unhappy, but he didn't say what he was thinking.

He didn't have to. Apparently, the Lizard could read minds as well as she could fly. She said quietly "I know, Captain—but this is one of Uncle Ira's jobs."

"Oh," said Duke. The subject was closed.

I'd met Colonel Ira Wallachstein—the day before he died. I'd brought down the worm that killed him. I hadn't exactly liked "Uncle Ira," but he'd been the Godfather of the Special Forces, so I respected his memory.

The Lizard let herself drop into a friendlier tone. "You'll be acting as spotters for this mission. You've been briefed?"

Duke said, "We got the mission book last night."

"Did you read it?"

Both Duke and I nodded.

"Good. I'm sorry you didn't have more time with it. Be glad you got it at all. Communications are lousy—and they're going to stay that way until we secure the rest of our ground stations. God knows when we'll do that." She looked strained and frustrated, but not defeated. She continued without hesitation: "Okay, we've got what looks like a major infestation in the lumber regions of Northern California. We're going to take them out—but we've got some anomalies. Second- and third-stage nesting—"

"Third stage?" Duke said.

Lizard looked annoyed at the interruption, but she nodded grimly.

Duke and I exchanged a glance. It was that bad? We'd seen skyball pictures of second-stage nests: hexagonal dome clusters, six around one.

Any child with a compass could draw the floor plan. But *third* stage? I couldn't imagine—

Lizard said, "You'll know when you see it. Captain, you take the left bubble; McCarthy, you take the right. You see anything red, fire a beacon. The cleanup crew will be thirty seconds behind us. They'll be dropping the appropriate detergents. Also short-life radioactive particles, taconite dust, poison vectors, selective X-agents, and degradable biocides. We are not using fire. We will use targeted explosives on medium- to large-scale dome clusters. These will be delivered by the second wave of ships, following sixty seconds after the first. Any questions?"

Duke said, "How far north?"

"An hour and a half."

Duke looked surprised. "That close?"

"It's worse than that. We also have renegade activity in the area."

"Near a heavy infestation?" Duke raised an eyebrow.

Lizard nodded. "It happens."

Duke scratched his head. "If you say so, but I find it awfully hard to believe."

"Most people do," said Lizard. "It started last year. We started finding Tribes in Oregon. Tribes with a capital T. There're pockets of survivors all over. We should have expected that some of them would bounce back at an odd angle. People do whatever they think they have to do to survive. But a couple of these groups were setting up their own governments.

"This one in particular," Lizard said, "had nearly three hundred members. They declared themselves an independent entity. They said the United States was now an 'invalid agreement.' " There was scorn in her voice. "That's what they call a government, 'an agreement of intention.' They said the intention of the United States was no longer valid, so it was their purpose to create the agreement for a new one."

"Did they say what the intention was?" Duke asked.

"It became obvious after a while," Lizard replied.

"It sounds like they were succeeding at something," I said. "At least to the degree that three hundred of them agreed with it. That's a lot of agreement." I was interested in spite of myself.

Lizard shrugged. "Yeah—well, that crap always sounds good to the simple-minded; but I don't buy that jargon. My uniform is still United States green—that's who signs my paycheck. I haven't seen any better offers."

"So you had trouble, right?"

"Both times." Lizard scowled. She rubbed her nose distastefully. "We asked them to move out of the area. For their own protection. They refused. We told them they didn't have any choice. They said that they refused to recognize the authority of the United States. Listen—" Lizard interrupted herself. "I don't care what people want to believe in. My parents were Shamists—Spiritual Harmony Among Mankind—so I've got 'space' to accept just about anything. If people want to paint themselves blue and mate with dwarves and elephants, it's all the same to me. And I tell you truly, you wouldn't believe some of the things these Tribes were up to. The problem was they had 'liberated'—read 'helped themselves'— to the United States property. 'In the name of the people' they said. Naturally, they were 'the people' they were referring to."

"What kind of property?"

"Military, of course. It was not a pretty operation. Somehow they'd gotten ahold of some very sophisticated ordnance. We had to call in a major air strike to take them out. I took in the first cleanup crews."

Duke looked startled. "There was no alternative?"

"They had ground-to-air missiles! And tanks! And they were moving toward a nuclear silo!"

Right. No further explanation was necessary.

"I'd heard the Tribes were gaining strength," I said, "I hadn't realized how bad it was getting. It must have been a difficult situation."

"You should have been there," said Lizard. "They'd taught their children how to use machine guns. Have you ever seen the effect on a soldier when he realizes that his enemy is a twelve-year-old girl? It's devastating."

Duke looked startled by that. He looked like he wanted to change the subject. He asked quickly, "Uh, why do they base themselves near Chtorran infestations—?"

Lizard said, "We think it's possible they're using the worms for cover."

"You mean they've found a way to coexist?" I couldn't help myself, I had to ask.

Duke snorted at me. "There's only one way to coexist with a worm: from the inside."

Lizard said, "It's very simple. The infested areas are no-man's-land, effectively beyond the jurisdiction of the United States government—at least for now, and probably for a long time to come. The Tribes know that if they come in out of the cold, the minute they step across the barriers and enter a Safe City they're accepting not only the protection, but the authority, of the United States government as well. And that means giving up their 'independence,' " she finished.

"But how do they defend themselves from the worms?" I asked.

"That's one of the things we'd like to find out," she said.

"Didn't you interrogate the survivors?" Duke looked puzzled.

"There weren't any." She said it like a door slamming.

Duke looked at her with new respect. She met his gaze coldly. It was obvious she didn't like talking about the subject; it made her hard. Duke dropped his eyes and studied the floor thoughtfully. He knew what she was going through. He'd been through it himself.

But I knew he didn't know how to say it.

Colonel Tirelli spoke first. She said, "We don't think it's the Tribes. We think it's the worms. There's something going on, some kind of shift in behavior. We're beginning to see a lower proportion of attacks on human beings. Some adaptation may be taking place.

"One of the theories is that now that a lot more of the Chtorran plant life has established itself, the worms might prefer to feed on their own ecology rather than ours—so humans might not be number one on the menu any more. But so far that's just speculation. I wouldn't want to test it personally—"

The radio beeped suddenly and she swiveled forward to answer it. "This is Tirelli."

"Banshee-6, we have you on visual. We'll fall in behind like good little children."

Lizard looked off to her left. "I see you." Then she frowned. "How many of you ducklings got into the air?" she asked.

"The whole wing, Colonel."

"How come I see only six?"

"The second wave is going up 101. We'll pick them up north of Santa Rosa."

"Whose good idea was that?"

"Cap'n Caswell's, Colonel."

"I got it. All right, you boys ready to go to work?"

"We're all bright and shiny, Colonel Ma'am, ready to spread death and destruction from here to Klamath."

"Just the target area today, please."

"Roger. Out."

I crossed to Duke's side and leaned down to look out the spotter bubble just behind his seat. I could see six dark gunships just dropping into line behind us. "Hey! Those are Scorpions!"

"Aye-yep," said the Lizard. "They sure are." She swung around to face us again. "You have a question about that?"

"Yes, I do." I looked to Duke, then back to Lizard. "I thought we had to give them up. It was part of the Moscow Treaties. We had to sink our gunships."

"We did. Every last one of them."

"But, how—?" I looked out the bubble again. Those were definitely Scorpions.

Lizard looked very pleased with herself. "Oh, we sank 'em all right. But first we sealed them in acrylic. It kept them nice and dry until we needed them. We started pulling them up last year." She glanced out her side window. "They sure look good, don't they?" She was grinning.

I couldn't deny it. They were big, they were black, and they were mean. With their red spotlights on, they would be terrifying.

"All right," said Lizard. "Let me give you the background. This is *deep* background. Uncredited. But one hundred percent reliable. Denver is getting too vulnerable. The military is looking at moving the federal government again."

"To where—?" I blurted. "Almost everywhere is vulnerable now."

"Hawaii isn't," Lizard said. "So far, there's been no sign of infestation on any of the islands, and we expect it to stay that way. To guarantee it, there won't even be any research labs allowed. Not even on the artificial islands or in the sea-domes."

Duke shook his head. "It'll never sell. It'll look like a retreat."

Lizard nodded. "If it happens, it *will* be a retreat."

"Hawaii's too small," said Duke. "Who gets left behind?"

"Hawaii's only Phase One. Phase Two is Australia and New Zealand. Neither of those land masses has been infested either. The negotiations are already underway. They'll actually be glad to have us—especially if we bring as much of our industrial capacity as we can crate and ship."

She reached down into the cooler next to her seat and pulled out a Coke. She tossed one to Duke and one to me, then took one for herself. "But the immediate goal right now is total centralization within eighteen months. The President will be announcing that before the end of the month. We're setting up a chain of Safe Cities, each one surrounded by a kilometer-wide defensive border. We think we can make each city self-sustaining within a year. We'll be using a lot of robot labor, of course. Each city can then function as a base for military operations in its surrounding district."

I said, "It sounds like you're abandoning the land."

She shook her head. "No. We're saving the people first. We can't fight a war without a front line."

Duke said, "So what does all this have to do with California?"

"Highway 101," Lizard replied. "It's the backbone of the west coast. We need to keep it clear. Seattle and Oakland will both be Safe Cities. We're hoping San Francisco. Probably Portland too, but that decision isn't final yet. The question is whether it's defensible. We also want to put some fortresses on the route. We're opening up a major campaign here. We need to keep our access to the sea. The Hawaii and Australia options both depend on it. Got it?"

Duke nodded. So did I.

"Good." The radio beeped then and Colonel Tirelli swiveled back to her controls. We were over Geyserville, and we'd picked up the second wing of choppers.

I dropped into the right side bubble and watched the ground stream past. We were flying low, not quite treetop level, but close enough to give me a good case of the queasies anyway. Lizard dropped us even lower, and now we began following the rolling texture of the country-side, up one hill and down the next. California had a landscape like a rumpled blanket.

The hillsides should have been green with April foliage, but they weren't. The trees and shrubs passing below us looked yellowish and sickly. There were patches of pink and red mottling the ground. "I know, it looks like lichen," said Lizard, "but it's not. It's another form of the sea sludge. Needless to say, its by-products aren't friendly to local life-forms. The redwoods are especially vulnerable. The stuff grows fast-est in puddles. Those bright patches are the places that were slowest to dry after the February storms. We've still got a lot of rain due. If it's bad, this whole area could be red by the end of summer. Denver is already testing specific biocides, but it doesn't look good."

"Thanks," I said. "Any more good news?"

"Yeah," said Lizard. "It gets worse ahead. Stand by. We're about to hit Clear Lake." She thumbed her radio to life. "All right, ducklings, this is Banshee-6. We're going in. Watch for beacons."

Suddenly we were over water. I could look straight down into it. The clear surface was as bright as the sky, a dazzling silver mirror. I could see the dark shadow of the Banshee rippling below us. Not too far behind were the shadows of the Scorpions. They were bigger and more ominous. They roared behind us like flying dragons. From the ground, they must have been terrifying.

We crossed the north shore of the lake and suddenly I was staring down at an animated nightmare. The brightness of it hurt my eyes—they started watering. I blinked in confusion. I couldn't tell what I was looking at. It was all a burning wash of color. I'd never seen anything so garish and bright. I fumbled my goggles over my eyes and dialed them down.

It didn't help.

All the colors were red—all different shades of red, a kaleidoscope of crimson and vermilion blossoms, scarlet trees and royal fireworks. The eye could not assimilate the information. The brain could not make sense of it. All the possible intensities of red were painted here—all splashed across a pink and almost fleshy-looking landscape. There was umber, orange, ochre and magenta—the colors seemed to hover without shape.

My vision blurred then and I saw the Earth as a gigantic living creature. Its bright pink skin was broken open, scored and lacerated. I looked down into deep and bloody eruptions. Here were open sores and festering wounds. Streams of warm dark blood came bubbling to the surface, ran and puddled into hollows.

I lifted my goggles, rubbed my eyes, and looked again.

Beneath the chopper was a dazzling vision of the floor of Hell. Bright orange bushes leapt upward like flames. Tall sequoias, smothered in red, looked like plumes of crimson smoke. Purple streamers hung from trees like shabby cobwebs. Below were large black spidery growths—they crouched in shadowy places. Red creepers stretched across the ground; they looked like grabbing claws.

The ground was pink.

It looked like it was tufted. It looked like it was made of cotton candy. The hills were sugary dunes. Welcome to wonderland—or insanity. The ground was patched with pallid streaks of blue—or erupting with yellow globular clusters—the colors delineated alien shapes. I couldn't tell what I was looking at. The hills were etched with purple threads—and white ones too; they looked embroidered; they were a crazy quilt of blinding hues.

The trees—what was left of them—were stark black spires, pointing accusingly up from the ground. They looked as if they had been burned raw. I saw the ruins of buildings—a scattering of hollow shells, crumbling beneath their coats of crimson ivy.

We'd crossed into a whole new world—a world from which the color *green* had been entirely banished. And everything else that lived in that green world too.

I looked and I knew. I didn't have to worry about renegade Tribes any more. I didn't have to worry about humanity at all.

I was staring into time. Beyond the bubble was a vision of the future of the Earth. How many years away? It didn't matter. We were not a part of it. Not even bones. There would be no place for humanity. Not here.

The roar of the Banshee's engines shifted then—we were slowing. We'd reached the target area.

ELEVEN

WE STARTED seeing dome clusters almost immediately.

And many of them were second-stage nests.

The pattern was standard: one central dome, six more the same size placed hexagonally around it. We'd seen that in the Rocky Mountain District too, but we still didn't have a sense yet how many Chtorrans a dome cluster would house. A single dome never held more than four; this was obviously an expansion—but for how many? These were the first clusters I'd seen where construction looked complete.

We tagged the first few, then gave it up. There were too many. "Save your markers," Lizard said. "There's a lot more to see."

"Jim!" said Duke, "Directly below us."

I leaned as far forward in the bubble as I could. There were at least a dozen bright red worms streaming across the ground below us, more than I'd ever seen in one place before—and they were *huge!* That one, chasing the chopper's shadow, had to be at least as big as a Greyhound Land Cruiser.

I had a horrifying realization. Every time the scale of the infestation expanded, so did the size of the worms. Was there no limit to their growth?

It gave me a queasy feeling to realize how puny we really were in comparison. How big were they going to get? And—how did they perceive *us?* The worms were turning to look up at us, often raising a third or more of their length off the ground. They waved their arms agitatedly, but I couldn't hear if they were screeching.

The scattered dome clusters were becoming frequent now. I had the sense of a village or a small town. There were domes and corrals and funny-looking spires. I remembered the totem pole I'd seen in front of the very first dome I'd ever burned. Were these the same thing? I wished I could have gone down to look at them firsthand. I wondered what a Chtorran town might look like when it was complete. Most of these structures were still in varying stages of construction. There were half-finished domes everywhere—and they were laid out in serpentine courses as often as they were circular. There was a hint of pattern in the layout—but it wasn't clear yet. I needed to see more.

But as we flew on, the sense of pattern became *less,* not more, obvious. As the density of clusters increased, so did the number of domes in each cluster—but the careful geometric spacing of the domes seemed to be disintegrating as if under pressure. It was as if some instinctual blueprint had broken down. There were extra domes jammed tightly around every core now, sometimes as many as nine or ten. They were squashed so tightly together, the individual domes were built mis-shapen, as if pushed out of round by the pressure. I could feel the *wrongness.*

Behind us, I could hear the first of the explosions. The Scorpions were going to work. They were dropping smart bombs to take out the large clusters. I could see the worms moving frantically beneath us. Was that a Chtorran panic? They streamed out of the domes. From the air, they looked like fuzzy pink caterpillars humping and flowing madly after us. I imagined I could hear their warbling cries over the noise of the jets. *"Chtorrrr! Chtorrrrrr!"*

The ship rocked as the blast waves passed us. Lizard hollered something and we bounced up higher. I looked back and saw an ugly yellow cloud spreading across the horizon behind us. A wave of twenty-four Scorpions was spreading a swath of death in our wake. The idea was to sterilize the ground, make it uninhabitable to worms—or anyone else, for that matter.

The truth was, we had no idea how effective any of our measures really were. The Chtorran ecology recovered too fast. Once the short-life radioactives expired and the biodegradables broke down, the Chtor-ran plants and insect-things were back in force in a matter of weeks. They established themselves faster than any Earth species could. This area would have to be sprayed regularly—until we could find something more permanent. Denver was talking longer short-lives.

Lizard was hollering something at me. "McCarthy! Coming up at two o'clock. What's that?"

It was on my side of the ship—the largest dome cluster yet! A cluster of clusters—the pattern was expanded again! The original hexagon of domes was the core of a larger wheel of hexagons—a Chtorran mandala! A third-stage nest! The sense of pattern was very clear here—there wasn't the same pressured feeling as we had seen elsewhere. It was as if this huge wheel of domes were some kind of model Chtorran village—and the other villages were pushing their growth in an effort to catch up *and doing it wrong!* The pressure was expressed as cancerous-looking domes.

As we came over the mandala, I could see that it was still growing. The central cluster of domes was being expanded into one huge dome—and other clusters were being laid out neatly around the perimeter. The mandala was adding yet another circle.

I hollered back to Lizard, "Bingo! We just found the Chtorran City Hall!" I fired a marker into it, and then another just to be certain. I leaned out into the bubble to watch behind. I wanted to see it explode. I could see the worms streaming out of it as it went up in flames.

The ground was erupting Chtorrans now—it looked like it was bleeding. There were too many of them. All sizes. Larger than I'd ever seen. Smaller than I'd ever seen. And all colors too, from bright purple to flaming orange. I saw everything from baby pink Chtorrans to huge scarlet worms. It was a riot of red! I couldn't see them as individual creatures any more. They were merely crimson streaks on a flesh-toned nightmare landscape. They flowed like oil. They looked like particles of fire. There were so many of them all flowing together that I could see the pattern of their panic as a vermilion river streaking horribly beneath us. It was insanity! Unreal—

The whole camp was on the move—they were a furious stampede. New worms kept joining all the time. In their blind fear, the larger ones tumbled the smaller ones aside, or flowed over them, leaving them writhing and injured in the dirt; the injured creatures disappeared beneath the maddened onrushing bodies of their fellows. I could hear them screaming. All of them. The sound was a high-pitched screech like metal being sheared. I could hear it even over the whuffling of the chopper's blades and the noise of its jets.

Now, as we came over them—and as the sound of the Scorpions behind us grew louder—the crimson river swirled in confusion, as if it were caught in the churning turbulence of the chopper blades. The shrieking worms turned this way and that in a bedlam of terrified disorder—until they were enveloped by the sulfurous yellow clouds from the Scorpions. The great black beasts came roaring on behind us like the avenging angels of death.

Suddenly the ground below was rockier. The clusters of huts vanished like a dream—as abruptly as if the worms themselves had drawn a border. No more of those crimson horrors poured out of the ground. No more paced the chopper's shadow. The last of them fell behind us and disappeared beneath the Scorpions' wrath.

A few miles farther and the festering red landscape vanished too. The hills gave way to green and brown again. There were pine trees here— and redwoods and sequoias.

For a moment, there was silence in the plane. Only the steady chuff and screech of chopper blades and the muted whine of jets filled the cabin, and that wasn't a sound any more; it was merely a presence, constant and unpleasant.

Lizard made a sound then—something like a growl, something like a shriek. It started low and quickly rose. It was a release of tension, a controlled scream like the whistle of a steam engine. Her face was tight—

And then she stopped and took a breath. And took us higher.

TWELVE

I TURNED around and looked at Duke. He looked away. He wouldn't meet my eyes. Goddammit. He did this every time we came up against the wall—every time we were reminded just how badly we were losing. He wouldn't share the pain, he kept it bottled up instead. He scared me when he got like this. "Goddamn worms." He said it bitterly.

I knew he'd have to go off somewhere to be by himself for a while—and then he'd be okay again. Until the next time. But until he had that chance, he would be bitter. And he'd take it out on the rest of us.

My own reaction—

I felt drained. Every mission only put me more in touch with the total hopelessness of the job. This one was the worst. I didn't know what I was doing here.

The worms confused me. I was horrified by them—and at the same time, I was fascinated. I wanted to know everything I could about them. I was attracted by the horror—and paralyzed by it.

And there was another feeling too, a darker more disturbing one. All that I could sense of it was an occasional hot red flash of memory—as if there was something I once knew, but had since forgotten; and yet the resonance of the experience still echoed in my head.

Whenever these feelings came over me, so did a profound disgust for my own species. Human beings were turning into something even more monstrous than the invaders.

It was all the killing.

I knew that there were people who looked at me with horror now—because there was death in my eyes. I could see it in Duke's face too. All of us who had met the worms head-on—we all wore the same expression.

We were killing machines. The only difference between us and the worms was that the worms didn't have a choice. We did. *We chose to kill.* We would even kill ourselves if it would hurt the Chtorrans.

I felt the pressure in my chest again.

The chopper bumped me out of my brooding. We were picking up speed. I looked at Lizard. Her face was military blank. Except for that one moment of screaming release, she was a perfect soldier machine; a pilot-thing, not a human being.

I wondered if she had ever been a real woman, then discarded the thought. Her face was set like steel. I couldn't imagine her laughing, or having a good time, let alone anything more intimate. She wore her body like armor and the effect was inhuman, almost repelling. I couldn't imagine her naked—nor could I see her trusting another human being enough to open up to him. No, she was just another monstrous machine. We all were now.

She was checking her flight plan. "All right, that's the worst of it. We'll let the navy finish cleaning this up. I want to look at Red Bluff before we turn back. Then we'll come back down the coast and look for sea sludge."

"Don't you have skyball overfights?" Duke asked. His voice and expression were normal again—hard and clipped.

"We did—but something's been knocking them down."

"And you want to go looking for it?" I asked. There was incredulity in my tone.

Lizard ignored me. She said to Duke, "We don't have enough skyballs left to schedule regular patrols. We won't until Lockheed starts shipping again."

"How about satellite eyeballs?"

"They can give us pretty good resolution, but they can't get under cloud cover. And they're not mobile on the scene. We need to find out what's going on."

Lizard thumbed her radio to life. "All right, ducklings. This is Banshee-6. You done good. I'm turning east. Fall in behind and keep your eyes open."

"Roger, dodger."

The horizon angled crazily as Lizard tilted the ship eastward. We were over crumpled hills again.

"This area looks green—" Lizard pointed. "But it's red on the map. We're spotting worms in these woods every day now. The governor has pulled the whole lumber industry out."

She added bitterly, "We're going to lose the northern half of the state. It's too wild to control. You won't get anyone to admit it officially, but it's just a matter of time. It's going to be a bitch just to hold the road open. We're running traffic in convoys now and it seems to work, but I don't know what it'll be like in two years. Hell, we don't even know what the worms will be like in two years." And then she added in a quieter tone, "Or even humanity, for that matter. Shit." She flew on in silence.

I looked at Duke. He was leaning forward, staring out of his bubble. All I could see was his back. He had his face in his hands. What was he remembering? He'd probably never tell.

I turned back to my window and stared out at the ground too. This pervading despair was infectious.

The hills were leveling out now. The slopes were lush and green and heavily forested. Some of the trees looked like they had a white sheen to them. I couldn't figure out what it was.

"Time to turn north again," Lizard said and banked the chopper to the left. I wondered if we were close enough to see the 1996 meteor crater, now called Red Lake. That was supposed to be around here somewhere. As we angled around and dropped into our new course, I strained forward to look—but the northern horizon was hidden by a line of pink clouds.

I looked back, but I couldn't see the Scorpions any more. I climbed forward and sat down in the copilot's seat. "Are the other choppers still with us?"

Lizard glanced at her controls. There was a screen in the center of the dashboard. She tapped it. "See those red dots. They're five minutes behind us. Don't worry about it, they're just making a wider turn. They'll catch up with us up here—" She tapped the screen. "If we have the fuel, we'll take a look around Redding too."

"Oh, I see. Thanks."

"Sure."

"Can I ask you something, Colonel?"

"You can ask anything you want. I don't promise I'll answer."

"It's about Denver. . . ."

Her tone was guarded. "Go on."

"Well . . . I remember thinking that the Special Forces people were all so—well, ruthless."

"Mm hm," she said. "That's what it takes to win a war."

"I know that now," I said. "In fact, sometimes I think we're not being ruthless enough. But that's not my question. What I want to know is—well, you were one of the first people there to be kind to me. In your own gruff way. Do you mind if I ask why?"

"I don't really remember—" She hesitated, frowning at the approaching wall of clouds. "Maybe I was having a bad day." Then she shrugged. "I used to take in a lot of stray puppies before I found out they all grew up to be sonsabitches." She glanced over at me. "Any other questions?"

"Uh, no—thanks."

Next time, I'd leave well enough alone.

The sunlight had turned a peculiar shade of pink—the sky was a funny bright overcast. "Are we heading into rain?" I asked.

"No." Lizard looked puzzled. "The forecast is for bright sun and strong winds off the ocean." She glanced at her instruments. "That's not moisture, whatever it is. It's too dense."

"Maybe it's sea sludge," I guessed. "Picked up by the clouds?"

"Not possible. There's no sea sludge this far north."

Duke came forward then, leaning into the space between our two seats. "Sandstorm?"

"Couldn't be. Where's it coming from? The northern part of the state is all forest and meadowland." She looked confused.

The clouds were a large fluffy barrier now, only a few kilometers away. They were rolling across the land like a bulldozer. The ground was darkening beneath them. They looked massive. They looked solid. They looked *too* pink.

"I don't like the color of that," Duke said.

"It looks like cotton candy."

Lizard did something to the radar and studied its display. "Whatever it is, it's rolling up awfully high."

"Can you go over that?" I asked.

"It's a little steep—"

"No," said Duke quietly. "Turn the ship around. Now!"

"Huh?"

He pointed past her shoulder. "Look—"

Something was spattering on the windshield. They were little round spots, red and sticky-looking.

"You're right," said Lizard. She angled the ship sideways into a steep turn. My stomach lurched. I grabbed for my seat belt.

More splotches appeared on the windshield. We were in the fringes of a cloud.

"What is it?" Lizard said. "Bugs?"

"I don't think so—" I leaned forward for a closer look. I couldn't see any details in the splotches. They were just little red pustules on the surface of the window. It wasn't rain. They didn't run. The window was rapidly filling up with red splatters. It was becoming opaque.

The sound of the engines shifted then, became a shrill whine. A red light went on in front of Lizard and an electronic voice said, "Engines overheating." Something started beeping. Lizard said a bad word and slammed a double-handled lever down. The chopper lurched as its jets cut back.

She pulled back on her controls and we hung in the air for a moment. The rotor *chuffed* stiffly through the air. "I don't know if we can get out of this without the jets." She checked something on her board. "I'm going to look for a place to set us down—"

Something screeched and went *SPANG!* on top of the ship. We rocked sideways—

"Shit! We lost the rotor!" Lizard pushed the double-handled lever up and pointed the ship skyward. "I'm going to need some height!" The jets roared—a wall of air pressed me into my seat. Behind me, I could hear Duke sliding and skidding toward the tail as we climbed.

Lizard unclipped a safety switch and slapped the first red button underneath it—and then everything happened at once! There was a *BANG!* from the roof of the chopper as the explosive cover blew off the parafoil. The chopper blades went flying away. Then there was a *THUMP* from the right as that side's engine exploded in flames.

Suddenly the ship was enveloped in fire! The air was hot and orange! Beside me, I could hear Lizard's startlement. "What the hell—?" But she was already hitting the release.

There was a *BANG!* that punched the ship like a bomb. I thought for a moment that our fuel was exploding—but it was only the explosive bolts going off as the engines were jettisoned. A smaller bang took off the tail rotor.

We were falling—I was too terrified to scream—Lizard released the parafoil, I heard it pulling away—something went *FWOMP!*—and then it filled with air and a giant hand caught us and we were sailing silently through the air, gliding forward through the reddish murk like a descending eagle.

"Duke! Are you all right?"

There was no answer.

"Worry about him later!" snapped Lizard. "Watch for a clearing!" She was speaking to her radio now. "Ducklings! Turn around! Stay away from *pink clouds!* This is Banshee-6! We're going down! Repeat—turn around! Stay away from pink clouds! It's some kind of dust! It'll seize your engines, and it burns like hell! I'm going in now. Stand by—"

I was pointing. "Sand dunes—I think."

"Good enough," said Lizard. "Hang on!"

She brought the ship around in a tight turn and aimed us at the long axis of the dunes. Too late, I saw the dunes weren't sand at all—they were pink! We hit with a *FOOF* and a *CRUNCH*—and a *BANG!*—

THIRTEEN

AND THEN everything was silent.

And pink. The light was pink. The windows were pink.

We were canted forward at a steep angle. We'd hit once on the belly of the ship, smacking against the pink drifts of whatever, then bounced up high as the wind-filled parafoil dragged us on—we came down again hard, skidding forward until the nose caught on something and we plowed our way in. But the tail didn't stop—it swung up and forward, tilting the ship even steeper. We were lucky we hadn't flipped all the way over on our back.

Something smelled sweet.

I wondered what we'd landed in.

The stillness was incredible—as if we were smothered in marshmallow. The sound of my breath seemed unnaturally loud.

"Colonel?"

"I'm all right. Yourself?"

"Yeah." I started pushing the still half-inflated airbag away from me. I could hear the air swooshing out of it as I pushed. "Duke?" I called.

He didn't answer.

"Can we get some light?"

"Hang on." There was the sound of switches. I could hear Lizard's hands moving across the console. "Let's try this—"

Whatever it was, it worked. The boards in front of us came back to life. The panel lights lit up, the screens began to glow. Several small alarms started beeping.

"Shut up!" Lizard said. She punched buttons. They shut. "Now, let's do a little fire prevention. . . ."

There was a hissing sound. Suddenly the air felt wet and smelled of menthol.

She thumbed her radio on. "Ducklings, this is Banshee-6. We're down and safe. Possible injuries to one of our party. Do not—repeat, do *not*—attempt to rescue us. The pink clouds are dangerous. Do you copy?"

There was static for a moment, then a military voice came back, "We copy." And then, more personal, "Are you all right, Colonel?"

"I'm a little annoyed."

"I got it. Keep your channel open. We're getting a bearing on you. What happened?"

"We hit a hard cloud."

"Yeah, we can see it. It's rolling south like a big pink carpet. Thanks for the warning. We're heading out over the ocean to get clear of it. What the hell is that stuff anyway?"

"I don't know yet—but it blows up engines. We lost the rotor and both turbines. We came down on the parafoil." She hesitated for a second, then added, "Listen, I'm pretty sure this is something Chtorran. You've got to let Denver know. This is what's knocking down our skyballs. It's just like hitting a wall of cotton candy." She sniffed. "It even smells like cotton candy."

"All right, we've got our fix. We'll be sending a rescue ship back as soon as the candy clouds pass."

"Thanks. I'll keep this channel open as long as I've got power. Out."

Lizard went fumbling beneath her seat. "Here—" she handed something across to me, a flashlight. "See what happened to Duke. And be careful. It's steep. I'm going to try to get the emergency power on."

I couldn't swivel my seat backward, not while the chopper was pointed so sharply downward. I guessed we were tilted at a thirty-degree angle. I unbuckled my safety harness and nearly pitched forward onto the controls.

"I told you, be careful."

"Yeah, I will." I angled myself around and swept the flashlight across the rear of the chopper. Duke was sprawled—no, caught—in the right side bubble. I couldn't see his face, his head was below the deck level, he was almost upside down in the seat. I started climbing toward him.

It was hard to find handholds. I had to use my seat and Lizard's to climb. Once I got past them, there were deck rings on either side for securing cargo. I grabbed for the ones on Duke's side of the ship. Half-way up, the chopper lurched—and shifted. The metal groaned. I thought I heard Duke gasp. I froze where I was—

"It's your weight," said Lizard. "You're bringing the tail down. Keep going."

I started climbing again, this time even more carefully. The chopper creaked once and lurched once—then it was still.

"I think that's it," Lizard said. "That last one felt pretty solid." I'd reduced the angle of tilt to fifteen degrees.

Duke's eyes were closed. I lifted him out of the bubble and stretched him out on the floor of the ship. There was blood on his face, streaming from his nose and a bad cut on his forehead—but he was breathing.

"Duke—?"

"There's a red-bordered panel on the floor there," said Lizard. "Open it. That's the primary first aid."

I found the panel she was talking about and pulled it open. There were three plastic boxes stored inside. One was labeled WATER, one was labeled FOOD. The third simply had a red cross on it.

I took out an ampule of ammonia and broke it under Duke's nose. For a moment, there was no reaction—then he twisted his face away and started coughing. The spasms lasted for only a few seconds. He coughed and looked up at me. Then he lifted his head and looked around the darkened chopper. He glanced toward Colonel Tirelli, then looked back to me. He coughed and said, "I sure hope she can fuck better than she can fly."

I glanced foward to see if Lizard had heard that. She was holding her earphones close to her ears and concentrating on something she was listening to. She hadn't heard. Good.

I turned back to Duke. "I'll let you know when I find out," I whispered.

He grinned at me. "No. I'll let *you* know when *I* find out."

I sat back. "I was going to ask if you were all right," I said. "Obviously, you are."

Duke closed his eyes for a moment, as if he were mentally counting something. "Taking inventory," he said. He opened his eyes again. "All here."

"You sure? It looked like you took quite a beating."

He levered himself halfway up. "I hurt a lot, if that's what you mean; but everything is working like it's supposed to."

Lizard came back to join us then. She squatted next to Duke and touched her fingers to his carotid artery. "Pulse is good," she said. She plucked a pocket light from her shirt pocket and peered into Duke's eyes. "Reflexes look normal. Hand me the medi-kit, Lieutenant."

Duke frowned as she applied the sensors to his forehead. They looked like little poker chips. "Is this necessary?" he grumbled.

Colonel Tirelli ignored the question—she just pushed him back down onto the deck and continued pasting the chips. She unbuttoned his shirt and applied three more to his chest.

I passed her over the console. "Shh," she said, as she thumbed it to life. She studied its screen thoughtfully. "Mm hm," she said. She looked at Duke as a person for the first time. "You took a few scratches, but otherwise you're fine."

Duke said dryly, "I could have told you that *without* the medi-kit."

"Yes, but it's nice to have a second opinion, isn't it?" She stood up. "There're clean jumpsuits in the back. I'll get you one."

Duke looked at me and shook his head. "This is not my idea of a good time." He sat up, grimacing, and started peeling off the poker chip sensors.

Lizard returned with a sani-kit and a plastic-wrapped jumpsuit. Duke thanked her for it. She nodded and returned forward.

"Do you need any help?" I said.

Duke gave me a look that made me sorry I asked.

"Right," I said, and followed Lizard forward. I climbed back into the copilot's seat. Even at this gentler angle, it wasn't comfortable. I still felt like I was about to be tilted out. I looked at Lizard. "How are *you* doing?" I asked. "Are you all right?"

"Only my pride is injured," she said. She was checking her controls with a sour expression. "I've never crashed a ship before."

"Really?" The word fell out before I could catch it.

She raised an eyebrow at me. "Is that a comment on my flying?"

"Um—uh, sorry," I flustered. I pointed to the controls. "How bad is it?"

"We broke the keel of the ship. That took out most of the cables. We have lights forward, nothing aft. There's no power for anything aft. I can run a bypass for the door, or we can pop it manually if we have to. Anything else, I don't know." She rubbed her eyes. For a moment, she looked tired. I felt sorry for her. I remembered what it felt like when I cracked up my first new car two weeks after I bought it. I'd wanted to die then. She probably felt the same way about this chopper.

I looked away politely. There really wasn't anything I could say that would help. Probably I should just keep out of her way for a while. I stared out the front window.

Now that the ship was canted at a gentler angle, we could see out the front windshield. We were staring at a frosty pink landscape. Frosty pink trees and frosty pink bushes—everything was covered by frosty pink snowdrifts. The world looked like the top of some gaudy baroque dessert—one of those Valentine's Day surprises my mother used to make; we never knew what was hiding under the thick pink whipped cream. We'd hated them. We thought they were tacky. That's what the frosty snowdrifts reminded me of. I felt there should be maraschino cherries on top of each delicious-looking mound. That made me think of breasts.

I looked at Lizard, speculatively. She was studying a radar scan on her screen. She had nice breasts. I wouldn't mind a better look at them.

She looked up and caught me studying her. "What's on your mind?" she asked.

"Um—uh, how long do you think we'll have to wait?"

"Depends on the size of the clouds and where they're coming from. We came down right at the leading edge, so we'll have to wait for the whole mass to pass over. I tapped into the weather net for satellite photos, but it didn't show anything we didn't already know. I expect we'll have to be lifted out, and probably not before tomorrow."

"Will we be okay until then?"

"Oh, sure. This ship will never fly again—but most of her equipment's still good. She'll sustain us." Lizard patted her console affectionately. "You done good, baby." Then she added, "A salvage chopper can pick her up and take her back to Oakland where they can strip her for parts. Then we can melt down the rest and try again." She slapped a wall with her hand. "Most of this is foamed Kevlar. The frame is the easiest part of the chopper to fabricate. During the Pakistan conflict, the Lockheed plant was putting out two hundred and forty frames a day. That's almost two thousand machines a week. Incredible. There'd never been a fleet like that before. You should have seen the dogfights. These birds are light, cheap and powerful—and quick to build. Most of the parts are modular, designed to be assembled by robots. That's good, because we're probably going to need a lot more of them—and very soon."

"Why do you think that?" I asked.

"Well—" she gestured toward the window. "For one thing the Chtorran ecology doesn't seem to like jet engines. For another—we'll need

them to control the spread of infestation. That nest we hit will be back
to normal within weeks. We're going to need ten times the number of
ships we had today if we're going to hold them back. And that infestation isn't the worst I've seen."

"We don't have enough pilots, do we?"

Lizard shook her head. "No, we don't. Probably, we'll have to start
flying drones. But these ships are programmable. A good pilot can
control a whole wing." She looked annoyed. "I've been recommending
it for a month. Maybe today's videos will convince them. God knows it
isn't a question of money any more." She snapped off the screen. "Well,
there isn't anything else I can do here now. I need to check outside."

We clambered into the back and Duke joined us at the hatch, zipping
up his jumpsuit. Lizard opened a hull panel, grabbed a lever, pushed
and—grimaced. "Damn! The frame must have bent." She braced herself and pushed again. The lever resisted for a moment, then snapped
loudly into position. "All right, we're on manual now."

She closed the panel and hit the large red button next to it with the
heel of her fist. The hatch popped open with a bang. It swung out and
up and out of the way. The ramp dropped into the fluffy pink dust and
disappeared. A puff of pink smoke rose around it.

We stared down at it. How deep was this stuff anyway? We could
smell the sweetness of it in the air. It was thick and buttery.

"Mm," Lizard said, "it smells like fresh bread."

"Nope," said Duke. "Too much sugar. It must be cake."

"So?" I asked. "Who wants to be first?"

Neither Lizard nor Duke answered. The intense pink landscape was
somehow intimidating. We studied it in silence. The drifts kept sliding
and collapsing under their own weight. We were in the middle of a
rolling sea of powdery dunes.

I realized I'd been making an inaccurate comparison. These weren't
snowdrifts—this was dust as fine as smoke, and piled as delicately as
spider silk. The rosy powder was so fine the light glittered and sparkled
as if the dunes were made of magic. It was impossible to see them
clearly. They were bright and vague and hard to focus on.

There were tiny motes floating in the air. I could feel my eyes starting
to water. But I had an odd thought about this stuff—I had to test it.

I stepped down the ramp, three steps, four—knelt and scooped up a
handful. It felt like talcum, smooth and powdery—but with a curious
silkiness. It was almost liquid.

I sifted a little more, till I was rubbing the last of it between my fingers. "It's very faintly gritty. There must be some larger particles in it too. I don't know." I touched a fingertip to my tongue. It was sweet. I glanced back upward. Both Lizard and Duke were watching me with curious expressions. "It tastes as good as it smells."

I scooped up another handful and blew on it. It puffed away like smoke—like dandelion fur. The motes drifted in the air like snowflakes. I was right in my guess.

I came back up the ramp and stepped back into the chopper, brushing the last of it from my hands. "I know what this stuff is—" I said it hesitantly. The realization was numbing.

Both Lizard and Duke looked at me.

"Remember Dr. Zymph's speech at the conference?" I said to Lizard. "—The one where she listed some of the different creatures in the Chtorran ecology? Well, these are the puffballs! Or what's left of them—they powder like dandelions."

"But so much—?" wondered Lizard. She looked out at the frozen pink landscape again.

I shrugged. "I guess they all blew up at once. The right combination of heat and sun and wind and who knows what else and you get puffballs. But they're practically pure protein," I said. "You can eat all you want. The stuff is harmless—"

"Harmless to everything but precision machinery," Lizard said. "Dammit. The one decent thing in the Chtorran ecology and it knocks airplanes out of the sky."

"Have you got a science kit here?" I asked. "I want to bag some of this."

"Yeah, wait a minute—" I followed her into the back. She opened another panel and dug out a pack for me. I returned to the hatch with a plastic bag.

"This stuff's a mess," coughed Duke, stepping around me. "We're going to need masks."

"I'm already getting them," called Lizard. "And goggles too."

"The puffballs powder as soon as they hit the ground," I reported. I stepped down onto the ramp again. There were fresh puffballs drifting down now—the great wall of clouds were just coming overhead. Some of the puffballs were as large as apricots—but so ethereal to look at they were hardly there. They were just spherical hints in the air, bursting like bubbles if they even brushed against each other, or anything.

"They can't even support their own weight," I called. "The stuff must be compacting under each new layer." I began filling the plastic bag.

"Here's a mask," said Lizard, reappearing in the doorway. I came back up the ramp to get it; she handed me an O-mask with goggles. And an air pack. "That stuff is pretty fine," she explained. "You'd better carry your own air."

"Good thinking," said Duke. He was already pulling his mask down over his head. "What about weapons?"

"What do you want?"

"What have you got?"

"Come take a look—"

Duke followed her aft. I heard the sound of a floor panel being pulled up. Then Duke whistled. "Holy Jesus! This ship is better equipped than a man with three balls!"

"I like to be careful," I heard Lizard say.

I wasn't surprised. I remembered her from my last visit to Denver. The woman was inhuman. What *would* surprise me would be seeing the famous Colonel Tirelli caught *un*prepared. I hoped I'd never be there to see it happen. I doubted there would be survivors.

I stepped out onto the ramp again and looked around.

Something moved.

On the far side of the dune, just behind that pink bush. Something small.

I thought I saw eyes. A face. Staring at me.

I wanted to call Duke, but I was afraid of scaring it off. Instead— I took another step down the ramp. Slowly.

The face didn't move. The eyes blinked.

I wondered what Duke and Lizard were doing. I wished I could warn them not to make any sudden moves or loud noises—

I took another step. Very slowly, I shaded my eyes against the sun and the glittering pink dust.

The eyes behind the bush were large. And gold. The face was pink. And furry. But it wasn't a worm face. Worms didn't have faces. Worms had two eyes, sort of, and a mouth, sort of—but that still didn't add up to a face. A worm had no more face than a snail. This was a face. Almost . . . human. I couldn't tell if the fur was really pink or just covered with dust. I'd bet the latter.

I took another step down. I was on the lowest step of the ramp. One more step . . . .

FOURTEEN

—AND THEN Duke appeared in the door behind me. "What do you want, Jim—the torch or the freezer?"

The eyes vanished. I caught a quick glimpse of a furry body and that was all. Something scuttled and there was pink smoke.

"Shit!"

"What was that—?" said Duke.

"There was something out there—" I pointed. "Some kind of humanoid!"

"Where—?"

"Over there!" I dropped off the bottom step of the ramp and sank chest deep in the pink powder. A great cloud of it swirled up around me. I ignored it and started pushing toward the bush the creature had been hiding behind. The powder was as light as cotton candy. It pushed aside like cobwebs. It was hardly there at all.

"Jim—wait! It might be a worm!"

"This was no worm! I know a worm when I see one! This was humanoid!"

"Here! Take the freezer!" He came down the ramp after me, but stopped on the bottom step. He was carrying a long nozzled rod and a pair of small tanks. Liquid nitrogen. The rod was almost as tall as I was and connected to the tanks by a stiff silvery hose. I'd used this kind of portable unit before. I grabbed it from Duke and shrugged quickly into the harness. The tanks sat on my back and I could use the rod to direct a soft-pressure spray of instant supercooling. It was a great way to gather specimens—

Duke reached up behind him and grabbed the flamethrower. "All right, let's go see—" He jumped into the dust. It came up in a cloud.

Lizard appeared in the doorway carrying a laser-gun. Duke waved her back. "No, you stay with the ship! Get on the radio. This might be something." I knew what he meant by that. We might not come back. But we could leave a clue for the ones who came after us.

Lizard got it; she nodded. "I'll cover you from the turret."

"Good. Let's go, Jim." We pushed off. The dust was almost waist deep.

I glanced back once and waved toward the chopper. I couldn't tell if Lizard waved back. I had to concentrate on my footing.

I was discovering something interesting about the pink powder we were trying to move through. It was only fluffy on the top. The deeper it was, the denser it got. The more I moved, the lower I sank—and I was sinking deeper with every step. It was like the lunar dust that almost killed that astronaut, "Free Fall" Ferris. The similarity was scary. I began to wonder if this was such a good idea. I started to lift the spray nozzle over my head to protect it—and then I had another thought.

I set the nozzle for wide-spray, pointed it forward, and touched the trigger lightly. A cold white cloud whooshed out, putting a sudden chill into the air. The pink powder snapped and sputtered and solidified.

"Hot stuff!" I shouted.

"Huh?" said Duke.

"I said, 'Hot stuff!' This liquid nitrogen is hot stuff!" I strode forward over crackling ice.

Duke followed me, grumbling and shaking his head. "Liquid nitrogen is anything but 'hot stuff.' "

"You know what I mean—"

He grunted something unintelligible in response. I didn't ask him to repeat it.

The liquid nitrogen had frozen a crust in the powder. Where the powder was lightest, it was just cracked and crumbled away, but deeper down, where it was almost dense enough to walk on, the supercold turned the dusty quicksand into a texture more like dry snow—and that we could walk on. There was resistance now. The frozen powder crunched under our feet. Every few steps I stopped and froze another patch ahead of us. We were carving a deep furrow through the high dunes.

We couldn't see anything but powdery drifts all around us. They were piled up like walls. Apparently, we had come down near the center of a large shallow depression—probably an old dry riverbed. We were in the center of it and couldn't see out—assuming, of course, that there was something to see that wasn't pink.

The bush we were heading toward was actually on a high rise of ground. As we climbed up through the dust toward it, we found ourselves climbing out of the powder as well. Toward the top it was only waist deep.

Perhaps this slope was the western shore of the riverbed, but it was hard to tell. Some of these California riverbeds could be as wide as a kilometer across. This felt like being in a deep desert. Or in a lunar crater. Or on another planet. I wondered if they had places like this on Chtorr?

The air around us was pink with smoke. The wind was stirring up small powdery whorls that rose and dissipated into the air. The clouds of it spread out and became a gentle haze. I looked up. The sky was turning rosy.

And it was impossible to see the horizon. Everything just blurred out in the distance. The only difference was that the sky was slightly brighter than the ground, and the sun was a bright pink glow in the middle of everything.

I glanced back at the chopper. It had carved a long uneven furrow through the pink dunes—I could see where we'd bounced. Already the sides of the soft pink scar were collapsing and sliding inward. The aircraft itself was canted gently forward, its nose halfway buried in one of the highest of the dunes. The silken shroud of the parafoil had draped itself across the slope ahead of the ship. Already, the pink dust was sweeping over it, burying it from view. Its lines were barely visible now.

And beyond the chopper—

—there was only more pink. Pink whipped cream dunes and rosy pink sky, all fading off into an oppressive, bright pink blur. Everything was pink.

We crested the slope—the powder was only knee deep here—and moved around to the other side of the bush. "Look—there're its tracks."

"Looks like some kind of paddlefoot," Duke said. "Four toes. The center two are the longest." He spread out the fingers of his hand and held it over the closest footprint for comparison. "He's a little fellow, whatever he is. My hand just covers this print."

"He went down that way," I pointed. I followed the tracks toward the trees.

"Jim—I don't think that's such a good idea—"

"Why not?" I paused and looked back.

"We'd better not get too far from the chopper," said Duke. "If we lose our way, we'll never get back."

"We'll follow our own path," I said.

Duke shook his head and pointed back the way we'd come. "Look—" Already the dust was filling in our trough. "It's still coming down. We're not aware of it, because we're stirring up so much of it, but if you watch something that isn't moving, you can see this crap is getting deeper. That cloud—" he gestured at the sky, "—is dumping most of its load right here. This stuff can't get past the Sierras. The wind can only carry so much of it. It's got to drop somewhere. This is the place."

"Damn," I said. "We'll have to hurry. Come on."

"That thing could be anywhere by now," Duke said.

"We've got to take the chance. We've got to see what that critter was! You can go back if you want—" I was already heading deeper into the pink forest. The creature had plowed a furrow through the dust, just like us. It zigzagged back and forth through the bushes.

Duke grumbled; but he shrugged, sighed, and followed. There are disadvantages to having a headstrong science officer. We twisted through the frosty trees, Duke muttering quiet obscenities.

"This is what I get for letting them assign you to me," he said.

"You *asked* for me." We'd had this argument before.

He waved it off. "You were the lesser of two evils. The alternative was a morally retarded sociopath who had fragged his commanding officer. The only reason they didn't shoot him was they couldn't prove he had actually tossed the grenade. Frankly, I just don't care to have that kind of man in my command." Duke changed his tone then; he became more serious. "Listen—whatever it was, it'll turn up again. Someone else will spot one. You don't have to be the guy who brings in all the animals. Besides, it's probably terrified of us and heading for the hills as fast as its fat little feet can carry it."

"I don't think so," I said, following the next turn. "It was studying us. That wasn't just an animal I saw. There was intelligence in those eyes. And where there's one, there're probably many. We're probably being watched from all sides right now." I stopped and pointed. "Look —I was right. There's another track—" A second line of paddlefoot tracks crossed the first. The dustfall indicated we were following the older set of prints. I turned to follow the newer furrow. It twisted and turned like the first.

"Don't these creatures believe in straight lines?" I asked.

"They must be descended from politicians," Duke replied.

"Or comedians," I said.

I came around what might have been a pine tree and stopped. Duke came up beside me. The furrow we were following headed straight into the center of a wide clearing—

—and into a whole switchyard of crisscrossing paths! It was impossible to tell one from another.

"Damn!" said Duke. "I knew it."

I looked at him. His expression was impossible to read behind the goggles and O-mask. I said, "What are you talking about? This is incredible! There must be a whole colony of these creatures."

"—Unless your critter doubled back over his own path."

"Why would he do that?"

"To confuse us," Duke said. "Are you confused?"

"Uh . . . I don't think so."

"Uh huh." Duke looked at me funny. "Then which way is back?"

I pointed past his shoulder. "That way."

"You sure?"

I looked at him curiously. "Do you know something I don't?"

He turned slowly, studying the dunes. "Remember Shorty? He and I were in Pakistan together. The black pajama boys used to do this exact same trick. They'd let one of their number be seen. As soon as he was spotted he'd take off into the trees. There was always at least one jackass stupid enough to chase after him, so he'd leave the most complicated, zigzag, twisty, serpentine trail he could—but he always made sure it was clear enough to follow. As soon as you were deep enough to be confused about the way back, the trail would stop. That's when his friends would come out to play. We lost an awful lot of jackasses that way."

I glanced around nervously. A steady breeze rustled the surface of the dust, stirring pink wraiths into the air. Everything looked pink. There was no horizon any more, no sky, no ground—just a fine pink haze. We had some bleak-looking bushes and dunes. Nothing else.

I shuddered. For some reason, frosty pink things weren't charming any more. I looked back to Duke. "Do you think that's what's happening here?"

Duke looked grim. "I don't know. I didn't see your creature and I can't guess what he wants or how his mind works. And this isn't Pakistan. But that's what I keep thinking of. Sorry, son—that's the only thing I have to compare it to—Pakistani Poker."

I considered it. Duke only called me "son" when he thought something was important and he wanted me to listen harder than usual.

"Let's head back," I said.

"I thought you'd agree." He pointed. "It's that way."

"You lead," I said. I fell in behind him.

Our path wound back through the bushes. I didn't remember making this many twists and turns—

Suddenly, Duke stopped and pointed ahead. "Look—"

Our path had been crisscrossed again and again by paddlefoot tracks, until our original prints were no longer visible. Something had been following behind us. "Urk—" I said.

Duke swung the torch around slowly, covering the bushes on all sides. "Well . . . now they know that *we know*." His eyes narrowed behind his goggles. "If they're going to attack, now's the time."

"Well let's not stand here talking about it. Let's keep going!"

"Just a minute—" Duke pulled a small plastic disc off his belt. "We're going to need the beeper." He studied it for half a second, then pushed off at a new angle. "Follow me."

The dust was coming down heavier now. We could see it floating in like snowflakes. The particles were bigger now—big pink clumps, turning as they drifted. They looked like dandelions. I reached out to catch one as it floated down. It disappeared when it touched my hand—it puffed into dust and was gone, it was that light.

"We're in the thick of the storm," I said.

"Uh huh—and the wind is rising. We'd better hurry. We'll be at the limit of our masks soon."

I nodded and followed him. The visibility was getting worse. I couldn't see more than twenty yards ahead of us.

"Jim, it's getting deeper. You'd better start freezing again."

"Right." I came up even with Duke and sprayed a quick cold cloud of chill ahead. The liquid nitrogen looked like steam when it hissed into the air. The dust crackled and broke as we moved through it. The frozen crust beneath crunched.

Duke checked his beeper and pointed. I moved ahead and sprayed again. We moved forward cautiously.

"You think they can attack in this dust?" I asked.

"It's their natural element," Duke said. "And they don't seem to have any trouble moving around in it. I won't feel safe till we're back in the chopper." He checked his beeper. "More to the left, Jim. We should be almost to the slope—"

"Urk—"

"What's that?"

I stopped and pointed. Duke came up behind me and peered through the pink gloom—

There were three of them.

They looked like flop-eared bunnies. Or puppydogs. They had little squat bodies covered with frosty pink fur. I couldn't tell if that was just the dust or if it was their natural color.

They seemed to have large round faces and short, blunt muzzles. The pink frosting that covered everything made it hard to tell. Their noses and mouths were invisible, and their eyes were narrowly slitted against the powdery dust. They were thoroughly covered with it; they stood waist deep in the bright powder. They looked like little Chinese bunnies in a cotton candy factory.

Bunny ears. Puppy faces. Not my idea of aliens from space. Certainly not my idea of a Chtorran intelligence.

I couldn't tell if they were friendly, hostile, or just curious. But they were staring at us. There was no question that we were the focus of their attention.

I looked at Duke—and then looked past Duke in horror. Five more of the little bunnydogs were just creeping up behind us.

I whirled around—there were more of them just coming out of the bushes behind me. They were coming out on all sides of us, too many to count.

There were bunnydogs to the left of us, bunnydogs to the right of us—

We were surrounded.

FIFTEEN

DUKE SPOKE first. "Well . . ." he said, very softly, "here's another fine mess you've gotten me into."

I looked over at him. "I must say, you're taking it rather well."

Duke ignored the remark. He was studying the bunnydogs, trying to figure out which one was the leader. He said, "You're supposed to be a scientist. What's the Chtorran word for friend?"

"The only Chtorran word I know translates out as 'lunch.'"

"Better not," Duke said. "Not until we know what these things eat."

"Well . . . they're not herbivores," I said.

"How do you know that?"

"Their eyes are on the front of the head. Predators need stereoscopic vision for tracking prey. Prey animals need their eyes on the sides of their head for avoiding predators. At least, that's how it happened on this planet. I could be wrong. But . . . if they're meat-eaters, then there's also a potential for intelligence."

"Why?"

"How much brains does it take to sneak up on a blade of grass?" I replied. I'd credit the joke later.

Duke considered the idea and nodded. During all this, the bunnydogs still hadn't moved. They just sat and stared at us.

I added, "Pray that these things are omnivores. According to the Cohen models, intelligence develops first in hunters, but it survives in creatures who aren't totally dependent on the hunt."

"So?" Duke asked, "Are we in trouble here or not?"

"Well . . . they're not carrying any weapons. If they're intelligent, then they could be just as curious about us as we are about them."

Duke turned slowly, studying the circle of little pink eskimo-things. They were remarkably patient little creatures. Duke said slowly, "You may be making a false assumption here, Jim."

I turned in the opposite direction, also studying. "What's that?" I asked.

"You're assuming that these things are sentient. What if they're not? What if this is just a wolf pack?"

The idea startled me. Duke was right. I'd been anthropomorphizing the bunnydogs from the very first sighting. I'd just naturally assumed that anything with a humanoid form would have to be intelligent. "You're right. I'm sorry."

"Apologize later. Let's get out of here first."

One of the bunnydogs moved then. He shifted his squat to one side, and languidly began to scratch his ear with a hind leg. For a moment he looked just like a fat little puppy. Dammit! These things were too cute to be dangerous!

I looked at Duke. "Still think this is a wolf pack?"

"No more assumptions," he cautioned. He started forward, crunching through the still-frozen powder. Parts of it had started to thaw and were turning muddy. I could hear his boots squelching in the ooze. He took three steps and stopped. The two bunnydogs directly ahead of him stood up, gobbling excitedly and fluttering their hands. Duke glanced at me—what now?

The two bunnydogs looked at each other. They began to gobble at each other like baritone chipmunks. One of them took a hop and a half closer to the other and began gesturing like a little cheerleader. He gabbled and squeaked at his companion. He wrung his hands—they were tiny monkey paws. He put his fists together and shook them as if he were making a martini. He hopped up and down, raising large clouds of pink powder around them both. At one point, he even grabbed his cheeks and pulled them out sideways in a grotesque comical grimace.

His companion made a funny expression and gabbled something back. It looked like a disagreement. He waved both his fists over his head and made nattering noises. He thumped his feet in the dust, sending up an even larger cloud of pink smoke.

The first bunnydog flounced its displeasure. He reached over and pinched his companion's cheeks. He pulled and stretched them into a sideways expression. When he let go, we could almost hear them snap back into place. The second bunnydog was unimpressed. He shook his fingers at the first, waving them like little tentacles.

It was turning into an argument. The pitch and tempo of their voices began to rise, like a recording being speeded up. Then abruptly the argument was over. The two bunnydogs began to make up like a pair of lovers. They touched each other's hands and faces, cooed like doves, glanced at us once, nuzzled each other's cheeks, chittered for a moment longer—but in quieter tones now—then finally turned to face us again.

"And I'm supposed to take them seriously now?" Duke asked. "After that little performance?"

I shrugged. "They do have us outnumbered." I glanced back. More bunnydogs had added themselves to the circle. More were arriving even as I watched. I said, "It's now or never, Duke."

"I agree." He took another step forward—

This time all the bunnydogs started chittering at us. They jumped up and down, gobbling and squeaking. The effect was ludicrous—and terrifying.

"Give 'em a puff of cold," Duke said. "See if they'll back off."

I nodded, pointed the nozzle at the space between us and the forward bunnydogs. I touched the trigger briefly, lightly—and released a *whoosh* of powdery cold into the air.

The bunnies leapt back away from it, startled and chittering—but they didn't panic, and they didn't flee.

They sniffed at the air, wrinkling their noses against the painful coldness of it; then they began to hop forward again, back into position.

"I could freeze a couple of them," I suggested. "But it might not be good for future relations."

Duke considered it. He shook his head. "Maybe a little fire instead." He armed his torch and raised it, deliberately pointing it high—

Something caught my eye. "Duke! Wait—"

Duke froze where he was.

Something large and dark was moving up through the dust toward us. I knew what it was even before it came out of the murk. So that's why the bunnies had held us here. They were waiting for this.

The worm was Papa-sized. It was five meters long, nearly two meters thick at the shoulder. Its eyes were shuttered against the dust.

And then I saw—

There were bunnydogs riding on top of the beast. The largest was perched on the brain-bump, and steering it with chirps and tugs and slaps. He was a chubby fellow—he looked and acted like a fat little bus driver. There were three other bunnydogs riding farther back on the worm. They looked like tourists. All they needed were cameras. If they hadn't been riding a two-thousand-kilo eating machine, they would have been cute.

The worm flowed to a stop and faced us. It blinked—*sput-phwut*—and warbled a soft sound. "Trllp?" Then it shuttered its eyes again. It looked like it was dozing.

I looked at Duke. I'd never seen a worm do this before. He looked back at me and shrugged. But he kept his torch at the ready.

The bunnydog on top of the worm gobbled something at the bunnies on the ground. They gobbled back. Several of them clambered up onto the back of the worm to confer face-to-face with the newcomers.

Duke lowered his torch, just a little bit. "Jim . . ." he said. "What are we looking at?"

"I don't know. I'd like to think that the bunnydogs are intelligent, perhaps even the intelligence behind the worms, but—" I said, "it could be the other way around too. The worm could be the intelligence, and the bunnies could be his dog pack. We might be the guests of honor at a fox hunt."

Duke accepted that thoughtfully. "Well, we need to make up our minds fast. One worm we can handle. We can't take on a whole family."

I nodded. "We're going to have to burn our way out, aren't we?"

Duke didn't answer. He just shifted the torch in his hands and steadied his stance.

Abruptly, the worm woke up. Its eyes popped open and stared directly at Duke. At the same instant, all the bunnydogs on its back yipped and leapt off. Were they commanding it? Or getting out of its way?

The worm said, "Chtorrrllpp?" It looked *questioningly* to Duke. It started to slide forward—

"No!"

—and Duke fired.

It was the dampness in the air that saved him, I'm sure of that. It was the lingering chill from the liquid nitrogen.

For a moment, the flame hung in the air—then it leapt *backward* and enveloped him—he didn't even have time to scream—he was a ball of orange fire—

It was the dust. It was so fine it didn't just burn—it exploded. It couldn't have been more dangerous if it were powdered hydrogen—

I didn't think. I just pointed the freezer at Duke and fired. The flames vanished almost instantly. Great clouds of cold steam whooshed up into the air, crackling and spitting. Duke was somewhere in the center of that.

I had to do it.

If I hadn't, the whole sea of powder would have exploded. It would have been a firestorm. I didn't have a choice.

There was a blackened burned thing standing where Duke had been. It toppled over into the powder—

The bunnydogs were gone—vanished into the bright pink haze. So was the worm—I hadn't even seen it move.

—there was just me and Duke, still crackling in the center of a smoldering black crater.

I started screaming.

"You goddam sonofabitch!" I was already pushing through the ooze toward him. "I told you to wait! Didn't anybody ever tell you about grain elevators? And dust! You stupid asshole!" I pulled his fuel tanks off him and rolled him over on his back. He was still alive. His breath was coming in great rasping wheezes. The O-mask had protected his face and lungs. He had a chance. Maybe.

I grabbed him by the tank harness, looped one of its belts around my forearm, and started dragging him forward. I couldn't carry him through this powder, but I could drag him. It would have to do. I cursed him every step of the way.

And then I stopped.

The whole world had become a fuzzy pink blur, vague and indistinct. Even the sun was gone. The sky and ground had vanished. There was nothing but pink. I couldn't even see my own hands. If I let go of Duke, I wouldn't even be able to find him again.

I'd heard of whiteouts in the Antarctic—this was worse; this was a California pinkout.

I didn't know where I was.

Worse, I didn't know where the chopper was.

SIXTEEN

I FROZE.

I knew I had to get back. But my sense of direction had totally failed.

I was afraid to take a step in *any* direction, for fear I would be going the wrong way. I could be only a few meters from the ship and unable to see it.

The wrong decision would kill us.

I stood there, trembling with the realization, paralyzed by my own terror. I had to do *something!* Duke needed attention *now*. And neither of us had much air left.

I didn't know where the beeper was. It wasn't in Duke's hand or on his belt. I'd looked for it when I grabbed him. That was before the pink closed in. And now, it was getting deeper. There was nothing but pink. It was waist-high now.

I had to do something. *Now*.

Even if it was the *wrong* thing to do.

I hadn't turned since grabbing Duke—I should still be pointed in the right direction. I didn't know what else to do.

I held the freezer in my left hand and sprayed it forward. I could hear the whoosh. I saw nothing—but I could feel the chill in the air.

This was crazy. It couldn't work. I moved forward anyway—slowly. I tested each step before putting my weight down.

Suddenly, the pink gave way beneath me. I let out a yell—I hung onto Duke—and we slid down a long slope of powder—

We came to rest at the bottom, buried in pinkness. I couldn't find the place where the ground ended and the air began. We were wrapped in spiderwebs. I wasn't even sure which way was up any more. I fired the freezer in the direction I thought was forward. The chill woke me up.

I caught my breath. I sat up. Somehow, I stood up. The belt of Duke's harness was still looped around my arm. My God! He was still with me!

I started pushing forward again.

I was frustrated—I was angry!

Dammit! This is Jim McCarthy here! I'm not supposed to die like this! Not this young! I'm only twenty-four! There's supposed to be *more* to my life! I'm important! I'm part of the war against the Chtorr! "Hey, God! Listen up! This is James Edward McCarthy! It's too soon! I haven't had the rest of my life yet!

"Hey, God, come on—let's be reasonable here." I staggered on, dragging Duke with me, spraying the air ahead with chill, and trying to hang onto my footing. I didn't know which way I was going. "Hey, God, give me a sign. Something. Anything. Please. Save me. Save Duke. At least save Duke. I've already got Shorty's death on my conscience. Isn't that enough? Let me save Duke—then you can have me if you want me. I'm scared of dying, God—" I gulped on that one "—and I'm sorry, I've been an asshole. Please—God, I thought you had bigger plans for me. This isn't the way it's supposed to work out, is it?" My throat was getting dry. My voice cracked. I didn't know why I was saying all this. It was just something to say while I pushed on.

And then, something happened.

Inside me.

Something shifted.

I realized what I was doing. I remembered something Duke had said to me. "You oughta try it sometime."

I gulped again.

This was stupid. But—

I could feel myself really *caring*. Really wanting to make contact. If it were possible.

"Um—I don't know how to do this, I really don't. I guess I should just talk, shouldn't I? So, um—let me start at the beginning. I'm really doing this for Duke. I've been selfish and—oh, hell, I know you can't save Duke without saving me too, but—"

My feet moved. My mouth worked. I pushed forward.

And I *prayed*.

"God—I don't even know if I believe in you. I don't know that you exist. I never thought about it. So—I guess I'm just another goddam hypocrite only believing in you now when there's no other hope—I'm going crazy here, God—it's just not fair. I'd always thought someday I'd have the chance to find out what it all meant. Are you listening, God?" I stumbled then and fell forward into the pink and somehow the belt to Duke's harness came off my arm. I felt it slip off.

It was gone.

I lay there in the powder, paralyzed.

Duke was only inches from me. If I moved, I could lose him. I had to be careful. Very careful.

I raised myself up to my knees. I reached backward, back and back— I fumbled in the dust. Please, God—let me find Duke. Nothing else—let me find Duke.

I ignored the sound in my ears. I had to find Duke. Carefully, I turned myself around, praying that I wouldn't slip sideways down another slope, or turn myself the wrong way. I felt around. I sprawled flat and felt ahead—my hand touched something—I grabbed it—

It was Duke's arm. Oh, thank you, God!

I felt around for his face. I found it. I was blind. The world was pink. I didn't care if I never saw again. Just let him be alive! I brought my face close to Duke's and listened. *Tried* to listen. Couldn't. There was too much noise. But his mask was making rasping sounds! He was still breathing! Oh, sweet heaven—thank you, God! Now, please—let me get him to the chopper!

The sound in my ears was getting louder. Annoying. Insistent. What the hell was that anyway? It sounded like a siren.

I stopped to catch my breath. And listened.

The sound was muffled by the dust. It was close by, yet sounded very far away. Some kind of whooping.

It *was* a siren! It came out of the pinkness as a steady series of short sharp rising yelps.

The chopper? It had to be!

What was it doing way over there to my left? I'd been heading wrong! I didn't care. Thank you, God! We could make it!

I tied Duke's belt around my wrist again. I stumbled back to my feet. I faced the siren. I pushed. I dragged Duke behind me. I focused only on the sound.

It was whooping like a demon. Like someone beating a bassett hound. The strokes were sharp and steady. A yelping purple sound. It was the only thing in the world that wasn't pink. And I pushed toward it.

I sprayed the liquid nitrogen ahead. I crunched through dust. I pushed through crackling spiderweb fluffiness. Everything was pink. But I could hear the siren and I knew that we were saved!

Thank you, God. Thanks!

There is a job here for me, isn't there!

SEVENTEEN

I FOUND the chopper by stumbling into it.

I don't know how I found the door. I just started feeling along the side of the ship, pounding and shouting as I went. The chopper was so deep in the powder that I was pounding on the roof of it. "Lizard! Open the goddam door!"

And then suddenly the door popped open in front of me and I fell in. I couldn't see it, I just fell in. I poured in, dragging Duke with me. The dust poured in on top of us. Somebody was pulling me forward. "Oh, my God—"

"Save Duke!" I was screaming. "Don't worry about me! I'm all right! See to Duke!"

"Wait! I've got to close the door!" Lizard was screaming back at me. "The dust is pouring in—" She coughed and disappeared—

I lay there on the chopper floor, listening to my heartbeat, listening to the insistent whooping of the siren, listening to my own sobs of relief. I couldn't move. I had to move. There was still something to do. I pulled myself to my knees. I heard the sound of the door hissing shut. There was something wrong with the sound. I still couldn't see. But at least it wasn't pink any more. It was dark and blurry. I wiped at my goggles—

"Keep your O-mask on!" Lizard was in front of me again. "McCarthy, can you hear me? Do you understand? Keep your O-mask on!"

I managed to nod and gasp, "Water—"

She put a bulb of something into my hand and was gone. I sucked at the moisture greedily. It was sweet. Everything was sweet. Suddenly I could smell the powder again. Fresh baked croissants. Bubble gum. Marshmallows. Something buttery. Sweet potatoes. Angel food cake. And cotton candy. Always cotton candy.

"McCarthy—!" It was Lizard again. "We've got a problem with the door! I can't close it! The dust is in the way! The door is jammed."

"Shit!" I scrambled around, felt past Duke—"I can't see a thing. Where's my freezer!"

"It's here—" She pushed something long and cold into my hands.

"Point me at the door and get out of the way. Get Duke out of the way too!"

I felt her hands on my shoulders, turning me, aiming me—"Wait a minute!" she said. I heard the sound of something heavy being pulled across the deck. "All right—"

I fired. The spray was too loud. The chill was terrible and bitter. Something crackled. This was not the smartest thing in the world. I could feel the clouds of cold steam billowing around me. The liquid nitrogen always reacted strongly to normal air temperatures.

Lizard pushed past me, moving to the front of the ship. I heard the sound of the door hissing again—this time, I could hear the powder crackling out of its way, even exploding as it came into contact with the warmer metal of the door.

And then the door was shut.

A moment later, Lizard shut the siren off.

And everything was black and silent.

"Is there any light?" I yelled. "I still can't see!"

"Just stay there—wait a minute!" I heard her doing something at the front of the ship. She came back almost immediately. I saw a bright glow in front of my eyes. "Can you see anything?"

"A blur. It's bright. It's moving."

"It's a flashlight." She wiped at my goggles. "Keep your mask on. I'm just blowing some of the dust away. Can you see anything now?"

"It's brighter. . . ."

"Just relax. There's a lot of smoke in here. I can't turn on the ventilators. They'll just jam. Give it a minute, I think your freezer is causing the stuff to settle."

"I think my sight is coming back," I said. "This is the eeriest experience."

"Yeah, a lot of fun—" And then she let out an involuntary yelp. "My God! What happened to Duke!"

I tried to focus. I could just barely make him out.

Duke was a mummy. Duke was a pink-crusted body. Duke was a cocoon. Duke was burned all over and frosted with pink powdered sugar. Duke was lying on the floor and gasping for breath.

My lungs hurt too. Despite the masks, we must have both inhaled a couple kilos of the dust. I didn't want to keep going. I wanted to lie down and die. But I didn't. Not yet. I started crawling toward the back, looking for the box with the red cross on it. Lizard came with me. We both knew the drill.

We didn't try to pull the jumpsuit off him. We had to cut it. Parts of it were burned. Parts of it were still frozen. Pieces of charred skin came away with the material. The dust covered everything.

I couldn't tell how badly Duke was injured. We got his shirt off him and I started pasting poker-chip-shaped monitors to his chest. I put the last three on his forehead and temples. Then we wrapped him in a medi-blanket. I found another probe and put it in the crook of his elbow. I attached a pressure-feeder to his upper arm and gave him a half-liter of artificial blood. Then I started him on glucose and antibiotics.

That done, I lifted his goggles and mask. His eyes were swollen. His nose was bleeding. Lizard wiped his face gently with a damp towel. I found a clean O-mask and carefully replaced his used one. We'd found the chopper just in time. The tank was almost empty.

The console said he was in shock. The ultrasonic scanner in the blanket gave a very confused reading. Then it gave up and merely flashed a simple red warning: WAIT FOR ASSISTANCE.

His brain waves were steady though. That was a good sign. So was his heart.

I sat back then, pulled off my O-mask and flung it at the back of the ship. Everything was covered with pink. A puff of dust billowed where the mask hit.

I still wanted to die "Give me one of those cloths—?"

Lizard peeled open a new packet and slapped it onto my palm. I unfolded it and buried my face in its cool freshness. "Thank you," I said. "Thank you for the cloth. Thank you for the siren. Thank you for being here. Thank you for saving Duke's life." I didn't know if I was thanking Lizard or God. Probably both. "Thank you." My voice cracked on the last one. Lizard handed me another bulb of water.

"What happened?" she asked.

I sank back against the bulkhead behind me. I sucked water from the bulb for a moment, then looked at her. She pulled off her mask. She was frosted all over with pink powder too—except for her eyes and mouth.

The effect was horrible. We both looked grotesque. She sat back against the bulkhead opposite me and waited.

I let out my breath. My chest hurt. I sucked more water. I didn't want to talk. I said, "You are looking at the biggest asshole on the face of the Earth. I screwed it up worse than I have ever screwed up anything—"

"That part I know," Lizard said. "That part is obvious. Tell me the part I don't know."

"I'm sorry," I said. "I led us into a trap. At least it looked like a trap to Duke. I'm still not so sure it was. But the effect was the same." I sucked at the bulb. God, I was thirsty! What was it about this dust anyway? I looked back to Lizard and continued softly, "Anyway, there *are* creatures out there. We saw them. They surrounded us. They look like little furry men. They're shaped like ducks. They waddle. They have round faces and slitted eyes and floppy ears. They talk like chipmunks. They make faces at each other. They use their hands when they talk. They're too cute to be real. I think they escaped from Disneyland. They surrounded us and wouldn't let us pass. They were keeping us for something. A worm. Three more of them—no, four—came riding up on a Daddy-worm. They held a conference. And then the worm moved toward Duke. It didn't look like an attack to me—but Duke fired anyway. And his torch blew up. It must have been the dust. It's too fine. It explodes—" I shuddered at the memory. I didn't want to talk any more, I didn't want to tell the rest.

Lizard didn't press me. She just sat and studied me quietly.

I studied her back.

I didn't know how to *be* with her. I'd fallen back into this chopper and I'd wanted to bawl like a baby. I'd wanted to cry into someone's arms. That's how I'd always thought of women—that they had an unlimited supply of hugs for the needy—because that's what I thought a woman should be. Because I'd always been one of the needy.

But there weren't any hugs here.

That wasn't Lizard. Lizard was all military. Lizard was as crisp as a brand new banknote. She scared me.

I sucked at the bulb of water again. It was empty.

Lizard went digging in the supplies and handed me another bubble. I took it and bit the nipple open. As I drank, she asked quietly, "Were you scared?"

"That's the *funny* thing. Not while it happened. Now—" I held out my hand to show her. "I'm still shaking—"

She nodded. "I'm familiar with the experience. People who don't know call it courage."

"Yeah," I said. "It wasn't courage. It was just—me doing what I had to do because I couldn't think of anything else."

Her eyes were too penetrating. I looked away. At the floor, the walls, the ceiling of the chopper.

Did she see how close to panic I still was? She began to speak again, quietly. "I saw an old air force hangar blow up that way once. I was only ten meters from the place where the fire started. It was just a little thing at first. It started in a trash can—some idiot tossed a lit cigarette into it, but the flames suddenly climbed up the wall. I turned for the door just as the fire touched the first catwalk. There was fifty years of dust in the rafters. By the time I finished turning, the fire had already raced ahead of me. In less than three seconds it had reached across the whole ceiling. Somebody yelled at me, so I ran. By the time I made it to the door there was a hot wind pushing me out. I got out of the building, ran twenty meters, turned around to look and saw the whole wall explode outward. I turned around and kept running. The next time I looked back, the roof of the building was just coming off in a ball of orange flame. The whole process of ignition took less than ten seconds. I've been terrified of it happening again ever since. I don't remember being scared at the time. But I've been scared ever since."

"Yeah—" I said. The bulb was empty. I put it aside. "That's what happened here. I didn't have time to think about it then—now I can't *stop* thinking about it. It's like a video playing over and over in my head and I'm stuck in the middle of it. And I don't know how to stop it. I keep seeing the flames. And the dust. And the worm. And the bunnydogs. I keep wishing I could have done something—"

A flicker of annoyance crossed her face, then she looked at me sternly. "What happened?"

"The flames didn't leap out from the torch like they should have. They leapt *back*. They enveloped Duke in a ball of fire. I didn't think— I just pointed the freezer at him and sprayed him with liquid nitrogen. The flames disappeared almost immediately. So did the worm and the bunnydogs. I don't know how they navigate in that stuff. I couldn't. I was lost. I grabbed Duke and started staggering in the direction I thought was the chopper. And I was wrong again. If you hadn't turned on the siren, I'd still be out there dragging him around. Or dead. We'd have been out of air by now," I added.

Lizard nodded. She said, "Actually, you did the right thing. That jumpsuit is flame resistant. So is the O-mask and goggles. There wasn't anything else you could have done. You're alive. He's alive. You did it right."

I shook my head. "But it doesn't *feel* right. It feels like a replay of Shorty—"

"Uh huh," she nodded. "That's what it looks like to you. Haven't you ever noticed? Nothing is ever just what it is? It's always like something else. Whatever happens, it always reminds you of something that happened before. Right?"

She was right. "Uh—yeah!" I found myself smiling.

"I do it too." She giggled back at me. Her laughter was liquid—and startling. "You told your story," she said, "—so I told mine. Do you know that most conversations are nothing more than two people telling their stories to each other?"

Something about the certainty with which she said it made me think of Dr. Fromkin. But I didn't get a chance to ask her—

Duke moaned.

We both looked at him, then scrambled to see if he was all right.

"Duke?" I put my face close.

He moaned again. "It hurts—"

"That's good, Duke. That's a good sign."

The medi-console beeped and flashed: PATIENT NEEDS SEDATION.

I found a red ampule and plugged it into the pressure feeder. After a moment Duke's breathing eased. "He's out of shock," I said. I didn't know if that was true, or just what I wanted to believe. I tried to convince myself. "The medi-kit wouldn't ask for sedation if he was still in shock. Would it?"

"I don't know," shrugged Lizard. "Let me put that console on-line to Oakland and see what they have to suggest." She climbed down toward the nose of the ship.

I sat with Duke a while longer, wishing there was something else I could do for him. I wondered if he was going to live. And if he did—what kind of shape would he be in?

I had to stop that train of thought real quick. That would be another good way to drive myself crazy. "Duke," I whispered to him. "I'm sorry. I didn't know what else to do. I love you, Duke. I never told you before, but I really do. I depend on you. Please, stay with me—"

I knew he couldn't answer. Probably, he couldn't hear me either. It didn't matter. I just knew I had to say it.

After a while, I got up and went down to the nose of the ship to join

Lizard. She was curled up in her seat, resting her chin on her fist, and studying a weather display. She looked grim. I sat down next to her in silence. The pink dust had risen almost to the top of the windshield. It was getting very dark in here.

"Did you raise Oakland?"

"Uh huh. They're monitoring. They'll let us know."

I pointed at the windshield. "It's still coming down, isn't it?"

"Uh huh. It'll be coming down all night." She pointed at the screen in front of her. "The main body of the cloud still has to pass over us. We're going to be buried in this stuff—and I have no idea how deep it's going to get."

EIGHTEEN

A SUDDEN thought came to me. "Will we have enough air?"

Lizard hesitated. "Yeah—we've got some oxygen tanks with the medical supplies. We can crack those. Theoretically, we should be able to hold out for a day and a half. I wouldn't want to have to depend on it though."

She pulled off her headset and tossed it onto the control panel in front of her. "Shit," she said.

"What now?"

"Oh, nothing. I had plans for tonight. Being buried alive wasn't part of them."

"Oh," I said. I couldn't imagine Colonel Lizard Tirelli on a date. "I'm sorry."

"What are you apologizing for? It's not your fault."

"Um, I was just expressing my regret."

"Yeah, well thanks for the thought then. I was thinking about steak and lobster all day."

"Lobster?"

"Uh huh. The Arizona farms are producing again. You should see some of the monsters they're turning out. This big—" She held her hands a meter apart. She added thoughtfully, "Arizona is an easy state to keep clean. There's not a lot of forage or ground cover for the worms. That's one place we should be able to hold the line against them for a long time."

"Is that part of the long-range planning?"

"Not yet. It will be though."

"Are you going to be on the Committee?"

"I've been asked. It's a question of . . . priorities." She shrugged. "What good is long-range planning if you don't take care of the present?"

"On the other hand," I said, "what you do in the present should be a function of your long-range goals, shouldn't it?"

She looked at me sharply. "Have you been talking to Dr. Fromkin?"

"Uh—no. Why?"

"That sounds like something he might say. That's a compliment by the way. But you're right. I have to go where I'm most effective." She smiled gently. "Which means I probably will join the Committee. I'm just afraid I won't get to fly as much. And I don't want to give up flying."

"I'd think being on the Committee would let you fly even more—you know, on-the-scene observations."

"It's a good idea," she acknowledged. "But I don't know that it would work out that way." She peered at the window then. "Hand me that flashlight—"

I passed it over, and she pointed the beam at the upper edge of the windshield in front of her. It was completely pink. "Yep. I thought so. The nose is completely covered. It must be coming down faster than ever."

She levered herself out of her seat and started working her way to the back. I followed behind. She dug around in a side panel and produced another flashlight and an emergency lamp. The lamp she hung from a hook in the ceiling. "There—that's better." She handed me the second flashlight.

She climbed past Duke and pointed her beam around the tail of the chopper. I didn't know what she was looking for. She stuck her head up into the rear bubble and pointed the flashlight around inside. "Uh huh. We are now completely buried. I sure hope this crap isn't an insulator. We could get awfully hot in here—"

"I thought that Banshees were tiled."

"They are—but if we're buried, there's no place for the heat to go." She climbed toward the back. "You hungry?"

"Yeah."

"Good. Get the emergency rations out."

I checked on Duke—no change—and then pulled out the ration box. We reconvened at the front of the chopper. We swiveled the seats around to face the rear. Better to have the fifteen-degree noseward tilt holding you in instead of tipping you out. I leaned back and put my feet up on the deck. The ration bars were chewy and required a little concentration.

Abruptly, she asked, "Have you ever been invited to a Blue Mass?" I shook my head. "Is that an invitation?" I asked.

She gave me a sour look. "I was just wondering if you knew anything about them."

"Sorry," I said. "I've heard that the members are pretty aggressive in their recruitment."

She nodded. "I was invited last week. They have them every weekend now. Hundreds of people attend, and pay a thousand caseys each for the privilege." Lizard's tone went softer then. She said, "I was just wondering—I've heard stories. But not from anybody who's been to one. Apparently there's some kind of confidentiality agreement. But I hear that . . . there's a lot of release. A lot of abandonment. I'm not sure what that means. There's supposed to be a lot of sex too."

She left that thought hanging between us for a beat, then commented, "I don't know that screwing yourself into insensibility is the best way to handle the madness, but obviously it works for some people. So . . . sometimes I wonder if it would work for me. I can't help but wonder if maybe all those people have really found something."

Her voice grew very soft then. I had to strain to hear what she said next.

"Sometimes I get tempted. What if it really does work? Wouldn't I be a jerk not to go? It would be nice to forget—even for a little while. That's why I would go. To forget."

I was embarrassed. I wanted to say something, but I knew that whatever I said would automatically be the wrong thing to say.

"Except—" Lizard continued, "I know that it's a trap. It's like drugs. Another escape. Once you start trying to escape, it isn't long before you're running. I've seen it happen to too many people already. I don't want it to happen to me." Abruptly, she fell silent.

I glanced over at her. She was staring at her ration bar moodily.

I looked at mine. "It sure isn't lobster, is it?"

"That's right—rub it in." She sounded bitter.

"I'm sorry—" I made up my mind then, I had to ask. "Colonel—?" She didn't look up.

"Uh—sometimes I get the same kind of feelings. And—uh, I figure that I'm probably not the only one. So I figure that the brass must know about it. I mean . . . there must be some—uh, outlet. Or something. Isn't there?"

She didn't answer immediately. I was beginning to wonder if she was going to answer me at all, when she said, "Yes, the brass knows that most of the men and women in uniform are this close to the edge. And no, there isn't a solution. At least, not the kind you're looking for—the easy one."

And suddenly, she was Colonel Tirelli again, crisp and military. Under control. "Remember Dr. Fromkin? He's working on that problem now. The President asked him to. So far, all he's said about it is that the only answer is an unsatisfactory one. He says that each of us is responsible for what goes on inside our own heads. Therefore, each of us is responsible for maintaining our own balance."

"But, how—?"

She shrugged. "That's what he's working on. I suspect it's a more advanced form of the Mode training, but I don't know. Listen—" she added, "you're in Special Forces, the Uncle Ira Group, so you can always call Dr. Davidson in Atlanta."

"Do you talk to him?" I asked.

"Now, you're getting personal," she said.

"Sorry—"

"There you go, apologizing again." She looked over at me, a funny look on her face. "Do you ever do anything else?"

"Oh, I'm sorry—I mean, uh, yeah—I screw up." I looked back at her. "So I'll have something to apologize for. Sometimes I think that's the only social transaction I'm good at." I grinned apologetically.

"It's called Schlemiel," she said. "It's a game. You win by getting people to forgive you. That's the payoff. You can play it forever—as long as there are people to spill soup on." She looked at her ration bar sourly. *"But it bores the hell out of me."*

I didn't know what to say. I opened my mouth anyway. Words fell out. "Well excuse me for being on the same planet with you. Excuse me for being in the same species."

"I'm not so sure that we *are* the same species . . ." she said. "I'd like a second opinion on that."

I flustered. If I could have gotten up and walked away, I would have; but there was no place to walk to. How was I supposed to *respond* to her? I said, "I don't know what to make of you! Just a few minutes ago we were talking like two human beings—now you're treating me like I'm some kind of a—a *thing!*"

She didn't answer immediately. She was chewing quietly. When she did speak, she kept her voice calm. She said, "I'm treating you like you're acting, *Lieutenant.* You're acting like a spoiled little brat. It's boring. I'm tired of listening to you apologize. I'm tired of you taking the blame for everything that goes wrong in the world."

"Well, but—"

"No. Just shut up and listen. You're not giving yourself any credit for the things you did right."

"I don't think I did anything right!"

"That's right. You *don't think* you did! You went out in that dust and got a good look at some previously unknown Chtorran creatures. You saved Duke's life—I grant that you did it with an extremely unorthodox and probably not recommended procedure, but you *did* save his life. You single-handedly dragged him back to the chopper. I know a lot of people who wouldn't have done that, they'd have given up first. You didn't give up! And when you did get here, you didn't stop. You didn't do anything for yourself until you'd first done everything you could for Duke. I was here too. Remember? I saw it! You know, they give out medals for that kind of stuff. You're a goddamned hero, McCarthy—"

"No, I'm not!"

"—but you won't believe it, because you have some picture in your head of what you think a hero is supposed to be, and that's not you! Right?"

"Uh—"

"Right?" she demanded. "Am I right?"

"Uh—I know I'm not a hero. Yes, you're right."

"Yeah," she nodded. "So you go around apologizing for being who you are. And in the meantime, you keep forgetting to notice that who you are is not such a bad person. You know, you'd be kind of cute if you weren't such a schmuck."

"*Huh?*"

She flushed and threw her hands up in the air. "Now you know my secret. I think you're cute. An asshole, but a cute one."

"Cut it out! I don't like being teased like that! I had my fill of it in high school!"

"I'm not teasing." She was dead-serious.

"Huh—?" This conversation wasn't making sense. "You mean that? You think *I'm* cute?"

"Yeah." She nodded. *"You."*

"Uh—no. I'm not. I have a broken nose that was never properly set. And I'm too short. And I'm too thin. And I'm—"

"There you go, doing it again. Can't you just let it in and say thank you?"

"Uh—" This was very hard. "I'm not—used to this. Compliments I mean. Nobody ever—I mean—uh—" I stopped. I felt embarrassed. And I felt good. Lizard was really a beautiful woman!

"Thank you," I said.

"Good." She beamed. "Very good." She looked at what was left of her ration bar. "But you're right about one thing, you know."

"Huh? About what?"

"It sure as hell *isn't* lobster."

NINETEEN

I WAS awakened by Lizard's voice. My throat felt filled with cotton. I tried to clear it and couldn't.

"—no, we're still buried. It's darker in here than the inside of a bear."

I opened my eyes. She was talking on the radio again. I tried to take a breath. My chest hurt.

"—no, I can't tell how deep. I think the sun's coming up though. There's a faint glow in the turret and at the top of the windshield, but I'm not sure that means anything. The stuff is translucent. And when it piles up in drifts it doesn't get very dense, so it passes a lot of light. We could be under ten meters of it and not know."

I'd heard this conversation before. Lizard and I had covered the same material all last night before we'd finally collapsed into separate makeshift bunks.

I pulled myself painfully into a sitting position. I was stiff. I was sore all over. Everything hurt. My lungs were the worst. Every breath was an effort. I wanted to cough, but I knew I didn't dare. If I started I'd never stop. I knew I had to keep my breathing shallow and my movements to a minimum. The pressure to cough was incredible.

But—first things first. I had to check on Duke.

He was still asleep.

He looked bad. Most of his hair was burned away. Parts of his scalp were peeling and blistered. The skin looked dead. He looked so bad I didn't want to look at him. I didn't want to know what he looked like under the medi-blanket. I felt queasy.

This wasn't Duke any more. This was burned meat. It didn't look like it would ever be Duke again. A thought crossed my mind—maybe he'd be better off if he died. I shoved it away. And prayed that God hadn't heard me. I didn't mean it, God, I said silently. I really didn't.

I punched the console for display. The medi-kit was continually monitoring his body functions and the level of sedative in his bloodstream was automatically maintained. It was probably dangerous to keep him out for this long—but what else could we do? They were reading the same information at Oakland. They knew what our circumstance was. If there was anything else to do, they would call us—or they'd reprogram the medi-kit directly. But for the moment, all we could do was wait.

And I hated waiting.

It made me feel useless.

Duke was starting to smell bad. Very very bad. The screen said his legs were infected. This couldn't go on much longer.

The chopper had a tiny lavatory at the very rear of the cabin. I stepped into it and threw up. And then I started coughing. It hurt like hell.

By the time I rejoined Lizard at the front of the ship, she was off the radio. She had turned her chair around to face the rear again and had just cracked open a new ration-kit.

"G'morning," she grinned. "Want some lobster?" She waved a stick of something gray at me. It looked unhealthy.

"No thanks," I said. I collapsed into my own chair. My chest ached.

"How about some prime rib instead?" She held up a sickly green-looking bar.

"Please—I've already thrown up once this morning. That stuff is not fit for human consumption."

"It depends on the wine you serve with it," she said over a mouthful. She held up a can of beer to show me.

I looked over at her. "When we get out of this," I said, "I will buy you the biggest fucking lobster in Arizona. And the best bottle of wine I can afford. Until then, I don't want to hear about food."

"You're on," she said. "With any luck, that'll be tonight."

"Really?"

She nodded. "Weather scan shows the cloud has dissipated—or spread out too thin to register on the scope. There were strong winds last night. The main body of the cloud passed us by around three in the ayem. Oakland says the last of it is still breaking up over Sacramento. They got a couple inches of cotton candy—but nothing like we got. There's also a chance of rain—with all these dust particles in the air, it's a very good chance. Weather service is adjusting their model now—but I'm betting that it rains before they can bring the new simulation up and running."

"Mp," I said.

Assuming that the puffball clouds hadn't left a permanent pink haze in the air, we still had to address the real problem. The chopper was buried in this crap. How were we going to get out of the ship? If we were under more than two meters of dust, we might as well forget it.

And that suggested *another* problem. Just how extensive *were* these drifts anyway? I already knew from experience that we wouldn't be able to move very far through them. No, it was too unlikely that we could get to clear ground—they were going to have to pick us up here.

And then there was the problem of Duke.

I sucked at a water bulb and looked at Lizard. She was lost in thought as well.

She caught me looking at her. "Yes?"

"How are we going to get Duke out of here?"

"You've gotten that far with it, huh?"

"Uh, I haven't gotten anywhere. I just figure that Duke is the hard part of the problem. If we can handle that, the rest takes care of itself."

She said, "I think we're going to have to wait for outside assistance. Right now, the best solution I can come up with is a Sikorsky Skyhook. It could just pull us out—if we could get the grapples in place."

I said, "If any part of the parafoil is accessible, they can hook onto that, can't they? They could use that harness."

"Hey! That's not bad—"

"Thanks."

"—except it won't work." She explained, "It's not your fault. The problem is the Sikorsky. No chopper can rescue us. It'll stir up too much dust. It'll ruin its own engines. They'll come down right on top of us."

"I wonder if this stuff could be washed away? My great-grandmother once tried to teach me a rain dance. You said there's a chance of rain. I'll call it down here."

She smiled sourly, "That'll turn this stuff into mud—and then it'll harden into concrete."

"But it's just—cake flour!"

"You ever try to eat a stale bagel?"

I threw up my hands in despair. "I concede the point."

"Got any other ideas?" she asked.

"Well, we know we can *burn* it away. . . ." I said it unenthusiastically.

"Now that's a thought," Lizard replied brightly. "You and Duke have already proven the dust is flammable. And this chopper is tiled. It'll make a wonderful oven." She grinned at me. "Do you like brick-oven cooking?"

"No thanks." I picked up the flashlight, switched it on, and swiveled forward. I stared at the pink barrier on the opposite side of the windshield. "I wonder what they do on the planet Chtorr?"

"They probably don't fly in cotton candy weather."

"Yeah, they probably have candy warnings."

"I can imagine the forecasts," Lizard said. "Tomorrow will be mostly fair with scattered high candy and a twenty percent chance of lemonade."

"Not lemonade," I corrected. "Wrong color. More likely strawberry soda."

"And instead of snow, they get syrup? Sounds like a good way to get your wicket sticky?"

"Actually," I mused, "that might not be so far from the truth. Everything is edible to something else. We're just another kind of snack to the worms. Maybe their own planet is one great big smorgasbord to them. It's all point of view. Maybe this is the season of candy."

"Well, we could sure use a couple of worms with sweet tooths along about now," Lizard said.

"Uh—I'm not so sure they're not already here," I replied very slowly.

"Huh?"

"Turn your seat around and look. I think something's moving out there."

TWENTY

"WHERE?" SAID Lizard.

"There. Up near the top."

"I don't see anything."

"Keep looking. It was just a flicker—right there. As if something's moving on top of the dust."

We stared and waited. Nothing.

After a moment, Lizard said, "Well, I don't see it."

"I'm sure of what I saw." There was an edge of anger in my voice.

"Yes, I'm sure you are," she replied quietly. "Last time you were that sure, you disrupted a conference."

I ignored the knife between my ribs. "And I was right, wasn't I?"

Lizard shrugged. "Being right is rarely a victory."

"Huh?"

"Never mind." She anchored one foot on the console, grunted, and swiveled her seat to the back again. "If there's really something out there, we'll see it soon enough."

I muttered something unprintable and grabbed the flashlight. I climbed past her to check on Duke again. The medi-console said he was stable. He looked a little less gray. I wished I'd taken more pre-med courses. I wasn't sure how to interpret any of this.

"Uh—Colonel?"

"Yeah?"

"Do you know anything about first aid?"

"A little."

"Come here and listen. Duke's breathing sounds funny."

She came to the back and squatted down next to Duke. She listened. Then she smiled. "His breathing's fine."

"But that wheezing—"

"He's asleep," she said. "He's snoring."

"Are you sure?"

Lizard looked me straight in the eye. "I know what a man's snoring sounds like."

"Uh—right. Thank you." I picked up the flashlight and went to the back of the tail to look and see if I could see anything out of the rear bubble. The cotton candy seemed a little more translucent there. I could feel my face burning.

How long would it be till we *really* started getting on each other's nerves? I wondered if I could get angry enough to kill her. I was afraid I might find out.

I climbed into the bubble seat, folded my arms across my chest, and faced the back.

What is it about women anyway? Why do they all seem to think that life is about challenging men? And then they wonder why the men are so touchy—

I was staring at it for several minutes before I realized what I was seeing. I came out of the chair so fast, I bumped my head on the Plexiglas. "Holy shit!—*Owwwl!*"

"Are you all right?" Lizard called.

"No—"

"What happened?"

"I bumped my head—" I could still feel the ringing. "Come here!"

"Why? You want me to kiss it?"

"I want you to *see* something. Come here!" I started coughing then, and couldn't think of anything for a minute. Every paroxysm was agony. I forced myself to stop, I don't know how.

When I opened my eyes again, Lizard was looking up at me with a concerned expression. She was holding out a bulb of water. I took it gratefully. "Thanks."

She came climbing past Duke with a sigh. "All right, what do you want me to see?"

I pointed at the window. "There *is* something out there."

She looked. She frowned. She looked confused. Then her eyes widened—

The entire surface of the bubble was alive.

It was still a solid pink mass—but we could see something through the pink. It was like looking through a layer of suds. There was something flickering behind it; the whole surface was flickering.

It was a seething movement, but the eye couldn't resolve a pattern. As we watched, the movement grew more pronounced than ever. The flickerings became scratchings.

"What is it?"

"I don't know. But it's getting bigger."

"Bigger? Couldn't you have chosen *another* word?"

"How about closer?"

"Not much improvement." She folded her arms around herself as if she were cold. "It's getting lighter in here, isn't it?" she offered. "Could it be the wind—blowing the dust off?"

"I wish it were. But I doubt it."

I moved as close to the window as I could and still keep my eyes focused. Something was moving the pink powder around—the way it shifted and swirled, it looked like thousands of tiny little shapes, all moving and scrambling at once.

And then it *resolved*—

"*Unh,*" I said.

"What—?" she asked.

"Look close."

She leaned into the bubble, staring. Her eyes widened in horror. "Bugs!"

The entire surface of the bubble was flickering and swirling and seething. We were looking at the bodies of millions and millions of frenzied insects.

"They're feeding on the powder," I said. I dropped back into my seat. I was starting to feel itchy.

Lizard dropped out of the bubble and scrambled forward. I could hear her stopping at the ports. "They're all over these windows too!" She checked the front of the ship. "They're all over us!"

I levered myself out of the seat and went forward to join her. She was staring at the window. Because this part of the chopper was buried deeper in the drift, the seething movement was still limited to the very top of the windshield. It wasn't as clear yet as it was at the tail, but it was clear enough.

Lizard shuddered. She couldn't tear her eyes away from that flickering pink wall. "They're all over us!"

I tried to imagine what the chopper must look like from above. A large pink sugary lump in the middle of a pink snowdrift—covered by a billion crawling insects, nature's perfect little machines, all of them feeding. I could imagine them working at the powder, their tiny mandibles flashing. I could imagine them chittering and scraping and jostling—

I grabbed her by the shoulders. "Listen to me! Is this ship airtight?"

"It should be—Oh, my God! The compartment—!" She looked to the floor.

"Does it seal?"

"Uh—yes, it should."

"Good. Now, we've got to find every other possible breach—every leak, no matter how small, has got to be plugged—"

"Plugged?"

"What? Is there an echo in here? When those bugs eat down far enough, some of them are going to get in. That's a feeding frenzy out there! They're going to be coming in hungry! You and I and Duke are the only things edible in this larder. What have you got that'll keep them out?"

"Uh, I don't know. Wait a minute—let me think."

"Come on—I thought these choppers were stocked for every emergency."

Abruptly, Lizard stiffened. She looked at me hard. "I suspect that *this* one isn't in the book. The army hasn't had much reason to bury choppers in cotton candy, so we don't really know what happens when bugs eat them out." She looked angry. That was a good sign. "Obviously," she continued, "you and I have been given the opportunity to research the subject."

"Terrific!" I said. "What an opportunity! What'll we try?"

Lizard looked at the floor of the chopper, frowning. She let her gaze travel slowly toward the back. She looked like she was using her X-ray vision to inventory each separate cargo compartment.

Abruptly she said, "Shelterfoam!" She was staring all the way back. "You'll have to move Duke—"

"What's shelterfoam?"

"It's in case you crash somewhere and need to build a shelter—especially in cold weather areas. First you inflate a big balloon, then you spray it with shelterfoam. You wait a half hour for it to harden, cut a door, and move in. It's like living in a pumpkin. We used it as quick-fix housing in Pakistan." She pointed. "Put Duke all the way in the back. He's lying right over the compartment I need to get at."

Duke moaned when I moved him, but he didn't awaken. The console suggested that I give him another bottle of glucose and I did.

As I settled him in, I noticed that the pink luminescence in the tail of the ship was growing stronger. I glanced up at the bubble. The morning sun was pouring directly down on us; I could see it as a brighter spot beyond the seething pink. I could even feel its warmth.

The layer of powder on the hemisphere of Plexiglas was growing noticeably thinner beneath the hungry insect-things. This cotton candy stuff was incredibly transparent to light. I could see the swarming bugs as darker bits ceaselessly churning and swirling. I wondered what they were.

But I didn't want Duke to wonder about it if he woke up and saw them. I pulled the shutter closed.

Lizard was busying herself with the shelterfoam. She wasn't paying any attention to me. So I took a moment to apologize to Duke. I peeled open a sani-pak and started cleaning his face with a moist towel. "I'm sorry, Duke," I whispered. "I'll get you out of here, I promise—" I wiped the dirt from his forehead.

"McCarthy . . ." he mumbled.

"Yes, Duke?"

"Shut up."

"Yes, Duke!"

But he was asleep again. I didn't care. He was going to live—I knew it!

I scrambled forward to tell Lizard. "Duke's going to make it!"

"How do you know?"

"He growled at me. He told me to shut up."

Lizard grinned. "Sounds like good advice. Here—" She thrust a tank into my arms. "The weak spots will be mostly under the floor, where we hit. Especially where we broke the keel. You'll need to empty each compartment, then foam it. Just point the nozzle and press."

"Does this stuff make fumes?"

"No, it's jellied Styrofoam. It's safe. You do the cabin, I'll get under the controls. I want to open the floorboards and get the nose-wheel compartment. If the bugs get in there, they could get into the circuit-pipes or the hydraulics or underneath the insulation. You ever spray for cockroaches?"

"Yeah."

"Then you know." She looked over my shoulder and lowered her voice. "Better pay special attention to the tail. You might just want to make a big cocoon back there."

I followed her glance. Duke. I realized how helpless he was. "Yeah. I see your point."

"Any questions?"

"No."

"All right, let's go to work."

"Uh—"

She stopped. "Yes?"

"I just had a thought, Colonel."

She waited patiently.

"What if these bugs eat Styrofoam too?"

"Will you stop thinking—" she said. "You're scaring the hell out of me."

TWENTY-ONE

IT TOOK us most of the morning.

Lizard stopped only to check in with Oakland and relay a data-chirp from the medi-console. Then she plunged back into her task. She opened up the whole floor of the nose of the ship and filled it with foam before replacing the deck panels.

By then, I had finished foaming the cargo compartments and had begun outlining every seam of the interior paneling. Lizard came back to join me. We set our nozzles for narrow jets and sprayed every corner, every crack, every seam, every seal on the interior of that ship. When we finished, the chopper looked like the inside of a wedding cake.

By the time we sat down in the nose of the ship again, the sun was high above us. And the chopper was starting to get warm. We could barely see the sun through the wall of pale powder, but we could feel its heat. I felt *trapped*.

And my body hurt worse than ever. My lungs felt like they were on fire. I was keeping an O-mask close now, and taking frequent breaths from it. It seemed to help. A little.

I forced myself to concentrate on the scientific opportunity here.

The front window was a bright pink glare. It flickered with a million tiny insect bodies. They were crawling all over it, but they were thickest near the bottom, where the pink powder was still piled up in drifts. It made me feel itchy just to look at them. I thought about a hot bath, one with hundreds of little pulsing jets, all throbbing in a steady underwater massage. I decided not to share that image with Colonel Tirelli.

"Brr!" she said. "I can't stand to look at them. What do you think they are anyway?"

"The Chtorran equivalent of ants maybe," I said. "But I wouldn't bet on it. I don't think we've scratched the surface of this ecology. Remember Dr. Zymph and her jigsaw-puzzle analogy?"

"Yeah?"

"Well, I think we're still at the point where we're just looking into the box. We still haven't dumped it out. We still don't even know how big the puzzle is or how many pieces there are. We just know there are a lot and none of them seems to make sense." I sipped at a water bulb and watched the seething mass of insects on the windscreen in front of me.

"I hate that analogy," Lizard said. "It's got too much *can't* in it."

"Yeah," I agreed.

Lizard picked up her headset and flicked the radio on. "Oakland?"

"Go ahead," said the radio.

"This is ELDAVO. Checking in. Our situation is unchanged. Except the bugs are getting closer."

"We copy, Colonel."

"Is there an estimate yet when someone can come and get us?"

"Nope. Sorry. Satellite shows that whole area is still hazy. The best we can do is pull a blimp out of Portland and let it glide over you."

"That's a little desperate, isn't it?"

"You want to wait a week for pickup?"

Lizard rolled her eyes. "Get the blimp."

"Oh, we do have some good news for you."

"Yeah?"

"Your patient is stable."

"Uh huh. And what are you *not* telling me?"

"Beg pardon?"

"Stable can mean a lot of things. How bad are his injuries?"

"Uh—is this line secure?"

Lizard looked at me, looked back at Duke. "Is he still asleep?" she whispered. I looked and nodded. Lizard said to the radio, "Go ahead."

"Uh—we're getting some funny readings off his legs. Like static. But we don't think it's infection. The monitor shows the antibiotics are holding. Maybe it's some effect of the dust. We won't know for sure until we get him home. Other than that, he's fine. Avoid moving him. We'll try and have a corpsman on the pickup vehicle."

"Oh, shit," I said.

"I copy," Lizard said. "Any more good news?"

"Well . . . it's official as of ten o'clock. The President's going to run again."

"Thanks. Do we get the ball scores too?"

"Dodgers lead the Braves, top of the third, two-nothing."

"Over and out." She hung up and looked at me. "What are you so unhappy about? You an Atlanta fan?"

"No, I'm worried about Duke." I started crawling toward the back.

"Didn't you hear? Oakland says he's doing fine."

"Yeah, I heard. They also said the Dodgers are winning." I sat down next to Duke. He'd been out all day. I didn't know if that was a blessing or not. Was it better to be unconscious—or in pain? If they didn't pick us up soon, there wouldn't be a choice. We were running out of supplies.

I looked at the medi-console. It was almost time to change his IV. We had plenty of antibiotics left—those were the blue ampules—but we were on the next-to-last bubble of glucose. I wondered what I could do when that ran out. These choppers were equipped only for basic first aid. The assumption was that the patient would be in transit and wouldn't be on the medi-console for long.

The real question was the red ampule. The painkiller. There was only one left in the kit. And I'd heard that burn wounds were the most agonizing. . . .

I reached for the medi-blanket, hesitated, then pulled it back and looked at Duke's legs.

They were burned and peeling. The flesh was blistered and scabbed. And then I looked again.

Duke's legs were—dusty.

No. They were covered with a light pink fuzz. What the—?

I stretched a finger out, carefully, and touched Duke's ankle. The fuzz didn't brush away. It was growing out of his skin.

And it tingled.

Like worm fur.

I sat down with my back against the hull of the ship and my knees up in front of me. I put my fists up to my mouth and sucked thoughtfully through them, all the while staring at Duke's legs, and trying to figure out just what the hell was going on.

I hardly noticed when Lizard came back to join me. She looked at Duke's legs and her face went gray. She pulled the medi-blanket over them again and looked at me with a question in her eyes.

I shrugged. "I don't know."

She picked up the medi-console and studied it. The answer wasn't there either.

I looked across at her. "How long before we know? I mean—if the foam is going to hold?"

She shrugged. "An hour. Maybe less."

"What if he wakes up? Do you think we should tell him?"

Lizard opened her mouth to say something.

But Duke interrupted. "Tell me *what*—?" he said.

"Duke! You're awake."

"I've been awake for some time. Listening to you birds jabbering. What'd you drug me with anyway? My legs itch."

Lizard shot me a concerned glance. Duke didn't see it. I said, "I don't know the name of it. It's the red cartridge."

"Oh," he said. "Where are we?"

"Near Red Bluff. As soon as the weather clears, they'll be coming to get us."

"The weather?"

"The dust."

"Is it still coming down?"

"No." And then I added, "But—we're buried. And there's haze."

Duke's face was puffy, but I could still see his eyes narrowing as he looked back and forth between me and the bag. "The light in here is pink," he said. "How deep is this shit?"

"Up to our ears, Duke." That was Lizard.

"Mmm," he said. "Then don't make waves."

"How are you feeling?"

"Cloudy." He reached up and grabbed my sleeve. "Jim?"

"Yes, Duke?"

"Do me a favor."

"Name it."

"Pull the red cartridge. Take me off the sleepytime."

"Sorry, Boss. No can do. Anything but that."

"I can handle the pain. I want to be awake."

"I can't! It's procedure! It might kill you!"

"Jim—" He coughed and for a moment I was terrified. It sounded like a death rattle. "Jim—will you pull that cartridge?"

"No, Duke, I won't."

He closed his eyes for a long moment. I had almost started to think that he had gone back to sleep when he opened them again. When he spoke, his voice was very faint.

"Jim?"

"Yes, Duke?" He was fading fast, I had to put my face close.

It came out a whisper. "Then fuck you. . . ." His eyes closed and he fell asleep again.

Lizard looked up from the console. "The machine put him out. He was straining."

"He hates drugs. I'm going to have a lot of apologizing to do." I realized what I'd said and looked up at her. "Sorry. Force of habit."

She didn't smile. "There's something else you want to watch out for."

"Huh?"

"You could have pulled that cartridge, you know."

I shook my head. "No, I couldn't. It's those bugs. If we're going to be eaten alive, he's better off not knowing."

Lizard looked at me sharply. "That's what I'm talking about. That kind of thinking is the first step."

"What kind of thinking?"

"Making other people's decisions for them. The next step is deciding whether or not they should continue living. And you know where that leads. I seem to remember you had a button on that."

"Yeah, well—" I stood up and climbed into the turret above Duke. "It's different when you're the person who has to do the deciding, isn't it?"

She didn't say anything immediately. She just studied me with an introspective look on her face.

Finally I glanced down at her. "Well, go ahead. Say it."

She shook her head slowly. "I don't have to. You already know what I would say."

"No, I don't."

"Yes, you do."

"God!" I said. "I hate conversations like this."

She sighed. "It's not important. I just wondered if *you* would have accepted that justification?"

I didn't answer. I turned away from her and pulled the shutter back. I stared at the uneasy surface of the bubble. The creatures were more active than ever in the afternoon sunlight. I could feel the sweat dripping down my sides. I didn't want to continue this conversation any more. I knew she was right.

And my chest hurt worse than ever.

TWENTY-TWO

IT WASN'T until late afternoon that the bugs finally cleaned off the turret bubble well enough so I could see them clearly.

The sunlight was slanting directly into the rear of the chopper and there were only pink streaks left on the clear canopy of the bubble to suggest that the ship had once been covered with the dust.

The insect-things were very tiny. Most of them were nothing more than little white specks. Few were big enough to have features. I had to strain my eyes to see them at all.

I called to Lizard, "Have you got a surveillance camera?"

"I've got a couple of electronics."

"That'll do. Let me have one, please."

She passed it up.

"Ah, good—it's a Sony. For once the army didn't buy cheap. I'll show you a trick I learned. You can dial these down for incredible closeups. We used to use them in school as portable microscopes." I braced myself and focused the camera on the insect-things on the surface of the bubble. The lighting was perfect. The afternoon sunlight was coming in sideways. The detailing on the image was perfect. The little bugs were white and powdery and—when the instant of recognition hit me, I felt my relief like a shot of Irish whiskey.

I started giggling.

"What's so funny?"

I closed the shutter and dropped out of the bubble. I was laughing so hard I started coughing. I had to sit down on the floor of the chopper to catch my breath. I hadn't realized how tense and anxious I'd been. Now, it was all pouring out of me at once.

"McCarthy!" Lizard was getting annoyed. "What is it?"

"Come on up front, I'll show you." The bugs were clearly visible at the top of the windscreen. I handed her the camera. "Look—do you recognize them?"

She peered up at the windshield through the eyepiece. "No."

"You should. You saw Dr. Zymph's slides."

"Will you just tell me what they are?"

"Those are baby pipe cleaner bugs! They are absolutely harmless to human beings! These and the cotton candy are the only two Chtorran species that are not directly dangerous to us—and we've been hiding here in the chopper terrified all day! By tomorrow morning, they'll have cleaned this entire ship off. There won't be a speck of pink anywhere on this aircraft." I sat down in the copilot's seat again, feeling terrific, a big silly smile on my face. "We're going to be all right."

Lizard sat down across from me, looking relieved and relaxed for the first time today. "We're really not in any danger?"

"Not in the slightest. I feel like such a jerk."

Lizard laughed. "We should celebrate. You want a beer?"

"You got more beer?"

"That cooler by your feet."

I pulled the top open. "Jeez—you don't travel light, do you?"

She spread her hands apologetically. "You never can tell when you're going to be buried in cotton candy. Hand me one, thanks."

We sat back in our seats and watched the bugs work on the windshield. We passed the camera back and forth.

Lizard said, "You're a biologist, aren't you?"

"I never got my degree."

"That wasn't the question."

"All right, yes, I'm as much a biologist as anyone is these days."

"Thanks. So, tell me—what's going on?"

"I can make a guess. The pipe cleaner bugs hatch on the same day as the puffballs explode. The puffballs are their primary food."

"But why so many? The scale of this—it's enormous."

"Uh huh," I agreed. "It's a good breeding strategy for bugs. Have zillions of offspring. That guarantees that enough will survive to breed the next generation." Another thought occurred to me then. "Of course . . . that's a Terran explanation. The Chtorran explanation could be something else entirely."

"What do you mean by that?"

"Just a guess. Remember how Dr. Zymph said that what we were seeing was really the advance guard—that some extraterrestrial agency was obviously trying to *Chtorra*-form this planet?"

"Yeah, so?"

"Well, I've been thinking. Suppose we humans were going to Terra-form Mars or some other nearby world. Would we take our *entire* ecology? Probably not. No, we'd only take those creatures suited for the kind of climate and terrain we'd be moving into. In fact, we wouldn't even take the full spectrum of creatures, we'd only fill the ecological niches that we need to support our own survival."

"What are you getting at?"

"Okay—we'd take a couple species of grass and grain, earthworms, rabbits, foxes to keep the rabbits in check, cows, ducks, chickens, and so on. That is, we'd take only those species immediately useful to us. We wouldn't bother with mosquitoes, termites, rhinoceroses, or three-toed sloths. I'll bet the Chtorrans have done the same thing. That's why the puffballs and the pipe cleaner bugs have experienced population explosions. There aren't the usual wide range of predators present to feed on them. At least not yet. Maybe they'll be here later."

"Mm," said Lizard. She took a drink from the can of beer, then leaned forward and tapped the window. "What's this?" she asked.

She was pointing at a larger, darker speck.

I looked. The speck was round and black and very busy. "That's the creature that feeds on the baby pipe cleaner bugs," I said.

"Well that didn't take long," she said. "There's your first predator." She peered through the camera. "It looks like a spider—only it's got too many legs."

"If it's Chtorran, it's a mouth on wheels. Here's another. And another. It's nearly dusk—the night feeders are coming out. I'll bet we'll be seeing a lot more of them."

"And this?" pointed Lizard. "What are these?" She passed me the camera.

I looked where she pointed. The creatures looked like red-striped silverfish. They made me think of millipedes—these were the micro-size. Or maybe the larvae. . . . I said, "Obviously, these are the bugs that feed on the bugs that feed on the pipe cleaner bugs." I shifted my attention to a thing that looked like a fingernail-sized amoeba. Incredible. It was enveloping one of the silverfish. "You know what we've got here? Box seats! We're seeing a whole slice of Chtorran ecology."

"I'm not so sure these are box seats," said Lizard. "We're seeing it from the bottom."

"Best place to see it from. None of the details are lost." I moved higher up the window. "Look—see that? Remember that one? That's a nightwalker."

"He looks like a little vampire."

"That's how he got his name. He lurks in corners. This one must be a baby."

"What's he eating?"

"I can't tell—but it's pink."

"Oh, here's another one—oh, my God!"

I looked where she was pointing. The creature looked like a tiny little human being. Its eyes were froglike, but its body was pink and as moist-looking as a baby and its proportions were almost completely human, only scaled down to the size of a baby's finger. It was feeding on the candy powder and the pipe cleaner bugs and whatever else got in its way. It had a tiny red tongue.

"This is incredible. Where are the memory clips for this camera? We're probably seeing a hundred new life-forms today."

"In that dark blue box." Lizard jerked a thumb over her shoulder. "And check the battery packs. You may have to plug it in up here."

I levered myself out of my seat. "Cokes, beers, medi-kits, shelter-foam, oxygen tanks, cameras—how come this chopper is so well packed?"

"All military choppers are now. It's standard issue. The robots check your supplies automatically and replace what's been used. It's all automatic. Obviously, it's for opportunities like this."

"Um," I said. "Hey! There's a Pentax-Pro in here! With eighty gigs of Zilog layered memory!" I held it up to show her. The batteries were fresh. "It's brand-new. You know, I used to dream about equipment like this."

"Help yourself. There's more where that came from."

"Huh?"

"The army wants you to have that equipment, McCarthy. Remember? There's a war on."

I grabbed the lantern and came back forward. "Here, hang this up somewhere so the light slants sideways. I'll get better contrast." I started shooting micro-closeups. The details visible just on the camera's preview screen were startling. "Are there any more of those little naked men?"

"Here's a couple—oops, you don't want to see what they're doing!"

"Yes, I do! No, I don't." I took their picture anyway.

"Voyeur," said Lizard.

"They're just licking the powder off each other," I said. "Besides, they might be female." I kept taking pictures. There was a thing that looked like a tiny pink cauliflower—or a walking brain. It was a gnarly little lump with red veins all over its surface. It looked dreadful. I noticed even the other creatures thought so—they kept out of its way too.

"This is incredible!" I said. I was probably repeating myself. I didn't care. I was too excited. "We're seeing things no other human being has ever seen! This is extraordinary! This must be the day everything hatches at once and feeds on everything else. This is wonderful. I don't think we've seen half of these life-forms before!"

Lizard said, "If that's true, then the joke's on you."

"Huh?"

"You just finished postulating that the Chtorrans would probably bring only their essential support species. Look at this zoo on the window! Do you still believe that?"

I lowered the camera for a second and looked. The window was totally covered with swarming Chtorran bugs and beasties. Long ones. Thin ones. Short fat juicy ones. Pink and black and purple—and red, all shades of red. They glistened in the reflected light of the chopper. Beyond was only darkness. It was already night outside. When had that happened? I'd been so entranced, I hadn't even noticed when the sun set. This closer spectacle was too overwhelming. The bugs were glittering little bodies now. The window fairly sparkled.

"Yeah," I said. "I do. This is still only a very narrow slice of an ecology. A planet might host a billion different species. We're seeing only a few hundred here. The Chtorrans probably haven't brought more than a few thousand altogether. Just what they need." I started to lift the camera to my eye again, then looked at it, stopped, lowered the camera and looked at Lizard again. Grinning.

"What?" she said.

"I take it all back," I said. "Well, part of it anyway. The Chtorrans haven't traveled any lighter than we did. We didn't pack just the bare essentials for this mission. We took everything we might conceivably need." I hefted the camera. "And so far, we've needed everything we've brought. They did the same."

Lizard laughed with me. She opened the last two beers and passed me one. She lifted hers high and toasted me. "Well, here's to the bugs. Here's to you."

I returned the toast. "It's a great show."

We watched in silence for a while.

I tried to imagine what the ground outside must look like. If the moon was bright enough, it would be covered by a shimmering carpet of night creatures and insects. I wondered if any Earth life-forms were part of that feast out there, and if they were diners or dinners.

Probably dinners. This was a feeding frenzy. These creatures were all so busy eating that they didn't even notice when something else came along and started eating them. I watched as new creatures kept landing on the windshield and joining the orgy. Where were they all coming from?

Lizard decided to call the little naked men "finger-babies." They reminded her of a set of tiny dolls she had owned a long time ago. The creatures had pale, nearly transparent skin, and they crawled along the window with slow deliberate motions. They had big bug eyes. It made them look expressionless—or perpetually frightened. It depended on your mood. They would open their tiny wide mouths and touch their tiny red tongues to the pink powder or the baby pipe cleaner bugs. Then they'd lift their heads while they swallowed and look slowly from side to side, before returning to their feast.

For a while, there were a lot of them. Many of them were licking the powder off each other. The window was covered with naked, squirming pink bodies. "It looks like you got your Blue Mass after all."

"There's something disturbing about the comparison," she responded. "Is that what human beings look like from above?"

As the night grew darker, more of the nightwalkers began to arrive. The little vampire creatures had pale faces and large mandibles. They grabbed the finger-babies with their upper pair of arms and pulled them into a disturbingly erotic embrace. The finger-babies didn't fight—not even when the vampires opened their mandibles and started eating. The vampires ate them like little plump sausages. They bit and chewed, bit and chewed, and the finger-babies died. They waved their little pink arms and kicked their little pink legs, but the nightwalkers kept eating. The finger-babies had bright red blood.

For a while, the window was covered with carnage.

"I think I hate them," Lizard said.

"Careful," I said.

"Huh?"

"You're anthropomorphizing. You're making judgments about these creatures. Your species prejudice is showing. What if the finger-babies are really embryonic worms?"

She looked at me, startled. "You don't really think so?"

"No, I don't—but I just wanted to caution you not to make assumptions. I already made one misassumption about the bunnydogs. I don't want to make any more. These things are probably some kind of newt-like organism with a coincidental resemblance. In their adult form, they could be vicious serpents. Or maybe not. Don't make hasty judgments."

Lizard grunted. That was her only answer.

We both fell silent again.

Something snake-like with a red belly slithered across my side of the window. It had a thousand flashing legs, and it plowed through the other life-forms like a vacuum cleaner. Oh no.

"Lizard," I said.

"Yes?"

"You'd better call for help."

"Huh?" She looked at me. "I thought you said we were safe."

"I may have to revise that estimate. You were wondering what comes next?" I pointed. "See that? That's a Chtorran millipede. If that's what comes next, we'd better get out of here. I don't think the shelterfoam will stop them."

TWENTY-THREE

WE GOT the call at twenty-two hundred hours.

The radio beeped. Lizard leaned forward and flicked it on. "This is ELDAVO."

"All right, here's the scoop. The blimp is on its way. They left Portland an hour ago. They've got a full rescue and medical team aboard. They should be over you by midnight. They're homing in on your beam."

"What about the dust?"

"They're aware of the problem. We all are. There isn't an engine running in the Sacramento Valley today—at least none that were left exposed. But Portland has the most experience with this kind of problem—you can thank Mount Saint Helens for that. They've already got the necessary technology on the shelf."

"I'll send a thank-you note to the volcano," Lizard said.

"They'll be monitoring the air all the way in. When they start hitting ten particles per million, they'll shut down the jets and drift with the wind till they're overhead."

"Drift?" asked Lizard skeptically.

"That's right. But they've jury-rigged a cold-rocket assist for local guidance. They can maneuver, and you won't have to worry about the fire danger. If they have to, they can fly on canned air for a short distance—at least far enough to get out of the pink if they head out over the ocean. It's all been thought out."

"I've heard that one before," Lizard said. "How are they going to hold their position over us?"

"They'll fire grapples into the ground and moor themselves. Then they'll lower a basket and pull you up."

"Listen—" said Lizard. "We've got a problem with that."

"What's that?"

"We're in the middle of a feeding frenzy here. Once we pop the hatch, we have maybe thirty seconds. If that. We've got a millipede swarm."

"We know about the millipedes. You're not the only ones down in the dust. We've been getting reports that would curl your hair."

I leaned forward at that. "How bad is it?" I asked.

"You don't want to know."

"Yes I do," I insisted.

"We think we lost Redding. All communications are down. We can't get anything into the area. You think you got it bad? The Northern California Eyeball scan shows nothing but pink desert—and there were some *tall* buildings in Redding."

"Redding?" But that was eighty kilometers north of here. A terrible suspicion was creeping coldly up my spine. "Just how extensive is the dust?"

"The whole northern half of the state is out. Everything. It's all been brought to a halt. Sacramento took another five inches this afternoon."

Lizard and I exchanged a glance. From Redding to Sacramento?

"You'll see it from the blimp. If the wind holds up, you might be in Oakland—or Sacramento—by tomorrow afternoon."

"Any more good news?" Lizard asked.

"The Dodgers blew it in the eighth."

"Thanks." She signed off, turned and looked at me. "So. No lobster tonight either." Then she noticed my expression and asked, "What's that about?"

"Nothing," I said. I climbed out of my seat and headed toward the back of the ship to look at Duke's medi-console. He was stable, but . . .

I pulled back the blanket to look at the pink fur on his legs again. The fur was noticeably longer. There were red and purple strands too.

Lizard squatted down opposite me; she searched my face. "Nothing, huh?"

"All right," I admitted. "I'm worried about Duke. He smells pretty bad—and I don't know what's going on with his legs. That fur is *growing*. Even if we could get him out of here tonight, we'd still be a long way from the kind of care he needs. And you heard the man. Tomorrow afternoon."

She picked up the medi-console and studied its display. Duke was on the last red ampule. There was no more glucose. I'd been waking him up periodically to give him sugar water laced with blue-series antibiotics. It was the best I could do. I couldn't think of anything else.

I knelt down for a closer examination of the pink fur on Duke's legs. It was growing out of his blackened skin like grass creeping back toward ground zero. Tentatively, I let it brush the palm of my hand. It was tingly. I pressed it gently flat—the tingly sensation got stronger.

"He's waking up—" said Lizard.

I straightened up again and took the console from Lizard. The display said Duke was still sound asleep.

"No he's not—" I looked back at Duke's legs. I stretched over and touched the fur again; I stroked a long length of it. The medi-console display went crazy. It said Duke was running up a hill—no, having a heart attack—no, it wasn't sure. PLEASE WAIT. It couldn't interpret. INCREASED NERVOUS ACTIVITY. And again, PLEASE WAIT.

I pulled open the medical supplies and studied the color-coded chart inside. There it was.

Terramycin.

I looked at Duke's legs again.

But it was such a long shot. It was a very stupid risk to take.

"What are you thinking?" asked Lizard.

"I'm thinking of doing something stupid," I said.

"How stupid?"

"It's never been done before." I popped the plastic ampule out of the kit. "That's worm fur growing out of Duke's legs. This stuff should kill it. Most of it, anyway. Remember the worm in Denver? That's what happened to it."

She frowned unhappily. "I don't know what to tell you, McCarthy. I'm not a doctor."

"I'm not asking your permission. I know more about this than you do. This is one I have to call."

"You're right," she agreed.

"I know." I closed my eyes. *Please God . . . let me be really right.*

I clipped the ampule into place on the feeder.

The medi-console beeped. TERRAMYCIN? it queried. I touched the CONFIRM button.

There was nothing to do now but wait.

We covered Duke up again and climbed back to the front of the chopper. The copilot's seat was beginning to get uncomfortable. It creaked as I sank into it. I picked up a flashlight and studied the bugs on the window again. I couldn't identify even half the creatures I saw. But the ones I could identify were enough to terrify me.

"The *real* problem," I said, "is I don't know how we're going to get him out of here. I don't know how we're going to get *us* out of here. I don't think it's safe to open that hatch." I pointed the flashlight toward the top of the windshield. The beam illuminated four red-bellied millipedes slithering down its curved surface even as I spoke. One of them curled itself around to point its eyes downward. It peered curiously at us, irising its eyes open and shut in confused blinks.

Lizard followed my stare. "Can you freeze them?" she asked.

I shrugged. "That's what I'm planning on—but that's not the problem. I'm worried about worms finding us. They're next in line at this cafeteria." I pointed at the millipedes. "See those? Those millipedes are the nastiest little monsters you can imagine. They'll attack anything that was ever remotely organic. They're as insatiable as an author at a free lunch, and they're almost impossible to kill. They bite like journalists, and they're as deadly as lawyers. They run in swarms and they can denude a forest in a week. They can strip a horse in minutes. Do you want to hear more?"

" 'And my point is . . . ?' " Lizard prompted.

"That," I said, "—is worm food. Those are Chtorran delicacies. Maybe it's their equivalent of lobster. The worms just pop them in their mouths and chew. Does that give you some idea about the personal habits of the worms? That's what I'm worried about. A worm could peel this chopper open real easy.

"And—" I added, "if that's not enough, we are effectively defenseless. Duke's torch is still lying somewhere out there in the dust—and even if we had it, it wouldn't be safe to use. Neither can we use grenades or bazookas—nothing that might ignite the dust. All we have is the freezer—and that is of very limited usefulness as a weapon against a worm. Believe me. I've tried it three times. No more. It is not recommended for people who are planning to die in bed. The first time I tried it, I didn't know any better. The second time, I figured it was just a matter of technique. The third time, I began to suspect it was impossible and stopped trying."

"Are you through, Perfessor?" she said.

"I'd be interested in hearing any suggestions you have to offer," I said. "I just wanted you to be clear about the problem."

"First of all—" Lizard gave me a knee-weakening, blue-eyed stare. "—I think you're making up problems that you don't have yet. The last worm we saw was forty kilometers on the other side of the mountains." She jerked a thumb westward.

"Right. That was the last worm we *saw.* How about all the ones we didn't see? Are you willing to bet your life that there aren't any worms in *this* neighborhood? I'm not." I jerked a thumb at the window. "Not a meter away from us, you have the clearest cross-section of the Chtorran food chain anyone has ever seen. That's a Chtorran smorgasbord out there. There *are* worms around. We just haven't seen them yet. But we will."

She looked skeptical.

I said, "A worm has a better sense of smell than a shark. We know that they are attracted to human beings. We don't know why—but we do know that a Chtorran gastropede will head for the strongest human scent it can detect. We've found this out the hard way. They've also learned to recognize the smells of our machinery. Like trucks and choppers. They'll home in on those scents too. I didn't want to say anything about this earlier—because I didn't think we were in a heavily infested area—but the millipedes prove that we are. This chopper is a goddam neon sign. It says FREE LUNCH to any worm in the vicinity." I realized I was getting a little too vehement and lowered my voice. "Sorry. I got excited."

Lizard didn't say anything. She was staring out the window.

I felt I ought to apologize, but—I'd promised I wouldn't do that any more—I shut my mouth.

But silence didn't work either. It just accentuated the feeling of discomfort. "Listen—" I said. "We do have one thing in our favor. The dust. Maybe it's so thick, it masks our scent. That's a very strong possibility. Really. In which case, we might not be in that much danger. We'd only have to worry about a worm finding us by accident. . . ."

"Like that one—?" Lizard asked slowly. She pointed forward.

I looked. I pointed the flashlight.

Something large and dark and red, with two huge black eyes like the headlights on an oncoming subway train, was peering in at us through the windshield. Its eyes shrank in the sudden light.

"I really wanted to be wrong," I said.

The worm cocked its eyes at us diagonally—a listening pose. It opened its mouth slowly and touched its mandibles to the glass. It was testing the surface.

"Oh, God—let it hold."

The glass creaked in its frame.

But it held.

The worm backed away from the window then and ran its fingers curiously over the surface. Its claws scrabbled politely across the glass, tapping and examining. I held the light steady. I was afraid to move it— or even turn it off.

The worm was huge. Four meters long. The dark purple and red stripes on its sides were definite enough to be visible even under the fine coat of pink dust caking its fur.

The monster put its face close to the glass again.

We stared at it. And it stared back at us.

I hoped to God it wasn't hungry.

TWENTY-FOUR

AND THEN the worm backed away from the window and was gone. There was darkness beyond the window. Where was it?

"Don't move," I said.

"I couldn't if I wanted to."

For a moment, there was silence. I wondered if this was the same worm that Duke and I had seen before. I couldn't tell—and it didn't really make much difference, did it? Then, from the side of the chopper next to Lizard, there came a gentle tapping, scrabbling sound.

The worm was still examining the ship.

Lizard's eyes went wide. This was worse than *seeing* what the creature was doing.

The sound moved down the length of the chopper. Slowly, ever so slowly, the worm tapped and scratched its way toward the hatch. When the scrabbling sounds reached the door of the chopper, they hesitated. It was as if the worm could tell that there was something different about this piece of hull. The examination went on for a long long time. I thought of a rabbit in a cage—

"I, uh—want you to know something . . ." Lizard said quietly.

Our attention was on the noise at the door.

"What's that?" I asked.

It almost sounded like a knock. Or like a dog scratching to get in.

"I meant it, what I said before. About you being kind of cute."

Now it was rattling the door handle!

"I know," I said. "Thank you."

Go away, goddammit! There's nobody home!

"No—listen, what I really wanted to tell you—" Lizard's voice was strained, "—I *can* fuck better than I can fly. You can tell Duke that—if you get the chance. . . ."

The rattle at the door stopped.

I said, "I, uh—wanted to find that out for myself. . . ."

There was silence again. Lizard and I listened painfully. Had the worm given up and gone away?

No. The scrabbling resumed farther back down the hull. Lizard gasped. She blurted quickly, "Me too."

The worm was at the tail of the ship now.

I said, "When we get back to Oakland . . ."

She said, "Okay. . . ."

Something went *bang*. The chopper lurched forward. Lizard yelped. Duke moaned.

And then there was silence.

"It went away . . . ?" she whispered.

"Wait," I cautioned.

The silence grew louder.

"Turn on the outside lights," I said. "All of them."

"Is that safe?"

"It knows we're here. There's no reason to hide any more. We might as well see what we're in the middle of."

She leaned forward slowly and touched a button on her console. The landscape beyond the window blazed suddenly bright. The ground glowed pink. The chopper's headlights were still under the dust—the light was reflecting upward through the powder. It created an eerie luminescence, a faerie landscape. A deep furrow led out of the trees, through the pink dunes and directly toward the chopper. The track of the curious worm. Where was it now?

The pink dunes were losing their pristine condition and collapsing into muddy-looking slush that pulsed and throbbed with swarming life. We couldn't identify the smaller creatures; they blurred into a glittering mosaic. Millipedes slithered through them everywhere, feeding like sharks; some of them were as huge as pythons.

But where was the worm?

Lizard switched on the overhead spotlights then—and gasped.

Outside, the air was filled with fluttery things. They looked like epileptic moths. They darted back and forth through the light pouring from the chopper. They dipped and dove and picked at the bugs in the powder. And now there were larger things that sailed through the fluttery things. They curled and swooped like silver ribbons. They were bizarre and graceful and beautiful to watch; they rippled and moved in perfect sine waves. Something like a kite darted through them, snatching them out of the air. What kind of creature fed on the kites?

The creatures in the powder were clearer now too. There were nightwalkers the size of terriers. There were things that looked like spiders on stilts. There were pipe cleaner bugs the size of rats. There were pink hairballs with mouths creeping through the dust, humping like inchworms.

Lizard stared in fascination. Almost without thinking, she switched on the outside microphones—

Cacophony!

Chirps and whistles! A thousand chittering, cackling, buzzing, warbling voices clamored in at us. The noise was horrendous!

Lizard turned the volume down—but that only made the sounds *more* ominous, not less.

Now, it sounded like chewing.

A million mandibles crunching, a noise like sizzling fat.

The night had brought out the biggest and the worst. The creatures beyond the window were functioning with a single biological imperative carried to its most horrifying extreme: eat as much as you can before you are eaten yourself.

It was hideous. And it was fascinating.

I glanced over at Lizard. She was pale and trembling—but she had the camera up to her eye again. I started climbing toward the back—

She yelped, "Hey—where're you going?"

"I've gotta find that worm—" I climbed past Duke.

She followed me back. "What in hell are you thinking?"

"I don't know yet." I was already pulling the weapon-bay open. "Have you got any cold explosives?"

"No—wait a minute. See what kind of rockets they packed with the rocket launcher—" She pointed.

"I found it—" I studied the warning labels.

"You're not going out there?" she said.

"If I have to—"

"That's crazy! You know what's outside—"

"Yeah—and I also know how worms like to solve puzzles with bait in 'em. Yeah, this'll do." I pulled out the "peace-pipe" and one pipe-filler, handed it to her to hold, then closed the compartment again.

"Just one?" she asked dryly.

"I'm only going to get one shot." I took the bazooka and loaded it. "You're going to have to cover me with the freezer. You know how to work it?"

"Point the trigger and press—?"

"That's close enough." I was checking the safeties on the weapon. Everything came up green. Good.

"Wait a minute—" she said. "Just wait a minute—" She held up her hands in front of me. "Have you considered all your options here?"

"Yes—and I am not a free lunch. That leaves only this." I hefted the pipe meaningfully. I stopped and looked at her. "Maybe I'll be lucky. Maybe the worm has already gone away." And then I added, "But I'll bet it hasn't. Here, hold this again."

She took it and said, "I could order you not to do this, you know—"

I was already climbing past her and pulling myself up into the bubble turret. "Go ahead—but court-martials are very time consuming." I opened the shutter.

She called up to me. "We don't court-martial lieutenants for insubordination any more."

"Oh—?"

"No, we just shoot them on the spot. It's cheaper."

I dropped down out of the bubble and jerked my thumb up at it. "Well, before you shoot, you better have a look yourself."

She handed me back the rocket launcher and climbed up into the turret. As she brushed past me I couldn't help but notice that she smelled . . . interesting. Had this woman *really* promised me a lobster dinner in Oakland?

"Oh!" she said; and then, after a horrified pause, "But what's it doing?"

"I don't know. Maybe it's considering all its options."

"It's just sitting there—staring at the hatch. . . ."

"Uh huh. And it can probably hear every word we say."

Lizard dropped back down out of the turret and stared at me. "Will this kill it?" she whispered.

"There's only one way to find out, isn't there?"

"Wait a minute. I have to think this out. Just wait a minute—"

"I can. It *won't*—"

The radio beeped.

We both looked forward.

Lizard looked at me. "It's waited this long, you can wait too—*that's an order."* She scrambled down to the front of the ship to answer the call. "This is ELDAVO." I let out a loud breath and followed sourly.

"ELDAVO, this is the *Paul Bunyan*—" came a male voice, "—on loan from Oregon Air-Lumber. Captain Peter Price at your service. You called for a tow?"

Lizard smiled grimly. "We'll be happy with just a lift. Of *any* kind. The sooner the better."

"Well, lift is what it's all about, ma'am. The *Paul Bunyan* has eighty tons of lift. How much of it do you think you'll need?"

Lizard glanced at me, then back at Duke, did a quick mental calculation, and said, "Oh, two hundred and twenty-five kilos ought to cover it." I shouldered the bazooka and dropped impatiently into the copilot's seat. How long was this going to take?

"Puttin' on a little weight there, ain'tcha, gal?" came a new voice. A deep male voice.

Lizard yelped, "Danny! What are you doing there?"

"Came along for the ride. How's my favorite redhead?"

"I can't tell you on an open circuit," she said with a laugh. I wondered who this Danny was and what his relationship was with Lizard. I wondered if I should be jealous. His voice boomed like a foghorn. He was too friendly.

Lizard glanced over at me, saw my eyes, and turned back to the radio. "Listen, Danny—what's your ETA?"

The man's tone shifted then, became more businesslike. "Well . . . your beam is loud and clear. We should be overhead sometime in the next two hours. How's your patient?"

"Not good."

"He can't ride in a harness?"

"No, we're going to need a basket."

I leaned forward then. "Ask him if they've got a zip line."

"Who's that?" boomed Danny. "Hey, hon—you got a boyfriend?"

"Don't be silly," Lizard said. "He's only a lieutenant." I felt myself reddening in reaction.

"Cradle-robbing again, I see," Danny laughed heartily. I decided I didn't like him or this conversation.

I leaned forward and spoke to the radio. "Can you rig a zip line?"

"Sure, we've got one, Lieutenant . . . uh—?"

"McCarthy, James Edward."

"Right," said Danny crisply. "McCarthy."

"And have you got a crab?"

"Excuse me," Captain Price interrupted, "Are you a blimper?"

"No—"

"Then why don't you let us handle the mission?"

"—but I did seven search and destroy drops off of gasbags in Colorado, so I had to learn this stuff the hard way. We've got some problems here—"

"And we've got some problems up here too."

"Are your problems bright red?" I snapped back. "Do they weigh three tons? And can they rip open a chopper with their teeth?"

There was silence for a heartbeat; you could almost hear the two men exchanging a glance. Then Captain Price came back on the radio. "You have worms?"

"We have one sitting right outside the front door."

Another quick silence.

"Uh . . ." That was Danny. "Lieutenant—" He was speaking very carefully now. "Whatever you do, *don't* annoy it."

"Colonel, I have no intention of *annoying* it," I replied, equally carefully. "I am going to *kill* it." Before he could argue with me, I added, "That worm is going to do one of two things. Either it's going to peel this ship open or it's going to go get the rest of its family—and they will peel this ship open."

"Lieutenant—" the blimp captain interrupted. "Are you an expert on the worms?" There was skepticism in his voice.

"As good as you're going to find in California," I replied matter-of-factly.

Lizard put in then, "Captain Price, he is. I specifically asked for Lieutenant McCarthy to be assigned to me because of his expertise with the Chtorran ecology. If he says the worms are going to shit soup, you'd better bring your bowl and crackers."

"If you say so, Colonel. My apologies for any offense. None intended. But we've had a few bad experiences with groundhogs today, so you'll understand if we're a little testy."

"No problem," Lizard said. She looked at me. "McCarthy?"

"I'm fine." I said to the radio, "But I've got a worm to kill and you're using up my time. Of course, if you've got a better idea, I'd love to hear it. But I'm still the guy whose ass is on the line—"

"Hold it, Lieutenant," came Danny's voice, very calmly. "Nobody's arguing with you any more. You made your point. It's your call. I just want you to be certain—"

Something went *thump* at the back of the ship.

Lizard and I both glanced back. "I'm certain," I said.

Again, a *thump*—this time louder!

Lizard said to the radio, "Danny—it's knocking on the door."

"Go do your job, Lieutenant. We'll keep this line open if you need to talk—"

I was already scrambling.

"—and Lizard, keep an eye on your patient for me." But she was already following me toward the back.

"Grab that freezer!" I pointed. "And a mask!"

"Here—" She tossed goggles at me—

Something *banged* loudly against the door. The handle rattled and clanged. Duke yelped in his sleep. I pulled the goggles down over my eyes, fitted the mask over my nose and mouth, then turned to help Lizard with the tank harness. "Who's Danny?" I asked.

"Colonel Danny Anderson. Northwest Liaison." She grunted as she pulled the harness into place. "—and whatever he says, he is *not* just along for the ride."

"Anderson?" I glanced back at Duke. "Duke's last name is Anderson—"

Lizard nodded. "Danny's his son." She stepped away from me to connect the freezer hose.

Duke was moaning now. He was half-awake, half-delirious. He was breathing very raggedly, and he looked worse than ever.

"Oh God—no."

And then the scratching began at the door again—

TWENTY-FIVE

"WHAT'S IT doing—?" Lizard asked.

I wasn't sure. "It sounds like it's chewing."

It was a quiet, steady sound—but it had too much *crunch* in it. The door protested loudly in its frame. It bulged and squealed. Something black broke through—a mandible? Pink dust floated in the air.

I motioned Lizard to the side. "Give me a clear shot." I braced myself against the opposite wall. "When I give the word, you pop the door—and then freeze it. The whole frame. Ready—?"

She nodded.

"Go!"

She hit the release. The door banged outward—

A very surprised-looking worm reared up and back and away. *"Chtorrrrr!"*

Lizard stepped in spraying—the worm disappeared behind a cloud of cold steam. "Get out of the fucking way!" I screamed. She stepped back—

The steam cleared just enough for me to see the worm dropping down into a charge—

What did they say in the comic books? *"Eat cold death, you purple slime!"* I squeezed the trigger.

The rocket streaked forward with a high-pitched scream and a cold white smell. The wall behind me *crackled*. I could feel the burning chill on the back of my neck.

There was a muffled *FWOOMP!*—

The worm's body puffed up for just the briefest of instants. It froze in surprise—and then it simply stopped and collapsed where it was. Within seconds, tiny white ice crystals were forming all over its fur.

And then there was silence.

"Did you get it?" Lizard peered out cautiously.

The body of the creature was trembling and twitching. A dark ichor was flowing from the creature's mouth and there was the faint sighing sound of air escaping from somewhere.

"Get that door closed!" I leapt forward and grabbed the handle—the door was stuck in its hinge!

Lizard grabbed too. "Goddam worm pulled it out of shape—"

"Keep pulling!"

The door came unstuck with a bone-rattling *BANG!* It swung shut with a slam and we tumbled backwards on the floor.

"Oh, God—we did it!" Lizard was laughing. She sat up and looked at me. "We really did it—didn't we?"

I gulped air and nodded. I held up a hand—

"It's one thing to bomb them from the air—" she marveled. She was almost delirious. "But it's quite another to meet one face to face! Oh, God—!"

I was gasping too hard to speak. I pointed at the door.

She followed my glance. "Oh, no—"

The hatch had a hole in it large enough to stick your head through—and you wouldn't have to remove your helmet first either.

"Shelterfoam?"

She managed to shake her head. "No good. The hole's too big. There's no support. We need a patch—" She looked around the cabin—

"No. You stay there with the freezer! Dust that hole and keep it dusted!" I scrambled to the back of the ship to a place where the frame had bent. Several of the floor panels had popped off in the crash. I'd had to shelterfoam the hull back here.

I scooped up the largest of the panels and the shelterfoam canister and headed back toward Lizard. As I passed Duke, he reached out and grabbed me—"Wha's 'oing on?"

"It's all right, Duke." I patted his arm, tried to disengage his fingers.

"My legs 'urt. M' legs. Feel all red. Burr'ng."

I pried his hand loose. "I'll be right back. Hang on." He didn't hear me. He kept on moaning.

"All right—dust it again!" I screamed at Lizard. She loosed a fine spray of liquid coldness at the hole in the door; she directed it all around the edges.

"All right! All right!" I screamed to stop her. I sprayed the edges of the hole with shelterfoam—it crackled against the frigid surface of the hatch. I waited ten seconds, then sprayed again, outlining the break three times over. I slapped the panel over it and held it in place, bracing myself for maximum pressure. "How long does it take for this stuff to harden?"

"Fifteen minutes—half an hour. I'm not sure."

"Terrific. Grab that canister. Spray the hatch. The hinges. The handles. Everything. Outline it."

"Right."

She had to work around me, but she was thorough. By the time she finished, the foam over the break was already hardening. Gingerly, I took my hands away from the panel I was holding. It stayed put. I took the canister from Lizard and gave it another *spritz* around the edges. Good.

I turned around and looked at her. She was giggling. She pointed at the door. "I always wanted a window—"

"Huh?" I turned back to the door. The patch had a glass window in it. And a warning: CAUTION. DO NOT OPEN THIS PANEL WHILE— The rest was obliterated.

I was too tired to laugh. I pointed toward the front of the ship. "Call whatsisname. Tell him we're okay. And—" I lowered my voice, "—tell him Duke's in pretty bad shape."

She searched my face. "As in 'Duke's on the roof and we can't get him down'?"

"Yeah—better start preparing him."

I pulled off my O-mask and goggles, and climbed into the back to see what I could do for Duke. He was still moaning about his legs being red and burning. I pulled back the blanket and looked. The terramycin had done its job. The pink strands were gone from his legs—but the purple and red strands were longer. It *was* worm fur! But—why? How—?

Duke's whole body was hot. The console said his temperature was 102. His face was dry. His skin was red and cracked. His eyes were puffed up so badly, I was sure he couldn't see out of them, but he turned his face toward me and managed to croak something.

I didn't understand. I had to put my face closer. "What—?"

"Ho . . . go ho . . . tay ho. . . ."

"Home? Right, Duke. We're on our way. Just hang on a little longer, okay?" I squeezed his arm in what was meant to be a reassuring gesture, but he writhed at my touch. "I'm sorry—just hang on, Duke. A little longer. Danny's coming to get you. Your son—"

He turned his head away from me.

There was nothing more I could do for him. I climbed back down to the front of the ship. Lizard was just signing off. She nodded to me. "They're rigging a crab and a zip line."

I grunted and sank down into my seat.

"Everything okay back there?" she asked.

"Yeah," I replied. I wasn't very convincing.

She reached over and patted me. "You're doing fine, McCarthy. Hang on just a little longer."

I looked at her sourly. "That's what I just told Duke."

"Sorry," she said.

"We're gonna lose him. I know it—"

"Jim—"

"I am tired of all this dying!" I said. "I hate it! I just hate it!" I could hear the raggedness in my own voice and how loud I sounded in the cramped cabin of the chopper, and abruptly I realized just how close I was to the edge.

I turned away from Lizard and buried my face against my arm, trying to create even a small private space for my frustration. I motioned behind me for her to just keep her distance and please not say anything. "No—just leave me alone for a while. Okay?"

"Sure. Okay."

The chopper was cold. There were tiny patches of frost on the walls where the freezer had sprayed—and ice crystals. It smelled of cotton candy and shelterfoam. There was a faint pink haze in the air, but it wasn't strong enough to cover the smell of our sweat—and the other smell too. The smell from the back of the ship.

We sat in silence. We listened to the eternal sound of the Chtorran ecology eating. We watched its myriad tiny forms scuttling across the windshield of the chopper. There were a lot less of them now. They probably didn't like the light and had gone elsewhere. The only critters left were the ones that didn't care.

One of the pink furballs was humping right across my field of vision. Almost mechanically, I picked up my camera and began photographing it. The creature had a tiny puckered mouth and it vacuumed up everything in its path. Maybe this was a larval worm. I wondered if I'd live to find out. I wondered if this would be my legacy—these pictures.

"Hey—" I lowered the camera and looked at Lizard.

"What?"

"I just realized. Duke's only a captain. How come Danny's a colonel?"

"You want the truth?"

"Yeah!"

"Do you know much about what happened in Pakistan?"

"Not a lot, no. That was a long time ago."

Lizard sighed. "Fifteen years is not a long time ago."

"I was only nine years old," I protested.

"I was in high school," Lizard replied. "Anyway, did you ever hear of the Rawalpindi Incident?"

"That I heard of."

"Well . . . your Captain Anderson back there—only he was Lieutenant Anderson at the time—was . . . ah, actively involved."

"How actively?"

"They gave him orders. He followed them."

"I must be stupid," I said. "I don't understand what you're trying not to say."

"Captain Anderson did his job. People got killed. A lot of them. Mostly on the other side. That happens a lot in a war. Captain Anderson deserved a medal. Instead, they gave him a court-martial."

"Duke—?"

Lizard nodded. "He was acquitted—but then so was Lizzie Borden, and look at how many people remember her."

"Jeez, I didn't know any of this—"

"Not many people do any more. I had to look it up myself. It's very interesting reading. Captain Anderson can have a promotion anytime he wants. All he has to do is retire."

"No way. Not Duke."

"Mm hm. A lesser man might have resigned his commission. Captain Anderson didn't. You ought to look up his statement to the court. That's the most interesting part. It's about the real meaning of service; he said, 'Commitment means not quitting just because the job got tough.' "

"But they never promoted him after that?"

"Right."

I thought for a moment. Her explanation made sense—except it didn't. I looked at Lizard sharply. "There's something else you're not telling me, isn't there?"

She didn't answer.

"Well . . . ?" I prompted.

"All right . . ." she sighed. "You'd better hear it from me, I guess."

"Hear what?"

"The *other* reason you were pulled out of Colorado is that Danny asked me, off the record, to find something a little less *dangerous* for Captain Anderson. You know, he's over fifty?"

"Duke?"

"Yeah, Duke."

I glanced to the back of the chopper. I'd never thought of Duke as really *old*.

"I told you I looked up his record. It's impressive. So I asked for him to be assigned to me. You were part of the package, so you got pulled too. But it could have happened anyway. We're pulling a lot of personnel out of the Rocky Mountain District right now for California."

I grunted a polite acknowledgment. I didn't like the implications.

Lizard reached over and put her hand on mine. She waited till I looked up at her. Her eyes were incredibly blue. "Listen, stupid. I did mean what I said about your expertise. I could have put you and Duke anywhere, but I asked for you in my section because the two of you are exactly what I need right now. I especially appreciate your sense of the Chtorran ecology. I've learned to appreciate it even more in the past two days."

"Thanks," I said grumpily. I even meant it.

"Are you unhappy about that?"

"Listen—" I said. "As long as we're telling the truth . . . the only reason I'm the best worm expert in California is that there aren't any others. You think too much of my abilities."

"You haven't done too badly here."

"There's no trick to that."

"Oh? Really?"

"Sure. You just ask yourself what could make this situation worse. Then plan for that. If it happens, you look like you know what you're doing. If it doesn't, you're still better prepared to handle whatever does happen."

"You're kidding."

"Nope. Try it." I gestured toward the windshield. "What could make *this* situation worse?"

She said, "Looking out the window and seeing a whole family of worms surrounding the chopper."

I glanced at my watch. "Probably within fifteen minutes."

"You don't need to be so cheerful about it."

I shrugged. "It's hard being right. You get cocky. Besides, what else can go wrong?"

She looked at me sharply. "You don't want this transfer, do you?"

"No, I don't," I said candidly. "I don't like the way it's been handled. It's been too abrupt. And I don't like leaving a job unfinished. We were making real progress in Colorado."

"Uh huh." She nodded. "You want to know something about that?"

"What?"

"Nobody's ever going to pull you off an important job unless the one they're putting you on is even *more* important. You might want to remember that. It's true even when there *are* other considerations."

She meant Duke.

Behind us, his breathing had gotten painfully loud. And it seemed even more ragged and uneven than before. I wondered if he was even going to last until the blimp arrived.

We sat in silence for a while.

Suddenly, Lizard said, "You son of a bitch."

"Huh?"

"You did it again." She pointed. I looked.

Outside the chopper, there was something moving through the edges of darkness—something just beyond the warm circle of our lights. Its eyes glimmered and flashed as it glanced toward us. It was that reflection that had given it away.

"Is the spotlight working?" I asked.

"The nose light is out, but I've got one overhead. Hang on." She touched her control panel. A bright beam sprang out across the clearing, suddenly catching the little silvery-pink figure by surprise—it was centered in the rosy pool of light. The creature blinked and froze in the sudden glare. It was round and furry and as cute as a baby abominable snowman. Pink dust hung in the air around it.

"Oh—" gasped Lizard. "Is that a bunnydog?" Her eyes widened in wonder.

"Yeah," I said sourly. I lifted the camera to my eye. The creature was only thigh-deep in the powder. That meant the cotton candy was settling.

"He doesn't seem scared of the light, does he?"

"No. Just curious. These creatures don't display much fear of anything. Do you see the others?" There were more bunnydogs in the dimness behind it. We could see them in the reflected glow. They were motionless too.

Lizard was grinning. "You just blew one. These are not worms."

I said, "I've still got ten minutes."

The bunnydog blinked and unfroze then. It scratched behind one ear, rubbed its face with its paws, made a face at us, then turned and ambled out of the spotlight.

"Well, I guess he told you," said Lizard.

"Yeah, but what?"

The other bunnydogs were getting curious now. One at a time, they began taking cautious little hops toward the chopper. They pushed through the powder in quick spurts of motion, stopping often to look ahead and ponder. They cocked their heads sideways to listen, their ears flopping open as they did so. I held my camera steady and recorded every moment of it. I thumbed the controls and zoomed in for closeups. These pictures were going to be *important*.

There was something funny about the shape of their mouths; they seemed permanently pouted—their muzzles were oddly blunted. As I watched, one of them straightened up and turned to its companion, pursing its lips as if kissing the air. The other replied with a kissy-face of its own. They looked like puppies who'd been pulled off Mamma's tit. Of course! Their mouths were shaped more for sucking than for chewing!

How very . . . odd.

I watched—and photographed—as the bunnydogs continued sniffing closer to the chopper. Every so often, one or another of them would lower its muzzle to the dust and suck and chew. Were they going for the powder—or the creatures feeding on the powder? I couldn't tell. But I knew it was important—it was part of the bigger question. Were these creatures sentient? Were they omnivores? Were these the sentients we were looking for?

Their nostrils and eyes were slits against the powder—but every so often, one of the creatures would pause and straighten and look at us, blinking its eyes wide for a quick curious instant; then we could see that the bunnydogs actually had very large round eyes. Puppydog eyes. Probably that was their normal configuration—when they weren't rump-deep in dust.

I said, "This is very very bad news."

Lizard glanced at me. "Huh?"

"We've been telling people that the Chtorran ecology is extraordinarily vicious, right?"

"Uh huh."

"And we've got pictures to prove it, right?"

"Go on. . . ."

"So—how long do you think we'll be able to sell that story after *these* creatures are seen by the public?"

"You're right," she said. "This *is* bad news."

I continued recording the bunnydogs' cautious inspection of the chopper. "We're going to have to put the lid on this. At least until we know what we're looking at. These creatures could be the most dangerous of all. And we might not find out what the danger is until it's too late, because we're so distracted by how cute they are."

The first of the bunnydogs reached the windshield then. It climbed up the side of the chopper and peered in at us, blinking owlishly. With its paws flat against the glass, it looked like a small child peering in the window of a candy store. It sucked at the surface—tasting it, no doubt.

"I keep wanting to say *awww*," whispered Lizard.

"It's a fucking teddy bear—a goddamned fucking teddy bear!" I growled. "What a dirty trick."

The bunnydog licked its chops politely. I wondered what that meant.

There were other bunnydogs climbing up the side of the chopper now. Within minutes, the window was full of tiny little faces peering in at us.

"I, uh—hate to say this," said Lizard, "but I'm starting to get scared."

"Me too. I never thought I'd be afraid of a herd of teddy bears."

"They just keep staring at us. What do they want?"

"I don't know." I was still recording. "I think maybe they're just curious." I lowered my camera. "I want to try something. Will you record this?"

"Sure." She took the camera from me. "Okay, go ahead."

I leaned forward in my seat and placed my hands up against the glass, opposite the paws of the first bunny. Its paws were no larger than a baby's.

The bunnydog blinked. It tried to sniff my hands through the windshield. It sucked at the glass. Then it stopped and frowned. It looked puzzled. It blinked and tried again. This time, it licked the glass. Its tongue was soft and pink. The other bunnydogs watched curiously.

"That doesn't seem very intelligent," Lizard said.

"It is if you've never seen glass before. It's testing."

The bunnydog blinked at me again.

I blinked back at it—a big oversized gesture.

The bunnydog showed its teeth.

I showed mine. As wide as I could.

The bunnydog—there was no other word for it—smiled.

I smiled too—a big ridiculous grin.

"I think you're communicating," Lizard said.

"I wonder what we're saying to each other?"

"It looks like, 'for better or worse, for richer or poorer, in sickness and in health . . .' "

"Bite your tongue," I said. But my face was frozen. I was still smiling broadly at the bunnydog. "Maybe we're negotiating a peace treaty. . . ."

The bunnydog made a face. It pulled its cheeks out into a grotesque expression. And held it.

"I dare you," Lizard said.

I swallowed. "The things I do for my species." I made a face back at the bunnydog. I hooked my fingers in my mouth and stretched it wide. I crossed my eyes and stuck out my tongue and touched the tip of it to my nose.

The bunnydog fell off the window in surprise. So did all the others.

"Oh, God—I think I've insulted them."

The bunnydogs were rolling around in the powder, stamping their feet and drumming up big clouds of pale pink dust. They looked like they were having a collective seizure.

"Or something," Lizard said. "Maybe they're laughing themselves to death."

I looked at Lizard; she had the camera still recording. She pointed it straight at me. "This—" I said angrily to posterity, "—is *not* the way Captain Kirk always did it!"

TWENTY-SIX

THE BUNNYDOGS climbed back up on the windshield and stared at us for a while longer. I made some more faces at them. They made some more faces at me. Gradually, they lost interest in that game and drifted away to explore other parts of the chopper. We heard them scrabbling across the top of the ship and scratching at the observation bubbles.

"I better see what they're up to—" I grabbed the camera and headed for the back. I stopped and peered up into the turret. One of the little cutenesses was peering back down at me. I waved at it facetiously—it waved back—then I closed the shutter in case Duke woke up again.

On a hunch, I peered out through the tiny accidental window in the door patch. "Holy Hannah—" I jammed the camera against the glass and started shooting. There were bunnies all over the dead worm! The ice had evaporated from its fur—now it was just a big collapsed bag of dead pudding—but the bunnies were climbing up onto its back, patting it curiously and chittering at it. They looked like they were trying to wake it up. One of them was even peering into its mouth—

Lizard called me then. "Hey, McCarthy—something's happening."

"Wait a minute—"

"I mean it! You better get down here!"

She was right. Something *was* happening. The bunnies were suddenly dropping off the dead worm and moving forward again. I swung down to the front of the chopper and climbed back into my seat.

Lizard pointed off to the left. "Over there. Look—the bunnydogs have all stopped to listen."

She was right. The little round creatures had fallen still—they were *listening* for something. They had their heads cocked sideways and their expressions were expectant.

Beyond, in the darkness, something was stirring up the dust. It rose brightly in the glare of our lights.

The bunnydogs stiffened expectantly. . . .

I could feel my heart rising. This was it.

And then the first worm poured over the dunes and down into the drifts.

And then a second worm, and a third—

There were more bunnydogs riding on their backs.

Lizard lifted her camera and started shooting. "Well, you got the worms right," she said, "but you missed the time."

I barely heard her. The worms were still pouring over the dunes. "Win one, lose one," I gulped.

Lizard was scanning the group with her camera. "I see six, seven, eight . . . no, make that ten, eleven—urk, fourteen worms."

They were all different sizes. The smallest was no bigger than a pony. The largest was the size of a bus. They swiveled their big black hand-puppet eyes at us, cocked them back and forth, up and down, locked them into place, and stared at the chopper. If they had expressions, they were unreadable.

We could see the coloring of the worms vividly. They were bright red and orange, striped with purple and all over frosted with pink powder. They left trails of glittering dust in the air. They sparkled as if they were made out of magic.

"I hate to say it," whispered Lizard, "—but they're beautiful."

She was right. As horrifying as the worms were, they were also *fascinating*. Each worm was a gaudy calliope of color. Their stripes had the confusing effect of seeming to shift even as we watched. If there was a pattern to the markings, I couldn't tell.

Despite the dust, this was the clearest and closest view of worms in the wild we'd had yet.

The monsters were shaped like stubby cigars, but with a bulge at the front like the nose of an old Boeing 747. That was the brain case, a thick shell of bone shielding the creature's gray matter (or whatever color it was—more likely purple). The monster's arms were anchored here. Mostly the worms kept their peculiarly double-jointed arms folded flat

against the brain case, reaching up and over the eyes only to grab or
hold something. Or some*one*.

The creatures' eyes rose up just in front of the brain case. The two
eyes moved independently of each other, as if they were mounted on
separate swivels, but both organs were enclosed in the same rubbery bag
of skin.

At the very front of the creature was the mouth.

When it was closed, it looked like a sphincter; but when it was open,
it was hideous—it was a maw, a grinding hole, a pit. Nothing godly was
responsible for this beast. No, Lizard was wrong. The worm was not a
beautiful creature. The mouth spoiled it.

The worms were moving around the chopper now, inspecting it,
looking at it sideways, but always keeping a cautious distance—at least
three lengths away. Several of them began moving toward the rear—

"Oh, my God—the dead worm!"

Lizard followed me back—I leapt over Duke toward the weaponbay,
she climbed into the turret—"They've found it! McCarthy, look at
this!"

I grabbed the box of rockets and scrambled back—I shoved my face
up to the accidental window. Three large worms were inspecting the
body of the dead one. The bunnydogs moved to keep out of their way.

One of the worms slid around then, bringing itself directly alongside
the body. It rolled up to it as if it were . . . cuddling? That didn't
make sense. Another worm was doing the same thing on the opposite
side.

"What are they doing—?" Lizard called quietly.

"I don't know. I've never seen this before. Are you still carrying your
camera?"

"Yeah. I'm getting it!"

Abruptly, one of the worms lifted its eyes and looked straight at me.
It was studying the door—the same door its colleague had been trying
to open when we'd killed it.

The worm slid forward—

I yelped and leapt for the peace-pipe. I fumbled a rocket into it, then
looked out the window again—

The worm was peering in at me.

I jumped backward, almost tripping, slamming into the opposite
wall. I braced myself and aimed the rocket-launcher straight ahead.

Something tapped at the door. It sounded *exactly* like a knock.

"Don't answer it . . ." squeaked Lizard.

The tapping continued for a long . . . long moment. And then it stopped abruptly.

I could feel my heart beating like a jackhammer—The silence was terrifying!

Abruptly, the door squeaked and groaned.

The worm was trying to work the latch!

It didn't rattle. The shelterfoam held—

And then silence.

"What's it doing—?" I whispered.

"It's backing away from the door—"

I jumped for the window. She was right. The worm was retreating a meter at a time. It was still studying the chopper door curiously. And then it—scratched itself right between the eyes. It looked . . . *puzzled!*

"Are you getting all this?"

"Uh huh—I don't believe it either. McCarthy! Look at the other one!"

The second worm to cuddle against the dead one had lifted its eyes to study the door now. It shifted its glance to the worm that was backing away—as if considering. Then it looked to the door again and apparently made a decision. It slid off toward the nose of the chopper.

Several of the other worms approached the dead one now. They looked like they were sniffing and inspecting it, but none of them moved up alongside it. "Nobody else wants to cuddle . . . ?" I guessed.

"Would you?" Lizard asked. She dropped out of the turret. "Come on! Something's happening up front."

The worms were forming themselves into groups. There were two groups of four and two groups of three. The bunnydogs looked like they were directing them, but I wasn't sure. I never listened to the person guiding me into a parking place either, why should a worm? The creatures were settling down quickly.

"Now what are they doing—?" Lizard wondered.

"I don't know," I whispered back. "Always before, we've seen worms only in groups of three or four. We've assumed those were family groups. We've never had a chance to observe a really large gathering." My voice cracked on the next-to-last word. I swallowed hard.

Lizard looked over at me. "How are you doing?"

"You mean, am I scared?"

"Yeah."

"I'm petrified. How about you?"

She said it matter-of-factly: "I guess you could say I'm handling it as well as can be expected."

I heard the quaver. I reached over and touched her hand. "Under the circumstances, there's not a hell of a lot of other options."

She squeezed my hand in hers—almost a little too hard. Then she let go quickly, as if she were embarrassed at having admitted her emotion.

I covered my own reaction by picking up the Pentax again. When in doubt, take care of business. I popped the clip and dropped the memory cassette into my lap. I reached down for a new one and snapped it into place.

I'd filled eighty gigabytes of memory with two hours of high-resolution video. No matter what else happened, what we'd photographed here tonight would make an incredible difference to the war effort. We'd seen things that no other human being had ever observed—and we'd made a record of them.

I expected the next hour to be even *more* interesting.

If we survived.

That thought hovered oddly.

I knew that we were very close to death here—

—and it didn't matter.

I realized I couldn't be scared any more. I'd moved beyond fear.

I'd passed into a kind of free-floating euphoria. It was the strangest feeling—I'd used up all my fear. All that was left was *interest.*

I supposed I'd run out of adrenaline—that was probably the medical explanation; but it *felt* like the freedom of madness.

And I didn't mind.

It was all right to be crazy. It was the best thing to be. I didn't have to be responsible any more. I was tired of being *responsible*—

I floated. I photographed the Chtorran worms, and floated above the land of fear.

The bunnydogs were gathering in front of the worm groups now. They were absolutely unafraid of the worms. The two species were obviously in partnership.

The question was . . . *which one* was the dominant partner?

The four groups of worms were arranged in a large arc in front of the chopper. Now, several of the bunnydogs hopped into the focus of that space and began stamping out a large circle, an arena several meters across. A cloud of pink dust rose around them as they moved. It glittered and sparkled in the air around them. They didn't act as if they noticed. They rabbit-thumped their big paddle-feet and pounded the powder into a hard-packed surface. They moved around and around the circle, spiraling out and then in again.

There were at least a dozen of them, and they went about their task with an almost grim determination. They were little round pink warriors trying to invent a war dance. As they continued, more and more of the bunnydogs entered the circle and joined the task—until all of them were there, determinedly stamping out an arena.

I glanced to the worms. They were paying very close attention to what was happening here. One by one, they were shifting to face forward. They moved up to the very edge of the circle, but did not enter it. Instead, they settled into positions of quiet readiness. They looked like giant red meat loafs; they folded their arms back and swiveled their eyes forward, and focused their attention on the stubby little bunnies in the circle.

They were *waiting* on the bunnydogs.

They were a monstrous tableau. Their large black eyes blinked rapidly against the spreading dust in the air. They watched dispassionately. If they had expressions, they were impossible to read.

Very quickly, the bunnydogs finished preparing their arena and stopped. As each one finished, he/she/it? moved to the center of the circle and waited. Finally, they were all of them gathered silently in the center in a loose jumble. For a moment, nothing happened. The bunnydogs were still. The worms might have been statues. The dust hung in the air—a silent pink haze. Everything was frozen.

"Now, what—?"

"Shhh."

We waited—

The first movements were imperceptible. We saw the dust, not the motion—it rose around the bunnydogs in a fresh pink cloud. They were stamping their feet again—but this time it had a *ritual* quality. They were trembling. They were shivering and shuddering. And finally, they were moving—all as one now—turning slowly around and around among themselves.

The cluster began to expand. Still stamping, still turning, they began to move outward toward the edges of their circle; at the same time they began to expand the size of their movements. They brought their arms out from their bodies. They lifted their hands over their heads. They opened their mouths wide and a shrill keening rose from their throats.

They had the *sweetest* voices.

The keening went on and on—and then suddenly, one of the bunnydogs let loose a rapid, high-pitched series of yelps. The other bunnies froze for just an instant and—

—then began to *dance.*

It was a wild and frenzied performance—an explosion of bright pink energy. The bunnydogs stamped the ground beneath their feet as hard as they could. The dust rose in thick billowing explosions, sparkling and churning around them. The bunnies whirled and pounded, jumped and bounced. They chittered and shrieked and whooped.

They flung their arms out wide and leapt into the air, screaming like sirens—they bounced like popcorn. Where one came down, five more leapt up. It was a chain reaction of giggling joyous energy. We could hear them growling like teddy bears and yelping like Indians.

There was no pattern to it that we could see. The dance was a celebration, an exuberant demonstration of enthusiasm and delight. I couldn't help myself, I could feel the grin spreading across my face. I glanced over at Lizard and she was smiling too. The bunnies were *funny.*

By now, they must have been out of control. They caromed off each other like ping-pong balls in a wind tunnel. The bunnies were shuddering and shaking and waggling their fat little butts like ecstatic puppies. I wanted to run out there and join them. I wondered if Lizard was feeling the same way. I glanced over at her.

"It's marvelous!" she said. "But what does it mean?"

"It looks like a *wraggle.* "

"A—what?"

"A dance. A communication dance. That's how bees tell other bees where to find the tastiest flowers. Maybe that's what's happening here. Maybe this is how you control or communicate with worms—by dancing. Dr. Fletcher is going to want to see this."

But—

No, it didn't make sense.

This dance couldn't be just for the fun of it—not here. Not now. *Now with all these worms watching.*

There was something else going on here, something I couldn't even begin to understand—and I knew I should.

It felt too *familiar.*

But the connection refused to complete—it hovered annoyingly beyond the edge of recognition. I could feel the frustration growing like a knot in my chest.

The bunnydogs were whirling now, not leaping. They twirled and spun like little fat dervishes—like plump pink pigs. They bumped into each other, fell into the dust, sputtering and gobbling, then bounced back up into the smoke and kept on twirling. They looked like chipmunks trying to describe a tornado.

A communication dance.

And then I realized—

"Oh my God."

"What—?"

"I've seen this before," I said.

"What!"

I added quickly, "Not exactly this, but something enough like it—" I swallowed hard. "In the herd. In San Francisco. Dr. Fletcher took me. The herd members do a kind of—dance. It looks like this." I shook my head. "I don't know. Maybe it's a coincidence."

"Why does the herd dance?" Lizard asked.

"Dr. Fletcher thinks—that it has something to do with communication. Nonverbal communication."

Lizard didn't reply immediately. She was studying the bunnydogs again. They were still bouncing. Their energy seemed inexhaustible.

"How do you decode it?" she asked.

"I don't know. I'm not a worm."

"You think the dance is for the worms?"

"Who else? Maybe they're telling the worms about us, about what they saw when they peeked in the windows. I don't know. Maybe—" I hesitated, then added, "I don't want to worry you with this thought, but—"

"Worry me," she said.

"Well—obviously, there's some kind of partnership here. And uh, it seems pretty obvious to me—by the shape of their muzzles—that the bunnydogs are meat-eaters, or at least, omnivorous. Their mouths look like they're good for sucking too. Maybe they use the worms to kill for them. Maybe they're telling them right now that this is a picnic basket."

"Right," said Lizard. "Listen, if you have any more thoughts like that . . . you don't have to worry me."

Outside, the frenzy was ebbing now. The dance was slowing. One by one, the bunnies whirled into the center and collapsed exhaustedly into the dust. They fell on one another, rolling and tumbling. The dance was deflating into a big pile of pink fur.

There was silence. The ever-present pink dust hung in the air.

"Now what?" Lizard wondered.

I didn't answer.

The worms had watched the entire dance without reaction. Now, they slowly turned their eyes toward each other. They almost looked . . . uncertain—as if they were waiting for the emperor's reaction before they allowed their own—

Only . . . which one was the emperor?

One by one, the worms were turning their attention toward the largest—*and most patterned*—worm in the group. It had narrowed the apertures of its eyes; it looked like it was brooding thoughtfully.

Caesar Augustus? Or Caligula?

Abruptly, its eyes bounced open.

And then it moved.

Ponderously, majestically, it flowed forward. Straight toward us.

And then *all* the worms flowed forward.

They surrounded the chopper—and began to examine it. All fourteen of them. They scratched and tapped and thumped the hull of the ship.

The chopper pitched and bumped ominously—

TWENTY-SEVEN

LIZARD WAS on the radio immediately, *"Houston! We've got a problem!"*

Colonel Danny Anderson replied immediately, "Go ahead, EL-DAVO."

"We've got worms. More than a dozen of 'em—" Lizard screamed, "—and they're reading the label on this package. Canned people!" She yelped again as something rocked the chopper.

I scrambled out of my seat and crawled back looking for the rocket launcher or the freeze gun. Maybe I could hold them off until the blimp arrived.

There were scrabbling sounds at the door. Something was scraping across the roof. The chopper bumped as if something else were pushing it from behind. It lurched so hard I stumbled against the wall—

Duke was moaning! He was waving his arms, trying to get up. He was mumbling and reaching—"Torsh—whah mah torsh?" A pair of giant black eyes was peering in at him through the left side bubble.

I didn't think. I grabbed the shelterfoam gun and sprayed the window. Did the worm look surprised? Did it back away? I didn't see. I turned and sprayed the other bubble.

I crawled over to Duke, pushing him back down onto the deck. "Stay still," I commanded.

"Huh—? Whuh—?"

"Stay still! That's an order, Captain!"

"Yessuhm—" And he lapsed back into unconsciousness.

As I scrambled back to Lizard, she tossed me a sidewise glance. "Gave yourself a little promotion, huh?"

"So court-martial me. Where's the goddamn blimp?" I looked at the clock. "They're overdue."

"I don't know—"

"We're eight minutes away," boomed Colonel Anderson's voice from the radio. "Keep your pants on."

"Why—?" I snapped back. "Will that taste better to the worms?"

"Listen up, Lieutenant!" Colonel Anderson had his father's same angry tone. "Anchoring a blimp is tricky. How you *feel* about it is irrelevant. It's going to take the same amount of time whether you're calm and rational or panicky and screaming. So it's up to you—how do you want to play it?"

Something in the rear of the chopper creaked ominously. It sounded like a Kevlar strut crackling under pressure. Something else went *thump* against the door. The door *bulged*. A piece of shelterfoam *spronged* off and ricocheted off the opposite wall.

I turned back to the radio. "That's real reasonable, Colonel, sir—but you don't have several tons of worm trying to climb into your ship. We do."

"I'm aware of your problem, Lieutenant. But we don't have any more time to talk about it. You'll have to have your little hissy-fit *after* we pick you up."

A worm was staring at us through the windshield—but it didn't push through. It just goggled its eyes and blinked. *Sput-phwut.* A second worm slid up beside it.

I opened my mouth to reply to Colonel Anderson—and then shut it. I realized how stupid I was about to be. I was going to argue for my right to be terrified and upset. The worms were still only inspecting us. If they'd wanted to come in, they would have. Time enough to scream then. "Go ahead," I gulped.

"We've got you on our horizon now. Stand by—" There was a pause. "Nope. There's still too much *schmutz* in the air. We'll have to do this on instruments." Another pause. "All right, we're dropping the crab. I'll give you the video—"

Lizard reached out and switched on the main display. She punched through the channels quickly. A bright clear image came up on the screen.

We were looking down from the blimp. A round, spidery-looking robot—it had a lot of arms and legs and attachments—was dangling

from four lines that looked too slender to support it. It was caught in
the spotlights of the blimp, and it flashed with spotlights of its own. The
only indications of motion were the pale and luminous clouds sweeping
past below.

Lizard touched her controls again and a second screen lit up to show
the view from the crab's camera. There were pink trees swinging wildly
below us.

I leaned forward to peer out the front windshield. "Shouldn't we be
seeing them soon?"

Lizard asked the radio, "Can you eyeball us?"

"Not yet. Stand by. We'll give you the computer-scan. Channel
three."

Lizard punched up a third display screen. The image was plastic-
looking, without detail; the blimp's computer had compiled all its sensory data—sonic, infrared, radar, visual and who knew what else—into
a single three-dimensional portrait. The landscape looked rippled and
uneven; the computer had painted it a dull orange. A wide depression
angled diagonally through the image; we were sliding toward it.

There! Just left of center—that bright white object! That was us! A
tiny gunship half-buried in a furrow of red. There were dark shapes
crawling all over it. I wished I hadn't seen that.

Lizard studied it for a moment, then pointed back over my shoulder.
"The blimp'll be coming in from that angle. You'll see them first from
the turret."

I climbed back to the turret and pulled myself up into it. I pulled the
shutter back—

—and I was suddenly staring into the large round eyes of a large
round worm. It blinked. I blinked. It blinked again. I made a face at it.
It blinked a third time. I shined my flashlight at it. It blinked.

But it didn't attack.

Why not—?

What was going on here?!

"Shoo!" I shouted. "Shoo!"

The worm blinked at me again.

"Goddammit! Get out of my way—! You big fat hairy bag of pustu-
lant pink pudding!"

The worm backed away from the turret.

I blinked. In surprise. I didn't know my own strength.

I swiveled around quickly. The worms were all over the chopper—
and all around it on the ground. They were huge dark shapes in the

night, moving quickly and silently across the pale glow of the dust drifts. The lights of the ship struck highlights off the powder crusted on their sides.

Another worm raised itself up to peer at me—one of the biggest. It leaned its weight against the chopper—and pulled us sideways! Lizard yelped. Duke moaned. I heard it over my own scream. The worm loomed ominous and black outside the turret. It swiveled one eye high and the other eye low to look at me from a very cockeyed angle. It only wanted to *study* me. It was *curious!*

These were not *ordinary* worms. They weren't hungry.

I'd never met a worm before that wasn't crazy with hunger—or rage. This was a whole new mode of behavior. We were going to have to rewrite the book.

We'd always assumed that the worms were like the millipedes—so much a victim of their own hunger that *everything* was perceived as food. But these worms were—beyond that.

How did that happen? How much food did a worm need to eat to be *satisfied?*

How much did it take to *stuff* a worm? Seattle? North Dakota?

Or maybe the answer was all around me. First, you bury California under two meters of cotton candy powder, so the worms are surrounded by food. Then let them out for a walk, so every time they take a step they get a mouthful. The issue of hunger is taken care of.

Maybe.

Maybe we were safe for as long as there was pink snow on the ground.

Or maybe that was just a false connection. Maybe there was something else going on here too—

We just didn't know.

A pink light in the sky pulled me back to the present. It looked like a warm glow behind a veil of smoke.

"I can see the blimp!" I hollered.

As I watched, the glow began to assume brilliance and color and even a hint of size and form. Then it became a cluster of lights. They grew brighter. The blimp moved out of the darkness and became a gaudy, cigar-shaped, rose-enveloped *presence.* The air glowed pink around it. Its brightest lights were banked along its belly; rows of spotlights, swiveling and pointing in all directions. The crab was a smaller cluster of beams and auras hanging just below.

The ship hung in the sky like a vision—like an angel. Its rays came

sweeping through the pale haze like fingers from heaven, turning everything *luminous*. The beams poured from the sky. They were beautiful!
One of them touched me in passing and it was almost too bright to look
at.

The whole world glowed with the light—the land, the drifts, the stark
and barren trees. Everything looked ghostly and iridescent. Even the
dark worms and the darker body of the chopper. A line from something
floated through my head. *God came out at midnight. I could see him
floating in my sky.*

All around us, the worms were stopping what they were doing, turning and looking upward. Some of them even backed away from the
chopper for a better view. They were puzzling at the light in the sky,
trying to make out what it could be—but there was no focus there. No
edges, no shapes, no lines—only the light. The beautiful, brilliant, dazzling *light!*

I felt a surge of joy in my chest and in my throat. My eyes started to
water. "It's beautiful," I said.

"What?" asked Lizard.

"It's beautiful!" I called. "I can see the lights of the blimp! It's the
most beautiful sight I've ever seen."

"How far are they?"

"Uh—" I brought myself back to reality again. "It's hard to tell.
Maybe a kilometer. Maybe two."

"They're past the trees," Lizard said. "They can fire the harpoon any
time now."

Something puffed from the bottom of the crab. It hit the ground with
a muffled thump and a large cloud of pale powdery smoke rose from the
point of impact. The crab slid down the line and disappeared into the
cloud, leaving four thin lines hanging in the air, stiffening against the
pull of the blimp.

"They got it!" I called. "They're moored."

"Not yet!" Lizard called back. "Two more to go."

The crab released the anchored line and scuttled sideways across the
pink drifts. Almost immediately, it disappeared into them, marking its
passage by the three lines still anchored to it. They cut through the
powder like fishing lines through water—they trailed a moving cloud of
brightly glowing dust.

Abruptly, the crab appeared again, coming up suddenly on a rise. Its
motion was mad—even comical—but it was *fast*. It scrambled quickly
across the ground, varying its gait to match the terrain: it bounced, it

crawled, it scuttled sideways; it paused, it backed up, it dipped and tilted; it *tiptoed* around a pink lump that once had been a bush—then dashed down the opposite side of the slope in a rapid spurt of action.

The bunnydogs were frozen. The worms *stared.*

The crab picked its steps like a ballet dancer. It moved like a lunar walker. It raced like a thoroughbred. If it could have cooked, I'd have married it.

It stopped inside another pink drift. The whole powdery area *glowed* with its light. There was another bright puff—another harpoon—and another line was anchored. This time when the crab came scuttling out, it was trailing only two lines back up to the blimp.

It headed directly toward the chopper now, directly toward two of the largest worms. Their eyes blinked as it approached.

It hesitated only a moment—then dashed directly between the two of them. Their eyes swiveled to follow this small presumptuous machine. It passed between them so rapidly they nearly twisted their eyes off. Only after it passed their tails did they remember to be surprised and leapt around to stare at it again. Was that a Chtorran double take?

One of the worms cocked its eyes curiously—the "hand-puppet expression" was getting very familiar—and started to follow the crab tentatively. The crab swiveled a spotlight toward it—and the worm backed away quickly. I started to giggle. It was *funny.* These monsters had to mass several tons apiece—and they were startled by a hyperkinetic machine?!

The crab had already scuttled sidewise around the chopper. I swiveled around to watch it disappear over—no, through—one of the steepest drifts of all. Its powdery light gleamed in the distance. It was moving as far from the chopper as it could to provide a long third leg for the tripod of mooring ropes. After a moment, I saw the now-familiar puff of smoke, and a few moments later, the crab scuttled back, trailing only a single line. Our lifeline.

"All right," called Lizard. "They're ready if we are."

"Wait a minute," I called. "Something's happening."

The worms were swiveling their eyes upward again—to stare at the blimp. The airship was moving onto station directly overhead. Mother! That thing was huge! And bright! The air around it didn't just glow—it *shimmered.*

The blimp was a giant pink egg that filled the sky. It hung there like a gorgeous UFO, pouring light down on all of us—the pale powdery drifts, the stubby bunnydogs, the darkened chopper, and the curious worms.

The worms—

I couldn't tear my eyes from them. They shone incredibly in the glare from above—they looked *luminous.* They looked like they were made of electricity. Their fur rippled in waves; the stripes on their sides seemed to shiver and shift with red and purple iridescence. They looked as if they were lit from within. They glowed with pink auras.

The airship was pulling itself into position by adjusting the length of its mooring lines. It was a tricky maneuver because the pilot also had to keep the ship pointed into the wind. The display boards on its sides were flashing with bright stripes and colored patterns and even a crawling message: HEAVY LIFTING IS OUR BAG. OREGON AIR-LUMBER. Then a moment later: PAUL BUNYAN RESCUES U.S. ARMY. PICTURES AT ELEVEN.

The worms were fascinated by the sight. They turned around and around under the blimp; their eyes were angled upward, blinking furiously. They circled in the clearing, oblivious to everything else; they bumped into each other again and again as they tried to track with the airship. The bunnydogs had to scramble to keep out of their way.

"They're going crazy," I called. "Something about the blimp—"

And then one of the worms *stood up.* It raised itself almost its entire length. I wouldn't have believed it if I hadn't seen it with my own eyes. It *reached* futilely, frantically for the blimp. It stretched its arms upward in a pleading gesture—

I thought of pictures I'd seen of New Christians trying to touch the robes of The Apostle.

—and then the worm opened its mouth and let loose the most incredible sound I'd ever heard from the throat of any creature—a long, high-pitched, warbling-wavering, strung-out-forever wail of hope, desire and *despair.* The sound was *maddening.*

And then the worm fell back down into the dust. It toppled backward, writhing; its two rows of pitifully tiny feet waved in the air for a moment; and then it scrambled around madly trying to right itself— trying to reach for the blimp again.

I felt sorry for it.

The other worms were trying to lift themselves toward the blimp too. They stretched their arms and cried. They wailed. They *worshiped.*

"I don't get it—" Lizard said.

"I do. The blimp looks like a worm. A big bright friendly worm—"

And then the second, *deeper* part of that realization hit me. "—A giant, floating, dazzling, *vision* of a worm! An angel hanging in the sky! Pouring light! In their own image! It looks like a *god* to them!"

"Oh, my God," said Lizard softly. She saw it too.

"Tell the blimp to cut their lights!" I called forward. "It's the lights that are doing it. We're going to have to do this in the dark."

I looked upward again myself. The blimp was beautiful. I could see why the worms were so crazy underneath it. How would you feel if an angel opened the sky and shone its light down on you?

And then the blimp doused its lights and disappeared. It vanished *completely,* cloaked by the night and the thick powdery gloom in the air.

The worms *shrieked.*

They screamed like all the tortured souls of Hell. The sound was hideous.

"Oh, no—" I'd made a mistake.

How would you feel if an angel opened the sky and shone its light down on you? How would you feel if—when you called to that angel—it disappeared and left you behind? *Alone.*

You'd feel damned.

Outside, the worms were raging.

TWENTY-EIGHT

WE WERE left with only the lights of the chopper and the crab. The worms were dark shapes in the night again.

The blimp was a darker shape overhead—not seen, just barely sensed.

The worms were moving again.

They circled and shrieked and raged at the sky. They raged at each other. They raged at the chopper. Something bumped us—*hard*. Duke began to moan again. I wondered if the worms were going to vent their fury on us.

A long dark shape flowed *over* the chopper just a few meters away from me. It startled me so badly, I tried to leap back in the turret and banged my head on the Plexiglas. The chopper creaked with the weight of its passage. The hull crackled and *complained*. Oh, God—

The monster poured down the opposite side and charged at the largest worm in its path. I wished for a spotlight. It shrieked and leapt. It attacked the other worm in a raging fury. The two great beasts wound themselves around each other like serpentine wrestlers and rolled across the powdery dust in a furious tangle. The smoke rose around them.

They broke apart once, then wrapped themselves up in each other again and wrestled off into the darkness, quickly disappearing in the ever-present haze.

I'd never seen that before. I'd never seen a worm attack another worm.

All around the chopper, suddenly *all* the worms were attacking each other. Or, at least, trying to—

They rushed at each other, then jumped away. They circled warily, all the time shrieking and moaning and making low, rumbling sounds. They were hellbeasts. They were terrifying.

Two by two, they paired off, writhing into the gloom. It didn't look like an attack any more—it looked like a ritual of some kind. It looked like—communion. The worms were withdrawing into each other's embraces—as if no one single one of them could figure this out by itself, as if they had to pool their brainpower.

And then suddenly, all the worms were gone. And there was silence. Stillness.

Nothing moved. Even the dust seemed frozen in the air.

The bunnydogs had disappeared. The millipedes were gone. There was nothing but the pale pink dust again.

"Is it over?" asked Lizard.

"I don't know." I made myself let go of the turret handles I'd been gripping. My fingers ached with the sudden release of tension. My chest hurt again.

"What were they doing?"

"I don't know—but let's get out of here now. Quickly! Before they come back!"

Even as I spoke, the crab was scrabbling up the side of the chopper. It poised itself next to the turret and pointed two spotlights and a double-eyed camera at me. One mechanical claw snapped upward in a crisp salute. Automatically, I started to salute back, then pulled my hand down in embarrassment. The crab bobbled its lights as if it were laughing—and waved. I glared back.

"That's cute, McCarthy. Real cute!" Lizard called from up front. She could see me through the crab's eyes—the video was relayed.

"Just what I need," I said. "A crab with a sense of humor. I'm going to kill the operator." I dropped to the cabin floor—

"All right," Lizard was saying, "get your ass out of the way—and Duke's too. I'm going to blow the turret."

I pulled Duke as far forward as I could—I had to ignore his moaning; there was nothing else I could do for him now—and fitted a clean O-mask over his face. Then I climbed up front again to join Lizard. She was just unlocking the trigger. I handed her a mask and hung my own around my neck.

"All set?" she asked the radio.

"You may fire when ready, Grisly."

There were three switches. Lizard flipped the first one. A quietly mechanical voice said, "The explosive bolts are now charged. You have three minutes to arm."

I glanced out the front of the chopper. Two of the worms were returning. They were moving solemnly back into our arena of light. They looked . . . thoughtful.

I pointed silently.

Lizard looked. She glanced sideways at me. "Will they move?"

"I don't know."

"Well, think—what could be worse?"

I didn't answer. I shook my head. I couldn't think of *worse* any more. We'd already gone beyond my capacity to imagine worse.

Lizard flipped the second switch. The mechanical voice said, "The explosive bolts are now armed. You have three minutes to fire."

Two more worms returned. Their eyes were blinking steadily, a sure sign of interest. I started to point—

"I see 'em," Lizard said, without looking up. "Put your mask on. We're getting out of here." The screen in front of her with the radar scan from the blimp was showing a ragged circle of cigar shapes closing in on the chopper again. *All* the worms were returning.

Lizard started pulling her mask on. She paused and grinned sideways at me. "Don't forget. You owe me a lobster dinner, buddy—"

She threw the third switch.

The turret blew off the back of the chopper with a *BANG!*

Almost immediately, a swirl of dust came filtering down through the hole. I started scrambling back. The crab was positioning itself over the escape hatch. Its lower eyes peered into the chopper, swiveling forward. Then, two of its claws dropped the fourth and last line into the cabin. Someone had painted ANCHOR ME on the grapple at the end of the line. I grabbed it and hooked it under one of the seats.

"Zip line's on its way down," said Lizard.

I looked up and saw something dropping from the sky. It was illuminated by a single red beacon. The crab stepped back out of its way. The object—it was a gurney basket and a couple of harnesses attached to a cable-rider—banged onto the roof of the ship. The crab grabbed the gurney basket and fed it down through the turret, then the harnesses.

I pulled the basket forward. "Come on, Lizard. I need your help." Duke's moans were louder now. We lifted him as gently as we could into the basket. I checked the seals on the medi-blanket while Lizard strapped him in, then I hung the console in the slot provided for it.

The crab was lowering three connector cables into the cabin. I snapped the first to the head of Duke's basket. I tossed a harness at Lizard and grabbed the other for myself. "The cameras—" I said.

"I've got all the recordings right here," Lizard said, patting her flight bag. She passed the second connector cable through its handles before snapping it onto her harness. "They're safe."

I finished shrugging into my harness and connected the third cable. "All right," I said. "Duke first, then you. I'll bring up the rear."

"Sorry, Lieutenant," she said. "The captain is the last to leave the ship. You go second."

"I'm going to cover your rear," I insisted.

"You'll wait until after dinner—and that's an order. All right—" she said to the crab, "—let's have a little help lifting this basket."

The cables began to retract. The basket pulled back, then upward toward the turret as the cable continued tightening. We guided it carefully up through the opening. I climbed up after it, then turned and pulled Lizard up after me. Then I started shivering. The night air was *cold.*

There were worms all around the chopper, sitting and watching us. Their black bulks were huge in the gloom. I couldn't tell how many there were, but there were more than fourteen of them now, that was for sure. There could have been thirty or fifty. I couldn't tell. But I could hear the sounds of their eyes blinking. *Sput-phwut. Sput-phwut.*

Lizard steadied herself on my arm, then leaned over and gave me a quick kiss on the lips. "Thanks," she said. She turned to the crab and gave a thumbs-up signal. The crab returned it with one mechanical claw.

And then the worms screamed again! *"Chtorrrrr! Chtorrrrrrr—!"*

—and swarmed in toward the chopper. One of them flowed up the front of the craft—the chopper's windshield cracked under its weight. It kept on coming anyway. It was on top of the ship now, pouring toward us—

—the crab swiveled all its spotlights and hit it with its brightest glare. The worm recoiled, blinking. The crab scuttled toward it, waving all its arms and legs and everything else—all its cameras, lights and attachments—in as threatening a manner as possible. The worm backed away, uncertainly—

—and then suddenly, the cable-rider was screaming up the line, yanking us with it! Duke screamed at the jolt as the basket leapt upward; he must have been in incredible pain. I gasped in surprise, and

Lizard yelled like a kid on a roller coaster. The chopper dropped away below us. It was an oasis of pink light in a sea of ink.

I could see that more of the worms were swarming up onto it now. The crab retreated before their onslaught. It clamped itself to the line and followed us up. A worm grabbed for it and missed.

And then the chopper was too far below to see anything else clearly.

I glanced upward. The blimp was an ominous hole in the night. Its lights were still off and we were hurtling toward a gigantic darkness. A square of yellow warmth opened directly overhead. The color of the light was startling. After two days of nothing but pinkness, it looked *alien.*

The square expanded, it became a hatch—we rose up through it and suddenly we were *inside* the blimp—first the basket, then me, then Colonel Tirelli.

There were men and women in jumpsuits to pull us aboard, to swing us away from the hatch, grab us and disconnect the cables from our harnesses. They were applauding and cheering. It was all a blur of faces and hands. I couldn't hear. I couldn't focus my eyes. They were too wet.

Someone was helping me out of my harness and O-mask. I kept blinking in confusion. All the light—all the noise—all these people! It was too dazzling!

And the room—it was *huge.* We could have put the chopper in it and we'd still have room for a dance floor. I saw the dust-covered crab come lifting through a great hole in the floor. The last of the line came up after it.

The hole closed up and a man with a headset said, "A2 is aboard and the hatch is *closed.* Retrieval is *complete.*" There was more cheering at this. Even I was cheering now—between paroxysms of coughing. I was having trouble breathing again.

"Release the mooring harpoons," the man with the headset said. "Let's go to Oakland." He grinned at me. "The lieutenant wants a lobster."

I looked at Lizard and blushed.

She *winked* at me.

TWENTY-NINE

FOUR MEN grabbed the basket with Duke and disappeared through a door. Two others led Lizard and myself out through another exit. We followed them down a long corridor and into a medical facility. They split us up then, putting Lizard in one cubbyhole and me in another.

A minute later, a teenage girl in a white jacket came in carrying a medi-kit and sat down in front of me. "How are you feeling?"

I took inventory and reported, "Hoarse. Sore throat from the dust. Pressure in my chest. Trouble breathing. Lots of coughing. Pain. Eyes hurt. Ears hurt. I want a bath. I'm still cold. I feel great!" I grinned at her.

She smiled sweetly but impersonally. "Okay, take off your shirt." She was already opening her kit.

"Huh? Where's the doctor?"

"I'm the doctor. Take off your shirt."

"Uh—" I shut up and took off my shirt. She stuck poker chips to my chest, my arms, my neck and my temples.

She studied her readouts, nodded, and blanked the screen before I could peek over her shoulder. She peered into my mouth, my nose, my eyes, and my ears. She nodded and said, "Mm hm. Wait a moment. I'll be right back."

She returned with a tray. On it was a pressure injector, a glass of orange juice, and a small plastic container with a handful of capsules.

"Antibiotics and vitamins," she explained. She touched the pressure injector to my arm. It hissed. I felt a cold wet sensation.

She handed me the capsules and the orange juice. I took them without complaint. The juice was sweet and cold.

"All right," she said. "You can put your shirt back on now." She left. The whole process had taken less than five minutes.

As I fastened my shirt, I wondered if I should wait here—or what?

I stuck my head out of the cubbyhole. A man in a jumpsuit with a *Paul Bunyan* patch over his heart was waiting there. "Lieutenant McCarthy?"

I nodded.

"Colonel Anderson requests your presence in the forward lounge. Follow me please?"

I followed.

The crewman led me to the forward lounge and told me to make myself comfortable. "Colonel Anderson will be along shortly. The bar is open if you want anything." Then he left.

The lounge seemed almost as big as the loading bay. It had tall, slanting windows circling in a vast horseshoe. I stepped to the very front and peered out.

The airship's running lights had been turned on again. There must have been a huge bank of spotlights just above the lounge, because the whole sky ahead glowed with the reflected light. It looked like we were plowing through pink fog. There was nothing else to see.

I could feel a faint vibration beneath my feet. We were under power. Captain Price must be using the cold-rocket assist. No other engine would function in this weather.

There was a well-stocked bar at the back of the lounge. I sauntered back and told the robot to make me a Staggering Buffalo and go easy on the soy. I found a seat by the window, still marveling at the sense of luxury in this airship. It was true; the heavy lifters had space to *waste*.

"Lieutenant McCarthy?"

I looked up. And up.

The man had shoulders the size of Ohio. He had a broken nose and a beefy grin. He stuck out a paw at me. I stared at it for a few seconds before I realized what he wanted. I leapt to my feet and saluted. "Sir?"

He returned my salute with something that looked more like a wave than a salute, then stuck out his hand again. I offered mine and he shook my hand gently. When he let go, I wanted to stare at my fingers. He *hadn't* crushed them.

"I'm Danny Anderson," he said. His voice resonated like the inside of a hangar. He had a smile as wide as the door. "I want to thank you for the job you did on my father. You saved his life."

"Uh—I hate to disagree with a superior officer, sir—" *Especially one as big as you.* "—But I didn't do half the job I should have—"

"Oh? Could you have done better than you did?" He raised a bushy eyebrow at me.

"Sir, I did the very best I could. It just wasn't as good as I could have done if I'd had the proper supplies. We ran out of everything—"

He started laughing. I stared at him. He caught himself and stopped, but the grin remained.

He put a hand on my shoulder. "I'm not laughing at you, son. Colonel Tirelli told me you would do this. I'm trying to thank you and you're too busy devaluing your contribution to hear me. You're going to have to knock that off, Lieutenant."

"Uh—" I was doing it again. "Right. Thank you, sir."

"Good. Now, let me tell it to you again. You did a good job. You saved Captain Anderson's life. Colonel Tirelli is putting you in for a medal."

I hardly heard the last. "Uh—thank you, sir. Uh, can I ask, how is Duke—Captain Anderson?"

Danny Anderson hesitated. He looked embarrassed, and his voice went curiously flat. "It—uh, looks like he's going to make it. His vital signs steadied out as soon as we got him on Code Blue Maintenance. But it's still too early to say what kind of shape he's going to be in." And then he added quietly, "He might lose his legs."

The balloon I'd been holding inside my chest suddenly lost all its air. I sank back down into my seat. "It's that red furry stuff, isn't it? I was afraid of this. I gave him terramycin, but I didn't know what else I could do—"

Danny Anderson sat down opposite me. He put his hand on my shoulder again. "Hey!" he interrupted. "I thought I told you to knock that off."

I gulped. "I'm sorry, sir. It's just—so damned frustrating! I mean—he's been like a dad to me, and—" I looked up at him. "Well—you know what he's like—"

"No," he said, coldly. "I don't."

"Huh—?"

"Don't worry about it, McCarthy." There was something hard in his voice. "That's not your concern."

"Oh. Uh—yes, sir. I—" shut up. And wondered.

"Listen to me," he said. "What's done is done. This is it. This is how it turned out. Like it or not.

"So stop arguing against me inside your head and let me congratulate you. The video that you and Colonel Tirelli brought back with you may be the most important recordings we've got. Those bunnydogs are incredible!"

I swallowed hard. I said, "I think they may be the next step of the invasion."

"I won't argue with you, Lieutenant. You had more opportunity to observe the creatures than anyone else."

"Yes sir."

"Now, I know you're tired and sore. I know you're probably hungry for a decent meal, a hot bath and a bed. We've got all of those waiting for you. But first—we want to debrief you while it's all still fresh in your memory. Can you manage that?"

I nodded. "Get me a pitcher of coffee and a straw, and I'm yours. No, better make that an IV bottle."

"Sorry, no coffee. We have tea and cocoa."

"No coffee?"

He shook his head. "Not at thirty caseys for a half-kilo of beans."

"The bean-rot?"

He nodded. "Congress closed the border. The only coffee you're going to get from now on will be greenhouse-bean. If you can afford it."

"I'll have the cocoa, thanks."

"Good. Now, we're going to set you up in one of the cabins with a standard ECO-6 debriefing program and two technicians. I'll try and stick my head in for a while too. Will that work for you?"

I nodded.

"Good." He clapped my shoulder. "Ready to go?"

"I'll need something for my cough. An O-mask?"

"I'll have the doctor bring whatever you need."

"Thank you, sir." I stood up and followed him aft.

I made it almost three-quarters of the way through the debriefing before I started coughing and passed out.

THIRTY

I WOKE up again in the ambulance. We were slowing. There was something happening outside.

I could hear someone with a bullhorn trying to give instructions to a crowd. They weren't listening. Scattered voices were hollering their defiance. I wondered if they were turning into a mob.

I wondered where I was.

I was flat on my back, staring at a plastic ceiling. I turned my head. A curtained window. I raised a hand. My chest ached. I pushed the curtain open.

The day was still pink, the air, the sky—

There were frightened people everywhere. On the lawns, on the driveways, and most of all, crowded around the emergency entrance. Some of them had been waiting all night for treatment. They looked tired and drawn. Their eyes were red, their faces were puffy. Was this turning into another plague? Would this be the one that finally destroyed our ability to resist?

And then the ambulance was stopping and the orderlies slid me out like a side of beef and onto a cart. Somebody in white grabbed hold behind me, and then we were moving—quickly—through a sea of painful, anxious faces. Somebody else was parting the crowds ahead of us. I turned my head to look at them. The people were huddling in the entrance hall, five deep. They were lined up in ragged formations, waiting. I thought I saw military guards. Were we under attack? No, those were riot helmets—

The hospital was a nightmare.

It was a wall of noise—children crying, people arguing, somebody screaming. The sound pressed in like an assault; each component voice was edged with hysteria. A woman was shrieking with rage—

—the cart lurched. And nearly toppled. The shrieking woman had grabbed it. She was screaming in my face. She yanked the blanket off me— "See! Another goddamn soldier! I knew it! The military is getting preferential treatment! They're going to let the rest of us die—!" And then they were pulling her off me, and the cart was rolling again, faster than before—

I didn't see what happened to her.

I heard voices. They were arguing about me. We were stopped again.

"—I can't do anything more for him than's already been done. Give him a shot and an inhaler and send him home to rest—"

"With third-degree pink lung?"

"When it turns into dust poisoning bring him back—"

"I'm not paid to take them home. I only deliver the meat—and this one's already signed in. He's got an army A-plus priority, and your Chief of Surgery already accepted delivery."

"Did they also tell you where the hell we're going to put him? The halls are already full of air mattresses—"

"That's not my problem. Here, read his chart—"

"I can't do this! I'll have to pull the plug on someone else—"

"That's not my problem."

Suddenly, someone bent her face close to mine. She looked tired and angry. "Open your eyes!" she demanded. "Can you move?"

I couldn't even speak. I made a noise—not even strong enough to be a moan. It turned into a cough. It came out pink.

I think I won the argument.

Now the cart was rolling again, this time faster than before—

—came awake again as they were sliding me onto a bed. I blinked through tears of pain, turned my head and squinted at the light.

This was a private room!

I tried to protest, but I didn't have even enough air to croak. I pointed toward the door, the unseen crowds, and waved my hand frantically—despite the pain it cost me.

The nurse just pushed me back down and said, "No, you don't. Your job is to be here now." He was a chubby little man with a well-scrubbed face. He could have been anywhere between thirty and fifty. He looked like someone's maiden aunt, but he had surprisingly strong arms. He held me down and pushed a breathing mask onto my nose and mouth. "Now, just relax—" he said. "I'll be right here the whole time."

I was dimly aware that something was happening. There were other people in the room now.

Something bit my arm. I let go and floated.

And waited to see if I was going to die.

I watched from above while they poked, they prodded, and they scanned. They set me up for DX studies and the Kelley series of broad-band vaccines, processes and affirmations. Then they "vacuumed" my lungs—which turned out to be nowhere near as painful as it sounded—and put me in an oxygen-helium tent.

And then they left me alone.

I floated and waited.

The reaction set in the next morning.

I woke up somewhere on the other side of death. I was trying to fight my way back, but I was smothering in marshmallow. I couldn't breathe.

There were alarm bells ringing all around me. Sometime in the night, my lungs had decided enough was enough and begun to inflame.

My chest was a balloon.

I was trying to breathe. Nothing was happening. I was trying to scream, but no noise was coming out of my throat either. There was no air to scream with. Even as I thrashed on the bed, I knew I was doing the wrong thing.

And then something cold touched my arm—and something bit me on the chest—and something wet was sliding down my throat—

I faded out.

And in again.

I still couldn't breathe. I faded out again—

And in. And out. I lost count.

And then one night, I woke up gasping. My throat was raw. And dry. I wanted water. I managed to holler—and my lungs screamed in agony! That was a mistake. I wanted to die, just to end the pain.

Somebody was saying something to me. "It's all right, Lieutenant. Just relax. See if you can relax." I tried to focus on the voice. All I saw was a blur. The room was too dim.

"Don't talk," he said. He held me up gently, cradling me and feeding me soup in small delicious doses. "Just eat. I'll talk." It was the nurse with the very clean face.

"Mmmf," I said, splurting soup.

He wiped my mouth with a napkin. "You're at Oakland General. It's Monday evening and you've already missed tonight's episode of *Derby*. Too bad. It was a good one. Grant is still looking for the missing robot, but now he knows it's still in the plant. Carrie found out about the last DV-sale—T. J. told her, of course—and now she's demanding a stockholders' meeting. Everything depends on Stephanie, but she refuses to leave Hong Kong, and nobody knows why. Ready for more?"

"Mmfl."

"Good. Open wide. So, compared to that, your problems are nothing, right?"

I didn't answer. My lungs hurt too much. Besides, Grant should have known from the beginning that T. J. couldn't risk having that robot's memory dumped.

"All right, one more slurp and we're done. There you go. Dr. Fletcher will be in to have a look at you in a little bit."

Dr. Fletcher was wearing gloves and a mask. All I could see were her eyes. They looked tired.

The first thing she said to me was, "Don't talk. You run the risk of destroying your vocal cords." She sat down on the edge of the bed and looked into my eyes, my ears, my nose. She studied the medi-console on her lap. Then, she looked at me and said, "Congratulations."

"Mm?"

"You'll live. We didn't expect you to. The tissues of your lungs were so swollen, there was no room for air. We had you on lung support for three days. You're one of the lucky ones. There were more than two thousand others who didn't make it—because we didn't have the machines for them."

I wanted to ask—but she put a finger across my mouth before I could speak.

"I said, *don't talk.*" She hesitated, then added, "You had one of the worst cases of dust poisoning in the state, Lieutenant. We should have pulled the plug on you—we needed the bed space—but your commanding officer wouldn't allow it. She said you owed her a lobster dinner, and you weren't going to get out of your obligations that easy.

"Besides, we needed to discover something, and you helped us do it. We now know that dust poisoning is reversible in even the *worst* cases. If we can save you, then we can save anybody. We're already preparing for next year."

"Umf," I said. I held up a hand to stop her from going.

"You're going to be all right," she said. "Don't worry. The worst is over."

I grabbed her arm. "Mmf?"

"Colonel Tirelli is all right too."

"Dmk!"

"And Duke. He's in intensive care and his condition is stabilized. We're watching him closely. You did a good job on him, Lieutenant. You can be proud."

"Mp."

"I'm going to put you back to sleep now," she said. "And then I'm going to put you back on maintenance. It'll be easier for you." She touched a button on the medi-console.

And I went out again.

THIRTY-ONE

THE NEXT time Dr. Fletcher came in, I was more coherent.

She picked up the console and studied it. Did all hospital personnel do that automatically?

"How am I?" I asked.

"You're fine," she said. "And I can say that with authority, because I am your personal physician. Only the president and movie stars get better treatment."

She sat down on the edge of the bed and put her hand on mine. "The truth is, all medical personnel in the science section were moved over to help with the emergency. But, even if that weren't the case, you'd still be under my care. You are not so much a medical case as a scientific one."

"Because I had the worst exposure to the dust?"

"You were one of the first," she said. "So if any weird effects were going to show up, we'd expect to see them in you first."

"And . . . ?"

"And I am disappointed to tell you that the dust is about as benign as a Chtorran life-form can be. The death toll is expected to remain below three thousand."

"Disappointed?"

"Mm hm. I was hoping you'd be an interesting case. Too bad. I guess I'm just going to have to go back to my worms."

"Worms? Plural?"

"Uh huh. We've got two more live ones."

"Dr. Fletcher?"

"Yes?"

"Have you ever put any of them together . . . ?"

"They're in the same tank, why?"

"Do they—I don't know how to phrase this—do they roll around together like they're making love?"

She looked surprised. "How do you know about that? We've only had them together for a few days. The whole thing is still very secret."

"You haven't seen the videos we brought—?"

She raised an eyebrow at me. "In all my spare time? In case you hadn't noticed—"

"Right. Sorry. Well, we saw the wrestling behavior when the blimp arrived. The worms got frantic. At first I thought they were attacking each other, but they weren't. They came back. They looked . . . confused—but I wouldn't even begin to guess what was going on."

"Mm," she said. She looked like she was considering something.

"I want to see your worms," I said.

She nodded. "I want to see your videos. As soon as you're ambulatory again, okay? I'll set it up." She stood up to go. "There's a wheelchair in the closet if you want to get out of bed. Please ask a nurse to assist you. Don't be proud."

"Thanks. What room is Colonel Tirelli in?"

"She checked out three days ago. But Captain Anderson is upstairs and you can visit him any time." She remembered something. "Oh—you have messages, quite a stack of them. Please read the priority ones first. And I think your mother wants to visit you. Handle that, all right?" And then she was out the door.

After a while, I buzzed for assistance and got myself bathed, shaved and transferred to a wheelchair. I found my way up to the twelfth floor without too much trouble.

Duke was still in an oxygen tent.

He looked dreadful. He looked like the guest of honor at a Texas barbecue. I couldn't look and I couldn't look away. His face was swollen. His eyes were blistered shut. His skin was blackened and peeling. His arms looked wet and putrefying. And he smelled bad.

I almost fled in horror. Human beings should not look like this. Human beings should not *smell* like this. But I didn't know how to put the wheelchair in reverse, and the little voice in my head was already bawling me out for being a coward. I steeled myself and stayed.

I rolled around to the foot of his bed and picked up the medi-console.

Duke was on maintenance. He was beyond consciousness.

For that I was grateful. There was not a lot to say. And I wasn't sure I could talk to him yet. Not with him looking like something out of a horror show. This wasn't Duke. I couldn't rectify this monstrous piece of meat with the man I had spent so much time with.

I didn't see how he could ever be human again. He might live. But his life was over. I don't know how I knew. I just knew it.

My mind brought up memories. Duke had taught me almost everything I knew about how to be a military man. He'd made it very simple, he'd boiled it down to two words.

Be certain.

"Here's how to know if you're certain," he'd said. "Can I rip your arm off if you're wrong? If you can't give me an unqualified yes, then you're still not certain.

"That thing that you ignore—that thing that you let yourself be unaware of, or unconscious of, or uncertain about—that's the thing that's going to kill you. So your job, whatever it looks like, is really this: you have to know everything about *everything* that you have to deal with.

"There are no accidents, Jim. If you get killed, the game is over. You lost."

Simple.

Except . . . what would you call lying in a hospital bed looking like a bride's first roast?

Duke had screwed up somewhere. He'd trusted *me*. It didn't matter what Colonels Tirelli and Anderson said. This was my fault.

I wished I could wake him up long enough to ask him to forgive me.

Except I knew he wouldn't.

THIRTY-TWO

TWO DAYS later, my chest scan came up clean and they checked me out of the hospital. They needed the bed space. "Go visit your mother," they told me. "She's been bugging us three times a day."

My mom was in Santa Cruz, doing something with maps—I wasn't sure what. She said she'd explain when I got there. I checked out a Jeep from the motor pool and headed south on I-117.

It was over an hour's drive, but I barely noticed. The whole way there, all I could hear was the argument inside my head.

I was considering resigning my commission.

It was something that Dr. Fletcher had said; it still rankled. "You and I have two different jobs. Your job is to kill worms. My job is to study them." I was looking at myself in a mirror and wondering how the hell I'd gotten *here*. This wasn't where I'd *wanted* to be.

What I really wanted to do was what Dr. Fletcher was doing—study the worms. But how could I do that with stripes on my sleeves? They kept putting weapons into my hands and that guaranteed that all I could do was kill worms. That was the thing about being in the army— there weren't a whole lot of options.

But killing the worms—at least the way we were doing it now—was *not* working.

The Chtorran ecology was eating us alive.

Its microorganisms alone had killed billions of people. Those of us who survived the plagues still had to deal with the sea sludge, the stingflies, the bladderbugs, the red kudzu, the oilworms, the "grab-grass," the binnies, the libbits, the meeps—and of course, always and inevitably, the worms.

Our ancestors had killed the dinosaurs. We'd sucked their eggs and eaten their children. We still ate their descendants today: chickens, ducks, and turkeys. If tyrannosaur and hadrosaur and deinonychus still walked the Earth, we'd find a way to eat them too. The Chtorrans would do the same to us. They couldn't see us as anything more than food. Do you talk with your sandwich?

And if this was only the first wave of the invasion—as Dr. Zymph kept saying—what horrors were *still* waiting to manifest themselves?

How long did it take to Chtorra-form a planet? How many waves of infestation?

There *had* to be an intelligence behind this madness—but it might not show up for centuries, perhaps not until long after the last human being was . . . what? In a zoo? In a museum? Did we figure at all in the equation?

I didn't think so.

But—

—if I really felt that way, then why did I bother to keep on fighting? If the situation was that hopeless, why not just lay down and die?

Because—I had to smile at myself—I still didn't really believe it. I *knew* it, but I didn't believe it.

But none of this had anything to do with the army anyway. The army was irrelevant. We were holding back the worms by sheer brute force because we couldn't think of anything else to do.

No, it wasn't the futility of the situation that was making me think about resigning. I'd fight the worms forever, no matter how ugly the odds.

No. This was really about Duke.

I felt responsible.

Damn it anyway!

It was Shorty all over again, but with a vengeance. I'd burned Shorty —and the worm that came down on top of him. Shorty had been lucky; he'd died quick; but Duke might take years—

If I did resign, I could probably go to work immediately for Dr. Fletcher. I already had the security clearance.

It was very tempting. I even went so far as to unclip my phone from my belt—

But I didn't call. No. I might be able to resign from the army; I'd fulfilled the basic obligation over a year ago; but I'd never be able to resign from the pain.

And that was the real issue.

I pulled off the freeway in Santa Cruz, but inside my head I was still in the same place. Stuck.

And I wasn't looking forward to seeing my mother either. I knew what that was going to be like.

She had an office-apartment in a private (read *fortress*) community called Fantasy Valley Towers, a sprawling complex of bubbles, domes, and spires like something out of a Hollywood fairy tale. The style was called Apocalypse Baroque. Inside the walls, it was a maze of arches, terraces and balconies. Before the plagues, it must have been very expensive. Now it looked run down—and even a little *wild*.

The front doors of Mother's apartment were twice as tall as I was, and they looked like they were made out of crystal. But the effect was spoiled by the unswept leaves piled up against the portico.

Mother answered the door with a flourish and a wild laugh. She was wearing a gaudy concoction of bright silks and feathers; she was a cascade of pink and scarlet—and around her neck, she had a silver and turquoise Navajo squash blossom necklace, with twelve jeweled squashes on each side. It looked heavy. So did the rings on her fingers.

"Ahh—here's my baby now!" she cried. She presented her cheek for a kiss. It tasted of powder. She had a glass in her hand. "I'm sorry we didn't come and visit you in the hospital, but they wouldn't let us—"

"It's all right. I wouldn't have been very good company anyway—"

She took my wrist and led me out onto the terrace, calling loudly, "Alan—! Alan! Jim is here! Jim, you remember Alan, don't you?"

"The surfer—?"

"No, silly. That was Bobbie—" Bobbie had been only two years older than me; when I met him he still hadn't decided what he wanted to be when he grew up. "—This is Alan Wise. You remember, I told you about him—"

"No, you told me about Alan Plaskow."

"I did?"

"Uh huh. I don't think I know this Alan."

"Oh, well—"

This Alan was tall and blond and graying at the temples. When he smiled, his eyes crinkled. His handshake was just a little too hearty, and his chest was in the process of migrating south toward his stomach.

There was another man on the terrace too. He was short and dark and of Japanese descent. He wore thick glasses and a dark gray business suit. He looked like a lawyer. Alan introduced him as Shibumi Takahara. Mr. Takahara bowed politely. I bowed back.

Alan slapped me on the shoulder and said, "Well, son—it must feel good to get home for a little old-fashioned cooking, eh?"

"Uh—yes, sir. It does." Except this wasn't *home* and my mother hadn't cooked a meal herself since before the *Hindenberg* went down.

"What are you drinking?" he asked. He was already at the bar, dropping ice into a glass. " 'Nita? Do you want a refill?"

"Do you know how to make a Sylvia Plath?" I asked.

"A what—?"

"Never mind. You probably don't have the ingredients anyway."

Mom was looking at me funny. "What's a Sylvia Plath, Jim?"

I shrugged. "It's not important. It was just a joke."

"No, tell us—" she insisted.

Mr. Takahara answered her. "It's a layer of mercury, a layer of salad oil, and a layer of crème de menthe. You drink only the top layer." I looked at him sharply. Behind his glasses, his eyes were twinkling.

Mom frowned. "I'm afraid I don't get the joke. Do you get it, Alan?"

" 'Fraid it's a little too deep for me, hon. How's about a Crimson Death?"

"Uh, no thanks. I've had enough Crimson Death this month. I'll just have a beer, if you don't mind."

"Don't mind at all," he said. He ducked behind the bar, muttering to himself. "Beer, beer . . . where's the beer—? Ah!" He came up with a slender green bottle. "Here we go—private stock. Imported especially for you from exotic, erotic, exciting . . . Topeka!" He poured with a flourish.

"Down the side, please—" I pointed.

"Eh?"

"You pour beer down the side of the glass, not the center—"

"Oh, well—it's too late now. Sorry." He handed me the glass of beer suds and the still half-full bottle. "I'll know for next time, right?"

"Yeah, right." There wasn't going to be a *next* time.

"I guess I'm just not used to pouring my own drinks," he said, sitting again. He patted the couch next to him and glanced toward my mother. She came over and sat down—a little too close. "I'm too used to being taken care of." He grinned and slid his arm around my mother's shoulders.

Mother said, "Alan—Jim's been off fighting those awful Chtorrans—"

"Oh? Really?" He looked interested. "Have you actually *seen*
any—?"

"Uh—first of all, it's pronounced 'Ktorran.' The 'Ch' is silent. It's
sort of a click before the 'T.' Just say the word 'victor' and leave off the
'vi-.' "

"Oh, well—" my mother said, excusing herself with a wave. "I never
watch the news. I only read about them in the morning papers."

"—And, yes," I said to Alan of the hearty handshake; I said it coldly,
"I *have* seen a few. Quite a few, in fact."

"Really?" he asked. "They really exist?"

I nodded. I sipped at my beer. I wiped my mouth with the back of my
hand. I was debating inside whether I should be polite or tell the truth.
My mother had the "dance for Grandma" expression on her face, Alan
Wise wore a big plastic smile, but Mr. Takahara was watching me
quietly. The truth won out.

I looked across at Alan Wise and asked, "Where have you been that
you don't know what's happening?"

He shrugged, "Right here. The good old U.S. of A. Where have *you*
been?"

"Colorado. Wyoming. Northern California."

"You're kidding! We have—how do you say it?—Torrans right here
in California?"

"One of the worst infestations I've ever seen. Just north of Clear
Lake."

"Well . . . I'll be damned." He looked at my mother and gave her a
little squeeze. "I didn't know that. Maybe we should drive up some
Sunday and have a look. What do you think, 'Nita?"

I blinked. He couldn't really have meant that! I put my glass down on
the end table, and said quietly, "That area is sealed off. And even if it
weren't, that wouldn't be a very good idea."

"Oh, come now—" He dismissed me as casually as if I'd just told him
the sky was pink. This far south and this close to the coast, it wasn't. "I
think you're exaggerating the case, son. It's just some more of that same
military thinking that got us into Pakistan thirteen-fourteen years ago.
Of course, you probably don't remember that. You were just a little tyke
then—"

"I know about Pakistan," I said. I'd had time to do a lot of reading in
the hospital.

"Well—let me tell you something, son. You're too close to the forest. You don't have the perspective. You don't have objectivity. Y'see, this thing with the Ch'torrans, K'torrans, whatever—it's overrated. Oh, now—" he held up a hand to keep me from interrupting "—I'll *grant* that there's really something out there. I'm sure that some old lady somewhere was actually frightened out of her panties by a big pink caterpillar; but when you look at the *whole* picture—like I have—you'll see that a young man like yourself needs to be looking toward the future."

"If there is one," I said dryly. Mr. Takahara's eyes narrowed thoughtfully.

"Oh now, don't give me that liberal-defeatist crap. That song and dance may work on a congressman—but you're talking to Alan Wise here, and you know your mother doesn't hang out with dummies."

"Mmm, if you say so."

"Listen, I know how the game is played. The military has to make the war look serious to justify all those heavyweight appropriations. Read your history, son! The more money they want, the worse the war gets. It's all about John Q. Taxpayer and his hard-earned Labor Standard Kilocalorie banknotes. The truth is, this is a terrific time for a smart man who knows how to read a newspaper."

"I beg your pardon?"

"I'm talking big money, son. Corporations. Licenses, Federal grants. I want you to know, there's an incredible opportunity here!"

"Huh—?"

"It's raining soup!" he said. "It's time to grab your bucket! I'm in the Reclamation Industry—and people are making fortunes every day! It's all there for the taking. There are huge areas still waiting to be reopened —whole cities. Somebody's got to go in and do the job—and whoever does it is going to get rich. *Very* rich. The government knows this. The *army* knows it. But all this war-scare stuff is keeping people from seeing the real problem—that big government has got its hands in our pockets again. *And* it's a very good excuse for the army to go in and nationalize the unclaimed property. You pay attention, son—read the papers! Not just that K'torran stuff. You'll see what's going on."

My mother gave his arm a squeeze and said, "Alan works so hard—" She looked across at me with an expression that said, Don't start an argument.

"Mr. Wise—" I said.

"Alan," he corrected.

I ignored it. "—Mr. Wise, I am a lieutenant in the United States Army, Special Forces Warrant Agency. We take care of those *special* challenges that are beyond the duties of the regular army. As such," I explained, "we are under the direct command of the President of the United States. The Special Forces is currently assigned to one task and one task only: the eradication of all Chtorran gastropedes—we call them worms—from the continental United States and Alaska. Hawaii is not presently infested.

"In the course of my duties, I have come in contact with over a hundred of the monsters. I have been personally responsible for the deaths of fifteen of them. I have one of the highest kill ratios in the Special Forces. If we had such classifications, I would be considered an ace. So I will tell you this about the worms—"

"Jim—" my mother interrupted. "I don't think this is the time or place for war stories."

I caught myself. I looked at my mother, and at Alan Wise. And realized something. They were both a little red-faced and happy-looking. They were both drunk. I couldn't tell about Mr. Takahara. He was a silent enigma.

What was it Duke had told me once? When a drunk and a fool get into an argument, you can't tell which is which. You have to wait until the drunk sobers up. The other one is the fool. How do you know when a drunk and a fool are in an argument? Easy. Anyone who argues with a drunk is automatically a fool.

Right.

"No, no, hon. Let him talk. I want to hear—" Alan Wise turned and nuzzled my mother's cheek, her neck—he nibbled her ear. She squealed and protested, but she didn't push him away.

I said, "Actually, I don't think we can have this conversation at all—"

"Eh?" He looked up at me.

"—because you really don't know what you're talking about, Mr. Wise. When you've done your research properly, then we can talk." I stood up. Their faces were gaping. "If you'll excuse me, I have to go to the bathroom."

THIRTY-THREE

MY MOTHER was waiting for me when I came out of the bathroom. I'd have been disappointed in her if she hadn't.

"What is the matter with you!" she whispered angrily. "All I wanted was a quiet little evening with the two men in my life! Is that too much to ask! Do you have to ruin everything? Now, I want you to go back in there and apologize—"

I headed for the front door instead.

Her voice went up an octave. "Where are you going?"

"Back to the military-industrial complex for a little more brainwashing," I growled.

Alan Wise of the hearty handshake was leaning up against the front door. I guess he thought that would stop me.

"Son," he said.

"I am not your son—" I warned.

"Whether you apologize to me or not is unimportant. But I certainly think you owe an apology to your mother. You're being rude in her house."

A half dozen possible replies flashed through my head, most of them having to do with the inhabitants of my mother's bedroom. I discarded all of them as being unworthy.

I opened my mouth. I closed it. I realized that whatever I said would only make it worse. The situation was a zero-sum game. I could apologize and be wrong, or I could remove Mr. Wise from the door and leave —and be wrong. It was a question of how wrong I wanted to be. I knew

I sure as hell wasn't going to apologize. I only apologized to people I *liked.*

I started to turn away. The hell with it. I turned back. I said, "Listen —I didn't mean to infer that you don't know anything. You may know quite a bit about your field—but you don't know anything about *my* field. I know the Chtorran ecology. I just spent three days buried up to my ass in it and three weeks in a hospital recovering. I know what we're up against. You can tell me anything you want about anything else, but I've seen the worms. I've seen what they can do. I've seen—"

And stopped in the middle of my tirade.

And realized something.

Three days buried in pink dust—and I hadn't seen the most obvious thing!

Those worms—every single one of them—from the first worm that Duke and I encountered to the congregation that clustered around the chopper to worship the blimp—those worms were the first ones I'd ever seen that had not *immediately* attacked a human being on sight.

I turned away from Alan Wise and my mother and my anger and walked out onto the terrace again. I held up my hand as a signal for them to leave me alone.

What if he was right—?

Not about all that political crap—but what if he was right about the worms? What if the truth was, they were *not* hostile?

I picked up my beer and carried it to the balcony rail. I looked out toward the Santa Cruz mountains. Were there worms up there? I wondered.

Look—I told myself—every worm I've ever encountered, I've had a torch in my hands and I've burned it. And that was because all the worms I'd ever seen—until the episode in the dust—had been hostile.

But then—I'd always had a torch in my hands. The episode in the dust was the first time I hadn't. And that was the first time I saw nonhostile worms.

Could it be that the worms were somehow sensing and reacting to my own hostility—?

It was a fascinating idea.

—If I could meet a worm in a situation with no hostility in it, would it still attack?

There was no way to test it. No, check that. There was no *safe* way to test it.

We'd made up our minds that the worms were a threat—so we were burning them. What if the worms were only a threat to us because we were a threat to them?

The other factor in that equation, of course, was the bunnydogs.

Based on the evidence I'd seen so far, you could make a very good case that the bunnydogs controlled the worms. If so, then we knew that the worms *could* be controlled. Now if we could find out *how*—

I needed to talk about this with Dr. Fletcher.

"Jim—" That was my mother. "Are you all right?"

I turned around. Alan Wise was standing behind her. They both looked concerned. Mr. Takahara had discreetly absented himself.

I nodded. "I'm fine. I really am. It's just—I just realized something very important." I looked past her to Alan Wise. "You were the catalyst. Something you said. It triggered an idea. Thank you. And—" What the hell, Lizard said it was the one thing I was good at. "—I'm sorry I flew off the handle, I really am—"

"Apology accepted." He waved magnanimously. He was still a jerk, but at least I didn't have to hate him for it any more.

I turned back to my mom. "I need to get back to Oakland—"

"Without eating—? You just got here!"

"Won't it wait?" Alan asked.

"Um—this is really important."

"Well, so is dinner. There's something Alan wants to talk to you about. I specifically invited you so he could—"

We started off with fresh tomato juice, pâté, and a spinach salad—where had she found spinach? Obviously, somebody had spent some money on this meal. This was *important.*

So I praised every course, and waited for the punch line. Had he finally proposed—? Was that what this was about? And who was Mr. Takahara?

Alan kept his dinner conversation polite. Apparently my earlier outburst had given him a healthy fear of the United States Army—or at least of my commitment to it.

He was also talking much more obliquely than before. "Listen, Jim—I wasn't kidding about the money to be made. For instance, do you know what July dollars are selling for right now? If you had bought July dollars last December, you could turn them over for a thirty percent profit right now. The market is galloping. It's a whole new ball game—and it's the best one yet. Now that the banks have been reorganized, this country can show a profit on the inflation of its currency.

And thirty percent is a very healthy rate. It's good for us. It guarantees a lot of economic growth."

I shrugged. "I guess you're right, Alan. I don't really know that much about economics."

He nodded at me enthusiastically. "That's the point. If you were to start turning your caseys into future dollars, you could double your money every eighteen months."

"So—?"

He looked over at my mother. She looked at me. "Dear—" she said, "—don't they pay you some kind of bounty for every Chatorran you kill?"

The punch line.

The United States government would pay one million caseys for every worm killed, ten million for every one captured alive. I'd collected two bounties as an individual and was owed a third. As a member of a team, I'd participated in 106 others. Last I'd looked, I was worth 9.2 million kilocalories. So what? What was I going to do with it?

My mother had an idea.

I looked at her. I looked at Alan. I was incredulous. "I don't believe this. That's what this is all about?"

Alan held up a hand. I held back. "Jim—wait a minute. Hear me out."

"No—" I said. "Absolutely not. Not half an hour ago, you were telling me you didn't even believe the worms were a threat. Now you're asking for the money the government pays for killing them. Excuse me, but that feels a lot like hypocrisy—" I could feel my tantrum shifting into high gear.

Alan said, *"Jim!* I didn't know that was the source of your money. I apologize—"

I looked at him. "Really?"

"Really. I apologize. I was out of line before. I didn't know—" He looked a little desperate. "—You had every right to get angry with me. If you have nine million caseys in bounty money, I guess that's proof enough you know what you're talking about."

"How did you know it was nine million? I never said how much I had—"

"Your mother told me you had a credit account. She didn't tell me where it came from. I'm sorry, Jim. Really."

Two apologies. The man *was* desperate. I sat down again, curious.

Alan looked to my mother. " 'Nita, honey—would you serve the coffee now?"

My mother nodded and left the table.

"Coffee? *Real* coffee?"

"No expense has been spared for the number one son." He grinned nervously, then allowed himself to relax a little. "I'd like to offer you an opportunity, Jim. I'd like you to listen, if you will."

I shrugged. "I'll listen, but I'm not lending any money—"

Mr. Takahara cleared his throat politely.

We both turned to look at him.

"If I may," he said. "The opportunity is actually mine to offer. Mr. Wise—" he bowed modestly, "—invited me here tonight specifically to meet you."

"Sir?"

"I am not going to ask you to lend me any money, young man. I already have all the money I need. May I tell you how this works?"

"I said I'd listen. . . ."

He took that as an assent. "My company is bidding on a major reclamation project—I can't tell you what—but it's one of the biggest ever. Now, I don't know if you know anything about the Reclamation Laws, but they're very strict. You cannot just set up a company and start bidding."

"Any gang of looters can do that—" interrupted Alan.

Mr. Takahara looked at Alan Wise politely.

Alan Wise shut up.

Mr. Takahara smiled and turned back to me. "This is the way it works. You have to put a deposit in escrow equal to one percent of your claim. So the amount of money you bring in determines the amount you can take out."

My mother returned with the coffee. Alan and I waited while she poured it. The aroma was intoxicating. I'd forgotten how much I missed coffee.

"So—" said Alan, resuming—yanking me out of my reverie over coffee. "Do you see what a terrific opportunity this is for you? You can put your money into a protected escrow account—and our company can then claim a very large and important piece of property. That's why I was suggesting that you invest in dollar futures. The federal government will accept that as a continually expanding collateral. You put it in a rotating account."

"Uh huh—and what happens when I want to take my money out again?"

Alan nodded, "But you won't want to—"

I said, "It sounds like I take the risk and you take the profit."

Mr. Takahara spoke again. He said, "This is very good coffee. My compliments."

My mother smiled and nodded and looked uncertain. "Why—thank you."

Mr. Takahara looked to me then. "There is no risk to you. You will own a pro rata share of the operation. That is better than you can get from any other reclamation company."

Alan Wise added, "You stand to turn your nine million caseys into ninety million." He looked at me expectantly. "That's quite a deal, isn't it?"

I hesitated. "If you say so. Um—what do you get out of it?"

Alan Wise spread his hands modestly. "I'm what they call . . . a participating agent. I put the package together and I take points."

"Points?"

"A piece of the package."

"Oh."

"Jim—" he added. "It's not just your money we want. It's your expertise as well. It's *you* we want. And—there's something else. I didn't want to bring it up, but it wouldn't be fair not to—" He glanced over at my mom and then back to me. "Your mother asked me if I could get you out of the army and into some place a little, well—safer. Your being in the hospital and all—well, you know how mothers are. She worries. I don't know what your present commitment is; but I know you've completed your basic obligation, so I know that *something* can be worked out. I know some people in Denver, and—well, you know; maybe it can be arranged. And certainly, if these worms, as you call them, are as dangerous as you say, then you *ought* to give serious thought to this. It's a safer, far more lucrative alternative. You've done your part for your country. Now it's time to do something for yourself, and for your mother too."

I glanced over at her. Too much makeup, too much jewelry, too much perfume—and too much hope in her eyes. There was too much desperation in this room. It made me very uncomfortable.

"This coffee *is* very good," I said. I put my cup down thoughtfully. All of them were watching me carefully. I picked up my napkin and patted my mouth. "I, uh—I'm going to have to think about this." My father had taught me that—the *polite* way to say no: "I have to think about it." Just keep repeating it until they get tired. It works on everyone except used-car and encyclopedia salesmen.

"Absolutely!" Alan Wise agreed, a little too enthusiastically. "You have to be sure that it *works* for you. I wouldn't want you to do anything that you're not absolutely sure of. But I just want to give you one more fact. Now, it's completely off the record, and you didn't hear it here—but it just might be the one piece of information you need to hear —" He looked at me, he looked at Mr. Takahara, he looked at my mother, he looked back to me. "Are you ready?" he asked dramatically.

"I think I can take it," I said.

"One word—" He whispered. *"Manhattan."*

"No way!" I protested. "Denver has been denying access to that real estate for three years. They say they won't even consider reclamation for another three. Even the Mothball Corps has to be bonded before they can go in. There's no way you're going to get a piece of that rock!"

Alan spread his hands wide in front of him. "Be that as it may. That's the word you need to keep in mind."

I realized my skepticism was showing. I picked up my coffee cup, but it was empty. I put it down again quickly. "Well—like I said, I need time to think it over."

Mr. Takahara patted his mouth with his napkin and said, "I understand your position perfectly."

Alan Wise I didn't trust—but Mr. Takahara was another story. "Is this true about Manhattan?" I asked him.

"I would be violating a confidence if I told you all that I knew," he replied.

"Yes, of course. But that doesn't answer my question."

He smiled—and he looked like Buddha. "What I can tell you is that there are extraordinary developments coming to fruition in the next eighteen months."

"Mm," I said. He'd told me nothing. "Thank you."

"I'm sure you understand what he *really* means," Alan said a little too quickly.

"Yes, but like I said, I have to think about it."

"Yes, of course. I don't want to push you." He wiped his nose with his napkin. "Here, let me give you my card. If you have any questions, call me—any time, day or night."

I slipped his card into my pocket without looking at it. I turned instead to my mother. "You said you were working on some project with maps—?"

She shook her head. "I've been working with the refugee relocation office. We're looking for places to establish colonies, that's all. We're using Family as the model—that's the one that takes care of the children, remember?"

"Uh huh. That's off the new peninsula, right? How is that doing?"

"Very nicely," she said. But she didn't really want to talk about it, I could tell. The light had gone out of her eyes. She excused herself abruptly and went into the kitchen and clattered the dishes around.

Alan and I and Mr. Takahara looked at each other embarrassedly. "So when will you let us know?" Alan asked.

"Oh, in a day or two. I just want to take a little time to think it over, that's all."

"Sure. Take all the time you need—but remember, this is one opportunity that isn't going to wait for too long."

"Yes, thank you. I'll keep that in mind." I smiled politely at them both. The subject was closed. In fact, it was dead.

We adjourned to the terrace then, Alan and I and the enigmatic Mr. Takahara. We talked about *Derby* for a while. The conversation was deliberately casual. Mr. Takahara advanced the theory that the missing robot was hiding on the assembly line. After all, who would look there? I admitted it was an interesting idea. I couldn't think of a better place.

When my mother finally came out to join us, I made my goodbyes and left quickly.

I realized I was humming all the way to the Jeep. I felt oddly satisfied. I had a brand-new thought about the worms—and my mother and her boyfriend had solved my other problem too.

Resign my commission?

Hell, no!

THIRTY-FOUR

THERE WERE voices in my sleep again.

They dropped out of a hovering pink sky, a wall of brightness—like God—and danced in circles around me. When I looked, they were bunnydogs. When I turned with them, they were men again. We took off our bunnydog suits and danced naked. We were happy there. When I looked at the singing sky, it was a worm.

There was something I wanted to know. I floated up toward the worm, but it sailed away and I couldn't catch it—and the dance was over now. I'd missed it. The herd was breaking up—

I woke up trembling.

I knew something.

There weren't words—I had this overwhelming sense that there were connections underneath the world—as if I'd heard the heavenly music, the great chords of reality, and the sound was still reverberating in my soul.

The weird feeling stayed with me all morning. It meant something. I knew it. There was something I had to do—something about that dream—

And maybe too it was another fit of delirium; but when they checked me out at the hospital, my readings came up green. "Forget it, Lieutenant," the doctor said. "You had a bad dream. Considering what you've been through, you're entitled to a few nightmares."

Except, it hadn't been a *bad* dream. It had been an extraordinarily *good* one. That was what troubled me so. I wanted to return to it.

I sighed, shrugged, thanked the doctor and headed upstairs to Intensive Care.

This time, Duke was conscious.

They were keeping him in a sterilized environment, so he was still inside a big plastic tent with odd little ventilation tubes and ultraviolet lights plugged into it.

He turned his head to look at me when I came in. His face was starting to look like a face again. But I wondered if plastic surgery would be able to make it look like a *human* face.

I dropped my gaze embarrassedly. I looked around for a chair, snagged one and pulled it up to the bed. "Hi, Duke—"

He didn't respond. He turned his head back to look at the ceiling. His breathing sounded labored. The shape under the sheets was disturbingly short.

Just to have something to do, I snagged his medi-console off the foot of the bed and studied it.

And then I wished I hadn't.

They'd taken off both his legs and his left arm. Dr. Fletcher's notes said there was too much nerve damage for prostheses.

Embarrassedly, I replaced the console. I looked to Duke again. "Uh, they said you were still having trouble talking—so, uh, if you don't want to talk, you don't have to. I'll do the talking—if you want—"

I waited a moment to see what he would do. I couldn't read his expression, so I continued, "—I don't really know where to start. Um, I guess I should tell you that we brought back some truly astonishing videos. They're being examined frame by frame. I've been debriefing almost every day since I was released. We really did discover something. I mean—nobody knows *what* to make of those bunnydogs.

"One theory is that they're worm-tenders—kind of like tickbirds and crocodiles. Or lieutenants and captains. The bunnydogs handle the paperwork."

He shifted his head slightly to look at me through the plastic. I wished I knew what was going on inside that skull. What was he feeling?

"Um—the other theory, Duke, is that the bunnydogs are the worm-controllers. We don't think that the bunnies are the intelligent species behind the invasion—although they could be—but we're wondering if perhaps they mightn't be the managers of this phase. Maybe they're some kind of sub-Chtorran intelligence.

"And—um, there's another theory—it's just a thought, nobody's advocating it seriously yet, it's just something to think about—that perhaps we're dealing with several different intelligences, or a compound intelligence. The worms are one part, the bunnies are another, something else is still a third part. What we're trying to do now is figure out how the bunnies and the worms communicate. If we can do that, then maybe we can find some way to . . . talk to them and negotiate or sue for peace or something—"

Duke made a rumbling noise in his throat.

"I'm sorry," I said. "I didn't get that, Duke."

He turned his head toward me and said it again. I had to strain to make it out. *"Bfllshmt,"* he said. The meaning was clear.

"Uh, yeah. I think so too. Listen, um—a lot of people have been asking me about you. I heard from the guys in Colorado. They send their best. And Dr. Fletcher says hello too. And—uh, I saw your son—"

Was it my imagination or did his expression harden? He turned his face back to the ceiling.

"I guess it's none of my business, but I think he wants to come and see you, Duke—I mean, he didn't say anything, I just sort of got the idea that he wanted to; he called me and asked how you were. But he didn't want me to say hi for him, so I don't know if I'm messing where I shouldn't. I just . . . well—"

"Shft fp."

"Huh?"

He didn't repeat it.

"I'm sorry," I said. "I guess I should go."

"Wfft."

"What?"

He struggled to make himself heard. *"Wait—"* he rasped. "I want . . . oo t' do smmfing. . . ."

"Anything, Duke!"

"Write 'own. Co' nummer."

"Write down a code number?" I was already fumbling for a pen. "Right. Go ahead, I'm ready."

He cleared his throat, coughed, and began hoarsely reciting digits. He was giving me his personal military code—and *password!*

"Duke—I don't think you should—"

"Shft fp, McCarfy—"

"Yes, sir—"

"I wan'—yoo ge' me . . . a grenay."

"A . . . grenade?"

He nodded; the gesture was difficult for him. "Sfuicide grenaye. Ffoice-actifvated."

"Duke, I don't think—"

"Fmk what you f'hink!" he said. He glared at me. This time there was no mistaking his expression, even through the plastic. "I don't want— be helfless—" He was interrupted by a spasm of coughing. It went on for a long moment. I wondered if I should signal for a nurse. No, if he was in real trouble, the medi-console would alert the nurses automatically. Duke caught his breath and continued, "—nft helfless . . . against wfrms—"

"Worms? Duke, there are no worms in Oakland—"

Somehow, he managed to turn halfway toward me. He tried to reach for me through the plastic of the sterile tent. His hand looked like a worm claw. *"Ge' grenay, Jhm!"* he rasped. "I don' wan'—to die— helfless!" There was terror in Duke's eyes.

I studied the code number in my hands. By rights, I should tear it up and forget it. This was insane. Duke wasn't being rational. A suicide grenade in a hospital? Defense against the worms *here?*

"McCarfy—promisf?"

"Duke, I *can't* do this—"

"Promisf me!" He looked wild. He couldn't hear a refusal.

I nodded. I swallowed hard. "I'll figure . . . something out, Duke. I promise."

He seemed to relax then. He sighed and sank back into his pillow.

"Duke—? Sir?"

"Mm?"

"Remember once, I asked who you cleared with—and you said you checked in with the boss upstairs? Do you remember that? Um—have you checked in recently . . . ?"

"Fmk'ff."

"I didn't get that, Duke. Could you say it again?"

He rolled his head toward me and rasped, "Ghod isf a lie—ge' grenay."

I sat there in silence, wondering what I should do. Should I tell his doctors—or what? I was churning up inside.

Damn it! This was Duke—

I owed him!

But—this was crazy! Where do you draw the line?

You son of a bitch, I thought. Haven't I got enough guilt already?

THIRTY-FIVE

I PROBABLY should have discussed it with my commanding officer.

Except I hadn't seen her in three weeks.

But she'd assigned me a terminal in the Science Section, so I knew she hadn't forgotten me. I guessed she wanted me to catch up on my paperwork.

There was a note from Danny Anderson thanking me for keeping him posted on Duke. I wondered if I should tell him about his father's request and decided not to. This was something I was going to have to handle myself.

And there was a letter from Dinnie, that nurse in Denver, asking me how I was doing and if I'd heard from Ted recently. No, I hadn't.

General Poole had sent me a congratulatory note. I'd been awarded a Silver Star. I wondered if I was supposed to send him a thank-you note. I decided to play it safe and did.

Dr. Fletcher had forwarded me a copy of her section's schedule. She'd highlighted the session on "Gastropede Communication." That was only an hour from now. Obviously, she meant that as an invitation.

And—*new orders from my colonel!* A search and devour mission. Two lobsters! Nineteen hundred hours. Jack London Square. I logged my confirmation with a grin. She hadn't forgotten!

And one last item. The paymaster had authorized the bounty check for the worm I'd flash-frozen from the chopper. One million caseys. I stared at the display screen for a long moment. I really was going to have to do something about all those credits. Nobody had ever told me I was going to get rich in the United States Army.

Maybe Alan Wise should join the Special Forces.

Nah.

The only position he was qualified to fill was bait.

But the money worried me.

It was too much.

According to the newspapers, the economy was in dreadful shape. Everybody said so—and they had the numbers to prove it. All I knew was that the President had committed to getting as much dead cash back into circulation as possible—and that meant lots of bounty and reclamation programs—but there were a lot of civilians screaming about that too. They said this was one more example of big government looting the private sector.

Translation: they weren't getting their share.

But, hell—the worm bounty wasn't limited to members of the military. Anyone who wanted a million caseys could go out and kill as many worms as he could find. The government would cheerfully pay up. The Montana office even paid in cash—all you had to do was deliver the mandibles.

No, it was something that Dr. Fromkin had said a year ago. He'd said that with a steadily shrinking labor force, the casey was doomed to inflate. I wondered if these big bounties were proof of it. I hadn't paid too much attention at the time because I hadn't had enough caseys to worry about. Now, however . . . I probably ought to do something with this cash while it was still worth something—but I wanted to do something with the money that made sense.

Something that would help the human race win the war.

Except—I already knew, better than most people, that the human beings could not possibly win this war. We'd already lost; most of us just didn't know it yet.

No, the best that humanity could hope for was not victory, but survival.

Hm. . . .

I punched for DIRECTORY. Yes, there was a local office of Lunar Five Enterprises in Berkeley. A white-haired woman answered the phone. Yes, she said, the Lunar Colony was officially reopened—and yes, construction on the two L-5 stations had resumed. As a matter of fact, the project was operating under the authority of the North American Unification Treaty, and as such was able to draw funding from public corporations in Canada, the United States, the nation of Quebec, both Mexicos, and the Isthmus Protectorate.

Did I care to invest? she inquired. She flashed me a list of the companies currently involved.

I could have climbed through the screen and kissed her.

I studied the list for half an hour—did some exploring through the network for background information—and eventually decided to buy a nice large piece of a Boeing Olympus-class high-orbit shuttle. The more spaceships we had, the better. There was stock available in the *Apollo,* the *Hercules,* and the *Vulcan.* No, those were already funded to the point of construction. I wanted this investment to make a difference. It cost just a little under three million to start a new shuttle. I decided to spread my cash three ways and start construction on the *Pegasus,* the *Athena,* and the *Ganymede.* I swept half of the rest of the money into the Kilimanjaro catapult and the other half into the Beanstalk Project. The latter looked like a long shot to me, but the payoff was very attractive. If the orbital elevator worked, the cost of lifting one kilo of mass into orbit would drop from five thousand caseys to five. All you'd pay for was the electricity, and you'd get most of that back on the way down.

The Paymaster's office could handle the necessary paperwork. The advantage to using the U.S. Army brokerage is that the commission is held to a scale rate, and your taxes are paid automatically. These particular investments, though, fell under the Resource Incentive Program and no taxes could be assessed on reinvested funds—so almost all that cash got put to work and Uncle Sam's share was limited to the handling charge. I set up a recycling trust with instructions that any and all future bounty payments were to be automatically invested in the same areas, authorized and confirmed, signed off and put the whole thing out of my mind. Alan Wise be damned.

I finished by dropping a quick note into my mother's mailbox letting her know that I had named her as beneficiary.

I logged off—realized I was already late to Dr. Fletcher's session— and headed down to the lab section. I slipped quietly into the back of the theater; all the chairs were filled so I found myself an inconspicuous place on the side to stand. There were a lot more uniforms in the audience than last time. This must be important. There was a lot of brass present.

Down below, Tiny was already hard at work. The worm's claws moved *thoughtfully* over the controls of the problem. This particular puzzle had a lot of interlocking rods and sliding blocks. It was almost too complex to visualize.

According to the outline Fletcher had sent me, these problems were designed by a computer program and could be manufactured to almost any degree of difficulty. So far, they had not come up with a problem that Tiny could not solve. The longest the worm had ever taken had been six hours.

Right now, an overhead clock showed the elapsed time was seventeen minutes. According to the agenda, this was supposed to be an "easy" problem.

The chime sounded, the cage popped open—and Tiny grabbed the rabbit. A white rabbit. Seventeen minutes, thirty-seven seconds. The rabbit did not have time to squeal.

Dr. Fletcher touched her controls and the panel with the puzzle slid closed. She said, "I know that many of you have seen our earlier demonstrations, you know what Tiny is capable of. If we were to give it this puzzle again, Tiny would remember exactly the sequence of moves to open it, and would probably take no more than thirty seconds. Now—" She typed something into her keyboard, waited, frowned, typed again and looked up.

"Our second specimen," she continued, "was captured near Superstition Mountain in Southern Arizona last month. It was close to death from dehydration and hunger. That area is not particularly kind to the gastropedes. We've found a number of their carcasses in the area. We think they wander down from the northern part of the state; there have been sightings in the high country. Had this one not been so weak, capture would have been out of the question, as the creature already massed nine hundred kilos. As it was, two men were killed and three others injured—and the creature was almost destroyed. We call this second specimen 'Lucky.' "

She added, "We think that Lucky may be a female—but we aren't certain." She touched a control and another panel in the chamber below slid open. "I am now going to introduce Lucky to the chamber."

There were audible gasps when Lucky appeared. According to the briefing book, this was the biggest worm in captivity. The beast slid into the chamber like a bus filling a row of parking places.

The two worms goggled their eyes at each other, chirruped and trilled. They circled each other like boxers—

"We believe this is a ritual behavior," said Fletcher. "Perhaps a kind of meeting dance."

The two worms suddenly leapt at each other and writhed together like snakes, turning and tumbling across the floor of the chamber. First one, then the other, was on top. It looked almost like a combat to the death.

"The first time we put them together," Fletcher noted, "we thought they were trying to kill each other."

Suddenly, the two worms froze in position. They were wrapped rigidly around each other. They held like lovers at climax; their bodies were as tense as steel.

"We call this state *communion*. It is as close to a sexual behavior as we have yet seen in the gastropedes." She looked like she wanted to add something else, but was holding back. "The length of communion tends to vary. So far, our experience has been that the more often two worms are exposed to each other, the shorter any individual episode of communion will be. We have four worms we're working with here. We've found that the first exposure is usually the longest. We have some theories about this, but none that we're willing to discuss at this point, let alone endorse." She glanced down into the chamber. "Ah, I see that they're complete—"

Lucky and Tiny were disentangling. They curled and chirruped, rolled sideways, trilled and broke apart.

Now Fletcher opened the passage to Tiny's cell and the smaller worm slid obediently into it. She remarked, "As I've said before, we have *not* tamed the worms. The creatures appear to cooperate, yes; but we rather think that they're learning the routine of our operations more than anything else. Even a kitten can learn to identify a refrigerator as the source of milk."

Fletcher checked that the passage was clear, then closed the panel behind Tiny. Lucky was now alone in the chamber. It twitched its hands impatiently—the *same* gesture that Tiny had used the first time I'd been here. The big worm slid up to the panel that concealed the rabbit puzzle and waited.

"You want to notice what Lucky's doing now," said Fletcher. "Every time we change the puzzle, we also put it behind a different panel. Lucky already knows exactly where this one is going to appear."

Lucky looked up at the glass then and issued a rapid, high-pitched trill. There were chuckles in the auditorium. "That's as clear a hurry-up as I've ever heard," someone remarked. Lucky repeated its cry, then returned its attention eagerly to the panel.

"What you're seeing now," said Fletcher, "is a very clear indication that the worm has learned not only to anticipate, but to actually *enjoy* these tests."

She opened the panel for Lucky then. The puzzle had been reset, this time with a spotted black-and-white rabbit. The rabbit was trembling in the cage.

Lucky burbled in delight and moved immediately to the panel. It unfolded its arms from its upper back, reached forward over its eyes, and began to work the knobs and switches of the puzzle with a swift deliberation. There was no uncertainty in the animal's movements.

Almost immediately, the puzzle chimed and the glass case popped open. There were gasps in the auditorium. Fletcher looked satisfied. So did Lucky. The worm grabbed the rabbit and popped it into its mouth. Again, the wet slobbery crunching.

Fletcher opened the passage to Lucky's cell, waited to see that Lucky was returning to its cage, closed the panel, and then closed the curtains of the theater. She paused for just the briefest moment, as if studying her notes, then looked out over her audience. The scientists looked excited. The soldiers looked grim. I could understand both reactions.

"There you have it," Fletcher said. "A very clear demonstration that the worms *do* communicate." She added, "I want to stress the importance of what you've seen here. Without this demonstration, a very good case could be made that a large part of the behavior of these creatures is instinctive and ritualized. We now have proof that they're capable of a lot more. How much more, we're still investigating.

"We do know that the communication between the two specimens— the transmission of information about the puzzle—occurs *in the communion state*. When the worms have visual and auditory access to each other, but are prevented by physical barriers from achieving communion, the transmission of information does *not* occur. It only occurs in the presence of communion.

"But . . ." and she paused to consider her next remarks carefully, "we still don't know what the mechanism of transmission is. We have extensively analyzed the chirps and trills of the creatures—and there is not enough patterning or modulation in the cries to indicate even a rudimentary language. At most, the chirruping calls are emotional indicators. We have identified a few calls to which we have assigned values corresponding to curiosity, interest, delight, impatience, anger, rage, anguish and despair; but we have not found any calls, patterns of calls, phonemes or patterns of phonemes, that are ever repeated with any correspondence to events in the physical universe.

"We have tested for chemical communication. The gastropedes have a very sophisticated set of pheromones which vary with their moods—but again, there is no pattern, and the bandwidth of the channel is too narrow to carry the necessary transmission. You don't send stereovision images by Morse code.

"We have measured the radio emissions of the worms, and the gastropedes *are* low-level transmitters. While the bandwidth of this particular channel *is* wide enough, all that we have been able to detect so far is static and noise. It may be that worms in the wild are capable of radio transmission, but these specimens are unconscious to it. We've tried broadcasting signals to them, but the only effect we've been able to produce is a nervous rigidity. It looks like—but we're not yet willing to say it is—a kind of insane terror."

She looked up at someone in the back of the room. "No—hold your questions for a minute. This may answer some of them. We wondered ourselves why the worms would have this potential if they don't use it. Our best guess is that it's a byproduct of the way the creature's nervous system is structured, and that it's too recent an evolutionary event for the species to have turned it into either an advantage or disadvantage. Just because the Chtorrans have a half-billion-year evolutionary head start on us doesn't mean that their evolution has stopped. In fact, we are very likely seeing their ecology in a state of severe chaos as it tries to adapt to this world.

"But I've strayed from the subject—the mechanism for communication. We've noticed that the worms begin every communion by touching their antennae at some point. We're not sure what this means either, but we've monitored the electrical pulses at the creatures' antennae and found some patterning—but again, it's not a communication pattern. It's too rhythmic and there's not enough variation. It looks a lot like an alpha wave.

"But we do know that communication *is* occurring during communion. We've attached sensors to both animals and discovered that all of their body cycles synchronize during the act. When that moment of synchronicity occurs, the creatures demonstrate a rigid and frozen posture. Our best present hypothesis is that the mechanism of gastropede communication is multi-channel. The trilling cries might indicate the context of the information to be transmitted. The radio noise might contain some modulation we've missed. The physical gestures may mean something, as might the creatures' pheromones. We really don't know."

A hand from one of the scientists went up. "If you could identify the channel of communication, would it be possible to jam it in some way?"

Fletcher shrugged. "Maybe. It depends on the channel. We've identified the problem here. We're still a long way from the answer."

"Can you give us a time frame?" asked one of the general's aides.

"No, I can't," Dr. Fletcher replied.

The general, with a thick Southern accent, spoke up then. "We wuh told, Doctuh Fletchuh, that you had infuhmation to present heah today that could be of vital military importance. Was that it? The wuhms talk to each othuh?"

"Yes, General, that was the point of the demonstration." She met his gaze with equanimity. "Was there something else?"

"Ah'm sorry, ma'am, Ah guess Ah would have preferred somethin' of *real* military importance. Like a weapon."

That was a mistake. Fletcher's eyes flashed angrily. "General," she said, looking directly at him, "I know you're here for answers. I wish I had them to give to you. But right now, the very best this section can do is give you intelligence about the enemy; there's still too much we don't know about the worms; we still have a long way to go before we can start suggesting ecological countermeasures."

She raised her voice to include the rest of the room. "Listen, the purpose of these demonstrations is to give all of you a better idea of what you're up against." And then she focused on the general again. "I don't claim to be knowledgeable in military procedures. I'm a scientist. But I asked you to be here because I think this could be important for you to know that our enemy is capable of a very sophisticated level of information transmission. It may be possible for the worms to spread the word about our procedures almost as fast as we disseminate our information about theirs."

The general smiled broadly, and a little too easily. He stood up and bowed a gentleman's bow. "Ma'am," he said with a shade too much graciousness, "Ah was raised to nevah ahgue with a lady. So ah'll just accept all of that at face value. Ah'm sure that the wuhk you're all doin' heah *is* very important to the war effort. Ah guess ah just wanted to see somethin' a little more immediate, a little more he'pful to mah own needs. So if there's nothin' else you want to show us, we do thank you for yoah time, but we do need to be gettin' back to ouah desks—" The man was *smarmy*. He'd just blown her whole demonstration right out of the water. He nodded politely and started for the exit. His aides followed quickly—as did most of the other men and women in uniforms. Several of those in lab coats assumed the session was over then and also started up the aisles.

Dr. Fletcher looked annoyed and frustrated. "If there are no further questions—" she began, but nobody was listening any more. Most of the audience was already filing out the door.

She switched off her console, took a long breath, and said, "Shit!"

THIRTY-SIX

DUKE HAD once given me a very interesting compliment.

It was after a burn, after the debriefing, after the usual bull and beer session; he and I had retired to the office to "hoist a jar" privately.

Duke didn't usually say much after a burn; he just sat and sipped. This time, however, he looked like he had something on his mind, so I nursed my drink and waited.

He had turned his chair to face the window and put his feet up on the little filing cabinet. He was holding his glass against his forehead, as if he had a headache and was enjoying the coolness of the ice.

"You know," he said, "you really impressed me this afternoon."

"Uh—thanks. What'd I do?"

"Amy Burrell."

"Oh," I said. "Yeah." I'd been wondering if he was going to say anything about that.

"You did right," Duke said. He lowered the glass from his forehead and glanced over at me.

I shrugged. "If you say so."

"I do say so," he said. "You didn't have a choice. You've known it for months that she's your weak link. I've seen it in your planning. And you knew it this afternoon. You did what you had to do."

"But I still feel bad about decking her."

"If you hadn't, it would be worse next time. Or it would be someone else. Think you can knock down José Moreno?"

"No way."

"Well, you'll probably never have to," Duke said. "Not now. Not after today."

"I hope so," I said. I shook my head. "But I keep seeing the look on her face—"

"You mean the tears? That's just the racket she runs on men. That crap doesn't work on officers."

"No, I mean when I jerked her back to her feet and shoved her at the dome. If she'd been carrying a weapon instead of a camera, I'd be dead now."

"That's precisely why she's carrying a camera instead of a gun. Because she can't be trusted with one." He sipped at his drink thoughtfully, then added, "Let me tell you something about integrity, Jim. It's like a balloon. It doesn't matter how good the rubber is; the air still goes out the hole."

"Uh . . . sure," I said. I still wasn't sure where he was going with this.

"Integrity means airtight. No leaks. No holes in the balloon. A hundred percent."

"So, what you're saying is—?"

"What you did was appropriate. You closed up a hole. It was a good lesson for all of them. You showed them that there's no alternative to doing the job. Your team will be a lot tighter the next time out. You'll see the difference."

"Thanks," I said, and I meant it. "But the truth is, I did it without thinking. I just got pissed off at her continual whining."

Duke raised his glass in my direction. "Absolutely. And you administered the appropriate response. I congratulate you. I salute you." And he drank to my health.

I remembered that now. I wondered what kind of a salute Duke would give me if I punched out a general.

Well . . .

At least, I could think about it.

I strode down to the front of the room and said, "Hi."

Fletcher looked up at me with a weary smile. "Hi, yourself."

I plunged right in. "I have a question for you."

"The answer is probably 'I don't know.' What's the question?"

"Well, your demonstration here was very impressive—despite General Whatsisname's reaction—"

"General Poole."

"That was General Poole? I didn't know they were so hard up for generals."

Fletcher allowed herself a hint of a smile. "What's your question, James?"

"Well, I was remembering something you said before, about the gastropedes' fur. You said it wasn't fur."

"Right. It's nerve endings."

"Well—that's my question. When two worms go into communion, isn't it possible that they're experiencing direct nerve-to-nerve contact?"

She nodded. "They very definitely are."

"Well—couldn't that be your mechanism? Maybe they're passing nerve impulses directly from one to the other."

She raised an eyebrow at me. "You think so?"

"You don't think much of the idea, do you?"

"As a matter of fact," Fletcher admitted, "I like the idea very much. It would explain a lot of things."

"But—?" I prompted.

"But—" she agreed, "it was one of the first things we tested for when we started putting Lucky and Tiny together. And it was one of the first hypotheses we had to discard. We kept finding arguments against it. Too many arguments."

"Really?"

"Really." She glanced at her watch. "All right, I'll have to give you the brief version. Here's what we know. Most of the Chtorran nerve-strands are sensory receptors of one type or another. We've identified at least seventeen distinct types of nerve-strands—different functions, different shapes of cross section, different colors, and so on. Each of those types are further divisible into categories of shade, length, and specialization of function. So far, we've identified over five hundred different sub-categories of nerve-strand. We presume that there is considerable overlap of function among the strand types, but we don't have the people available to do the necessary research.

"We do know that most of the strands are sensory receptors of one type or another—but maybe one strand in a thousand is a 'tickler nerve.' It's a little transmitter; it can trigger any nerve it touches. That accounts for the tingly feeling of the fur. So, yes—it does look like a very good mechanism for communication. Pat yourself on the back for recognizing the possibility. Now here's the bad news. It can't possibly work. Do you want a minute to figure it out yourself?"

I thought about it. "It's a connection problem?"

"Not quite. The worms have no problem connecting. When they're in communion, they're connecting at least twenty percent of their surface area. But you're on the right track. It's a networking problem."

"Huh?"

"When you plug one computer into another, how many lines are you connecting?"

"Just one—oh, I see what you mean. There are one thousand and twenty-four individual channels in a standard lux-cable."

"Right. Now suppose you were working with wires instead of light and you had to connect each wire by hand—and suppose also that you didn't know which one went where. What are the chances of you plugging each of those lines into the right socket?"

"None, and less than that," I said. "There're billions of wrong combinations, and only one right one."

"That particular problem," she said, "would take longer than the life of this universe to solve. Now, raise it to the power of itself, and you have the odds against two worms forming a direct nerve-to-nerve contact for communication. Don't take my word for it," she added. "Run a simulation on the nearest terminal."

"No, it's all right. I'll take your word for it. But couldn't the worms have some kind of internal decoding?"

"We thought of that too," Fletcher said. "We had two fellows from the Minsky Foundation looking into that very problem. They said it was possible only if the creature was almost entirely brain and very little else. So far, we haven't found the evidence of that. Have you had the opportunity to see any of the photo-isotomographs?"

"I've seen the demonstrations, but I haven't had the opportunity to poke around on my own." A photo-isotomograph was a three-dimensional map. Easy to make. You thin-slice a frozen worm, taking a picture of the cross section after each slice. You store all the pictures in a computer—the computer holds the data as a three-dimensional array that can then be explored as a visual display. You can examine any part of the worm's body, inside or out, from any angle. With a joystick you can move around through the entire body, tracing the paths of blood vessels, nerves and other structures. So far, most of what we'd seen still fell into the category of "other structures." There were organs inside the worms with no apparent function. Were they evolutionary leftovers, the equivalent of the human appendix—or were they something else, on biological standby and still waiting to be activated?

"I'll get you lab time if you want," Fletcher said. "If you can prove they have the computing power to do that kind of encoding, I'll dance naked with a big pink worm."

"You're that sure, huh?"

"I'm that sure, yes."

"Hm—" I said. "But that still raises another question—"

She glanced at her watch again. "It'd better be a short one."

I said, "If not for communication, then what *are* the tickler nerves for?"

Fletcher smiled. "Stimulation. Very *intense* stimulation. Probably very sexual. Communication is a kind of hug. The density of the strands, plus the tickler nerves, must make it a very intense experience. You saw the rigidity of their 'climax,' didn't you?"

I nodded, but I asked, "Now is that one a theory or a fact?"

A flicker of annoyance crossed her face. I was immediately sorry I'd asked the question; it was the kind of thing General Poole might have said. But Dr. Fletcher let it pass. "It's an *extrapolation,*" she corrected. "In our own ecology, we know that as life-forms become more sophisticated, the sexual experiences become more intense. So do the rituals, so do the mechanisms of communication. Humans are the best example of all. The worms may be a good half-billion years further down the evolutionary line than anything that's evolved on Earth, but it doesn't mean they're necessarily more intelligent; it *does* imply several orders of magnitude of adaptation. Who knows? The worms could be what Terran earthworms might evolve into. You ought to know that sexual reproduction not only encourages evolution, it also self-selects for more sexuality in the species."

I grinned. "Okay, I concede the point."

She looked at her watch once more, looked annoyed, but didn't leave —not yet. "Listen, James—" she said to me. "You're asking all the right questions. If you ask enough of the right questions, you'll probably retrace most of the steps we've taken in the last eighteen months. Right now, we're bang up against this communication thing—and I'm terribly afraid we're overlooking something so obvious that even a lieutenant could see it." She gave me a speculative smile. "Have you been noticing anything?"

"Well . . ." I began cautiously, "there is something. Um—you've seen our videos, haven't you? The ones from the chopper?"

"I have, yes."

"Did you notice anything about the bunnydogs and that little dance they did?"

"You mean, did it remind me of the herd?"

"Then you recognized it too."

She said, "It's an obvious comparison."

"I think it's more than that. You were the one who gave me the clue. Remember what you called the clustering phenomenon in the herd? You called it an 'enrollment process.' "

"It's a lot more than that," Fletcher said. "It's an essential way for the herd to mortar its identity. It's the glue that holds the members there."

"Yes, of course—but to someone who isn't a member of the herd, it's something else. It's an . . . invitation."

"All right. So?" And then it hit her. She looked up at me in surprise. "The bunnydogs?"

"Uh huh. Exactly. I'm thinking that their dance was an invitation to Colonel Tirelli and myself to come out and join them?"

A thoughtful expression appeared on her face. "Wait a minute." She unclipped her phone from her belt and punched a number. "Jerry? Fletch. I'm going to be late. Can you handle—?" She listened a moment. "Oh, good. All right. Thanks." She refolded the phone and reattached it to her belt. "All right—you've obviously been thinking about this. Give me the rest."

"Well, while I was in the hospital, I did a lot of reading. I looked up Dr. Fromkin's essays on communication." She frowned when I said the name. "Is there something wrong?" I asked. "I thought you were one of his students. You once told me that you'd done the Mode training."

"Yes, I did—and I got a lot out of it—but . . . I don't like what it's become. I don't like the—Never mind. Go on with what you were saying."

"Well—the point of his study seemed to be that human beings don't very often experience true communication. In fact, most of us don't even know what true communication really is. If you look it up in a dictionary, communication is defined as an exchange of agreed-upon symbols. Fromkin says that's an inaccurate description of communication. He goes on at some length to demonstrate this—"

"I'm familiar with the essays," Fletcher interrupted. "You don't need to do the whole recap."

"All right, well—Fromkin makes the point that true communication is actually the transmission of experience. If I could take a feeling out of my head and pour it directly into yours, that would be true communication. He says if we could function with that kind of communication, our

perception of ourselves, the universe, everything, would be transformed.
A race like that would be like gods. That's why I was thinking about
the worms."

Fletcher nodded. "We went down that tunnel. So far, we haven't
found any cheese. But go on."

"Well, that was only my first thought. The thing that really blew me
away was what Fromkin said about language. He said that language is
ineffective for transmitting experience. A language is really just a set of
concepts—so while it's terrific for describing the *physical* universe, it's
totally inappropriate for describing the *personal* universe; that is, the
universe of individual experience. I mean, try to describe love, right?
The best that language can do is *evoke* experience. That human beings
do so well is testament to our commitment to communication more
than our ability.

"What he said absolutely has to happen before a transmission of
experience can occur is a *relationship* of communication. Communion.
Right? Well—that's what the herd clustering is, isn't it? A relationship?
It's a willingness to be together. And that's what the bunnydog clustering is too, I'll bet." I studied her face eagerly. "What do you think?"

She said slowly, "I think . . . you've done very well." She took my
arm. "Come on, let's go for a walk. I'll buy you a cup of coffee. *Real*
coffee. My office."

"Uh—? Sure." I was a little puzzled. Usually she answered a scientific question right away.

She made small talk as she brewed the coffee. "Remember those eggs
you brought in to Denver, the ones that hatched into millipedes?"

"Yeah?"

"We kept them alive because they were the only red-bellied millipedes
we'd ever seen—at least until recently. The ones up north all had red
bellies. Do you take milk? Sorry, I don't have any sugar. Anyway, you
might be interested to know that the red-bellies aren't as voracious as
their black-bellied cousins. They grow a lot slower too. And—if you'll
accept an undocumented opinion—I suspect they're also smarter. We
were going to do some maze tests, but we never had the chance, what
with the hassle of moving the whole operation here. I think we brought
your three bugs—I'd have to check—if you want to see how they're
doing." She handed me a heavy white mug.

"Later," I said. "What about my idea about the bunnydogs?"

She sat down opposite me. "Is the coffee okay?"

I tasted it politely, then started to ask the question again—then stopped and looked back into the mug. The aroma was *heavenly.* I inhaled deeply. "Mmmm—this is terrific. Thank you." I decided to shut up and just enjoy the terrific smell.

There were loose strands of hair hanging down over Dr. Fletcher's forehead. She brushed them back and I realized how tired she looked. There were tiny lines around her eyes. She must have been under a lot of strain these past few weeks.

She sipped at her coffee and said, "We've been planning another mission, James—up north, the same area—specifically to try to establish contact with the bunnydogs. We think there's a chance that we're looking at the next step here—we're not sure. There's been a lot of discussion about that clustering dance and what it might mean. We've spent a lot of time looking at those videos." She paused, swirled her coffee mug, took a careful drink, and then said, "And we've covered a lot of the same ground you have. . . ."

I could feel my balloon deflating. "So—this isn't news, is it?"

She shook her head. "No, it isn't. The thing about the dance being an invitation, though—that's very interesting. We hadn't realized that." She studied my face.

I sighed and looked into my lap. I rolled my coffee mug between my two hands. "You're trying to let me down easy, aren't you?"

"Not at all. The fact is, you not only saw the resemblance—you also did the appropriate research, and you came up with a pretty damn good hypothesis. It makes more sense than even you may realize." She scratched her head bemusedly. "I think I'd better offer you a job, James."

"A job?"

"Mm hm," she nodded. "We're going to need a mission specialist. I think you might be right for the position—"

THIRTY-SEVEN

THERE WERE eight people in the room, all seated around a huge shiny-topped conference table. I knew Colonel Tirelli, Colonel Anderson, Jerry Larson, Dr. Zymph and Dr. Fletcher. General Poole was flanked by two of his aides. The three of them looked about as pleasant as a bowl of cafeteria chili.

"Based on the evidence of your videos," Dr. Zymph was saying, "we have to assume that communication with the bunnydogs *or* the worms may actually be possible." She still looked like a truck driver—she was a squat barrel-shaped woman with the expression of a bulldog and jowls to match. There was more gray in her hair than I remembered from Denver, but her voice was as fierce and gravelly as ever. "We were able to identify over a hundred and forty-three specific interactions among the creatures we are now calling 'bunnydogs' and another eighty-seven interactions between the bunnydogs and the worms."

"And based on that evidence, you want to drop a man in their midst. Is that correct?" I asked.

"The mission specialist will be given every protection possible," grumbled General Poole. "You'll have two full squads behind you."

"But—essentially, what you're asking me to do is step out of a chopper and walk up to the first bunnydog I see and offer to shake hands, right?"

Dr. Zymph admitted it. "We want to put a man and a bunnydog face to face and see what happens."

"And if I don't get eaten, then you'll know it's safe for the real scientists to come out and talk," I finished.

"Not exactly, but—"

"But exactly!" I interrupted. "You want to stake me out like a goat. That's what you've outlined here."

"Lieutenant," said the general warningly.

"Excuse me, sir. I think it's time I said something about this idea. It's not going to work. At least not the way it's been explained here. I know I'm only a lieutenant—but I've had more experience with the worms and the bunnydogs—face to face—than anybody else in this room. That makes me the expert."

"That's right," said General Poole. "That's what makes you so important to the success of the mission. We want the benefit of your experience." He was wearing his plastic smile.

"If you really do mean that, General, then you'll listen to what I have to tell you. I've seen a lot of cute ideas come down from Denver and everywhere else about how we should deal with the worms. Some are—interesting. Most are dangerous. A few are damned foolish. But almost all of them require some dogface like myself to go out there and put his ass on the line to test somebody else's theory. If the mission fails, you don't lose anything but face—but the asshole who trusted you finds himself on the inside of a giant pink appetite with hair."

"So you are sayin'—?"

"—That if someone has to put his head in the lion's mouth, he should be allowed to choose his own lion."

Dr. Zymph cleared her throat. We all looked toward her. "I think you're exaggerating the situation a bit, Lieutenant—"

"No, I'm not! I'm the guy who froze three worms before we found out it was impossible. This makes even less sense than that. I admit I'm unpopular, but couldn't you find something a little less transparent?"

"Are you through?" she asked.

"For the moment. If I think of anything else," I growled, "I'll interrupt you again."

General Poole said quietly, "Lieutenant! Ah'll be glad to acknowledge the contributions of the Uncle Ira Group any day or night—but let me remind you that you are still part of Uncle *Sam*'s army. When you took your oath you were signifyin' your willingness to give your life, if need be." He gave me his famous intimidation stare.

I gave him my defiant look. "I took an oath, not a suicide pact. Sir."

"Ah'm talking about service and commitment, Lieutenant."

"I hear you. And if I'd wanted to talk about service and commitment, I'd have joined a Tribe and played follow the leader."

"Ah take it that's your answer? You don't want this opportunity, after all."

"On the contrary, sir. I want this opportunity very much. But—if I'm the guy who's gotta get out of the chopper and say howdy to the bunnies and the worms armed only with my own good looks and sparkling personality, then it's my responsibility to make sure this thing is actually *do*able."

General Poole looked around in disgust. "This isn't getting us anywhere. Who else have we got? Preferably someone with balls."

"No one else who's qualified—" said Dr. Fletcher. "If we don't use McCarthy, then it'll have to be me or Jerry here—"

"That's out of the question," said Dr. Zymph.

Lizard said, "Excuse me—but I've seen McCarthy in action. He's neither a coward nor a fool. I'd like to hear what he has to say."

Poole glowered at her—

"General," said Colonel Danny Anderson, "so would I."

The general shifted his glower to me. "All right . . . if you have something else to say, Lieutenant, let's hear it."

"Sir—you have me at a disadvantage. I've only had a half hour with this proposal, just enough time to recognize that it's seriously flawed. My apologies to those who wrote it." Jerry Larson looked grim. I mushed on. "But I don't think it takes into account who or what we're really dealing with."

Larson raised his hand. "If I may—" General Poole nodded; Larson continued, "I disagree! This proposal takes very much into account who or what we're dealing with." He opened his copy of the briefing book and turned it around for me to see. "We know how dangerous the worms can be. We're sending in enough firepower—"

"That's the *first* mistake," I said. "You've set this up as a *military* operation. You want to put men and machines down in the thickest part of the infested region to see who'll come and say hello. The worms have got to have some very bad feelings about choppers by now. We spread death from the sky. You're not even going to get close to them or the bunnies until you demilitarize the mission. You're going to have to put the team down and get the choppers out of there fast—or hide them. And hide anything that looks like a weapon. Maybe take no weapons at all.

"What if the bunnies or the worms are telepathic or have some other way of sensing hostile feelings? We're doomed before we start."

General Poole looked to Dr. Zymph. "Is that possible?"

Dr. Zymph pursed her lips sideways in a thoughtful grimace. "As a matter of fact, it just might be."

General Poole made it clear by his reaction that he did not like that answer. "Would you clarify that please?"

"Yes, of course. This information has not been made generally available yet, because we're not sure how to interpret it, but there is some kind of communication going on between the worms that we cannot explain. I believe you've seen Dr. Fletcher's demonstration—"

General Poole made an affirmative-sounding snort.

"Well—" said Dr. Zymph, "you should find this very interesting. In January of this year, we introduced three new weapons against the worms on the Cumberland Plateau in Tennessee. That's a fairly isolated area of infestation, so it gave us a pretty good test of the effectiveness of our operations.

"We tested three kinds of biocide capsules, two types of gas mines, and four different worm barriers. Within two months, the worms in the region had learned to recognize and avoid the mines—even when they were buried. They learned to ignore the heifers wearing the biocide collars, and they learned how to neutralize two of the fences.

"We then moved our region of testing to Western Canada. Within one *week*, we had established that the worms in the Canadian Rockies already knew how to recognize our gas mines and how to neutralize two of the test barriers. They did not take a single heifer we staked out. They took two ponies wearing biocide collars and none after that. When we went back to Tennessee, the worms there would not take ponies. They learned to recognize the biocide collars and they learned to pass the information on. Would you call that pretty fair intelligence, General?"

General Poole scowled. I could have kissed Dr. Zymph.

I said quickly, "So, the point is—we don't dare bring in anything that is identifiable as military hardware. That's one. The second point is—"

"Wait a minute. Ah still haven't digested the first one," said General Poole. He frowned at me. "First you tell me that it's your butt on the line, then you tell me you don't *want* any protection—"

"I don't want it *visible,*" I said. "That's my second point. This proposal makes too many assumptions about the behavior of the worms and the bunnies, and I don't think we should even try to structure a

contact like this proposal suggests. It would make sense only if we were
trying to contact another *human* species. It doesn't make sense here."

"Ah'm sorry, Lieutenant." General Poole looked annoyed. "You've
lost me. Ah understood the proposal clearly: set down and talk."

My annoyance must have shown visibly because Dr. Fletcher reached
over and stopped me with a touch on my arm. "I think that what
Lieutenant McCarthy is saying is that we're not completely sure about
the relationship of the bunnydogs and the worms. It's clear that we're
seeing a level of partnership that doesn't exist on this planet, because
there hasn't been enough time on our evolutionary clock for this kind of
thing to happen.

"In our lab experiments, we have been able to *train* worms. We have
not been able to talk to them. This suggests that we are dealing with an
essentially *un*intelligent life-form. But—the other side of that argument
is that we may have been dealing with immature or feral individuals, so
there is as little possibility for communication as there would be with a
three-year-old baby or a wolf-boy. So—that whole area of investigation
is still unresolved.

"Now, as for the bunnydogs—well, the evidence of Lieutenant Mc-
Carthy's very extensive video record is that the bunnydogs do exert
considerable influence, perhaps even *control,* over the worms. We very
much need to know the source of that relationship and if it is possible
for human beings to create a similar relationship with the worms.
That's *our* goal in communication. Lieutenant McCarthy is suggesting
that the bunnies and the worms may have goals or methods of their
own that could be way beyond our best ability to extrapolate, and we
need to allow for that in our planning. We need to be flexible."

General Poole looked around the table. He rubbed his jaw thoughtfully. The rest of us waited. Finally, he returned his attention to Dr.
Fletcher. "For once, you make sense," he said.

Dr. Fletcher did a better job of concealing her annoyance than I
would have. She merely said, "General, it's the same thing I've been
saying all along."

General Poole shook his head and looked around the table. "When
Ah walked in here, Ah thought this operation was all settled and
needed only a Go-date, but the more Ah let you people talk, the more I
wonder."

Dr. Zymph looked like she wanted to interrupt, but General Poole
held up a hand to stop her. "No—it's mah turn now! Rank still has
some privilege. You people are the most confused operation in this en-

tire effort. Mah orders are to provide the Science Section with total support. So Ah have to give you what you need. But Ah can't work like this. You people don't know what you want. First you want military backup, then you don't. Next you'll be telling me that the lieutenant here has to dance naked with the furballs—"

"That's not a bad idea either," I said softly.

The general heard me and shot me a withering look. "Before this goes any further, Ah want to see some agreement about what you want to do and *how* you want to do it. Now Ah'm through listenin' to you people squabble. Ah've got some *real* work to do. Don't come back to me until you're sure about what you want to do. Understand? This meetin' is adjourned."

The general stood up and walked out, followed by his aides. Lizard traded glances with Danny Anderson and then the two of them followed quickly. "General Poole—" She hadn't even glanced in my direction.

Dr. Zymph looked across the table at me. "You know, Lieutenant, you're even more deadly *without* a gun in your hands." Then she got up and walked out. Jerry Larson muttered something unintelligible and followed.

I looked to Dr. Fletcher. "I don't get the job, huh?"

She touched my arm again. "James—you said what had to be said. Thank you for saying it."

"But—?"

"But I think you'd better make yourself scarce. This is going to take a while."

THIRTY-EIGHT

JACK LONDON Square in Oakland was not square.

It might have been square once, but now it was a great sweeping arc that encircled a sheltered lagoon. Along the shore, tall trees strung with glittering lights overlooked wide lawns bordered with pink brick paths. Beyond the lawns was a long row of elegant three-story neo-Victorian buildings. There were clusters of tiny shops and open-air restaurants, all bathed in soft gaslight.

I felt as if I'd stepped into another world, an old-fashioned fantasy of another era. It looked like a fairy tale. Everything was too beautiful. There were wide avenues for strolling couples, shaded arcades and even a summery gazebo. The only vehicles were occasional pedicabs. Silvery music—like faint fairy-bells—came drifting across the water.

I was staring at a big bronze plaque set in a concrete marker. It had a huge arrow pointing directly at the ground, and the legend above it said: "YOU ARE THERE!"

Below, in smaller letters, it said, FOR GERTRUDE STEIN.

I guessed I was going to have to have someone explain it to me.

I shouldered my rifle and started walking.

The restaurant was at the end of the strand. It was called This Crystal Castle and it was a gaudy pastiche of baroque gables and cupolas, gingerbread ornaments and stained-glass windows. It shimmered in a glow of opal, gold and rose-red light. It looked like something out of a dream. As I approached, I could hear the gentle sound of a playful string quartet. Mozart? I wasn't sure.

Inside, the lobby was done in shades of emerald and gold. It was deliberately overdone to let you know that it was elegant; but I already knew this place was expensive—it had human waiters. The maître d' was wearing a green Doorman-of-Oz suit. He asked me to check my rifle, but I glared at him and told him I was on twenty-four-hour duty; he bowed subserviently and got out of my way. Lizard wasn't here yet, so I stepped into the bar. It was interesting the way people reacted to the red beret of the Special Forces.

The bar was subdued and suggestive. The walls were polished oak and purple velvet wallpaper. The chandeliers glowed with the soft golden color of candlelight. The mirrors behind the bar were smoky, so you couldn't see yourself drinking.

While I waited, I studied the cocktail menu. There were drinks here I'd never heard of before. What, for instance, was a Rubber Worm? Or a Leather Helper? Or a Plumber's Revenge?

My phone beeped.

I pulled it off my belt and flipped it open. "McCarthy," I said.

"Jim?" Lizard's voice.

"Hi. Where are you?"

"Stuck in a meeting, thank you." She sounded annoyed. "This is going to be resolved tonight."

"What time will you be out? I'll wait."

"No good. They're sending out for sandwiches. We'll be here for hours. Unfortunately, you've opened a real—you should pardon the expression—can of worms. We're going to have to cancel our date."

I couldn't think of a single polite thing to say—

"Jim—? Are you there?"

"Uh—yes. You've just won the undying gratitude of a couple of very large lobsters."

"I'm sorry, Jim, I really am." She didn't sound sorry—

"How about tomorrow night?"

"Um—no, that won't work. Listen, let me call you. All right?"

"Yeah. I guess so."

"It's not all right, is it?" she said. "I can hear it in your voice."

So I admitted the truth. "Yeah, I'm disappointed. I was really looking forward to this."

"Jim—I've gotta run now," she said quickly. "I promise you, we'll work it out. I do care." She clicked off.

I stood there marveling at my peculiar mix of feelings. I felt disappointed and wonderful at the same time. I refolded my phone and stuck it on my belt. I replayed her words over and over in my head. "I promise you, we'll work it out," she'd said. "I do care."

I could feel good for a long time on those three words.

Except—what was I going to do *tonight?*

Me and my big mouth.

I turned to the bartender and ordered a Green Slime. It was tall. It was green. It was tart. It turned my knees to jelly. I had to sit down. I wondered how many it would take to turn the rest of me into a slimy green puddle. I ordered a second one. While I waited, I looked around the bar.

The Chinese girl had shining eyes.

That's what first attracted my attention—the way she was looking at me. Then I noticed her waist. She was deliciously slender. And her hands—as delicate as orchid blossoms. Then I noticed her eyes again. She looked as if she knew something I didn't.

She floated in my direction. My heart popped and missed a beat. Every male eye in the bar—and several female ones as well—swiveled to follow her. She was wearing a silk dress so red they'd have to retire the color after tonight. Just the way she walked was illegal in thirty-seven states. One fellow leaned out so far he nearly fell off his stool.

She stopped directly in front of me. I wondered which of the gods was smiling on me. "Something I can do for you?" I asked.

Her smile grew sweeter. She wet her lips and said, "I was wondering what caliber your gun was . . . ?" She touched the barrel suggestively with one exquisite finger.

My mouth went dry. My throat wouldn't work. My tongue was paralyzed. "Uh," I finally said. "Well—uh, properly speaking, it doesn't have a caliber. It fires eleven-grain needles, four thousand per minute. Its focus isn't as precise as the two eighty—" My mouth kept making words—automatically. I was impaled on her smile. She never took her eyes off me. She was *fascinated*. "Uh—it tends to shred the target, but that's more effective. Against the worms, I mean."

"You have the *greenest* eyes," she said.

"I do?" I swallowed.

"Mm hmm." She slid onto the stool next to me. Somebody at the end of the bar moaned. I wondered if I were about to pass out from lack of blood to my brain.

The bartender rolled up to her immediately and beeped. "Your order, ma'am?"

She didn't even glance at the robot. She said, "I'll have a . . . *Pink*

Butterfly." She held her eyes on me—I was paralyzed by her spell. I wondered if I was drooling on myself.

The robot returned and put something pink and frosty in front of her.

I didn't know what to do, so I just grinned embarrassedly, and said, "You'll pardon me for saying this, but all of the Chinese girls I've met in the past have been extraordinarily . . . ah, demure. I mean—not quite so . . . uh, forward. Are you sure you're Chinese?"

"Chinese?" She blinked in sweet confusion. She flipped open her purse and looked into her mirror. Her eyes went round. "My God— you're right! I *am* Chinese!" She closed her purse again. "Wow!" she said wonderingly. "Chinese! Wait'll I tell my mom!"

"Your mom? Right. She doesn't know?"

The girl laughed. "Well, how could she? I mean—I just found out myself."

I stared at her. This was too confusing. I felt as if my reality were starting to shred. I said, "I—uh, don't think that . . . I know what's really going on here, Ms. . . . ? I mean, maybe—that is, I was just going—"

"No, wait—" She touched my arm to stop me. "I'm sorry, Jim."

"Huh?" I stopped. I looked at her again. "Do I know you?"

She met my puzzled stare with embarrassing directness. "We've met."

I studied her face. It was almost a perfect oval. She had high cheekbones and bright almond-shaped eyes. Her mouth was wide, but not too wide. Her hair fell to her shoulders like a wave of sheer black silk. I'd never seen her before. I'd have remembered this face. And yet—

I couldn't shake the feeling that there was something else going on here. "Who are you?"

She smiled. "If I'm Chinese, I'm supposed to be mysterious. You know, inscrutable. You figure it out." Her smile was impish.

All my alarm bells were ringing now, and I still didn't know why. I said, "What's your name?"

"You can call me Tanjy."

"Tanjy. Is that Chinese?"

"No," she said. "I'm not Chinese."

"You're not? I think you need to look in that mirror again."

"You still haven't figured it out, have you? I'll give you a hint."

For just the briefest moment her face went blank, then she was back again. She said, "Do you get it now?"

I pointed at her. "What was *that?*"

"I was communicating with my terminal."

I frowned. "You're a—?"

"Telepath, yes. Something wrong?"

"Uh, no. You just caught me by surprise—" And then I realized—

She said, "You ought to have your face checked. It does the most curious things when you're caught by surprise."

The realization was still sweeping over me. I grabbed her by the shoulders. "You *son of a bitch!*"

"Hi, Jimbo!" she said broadly.

"I should have known!" My mouth was working like a fish out of water. I managed to make some words with it. *"Ted!* Tanjy! Theodore Andrew Nathaniel Jackson! You creep!" People were staring at us. I didn't care.

She—he?—grinned at me. "Don't you even kiss an old friend hello?"

"Kiss you? I oughta—" I unclenched my fist. I sputtered helplessly. I didn't know what to say.

"Gee, Jim!" He—she?—twinkled. "You're *cute* when you're angry!"

THIRTY-NINE

LISTEN, I'M no bigot.

At least, I don't think I am.

But I was raised old-fashioned, so I never held much with people shifting their sexes around—but then again, whatever one or more consenting individuals wanted to do in the privacy of his or her own body was his or her own business. Certainly not mine.

I was able to achieve the enlightenment of that position by dint of an adolescence uncontaminated by any experience other than theoretical. That is, I didn't know anyone who had ever changed sex—or even gender-identity.

It is one thing to hold an enlightened position in a vacuum. It is quite another to be confronted by your ex-best friend wearing a body that can turn parts of men to stone.

I hadn't realized the Telepathy Corps worked like this.

"Um—" I couldn't find the words. "This—this is going to require a lot more explaining than usual, Ted."

The way I'd always understood telepathy, it was like having a computer terminal in your head; the same microtechnology that made it possible to graft the artificial nerves in a prosthesis also made it possible to graft a prosthetic lobe into the human brain, a lobe that could be programmed for any multitude of data-processing and communication functions. I'd heard that the new generation of implants made full-sensory transmission possible, but I'd thought it worked like a mental movie screen—like looking through the remotes on a spider.

Ted—Tanjy?—corrected that misperception quickly. "The transmission of experience is *total*—at least it *experiences* that way. I think they drop out a lot of the hash at the bottom, because the experience feels somehow cleaner, *purer*. When you become an operator—like I am— control is also assigned. That's when your soul moves out of your body. It feels just like being here. It's like—being able to change bodies as often as you change your underwear. Or in your case, even more often."

He—she?—I really was going to have to figure this out—was a kind of courier. Sort of. There really wasn't a word in the language yet. His (her?) job was to gather experience and put it into the telepathy network, where it was recorded and made available to the—again, there was no word—*synthesists,* the people who experienced the data, assimilated it, and looked for patterns. It was so high-level even Ted/Tanjy didn't understand it. Yet. Perhaps eventually, she said.

Over dinner—well, it would have been stupid to waste the reservations—I asked her, "Where's your own body now?"

"You mean the one you think of as Ted?"

"Yeah."

"It's in Amsterdam. I think. I'll have to check."

"You're not sure?"

"Jimmy," she explained, "when you get certified, you donate your body to the network. In return you get access to every other body in the network. Pretty soon, you give up the *attachment* to the body you grew up in. In fact, attachment is considered . . . disloyal. That's the closest referent. Um—individualism is disloyal to the massmind in that it makes fragments. Hidden agendas pull the mass off center. Never mind —these are experiences that are beyond your referents. I'm sorry. I'm not used to communicating in such a narrow bandwidth."

"Uh—right."

"Well—" she said, "hard work must agree with you, Jimmy. You look terrific."

"I, uh—wish I could say the same for you, Ted—"

"Tanjy," she corrected.

"Uh, yeah, Tanjy. As a matter of fact, I can. I think I can truthfully say that I've never seen you looking better. Um, didn't they have any male bodies available?"

"Sure. But then you wouldn't have been willing to buy me dinner." She added, "Except for that, gender is really a very arbitrary definition."

"Not to the gend*ee.*"

"Not sex," she said. "Gender. Mundanes have trouble with that one, I know. Trust me. Gender is merely a role to play. Like all the other roles. A large part of the telepathy training is about overcoming your gender identification, your age identification, your racial identification —and all the other *arbitrary* identifications that you've wired up while you've been trapped in a single body. By the way, you'd love the section on personal hygiene. I discovered things I never knew about the female body. And the male."

"That must have been quite a revelation."

She ignored the jibe. "It's part of the basic agreements. You have to leave the body in as good condition as you found it. Proper food, proper exercise, enough rest, and so on." The Chinese girl grinned, but it was Ted's grin on her face. "It also means I'm not allowed to get pregnant or go out with sadists." She looked at me speculatively. "You want to keep that in mind?"

I could feel my face reddening. "I uh, think—that you can trust me," I said.

So, of course—naturally—we ended up back at her place. The body's place. The apartment was furnished with surprising luxury. An indoor garden. A lawn. A pool. An overhanging bedroom. A bed the size of Rhode Island.

"Well, why not?" Ted/Tanjy asked. "Think about it. Money is irrelevant to a telepath. It's difficult—not impossible, but difficult—to take it with you. But you don't become a telepath for the money anyway. All that's left are the local perks and privileges. A silk dress is easier to experience than a thousand caseys." He ran her hands up her body. I stared at the gesture. I'd never seen anyone fondle a woman from the inside.

Ted/Tanjy seemed to keep shifting from male to female. The body remained the same, but the personality inhabiting it was a chameleon, sometimes male, sometimes female, sometimes neither. It gave me a peculiar double vision. There were moments when I was conscious only of the person, not the body—and there were moments when I was *acutely* conscious of the body. It was gorgeous. I could have watched it for days. My erection was killing me. I would never wear tight underwear again.

Ted/Tanjy sat the body down on the couch. She left room for me.

I sat down on the chair opposite. "I have to admit—this is still very unnerving."

"I really do understand," she said. "The first time I found myself in a girl's body, I was so caught by surprise, I started to cry."

"You? Really?"

"It happened during my training," she explained. "Mostly, you spend the first part of your training in the body pool. You're always on call. They loan your body out to whoever needs a body to wear. Sometimes you get to ride along, most of the time not. When you can't, that's when they turn you loose in the library. You get to play a lot of recorded experiences. Pretty soon, you start to get a sense of the range of human experience that's available to you. It's mind-stretching, Jim. It really is. You're never quite the same afterward."

"I remember how you were at the bus stop in Denver," I said. "You were a little dazzled."

"That's an understatement, Jim. I was mindfucked. Everybody goes through it. You have to. It's part of the process. Suddenly you find out all kinds of amazing things. You get to look at the same incident from a hundred different points of view and pretty soon you start to get a holographic perspective. Your whole mind-set is destroyed and reformed and destroyed, over and over and over—and each time, it's more exhilarating. It's like the first time you learned how to masturbate. It feels so good, you can't help but suspect there has to be something wrong with it, but you sure as hell aren't going to stop. You are definitely not the same person afterward."

"You certainly weren't," I said. "Not then."

She nodded. "It's one of the very first tests. Becoming a telepath is like running an obstacle course. You have to make it past all the barriers. The first one is to simply find out if you can handle it. I nearly blew it. I almost disappeared into the network. It happens. People get lost, leaving their bodies behind. I was lucky. I came back.

"Somehow, I got past the initial exhilaration. You have to do that on your own. There's no help for that. If you do, that's when your *real* training starts."

"The *real* training?"

"Mm hm. They put you in a training class with thirty other men, and you start trading bodies with each other for short periods. This goes on for three or four weeks, and you still return to your own body at the end of each training session. That's so you can begin to appreciate what happens to a body when it's worn by someone who's unfamiliar with it. That teaches you respect for the equipment real fast.

"Then they start leaving you in your traded bodies for longer and longer periods, so you can start to learn how to fit into a new body comfortably, how to work with it instead of against it—and also so you can begin to give up the attachment you have to your own body. After all, you may never see it again. You end up being *everybody* in your training class. Once—after we'd had a chance to get to know each other —they scrambled us around and we had to figure out who was wearing whose body. It was really eye-opening. We discovered a lot about the signals that we project unconsciously. One boy gave himself away because he didn't realize how often he wiped his nose—even when it wasn't running. We always knew which body he was in.

"Anyway, I guess I got cocky. I started to think I could handle anything they threw at me. After all, I'd already experienced so much in the library, I thought I was an expert. God, I was a jerk."

"No!" I said, grinning.

"Oh, yes!" she laughed back. "I was even a bigger jerk than you." She grabbed my shoulders and stared into my eyes. "Listen to me, Jim —there is an incredible difference between being the recipient of an experience and the author of it. They really set me up to discover that.

"It was my first prolonged solo, although I didn't know it at the time. They just told me I was to take a walk through the woods and smell the flowers. I didn't think anything about it—they had started bouncing all of us around on odd little errands. They never told us the purpose of the assignments until afterward. Sometimes it was a test, sometimes they wanted to record a specific experience, sometimes they wanted to see what we would discover on our own.

"Anyway, you're going to laugh when you hear this. I found myself on a hillside. I was alone. I was wearing a sweat shirt and jeans and tennis shoes. The background feel of the body was different of course, it always is, but this one felt funnier than usual. I had a lower center of gravity and I felt kind of soft. I'd had the opportunities to wear a lot of different bodies by then, so I knew it took a little while to get adjusted, so I didn't think too much about it. I just sort of took it for granted. I assumed they'd given me one of those flabby effeminate little-boy bodies that we used to call capons. I figured they wanted this body exercised and that was the purpose of this assignment. I was so *naive*.

"So, I started walking. It was a beautiful day. The air smelled of flowers, everywhere. I think I must have been in Hawaii or the Bahamas, or someplace tropical. The closer you get to the equator, the more intense the light is—well, the colors here were just incredibly bright and beautiful.

"The day was hot, a little muggy, and I thought I could smell the sea. And my skin was darker than I was used to—and smoother—so I figured they'd given me a native body. Once, I reached into my shirt to scratch a nipple and I was amazed at how soft and sensitive I was. But I still didn't put it together. Still not yet. To be fair, the body was young —maybe thirteen or fourteen—and not all that well developed. In fact, it was quite boyish. But still—you'd think that I, one of the great breast-strokers of our time, would have figured it out, wouldn't you? Well, I didn't. Not from the inside.

"The body was wearing a pack. There was food in the pack, and a canteen, but no mirror or ID card. Nothing to let me know who or what I was. That's part of the training too. You can't take on the identity of the host body. You have to create a new one, your own.

"After a while, I realized I had to pee. There was no one around, so I just unzipped my jeans and reached in—and reached in—and felt around and felt around—It was funny, I still hadn't quite figured it out, I thought I was tangled in my underwear. You know how you'll think anything to avoid confronting the truth? I finally got annoyed, I figured there was something wrong with this body—I yanked down my jeans and my underpants and—just stared at myself. I can still remember the feeling of . . . there's no other word for it—horror. Everything contracted at once. It was like something squeezing me in the balls—except I didn't have any balls! No penis, no nothing! Just hair! I forgot who I was, where I was, everything! I felt betrayed! It must have been terribly funny to the monitors. I started feeling around in my crotch looking for myself. I still couldn't quite accept the truth yet. There was all this loose skin—and it was all wet and skwooshy—and it was so sensitive— and then I touched my own clitoris—and I *knew*—

"I think I yelped in surprise. I can't tell you the *shift of identity* I experienced, Jim. It wasn't just the body that was female—*I was!* When I realized it, I nearly *came!* My nipples came instantly erect, I could feel them hardening against the material of the sweat shirt. My skin flushed. My face got hot. It was an incredible wave of feeling that swept up through me. I felt dizzy. I nearly fell down. It was the most exquisite flash of excitement and discovery and shock. You can't imagine it.

"They hadn't told me on purpose. It was a setup. The point of the exercise was for me to discover the assumptions that I brought to a circumstance. Oh boy, did I feel stupid—and flustered. The physical waves of shock—and pleasure—were still sweeping through my body. That's when I started to cry. It was such a *basic* mistake! I felt so *embarrassed.* I'd wanted to be the perfect trainee and instead I'd just demonstrated how pompous and naive and airheaded I really was. The monitors were probably laughing their heads off over me.

"After I stopped crying, I started feeling silly. And after that, I realized that they wouldn't have done this to me if they hadn't had a purpose. So I tried to figure out what the purpose was. I decided they'd wanted to teach me a little humility. Well, they'd certainly done that. Learning how to pee from a squatting position doesn't sound difficult, but if you're not familiar with how the equipment works—well, never mind."

"So what happened?"

She shrugged. "I cleaned myself up and waited for my recall. I thought that now that I'd figured it all out, the exercise was over. Only it wasn't. Nothing happened. They left me waiting. After a while, I figured it out again. They *weren't* going to recall me. There was something else I had to discover. Are you sure you want to hear the rest of this?"

I said, "If you don't finish this story, I'll kill you."

"Right," she said. "So I took off all my clothes and started examining the body as thoroughly as I could."

"Huh?"

"Well, wouldn't you?"

"Uh—" I thought about it. "I guess so."

"Of course," she said. "As soon as you're sure it's safe, the first thing you do is explore the most unknown thing in your environment." She added, "But there was something else going on here too. I didn't want to be caught by any more surprises. You see, I'd heard stories about people flunking out during training—"

"I didn't know it was possible to flunk out of the corps," I interrupted.

"It isn't possible. But it happens. What they do is, they put you in 'maintenance.' It means they transfer you into some old body that they're not currently using, or have no plans to use, or no need for, and let you stay there. Your job is to maintain it. Right? It puts you out of the way.

"Anyway, we were in that part of our training where we were starting to lose some of our fellows, and they never told us why, so I couldn't help but wonder. I'd had a little run-in with a captain during my training and she'd threatened to send me to a leper colony—or something equally unpleasant. Maybe she'd made good her threat, I didn't know. This could very well be my body for the next umpty-leven years. I'd already made one mistake with it. I didn't want to make any more. I figured I'd better find out exactly *who* I was—or who I was wearing, that is. You know, Jim, the English language is really inadequate for this kind of discussion."

"You're doing okay," I said. "Go on."

"Well—it was like being a kid again. You know how when you reach a certain age, a certain point in life, you start getting really curious about your body and what it can do. Some of it is sexual, some of it isn't. You explore all your nooks and crannies. You find out what you feel like. You see what parts of you are smooth and what parts are hairy. You touch the places that are sensitive to find out just how sensitive you are. You do a lot of masturbating for a while. You have to do it. It's part of the job of moving in and getting comfortable and finding out how the body works.

"We'd had that in the training—we'd had to trade bodies and then explore ourselves from the inside. You can't imagine how silly it looks to see a room full of naked men sitting on the floor and playing with themselves, examining their hands, their fingers, their toes, their etceteras. But it's part of the job of developing your sensitivities.

"This was the first time I'd ever really been a female, so I went through the steps as completely and thoroughly as if I had a manual in front of me. I knew I was being *really* tested now, so I explored that body as if I were going to spend the rest of my life in it. I found out everything I could about what it meant to be a female. I suppose someone who'd grown up in a female body would think most of what I discovered was terribly naive, but I was excited. I felt like I was discovering a new continent. I guess, in a way, I was.

"Of course, I did all that stuff that you see in the movies. I pinched my nipples, I stroked my breasts, I rubbed the insides of my thighs—do you know the inside of a woman's thighs are extraordinarily sensitive? Most men don't. That's why they're such uninspiring lovers. There's a lot you can learn if you just listen to the body.

"It was a remarkable afternoon for me, Jim. My whole sexual identity was destroyed—and rebuilt. You see, always before I'd been a guest at a woman's body, a visitor. Now, I was the . . . host. Hostess! I gave myself permission to do everything I'd always been curious about, but too polite to ask. It was like being given a wonderful, delicious toy to play with.

"I spent the whole afternoon playing with myself, Jim. I had a great

time. It was terrific. I found out later that almost all men do that the
first time they're turned loose in a female body. They can't resist their
own curiosity. The women tend to be a little bit shyer their first time in
male equipment. You figure it out. But it was an incredible experience,
Jim. Do you know that female bodies don't experience orgasm like male
bodies? A female orgasm comes in waves—wave after delicious wave
that sweep up inside of you. It was incredible. I fell in love with myself
five times over." Her face was glowing, her eyes were shining. Even the
retelling of the experience had aroused her.

I felt momentarily embarrassed at her—his?—revelations. It wasn't
just the information—it was the candor with which he shared it. It was
too intimate. I was embarrassed because I was aroused—and fascinated.
I wanted to hear every bit of his story. Her story.

"Do you know what they did to me?" she asked.

"What?"

"They left me in that body for three weeks."

"In the forest?"

"In the forest," she said.

FORTY

"THERE WAS an old navy weather station nearby," Tanjy continued. "The Telepathy Corps used it as a retreat. Robots ran everything now, so the human quarters were completely available. It was the perfect place for this kind of exercise. We were on an island somewhere, completely isolated. There were three male bodies and four female bodies besides the one I was wearing. They greeted me as I came up the path.

"They must have been able to recognize that I was a new operator. Before I could even say hi, they led me inside into the main lounge. One wall was painted white and was covered with big black lettering—the ground rules for the retreat. They were very simple. The first one was you couldn't tell who you were. You couldn't tell your name or anything from your past experience. You had to make up a new name for yourself that didn't have any gender attached to it—I used my initials.

"You couldn't say anything that might reveal any past identity you might have held. No personal histories were allowed. Also, you couldn't speculate on the purpose of this assignment, and you couldn't ask other people how long they had been here, or any other question the answer to which would break any of the agreements.

"The point is, you couldn't go around explaining, 'This isn't my *real* body, you know. I'm not really like this.' That's hiding out. That's pretending it isn't really happening to you. You had to be a person in the body you were wearing—nothing else. The only identity you could have was the one you created in this situation—whatever you made up in the here and now. I tell you, it was a very crazy time. I knew I wasn't really a girl, at least not inside—but I had no way of knowing I was a boy either, except by my own say-so. I didn't know what I was for a while. And neither did anyone else, I think. I gave off a lot of conflicting signals; come-hither mixed with bug-off, please-help-me, and I'm-all-right-Jack. They were real patient with me though—or else they knew what I was going through.

"Eventually, what I found out was that I had an incredible investment in my sexual identity—and I had to give it up. Not the identity, the investment. I had to stop being a visitor in the body and start being the owner. I had to *be* a girl, as completely as if it were the only thing in the world I knew."

Abruptly, she shivered. "I still get cold chills thinking about it. It was an adventure. And the others—they were so . . . supportive. Because they knew. They were going through it too. I think at least one of the other women had been a man before. I'm pretty sure—because of the way she spoke, the way she taught me how to be a woman, she was almost clinical—and by the way she made love. Oh, yes—there was a lot of lovemaking. A *lot.*" She laughed and added, "There wasn't much else to do on the island. So we played combinations. The first time a man entered me I wept. I still don't know why. It was very intense. He was extraordinarily gentle."

She fell silent, remembering.

I was at a loss for words. I picked up my drink and held it in my hands. I looked at Tanjy, I looked at my glass again. I felt embarrassed —and I felt privileged. I'd never heard a telepath speak so candidly about his or her experiences before. And I felt even a little envious.

She looked up at me with those large Chinese eyes and smiled. The expression on her face was mysterious—as if she were looking at me from far, far away. It gave me a weird feeling of transparency—as if she were reading my mind. As if there were no secrets I could keep from her. I could feel myself stiffening. I wanted to be known—and I was scared of it too.

And then, abruptly, she grinned with Ted's old grin, and I knew it was all right.

"Hey—mix us a couple of Crazy Marys," she said. "I want to get out of this dress." She came back in a red silk robe that was probably illegal in some parts of the world, and sat cross-legged at one end of the couch.

I handed her a drink and parked myself at the opposite end. I wanted to hear the rest of her story.

"It was that *willingness to experience* that they were looking for," she continued. "That was the whole purpose of the retreat. They were tapping into me. They knew when I had broken through. When they picked me up again, they told me I'd graduated to the next level of my training. I'd demonstrated that I could assimilate. Now I was ready to be *trained* in assimilation.

"You can't imagine the classes, Jim. We wore the most incredible bodies, different bodies every day, bodies we'd never seen before. The paradox was that it was so we could be trained as *beings,* not identities. You see, identities and bodies are all tangled up together. You can't detach from one unless you also detach from the other.

"Do you know—no, of course, you couldn't—but after a while, when you know your body is just a transient phenomenon, you realize that bodies are *irrelevant.* Very quickly, you get detached from the physical universe that way; you lose all identifications and you begin to exist only in an experiential universe—a universe of pure beingness. I mean, the physical stuff is still there, of course, but it doesn't have any significance any more. It's just another piece in the game.

"And then after that, they started making us stay in the assigned bodies for longer and longer periods of time, so we wouldn't get *too* detached. Sometimes we had bodies as young as six, sometimes as old as seventy. Once I wore a Down's syndrome. Another time, I wore a little-girl body that still wet the bed. Once I was a football player. I felt like I was made out of bricks. They wanted us to know—and appreciate—the operating equipment that the rest of the human race is . . . trapped in. So we could . . . sympathize with their condition.

"Then—and only then—did we start the classes in how to act like a male or a female in different cultures. I was amazed at how much I didn't know about how to be a man. I knew I didn't know how to be a woman—but there's a lot about manliness that most men don't know either. And we don't take the time to learn, because we think we already know it by the mere virtue of having been born male. The roles that we play—including *gender*—are almost all learned behavior. We make it up. Really! It's all an act, a performance. We had to learn those performances. We had to learn how to be actors putting on our parts so thoroughly we became them. Just like you mundanes do—except you mundanes don't know you're doing it. That's the trap—and we escaped. We learned how to let go again too, so we could move onto the next identity.

"They told us we would probably change sex so often that we'd eventually lose any identification we had with either gender. And with that we'd also lose whatever investment we might have in a specific sexual identity. They said that ultimately we'd become *omnisexual.* I think I'm beginning to understand that now. Sex has become a totally different experience."

"I can imagine . . ." I started to say.

"No. Unfortunately, you *can't.* I'm sorry, Jim—I feel like I keep excluding you. But this is beyond imagination."

"Try me," I said.

She sighed and waved a hand in frustration. "What I've experienced, Jim, is so . . . incredible, I *can't* put it into words. It's that *different* when you don't have an identity attached. See, Jim—that's what I really learned—that I don't *have* to have an identity!"

"I beg your pardon?"

"Normal people need identities. Telepaths don't. We're detached!"

"Uh—" I said. "I'm sorry, Ted. I don't get that."

"Oh." Her mood collapsed. Her effervescence disappeared. "You missed a step along the way, huh?"

"I guess so."

"Sorry." She scratched her head, a very unfeminine gesture. "Um, let's see—I guess I'm going to have to define my terms. Look, Jim," she said patiently, "the problem is the word 'identity.'

"See if you can get this. Your identity is really a concept that you carry around. It's all attachments. You attach yourself to your name, to the cards in your wallet, to your job, to everything in your life—the car you drive, who you live with, who your parents were, what your rank is, where you come from, what school you went to, what your ambitions are, what your zodiac sign is, what church you go to, what branch of therapy you're currently in—did I leave anything out?"

"Doesn't sound like it."

"But that's not who you really are, is it? You could change any of those things—or all of them—and you'd still be the same self, the same person experiencing. Right?"

"All right, yeah. I got that."

"The self is what *experiences* the identity, Jim. Identity is only memory. It's the cumulative sense of all that stuff in your data banks. If I were to take away your memories, I'd be robbing you of your identity, but you'd still be the same person experiencing."

"But—I know I'm me *now,*" I said, tapping my chest. "I know who I am—"

"You know your attachments. When I ask you who you are, where do you go to look? When I ask you where you went to school, who your parents were, what kind of terminal you work on, where do you look?"

"Uh—oh, I see. In my memory."

"Right," she grinned. "So if I took away your memory, you wouldn't know who you were, would you?"

"I'd be awfully confused."

"Sure. In your case, that'd be just like normal. But you see the point. If you had no memory, you'd have no identity. You'd have to build a whole new one, wouldn't you?"

I shrugged. "Yeah, sure."

"Now if I gave you all of my memories, if I could just pour them into your head, you'd think you were me, wouldn't you?"

"Yeah. I can see that."

"But you'd still be you, the same person experiencing it all. You'd just be experiencing a different identity now, right?"

"Okay, I got it."

"Good." She leaned back against the sofa and relaxed. "Well, that's what this whole thing is all about. The *self*—that being inside—that's who you really are. A telepath needs to know that or he'll go crazy. That's what all that training is really about. I had to experience my identity as a thing apart from my *self* so I could know my *self*. Jim," she said, with frightening candor, "I can never be my old identity again—because I know how artificial it was in the first place. In my training, I learned how I made it up. I looked at all my old memories. I saw how it all happened and it freed me!

"They tell you when you start your training that you're going to have to give up that thing you'd rather die than give up. I didn't know then what they meant—but it's the attachment to your identity. I had to give up being Ted. I am not Ted any more. I will never be Ted again." She stopped abruptly and looked at me—as if waiting for a reaction.

I stared at her. For a moment, I had the bizarre sensation that I was sitting with a total stranger again. "But I know who you are—" I protested. "Or do I? Is there any of Ted left?" I asked.

"All of me is left," she laughed. "What's gone are the 'foo-foos'—the arbitrary attachments to being a *specific* person."

"This is very confusing," I admitted. "I keep thinking they've done something *weird* to you. I mean, weirder even than you're telling me."

"Of course it's weird!" she laughed. "That's the only reason for doing it." And then she turned serious again. She took my hand in hers. There was a hint of—was it sadness?—in her voice now. "The difference between us is that I *know* that identities are *all* artificial. That's a terrifying thing to know. An identity isn't just threatened by that fact—it's *destroyed.* Of course, you're going to resist knowing that. Because then you have to start being responsible for the identity you've created, are continually creating!"

"Uck," I said.

"That's exactly what I said when I found out—but there's something else on the other side of that—a whole new way of experiencing people. It was like discovering a new species! I stopped seeing—that is, I stopped focusing on all the shallow, physical, temporal attachments that people surround themselves with, and started seeing beyond the identity to the *being* who'd created it in the first place! It is an eerie—and wonderful—experience."

"You did that to me before, didn't you?"

She nodded.

"Yeah—I had the strangest feeling that you were reading my mind. Or something."

"I was. Sort of. Only not quite the way you think. I was reading the physical expression of your mind."

"Huh?"

"Jim." She put her hand on my arm. Her tone was serious and intense now. She captured me with her eyes. "People build identities out of fear. You build an identity because you think you need it for survival. You use it as a wall. Telepaths know how to read the walls. You think your life is a secret? It never has been. We can see how it turned out on your face."

I didn't know what to say. I felt as if I'd been slammed against the wall—my wall. Why was she telling me this? What did she want from me?

She must have seen it in my expression. She stroked my arm gently. "A telepath has to know all this, Jim, because part of the job of the telepath is to *build* new identities. Every time I shift into a new body, I have to create a persona that's appropriate. It's not about acting—it's about *being.* I know this is hard for you to understand, Jim. I'm trying to condense months of training into a single conversation."

"I really do want to understand," I said.

"I know. I can see it. That's what makes this so hard for me. All I can tell you is that when you lose your body *and* your identity, what you gain is an incredible *freedom.* You can't imagine it. Really. There's a—a thing that happens, a point you reach, like an airplane racing down a runway, where you become airborne, and then you're flying. You know when you reach it, nobody has to tell you. That's the experience, Jim. I wish I could take you with me. I wish I could share it with you."

I said, "So do I."

She didn't reply. Neither of us spoke for a moment. The moment stretched out—became an uncomfortable silence. I looked at her eyes again. I felt myself drawn—and I felt uneasy too. She was my boyfriend who'd become a goddess, and I didn't know what that made me.

"What's the matter?" she asked. She touched my hand gently.

"I, um—" I shrugged and pulled my hand away. "I'm a little overwhelmed, I guess." I took a breath, I exhaled loudly, I put my drink down. I wondered if I should say good night and go.

She sat up a little straighter then, she became more purposeful. She said quietly, "I'll tell you the truth, Jim. I had a very simple intention for tonight. I was going to bring you up here and fuck your brains out. Nothing more. I didn't really intend to have this conversation. I just wanted to complete some old business for myself and have a little fun with an old buddy and pay you back for all the hard times I gave you in the past. Stupid me—I guess I really do love you too much to take that much advantage of you."

"Huh?" I picked up my jaw and fitted it back in place.

"Well, yeah," she admitted. "Hell—the one time we did it, you were so intense, it was like touching a high-voltage line. Don't you wonder why I kept trying to get you back in the sack—or the shower? That was my hidden agenda for tonight. But then we started talking. And there was just too much to talk about. And I realized how much *mis*information there was between us. And I wanted you to just know me as I am now."

Her face was shining again. I thought of Ted. I remembered how he was always like a big silly kid—and the whole world was filled with fascinating toys. He was always grinning—like this. I'd never realized before how *innocent* his grin had been.

That smile was so sweet, so infectious . . . and Tanjy's eyes were incredibly fascinating. I could look into them for hours, years, the rest of my life. I forgot all about Ted. That was a couple of lifetimes ago. This was a beautiful woman; this was now—

Something—happened. A throb of dizziness and—

The way I saw her *shifted*. The easy personality that was Tanjy was gone—the *performance* of Tanjy, but not the *self*. It was like a veil being pulled aside, revealing the light behind as clearly as a rosy vision hovering in the sky. The smile was a window—and her drowning eyes were bottomless—I fell upward into them. She glowed like a god—she was radiant. And I felt beautiful, just basking in her reflection. The delight rose like a bubble, I surged with it—

And suddenly, I knew what she meant.

I had to blink and pull myself back out of her eyes. I didn't want to, but I had to ask. "Tanjy—there's a kind of telepathy that doesn't need an implant, isn't there—?"

Without taking her eyes from mine, she nodded slowly. "The corps thinks so. We know there's something that happens between two people that can't be explained." She took my hands in hers and held them warmly. Her face was angelic. I wanted to drown in her eyes again. "It's a kind of communication without words . . ." she whispered.

"I've heard of such a thing . . . I've never really experienced it . . . until now."

For a moment, we sat there looking at each other. She wasn't Ted—she wasn't Tanjy. She was just—beautiful.

The room, the world around us, ceased to exist. We were alone in an island universe, just the two of us. Her bright eyes had swallowed me. I had the weirdest feeling that the person opposite me was a mirror of my own soul.

In that moment, I loved her. Him.

I shook my head slowly. "None of this makes any sense to me," I said. "I don't understand any of this—and at the same time, I think I know exactly what you mean. There's a kind of tension between us, an electricity in the air. And I don't think it's just my hormones either."

"Uh huh." Her eyes were immense. "Don't try to explain it," she said. "Just . . . enjoy it."

"I have to know—"

She placed a finger across my lips. "Shh. Let it be mystical." And then she added, "Non-telepaths might call this love. It is, of course—but not the kind of love you think of when you use that concept-symbol. It's the experience of love without the attachments."

"I do . . . love you. . . ." Or did I? Who did I love?

"Listen to me—" she said abruptly. "You're going to be involved with some very big stuff, very soon now. I want to tell you something about communication. *True* communication. You're going to need to know this. It's not about talking—it's about *listening*. Listening with your *whole* soul. It's about listening so hard that you *become the person you're listening to.* Like you're doing right now. Can you remember that?"

"Yes, I will. I promise."

She looked thoughtful then. Even a little sad. She was Ted—or Tanjy —again. It didn't make any difference. She allowed herself a small smile and touched my hand. "Good. Your life may depend on it. And—I love you too much to want to see you wasted."

And then there was nothing else to say. We just sat and looked at each other until the clock beeped. Three in the morning.

"It's late," I said.

"Do you want to spend the night?" she asked.

"Sure."

She stood up then and offered me her hand. I got up off the couch and she led me into the bedroom.

I was surprised at how easy and natural it was.

FORTY-ONE

THE FIRST part of me to wake up was my smile.

I said, "Mmmm," and curled affectionately around the warm female body next to me. I slid my hands around her waist and up to cup her breasts.

She said, "Excuse me," and slipped out of bed. I heard her pad barefoot across the floor and into the bathroom. I heard the sound of a toilet flush. I waited for her to come back.

Instead, there was the sound of water running. A bathtub?

I opened my eyes. I sat up. Wasn't she coming back?

She came back into the room, wearing a long dark robe suitable for a convent. She glanced around and made an expression of distaste. "What happened here last night? What is this—? Marshmallows?" She gave me an odd look. Almost hostile.

She wasn't beautiful any more. She was small and mean-looking. She seemed scrawny.

She wasn't Tanjy.

"We had—a marshmallow fight," I explained. "We were going to pick them up—"

She looked at me as if I were a cockroach in her bed.

"Um—I'm sorry. . . . It wasn't *my* idea."

"Mm hm," she said, picking up marshmallows from the floor. "It never is."

"Are you the, uh—owner here?"

"The host? Yes, I am." She was making no secret of her annoyance.

"Oh," I said, feeling suddenly very weird. Like an intruder. I felt like I should pull the blanket up in front of me. Like a shield. "I, uh, guess I should be going then."

"Yes, you should."

I still didn't move. I said, "I'm sorry for the mess. Can I help you clean up?"

She stood up then and faced me. "No. I'd rather you didn't. I'd rather you just got out. Now, please."

I slid out of bed. I stepped on marshmallows. I started gathering up my clothes and pulling them on as quickly as I could.

As I was buttoning my shirt, I looked over at her. "Can I ask you something?"

She dumped the marshmallows into a wastebasket and straightened, brushing the powdered sugar off her hands. She waited for me to continue.

"What happened to Tanjy?" I asked.

She shrugged. "She went on to the next."

I said, "Look—I know this is difficult for you, but I get the feeling that there's something very wrong here, and I don't understand."

The Chinese girl said, "Wait a minute." She stepped into the bathroom and shut off the running water. When she came back, I was just tying my tie. She said, "Do you know what we call telepaths like Tanjy?"

I shook my head.

"Carpetbaggers."

"Carpetbaggers?"

"Mm hm. They take over your body, your house, your life for an evening. They get your body drunk, they take your body to bed with strangers, they get stains on your best silk dresses, they get sticky marshmallows all over your sheets and rugs, and then they disappear in the middle of the night, leaving you with a hangover, scraped legs, chafed elbows, a sore back, and three days of cleaning. Not the least of which is explaining it all to last night's trick."

"Can I help pay for the damages?" I asked, reaching for my wallet.

She stiffened. "I am not a whore, thank you. No, you may not. The service will cover any costs. Besides, it's not your fault. You're as much a victim of the carpetbagger as me."

I shoved my wallet back into my pocket. "Can I ask you one more thing?"

"Go ahead."

"Well—maybe this will sound stupid, but I thought—that is, Tanjy said that telepaths don't have much identity. That is, you don't have much attachment to body, house, clothes, that kind of stuff. But, you . . . ?" I pointed around the room and shrugged and looked at her.

The Chinese girl looked annoyed again. "Right. That's the carpetbagger's justification again." She said, "The truth is that some telepaths do and some telepaths don't. My duties require me to stay local. Twice a month, I rejoin the network and go worldwide. I have work that has to be done on-site. That's the limit of my telepathic participation. I hate leaving my body in the pool, because I never know who's going to be in it while I'm gone or what damage they're going to do."

I stood there, feeling very guilty. I wanted to apologize, and at the same time—I didn't want to. I didn't want to admit that Tanjy—Ted—and I had been like two small boys playing with a girl's body while she wasn't home. I felt like the time my cousin and I had been caught looking in my sister's underwear drawer—only this was worse. Far worse. This time I didn't have a cousin here to share the blame. And we'd been playing with far more than her underwear.

I said, "Um, I understood—I mean, I was told that there were certain . . . agreements between telepaths."

Her eyes narrowed. "You don't understand anything, soldier."

"I guess not," I said. I picked up my hat. This Chinese girl was *nasty*. "Well, I'm sorry," I said. "I really am."

"Yes, you said that. You boys *always* say that. Now, if you don't mind, I'd like to take my bath. I want to feel *clean* again."

Outside, on the street, I could feel my anger smoldering. Dammit! I felt dirty now too.

I should have punched him when I'd had the chance—except it still would have been the Chinese girl who woke up with the bruise.

It wasn't fair!

Dammit! He'd done it to me again!

FORTY-TWO

THERE WAS a large security lockbox sitting on my desk. It opened to my thumbprint. Inside were three very fat mission books.

Somebody had done a lot of work last night.

I spent most of the morning going through the books, my astonishment growing as I did so.

They'd listened to what I'd said.

The first book outlined how the military would deliver the presentation team to the target site and provide protection without being a physical presence. The choppers would be extensively camouflaged.

The second book described the duties of the observation team and how they would keep the physical presence of their monitoring devices to an absolute minimum.

The third book discussed what was known and wasn't known about the worms and the bunnies.

But it didn't say much about how to contact them.

I had an idea about that. It was something Ted/Tanjy had suggested. Listen with all your soul.

I tried to imagine sitting down and talking to a bunnydog. I couldn't. The best I could imagine was joining their cluster.

Finally, I went to see Dr. Fletcher.

I stuck my head in her office door and knocked, "Got a moment?"

She looked up from the report she was studying. She had a sandwich in one hand. "Oh, James. Come on in. Did you read the books?"

"Yeah, that's why I'm here." I snagged a chair and sat down opposite her. "I assume I got the job."

"That was never the question," she said. "Do you want some tea?"

"Oh, today it's only tea, huh?"

"Hey—coffee's for special occasions. You're on the team now. I don't have to be nice to you any more." And then she asked, "What's the problem?"

I explained to her about the briefing books. There was nothing in them for me.

She put the last bite of sandwich into her mouth, nodded thoughtfully, waited until she finished chewing and wiped her fingers on a napkin. "Uh huh—and how would you make contact with the bunnydogs?" she finally asked.

"This is going to sound real weird, but I think General Poole was right. Dance naked with the bunnydogs."

"An interesting idea—" she said. She patted her mouth and tossed the napkin aside.

"I can justify it—"

"You don't have to. I know the reasoning."

"Huh?"

"We talked about this for a long time last night. We pretty well explored the subject."

"Really?"

"The military sat the meeting out. We accomplished a lot. I didn't put it in your book because I wanted to see how much of it you'd figure out yourself. You did good. Now let's see if you can get the second half of it. How would you prepare for such a dance?"

"It's obvious. Go into the herd."

"Mm."

"You're not going to argue with me? I've given this a lot of thought."

She shook her head. She stretched over to her desk and picked up her clipboard. She settled it in her lap and switched it on. "When do you want to go in?"

"The sooner the better, I guess."

"Mm hm. Tomorrow morning?"

"Sure, I could do that."

"And how long do you want to stay?"

"Two days, three. Just long enough to get the sense of it."

"Mm hm." She was writing all this down.

"I figured I could wear a beeper collar, so you could track me."

"And—" she looked up, "—how do you figure we're going to bring you back?"

"Well, you could always break my leg?"

Fletcher smiled. "As a matter of fact, we might just have to do that. Let me give you some bad news about the herd, James; some things we've been finding out.

"We've been doing enzyme analysis on various herd members, and we've found that the brain chemistry is slightly skewed. There's a shift in the body's ability to produce certain memoreceptor activators. In other words, there's a chemical basis for the lack of timebinding. To some degree, it's a self-induced drug experience. But—" She hesitated. "It's the permanence of the effect that we can't understand. We have a . . . theory, but—"

"Go on," I prompted.

"Well, you're not going to like this. We think it's another plague, only —not quite. It's not a fatal one. We think that there are some low-level Chtorran viruses spreading through the biosphere. The suspicion is that these viruses do not produce diseases as much as they shift out body chemistry—and as such shift our state of consciousness."

"Like a drug experience?"

"Mm, maybe. Maybe not. We think that the human species has always had this herding potential, but we've always been so acculturated that we've been able to channel the herding instinct into the service of the culture; but this viral effect so damages our chemoreceptors that we're—all of us—functioning right on the edge all the time now. The slightest stimulus can push us over. In other words," she said somberly, "—it is now an act of deliberate will to be an intelligent and rational being."

"Hasn't it *always* been?" I asked.

She smiled. "I appreciate your cynicism—but, James, you need to appreciate the danger here. The process may be irreversible."

"Isn't there a counter-enzyme or a vaccination or something—?"

"We don't know. We don't have the people to do the research. Listen, I've given you the bad news. Now, let me give you the worse news. We suspect that the viral agent that unlocks the herding capacity is already so widespread in the human species that for all practical purposes it's transparent. We're all infected. Did you see the news this morning?"

"You mean the cleanup of the Capetown riots?"

"Mm hm. There was no reason for that madness—all that rage. It was as if all those people just went berserk at the same time. Could that have been another effect of the same virus? We don't know. I'd love to do a dozen autopsies, but with the political situation the way it is—anyway, you get the point, don't you?"

"We could all fall into herds tomorrow, couldn't we?"

She nodded. "Just waking up human is a victory."

"So . . . what you're saying is that if I go into the herd, you don't know that you can bring me back, right?"

"That is the risk," she admitted. "Do you still want to go—?"

"Wait a minute. I thought this was all theoretical—"

"Then you *don't* want to go?"

"I didn't say that either. You've already got this approved, haven't you?"

She nodded. "We have conditional authorization, if we can find a suitable volunteer." She looked at me pointedly. "Someone who understands the real nature of the problem.

"Here's what we realized last night. The whole question of sentience is premature. We can't even consider it until we know if our two species are compatible. Can humans and bunnydogs even herd together? Forget communication until that question is answered."

"So, you were already planning a dance—?" I said.

"None of this was in your briefing book because I wanted to talk to you about it privately. I know your sensitivity to the herd, James. This whole thing could be very dangerous to you personally."

"I came to you, remember?"

"James—I'm not trying to talk you out of it. I *want* you to go. I argued for this opportunity all last night. But it has to be *your* choice. Before I can authorize this, you have to know what all the risks are, so you can choose responsibly."

"I know the worst that can happen," I said. "The bunnydogs could be the worm predators. I could get eaten. But I have to deal with that possibility every day I get out of bed."

"The *worst* that can happen," Fletcher said, "is that we can lose you to the herd."

I stopped my reply before it fell out of my mouth and reconsidered what she'd just said. I looked at her thoughtfully. "You've put people in the herds before, haven't you?"

Fletcher nodded. "And we've lost some of them too."

"How long can a person stay in the herd before he's lost?"

"It varies. It happens fast. Four or five days is the maximum safe

The War Against the Chtorr

time. Even that's pushing the margin. The experience is too intense. It's a mindwipe."

"All right—so all I want is two days. A day and a half. I'll go in tomorrow morning, spend the day getting acclimated, spend the night and participate in the next day's gathering. You can pull me out around dinner time. That'll give me a day to debrief and the weekend to assimilate the experience. Monday, I can get back to work on the mission."

She switched her clipboard off and put it back on her desk. "You're clear this is what you want to do?"

"I'm clear this is what I *have* to do."

"All right," she said, picking up her phone. "Jerry? It's a Go for tomorrow. Right. No, not at all. Thanks." She hung up and turned back to me. "Okay, we've got a lot of work to do this afternoon."

"Huh?"

"I'm going to train you."

"Train me? How do you train for a herd?"

"There are exercises we can do that will strengthen your sense of *self*. It might help."

"Meditation?"

"Mm, not really. Call it *soul-centering*. It's something from the Mode training—"

"I thought you were down on the Mode training."

She shook her head. "Nope. Only some of the people. I don't like what they're doing with it. But the training is one of the most valuable things I've ever done. It was the thing that kept me . . . rational . . . during the worst part of the plagues. I think it's what keeps me rational today. The truth is, I don't know if it will help or not. I just want to give you every advantage I can."

"I'll be fine," I said. "Really."

She didn't answer.

"What's the problem?" I asked.

"I know you're confident. I know you've thought this out carefully. So have we. But I'm still scared. I know how easy it is to miss something. And I really would hate to lose you *too*. . . ."

FORTY-THREE

"ALL RIGHT. I'm going to activate the collar," Fletcher said. She turned to the monitor in the back of the Jeep and typed something into the keyboard.

The collar around my neck beeped. Loudly.

"How's the signal?" I asked.

"It's good," she said. "So's your heartbeat and your respiration. All right, I'm going to lock it on." She stepped over to me and did something under my chin, I couldn't see what.

When she stepped back, I tugged at the collar experimentally. It was locked and operating. There was no way I could get it off or turn it off. Not until I was retrieved.

I had the feeling that there was something she wanted to tell me, but when I looked at her she glanced quickly to her watch. "You'd better get going."

"Yeah," I said. I took a breath. I began pulling off my shoes and socks. The herd was already starting to form in the plaza. It was going to be a warm day.

I was wearing shorts and a T-shirt. Was that too much? I wondered if I should take the T-shirt off. I glanced to the herd again. There were far more naked bodies than I remembered. I decided to take my cue from the group; I pulled my shirt off and wondered if I should abandon my shorts now too.

I glanced at Fletcher. She looked pensive. "You okay?" I asked.

"Uh huh," she said.

"You don't look it."

She shrugged. "I was just thinking."

"About?"

"I wish we'd had more time."

I took her hands in mine. "I'll be all right," I said.

"I know you will. I guarantee it."

"No, I mean in here." I tapped my head with my forefinger. "I won't get lost. I promise."

She squeezed my hands and searched my face. "You'd better be right, because I'll break your leg if you're wrong."

"I'll remember that." I glanced over at the herd. Too much nudity. Modesty prevailed. I'd keep the shorts on. For now, anyway. "Well . . ." I said, "I guess I'd better . . ."

"Yeah," she agreed. Suddenly, she put her hands around my neck and pulled my face down to hers. Her lipstick tasted of roses and apricots and sunshine.

I broke away, embarrassed. Her kiss had been a little too intense. I turned away quickly to face the herd. If I didn't do it now, I never would.

The herd was a great milling mass of humanity.

They were so dirty, I could smell them from here.

I started walking. The dry grass was scratchy under my feet. The sun was hot on my back. My mouth was dry.

I stopped just before the fringes of the herd.

And studied.

I didn't know what I was looking for yet. Some clue. Some *cue.* Something that would tell me how to act.

A group of young bulls was posturing on the lawn. Two of them were casually wrestling. Some of them glanced over at me. There was a knot in my stomach.

I knew this feeling.

It was the first day of kindergarten all over again. The first time having to shower naked with the other boys. The first time with a girl. The first time I saw a worm.

It was the feeling of walking into a roomful of strangers and having them all look at you. Only, it was worse than that. I didn't know if these were animals or people.

They looked like people. They acted like animals.

Apes.

If I could act like an ape, the *right* kind of ape, they'd accept me.

So . . . now I had to figure out how to act like an ape.

"The problem is," I said quietly, "that nobody around here is giving ape lessons."

And then I realized the joke. Nobody ever taught me how to be a human either.

You just are.

I circled around the young bulls wrestling and headed toward a clear space in the center of the plaza. There was a long wide wading pool there. It was the water hole. Some of the children were playing and splashing in one end of the pool. I moved away from them. I found a place away from everybody else and dropped to my hands and knees. I looked to see how the other apes were drinking. Did they cup their hands or did they just lower their faces?

No. I had to find it out for myself.

I lowered my face to the water and drank. The water tasted horrible. Chlorine? And what else? I couldn't tell. I was glad I had my shots.

How do you act like an ape anyway?

This was the same problem I *always* had with my own species. I never knew how to act.

Other people always seemed to know exactly who they were. I always knew that I was pretending to be who I was. I wanted to stop pretending. I wanted to just *be* a human being. Or an ape. Or whatever it was I had to be.

How did these apes feel about human beings anyway? Did they resent us studying them? Watching them? Or did they tolerate us? Did they appreciate us feeding them? Or did they even make that connection?

Did they want us to join them? Or did they just allow us to join them because they had no way to keep us from joining them?

Or was it that there was nothing to join?

I started giggling. Wouldn't it be funny if everybody here were trying to act like an ape, just like me? Wouldn't it be funny if we were all pretending?

I wished I could stop thinking. My mind was chattering like a machine. "Chatter, chatter, chatter, chatter . . ." I said. "My mind chatters. Chatters. Chatters. Lumpty lumpty lump."

Nobody even looked at me. None of the apes noticed. Cared. The words were all meaningless. All words were meaningless.

And who made up the meanings for the words in the first place? I had. Who else? All the words and all the meanings in my head were connected with connections I had made. They could all be false. Or worse—just some of them might be false connections. But how could I tell which was which?

Where did it all start anyway? "Ma, ma, ma, ma, ma . . ." I said. A baby makes noises and gets a warm tit shoved in its face. That's such a powerful lesson that we spend the rest of our lives trying to find the right noises to make so we can keep getting warm tits to suck on. We spend years shrieking and yammering at each other, looking for the right control phrases. Humans have more control phrases than robots. Say, "I love you," and you can get laid. Say, "Fuck you," and you can have a fight. It's as simple as any other machine—

—it clicked.

We treat each other like machines.

We manipulate.

When the apes gave up language, the control phrases didn't work any more. You could push the buttons all you wanted, but the machinery was broken. "Blabber . . . blabber . . . blabber. . . ." I felt the grin spreading across my face. This was *very* interesting.

If you said a word over and over and over, and did it long enough, it lost all its meaning. But how do you lose a whole language? How do you detach all the meanings from all the words, the sounds, when you've spent a whole lifetime putting them together? How do you lose even the capacity for language?

"Blabber . . . blabber . . . blabber. . . ."

I had the feeling I was doing it wrong.

I was sitting here trying to figure it out.

Maybe this wasn't something you figured out. You just . . . did it. That didn't make sense, but then—figuring it out wasn't making any sense either. I just didn't *know* enough. Maybe if I—

No. Stop figuring it out.

I was a part of the herd now.

Because I said so.

I was the part that was sitting here in red shorts trying to figure out how to be a part of the herd. I was the stupid part. I was trying to figure out how to be what I already was.

I could let go now. I was here.

A teenage boy squatted down in front of me. Uncomfortably close. He was dirty and naked. He had stringy black hair and a large narrow nose. His eyes were extraordinarily wide; they were a startling shade of liquid blue. He stared at me curiously.

"Hi," I said, and smiled. Almost immediately, I knew it was the wrong thing to do. There was too much meaning in the words, and not enough of that *other* quality.

The boy blinked and kept staring at me.

I felt as if I were being tested. As if the herd were some kind of macro-organism looking to see if I had been *assimilated* yet.

The boy scratched himself absentmindedly. His nails were long and dirty. Ape hands. That's what his hands reminded me of. He was skinny, like an ape, too. He squatted on his haunches, studying me. I studied back. I stopped trying to figure him out and just focused on him like a camera, watching him. His eyes were remarkably interesting. Too blue to be real. He had thick dark lashes that shadowed his expression with mystery.

But why was he so interested in me? I couldn't tell what he was thinking by looking at his face. He was there—and he was unreadable. His soul was home, I could sense that—somehow—but there was nothing else going on. No . . . thoughts. No . . . identity. It was compelling, just to sit there and look at him looking at me. It wasn't a staring contest. It was a . . . a being with.

Fletcher had had me practice this. Being with. Intensely. I couldn't look away. I didn't want to look away. It was a strangely reassuring encounter.

I realized what it was about his eyes that disconcerted me—they were too *feminine*. If a woman had eyes like that, she would be a model or a movie star. On a boy . . . they were simply overwhelming.

There was a strange kind of peace here.

I could drown in it.

The boy reached out and touched my face. Like an ape, exploring a strange object. He touched my hair, patted it. His hand moved cautiously, drew back quickly. He smelled of dust.

And then he dropped his hand again. And waited.

I don't know how I knew what he was waiting for, but I knew that it was an invitation.

I touched his face as he had touched mine. I touched his hair; I let my fingers drift across his cheek. A smile spread across his face. He reached up and took my fingers in his hand and looked at them. I could see how clean my hand was in his. He sniffed my fingers. His pink tongue flicked out in a tentative, delicate movement and tasted my fingertips. He smiled at me again. He liked the way I tasted. He let go of my hand. And waited again.

Was I supposed to taste his fingers now?

I took his hand in mine. And sniffed it. And tasted. Dirt. I smiled at him.

He smiled back. It was good.

Complete.

The boy stood up then and walked away. Didn't look back to see if I was following. I didn't know why; I followed. Realized I wasn't used to going barefoot. The dry grass hurt my feet.

My body felt . . . held back. Not free. I knew what it was. I stopped and dropped my shorts, stepped out of them. Felt myself begin to disappear. Into the crowd. The herd. All bodies. Had to let go of bodies first. Be naked. Free. Vulnerable.

Accessible. Available.

Beginning to feel enveloped. Like sunshine. Bathe in it. Withhold nothing. Let it go. Giggling. Feeling. Silly.

Crazy. Mind-noise. Wondering what patterns. Meaning. Applying. Here. Confusing. Concepts. Silly. Feeling—

Shook my head. Puzzled.

Startled myself back to reality—

—turned around slowly in confusion.

Looking for?

I wandered in a daze, I wasn't sure how long. I remember stopping to drink at the wading pool again, and I remember emptying my bladder in a sodden ditch at the east end of the park.

I remember getting hungry and finding my way over to the trucks when they rolled into the park. I pulled off a piece of the loaf and found a place to sit and eat.

Blinking. What was—happened?

Moment after moment after moment, but none of them bound together—so none of them are remembered. All lost as soon as they occur. A roller coaster.

No control.

I'd thought I'd understood. I'd thought that I could get a sense of it. I was mistaken.

I had to get out.

I stood up and headed toward the Jeep. Toward where the Jeep had been parked. And Fletcher. "I'm coming out," I said. I touched the collar. "This isn't going to work. Fletcher, are you listening? I'm coming out. This is Jim." I touched the collar like an icon. My life depended on it. "Fletcher?"

There was no reply.

Was the collar still working?

It didn't matter. I'd just go straight to the Jeep.

I realized I was naked. Where had I dropped my shorts? I should look for them. I moved through the milling bodies with a purposefulness they lacked. Some of them turned to look at me. Then they turned back to their own concerns. Their food. Their mates. Their games. Most of them were naked. Turning.

I didn't see my shorts. I gave up looking. There'd be a blanket at the Jeep anyway, or a coat. I stopped and turned around slowly, scanning the edges of the plaza. Now, where—?

—am I?

No, don't panic. It's all right. She's probably monitoring from a distance. That's all. She said it herself, it wouldn't be a good idea for her to stay too close to the herd.

A note in the air. I turned to look.

Children, humming. A tuneless hum, but—

—and the females humming too. Chorusing. An odd atonal wail. All vowels.

Oh, no. No. That wasn't supposed to happen until tomorrow. Oh, God. The gathering. The tuning. It's accelerated again. Two days in a row now!

Others picking up the hum. Discordance. Babbling. Trying to find the note—

I have to get out of here. Now. I turned around in panic.

It was building rapidly. Much too fast. Remember what happened to me last time. I have to get out of here while I still remember.

And now, the males—the voices deep growling at the bottom end of the scale. And the females are unearthly, an almost heavenly chorus. The cubs' voices are high and sweet . . . and curiously musical.

And . . . I could hear what they were trying to do. All of them. It was a resonance in the air, and each one of us was trying to fit his or her own particular note into that resonance.

I turned around and around, looking for the way out, feeling like I was about to dissolve. Turning—

I could feel my own body vibrating in response. I wanted to add my own note. It was in my throat. It came welling up, rumbling like two heterodyning engines. "Mmmmhhhmmmmhhhmmmm. . . ."

And I found it. It clicked into the chorus and I disappeared into the sound. The sound was larger than the universe. There was no me any more. Only the sound. The incredible sound. All the voices. All to-

gether. And. All of us. Echoes of me. I put my note out and it echoed in
all those other throats, all those other bodies.

All the bodies, all the hands, all the bodies turning, not

not lost at all, not

and

turning

found

home

here

cry

happ

ing

FORTY-FOUR

THE FAT black lady was naked.

She was sitting on an old toilet, laughing and rocking happily. She saw me and began to laugh even harder. Her eyes were twinkling.

I couldn't help myself. I moved closer.

Her breasts were large and voluminous. They shook like jelly with her every movement; when she laughed, they rippled with waves of hilarity. Her nipples were large and black against her chocolate skin.

Her arms were immense, thicker around than my legs. They shook too with great masses of flesh. I found myself grinning. Her thighs were massive. Her hands were balloons. I loved her. Who wouldn't?!!

I could feel her joy. It poured from her like light—I wanted to bathe in the light—

She knew I was standing in front of her, watching her. She knew I was smiling with her, but she didn't do anything except watch me and rock and laugh.

I wanted to ask her who she was—except I already knew. She couldn't hide it.

She saw it in my eyes that I knew—and she laughed even harder. She laughed and laughed at the joke. Her joke. *Our* joke.

I laughed too. It was a terrific joke.

We looked at each other and we laughed like crazy. It was the craziest joke in the universe. There we were, the two of us, knowing what we knew about each other, each knowing how silly the other looked, each knowing how silly we looked to the other, each knowing how silly all of everything was—and we laughed and laughed . . . until we fell into each other's arms.

When the fat black lady hugged you, you stayed hugged.

I was happy in her arms. She loved me. She would hold me forever. I was happy here. She laughed and held me and rocked me and cooed at me.

I whispered, "I know who you are. . . ."

And she whispered back, "And I know who *you* are—"

I glanced around at the others and giggled; I looked back to her and whispered again, "We're not supposed to be talking here, are we?"

She boomed with hearty guffaws then and hugged me to her massive breasts. "S'all right, hon-bun. None o' them can hear us. Not 'less we want 'em too." She stroked my hair.

Her nipple was near my mouth. I kissed it, and she laughed. I looked up at her, sheepishly. She leaned down to me and whispered, "Don't you stop that, hon-bun. You know your mamma likes it." She lifted her breast toward my mouth and—

—for an instant, I was a baby again, safe and warm and rocking in my mother's arms, happily enraptured—

Mamma loved me. Everything was all right by Mamma. Mamma says yes. Come here and let your mamma hug you, honey-bunny—

The tears were rolling down my cheeks again—

I looked up at Mamma and asked her, "Why—?"

Her face was kind, her eyes were deep. She brought her hand up to my cheeks and with her massive thumb, she gently wiped my tears away.

"Mamma," I repeated. "Why—why did you let this happen *here?*"

Mamma's face was sad. She whispered to me—something, but I couldn't understand the words—

"Say what, Mamma? I didn't understand—"

Her mouth was moving, but I couldn't—The sounds weren't turning into words—

"Mamma, please—! Why?"

"Baba-baba-baba—" The black lady was babbling. She wasn't making sense.

"Mama-Mama—" I begged—

But she wasn't Mamma any more. She was just a fat black lady, dirty and smelly. Not laughing, not Mamma, not anyone I knew or wanted to know or—

I was crying again. Again and again for everything I'd lost—but especially for losing my mamma again.

Mamma, please don't leave me—Mamma—

FORTY-FIVE

WHEN I was fifteen, I discovered chess.

We had at least thirty different chess-playing programs in the house, including a copy of Grandmaster Plus, the one that finally won the title and held onto it until they changed the rules to exclude artificial intelligence. Most of the programs were public domain, or review copies that had been sent my dad.

One of the programs, Harlie, allowed you to redefine the pieces and the board, so that you could play "fairy" or nonstandard chess. I remember, I'd never wanted to get involved with chess before, because it had seemed so rigid; but with Harlie, I could redefine the game the way I thought it *should* be played. In my own image.

I spent my fifteenth summer inventing new chess pieces and new playing fields.

One piece was the Time Traveler. It leapt forward in time, any number of moves—but they had to be specified at the beginning. If there was a piece on the square when the Time Traveler materialized, both were destroyed. That was how you destroyed a Time Traveler. You parked a pawn on his arrival point.

Another piece was the Gulliver. Gulliver was a giant. He stood on two squares at once—but they had to be the same color, so there was always another square between them. Because the Gulliver straddled, he could only move one leg at a time. You could only kill him by moving an enemy piece between his legs. Preferably the Time Bomb.

Two other pieces were the Magician and the Troll. The Magician moved like a Bishop, but couldn't capture. It moved into position so that another piece was attacking it. If a piece attacked the Magician, even inadvertently, it died. The Troll was the only piece that was safe from the Magician because it couldn't attack anything. It was just a big inert block that could only move one square at a time. It couldn't attack and it couldn't be attacked. It was useful for getting in the way.

I also invented Ghouls and Vampires and Zombies. Ghouls moved through tunnels under the board. Vampires attacked enemy pieces and turned them into Vampires too. Once you started a Zombie moving, you couldn't stop it. It just went on forever.

In order to play a game with all these new pieces, I had to redesign the chessboard. I invented a gigantic spherical playing field with the opposing armies starting the game at opposite poles. I found I had to put in oceans then—blank areas that no piece could move through to allow for edge strategies. Very quickly, I reached the point that the game could only be played on multiple high-resolution terminals. It was the only way to keep track of what was happening on all sides of the globe at once.

Then I added civilians—pieces whose loyalties were unknown until they either enlisted on one side or the other—or were drafted. Civilians always started out as pawns.

I also randomized the initial setups and board layouts to confuse opening-book strategies. It made the opening hundred moves far more tentative.

By the end of the summer, the game was so big and so complex that the strategy part of the program was taking almost five minutes to compute its options and report back its move. And I was running the program on Dad's desktop Cray-9000 with the 2-gigaherz, multiple-gate, 256-channel optical chip, with pseudo-infinite parallel processing. I was more proud than annoyed. I was the only person I'd ever heard of who'd produced a noticeable delay out of a Cray logic processor. But when I showed it to my dad, he pointed out that most of the delay was due to unnecessary branching. I was letting the program test every possible move, sometimes as many as ten moves ahead to see if there was an advantage, before it made its choice. That was when my dad taught me about orchards—in other words, how do you grow a self-pruning matrix of logic trees? He showed me how to implement the search for live and dead branches.

The rewritten version of my fairy-chess program was reporting back its moves even before I'd lifted my fingers from the keyboard. I was very annoyed at my dad for that. Sure, he was only trying to help, and yes, I appreciated the increased speed—but the total absoluteness of the machine's response was ultimately just too intimidating. It made me feel . . . stupid. As if the answer was so obvious, the machine didn't even have to consider it. I finally had to put in a random delay—but it wasn't the same. I still knew.

When I finally sat down to actually *play* the game, I realized that something very interesting had happened.

My perception of chess had shifted.

I no longer saw the game as a board with a set of pieces moving around on it. Rather, I saw it as a set of arrays and values and overlapping matrices of shifting dimensions—and the pieces merely represented the areas of influence and control. The game was not about tactics and strategy any more—it was about options and relationships.

I had a bizarre experience of looking at a chessboard and realizing that it and the pieces were actually unnecessary. They didn't need to exist at all. They were only placeholders in the physical universe—something with which to annotate the actual relationships which the game was truly about.

The pieces weren't the pieces any more—they were their move patterns. A King was a square block, three squares by three. A Queen was a star-shaped radius of power. A Rook was a sliding cross. A Bishop was an X-shape. And I didn't play chess by just studying the pieces any more. I looked instead at the overlapping relationships.

I rewrote my program one more time.

I added an option to display the relative strength of the opposing sides. The pieces were black and white, the areas they controlled were colored red and green. The more a square was under the black control, the redder the square was shown. The more a square was under white's influence, the greener it was displayed. Squares that were equally contested showed up yellow. It became possible to look at the sphere and see all the strong and weak points all at once.

The game was no longer chess. It had become something else. You didn't move your pieces to move pieces, but to change the coloring of the board—to control space. Controlling space was more important than capturing it. Capturing a piece tended to *decrease* the amount of area controlled. The game was won by juggling threats, not actions.

That realization transformed chess for me. The game took on a whole new dimension.

It became a game of balance more than one of action. There were very few actual battles in this game. Mostly it was minor skirmishes. When the end did come, it often came as capitulation before the inevitable. Or sometimes not. Sometimes, there was a flurry of battles that decimated *both* sides. That was usually quick and violent.

I remember, my dad was impressed. He spent more time play-testing the game than I did. Then he sent it out to a play-testing company for their evaluation. I'd almost forgotten about the game when he got their report back. I had already gone back to school, so Dad made a few minor modifications according to Playco's recommendations, named the game Globall, and put it on the network. I made eighteen thousand caseys the first year. Not too shabby. After that, it tapered off to a few hundred caseys a month, which Dad insisted I put in a college trust.

The point is that there was a moment when chess stopped being chess for me and turned into something else—a perception of the relationships that chess was actually about. The pieces disappeared and all that was left were the patterns.

That's what happened to me in the herd.

I learned to see patterns.

FORTY-SIX

I KEPT fading in and out of consciousness.

My mind was like something else in my head. It was a voice that wasn't me. I had the weird sensation of not being my own mind any more. Instead, I was just a disembodied listener. All that babbling—it didn't have anything to do with me.

It was a network of connections. A computer made of meat. A reaction machine. Something with a hundred million years of history attached to it. A reptilian cortex. A monkey's reactions.

I remember, I started laughing, "Help me! I'm trapped inside a human being." And then I cried because it was so sad. Why a human being? Why did God make us into these things? Why hairless apes—!!

I could see the horror of it. I had a computer inside my head. A computer that I couldn't shut off. It was a vast, uncontrollable memory-storage-and-retrieval device. It kept bubbling up with thoughts and images and emotions—all those emotions—like bubbles in a tar pit. I felt as if I were drowning. I couldn't escape from it. I wanted to stop listening to it.

And then I did.

All that noise—that wasn't me.

It was as if I could see my own thoughts—so clearly—and how my body automatically followed each thought without question. The mind and body were one. The body was a robot—and I was just the soul trapped inside, watching and listening. I had no control at all. I never had. It was the machinery that ran—even the freewill machinery was automatic.

At first, I thought—

Thought. Hmp. That's funny. Thought. How can you think about thinking without thinking? Thinking is its own trap. But I wasn't thinking any more. I was just . . . looking. Looking to see what was happening.

It was very peaceful. . . .

It was . . .

Like—

When I was sixteen, my dad took me to a programmers' convention in Hawaii. Globall paid for it. That was Dad's rule. You could do anything you want, if you could afford it.

The first night we were in Hawaii, we were taken out to dinner by three of the members of the convention committee. We went to one of those revolving restaurants that they always have on top of the tallest hotels. I remember, one of the ladies asked me what I thought of Honolulu, and I told her, I couldn't figure out what it was—but it was *different* somehow. But I couldn't figure out what the difference was.

She smiled and told me to look out the window. I did. I spent a long time studying the twilit streets of Honolulu below us. The cars were the same cars. The buses were the same buses. The street signs, the streetlights, all looked the same as I was familiar with in California. Even the style of architecture was familiar. It could have been a suburb of Oakland or the San Fernando Valley.

"I'm sorry," I told her, "I can't tell what it is."

"No billboards," she said.

I turned back to the window and looked again. She was right. There was no outdoor advertising of any kind.

She told me that there was a state law prohibiting signs larger than a certain size. She said that was one of the reasons Hawaii always seemed so quiet to tourists. You walk down a city street anywhere else in the world and you're bombarded with advertising, so you learn to "tune it out." All that advertising is like a steady chattering noise in your ears. In order to function, we have to make ourselves deliberately blind and deaf to that part of our environment. The advertisers know that we do this, so they increase the size, the color, the intensity and the repetitions of their ads. They give us more, better, and different ads. And we tune them out even harder.

But . . . when we get to a place where that channel of mind-noise is missing, the silence is suddenly deafening. She told me that most people don't even notice that the signs are there, but they notice that something is wrong when they're not. Like you did, she said, they experience it as quietude.

"I like it," I said.

The herd is quietude.

Until you've experienced quiet, you can't know how loud the noise is. It's all the mind-noise in the world that keeps us crazy. All that constant mind-chatter is so distracting that it keeps us from seeing the sky, the stars, and the souls of our lovers. It keeps us from touching the face of God.

In the herd, you detach from all that noise—it floats apart from you —and all that's left is a joyous feeling of emptiness and light. It's so *peaceful.*

I think that's why people go to the herd. For the peace. That's why I did. That's why I want to go back.

FORTY-SEVEN

I REMEMBER the screaming.

All that screaming. Everyone. And running too. I remember the running. All of us. Why? Melted canyons. Broken pavements. Scattering. Gunshots. Sirens. Roaring sounds. Purple sounds.

I remember hiding.

I remember a dirty place, bad smelling. Brackish water, gathered in pools. I remember hunger. Wandering. Searching. Looking for the herd again.

I remember someone screaming at me. Making loud sounds in my ear. Slapping my face. Hurts! Piled-on hurts! Don't slap me!

I remember crying—

And slaps—more slaps—

Until finally, I screamed—"Goddammit! Stop that!"

"Oh, thank God! He's coming back."

I remember—

"Jim! Look at me!" Someone grabbed my chin, tilted my face up. A female. Dark hair. Grim face. "Jim! Say my name!"

"Wha—? Wha—?" Make sounds. Drown out meaning. "Wah—?"

Slap! Tears in my eyes.

"Wah—?" I try again. "Wah—?"

Another slap!

I remember screaming.

She holds my face and screams right back at me.

If I can only find the *right* scream—I had it once—"Goddammit, Fletcher! Stop it already! You're hurting me!"

"Who am I?"

"You're—Fletcher! Now leave me alone!" I want to climb back under and pull the covers over my head again.

"And who are you—?"

"Uh—"

"Come on, James! Who are you?"

"I—I . . . name?"

"Come on, you're doing fine! Who are you?"

"I was . . . Jame—"

"Who?"

"Jame—no, James. Edward."

"James Edward who . . . ?"

"Who?"

"That's right. Who?"

"Who? Who?" It's soft and warm down here. "Hoo? Hoo. Hooo—"

Slap! My face rings, stings—

"Who are you?"

"James Edward McCarthy, Lieutenant United States Army, Special Forces Warrant Agency, on special assignment! Sir!" Maybe that will satisfy her. Maybe now she'll leave me alone.

"Good! Come on back, Jim. Keep coming back!"

"No, goddammit! I don't want to come back! I want to finish my dream!"

"It's over, Jim! You're awake! You can't go back to sleep!"

"Why—?"

"Because it's Saturday."

"Saturday?!! You were supposed to pick me up on Thursday."

"We couldn't find you!"

"But the collar—?" I looked at her. Confused.

"Yes, the collar. Where is it, Jim? Do you remember?"

I reach for my neck. The collar is gone. I'm naked. Shivering. Cold. "Um—" More confused now.

Fletcher is wrapping a blanket around me. I'm starting to fade again. I have to say something, quickly. "I—uh—how did . . . you find me?"

"We've been watching the herd. We've been hoping you'd find your way back. Luckily, you did."

"Find . . . my way *back?*"

"Some yahoos from down the coast came in looking for some cheap and dirty sex. They ended up stampeding the whole herd. We've had deaths and injuries. It's the worst. Are you following this?"

"Yes!" I say quickly.

She lowers her hand. Lowered her hand. My time sense is—was coming back.

Somebody put a mug in my hand. It was hot. I drank automatically. Bitter. Coffee? No. I made a face. "What is this shit?"

"It's ersatz."

"Ersatz what?"

"Ersatz shit. We couldn't afford the real stuff."

"This is offal," I said. And grinned suddenly, "Hey—I'm alive again. I made a pun. This is offal. Get it? O-F-F-A-L?"

Somebody behind me groaned. Fletcher grinned. She said, "I never thought I'd be *happy* to hear someone make a pun that bad. It's a good sign. You're coming back into the language again."

I looked into Fletcher's eyes. As if I'd never seen her before. They were bright and deep. I spoke directly to her. I said, "Fletch. I *understand* what's going on here. I don't know if you can understand it without experiencing it, but I know what it is now because I've been through it. It's terrifying—and it's wonderful—and I want to go back— and I want you to keep me from going back. It—" I pointed at the milling bodies behind us. "That—could be the end of the human race. That could get out of control. Very easily. It's got to be broken up, Fletcher. I don't know how, but it's got to be broken up."

"What is it? Can you explain it?"

I took a breath, I looked at the herd, then looked back to Fletcher. "No. I can't. I can make some guesses. I can describe what happened to me. But—any explanation would only be a tiny slice of the truth, not even a cross section of it. But—somehow, when you're in the herd, you know that words don't have any meaning any more. They're just sounds. All the meaning falls away. It gets detached. You can find the meanings if you have to, but—no—" I shook my head and waved my hand as if to erase everything I'd said. I took another drink of the terrible ersatz. "That's not right either."

I looked back up into her eyes. She was beautiful. I could mate with her. Now why did that thought come up? "It's—it's a kind of primal humanity, out there. Listen—there's a . . . space that's been created and defined over there. And in that space, you stop being a human being like we know human beings and start being a human being like *they* know human beings. Over there, the apes have the agreement.

"It's like—humanity has decided that thinking *doesn't* work and has abandoned it. To try something else instead. It's like a kind of telepathy, Fletcher—it envelops you. The closer you go, the easier it is to escape from the language. It's like letting go of a particular madness. Like language is a mental disease that we all agreed to share. Over there, they've created a new agreement—that they can be a species without thinking, without language, without concept. They exist totally in a moment-to-moment state. It's—I'm explaining it again, aren't I? We keep getting trapped in our explanations. That's our minds."

She stopped me with a finger on my lips. "Shh," she said. "Catch your breath. Take your time."

I ran a hand through my hair. It was matted. God knew what I looked like.

"What did it *feel* like, Jim?"

"It felt like . . . this is weird. . . ." I looked at her and I could feel the tears coming into my eyes. "It felt like . . . freedom. As if my mind were a parasite in my body, somehow. And for a while, I'd gotten free of it. And now, that it's recaptured me, I have this . . . terrible grief, this . . . profound sadness." I looked back to the herd again. "They're so . . . happy over there." The tears burst from my eyes again.

She hugged me to her. I was oblivious to everything else except the warmth and the smell of her. She smelled like flowers. There were men standing around us. I didn't care. I let the tears flow. I buried my head against her breasts and sobbed. Why? Why the tears?

She stroked my hair. I could feel how greasy I was, but she didn't seem to mind. She said, "You want the official explanation?"

"What's the official explanation?" I asked.

She wrapped her arms around me and said, "The official explanation is that we haven't finished grieving for the world we've lost. The pre-plague years. How do you deal with the death of a whole planet?" She left the question echoing in the silence.

I found the mug again. The ersatz was cool enough to drink now, cool enough to taste. I could almost get used to the taste of it. In another hundred years or so. I pulled the blanket around me.

"How are you feeling now?" Fletcher asked.

"Fine," I said. "Really." I looked at the sky, I looked at the herd. They were starting to head into what was left of Brooks Hall, their stable for the night. "I should be going to bed too. . . ." I looked to Fletcher, hopefully.

"Yes," she agreed. "But not with them. Not any more." She nodded to someone and they helped me into the ambulance and we headed back to Oakland.

FORTY-EIGHT

THEY KEPT me up the whole night, talking.

They filled me full of coffee—someone found some of the real stuff—I threatened to clam up if they handed me another cup of the ersatz—and they kept me talking.

I kept begging Fletcher to let me go to sleep, but she kept saying, "Not yet. Just a little while longer."

"Why—what are you waiting for?" I could hear the whining in my voice. I hadn't whined since I was five.

Finally, she admitted, "We want to make sure that you'll wake up human. We need to see that your brain is responding to language again. When you sleep, you let go of language. In the morning, we want to make sure you pick it up again."

"I'll be—all right," I said. "I think you can trust me now."

"Would you bet your life on it?"

"Huh?"

"If you don't wake up human tomorrow, can we kill you?"

"Say again?"

"I said, 'If you don't wake up human tomorrow, can we kill you?' Are you that certain?"

"Uh—" I held out my cup. "Can I have some more coffee?"

Fletcher grinned and took the cup from me. "You're fine." But she refilled the mug anyway. "We were thinking about leaving a radio on for you, low-level—but there're two schools of thought on that. One is that it will help keep you tuned to language. The other is that it will be just another babbling voice in the background and will encourage you to start tuning out again." She sighed. "Ultimately, it comes down to this—it's up to *you*. At some level, James, it's going to be your choice."

She turned my face to hers. "Do you understand? I know that you want to go back. You're going to have to resist the pull. Can you? Will you?"

I lowered my eyes. Her gaze was too intense to look at. I wanted to hide from it. "I think I can," I said. I looked back up at her. "I'll try."

"Don't try. Do it." She took my chin and turned my face to hers. "I am *not* going to lose you, do you understand?"

I nodded. All the words seemed so feeble somehow, but it was words she wanted most from me. I felt trapped.

"Do you want some help?" she asked.

"What kind?"

"Just a trick. Use your name as a mantra. Do it as you're falling asleep. Chant your name over and over again. I am James Edward McCarthy. I am James Edward McCarthy. And so on."

"Why? What will that do?"

"It'll set some instructions running that will help you tune back in tomorrow. Every day it'll get a little easier. Will you do it?"

"Yeah," I said. "I'll feel silly, but I'll do it."

"Good." She leaned over and kissed me on the forehead. "I'll let you sleep now."

As I drifted off, I found my body curling familiarly around a pillow. I wondered who I was missing. Who had curled up with me in the herd? I remembered the curve of a spine. The feel of skin. Liquid eyes. I missed—

I drifted back into wakefulness, missing my mate. Finding myself in a strange white place. Wearing a stiff white cloth. And—

"James Edward McCarthy!" I said. "My name is James Edward McCarthy!" And started laughing. It worked.

I found a jumpsuit in the closet. The ubiquitous army jumpsuit. And a pair of slip-ons. Good enough for what I had to do.

First thing, I had to let Fletcher know I was back.

Second. I had a dance to plan.

FORTY-NINE

BUT BEFORE I could do anything, General Poole summoned me to his office. I felt embarrassed wearing just the jumpsuit.

General Poole didn't get up from his desk; he just pointed to a chair and asked, "Whose idea was it for you to go into the herd?"

"Mine," I said.

He shook his head. "In mah day, Lieutenant, that little stunt would have bought you a Section Eight discharge. Ah expect better behavior than that from mah officers."

"Yes, sir," I said. I resisted the temptation to tell him his day was past.

"However . . ." he continued, "this particular operation comes from the Science Section, so perhaps you feel that the opinions of your superior officers in the military aren't applicable. Is that correct?"

"No sir." I wondered what he was getting at. "It was my understanding that I'd been authorized by the mission commander, Colonel Tirelli."

The general didn't respond to that. He adjusted his glasses on his nose and peered at the file on the desk in front of him. "You are a science officer, is that right?"

"Yes, sir."

"You have your degree?"

"No, sir. Not yet."

"Do you have a target date?"

"Three years, sir. I've been averaging one course every six to eight weeks. Three hours a day at a terminal, six days a week, I think I'm making pretty good progress. I'm a little behind right now, but I intend to get caught up right after this mission."

"Mm hm. The mission." General Poole closed the folder and raised his face to mine again; his glasses made his eyes look small and mean. "Let me be candid, Lieutenant. Ah wouldn't start any trilogies if Ah were you."

"Sir?"

"This mission tomorrow—it looks like suicide on a shingle to me."

"With all due respect, sir—I don't agree."

"Of course not. But the fact remains, this mission is . . . of dubious military value. Do you understand what that means? That's why Ah let you volunteer."

"Huh?"

He tapped the folder with one forefinger. "You've got an asterisk."

"Yeah," I agreed. "I'm sitting on it." I regretted the pun instantly.

General Poole looked annoyed. "An asterisk is a little star-shaped mark. In this case, it means that you can be put in life-threatenin' situations."

"Terrific," I said. "How did I earn that?"

"Couple of ways." He ticked them off on his fingers. "One—you could be a telepath—are you?"

"Not that I know of. Not unless someone snuck up behind me when my back was turned and gave me a secret implant."

"Hmp. Not bloody likely. Two—you got someone pissed off at you. Have you done that?"

"That I've done," I admitted.

"Or . . . three, you've demonstrated that you're a survivor. And that you can be trusted to produce results. Unfortunately, not all the asterisks are annotated. We'll have to find out which kind you are by sending you north."

"Yes, sir. Thank you, sir."

"Not so fast, Lieutenant. The purpose of this meetin' is a little old-fashioned fine tunin'. Call it an . . . attitude adjustment." The general picked up a pencil and held it delicately between his two hands.

"An . . . attitude adjustment?"

"That's right. How well do you think you can do your job if your loyalties are divided?"

"Sir? I'm afraid I don't understand."

General Poole looked across his desk at me. "Ah'll say it in English, son. I appreciate your scientific contributions, but—Ah want you to remember also that you are *still* a soldier in the army of the United States of America."

"I don't see the conflict, sir," I said hesitantly. "It seems to me that both the Science Section and the Military are committed to the same thing—"

The general looked skeptical.

"—aren't they?"

"You tell me, Lieutenant. What's the purpose of this mission?"

I quoted from the briefing book: " '. . . to establish a contact relationship with the bunnydogs and/or the gastropedes with the eventual goal of opening a channel for communication.' Sir." I added.

"Mm hm," he said thoughtfully. "And what's the usual purpose of a military mission."

"Uh—" I suddenly realized what he was getting at. "The destruction of the Chtorran ecology."

"That's right." He looked at me calmly. "Some people want to talk to these creatures—and some people want to kill them. Ah'd like to know, Lieutenant, what your feelin's are on the matter."

I was staring down the barrel of a 45-caliber loaded question. "I— I'm on the side of humanity, sir."

"And what does that mean? Are you committed to killin' worms or not?"

"It means, I want to do what will save the most lives."

"And you think that talkin' to the worms or the bunnies might do that?"

"I don't know. That's what we want to find out—"

"But you do think there might be an alternative to killin' them? Isn't that so?"

I swallowed hard and met his gaze. "Yes sir—I'm willing to try."

"Ah see. Well, let me tell you somethin', Lieutenant. The trouble with that kind of thinkin' is that it diverts precious resources of time and matériel. 'If we can just talk to the agency that's behind the Chtorran infestation, p'haps we can work out some kind of *negotiation.*' Ah've even heard some people talkin' about *sharing* the planet with them."

"Sir—?" I started to say.

"Share!" he continued over my protestations. "Why the hell should they? They're already winnin' the whole ball game! Why should they stop to negotiate a draw?"

"Maybe they don't know we're here!" I flustered. "Maybe they made a mistake. Maybe—"

"You don't kill four billion human beings by mistake."

"We don't know that—"

The general looked astounded. "You don't think we're at war?"

"I know we're at war, sir! I just—"

"And you want to *talk* to the enemy?" Was he deliberately baiting me?

"Yes! I do! I want to find out who the enemy is! Maybe they're just as curious about us—"

"Y'know, that's the trouble with you—and with the rest of your so-called experts. You want to study everythin'. You want to question it. And you want to piss away our time! Sometimes Ah wonder just who's side you're really on—"

I stood up. "Goddammit! This may cost me my assignment—but if you're mad at someone, tell them! Not me! I just want to do the job I was trained for! The United States Army wants me to study the worms and the millipedes and the bunnydogs and all the other Chtorran creatures. Yeah, I'll admit it—I'm fascinated by them. These are the first extraterrestrial life-forms that humanity has ever encountered. But don't you go making assumptions about my loyalties, sir! That offends me. I want the Chtorrans off this planet just as much as you do—but I'm also realistic enough to recognize that might not be possible. If it isn't, I want to know how to survive among them. And if it *is* possible to neutralize the Chtorran infestation, you won't find anyone more dedicated than myself. I'll burn worms till you pry the torch out of my hands! You've got my record there on your desk—you look and see! But I can't stand people making up their minds about a subject before all the facts are in!" I added politely, "Sir!"

And sat down.

The general applauded. He grinned. "Not bad. You throw almost as good a tantrum as Ah do. You could use a little polishin'—but experience will take care of that."

Blink. "I beg your pardon, sir?"

"Son, sit down and listen for thirty seconds. It doesn't matter how Ah feel about this joyride. Nobody's listenin' to my opinion. Ah think you're a damn fool and Ah think this is a waste of valuable time. But the Science Section has given this a triple-A priority, so like Ah said, it doesn't matter what Ah think.

"But—" he continued, "you are still under mah command—and Ah

am responsible for your life. So, if nothin' else, Ah want to know that
you're sure about what you're doin'. Ah don't have to be sure, but you
do. Ah've found that a little bit of certainty makes a lot of difference in
the results you produce."

"Yes, sir."

"It looks to me like you're actually willin' to put your life *and your
career* on the line. Ah'm impressed, Lieutenant. With that kind of intention, you just might have a chance of comin' back. But—" he added,
"Ah still wouldn't start any trilogies."

"Yes, sir. Thank you, sir." I felt like I should be looking for the
Dormouse and the March Hare. "Uh—would you like to hear about
my plan? I'm very well prepared."

He shook his head. "No. Ah'm going to trust you."

"But I really think you should."

"Lieutenant, don't press your luck. It might be a very stupid plan.
And then Ah'd have to reconsider mah decision. No. Ah think Ah'll bet
on your certainty more than your intelligence. And Ah will trust Colonel Tirelli's faith in you. Have a nice trip."

He stood up and reached across the desk to shake my hand. I had to
stand up again to grab it. "Uh, thank you, sir."

"Oh, one more thing. It might be some small comfort to know. If you
get killed, you'll be automatically promoted one rank. It'll be a consolation for your family."

"Uh, thanks. What about if I live?"

"We'll talk about it when you get back. Now, get the hell out of here.
Ah have some real work to do." He sat down again and I left, shaking
my head and marveling.

FIFTY

FLETCHER SPENT most of a week training me.

On the morning of the first day, she showed me how to listen.
"It's about listening with your whole soul—" she began.
"You have to listen so completely," I said, "—that you become the person you're listening to."
She looked at me surprised. "Who told you that?"
"A telepath."
"Well, he/she was right."

On the afternoon of the first day, she defined *bullshit:*
"You use that word all the time, James—but you don't even know what it means. 'Bullshit' is a colloquialism. We use it to mean that something is inaccurate. A lie is bullshit. An excuse is bullshit. A justification, a rationalization, a reason, an explanation. All bullshit. Anything you use to excuse yourself from being responsible.

"From this moment on, any time you are inaccurate, any time you let bullshit fall from your mouth, I will bust your chops. You got that?"

On the morning of the second day, she showed me how to listen even deeper than before.
"Close your eyes and actually *look* at how you're feeling. Look at your emotions. Look at what your body is doing. Look at the memories that come floating up to the top. Pick an incident from your memory, or

make one up. Look at the incident—and notice what your machinery is doing. Notice how you feel. Notice what your body is doing. Notice what memories are connected—"

We did that all morning.

On the afternoon of the second day, we talked about righteousness:

"Do you know that most people, when they tell you something, they're really just second-guessing. They're trying to figure it out afterward, explain it or justify it—and ultimately, prove themselves *right*. Listen, that kind of *right* is the enemy. When you try to be right like that, you add inaccuracy. The specific word is righteousness.

"You can't make yourself right without making the other person wrong—that automatically makes him your enemy. It doesn't give him room to do anything else. You can't go out into that circle being right about being human. You can't take your pain and grief and rage into that circle. The bunnies want to *communicate,* not have a shrieking match with the monkeys at the waterhole.

"You cannot have enemies in that circle, James—only partners—"

On the morning of the third day, she showed me how to center my sense of myself.

"Did your telepathic friend tell you about identity?"

I nodded.

"Then you know that you are not what you *think*. You are the person who hears the thoughts. The question is whether or not you're really listening.

"Do you know there are three levels of listening? First, you hear the sound. Second, you hear the meaning. And third, you hear the meaning under the meaning. You can't be 'centered' unless you're listening on all three levels—"

"This is starting to get confusing—"

"I know. A lot of it comes from the telepathy training, and more of it comes from the Mode training. I know it's a break in your reality—the reality that you've made up for yourself. You can't get out of that reality, James; all you can do is learn how it works. That's the point here. All of this information comes from looking at how people experience things and how they react to them. Call it the technology of living. You've been running your machinery without an instruction book—"

On the afternoon of the third day, we talked about concepts:

"Your *name* for this object is 'chair.' This is not a chair. This is a collection of molecules, a focus for your attention. This is a *thing* that you use for the purpose of *chair*, but the chair*ness* of it exists only in your mind. It's a concept.

"This object is a chair only to the extent that it matches that concept. If you were cold enough, this would not be a chair any more. It would be firewood—well, not *this* chair, but you know what I mean. Do you follow this? See, you think the connections you've made between your concepts and the physical universe have meaning. They don't—only in your head. If you believe the world is flat, does that make it flat? No, of course not.

"Now I'll ask a hard question. If you believe the world is round, does that make it round? Take your time. Right—what you believe is irrelevant. The Earth is an oblate spheroid; and it doesn't care what you believe. You don't get a vote on the physical universe. It is what it is, regardless of your opinion about how it should or shouldn't be. The only thing you have any control over is what *you're* going to do about it—"

On the morning of the fourth day, we talked about *creation:*

"Creation is *not* making something up out of nothing. You can't create in the physical universe—the best you can do is reorganize its molecules. No, real creation happens in here—" She reached over and tapped my head.

"Creation is the act of discrimination. You separate this from that and you have created a space between them. Creation is also the act of connection. You connect this *to* that and you have created a new entity or a new relationship. Creation is the act of drawing a line. You use the line to connect or separate or enclose; but you're the one who drew the line in the first place.

"The question is, what do you want to create? What kind of line do you want to draw? Do you want to draw a circle around humans and bunnydogs? Do you want to draw a line between humans and worms? How are you going to make it up? You need to be clear about the circle you're creating before you walk into it."

And in the afternoon of the fourth day, we *created.*

"Are you ready for the last lesson, James?"

"Yes."

"It's bad news."

"I can handle it."

"All right. This is it. You're a monkey."

"Huh?"

"I'll get you a mirror. Your umpty-great-grandmomma and umpty-great-grandpoppa swung naked in the trees and lived on bananas and coconuts. You're their umpty-great-grandson. You live in a house, but you still like bananas and coconuts. And if we took away your clothes, you could climb back up into the trees and nobody would ever know the difference. Are you getting this?"

"I'm not sure. What's the point?"

"The point is, you're a monkey. You are—or at least, you think you are—the dominant species on this planet. That may be a conceit. It's ultimately irrelevant. You can't go out there thinking that. You can't go out there being anything but a monkey, because that's all you are. A monkey. You are not a representative of all humankind. Most humanity doesn't even know you exist, and if it did know, it probably wouldn't want you as its representative."

"You have a great way of pumping me up."

"Listen, you have to operate in the real world. Out there it will be a circle and some bunnydogs. And you are a monkey. A naked monkey. You have to go out there and be a monkey meeting a bunnydog. That's all you can be. You can't speak for any other monkey on this planet. Are you getting this?"

"Yes, I think so."

"Good." She looked at me. "So what are you?"

"A monkey." I scratched myself in a monkey gesture and made an "eee eee" sound.

She grinned. "Mates and bananas, James. That's the bottom line. Remember that. There's not a lot much else for monkeys."

"So, do I eat the bunnydogs or screw them?"

"That's up to you," she said. "Now—look, you need to be clear about what monkeys do. What happens when a monkey comes up against something new, something outside of its experience—what's the very first thing that happens?"

"Um . . . it shrieks. I shriek."

"Yeah—startlement. That's where the human race has been with the infestation. We're still running around startled. What comes after startlement?"

"Fear. Obviously."

"Mm hm. Good—you did your reading. A monkey has only two responses, James. Yipe and Goody. There aren't any others. Everything is variations on that. There isn't an animal on this planet that doesn't have that basic mechanism hard-wired into its cerebral cortex. That's your machinery. You can't *not* react with yipe or goody. And most of the time, just to be on the safe side, you react with yipe. So you spend ninety-nine percent of your life running your yipe machine. And it doesn't matter how much intelligence you've superimposed on it, James. The intelligence doesn't control the machine, it serves the machine. The intelligence only expresses the yipe on a higher level."

She pointed forward. "Those creatures out there—those bunnydogs—no matter what kind of animals they are, no matter what kind of culture they operate in, no matter who they pretend to be—they have the same machinery. Or equivalent machinery. Or they wouldn't be there. I'm talking about basic survival machinery. If you don't have a yipe machine you don't survive. Evolution automatically produces a yipe machine. So, what you need to know is that those creatures out there are as scared of you as you are of them."

I nodded my agreement.

She continued, "What comes after fear?"

I thought about it. "Running?"

"No—let's say you can't run from the thing you're afraid of. What do you do next?"

"Um—I get angry?"

"Are you asking me or telling me? What happens when someone threatens you and threatens you and threatens you—?"

"I get angry."

"Right. Anger. After fear comes anger. How do you act out anger?"

I bared my teeth at her. I growled.

She grinned. "Right. You counterattack. You start by baring your teeth and growling and making terrible faces. If that doesn't work, you start screaming and shrieking. And if that doesn't work, you start throwing coconuts. In other words, you put on a performance of rage. All monkeys do. You do it when your survival is threatened—or the survival of anything you identify with, anything you consider as part of your identity.

"It's all part of the automatic machinery. If you scare away the thing that you're angry at, then the machinery worked; you survived. At the very worst, you might have to fight—but most of the time, though, a

good performance of anger can prevent a fight. I've just told you everything you need to know to understand international politics."

She let me appreciate the truth of that joke for a moment, then she
continued, "That may be fine for monkeys, James. It may even be fine
for human beings, though I doubt it. It is definitely *not* fine for dealing
with worms. That's what you need to know.

"Some of us are moving through fear and are starting to move into
anger toward the Chtorrans. It could be a fatal mistake. Our monkey
machinery is stuck in yipe. There's no escape. Running doesn't help.
And there are no goodies. So, the next step is rage."

"I know—I've seen it—"

"Go on. Tell me, what's rage."

"Rage is the fighting machine gearing up."

"Right," she said. "And we know we can't fight the worms, can we?
They've already demonstrated that we can't outfight them. So, what
comes next, James?"

"Uh—"

"What comes after rage, James?"

"I don't know—"

"Come on, what happens after you've been arguing the same argument for a week?"

"I don't know about you, but I get bored—"

"Right. Boredom." She nodded with satisfaction. "After you've
raged and raged and raged and used up all your energy and frustration,
suppose the thing you're frightened of, angry at, raging at, is still sitting
there picking its teeth and grinning at you. That's when you get tired of
being angry. We call that boredom. Or annoyance. But now that you've
given up being angry, there's room for you to actually become *interested*
in that thing—whatever it is—that scared you in the first place. That's
how the machinery works. It isn't until you let go of the yipe that you
have room for the goody, right?"

"Right."

"That's the machinery, James. That's what you're operating on top
of. You can't stop it from running. You never could. Now, why do you
think I'm telling you all this?"

"So, I can—uh . . . well, the object of this is to establish communication, so this is about not letting the monkey machinery get in the way
of the communication . . . right?" I grinned, I knew it was.

"Right." She grinned right back. "I want you to finish being afraid
and angry and bored in here. Don't take that into the circle or that's

what the circle will be about. When you give up all that stuff—what can you do?"

I shrugged. "Nothing, I think."

"Don't be flip. What can you do after you give up all those monkey-machine reactions?"

I shrugged again. "Have a party?"

"That's exactly right. After all that other stuff is taken care of, there's nothing left to do but play together. You make up a game—call it business or marriage or United States Congress—but it's still only a very fancy game played by very fancy monkeys. So . . . do you know what you have to do in that circle?"

"Make up a game for monkeys and bunnies."

"You got it. That's all you have to do. If you're fun to play with, the communication will take care of itself."

"Yes, I see—I really do." I was marveling at the simplicity of it. "I have to leave my rifle behind. I have to leave my military mind-set behind. I have to even leave my scientist act behind. I have to just—I see it!—I have to just go in there as a monkey who wants to play, don't I?"

"Congratulations." She beamed at me and shook my hand. "As Chief Medical Officer of this operation, I hereby pronounce you fit for duty. You are the *best* chimpanzee in the United States Army." She handed me a banana.

"Only a banana?" I asked. "I don't get a mate?"

"That, James, is part of the graduate course."

FIFTY-ONE

THE FINAL meeting of the presentation team took place at eighteen hundred hours.

Colonel Tirelli, Dr. Fletcher, Dr. Larson, three staff members I didn't recognize, the two women on the audio-video team, five observers, three mission specialists, six pilots, two programmers, two spider handlers, and the weapons team. I almost felt crowded.

There wasn't a lot of business that needed to be handled. Even Dr. Fletcher admitted that. We checked the weather forecasts, narrowed our choice of target sites—we'd make the final selection tomorrow morning—and then opened it up for questions. There weren't a lot.

Colonel Tirelli took over then and asked if anyone wanted to reconsider their decision to participate. This was a strictly volunteer operation and if anybody present wanted to drop out, they could do so now— or they could see her privately if they preferred. "You have until—" she looked at her watch, considered, and said, "—twenty-one hundred hours. There are backup people available, I assure you—so don't feel that you *have* to do this. The operation is dangerous, so do consider your participation carefully. If I don't hear from you by twenty-one hundred hours, I will assume that you have made a complete and total commitment. Did everyone understand that?"

Affirmative nods.

"Well, then—that seems to be it. Does anyone here have anything else to add?"

No. No one.

"Good. Thank you—and good night! Get yourself a good dinner, get to bed early, and get a good night's sleep!"

Most of the team headed for the doors. I headed for the front of the room. Colonel Tirelli was conferring softly with two of her pilots, so I waited politely to one side. When she finished, she looked up and saw me. "Yes, McCarthy?"

"May I talk to you privately?"

Her eyes shaded. "You want to drop out?"

"No! It's just—"

"If it's not about the mission tomorrow—"

"It's something that could *affect* the mission tomorrow." I said it as pointedly as I could.

"Mm hm. Wait a minute—" She handed her clipboard to one of her aides and then took me out into the hall, around the corner and into a deserted office. She closed the door behind us and leaned back against a desk, leaving an uncomfortable distance between herself and me. "What is it?" she asked. Her expression was polite, curious—and very very cold.

I felt myself flushing. "I—I guess this is a personal thing," I started. "But it's really getting to me. I mean, what's going on?"

She blinked as if she didn't know what I was talking about. "I don't understand."

"We had a date planned, remember? You and I and the biggest lobster on the west coast, remember? I mean, you said some things in the chopper—and I don't know if that was for serious—or if it was just . . . well, you know, real casual, or what?"

Lizard noticed an ink smudge on her palm. She rubbed at it with her thumb. She wasn't looking at me as she remarked, "That's what I like, a question with a lot of certainty in it." She shoved her hands into her pockets and looked up at me. "Listen, McCarthy. Everything I said to you in the chopper was true. You're cute. You're probably fun in bed. And you're also a lieutenant. One thing I know about lieutenants is that they have permanent erections. It's convenient at times. Most of the time it's not. Your problem is that you're trying to think with your erection. Please don't. It wasn't designed for that."

I stared at her. I wanted to ask, "Who are you really and what have you done with Lizard Tirelli?" Instead, I merely opened my mouth and said, "Is that it—?"

"For now." She looked at her watch. "Don't you have one more meeting tonight?"

"I have some kind of counseling session, yeah—"

"Well, I suggest you get to it." Her expression was impassive.

I could see that even being confused would be a waste of time here. I shook my head and stepped past her to the door. Halfway through it, I turned back to her. "This does not make sense to me. And it sure doesn't make me confident about tomorrow."

"I'm sorry, McCarthy—but that's the way it has to be."

"Yeah, sure." I closed the door behind me. Colonels! I'd never understand them.

I found Fletcher back in the meeting room. "Listen, about this counseling session—"

She shook her head. "I'm not your counselor, James. I have nothing to do with that."

"Well—listen, I just want to skip it. I don't feel—"

Fletcher's face hardened. "You do and you don't go tomorrow. You get your ass downstairs, right now!" She turned to one of her assistants. "Jerry—will you escort Lieutenant McCarthy down to the basement? Make sure he gets there."

I remembered Jerry Larson from Denver. He'd lost some weight and cut his hair; it made him look more intelligent than I remembered.

He led me down three flights of stairs (it was faster than the elevator), past the holding tanks (four worms), and into the specimen section, through the greenhouse.

The air smelled overpoweringly sweet. On either side, behind thick glass walls, I could see banks of purple and red plants.

"See that one?" Larson pointed to a shapeless black bush as tall as a man. Its leaves were ragged and shaggy. Whatever form or structure the plant had was impossible to see; it looked like a big pile of dirty laundry. "That one walks. Very slowly. We call it a shambler. It feeds on carrion. It's probably a scavenger. I don't think it kills—but we've got it isolated just in case."

"What're these?" I pointed to the opposite side. The plants there were more colorful. Banks of red and yellow blossoms cascaded across the tables.

"Oh—" said Larson. "We call those mandala vines. You have to look at them close up. You see those blossoms? Each one is made up of hundreds, perhaps thousands, of miniature blossoms all clustering together."

"They're gorgeous—" Even from this side of the glass, I was dazzled.

The blossoms were pink and scarlet and purple; but they were speckled with yellow and orange and white.

"Here—you can see this one a little better." Larson pointed to one of the smaller vines, hanging against the glass.

He was right. The miniature blossoms were easier to see. They gathered in groups to form clusters. Each little cluster had its own bright pattern of colors, lightest at the center, brightest and gaudiest at the edges.

Lower down on the vine, I could see how the clusters expanded and gathered around a central one. "I see where it gets its name," I said, grinning. The vines were beautiful; the clusters of clusters formed a dazzling mandala. There was even a sense of a pattern. "How big does it get?"

Larson shrugged. "We don't know. We haven't got the room to let it grow. I'll tell you this—it drives the bees crazy."

"Is that its danger?"

"We don't know. It's here. We're observing it. It's pretty, isn't it?"

"Yeah, it really is."

"You should smell its perfume—it smells like all the good things in the world all rolled together. Honeysuckle, fresh bread, the inside of a new car, you name it; it smells different to everybody."

I followed Larson through two sets of double doors, out of botany and into biology. We moved through a vast white warehouse full of cages and terrariums. The air was full of dark animal smells. I couldn't identify any of them.

"We discovered something very interesting about the meeps," he said.

"Meeps—those are the weaselly-looking red-brown things, aren't they?"

"No, you're thinking of libbits. A meep is a mousy pink furball. Here —these are libbits."

I looked into a large glass enclosure. The libbit looked like a small polite worm, except it had no eyes, no arms, and only the finest coat of downy brown fur. It was about the size of a mole or a badger. There were four of them in the terrarium.

"They burrow," said Larson. "They eat small rodents: rats, mice, chipmunks, bunnies and meeps. Here—up here. These are meeps." He pointed at a row of cages.

"Oh, right—we saw some of those on the chopper windshield. Kinda cute. What about 'em? I bet they breed like crazy, right?"

Larson shrugged. "We don't know yet. This is what I wanted you to see. We put three of 'em into a cage with a mamma rabbit and her litter. Mamma rabbit rejected her own babies to nurse the meeps instead."

"You're kidding!"

"Nope. The same behavior has been repeated with a dozen other rabbits. If the babies are small enough, the meeps will eat them, but they prefer to nurse on Mamma."

"Yick. I wish you hadn't told me that."

"Oh, you haven't heard the worst of it. The meeps will nurse a mamma rabbit to death." He added somberly, "And she doesn't appear to object, either. She dies happy."

We passed out of the specimen section into a storage area; we walked past bags and bags of various animal feeds. The air was fresher here.

"Listen," I stopped him. "I want to apologize for shooting down your plan. I guess I came on a little strong—"

"You want to hear my theory about the bunnydogs?" Larson asked. He looked me straight in the eye. "I think they're like the meeps—only for humans. The bunnydogs are so cute, they're irresistible. The first time people see those videos, they all go, 'Awwwww.' Especially women. They all want to pick the bunnies up and cuddle them. I'll bet a woman would put her own baby down to cuddle a bunnydog. I'll bet tomorrow you'll find out just how friendly the bunnydogs *really* are—"

"Thanks. I think I can find the rest of the way myself," I interrupted him deliberately.

"It's just down there." Larson pointed. "Past those steel doors. Follow the red stripe to the security section."

"Security?"

"It's an isolation block. It sits on springs. It's earthquake-proof and self-contained. That's where we control the whole operation. All our files are stored there. It can be locked down tighter than the Iron Mountain. It's got an independent air supply, power supply, and a six-month supply of food. It's safe against the entire electromagnetic spectrum, including lasers, masers, xasers, all kinds of radiation, magnetism, and television reruns. It's blanketed by scrambler fields. *Nothing* goes in or out without permission. Oh—and you'll have to decontaminate too."

I looked at Larson. "Isn't all this a little extreme for just a counseling session?"

He shrugged. "It's the best place in the world for privacy." He turned and headed back the way we'd come.

I followed Larson's directions: through the steel doors, past a security scan, detoxification, through a security tube—through a triple air-lock—then through another security tube and a final scanning station.

The robot at the desk directed me down a hall to a corridor of personal apartments. Room fourteen, please.

I knocked on the door politely.

A woman's voice: "Door's open. Come on in."

I pushed it open. The first thing that struck me was the smell of lilac perfume.

And then, Colonel Lizard Tirelli came out of the kitchen wearing an apron and an embarrassed smile. "Come on in, Jim."

FIFTY-TWO

"I GUESS I owe you an explanation—and an apology," she began.

"I should think so." I was still standing in the doorway.

"Come in, Jim, and close the door behind you." When I didn't move, she stepped past me and pushed the door shut herself, then she took me by the hand and led me into the room. "Lieutenants," she muttered. She pointed at the couch. "Sit down and listen."

I sat. She pulled up a chair and sat down opposite me.

"Do you want something to drink?" she asked.

I shook my head. The apartment was furnished very comfortably. There was nothing at all to indicate that it was eighty feet underground.

Lizard began softly. "I treated you abominably, I know. Believe me, I feel terrible about it—but there's a very good reason why it had to be this way."

"A good reason? Yeah?" I waited.

"The problem is . . ." she continued, "I can't tell you what that reason is. All I can do is ask you to forgive me." She searched my face expectantly. "Jim?"

This did not make sense.

I shook my head. "I don't know. I'm confused." I rubbed my forehead, my face. I looked back at her. I couldn't think of any words to say. "I—just—You're crazy! You know that?"

She sighed and nodded her agreement. "Very probably, I am. But this is the only way I could make it work."

"Make *what* work?"

She looked unhappy. "My promise—to you."

"Your promise—?" I crossed to her and pulled her to her feet. I held her arms and demanded, "Just what the hell is going on?"

She went rigid in my grasp, but her expression wasn't angry—it was *frightened.* Of me? Abruptly, she burst out in frustration: "I'm being monitored! You're being monitored! By the military! This is the only place where we're guaranteed any privacy. I think."

I let go of her in surprise. I could still smell her perfume. Lilac. "Monitored—? Why?"

She shrugged helplessly. "Why not?"

I stared at her. My mind was whirling. "So that little performance upstairs—that wasn't for me? Was it?"

"I am so sorry about that . . ." she said.

"You did that to me without—?" I could feel the fury rising into my face. "I don't understand. I've been monitored before. Everybody on the goddamn base knew about the time Ted got me drunk. They're already gossiping about you and me. So what does it matter if somebody sees us or looks at a tape or something—?"

"You don't know. It matters to me!" she said.

"Why didn't you tell me—?"

"I *couldn't!*"

"Why? What am I—some kind of a cretin, or a thing—that you'll only be my friend if you can keep it a secret from me?"

"Y'know, it isn't easy being your friend!" she snapped back. "Sometimes you *are* a jerk."

"And you're a stuck-up, fat-assed, iron-clad, dragon-faced, red-headed gorgon who can't even keep a plastic eggbeater in the sky! But you're the one who wants to go to bed with me!"

"My ass is not fat! And I thought it was mutual—"

"It was!" I shouted back.

"Well then—" And suddenly, she was flustering close to tears. Lizard? "—Can't you just accept it? Jim, please?"

"And wake up tomorrow and find you've turned back into Medusa? Dammit! That *hurt!*"

"Jim—" She took my hands in hers. Her eyes were incredibly blue. "I am so terribly sorry and unhappy to have hurt you. You are an extraordinarily precious human being. Please believe me, if there had been any other way—but this was the only way I could manage it."

"I want to believe you," I said. "I really do. . . ." I kept on holding her hands in mine. They were very warm. "But I—I just don't know—"

"I wanted to be with you tonight," she said. "That was the whole purpose of this—"

"I want to be with you too!" I felt my throat tightening. "I just want to know that you *care.*"

"I do care." Her voice was very soft. "Believe me. I really do."

I couldn't deny it. She was telling the truth.

And I wanted her so badly—

I leaned forward and touched my lips to hers. She tasted sweet.

After several eternities, we broke apart and looked at each other. We were both relieved—and embarrassed.

"So you'll stay for dinner?" she asked.

"Well . . . maybe. What are you making?"

"C rations and bottled water."

"You promised me a lobster."

"Listen, it was hard enough to reserve the apartment—"

"I'm sorry, it's lobster or nothing."

"Well . . . all right." She led me into the dining room.

The lobster on the table was large enough to have been a threat to dogs, cats and small children when it was alive. There was a bottle of wine chilling in the bucket.

"Pretty sure of yourself, aren't you?"

She shrugged. "When the day comes that I can't outthink a lieutenant—"

I pulled away from her. "Hold it! Before we go any further—no more military stuff, okay?"

Colonel Lizard Tirelli of the United States Army, Special Forces Warrant Agency nodded her head in agreement. She unpinned her long red hair and let it cascade down to her shoulders. "Deal," she said.

Dinner passed like a dream.

She was too beautiful. I couldn't stop watching her. We traded a lot of embarrassed smiles and kept our conversation deliberately casual.

"I have to admit something," I said.

"What's that?"

"I—was jealous of you. I thought that you and Danny Anderson were—you know—lovers."

"Really?" She laughed. "Don't be silly. Danny's gay."

"Huh? You're kidding! I'll be damned. Is that why Duke—?" I shut my mouth.

"Probably."

"Well. Gosh." I shook my head unbelievingly.

"I have to admit something too."

"What?"

"I was jealous that you were spending too much time with Lois Fletcher."

"No!"

"Yes."

"But she's—" I shrugged. "I just never thought of her that way."

"I'm glad—"

Eventually we moved to the bedroom and I started to tense up again. I didn't know why.

While I waited for her, I busied myself with bridegroom things. I turned the lights and the music low. I turned back the bed. Finally, I pulled off my clothes and slipped between the sheets to wait.

After all this time—

She came out of the bathroom wearing a nightgown so sheer two silkworms couldn't have spent more than an afternoon on it. She got into bed next to me and I wondered if I should reach for her. I wanted to.

I looked over at her.

She looked back at me expectantly. "Are you going to make the first move?" she asked. "Or should I?"

"Uh—" I said. This wasn't going to be as easy as I thought. "You are so beautiful. . . ."

She stroked my cheek. "You don't need the compliments any more, Jim. We're beyond that." She added gently, "Now we're at foreplay."

I said, "I—I know this is going to sound stupid, but you're *too* beautiful. I don't know if I can make love to a woman as beautiful as you."

She looked like she was about to laugh—she smothered it quickly, compassionately. "I'll let you in on a secret," she said. "I'm really very plain. I walked into that bathroom and looked at myself in the mirror and said, 'Ick. What a mess.' Really. But then I said, 'But Jim deserves the best, so I'm going to pretend to be gorgeous, just for him.' And see, you believed it."

"I think you *overdid* it," I said. "I hate to admit this—but I'm scared as hell!"

"You're kidding." She said it straight out.

"I am twenty-four years old," I said. "I lost my virginity when I was nineteen. I have been with three different girls in my life—four, if you count Ted. That's it, the sum total of my experience. I have never been with a woman as *intensely beautiful* as you are. And—" I added, "I have *never* been with anyone I cared about as much as you."

She was studying me thoughtfully. "You *are* scared, aren't you?"

"I'm terrified . . . that I won't be good enough. . . ."

"Thank you," she said. "For being so *honest.*" She reached over and put her hand on my chest. It felt like fire—like electricity. For a moment, all I could feel was that hand, those delicate fingers, the fingernail tracing a circle in the little patch of hair over my breastbone. After a moment, she said softly, "Listen, sweetheart. This isn't an audition. You're not being graded. Let me play Mommy for about two seconds here and I'll tell you something. The only thing that you need to do a good job is *enthusiasm.* You got that?"

"I've got *lots* of enthusiasm," I said. "So much so I'm afraid I'm going to burst a blood vessel."

"Good," she said. She shifted her position so we were lying side by side. "There is no right way to do this, Jim—so you can't possibly screw it up. And if you do anyway, I forgive you in advance."

I moved my hand to her breast. She was warm. My hand was cold. I was afraid to move it. I said, "I, uh—I can't help it. I feel like I should ask permission."

She didn't laugh at me. She took my hand in hers and held it. She kissed my fingers. She took a breath and whispered, "Sweetheart, you are so caring—but you have to stop thinking of sex as something you do to another person, and start thinking of it as something that two people share together."

"I'd really like that—" I said. "But I've never experienced it that way."

Lizard's expression remained open. She wasn't judging me. She was just hearing what I had to say. She squeezed my hand again. "Listen to me, stupid—" The way she said it, it was a term of endearment. "I'm going to tell you everything you need to know about sex."

"I don't think we have that much time," I admitted.

"It's all right. There isn't that much you *need* to know. It'll only take a minute."

She lifted herself up on one elbow and put her finger on my lips. Her fingers were exquisite. I kissed them.

"The only thing in the world that you *really* own," she began, "is the body that you live in. So that's the only thing you really have to share."

"I never thought of it that way," I said.

"Hush, child—I'm not through. Have you ever noticed that you never go to bed with anyone unless you're interested in their body?"

I nodded.

"Well, nobody ever goes to bed with you either without being interested in *your* body. Sex is about bodies. Either you like bodies, my dear, or you don't have sex."

"I like bodies," I said. "I like yours." I put out a tentative hand and let my fingers touch her arm.

"And I like yours," she smiled back at me.

"See—" I said, "that's the part I have trouble with. I never knew that."

"I know," she said. "That's why you're such an asshole. Cute, but still an asshole. Why do you have such a low opinion of yourself? Do you know that's an insult to the people you go to bed with? It means you don't think much of their taste either. It also means that you have to con people into your bed, and when you get them there, the best you can do is use them. Here's what I'm trying to tell you, my sweet lover— you can't have good sex with anyone else until you let yourself experience your own wonderfulness."

"My own wonderfulness . . . ?" I squeaked. I cleared my throat. "I, uh—always thought that a person should be . . . um, modest."

"Hmp," she said. "Modesty is the most arrogant form of conceit. Modesty is an excuse to hide yourself, and that rips people off. If you're wonderful—and you are—then, share it. Don't you think people like being around wonderful people? Don't you?"

"Sure. But I'm not—what you said—wonderful."

She sat up and stared at me. "Who made up that shit?"

"Huh?"

"I said, 'who made up that shit?' That you're not wonderful. Trust me, sweetheart—you are positively terrific."

"No, I'm not."

"Yes, you are."

"This is making me very uncomfortable—" I said. "Couldn't we just get on with what we set out to do . . . ?"

"No, we can't. Not until you let it in. I think you're wonderful."

I looked away. She was too beautiful.

She put a hand on my chin and turned my face back to hers. "It's all right for you to think I'm gorgeous, huh? But not for me to think you're terrific?"

"But, I'm not—"

"I. Say. You. Are." Her tone of voice left no room for argument.

"I hear you—" I managed to say.

"Do you? Do you really? You need to let this in, stupid. I don't go to bed with losers. I *chose* you. Did you ever stop to think *why?*"

"Bad eyesight?" I joked.

She slapped my face. Hard.

When my vision cleared, I was lying on my back and she was on top of me, glaring down at me. "Now that I have your attention," she said, "—don't ever do that again!"

"Do what?"

"Insult my taste in lovers. You're so busy denying your own sexiness you can't even see how horny I am for you. Will you let it in?" Her face was very close to mine. Her eyes were almost too close to focus on. I felt like I was staring into an abyss that I wanted to jump into.

I wanted to tell her something, but I didn't have the words for it. I wanted to ask for help, but I didn't think she could help me. I felt her fingers on my shoulders. I felt her weight on my chest, her legs around mine. I felt myself stiffening with desire—and I was terrified.

She must have seen it in my eyes. She raised herself up and looked down at me.

"Something's the matter, isn't it? There's something deeper, isn't there?"

"I don't deserve you," I said.

"Of course, you don't," she agreed. "I'm a gift, not a payment." And then she stopped in mid-thought and studied me. "But you don't know how to *enjoy* sex, do you?"

I didn't answer. She was right. I'd seen other couples laughing and playing together. I'd always wondered how they managed it. I always felt . . . left out.

"All right—I give up," she said. "We'll do it your way." Abruptly, she rolled off me and out of bed.

"Where are you going?"

"I'll be right back—"

She padded back in carrying an American flag. Fifty-two stars, thirteen stripes. I remembered there had been a small meeting room next door.

She climbed back into bed and began settling herself with exaggerated care. "I'll tell you what," she said seriously. "I'm going to put this flag over my face—" she pulled it up over her head like a sheet "—and you can do it for love of country." And then she lay there and was very very still.

"What—?"

She didn't answer.

I pulled the flag down off her face. She was grinning up at me. "I don't know what else to do," she said, and pulled the flag back up.

"You come out of there!"

"What's the matter!" Her voice came up through the stars and stripes. "Aren't you patriotic?" She cradled her breasts. "Here—pretend that these are the tits of liberty!" And then she jiggled them.

"Lizard—!"

She jiggled her tits again—harder this time.

"This is not funny!" I said.

The flag started shaking. "Then why am I laughing so hard?" she asked. She was making little squeaking noises in her throat. Her chest shook.

I reached to pull the flag away. She grabbed it and held on. I poked her in the ribs instead. She shrieked and jerked her hands down to her stomach. I reached for the flag—she grabbed it again—I gave her another poke in the ribs—and another—"Here! You want patriotism? It's Pearl Harbor Day!" I made explosion noises to punctuate each poke. She yelped each time, but she wouldn't stop giggling—she pulled her knees up to her chest. I hollered, *"Banzaiii!"* and smacked her on the bottom!

"Oh, you're gonna get it now—" she started.

"Yeah! You and what army?" I pulled the flag away and poked her again; she doubled up on her side, giggling too hard to resist. I grabbed her and rolled her over on her back. "Tits of liberty, huh? It looks more like the two-party system to me. First I'm going to party here—"

"Jim—!" she shrieked in surprise.

"—and then I'm going to party over here! And what's this? A cleavage in the body politic?" I put my face between her breasts and made a big wet razzberry sound. She was laughing like crazy now. She pulled her legs up to kick me away, but I pinned her knees under my chest and held her shoulders down with my hands. I was laughing as hard as she was. "And what's this down here—? The crack of doom?" Her eyes met mine.

And in that moment—I knew. And grinned. I could feel my face splitting in joy. I could see the laughter reflected back in her eyes.

I couldn't catch my breath. I was giggling too hard. And so was she.

We giggled and laughed together and in the middle of it, I bent my face down to hers. Her knees parted, her legs opened beneath me and I lowered myself onto her and into her. She wrapped her arms and legs around me and held on tight. We both did. I gave myself to her, and she to me—and we were joyous.

She was right. I was wonderful.

FIFTY-THREE

SATELLITE RECON gave us the morning pictures: three primary targets and seven backups.

I voted for the one closest to our original crash site. Both Colonel Tirelli and Dr. Fletcher agreed and that settled that.

We reconfirmed our choice a half hour before liftoff, and then we were on our way. Three huge choppers clattered into the air like malevolent insects and turned north across the bay. I remembered this view from before.

I glanced around the chopper. Dr. Fletcher was conferring with Jerry Larson about the layout of monitor probes and sample traps. The crew in the back were sleeping. It was a good idea. We'd been up since before dawn. I made myself comfortable—

—and was awakened by the beeping of the autopilot. The chopper was dropping. "We're there," called Lizard. I straightened up and looked out the window.

We were falling toward a wide grassy pasture. It was overgrown with tall blue-green grass. I could see it waving in the wind. I glanced backward. The follow-choppers were still in formation, coming down with us.

The three ships settled down into the soft ground right in the center. There was at least a kilometer of clear space on every side of us. Good. Nothing would approach us undetected.

"All right," growled Lizard, "everybody stay in your seats until the ground crew declares the area secure."

I peered out the window. A security team, armed with torches, caustic sprays, and bazookas was just fanning out. I envied them. At least they knew what they were doing.

As soon as security declared the area yellow, the science team hit the ground running. Their job was to put out probes and sensors. I saw several small mobile units rolling out through the grass, including two walkers and a spider.

My orders were to stay inside until we went to condition green. I climbed forward and parked myself in the copilot's seat again. Directly ahead, the walkers were beginning the process of clearing a wide circular area. A gathering circle. A friendly sign for the bunnydogs. An invitation.

I thought about a beer. I opened a Coke instead.

The afternoon got suddenly dark. The camouflage dome was being pulled into place over the chopper. Soon it would be inflated and sprayed. The whole process would take less than an hour. The theory was that the choppers would have negative associations for the worms and bunnies. So we'd hide them. If we needed to scramble, the camouflage domes could be blown away in seconds.

Somebody switched the cabin lights on. I glanced back. Colonel Tirelli was just climbing forward. She dropped into the pilot's seat.

We were alone in the chopper.

I turned to look out the opposite window. I made sure she saw that my studied nonchalance was deliberate.

She ignored me. She clicked her controls this way and that and looked very busy. I wondered if she had anything to say to me.

Either she didn't—or she wasn't ready to say it yet. The silence stretched on.

Maybe I should say something. I turned to her—

—and noticed a tiny American flag pin on her lapel. I nearly cracked up laughing. I had to bite my tongue to keep control.

Lizard looked at me curiously. "Are you all right, Lieutenant?"

"I am fine," I grinned. "Just fine!"

FIFTY-FOUR

THE TWO robots had stamped out and cleared a wide, mathematically precise arena. A perfect circle.

I stripped down to my shorts and sat in the center and . . . imagined. I closed my eyes and imagined what it would be like to be surrounded by bunnydogs. And worms.

I tried to imagine sitting naked before a curious worm.

I shuddered. And not because the wind was cold.

I tried to imagine the smell of the animal. The look of it. The feel of its fur. I had touched a living worm's fur once. It had *tingled*.

I tried to imagine what it would feel like to stand naked before a worm. I couldn't imagine myself feeling anything but terrified.

No bunnydogs showed up the first day.

Or the second.

We kept close to the chopper domes and worried.

Fletcher and I practiced. We did communication exercises, clearing exercises, confrontation exercises—things that seemed to make no sense at all, and yet . . . I began to feel as if I were the center of the world here. I began to feel . . . *focused*. There was a clarity of purpose developing here.

Every moment was preparation. Every moment was a drill.

Fletcher would ask me, "What are you doing now?"

And I would reply, "I'm eating."

She'd ask, "And *why* are you eating?"

"Because I'm hungry."

"What's your purpose in eating?"

"Taking care of my body, so I can do the job." It felt like a cate-chism, but—I could feel the meanings under the words. It was true.

"And what job is that?"

"Creating a relationship with the bunnydogs, a space in which com-munication can occur."

"Good. Do you have any other purposes?"

"I did want to . . . have a relationship with Lizard—but I've let go of that now."

"Good, James. Anything else?"

"No."

I felt myself entering a *different* state of consciousness. The difference was *profound.*

I felt—in control.

As if I were creating it.

All of it. The forest. The meadow. The domes. The quiet, distant faces.

Especially the faces—they were all so *detached* from me. They were my herd. And I was—the leader? Not . . . quite. I was the . . . ma-gician.

The feeling was curious.

I told Fletcher I wanted to walk in the forest.

She shook her head no.

I insisted. I said it was necessary—for me to be clear.

She said all right, but only if she could send a security team with me.

I told her I needed to be alone. I needed to feel *ownership* of the land —especially if I were going to invite a bunnydog family to *share* it.

I insisted.

She gave in. She let me walk.

I knew the team was following me at a discreet distance. I didn't mind. As long as I wasn't tripping over them.

The forest was a cathedral, green and gold.

Its ceiling was so high it was invisible—a canopy of lofty branches and dark broad leaves. God's light slanted down through the pine and the redwoods, turning the tree trunks ruddy. The beams were so solid you could feel them with your fingers. They struck sparks of golden dust in the air.

High above, a cold wind played across the roof, letting the bright blue sky peek through in tiny patches here and there. The breeze rustled the leaves like an organ and dappled the light that fell to the soft brown earth below. My footsteps fell lightly on a carpet of fresh green pine needles.

I breathed deeply—and the air smelled like heaven: pine and honeysuckle and cascades of beautiful growing *green* things. There was no pink left anywhere.

I could have stayed here forever.

Somewhere ahead, I heard water—a stream. I followed the sound and—

The forest opened out onto a meadow.

A riot of color, gaudy brilliance, dazzling to the eye!

But such a meadow! Nothing like this had ever been seen on the Earth before!

I stepped forward hesitantly.

Purple ivy, streaked with lavender and white, curled away from me. Black shambler bushes struck silver sparks in the air. Slender red growths rose like fountains, exploding into feathery black and pink fronds.

And over everything—mandala vines.

They captured the eye, they overwhelmed the senses. They were a carpet, they rolled away in endless waves. The mandala flowers piled themselves high; they dripped from stumps of rotted trees; they hung from branches in a riotous celebration of color, a royal display.

I stood and gaped in awe and wonder. Silver and crimson, orange and indigo so dark it was black, magenta, yellow and blue, cascades of hue and shade beyond the eye's ability to differentiate.

And, oh—the smells!

Waves of scent swept over me—fresh baked bread, strawberry jam, thick fresh cream, apple cobbler, peaches—and scents for which I had no names at all. Dark purply scents laced with scarlet overtones: sweet chords of gold and opium perfume. Heady aromas of magic, sparkling spells; doorways into crystal heavens and beautiful trips through Hell.

The forest behind me was forgotten.

Dammit! Why did the invasion have to be *beautiful* too?

On the morning of the third day, the sensors picked up a worm on the east edge of the meadow.

A quiet voice on the radio said, "I think I've got something."

We crowded around the monitors. The big display showed a smallish-looking worm poised on the high end of the slope. It seemed *confused*. Its eye-stalks swiveled back and forth as it studied the three mottled domes in the middle of the pasture below it. It flowed a few meters forward—

—and stopped. Hesitated. Swiveled its eyes. Backward. Forward.

We went to full magnification. The eyes irised shut and open again. *Sput-phwut.*

The worm half turned and looked behind itself. Then it swiveled its eyes toward us again.

I felt as if I could read its mind. It was a five-year-old child, seeing something very interesting, but not knowing if it should investigate by itself—or go tell Mommy first.

It made up its mind. This was a well-trained five-year-old. It completed its turn and headed off to the east as fast as it could go.

Nothing else happened for the rest of the day.

During the night, the sensors picked up movement on the ridge, but it could have been deer or coyotes.

FIFTY-FIVE

LIZARD WOKE me up. "Jim—"
"Huh? What?" Everything was dark. "What time is it?"
"Shh. Be quiet. It's almost dawn. I want you to come forward."
I rubbed my eyes and fell out of my bunk—
"I said, 'Be quiet!' " she whispered again.
I followed her forward. "What do you want?"
"Look—" She pointed.
I looked to the monitor screen on the console. I looked out the window. Through the netting, I could see—
There were three bunnydogs sitting on the opposite side of the circle.
"This is it," I said. I looked at her. "Isn't it?"
She nodded.
I started unbuttoning my shirt. "We should get started—"
She put her hand on my shoulder. "There's time. We'll do it by the mission book."
"But they could leave."
"I doubt it," she said. There was certainty in her voice.
I turned to her. "How long have they been there?"
"For an hour."
"And you didn't wake me?"
"As mission commander, I felt you needed your sleep. If they're here to communicate, Jim, then they'll wait. And if they're not, then it's a mistake to rush into anything. We'll follow the checklist. I'm calling condition yellow. I have to open two separate channels to Oakland,

satellite and direct. I have to wake the observation team and the defense team; I have to activate the high-level monitors. You might as well have breakfast and go through your exercises with Fletcher again. It'll be at least ninety minutes before I'll go to condition green. Probably longer. Until then, my *friend,* you're still under my command. Got that?"

"Yes, ma'am."

"First thing, I want you to put on a medical harness. I want you to stabilize your heart and respiration before you go out there."

"Is it that obvious how excited I am?"

"Just do it," she said, hooking a thumb over her shoulder. "I've got work to do."

I moved. I went and woke up Fletcher, showed her our guests and then the two of us fell into the familiar routine of preparation and clearing. The excitement was growing in me like a bomb. This was worse than Christmas.

Fletcher took me to the back of the chopper and began talking to me low and quietly. At first, I couldn't hear a word she said. All I could think of was the bunnydogs.

"Jim!" Her tone was urgent. "Pay attention."

"Yes, ma'am."

"What are you here for?"

"The bunnydogs. Um, creating a relationship with the bunnydogs so communication can occur." The words fell out like a recorded phrase.

"Sorry, I don't get it. Where are you, James—because you're sure not here with me."

"I'm—sorry. I—guess I'm just excited."

"I know. All right, strip down and put on the harness. Let's see what's going on."

The decision had been made that the contact—me—should be naked. Or as close to naked as possible. To allow the bunnydogs to experience the *animalness* of the individual first. The physical beingness. I'd voted in favor of shorts. We'd compromised on a loincloth.

As soon as I'd stripped, Fletcher had me slip into the medical harness. She studied her console and frowned. "Is there any part of you that *isn't* elevated?" she asked.

"Well, there is one," I said, glancing down. "But, if you want—"

"Knock that off." She was all business. "Close your eyes, James. Good. All right. Here's the exercise. Thirty deep breaths. Like I taught you. See how long you can take."

I closed my eyes and concentrated on my breathing. Breath number one. Breathe for your toes. This oxygen is for your toes. Take in as much as you can. Take care of your toes. Hold it as long as you can. Now, let it out. Breath number two. Breathe for your left foot. This oxygen is for your left foot. Take in as much as you can.

I could hear Fletcher and Colonel Tirelli conferring softly in the front of the chopper. I couldn't hear what they were saying, but I knew it was about me. I could sense the concern in their voices.

This breath is for your right knee. Take in as much as you can. I was going to go through my whole body this way. I was going to be thoroughly oxygenated. I knew I was letting myself be distracted.

The sounds from the front of the chopper were too negative. If I wasn't ready, they weren't going to let me go. That's what they were discussing. If I was too *excited,* I wouldn't be able to hold my focus.

Breathe for your stomach. This oxygen is for your stomach. Breathe for your chest.

They stopped talking then and the only sound in the ship was the sound of my own breath.

Breathe for your brain. Take in as much as you can. Hold it for as long as you can.

When I opened my eyes again, Fletcher was sitting opposite me.

"How are you feeling now, James?"

"Better." I added, "But I'm still not ready. I can feel it. I'm too giddy."

"You're doing fine," she said. "It's just that you think this is important. It's not. It's only an oddball little experiment that no one is taking seriously. So there's nothing at stake here. You got that?"

"Yes."

"Good. So that means you're off the hook, Jim. No matter what happens out there, you can't screw up. Whatever happens, we still learn something. The experiment is already a success. All that's left is to find out the results."

"I wish I could believe that."

She shrugged. "It doesn't matter if you believe it or not. It's still true. Listen—" she added, "that circle that we cleared out there is an invitation to a party. It's the same invitation that they offered you and Duke and Colonel Tirelli three weeks ago, only you couldn't recognize it for what it was. Now that we know what it is, we can return the invitation. And they want to accept it. They're waiting for us. The *hard* part is over." She studied me intensely. "So, now what's the next move?"

"I go out there."

"And . . . ?"

"And—" I stopped. "Uh—I know the answer, Fletch—but knowing the answer doesn't change anything. I'm still running the monkey program. I'm excited—and I'm *scared.*" I looked at her, frustrated, "How do I let go?"

"Right. That's why you can't go out there, James. Not yet. You're still not ready to just *be* with them and play with them. You're still too busy being with your own feelings." Without missing a beat, she said, "Tell me a dirty joke."

"Huh?"

"Tell me a dirty joke. Any joke. Make one up."

"Why?"

"No reason at all. Tell me a joke!"

"Um—okay. What do you call a Chtorran who farts in the bathtub and bites the bubbles?"

"Well adjusted. Tell me one I haven't heard."

"What do you say to a Chtorran who's eating a Revelationist?"

"I give up, what?"

"Bon appetit!"

She smiled. "Okay, my turn. What's the Chtorran word for midget?"

"What?"

"Hors d'oeuvre. What does a Chtorran call a jogger?"

"Fast food. I've heard that one."

"All right. One more. What do you get when you cross a Chtorran with a grizzly bear?"

"What?"

"A very cross grizzly bear." She glanced at her console.

"How'm I doing?" I asked.

"Better." She grinned at me. "We may make it after all."

I felt myself surging with excitement. And immediately tried to suppress it.

"No, it's all right," she said. "You're excited. Let yourself be excited. If you try to stop being excited, it'll just keep building. Just let it run itself out." She pushed the console aside and turned to me. "Okay, here's what I want you to do:

"I want you to go up front, sit in the copilot's seat and study the bunnies. Just watch them. Watch them until you are tired of watching them. Until you are bored silly with watching them. Watch them until there is nothing left to do but watch them. Remember your herd experience. There's a point at which you will feel a shift in your experience of the bunnydogs. I can't explain what it will feel like, but you'll know it when it happens.

"I don't want you to move until you know that you're absolutely ready. When you are, get up quietly, take off the medical harness, and go out and do whatever is appropriate. You'll know what that is too. Have you got all that?"

I nodded.

"Good." She pointed me toward the front of the chopper.

I slipped into the copilot's seat and stared out at the bunnydogs. There were still only three of them. Papa, Mama, and baby? Maybe.

I remembered what Tanjy had said. Listen with your whole soul.

The bunnydogs were sitting patiently on the far side of the circle. Occasionally one or the other would scratch itself behind one ear. The littlest one had curled up and gone to sleep. It looked like a little pink pillow. That was interesting. The bunnydogs were naturally pink, even without the dust.

I remembered what Fletcher had taught me. Look beyond what you're seeing. Look at the surface. Look beyond the surface. And look inside yourself to see how *you're* seeing.

I was beginning to get a sense of the bunnydogs' patience. It wasn't their circle. It was *ours.* They were waiting to see what kind of a game we were inviting them to play.

And . . . we were too scared to play.

We couldn't even offer an invitation without hiding guns behind it.

The invitation lay empty.

The game hadn't been created yet.

Once you step into the circle, the game begins. So, the question is—what kind of a game did I want to create with the bunnies?

No.

The question was—what kind of a game could all of us create together?

I looked across at the rabbity little puppies and wondered—could these creatures play the game of *sentience?*

It was time to find out.

I levered myself out of my seat.

There was no one else in the chopper. They had left me alone. They were probably sitting in Colonel Anderson's command ship, watching the monitors.

The door was open. I stopped and removed the medical harness. I was wearing only a loincloth and a neck chain with a small transceiver hanging on it.

I stepped down out of the gunship.

I crossed to the wall of the camouflage dome and stepped through the netting.

FIFTY-SIX

THE BUNNYDOGS sat up straighter as I approached.

I stepped to the edge of the circle opposite the bunnies and sat down cross-legged. They needed the chance to study a human.

The two larger bunnies began to chirp and gobble at each other. The littlest bunny sat up, yawned, stretched and scratched himself. He looked around and saw me—and jumped nearly a meter in the air in startlement. His eyes went impossibly round. He was probably only a child. He edged sideways until he was hidden behind the largest bunnydog. Then he peered around curiously and blinked at me.

I waved at him.

He pulled his head back quickly, disappearing again behind his— what, his papa? No, that was a human assumption. Maybe the females of this species were the larger.

The two adult bunnies ceased gobbling and reduced their conversation to a series of coos and chirps.

They reminded me of something I'd seen in the herd. There were two young women who liked to sit opposite each other, cooing and gobbling nonsense syllables. If you didn't know the language—or the lack of it— you could almost think that they were really talking. It looked like they were totally engaged in some happy casual chatter—and in one sense, they were. But there were no agreed-upon symbols, and there was no transmission of any experience at all beyond the shared one of sitting and gobbling.

If an alien didn't know human language, would it assume that they were communicating?

And then, having made that assumption, if it had turned and looked to the observers of the herd, Dr. Fletcher and myself, and studied our quiet sidewise exchanges, could that same alien have perceived a difference? If anything, the two gobbling women would have looked *more* in communication than Fletcher and myself. At least it was obvious that they were acting in relationship.

This was the real question.

If two creatures are sitting and gobbling at each other, how do you tell if they are talking—or just gobbling? Were these bunnydogs actually using a language? Or were they simply making noises at each other?

It sounded like a language. But then, so did the herd noises.

Two more bunnydogs were hopping down the slope to join the three sitting opposite me. They bumped noses with Mama, Papa and baby bunnydog. They patted each other's fur. A greeting ritual?

The two newcomers looked older and more cautious than Mama, Papa and baby. But they took up their places at the edge of the circle and waited also.

I felt a little like a guru. Naked. Patient. Mysterious.

A sixth bunnydog joined the vigil.

There were other bunnydogs hopping and waddling toward the circle.

There were more up on the hill. Some were just sitting and watching. A few were advancing.

I waited until the gathering was complete—they gobbled and greeted each new arrival; there was much exchanging of nuzzlings and nose bumps, even a few pats and hugs before settling down—and then I stood up.

The bunnydogs sat up alert.

I stepped to the exact center of the circle.

I could feel their eyes. This was the center of the world.

Every bunnydog was watching me; so was every human. Everything I did was being monitored from the choppers hidden in the domes. Recorded. Photographed. Analyzed.

I stopped and waited. I allowed myself to feel the wind on my body. I let myself smell the grass and the scent of pine in the cool afternoon air. There was another scent on top of the pine. A sweet peppermint smell. The scent of the bunnies? It would be appropriate.

The bunnies were watching me attentively, but none of them had entered the circle yet.

They were waiting for me to do something.

I remembered what the bunnies had done before.

They had danced.

I touched the transceiver at my neck and said, very softly, "I have a problem. I don't know how to dance."

Fletcher's voice, just as softly, replied, "They don't know that. They've never seen a monkey dance before. Whatever you do is the right way."

"Oh, yeah. Thanks for reminding me."

I took a breath.

I started dancing.

I capered, I bounced, I shouted. I made Indian whooping noises with my hand over my mouth. I did a jig, a Charleston, a freddy, and a break. I jumped and hollered and shook.

The bunnydogs looked at each other curiously.

"Well, come on—!" I shouted. "Don't you want to dance?"

Several of the bunnies took a hop backward. Oh, shit. I was going to lose them.

I dropped forward in a somersault, came up on my knees, hooked my fingers in my mouth, crossed my eyes, stuck out my tongue, and said, "Boola-boola-boola! Labber-labber-labber—"

Two of the bunnies started giggling. The littlest bunny came charging into the circle then. He stopped in front of me and shook his head rapidly back and forth. He let his floppy lips and tongue shake like an ape. "Lubber-lubber-lubber—" he said in a high squeaky voice.

In seconds, I was surrounded by bunnies, all of them making incomprehensible gobbling sounds. They were bouncing and hopping all around me, somersaulting and turning upside down, shrieking, bubbling and shouting. They danced and jerked like little spastic puppets. I looked up the hill and it was covered with fluffy pink bodies bouncing down toward the circle. They were coming to join the party too. We had won!

A bright red worm came over the crest of the slope. Two more followed after it. And then two more. And another—I didn't care. The bunnies saw and began cheering and shouting. It was beginning to sound more and more like a language.

"I think we've done it!" I laughed. "We've done it! I don't know what we've done, but we've done it!"

The bunnies were all around me now, patting me and touching me affectionately. Their fingers were soft and furry. And they tickled.

I dropped to my knees. The bunnies came up close to inspect my face. Their tiny hands touched my cheeks, my nose, my hair. They were fascinated by the hairlessness of my body. They stroked me curiously. Their eyes were huge and round. They looked like little toy animals, pink and cuddly. But when they yipped, I could see that they had sharp white teeth. But then—so did puppies.

One of the bunnies took my hand and began licking my fingers. He put my middle finger in his mouth and sucked on it thoughtfully. Then he let go and looked at me and . . . giggled. I reached over and tugged his ear gently and we both knew it was all right.

The new arrivals plunged into the circle and joined the curious crowd. All of them wanted to get as close as possible. I reached out and touched as many of them as I could reach. I began to tickle them and poke them affectionately. I patted their heads and skritched their ears— they really loved that. I even picked up the baby bunnydogs and gave them little hugs and kisses. They shrieked and giggled with delight.

My transceiver started beeping. The bunnydogs cocked their heads at it curiously. I held it up for them to see—a tiny little button on a chain around my neck. I said, "See, it's nothing. It just makes noises. Make a noise, button."

The button said, "Oh, great and powerful god of small pink things, look around you now."

The bunnies were fascinated. One of the babies sniffed the button. Another tried to put it into his mouth. I had to take it away from him.

I looked up, beyond the small pink bodies.

There were worms here.

I was surrounded by worms.

Nineteen. Twenty. Twenty-three worms.

All sizes. From the smallest I'd ever seen—about the size of a St. Bernard—to three huge monsters the size of Greyhound buses.

"Well, hi guys . . ." I said. I stood up and looked at the worms. The last worm was just being herded into place by three energetic little bunnies. Again I thought of a jumbo jet being directed to dock by the ground crew.

All right—assume that the bunnies control the worms. The question was why? What did the bunnies use the worms for?

We were about to find out.

FIFTY-SEVEN

SOME OF the worms swiveled their eyes to study me. Some of them closed their eyes and looked like they were dozing.

And that was it.

They stayed outside the circle. Why? Did that mean something? Or not—?

Most of the bunnydogs were ignoring the worms. They were here to party. The worms were just . . . wallpaper. Or protection. Or . . . what? I couldn't even guess.

Several of the bunnies were tugging at me. I allowed myself to be turned away from the worms. They wanted to play some more. I let myself be pulled into a cluster of them. I grinned. I giggled. I laughed out loud.

The bunnies laughed with me. They bounced and hugged and fell all over me, screaming and giggling like children. They seemed to be asking for something. They tugged at me and made little begging noises. I had the weirdest sense that they were wondering where the rest of my . . . family was.

I touched the button at my throat and laughed. "I think there's room in this circle for a few more monkeys."

The button didn't respond.

I repeated my request. "I think we need some more monkeys out here."

"It's not part of the mission—"

"But it's *appropriate,*" I said. "It's what needs to happen next. We need to prove we're safe—as a species."

The button was silent.

I chuckled a bunny under his chin. We giggled together and made funny growling noises. I batted him gently, and he rolled and somersaulted backward like a happy little croquet ball. He scampered back for more.

I said to the button, "Come on, guys. I think, if a few more monkeys don't join us, it might be an insult to our guests."

The button said, "Hold your shorts on, Jasper. We're picking volunteers—"

I stayed with the bunnies. I started talking to them, seeing if I could create the beginnings of a common language.

"Jim—" I said, and pointed to myself. "Jim—"

"Ch'ch'ch—" chittered one of the bunnies, and that was as close as we got. There simply was no interest here in exchanging concept-symbols.

The bunnies were sitting up now, turning to look at the domes. I turned to look too—

Six more apes were coming out to join us. I recognized Jerry Larson and Roy Barnes, and two of the observation team, though I didn't know their names. And Fletcher. All had stripped to their underwear.

The bunnydogs welcomed them into the circle, touching the newcomers as curiously as they had touched me. One of them tugged at Larson's shorts, sniffing and even biting. Another reached up and touched Fletcher's breast. She laughed and squatted down so the creature could examine her close up. She examined it right back. There was no modesty here.

I called to her, "They must be mammals—"

She grinned and called back, "Don't bet on anything yet—"

The bunnies circled around all of us, clustering and gobbling and petting and touching. I looked to the worms—they looked bored. I felt curiously exultant. This was it! The breakthrough! We didn't need to be at war—!

I noticed that the bunnies were calming now, turning and also noticing the worms.

And then they began to—*sing.*

It was an eerie sound, but high-pitched and sweet. No two of the little creatures were singing in unison, yet the effect of the whole crowd of them singing all at once was that of a chorus. Their voices blurred in a way that was distinctly otherworldly and oddly pleasant.

I looked to Larson, to Fletcher, and to the others. Their eyes were bright with wonder. They were as enchanted as I was by this little miracle.

"It's just like the herd!" I called.

Fletcher laughed back, "I know—I can feel it!"

Now, the bunnies began turning back and forth in little quick hops. They bleated as they bounced. They cooed and bubbled and chirruped at each other. It sounded like song, like a conversation, like a bubble of delighted laughter.

I turned around in the middle of it all, turning to get a sense of the entire group. As I did, I noticed the bunnies picking up my motion. They were turning too. The gathering was a reflection of myself.

I noticed the other monkeys, humans, turning too—all smiles and delight. A couple of them were humming lightly.

We turned together. Individual bunnydogs circled to me, then swirled away. There seemed to be no pattern at all to their movements, and yet there was a sense of harmony and wholeness in this gathering. I could feel it enveloping me like a big warm fizzy bubble bath.

It felt like *home*—

The bunnies were moving out of the circle now—moving to the worms.

They began climbing on the worms and patting them, grooming them, nuzzling them. Even the largest of the worms was covered with little pink shapes, patting and stroking at its dark purple fur. The fur seemed to shimmer with color as I watched; its stripes rippled and flowed along its sides. The movement was clear and distinct.

I realized that the humans were being left alone in the circle. Were the bunnies abandoning us—?

No—one of the bunnies had grabbed my hand and was stamping its feet impatiently. It tugged at my arm, and looked at me with its large cookie-button eyes. Its expression was *expectant.*

I said to the other humans, "I think they want to introduce us to the worms—"

"You go first—" called Barnes. He was grinning, but he also looked terrified. Fletcher shushed him.

I let myself be tugged toward the edge of the circle.

I looked to the worms. Most of them were preoccupied with their attendants. Were the bunnydogs grooming the worms? Or were the worms *mothering* the bunnydogs?

What was happening here? Had the bunnydogs rode in on their worms like cowboys riding to a square dance? Or had the worms brought their bunnies out to play, like nannies in Central Park?

I looked around the circle. Some of the bunnies were staring into the worms' great eyes. One of them tapped a worm on the side and it lowered a hand and lifted the bunny up before its face.

Was it that simple? Eye contact?

One of the worms was studying me now. It was a medium-sized creature, only three meters long. Its fur was bright red, striped with shades of pink and purple. Its giant black eyes—were focused right on me.

The worm goggled its eyes sideways, the inevitable expression of curiosity. Those eyes must have been a third of a meter across. They were hypnotic.

I took a step toward the worm. And another.

The worm straightened its gaze. It studied me head-on. It shifted its arms.

I took another step toward it, and another. There were less than three meters between us now.

I stood before the worm and looked deeply into its eyes.

The creature was fantastic.

For just a moment, I felt as if I could hear its thoughts.

It blinked. *Sput-phwut.*

How odd. I felt perfectly safe looking into its gaze like this.

I lifted my arms and spread my hands out before me.

The worm unfolded its arms. They were jointed like wings and attached to the sides of the bony brain case behind the eyes. The arms came over the creature's eyes and then downward. I was reminded of a scorpion's tail.

The worm opened its hands toward me. It was echoing my gesture.

"It's intelligent," I said. "I don't know how I know, but I know. It's intelligent. Too intelligent to be just a domestic creature. . . ."

I took a step forward, my hands still out.

The worm hunched toward me.

Our fingers touched. The worm took my hand in its claw and turned my hand this way and that, studying it. It dipped its eyes close, refocusing. It saw me studying the way its eyestalks moved and peered into my face. Then it turned its attention back to my hand.

When it finished, it let go of my hand, but it left its claw in front of me. It was offering itself for mutual inspection. I took the claw in my hands and lifted it up to my face. I turned it over, back and forth, and studied it as the worm had studied mine. There were three digits, all opposed. There were three joints to each digit. I moved the fingers around. The worm could use any of its digits as a thumb opposed to the other two. Convenient.

I let go of the worm's hand. I met its eyes again and said, "Thank you."

The worm dipped its eyes—that gesture, it was an acknowledgment of some kind—and made a burping sound. "Ctrlp?"

"You're welcome."

The worm extended both its hands now and touched my shoulders. I flinched at the contact—but I looked into the creature's eyes again. "It's all right. Go ahead."

The worm began patting me, stroking me, and touching me as the bunnydogs had done. It was fascinated with my body—as the bunnydogs had been.

The worm's fingers touched my transceiver curiously. It lifted the chain, then let it drop. It looked at me as if wondering why I was wearing such an obvious piece of *technology*. It lowered its fingers to my loincloth and tugged at that. I wondered if I should take it off—but the worm was already ahead of me. It snapped the cord with its claw and dropped the loincloth carelessly to the ground. It blinked curiously at my genitals, but made no move to touch me there. It turned me around to examine my back.

Around me, I saw that the other worms were watching us. So were the other humans; they remained scattered across the otherwise empty circle. But the bunnydogs had completely forgotten about us, they were so engrossed in grooming the worms. The activity was almost *sexual.* Many of the bunnies had climbed on top of the big red monsters. Two of the bunnies even appeared to be . . . copulating? No. I must have been misreading the behavior.

The air was cold on my body. I could feel the worm poking at my buttocks. I said, "It feels like a medical inspection—"

Barnes giggled nervously. "It looks like a meat inspection. My uncle used to be in livestock and—"

Fletcher jabbed him sharply in the ribs. "Don't bring that into this circle."

Abruptly, the worm grabbed one of my feet and yanked, lifting me upside down. I managed to holler, "Hey—!" Then the worm goggled its eyes sideways at me as if to ask, "Yes?" And then it resumed studying my foot with its giant eyes. It poked and stroked, and once even drew one dark finger across the soft flesh of my arch. I couldn't help it, I started giggling.

The worm grabbed one of my hands and lifted it up beside my foot. It was comparing.

"It's intelligent! It has to be!" I was still hanging upside down. "Do you see what it's doing?"

Abruptly, the worm let go of me. I tumbled back to the grass. I climbed back to my feet, grinning. "You ought to ask first," I said to the worm.

It blinked at me.

I said, "I know this doesn't make sense, but I'm actually beginning to feel . . . friendly . . . toward these creatures."

The worm lifted its arms high then. A stretch? Its mouth opened in front of me. I squatted to my knees and peered in. Huge. Dark. And it smelled awful.

But I was grinning. I was the first human being on the planet to look into a worm's mouth without being pushed. I was actually feeling cocky—

—that's what saved my life.

I was turning around to look back toward the domes, I was about to say something stupid, when one of the bunnydogs let out a yelp—a yelp cut suddenly short—

I turned and saw—

One of the worms just crunching a bunny into its mouth.

I turned back toward the worm I'd been with—it was just rising up into an attack position—

I stabbed a finger at it and commanded, "No!" I didn't know what I was doing, I just bellowed, "That's very bad manners!"

The worm hesitated.

"Down!" I shouted. And pointed. "Down!"

The worm came down.

It looked confused.

I started backing away. "Get ready to scramble!" I said quietly. I glanced behind me. Barnes had dropped into a karate position—a cat stance. The others were backing away slowly. Fletcher's eyes were wide. She looked ready to bolt. "Slowly . . . !" I commanded. "Don't break . . . !"

The worm started to follow me. It started to flow after me.

I pointed at it and said, "No! Stay!"

It worked.

And then—

—another bunnydog yelped. Another worm was feeding.

And then another, and another—the air was suddenly filled with yelping!

The worm moved—

I broke sideways—I ran for Fletcher, leaping and knocking her flat to the grass—

Something purple chirruped behind us. Something roared close over our heads and exploded! The blast blew us sideways—we bounced against a furry wall—Fletcher gasped and started screaming! I rolled her over on her belly, rolled on top of her—

More explosions—the blast slammed into us—a wall of heat—

Larson was screaming—Barnes was shrieking—There were flames—

—and pulled Fletcher to her feet and ran, scrambling toward the chopper. A worm was burning. Something small and pink and flaming rocketed past us. Another worm was skidding, turning toward us—

The dome was already exploding off the chopper—the door was open —a man was on the ground before it, firing past us! I saw the streaks of incendiary bullets—

The door was open. We pounded up into it—past the man with the rifle—he gasped as something grabbed him—and then we were airborne —the open door looked down on Hell—backside.

FIFTY-EIGHT

I WENT to see Duke.

He looked better. And he looked worse. The bitterness was obvious now. When I sat down next to his bed, he turned his head away from me.

I said, "I won't stay long. I came to deliver something."

He still didn't look at me.

I waited till the nurse was out of the room. I said, "I don't know how you're going to hide it Duke, or where—but . . . well, *here.*" I slipped the grenade into his hand. His one remaining hand. The grenade was small but lethal. It would do the job.

Duke didn't move. The grenade sat in his hand like a rock.

Had I made a mistake? Had I reminded him again of his own fear? Perhaps I should just go.

Duke turned his head.

The hand with the grenade lifted up as if it had a life of its own. It carried the grenade painfully upward to where Duke's eyes could focus on it. They blinked and cleared and looked at the grenade dispassionately. The hand turned the grenade over and over. The thumb found the safety catch.

Duke's mouth opened. The hand brought the grenade forward so he could grab the ring with his teeth. Was he going to detonate it now?!

No. He wasn't. He let go of the ring. He was just testing the feel of it. He looked at the grenade again, and there was just the slightest hint of a smile on his face.

And then the hand holding the grenade disappeared beneath the covers.

Duke still hadn't looked at me. Still hadn't met my eyes.

I waited, but he turned his head away again, toward the wall. Not even a thank you.

It was all right. He knew. *There was no better way.*

After a while, I got up and left.

That was the last time that I saw Duke.

ABOUT THE AUTHOR

DAVID GERROLD began his science fiction career in 1967, as a writer for *Star Trek*. His first sale was the episode entitled "The Trouble with Tribbles," one of the most popular episodes in the show's history. Gerrold later wrote two nonfiction books about *Star Trek: The World of Star Trek*, the first in-depth analysis of the show, and *The Trouble with Tribbles*, in which he shared his personal experiences with the series. Gerrold has since written many other TV scripts, including episodes of *Logan's Run, Land of the Lost*, and the *Star Trek* animated TV series. He has served as story editor for *Land of the Lost* and *Buck Rogers*.

Gerrold is also a well-established science fiction novelist. His best-known works are *When Harlie Was One* and *The Man Who Folded Himself*, both of which were nominated for the Hugo and Nebula awards. He's published eight other novels, five anthologies, and a short story collection. In 1979, he won the Skylark Award for imaginative fiction.

David Gerrold is forty years old and lives in Los Angeles with three peculiar dogs, two and a half cats, a computer with delusions of sentience, and a butter-scotch convertible. Gerrold is a skilled programmer and contributes occasion-ally to *Creative Computing, Info-world*, and other home-computing periodicals. He also writes a monthly column on science fiction for *Starlog* magazine.

Gerrold is currently at work on Book Three of *The War Against the Chtorr: A Rage for Revenge*.